LA
GUERRA

LA GUERRA

A SPANISH SAGA

STEPHEN D. FRANCES

3-23-92

DELACORTE PRESS / NEW YORK, N.Y.

BOOK I

1

It was dark when Rafael Ledesma and three other cadets in mufti parked their cars in Madrid's Plaza del Sol and set off with their brief-cases.

The iron-grill door to the block of offices was closed but persistent ringing summoned the caretaker. He knew Cadet Claudio Ferraz whose father had an office on the sixth floor, so he allowed them inside and retired to his quarters. The four youths took the elevator to the sixth floor but they did not enter Claudio Ferraz's office. Instead, they climbed to the roof terrace. The flat roofs of other office buildings adjoined and the young men clambered across them until they overlooked a large, tree-lined plaza.

They settled down to wait, Cadet Castro took from his briefcase a bottle of sparkling wine, bread, caviar and fois gras. They drank and ate and jested coarsely while they watched the preparations in the plaza below. A rostrum had been set up and bedecked with red flags; microphones were wired up to loudspeaker vans; banners were being unfurled; and the plaza was slowly filling with contingents of marching demonstrators, brandishing clenched fists.

The cadets upended their briefcases, and big potatoes rolled out. Rafael Ledesma unwrapped razor blades and set them out in a neat row.

"We were born at a bad time," complained Claudio Ferraz sourly. "Spain is corrupted by primitives. A handful of troublemakers are trying to disrupt our way of life."

"We'll give them trouble!" vowed Cadet Castro grimly.

Rafael Ledesma picked up a potato and partially embedded three razor blades in it. "Hitler's got the right idea," he said. "Germany for the Germans and Spain for the Spanish."

"The Trade Unionists are the worst," said Cadet Redondo.

They worked swiftly, building mounds of potatoes that bristled with razor blades.

3

"All Anarchists are Russian-dominated," said Redondo. "Hitler would teach them a lesson!"

"He'd teach them death."

"Long live death," said Rafael piously.

"Free love is all right," said Cadet Castro slyly. He sniggered. "For the Red daughters of Red whores!"

Rafael Ledesma was thinking of a common shop assistant who had once rejected him. "These Red bitches are all the same," he said. "They think they're as good as we are!" He remembered the contempt in her voice as she tore free from him. "They're just crap," he said furiously. "They're anti-Christ." His fingers had stung against her cheek, and there had been fear in her eyes. "They all ought to be flogged!"

"Who?" asked Claudio Ferraz, hadn't been listening.

"Those Red bitches who want free love and sex equality!"

Cadet Castro's eyes gleamed. "If they want free love . . . we'll give it to them!"

"Why don't we give them a taste of their own philosophy?" urged Redondo.

"How?"

"Grab one of those Red bitches and give it to her. What's the name of that secretary of the CNT in Toledo? Charugin? His bitch of a daughter is always flaunting herself at meetings! What about her?"

They had fixed all the potatoes, and now they leaned over the roof parapet and stared down at the meeting below. The loudspeakers were defective and the orator's voice so charged with static they caught only isolated words. *"Comrades . . . workers' state . . . land for the peasants . . . solidarity . . ."*

The listening crowd roared approval and flourished clenched fists.

"How about a little action?" suggested Claudio Ferraz.

They lobbed the potatoes high out over the crowd, throwing quickly to complete their work before the close-packed crowd realized the danger and scattered.

Slicing steel fell from the night sky and caused a panic-stricken stampede. But long before the injured reached the hospital, the four cadets were on the outskirts of Madrid and driving on to Toledo.

Teresa's father called from the beach to awaken her. She threw back the sheets, swung her legs off the bed and ran across the cold tiles to the window.

"Teresa!"

She swung open the shutters and leaned out over the sill, shivering in the chill winter air. "What is it, Papa?"

"Come quickly, daughter. Awaken Pepita. Miguel set the *alma-draba* before dawn and it's time to haul."

The sea gleamed like polished lead as Miguel rowed along the line of floating corks. Teresa saw him drop his oars and peer through the glass-bottomed *mirafondas* to see the fish trapped in the fine mesh net that curtained the seabed.

"I'll be down in two minutes, Papa."

Teresa goose-pimpled as she stripped off her nightgown and snatched up her work frock.

"Pepita!" She shook her younger sister and ripped off the top sheet. Pepita yelped bad-temperedly and rubbed sleep from her eyes. Teresa rumpled the younger girl's hair. "Quickly! Father wants us for the *almadraba*."

They scampered downstairs to the kitchen where Elisa Barras was brewing chocolate over a charcoal fire. "Hurry, girls," she urged, pouring the steaming liquid into large cups. "Your father's impatient."

Pepita, still half-asleep, hadn't buttoned her dress, and it exposed her childish, unformed breasts.

"Such laziness!" scolded her mother affectionately, buttoning while Pepita gingerly sipped the scalding chocolate. Teresa cut a slice of bread and wrapped it around a salted anchovy as their father's shadow darkened the doorway.

"Take your time, girls," he said.

"Listen to him!" scolded his wife. "You told them to hurry."

Paco Barras chuckled. "Getting them out of bed is the big difficulty. But the fish will wait for them to fill their bellies."

He stepped outside again and stood with legs astride and toes digging into the sand. He was stocky, forty years of age, blue-eyed, and silvery blond. Everyone called him El Rubio, the blond one. But his son, Miguel, had the swarthy skin and curling black hair of his mother.

Miguel looked up from his *mirafondas* and gestured that he had seen many fish in the net.

Paco Barras nodded and breathed deeply, relishing the tang of the sea air and the scent of the pines that grew on the sandy slopes.

Teresa joined her father, cramming the last of the anchovy into her mouth and wiping her greasy fingers on her skirt. She was as blond as her father.

"We'll have the Tramontana," prophesied her father, nodding toward the north as though he could see the wind gathering its strength to hurl itself upon the village.

"It is still not cold enough, Papa," disagreed Teresa. She too stood with her legs apart and toes curling over into the soft sand. The down on her brown limbs was silvery. She shivered in the chill air and her father chuckled. "You'll grow warm when we start."

A seagull skimmed over the still surface of the water, swooped and hit with a splash. The gull cried loudly, snapped up a tidbit and beat its wings to become airborne. It wheeled, climbed swiftly and floated high on unseen wind eddies.

"Here comes Hernando to help," nodded Paco. They watched him approach along the sea's edge where the sand was hard-packed. When he drew close, he angled up toward them, his brown feet sinking into the soft sand.

"*Bon día,* Paco."

"*Bon día,* Hernando."

Hernando's blue eyes laughed at Teresa. His walnut-wrinkled face was tanned dark brown and his silvery hair was carefully combed. His waxed moustache bristled fiercely above the grave dignity of his neatly trimmed goatee. "Up early, yet still half asleep, Teresa," he teased.

"Away with you, old man. I arise before you *every* morning."

"You won't die of it, girl."

Hernando was ageless. He had fished and traded his catches for wine, bread and tobacco longer than anyone could remember.

Paco Barras sniffed the air. "I smell wind from the north."

Hernando shook his head. "It's too warm for the Tramontana."

"I agree," said Teresa.

Hernando chuckled. "So! Now you're a weather expert!"

"Your shirt sleeve's torn," she criticized. "I'll mend it later."

"That'll be the day! When I can't mend my own clothes!"

Teresa smiled. He wore his patched rags with the air of an aristo-crat.

Pepita ran out to join them, laughing at Hernando and shamelessly scratching the inside of her thigh through her frock. "I'm ready."

"Miguel!" Paco Barras's voice floated out across the still water and echoed around the moored fishing boats. Miguel bent to his oars, his little boat leaped forward and silver-crested ripples arrowed from its stern.

Teresa heard the whisper of scattered sand and glanced over her shoulder. Her heart stood still.

"Anselmo!" she whispered.

His eyes crinkled when he smiled. *"Bon día,* Señor Barras. *Bon día,* Señor Hernando." He looked at Teresa. "How are you?" The breathlessness she noticed in his voice started her heart beating again.

"Welcome, Anselmo," said Paco Barras. "Are you staying long in Escoleras?"

"This is a quick visit. A friend gave me a lift home. But nobody is awake yet."

"Have you had breakfast?"

"It is of no importance."

Paco Barras stepped to the kitchen doorway. "Elisa. Prepare breakfast for the son of neighbor Ledesma."

"You are very kind," said Anselmo. He could not take his eyes off Teresa. Her cheeks glowed.

Hernando and Paco waded into the sea to help Miguel draw up the boat.

Anselmo asked: "Are you pleased to see me?"

"Very!" breathed Teresa.

"It's a nice surprise?"

"Nothing I wanted more."

Pepita complained loudly: "Aren't you going to say hello to *me?*"

"Forgive me, Pepita. How tall you're growing. And prettier than ever."

"You're very handsome, too."

Teresa said: "Why don't you help Papa beach the boat."

"Why don't *you?*"

"Do what I say, Pepita."

"Why should I?"

"Do you want me to help you embroider your new dress?"

Pepita was delighted. "You will?"

"Later. Now run and help Papa."

Pepita sped down the beach, white sand spurting from her bare heels.

There was a long, shy silence.

"How are your sisters, Antonia and Pilar?" she asked.

"Well."

"And your brothers, Manolo and Rafael?"

"They are well, too."

"Will you stay long?"

"I must be back at the university tomorrow."

"I . . . I've missed you."

"I've missed you, too." His honey-brown eyes stared intently. "I haven't stopped thinking . . . about you, Teresa."

"I've thought of you too, Anselmo." She was remembering Carnival night, a shy kiss stolen in a joke which could become much more.

Elisa Barras came to the door with a slice of bread and three salted anchovies. "For you, Anselmo. Will you drink chocolate or wine?"

"Wine, please." He doubled the bread to make a sandwich and bit into it. The corners of his eyes crinkled again as he ate.

"Don't stare so intently," Teresa pleaded. "I've just got up . . . no time to wash. And . . . this old dress." She looked down ruefully at her black frock, stained white with sea salt.

Anselmo reached for the *porrón* and threw back his head. As he drank the purple wine, Teresa's eyes adored the rhythmic pulse of his throat.

He put down the *porrón,* wiped his hand across his lips and bit into the sandwich. His honey-brown eyes danced. "Do you remember Carnival?"

"I . . . I was thinking of it."

"I've thought about it ever since."

"You have?"

Her father called to her.

"I must go," she said and ran down the beach.

The line of corks floated like an enormous horseshoe. Hernando and Miguel grasped one end of the line while Paco Barras and his daughters hauled on the other end. The rope came in easily, hand over hand, steadily trawling the net across the seabed, stirring up mud and the feeding fish.

Anselmo stood watching Teresa, wanting to help her but concerned about his good clothes.

"Let me help," he offered.

Paco Barras refused with a chuckle. "We're used to it. We won't take long."

They hauled steadily, coiling the line and net neatly. But then the net resisted as though snagged on a rock. They dug in their heels and strained until their shoulders creaked. The net would not yield.

Teresa and Miguel waded into the sea and renewed their grip on the rope. Teresa's skirt floated up around her waist on a bubble of air and she pushed it down and clamped it between her thighs. The cold sea stung her flesh and numbed her toes. She dug in her heels and threw her weight back upon the rope.

Anselmo stripped off his jacket, kicked off his shoes and rolled up his trousers.

"We will manage," grunted Paco Barras.

Anselmo gestured at Pepita. "Change over," he ordered and as Pepita ran to help Miguel, he waded into the sea, joined Teresa and grasped the rope alongside her.

"Heeeeave!" cried Paco Barras, so they pulled in unison and the net yielded.

"Heeeeave!"

The reluctant rope gave slowly.

"Heeeeave!" shouted Miguel and the net was suddenly free. They hauled it in through the shallows, boiling furiously and flashing silver. They drew it up onto dry sand and fish leaped within the net, flapping seaward. It was a good catch.

While the men picked fish out from the slush and seaweed and cut the poisonous stings from the scorpions and water-spiders, Teresa shook out her soaked skirt. The thin cotton clung, and she was embarrassed by Anselmo's steady gaze as she peeled the skirt away from her.

"Thank you for helping," she said.

"The water was cold, was it not?" There was laughter in his voice.

Miguel untangled the net while the catch was divided into separate heaps.

"None for me, Señor Barras," protested Anselmo.

"Nonsense. You earned a share."

"But not so much. Please. My help was little."

Paco slightly reduced the generous heap of flapping fish. "This is yours," he stated flatly.

Hernando rolled a cigarette and contemplated his own share. "You have a strong fishing line, Paco?"

"I bought a reel last week."

"I don't need fish, Paco. I need a fishing line; about thirty meters."

"As you wish, Hernando. Do you want hooks also?"

"Hooks for two-kilo fish."

"I'll give you half a dozen."

The north wind gusted suddenly. It whistled down over the far-off ice-capped Pyrenees and molded Teresa's wet skirt against her thighs. She shivered.

Anselmo frowned. "The Tramontana!"

Paco Barras nodded wisely. "I predicted it."

Hernando grumbled. "The air is too warm for the Tramontana to blow strongly."

Anselmo's well-pressed trousers were now wrinkled and wet-stained. He shrugged his shoulders and straightened up, holding his shoes. "Will I see you later?" he asked Teresa.

"Don't forget your fish," said Paco Barras.

"You keep it, Señor Barras."

"You *must* take your share," insisted Paco.

Teresa flapped her wet skirt. "I'll take the fish to Anselmo's house later."

Anselmo smiled gratefully. She asked him impudently: "Will you walk barefooted then through the street?"

He was unaware she was teasing. "Of course not." He wiped his wet legs with his socks and thrust his bare feet into his shoes.

"What's the matter with bare feet?" asked Pepita innocently.

"Nothing," said Anselmo and looked puzzled.

They watched him walk away.

"He's just like his father," said Paco Barras and sighed.

"What's wrong with his father?" flared Teresa.

Paco Barras glanced sharply at his daughter. A slow smile spread across his face and he chuckled.

Teresa stamped her foot. "Anselmo's not for you to criticize, Papa! He's *my* friend."

Paco Barras spread his hands. "As *you* wish, daughter. As *you* wish."

After she had helped her mother clean the fish, Teresa carried a bowl of water upstairs and washed away her salt-water stickiness. She brushed her hair until it shone and tied it in a ponytail. She put on a white frock with a pleated skirt, and a suede belt with a large buckle that emphasized her slender waist, and rope-soled *alpagartas* with ribbon laces that crisscrossed over her ankles.

Her father was in the kitchen splicing hooks onto fishing lines when she came downstairs. He looked up and laughed. Teresa tossed her head and snatched up the fish she had gutted for Anselmo.

Miguel's dark eyes were solemn. "Why dress up?" he said. "Let them see you as you *really* are!"

"He's seen me working," she retorted.

"Don't interfere, Miguel," said his mother. "All girls like to look their best."

The sun blazed down onto the hard-packed earth of the main street, but in the shade the winter air was numbingly cold. She walked briskly toward the Ledesma residence at the far end of the village and her neighbors greeted her as she passed.

Manuel Coruna was setting out baskets of vegetables in front of his shop. *"Bon día,* Teresa."

"Adeu."

The men were away working in the fields or fishing, but their womenfolk sat in the doorways of their cottages warming themselves in the sun. Many had propped lace-making pillows against their walls, and bobbins flew through their fingers. They all greeted Teresa.

"Bon día, hija."

"Adeu."

Black-bearded Jesus Guitart was making a length of rope in the plaza. His youngest son turned the big wheel which twisted fiber into fine cord, while the boy's older brothers stretched a finished rope between two trees. José Guitart winked slyly at Teresa, but she tossed her head and hurried on.

Her friend Rosalia sat outside her house, embroidering initials on a pillowcase, but she put away her work and walked alongside Teresa.

"You're going to see Anselmo?" she guessed.

"He arrived this morning," Teresa confided. "I looked a sight, helping Father and wearing my work frock. But Anselmo didn't care. And he helped too, waded in up to his knees!"

"What's in the basket?" asked Rosalia.

"Anselmo's share of the catch. He wouldn't take it. It gives me an excuse to call."

"He was too proud to walk through the village carrying it," said Rosalia. She gave Teresa a speculative glance. "Do you truly love him?"

Teresa's eyes shone.

"You'll have lots of . . . problems!"

Teresa sighed. "I know."

"His father will want him to make a good match."

Teresa bridled. "I'll be a good wife!"

"It's not you. It's *them*. Will they let their oldest son marry a fisherman's daughter?"

A canvas-hooded cart rattled past, its iron-rimmed wheels singing over the cobbles. Benito Vigon peered down over the heap of manure he was carting and shouted: *"Bon día,* Rosalia."

She ignored him.

Teresa nudged her. "It's Benito."

Rosalia sniffed.

"Bon día," Vigon called again.

"Answer him," urged Teresa.

"He bores me!"

Vigon smiled wryly at Teresa and the cart clattered on, leaving the pungent odor of manure hanging on the air.

"He's crazy about you," said Teresa.

"I can't help that."

The tree-lined plaza at the end of the main street separated the fishermen's cottages from the residences of wealthy people who lived in Barcelona and owned summer villas on the coast.

"I won't come any farther," said Rosalia. She smiled encouragingly. "I wish you luck."

Teresa crossed the plaza, skirted the fountain and walked up the gravel drive of the Ledesma residence. It was a two-story mansion. Towering palm trees kept the house cool in summer and closely planted cyprus trees broke the force of the winter gales. Teresa climbed the marble steps to the mosaic-tiled terrace and rang the bell.

"They're at breakfast, Teresa," said the maid, who had worked for the Ledesmas for many years. "But come in. They won't mind *you*."

Anselmo leaped to his feet and met her at the doorway to the dining room. Baudillo Ledesma rose courteously and smiled. *"Bon día,* Teresa. Do sit down. Have you breakfasted?"

Cornelia Ledesma stretched out a frail hand and rang the service bell. When the maid appeared, she ordered: "Set another place, Carmen." Then she smiled at Teresa. "I'm so pleased you've called, my dear. We see little of you these days."

Anselmo drew up a chair for Teresa.

"What *lovely* hair you have, my dear," said Cornelia Ledesma.

"Thank you, Señora."

"It's bleached," said Anselmo mischievously.

The windows were shuttered against the sun, and in the subdued light of the dining room the pearls around Cornelia's throat glowed warmly.

"Your pearls are lovely, Señora!"

The older woman fingered them. "A present from Baudillo. Yesterday was our thirtieth wedding anniversary."

"And may you have many more."

Baudillo Ledesma nodded contentedly, pushed away his coffee cup and took out a cigar case. He glanced at Teresa. "With your permission?"

"Havanas, Father?" asked Anselmo.

"You want one?"

"I can't say no!"

Father and son lit up, giving to the act all the careful ritual that good cigars require. Señora Ledesma watched with the serenity of a woman who has her menfolk around her. Teresa was, as always, impressed by the grace of her bearing. Señora Ledesma was not beautiful, but her appearance was striking. Her hair was a mass of tight, iron-gray curls, and she wore a large, fan-shaped tortoiseshell comb in her back hair. Her forehead was high, her face proud, her lips firm and her eyes startlingly clear.

Carmen poured coffee for Teresa and refilled Anselmo's cup. Above them the enormous chandelier's glass teardrops swayed and chimed musically in an eddy of wind. Baudillo rose quickly to shut the window. "We're going to have the Tramontana," he sighed.

"Father forecast it this morning," said Teresa.

"What a pity," grumbled Anselmo. "I wanted to launch my Snipe." He smiled wryly at Teresa. "I planned to take you sailing." The north wind whined through the house and sandy dust buffeted the windows.

"Teresa," said Señora Ledesma softly. "I'm having trouble with my lace-making. Will you help me with it?"

Teresa knew then she would be invited to lunch. "Of course, Señora, I'll be delighted."

The north wind blew with unrelenting fury. It bowed double the tall canes in the hedgerows, uprooted electric-light posts and stripped leaves from the olive trees. It whined in the telegraph wires and moaned through the narrow streets. The villagers huddled around charcoal braziers, listening to rattling doors and banging shutters. Those who went out lowered their heads to the gale and leaned against it.

The wind howled down over snowy mountain slopes to the sea; water froze in the fountains and the villagers threw more kindling on their fires, toasted bread and spread *all-i-oli* on it thickly.

Over the bay the sea was whipped into a tempest of white-crested waves; flying spray rolled like smoke across its stormy surface. It was a cold wind and a dry one. It sucked the moisture from the dunes and turned the sand into dark clouds scudding across the water. Fresh-baked bread turned brick-hard, root vegetables shriveled in their skins, and the weathered faces of the fishermen became more deeply lined. The racing waves, driving against the jetty, exploded like bombs, blasting spray high into the air to freeze on the flagstones in delicate lacework patterns.

Nobody ever knew how long the Tramontana would last. Once it had blown for two months. This time it lasted a week. Then the wind died, the sea became transparent, the sky blue, and the air was so clear the distant, ice-capped peaks of the Pyrenees were clearly visible. The sun burned fiercely as though to warm the cold earth.

Linesmen repaired the cable poles, fishermen mended their torn nets and the women swept away the sandy dust that had invaded their cottages.

The ripening olives had fallen and had to be gathered quickly.

All day the Vigon family had been gathering olives, collecting them in baskets and pouring them into big sacks. The sacks were loaded on their two-wheeled cart, ready to be driven to the village cooperative store and pressed. The crop was good and the olives fat and rich with oil. Their yield would be copious.

By evening the cart was loaded.

"I will walk home," said Benito Vigon.

"You must be mad," said his father. He grimaced with the ache of his back as he pulled himself up onto the cart.

"I like to walk," said Benito sullenly.

His sister Camila held the bridle rein to steady the mule while her mother climbed up onto the cart. "Walking home; *along the beach!*" Camila mocked.

Benito Vigon flushed.

"What's that? Eh? How's that?" demanded her father.

"Leave the lad be," soothed his wife. She looked around at Edita who was perched precariously on the back of the cart. "Hold tight," she warned.

"I know where Benito's walking," chanted Edita tauntingly. She was precocious for her ten years. "I know where Benito's walking."

"Hold your tongue," snapped her mother.

Edita lapsed into silence, but smiled slyly at Camila.

"You will walk along the beach?" José Vigon asked incredulously.

Benito nodded reluctantly.

"What else?"

"I will call upon Señor Barras."

"So?"

Edita giggled then clapped her hand over her mouth.

"What happens with Paco Barras?"

"I . . . I . . ." Benito invented a reason. "I . . . will give him some olives."

"The boy's mad," his father told the air. "He will walk a kilometer to give his neighbor olives!"

"I like to walk," insisted Benito stubbornly.

"Let him alone," pleaded his mother. She motioned to Camila, who led the mule toward the path. The high wheels turned and the cart lurched wildly over the uneven ground.

Above the clop of the hooves, the older man's voice grumbled: "The boy's out of his mind!"

Benito waited until the cart was some distance away before he picked up a basket and gathered olives. When the basket was full, he balanced it on his shoulder and set off across country, jumping ditches and climbing over rock-built boundary walls until he reached the sand dunes and the sea.

His pace quickened when he came within sight of the cluster of whitewashed fishermen's houses that was Escoleras and his mouth turned dry when he thought of Rosalia. He strode on more swiftly, sand smoking from the heels of his *alpagartas*.

When he reached Hernando's stone-built hut, the old man was seated outside slicing cane into thin strips to make lobster pots.

"*Bon día,* Hernando."

"A beautiful evening indeed," replied the ageless old man. He wiped his knife on his sleeve as Benito swung his basket down from his shoulders.

"You have a bowl, Hernando?"

"I will get one."

The fat black olives flowed and filled the bowl.

"They're beautiful," praised Hernando. He polished one on his sleeve and bit into it. His moustache bristled like a bull's horns as he sucked the flesh from the stone. "They are as swollen and as rich as a capitalist from Madrid," he chuckled and turned his head politely to one side to spit out the kernel.

"The Tramontana did not blow until late this year. They remained ripening on the trees," explained Benito Vigon.

"You will drink wine?" invited Hernando. He handed Benito the *porrón* that rested on the sand beside him.

Benito threw back his head and drank deeply. Then he nodded farewell and swung the basket up onto his shoulder.

The Barras's cottage was the last but one, and when Vigon drew close he saw that Paco Barras was preparing his fishing *palangres.* Teresa and Rosalia were lace-making. He stopped before Paco Barras and swung the basket down off his shoulder to the sand. *"Ola!"* he greeted.

"*Bon día,* Benito." Paco Barras smiled up, crinkling his eyes.

Benito glanced shyly at the two girls. They sat on three-legged stools with their lace-making pillows resting against the cottage wall. The girls' fingers flew and the bobbins danced while on the pillows, delicate, gossamer-fine lace edging took form.

"*Bon día,*" Benito called toward the girls, his voice hoarse with nervousness.

Teresa glanced around briefly. *"Bon día."*

Benito waited. For a terrible moment, he feared Rosalia would ignore him, and he flushed, dreading the humiliation. Then Rosalia's gray-green eyes flicked toward him and her lips smiled mockingly. *Bon día,* Benito." Her voice was low, its unusual huskiness curiously melodious. His palms were so moist he wiped them on his trousers.

"The olive crop is bountiful this year," commented Paco Barras.

"I've brought you these."

"Thank you," said Paco Barras. At his side was four hundred yards of tangled fishing line and hooks. Paco Barras looped the mother line around his big toe and strummed it like a guitar string. The finer line bearing the hook vibrated and danced until it hung straight down from the mother line. Paco Barras coiled the unraveled line onto a wickerwork mat and left the barb hanging over the side of the mat to be baited later.

"How was fishing today?" asked Benito, not taking his eyes off the girls.

"Middling. Middling." Barras held his hand palm down, moving it slightly as though it floated in mid-waters. "Do you like sea pike? We caught a big one . . . three kilos. Take it when you go. It makes fine soup."

"Thank you, Señor," said Benito absently. After a pause, he asked, "Have you news of your son Isidro?"

"He wrote last week. All is well except the food."

"The army has always lived on beans," said Benito.

Barras looked up at him and saw he was watching the girls. He smiled as he looped the mother line around his broad toe. "The girls are clever at their work, are they not, Benito?" He strummed the taut fishing line with his blunt forefinger.

"They are indeed," said Benito breathlessly.

"Have you seen what they are making?"

It was the excuse Benito wanted. He walked across to the girls and stood behind them. Their fingers flew and the boxwood bobbins tinkled against each other.

The hard, angular boniness of Teresa's shoulder blades showed through her linen blouse, but Rosalia's body was like a ripened fruit. Her black hair, plaited in two long tresses, hung down before her and the soft skin at the nape of her neck was uncovered. Benito Vigon longed to touch it.

"What's new?" asked Paco Barras.

"There's talk about land reform," said Benito Vigon.

Barras clucked his tongue.

"Land reform could be a good thing," said Benito.

"It is confiscation of private property."

"That is a good thing!"

"You think so, son?"

Benito wanted to impress Rosalia with his knowledge. "Land reform is necessary."

"Why necessary?" asked Barras, who liked to talk.

"There are many poor people who have nothing. Yet there are a few rich men who own all. It is justice that some should be taken from the one and given to the other."

Barras sighed. "Tell me, son. Who do you know who has nothing? We do not allow anyone to go hungry. We have our land and grow our vegetables. The sea provides and we are rich in oil and wine. If anyone lacks, he has only to ask and he will be given."

"Thus it is in Cataluña, Señor," agreed Benito quickly. "But I speak of the south of Spain where many starve."

"In China there is famine. In India many die of hunger. But must everyone live unhappily because of all the misery in the world?"

"I do not say what should be done," said Benito quietly. "I say only that I believe land reform is good and necessary."

"These are not matters for our heads, son."

"I disagree, Señor Barras. Our People's Front Government has promised land reform. In Estremadura, more than fifty thousand farm workers have already settled on land that has now become their own."

Barras laughed mockingly. "What great wisdom you possess, boy. Next you will become a state minister. What a marvel you are! So young and yet to have so much knowledge!"

Benito said doggedly: "It is what I heard on the radio, Señor Barras." He changed the conversation and spoke to Teresa. "Do you never mistake a bobbin and spoil the pattern?"

Teresa's forehead crinkled with concentration. "Sometimes," she said absently. The bobbins clicked musically. The balls of her toes braced against the sand and her skirt scalloped down between her bony thighs as she gripped the pillow with her knees.

"I am astonished you are not confused by so many bobbins."

Teresa pinned a guide needle through the pattern, the bobbins flew through her fingers again, and as she brought her work to an end, she said: "You get used to it." She bound the hanging bobbins to the pillow with white tape, put it aside, rose to her feet and stretched lazily. She displayed the thinness of her arms and the flatness of her breasts.

Rosalia pressed her hands to the small of her back. She spoke to Teresa, ignoring Benito. He stood apart from them, shy and uncomfortable, waiting for Rosalia to be ready to leave. Then he blurted quickly: "Rosalia!"

She raised one eyebrow.

"May I walk you home?"

She studied him. "How do you know I'm going home?"

"I . . . that is . . . *if* you are going home?"

Rosalia sighed. "Very well."

"Don't forget the sea pike in the kitchen, boy," called Paco Barras.

Behind the fishermen's cottages, the village spread upward along the slopes of a steep hill. The narrow streets were sharply inclined and paved with natural stone. Rosalia walked ahead of Benito and answered his questions over her shoulder.

He pleaded: "Come walking with me, Rosalia."

"What are we doing now?" Exasperation was in her voice. "Everyone knows you call at the Barras's house to walk me home."

"Are you ashamed of it?"

"Yes," she said bluntly.

He flushed. "I'm sorry, Rosalia."

She stopped to drink from the plaza fountain and held her braids so they would not fall into the stone basin.

"Don't you like me to walk you home?"

"No," she said. She straightened up and wiped the back of her hand across her mouth.

He was sweating. "Why not?"

Her wet lips were very red. She ran her long pink tongue across them before she spoke.

"Who could wish to walk with *you?*" She looked at his sweat-stained shirt and earth-soiled trousers. "You're dirty. Look at your feet!"

He stared down guiltily. He wore no socks and his rope-soled *alpagartas* showed his bare feet stained with moist earth.

"Your hands are filthy and you're sweaty."

"I . . . I . . ." he choked.

"Also . . . you *smell!*"

His face showed his hurt. "It is the fish that smells." He held up the sea pike, dangling from his forefinger.

"No. It is *you* who smells."

"I smell?"

"Strongly. Of horse dung and stale sweat."

"The dirt of honest labor is not shameful."

She narrowed her eyes mischievously and the intimate huskiness of her voice soothed his annoyance. "What you say is true, Benito. But . . . it does not stop you from smelling!"

"If you will go walking with me, Rosalia, I will not smell. I will wash and be clean and wear a white shirt and my best suit . . ."

She started walking again, swinging her hips. "I will think about it."

"When will you let me know?"

"Tomorrow. Or the day after."

"Tell me *now.*"

"I'll see."

"Next Sunday," he urged eagerly. "In the evening?"

"Perhaps."

"I'll meet you at seven o'clock. At the fountain."

"Don't be surprised if I don't come."

"I'll wash and shave and put on my best suit."

She giggled.

"I can't wait for Sunday," he confessed.

"Don't accompany me any farther," she warned. "Father doesn't like boys to walk me home."

He watched her as she walked on, swinging her hips until the hem of her skirt flicked.

Teresa switched on the electric light, but the bulb glowed only dimly. The doctor and the mayor, who were strolling along the beach, noticed this and stopped to talk to Paco Barras.

"We are talking about the lighting, Paco," said Federico Morales, the mayor.

Paco strummed the mother line. "Lighting?"

"Shall we install street lamps? Or is another public fountain more useful?" summed up Doctor Aldo.

"By day there is the sun and on many nights the moon shines strongly," said Barras slowly. "Whereas on hot, dry days in the summer, there are many who stand in queues at the fountain."

"He agrees with me," said the mayor triumphantly.

"But on dark nights is not light useful, Paco?" asked the doctor.

Barras shrugged his shoulders. "Is a wine barrel useful without wine? Does a car run without fuel?" He gestured at his cottage. "Will street lamps give us more light?" His blue eyes laughed at the mayor. "What use a dozen fountains if we have water for only one?"

"We cannot do *everything* at once," said the mayor, puffing out his fat cheeks. "Do you favor nationalization of the electrical industry?"

Barras shook his head dubiously. "Such matters are for bigger brains than mine."

"Our new People's Front Government is granting local authorities many useful concessions," said the doctor. He took out his watch and glanced at it. "I can't stop. Pairet is due for an injection." He hurried away, a tall, earnest, middle-aged bachelor in a neat but old-fashioned black suit.

The mayor sank down onto the sand alongside Barras and drew out his tobacco pouch. "Smoke?"

"Please."

The mayor rolled two cigarettes. "We Spaniards are too temperamental to have good government," he sighed. He held a match for the fisherman. "Twenty-six government crises since we deposed the king. Seventy-two new ministers in the past four and a half years!"

Barras brushed away glowing tobacco particles that dropped from his cigarette. "Bread, wine and a smiling face are all any man needs," he said philosophically.

The mayor nodded sad agreement. He was an easygoing man, and small problems worried him. Politics disturbed him deeply.

"It's the hotheads who cause the trouble," complained the mayor.

"We've no hotheads here," said Barras gently.

"But in Madrid and Barcelona, there are shootings and killings every day." The mayor saw his younger son trudging over the sand toward him and rose to his feet.

Juan Morales was breathless. "We've got a rush job in the shop, Papa. Can you come?"

When it was too dark to see, Paco Barras put away his fishing lines and stood staring out across the sea at the golden rim of the sun edging down behind the mauve horizon. He breathed deeply and rapped his knuckles on his chest. He turned, walked to his cottage and thrust his head in through the doorway. "How are we doing, beautiful?" he shouted at his wife and chuckled delightedly when she snapped at him.

"Get away with you, old man," she scolded. "Be your age." But she flushed happily.

Miguel was left with three large lobsters after auctioning the rest of his catch in the fish market. They had died before he had landed them and nobody would buy dead lobsters.

Teresa heaped charcoal under the kitchen grill and fanned until it glowed white-hot. Her mother placed the lobsters, still in their shells, on the hot embers and soon the pleasing smell of broiling shellfish filled the cottage. Teresa turned the lobsters so they cooked evenly, while her mother peeled garlic and pulped it with mortar and pestle. She poured olive oil on the pulp and whipped it into a yellow custard.

Pepita spread the tablecloth, set out the plates, the bread and a *porrón* of black wine. Miguel and his father seated themselves and waited for their womenfolk to serve them.

The lobsters were split open, the meat removed from the shells and served with the *all-i-oli*. Squid were sliced into rings and dropped into sizzling olive oil.

"The Medinas have bought a radio," Miguel said.

"Was it expensive?" asked Teresa.

"I don't know," said Miguel and lapsed into sullen silence. His dark eyes, black hair and swarthy skin were such a contrast to his father's blondness that they did not seem related except for the obstinate jaw they shared in common with Teresa.

"Have you seen it, Miguel?" asked Pepita.

"Of course."

Pepita asked, "Why can't *we* have a radio, Papa?"

"Don't pester Father with your nonsense," scolded her mother.

But Miguel said bluntly, "She's right. Why *can't* we have a radio, Father?"

His father finished chewing, drank deeply from the *porrón* and then looked levelly at his son. "How will we pay for it?"

"It's easy, Father. You can pay for it over two years. That means so little each week that we'd never notice it."

"No!" said Paco Barras flatly. He cut a hunk of bread and lavishly spread *all-i-oli*. "I owe nobody," he said proudly. "When I need anything I save until I can buy it."

"Well then. Why don't we save for a radio?" asked Pepita.

"Don't interrupt, child," scolded her mother.

"Because we're saving for Miguel's wedding," Teresa said.

"Of what use is a radio?" demanded Paco Barras.

"We can listen to music," said Pepita quickly.

"And we'll know all the news as it happens," said Miguel.

"Are you so anxious to learn of all the tragedies and miseries of the world then?"

"Perhaps Miguel would stay at home and not go out to the cafés so much," interjected his mother.

"After the fourteenth of July he'll have other things to do with his evenings," said Paco Barras.

Miguel turned pink. He was to marry Helena Medina on the fourteenth. Since the Barras cottage was too small for his wife to live at home with him, he had rented the top half of another.

"Where will you go for your honeymoon?" Teresa asked.

Miguel broke bread and scooped up *all-i-oli*. "Helena says she'd like to go south," he said with his mouth full.

"I envy you," sighed Teresa. "I'd love to see the south: Sevilla, the mosque of Cordoba, Granada, Cadiz, Malaga . . ."

From the open doorway came the whisper of sand kicked up by bare feet, and Hernando smiled in at them. His silvery locks were sleeked flat and his waxed moustache bristled fiercely. He carried a torch and a rusted airgun. "I'm hunting sparrows," he said. "Anyone like to join me?"

Miguel offered him the *porrón*. "Step inside and drink," he invited. "I'll go with you when I've finished eating."

2

After lunch, Pepita washed the dishes while Teresa and her mother laundered. They stood at the stone washtub slapping soaked linen on the sloping sill. The clothes line bowed under the weight of wet sheets.

The mother of Miguel's financée came by.

While her mother chatted with Señora Medina, Teresa poured out the dirty water in the washtub and refilled it with clean water.

Señora Medina mentioned that the postman had told her the Ledesma boy had arrived on the afternoon bus from Figueras. Teresa looked up quickly and caught her mother's eye. When their visitor left, her mother said, "I can manage the rest, Teresa. You run along."

Teresa hurried upstairs with a pitcher of water, stripped off her black dress, washed, and then brushed her hair until it shone. She tied it with a strip of black velvet. Then she put on her white dress and high-heeled sandals. Her heart was beating excitedly when she ran downstairs and called a farewell to her mother. She hurried through the village and across the plaza and almost ran up the gravel drive leading to the Ledesma residence.

The quick rap of her high heels was heard inside the house as she crossed the terrace, and the door opened.

Teresa's smile withered when she saw Anselmo's sardonic younger brother, Rafael, who had been away for almost a year. His voice was cold and metallic. "*Ola,* Teresa! You've come to welcome me home?"

She concealed her disappointment. "*Ola,* Rafael. It's good to see you again; but how you've changed. You're much taller!"

"More handsome, too?" His black eyes gleamed.

"Oh yes, Rafael. *Much* more handsome!"

"Come in," he invited. "It's cooler in the patio."

Teresa hesitated.

"Oh, come in!" he said irritably. "You can surely stay five minutes."

She followed him along the cool corridor into the garden. It was shaded by palm trees and smelled of moist earth and pine needles.

As they strolled around the garden, she studied him slyly. He was only seventeen but he seemed much older. His cadet training at the Alcazar had squared his shoulders; his high forehead, pale face and fashionable wisp of moustache showed an officer's bearing. Despite his civilian clothes, his crisp movements betrayed his military background. He carried a leather riding crop which he slapped against his calf.

"Is this a long visit, Rafael?"

"A short leave. Only ten days." He slashed with his riding crop and neatly lopped the head off a plant.

"Don't do that, Rafael," she scolded. "Your mother will be angry."

"Don't tell me what to do!"

She was silent.

"I suppose all the village is talking about me being home," he said smugly.

She said tactfully, "News travels fast."

"Everyone will want to know how I'm making out in Madrid."

She nodded solemnly. "Naturally."

"I can't stay here long," he said with studied casualness. "I have many important matters to attend to in Madrid."

"Indeed, Rafael?"

"Indeed!" he mocked.

"Tell me about them," she encouraged.

"It's politics," he said importantly. "An officer and a gentleman has a political duty to his country." His pale face was bitter. "The Red scum have arrested José Antonio!"

"Is he one of your friends?" she asked innocently.

"Stupid!" he flared. "José Antonio Primo de Rivera is Spain's savior. He's our natural leader."

"Leader!"

"He's the head of the Falangists." Rafael held himself erect. "I *too* am proud to be a Falangist."

"Forgive me. I know nothing about politics, Rafael."

"But you surely know that the Red swine in power are corrupting our country? Anarchism and madness are running riot. The so-called People's Government has set loose a Red menace that has Spain by the throat!"

Teresa allowed his tirade to wash over her, and he concluded: "And now they've arrested José Antonio!" He paused for breath.

"Why?" she asked automatically.

"It's a frameup. They're afraid of José Antonio. They want him under lock and key."

"But *why* was he arrested?"

He sneered. "A bomb was planted in Largo Caballero's house. The Falangists are accused of doing it."

"Who is Largo Caballero?"

"He's a government minister, a puppet for the Reds!"

Teresa was bored. "Anselmo didn't come with you?"

His dark eyes studied her. "You didn't come to see me," he accused. "You were expecting Anselmo?"

"I hoped he was here," she admitted. "But it's nice to see you too, Rafael."

He glared and strode on ahead of her, slashing with his riding crop.

Teresa said timidly: "I'll tell Rosalia you're here."

He wouldn't look at her.

"Rosalia . . . likes you, Rafael."

"She's scum!" he spat. "Just cheap scum!"

Teresa was deeply shocked. "Rafael!"

He spun around. "You're scum, too! You're both scum, living like Gypsies, soiled clothing and unwashed bodies." His voice became high-pitched. "One glance shows what you are. You don't know what it means to be well-bred! Look at your hands—rough and calloused. What gentleman could tolerate a caress from such hands? You're dull and uncultured."

Teresa stepped back, shocked by his vehemence.

Then the loud, clear voice of Señora Ledesma rang out sharply.

"Rafael!"

He turned to face his mother. They stared at each other for long seconds. Señora Ledesma held herself proudly, leaning upon her walking stick, and presently her son wilted beneath her steady gaze and looked away.

"I never thought my son could behave in such a way," she said icily.

He hung his head.

"Go!" she said in a low voice. Then angrily: "Get out of my sight!"

He hesitated and then, without glancing at either of them, strode away.

Señora Ledesma's hurt sounded in her voice. "He is stupidly stubborn and has not the grace to apologize, Teresa. But I beg of you to forgive him. He is young and often the young have strange ideas." She held out her hand. "Come, Teresa. Help me with my knitting."

Within the sanctuary of the sewing room, Señora Ledesma talked frankly while she wound a ball of wool from the skein Teresa stretched between her hands.

"Try to forgive Rafael," she said. "He is the strange one of our family. Pilar and Antonia are in Madrid, yet he never calls on them. He is so different from Anselmo and Manolo."

Teresa still could not trust herself to speak.

"The boy has wild notions. Take no heed of him, Teresa."

Teresa nodded numbly.

"The Ledesma family has always been wealthy, Teresa. Our farms, olive groves and vineyards have been in the family for generations."

Teresa nodded. "I know."

"But I am not a Ledesma, Teresa. I did not come from a wealthy family." The older woman sighed. "My family was poor. I was the youngest child of six and my parents died when I was still very young."

Teresa's eyes widened and she studied the other woman with new interest.

Señora Ledesma wound the ball of wool so that the strands lay evenly. "I scrubbed, washed and cooked for my brothers. My hands were rougher than yours and the only frock I owned was a work dress."

"I did not know this, Señora," said Teresa. She added with a faint smile: "Nor would anyone suspect it."

"You are a good girl, Teresa."

A warm bond of understanding united the two women.

Señora Ledesma said: "I do not want for my sons wives who are pampered cats, who wish to be displayed on silken cushions, sleek and well-groomed but useless in the home."

Teresa kept her flushed face lowered.

"I want good wives for my sons; women who will know how to wash and clean and mend even when they have no need to do so."

"It is a woman's instinct to care for a man," said Teresa.

"It is . . . when she loves him."

Teresa flushed more deeply.

"There are wives who do not love their husbands but only themselves. Such women cannot give to a man . . . they can only take."

Teresa nodded.

"You are a good girl, Teresa. I've loved you since you were a child. You're kind and thoughtful and a wonderful help to your mother. You have all the qualities of a good wife."

Then after a pause she said: "Anselmo will be home again soon."

The mayor met Doctor Aldo on his way to the café casino for his evening game of chess with the priest.

"What's worrying you, Juan?" he asked, puffing out his fat cheeks.

The doctor frowned as he drew his watch from his pocket and glanced at it hurriedly. "Illness can be treated. But I cannot cure stupidity."

"What's the trouble?" Federico Morales's tufty gray eyebrows arched in curiosity.

"That ignorant Serra and his wife."

"What have they done now?"

"They're both chronically undernourished! They have a storeroom crammed with food, wine and oil. They've crates of salted anchovies, last year's potato crop and a dozen salted hams hanging from the rafters. Yet . . . they're undernourished!"

The mayor shrugged his shoulders. "What can you do. The Serras will starve to save a peseta."

The doctor scowled. "Are they greedy or stupid? She does all the scrubbing and washing she can get and he labors sixteen hours a day. Why do they kill themselves with work and starve themselves?"

"They had spendthrift parents. People who've known poverty are scared of it."

"I fear for the woman's lungs," confessed the doctor. "Last week a fisherman gave her a basket of fish because she looked hungry and she took it to Figueras to sell in the market. She walked there barefooted to save the bus fare and was caught in that downpour. Now she's got a temperature of over a hundred and two."

"She's gravely ill?"

"She had to be bad before her husband called me in. He's worried about my fee . . . although he's never paid me yet!" The doctor took out his watch again. "I must run."

"I'm going your way," said the mayor. But he walked slowly and irritated the briskly walking doctor. "José Antonio's been jailed," added the mayor.

"When bombs are planted in a minister's house, some action must be taken."

"Do you think the Falangists are fomenting trouble, Juan?"

"Everybody's making trouble. This government can't last long. Too much public unrest."

"Do you know any Freemasons, Juan?"

"One or two."

"Do you believe they were behind Portela? Did they want a People's Front politician to become president?"

"The appointment of Azaña as president was constitutional procedure," snapped the doctor. He was fretful to be on his way, and with relief saw the benign face of the elderly priest approaching. "Here comes your chess partner," he said. "I'll leave you now."

The doctor hurried away.

The two stout men paced on side by side. The mayor wore a collar and tie as a sign of respect for his public position and the priest's dusty shoes whispered out from under his dusty skirts like seal flippers.

"Juan was in a hurry," commented the priest.

"He's always in a hurry. The wife of Serra is ill."

"Ah!" nodded the priest, as though it was exactly what he expected.

"They starve themselves."

The priest sighed. "In some ways that is the story of our Church.

We receive many gifts. But the money is hoarded. Gold inlays enrich the domes of our cathedrals, but nuns and priests live modestly and the poor go on being poor."

"Sometimes I wonder if you are for your Church . . . or against it!"

The old priest chuckled, holding his paunch to steady it. "I was born a man without faith and became a Catholic by conversion. Birth is an inescapable fact, but the religion of Catholicism is debatable."

They walked on toward the casino. The priest pulled out a handkerchief, raised his round black hat and mopped his forehead.

"Have you heard that José Antonio has been arrested, Don Carlos?"

"Who has not heard?"

"Do you think it is just?"

"Who knows what is right?" sighed the priest. "We say *this* is a good thing or *that* is a bad thing. But always somebody will ask *why* we think it is a good thing, when it is so clearly bad. I can only reply, *this* is a good thing because God says it is a good thing. Then they answer, *your* God says it is a good thing; but *our* God says it is a bad thing!" The priest sighed again. "There are so many Gods with conflicting opinions. *Who* can know what is right?"

"In Madrid there is shooting in the streets. The Anarchists fight the Trade Unionists and the Falangists fight them both."

"I will pray for peace," said the priest and chuckled.

"The political situation does not worry you, Don Carlos?"

"It does. And with good reason." The priest's round face wreathed in a smile. "Spaniards are Catholics; but the first thing our people do when there is unrest is burn the churches. Still, the mob can burn only substance. Goodness cannot be destroyed by fire."

They stood to one side of the narrow street to allow Hernando to pass. His wrinkled face smiled a greeting. A shotgun was slung over his shoulder and a rabbit and a brace of partridges hung from his worn cartridge belt.

"A good hunt, Hernando?" praised the priest.

"Would you like a partridge, Don Carlos?"

"Thank you. No."

"And you, Federico?"

"No, thank you, Hernando."

"How about the rabbit?"

"You cook it, Hernando."

"Then a good day to you both."

"Plenty of onions with the rabbit," the mayor called after him and Hernando waved without turning his head.

"There goes a truly happy man," said the priest. "When he is hungry he hunts. He asks nothing from anyone, but will give all if asked. He works when he wishes or sits in the sun drinking wine. He takes orders from nobody and dictates to none. He's a good man but has never once set foot in my church."

"He's an Anarchist," said the mayor.

"Catalans are natural Anarchists," said the priest.

The mayor gave the priest a sly glance. "Is anarchism a bad thing?"

"I long ago ceased to believe I know what is right or wrong." Don Carlos chuckled. "Although at times I have thought there may be some justification for the extraordinary claim that Jesus Christ was the first Anarchist."

They had reached the casino where the men of the village gathered to play cards or billiards, and as they drew back the mosquito netting across its doorway, Teresa and Rosalia passed them.

"Pasiu be, Padre," they said to the priest.

"Bon día," they acknowledged the mayor.

The two girls carried a rafia basket containing twenty kilos of crude soda. Teresa's mother would use it in rendering down olive oil to make soap. The girls strained apart to prevent the basket rubbing against their calves. Their arms ached but they chattered excitedly.

"I don't know what you see in him," said Teresa.

Rosalia's eyes glowed. "What else did he say?"

"That . . . that we're Gypsies!"

One morning Rafael arose at dawn, strapped on leggings and took down his shotgun.

He left the village and walked inland, traversing the olive groves and vineyards terraced on the mountain slopes. The sun was hot and he sweated as he climbed. The scent of pine trees and gorse was strong. Twice he flushed partridges and was so startled by the fierce beat of their wings that they were beyond range of his gun before he got the butt to his shoulder. At midday he reached a rock-strewn plateau and looked out over the plains of Ampurdan and saw his village, a gleaming cluster of white specks against the hazy blue of the sea.

The long walk had tired him and he sat down and took from his haversack a goatskin of wine, bread and a hunk of salami. There was no shade and his chest was wet with sweat. He inhaled the smell of sage and remembered picnics as a child with his parents. When he drank from the goatskin bottle, it revived memories of the heady tang of fermenting grapes in the family's large store-barrels. The wine was so thick it furred his tongue and stained his handkerchief purple when he wiped his lips. Such wine was unavailable in Madrid, he regretted, as he sliced bread. He ate with relish and drank until the wineskin was half empty. The remains of the bread he crumbled and spread out on a flat rock, and ten minutes later when half a dozen sparrows were pecking at the crumbs, he raised his shotgun and fired both barrels. When he could see through the haze of smoke, the flat rock was swept clean. Around it was scattered feathers and bloody shreds of flesh. He chuckled, stretched out lazily and dozed.

He awoke with a start. It was late afternoon and at this altitude it was chilly when the sun set. He set off briskly to the village and soon a partridge flew out from under him when he all but stepped on it. He threw up his gun and snapped off a shot. The bird faltered in flight and wheeled. One wing beat the air furiously while the other trailed, dragging it spiraling downward.

He took careful aim, fired his second barrel and the bird fell like a stone.

It was a plump partridge. He fingered the warm body with pride before he hung it on his cartridge belt. But as though the shots had warned all other prey, he walked down the mountain slope toward the village without seeing another sign of wildlife. When he neared the village, he unloaded his gun and carried it slung across his shoulder. He plodded across neatly terraced vineyards and olive groves, using a shortcut to the village.

It was a sixth sense that warned him of another's presence. He stood still and listened, then walked on stealthily through the olive grove to the edge of its terrace. From the cover of a cactus hedge he looked down into a gulley where a shallow stream flowed lazily over flat rocks. Rosalia Prada sat dabbling her bare feet in the water. A bundle of pruned olive branches showed she had been gathering firewood. With an oval of pumice stone, she rubbed away the calluses on her heels. Then she turned her attention to her calves, hunting diligently for truant hairs, rubbing gently until her legs were smooth.

Rafael was strangely stirred by the girl's movements as she stroked her legs, her fingers searching for imperfections. Presently she was satisfied and smiled secretly as she put away the pumice stone. She sat with her skirt in her lap and dabbled her toes in the stream, kicking golden droplets of spray across the gulley.

He retraced his steps to a break in the cactus hedge and picked his way along the gulley. She did not hear him until he was almost on her. She glanced up with startled eyes and her hands flew to the hem of her skirt. But when she recognized him, her hands fell to her sides. She leaned back, staring up at him impudently. Moist wisps of black hair curled out from the armpits of her sleeveless frock.

He leaped the stream and stood over her. *"Ola,"* he greeted.

"You walk very softly, Rafael!" She stared so intently he feared she knew he had spied on her. He was disconcerted by her parted thighs.

"You have been fortunate with your gun, Rafael?" She nodded at the partridge swinging from his belt. When she smiled, her red lips were full and pouting.

"Yes," he said huskily. The softness of the skin on the inside of her thighs stirred him deeply. She smiled lazily and with a shock he realized his gaze didn't embarrass her.

"Would you . . . would you like this partridge?" he stammered.

She chuckled. "The prey should be enjoyed by the hunter."

"Why do you laugh?" he asked.

"I am honored you wish to make me a gift."

He wondered if he should offer her money. It was a mad thought, but her brazen thighs and the inviting pout of her lips provoked it. His hands were shaking as he placed his gun on the ground and took off his cartridge belt.

Her cool eyes mocked him, and he picked up a birch wand and slashed the air.

"Will you stay home for long, Rafael?"

He sat down beside her. "I'll stay a few weeks." He hoped he sounded casual. "I was lucky to meet you here, Rosalia."

She studied him intently. "Why do you say that?"

The peppery tang of her perspiration blended disturbingly with the warm-milk smell of a young girl.

"You . . . you attract me."

"I attract you?" she stretched her long legs and relished the caress of his hot eyes. "How?"

"You've *always* attracted me."

"But . . . how? Tell me."

"You're beautiful."

"Beautiful? Dressed like this?" She gestured at her black work frock, washed threadbare and sunbleached.

"Clothes do not make a princess," he said.

She gave a husky chuckle that made him long to seize her.

"Why laugh?"

"Clothes can make a girl a Gypsy!" she said.

"You were born to wear beautiful clothes."

She gave him a strange, sideways glance. He took her hand, but she pulled away.

"Please," he said.

"Don't."

"Does my touch anger you?"

"It can be no pleasure to hold callused fingers."

"You have soft hands," he said, while at the back of his mind stirred the memory of a forgotten conversation.

"I'm coarse and dirty, Rafael."

"You're full of grace," he said solemnly.

Abruptly she climbed to her feet. He arose quickly and stood watching her shake out her skirt.

"Have I angered you?" He slapped the birch wand against his leggings.

"You arouse emotions which are dangerous."

"Such as?" he asked quickly.

"Thoughts of you . . . and me!"

"Why are they dangerous?"

"They can become dangerous, Rafael." Her eyes were wide as she stared up into his face.

"What is natural is not bad!" He moved closer to her. The moist scimitars of hair curling out from her armpits exhaled her musky, intimate smell.

She continued to quote Teresa. "I am not clever, Rafael. I am dull and uncultured."

"It is important only that we desire each other."

"I feel desire for you, Rafael," she whispered.

He pulled her hard against him. She resisted, making him aware of the sturdiness of her hips. Then her hair brushed against his hand and he seized it and tugged her head back until she cried out. His lips went to the hollow at the base of her throat. He scored her flesh with his teeth and bit at her neckline.

She broke away from him and they stood facing each other, breathless.

"Come to me," he pleaded.

She held together her torn neckline. "Please go away."

"Are you afraid of love?"

"You have no love for me."

"I adore you, Rosalia. I . . . need you."

"Do . . . you want me to be your . . . betrothed?"

He did not hesitate. "I do, Rosalia."

Her eyes shone and he took her in his arms again. The bracing of her loins stirred him uncontrollably.

"Say you'll marry me, Rafael; say it."

"Marry me, Rosalia. I love you." His hand found the fullness of her breast and twisted. She cried out and tore free.

He reached for her again. Her hand flashed and her palm cracked across his cheek. "You beast! Don't soil me with your touch!"

He struck her, and the blow hurled her to the ground. She propped herself up on one elbow and a trickle of blood ran from the corner of her mouth. He was trembling violently and when she screamed, her cry was a spur. His fingers locked in her hair, and he slashed at her shoulders with the birch wand again and again. When she writhed to escape he flipped up her skirt and struck at bare thighs. His passion flamed higher as the birch wand cut red lines across her brown skin. He whipped frenziedly until dammed-up desire surged free, its spurts of emotion draining him of strength.

He stopped, panting, his senses swimming. There was a sticky emptiness within him, and he looked down upon the whimpering girl and knew a terrible guilt. He threw away the birch wand, slung his shotgun across his shoulder and stumbled away blindly.

Rosalia clawed at the black earth. "Ayee! Aaaah! Holy Queen, Mother of Mercy, save me! Aaaahhh! The pain, Holy Mother. Dear Holy Mother . . . the pain!"

It was dark before Rosalia found the strength to climb to her feet.

She limped to the high-wheeled cart and fell into it. Her command to the mule was a whimper. The animal strained against its collar, and the cart rocked along the uneven track. Rosalia lay on its floor, grateful for the coming darkness that would cloak her humiliation.

The mule trotted briskly, lured by the straw-filled trough in the stable. But with no hands on the reins the high cartwheels jolted over rocks and bumped down into potholes, making Rosalia cry out. When the mule reached home, it came to a standstill with its head hanging patiently. Rosalia climbed out. She was a living torch. Only vaguely aware of what she was doing, she opened the door and stared unseeingly around the living room. She stumbled toward the narrow stairway leading to her room.

She was almost there when her mother screamed.

Rosalia's legs suddenly failed her. She fell, her hands partly broke her fall and her cheek split against the lower stair. Through a gray mist she sensed her parents stooping over her, their voices persistent.

"Who did it?" thundered her father. "Who?" Through a mist his red face bleared down at her. A great vein on his temple throbbed violently.

"The shame of it," wailed her mother. "Aaaah! The shame of it!"

Her father shook her furiously. "Tell me his name, you stubborn bitch. Tell me his name or I'll fetch the Civil Guard."

"Answer your father, child," pleaded her mother. "Merciful Holy Mother, make her tell her father!"

Rosalia's lips were shriveled by the fire that consumed her. "Ledesma," she whispered.

Her father understood instantly. "Rafael! That son of a great whore!" He strode across the room and tore down his jacket.

"Watch your tongue, foul mouth," screamed his wife. She stooped over her daughter. "Don't cry, dear one. Mother will comfort you."

Baudillo Ledesma sat in his favorite armchair reading *La Vanguardia*. When the doorbell rang, he looked at his wife over the top of his newspaper and raised his black eyebrows.

Without looking up from her crocheting, Cornelia said evenly, "It's nobody I'm expecting."

Carmen was setting the table. "Shall I go to the door, Señora?"

"Leave it to Maria."

Baudillo turned to another page and listened to the murmur of voices at the front door.

Presently Maria entered. "It's the Pradas," she announced.

"They want to see me?" Baudillo's eyebrows arched high.

"They ask for you *and* the Señora."

Baudillo looked at his wife. She crocheted placidly. "What do they want, Maria?"

"They say it's a very private matter, Señora."

Baudillo dropped his newspaper and got to his feet slowly. He was not tall, but he looked big. He had an ugly, bulldog face and thick, sensual lips. But honesty and kindness were in his eyes. "Show them into the waiting room."

"What's this about, Cornelia?" he asked when Maria had gone.

His wife carefully placed her crocheting on one side. "It's probably about money. Did they pay last year's rent?"

He scowled. "Nor the year before. They're lazy. They neglect the vineyards and plead poverty when the crop is bad. Come. Let's see what they want."

Marcel and Isabel Prada flanked their daughter. Marcel was ungainly and moved clumsily. The gray stubble on his face emphasized its redness. He liked wine too much and work not enough. His drab and mousy wife was thought a fool to have married him.

Rosalia stood unnaturally stiff. Her face was white, her lips colorless and her eyes dark-rimmed.

Baudillo Ledesma frowned. *"Que hay?"*

"Shut the door," ordered Marcel Prada. Then, after a long pause, he dropped his eyes from Baudillo's indignant glare and whined: *"Por favor."*

Baudillo gestured and Cornelia closed the door.

"Now!" breathed Baudillo. "What's this about?"

"Turn around, child," Marcel Prada told his daughter.

Rosalia turned stiffly and her father removed the black shawl from her shoulders.

After long seconds of shocked silence, Baudillo Ledesma asked: "Who did it?"

"Your son Rafael!"

Marcel Prada backed nervously when Baudillo's face blackened with anger.

Cornelia Ledesma interjected quietly: "Have you sent for the doctor?" Her face was pale and seemed to have shrunk.

"We thought . . ." began Isabel Prada, and broke off.

"We think it's better for *you* to decide what shall be done," said Marcel bluntly and then stared hard at the floor.

Cornelia crossed to the door and opened it: "Maria. Send Carmen for the doctor. It's urgent. Then bring a bowl of hot water, gauze and cotton wool."

Baudillo said disbelievingly: "My son did *this!*"

"Rosalia should know!"

Cornelia led Rosalia across to a settee. "Lie face down, my dear," she soothed.

"I should denounce him to the Civil Guard," said Marcel Prada, staring intently at the floor. "But when Rosalia said it was Rafael . . . !"

Baudillo's voice was toneless. "Do you wish me to send for the Civil Guard?"

Marcel was startled. "I don't unless *you* want it. This is a bad thing. It's better there's no talk about it."

Maria knocked. Cornelia opened the door, took the bowl of hot water and shut the door again. She went back to Rosalia. "Help me, Isabel," she said crossly. "You shouldn't have waited. The wounds must be cleansed."

"You are known to be a just man, Baudillo," said Marcel. "I *know* you'll do what is . . . right." He looked up then and stared boldly at Baudillo.

Baudillo's broad shoulders braced themselves to accept responsibility for his son's act. "If Rafael did this terrible thing he will pay."

Rosalia whimpered.

"There, there, child!" soothed Cornelia. Her delicate hands moved gently.

"Justice is not simply an eye for an eye," said Marcel Prada and studied the floor again. "Innocence has suffered and there should be atonement." He glanced up quickly to make sure his point had gone home. "This is a shameful affair, Baudillo. We will keep it a secret between us."

Baudillo said bleakly. "This is a deed that hurts all my family."

"Doctor Aldo is discreet. He will not talk."

"He can be trusted," agreed Baudillo.

"But my daughter has suffered grievously . . ."

"We will reach agreement, Marcel."

"My daughter is scarred. Who will want her now?"

"My son will marry her."

"We understand each other well enough, Baudillo."

Rafael did not come home for dinner. His parents sat up until the early hours of the morning before he arrived. He had lost his gun, his face was streaked with earth and his hair was moist. There was a wild glitter in his eyes.

Baudillo stalked across to him, jaw jutting and hands clenched into hard fists. "Marcel Prada was here with his daughter!"

Cornelia sat erect, her delicate hands clasped in her lap, her set face concealing her misery.

The skin was stretched so tightly over Rafael's high forehead it seemed it would split. His eyes were defiant, and he sneered. "What did they ask . . . money?"

"You admit you did this shocking thing?"

"I would do it again!"

"How can you justify your deed, shameless one!" Baudillo's forefinger stabbed accusingly.

"Is our family name to be insulted?"

Baudillo took a slow breath. "Whatever your provocation, you have behaved like a . . . a monster!"

"She's a slut, that one. She threw herself at me. I could have taken her if I had wanted. But she's cunning. She seeks to get herself with child to make a good match. But she's scum. So is the rest of her family. I rejected her. Then such a storm. Such language. It was terrible to hear such words on a girl's lips."

"Rosalia tells a different tale."

Rafael shrugged his shoulders. "What do you expect?"

"If she lies, it changes nothing! Your deed was monstrous. I thought I had reared a son. But I have nourished a wild beast."

Rafael bit his lip. His eyes glittered.

"I want my sons to be men . . . not animals!" blazed Baudillo. "What you have done is inhuman . . . the work of a devil!"

"I am not a child," Rafael said fiercely. "I will not suffer insults from common sluts."

"No insult can excuse your shocking brutality. Tomorrow you will call and express your regret . . ."

"Never!"

"You will do as I say. You will learn to be ashamed." Baudillo's stubby forefinger jabbed emphasis.

Rafael's lips became a thin line.

"When you have apologized, you will ask for Rosalia's hand . . ."

"No, Father. I will *never* apologize and I will *never* marry a common slut."

Baudillo's face reddened. He said slowly:. "Listen carefully. Your mother and I have made many excuses for you. But this disgrace you have brought upon us we cannot forgive if you refuse to admit your wickedness. That's all for now. Go to bed and think about it. Tomorrow we will talk again."

Rafael sneered. "And what of you, Mother? Do you too want me to humble myself to scum?"

Cornelia said quietly: "You are my son, Rafael. I love you. But I agree entirely with your father."

Rafael's eyes were bitter. "*This* is the family I protect from insults!" He laughed scornfully. "Am I to be shamed by my parents' lack of pride?"

His father trembled. "I warn you. Be careful of your tongue."

Rafael stared at him defiantly and then spun on his heel and strode away. He ran upstairs and slammed his bedroom door, awakening the servants.

Rafael did not sleep. He emptied his desk and bundled together his personal papers, school certificates, bank accounts, a hunting license and other documents. He packed his bag, washed, shaved carefully and changed into his cadet's uniform. As dawn was breaking, he slipped silently out of the house.

He woke up the taxi driver and arrived at Figueras in time to catch the milk train to Barcelona. He left no farewell note for his parents.

3

Emil Znadlon Serra awoke in strange surroundings, and it was some seconds before he remembered he had booked into a *mueble* the night before.

He yawned, turned on his back and stretched. The large ceiling mirror reflected him and the girl lying beside him, and for a wild moment he thought he was looking down upon himself.

His watch showed it was half-past eight. This was early for Madrid, but he had an appointment at eleven. He sat up, scratched his fleshy chest and studied the girl curiously. She was a Canary Islander with swarthy skin and bee-stung lips. She slept soundly, her cheek flattened by the pillow which bore a wet saliva stain under her mouth. Her perfume was body-heated and potent.

He eased out of bed, shivered in the morning freshness and padded to the bathroom. He turned on the shower and eyed himself in the mirror with distaste while he waited for the water to run hot. He was overfleshed and paunchy, his ankles swollen from too much alcohol, his jowls fleshy. Only thirty-five years of age and already dissipated! He cupped his breasts, wrinkling his nose in disgust at his flabby flesh. He would have to do something about it, he decided, and knew he would do nothing.

He showered as hot as he could bear it, sluicing himself clean of the smell of drink, sweat, sex and cigar smoke. When he dried himself the mirror reflected the red-splashed shrapnel scar between his shoulder blades, and for a moment he was back in Vienna amidst the whistling of shells, the thunder of artillery and the crumbling state-built blocks of working-class apartments.

The girl slept soundly and while he dressed he tried to recall her name. Most of the previous evening was shrouded in alcoholic mist. He gripped the girl's shoulder and shook her gently. She awoke reluctantly, but when she saw he was dressed, she leaped out of bed. "You're *not* going!"

"I must."

The morning air goose-pimpled her flesh and her dark-skinned breasts jutted. "You should have awakened me," she protested.

"It doesn't matter."

"I don't want you to be *disappointed,* darling." She took his hand and rubbed it against herself intimately. "Don't you want to stay?"

"Very much. But I must go."

"I'll make you change your mind." She caressed him shamelessly, but he chuckled and pushed her away.

"You've been a good girl," he said.

"I've made you happy?" she asked anxiously.

He took out his wallet. "You've made me *very* happy." Her eyes glistened as he peeled off notes from his wad. It was much more than she had hoped for.

"Thank you, darling. Oh *thank* you!" she whispered as with unnecessary delicacy he dropped the notes onto the bedside table. She pressed against him. "Are you *sure* you have to go?"

"There'll be other times. Jump back into bed and rest." He picked up the telephone: "Room Twenty-seven waiting to leave."

When the knock came at the door he slipped outside and followed the steward to the elevator and down to the ground floor. In these

Spanish houses of assignation, every precaution was taken so no guest could be embarrassed by encountering another. All the background facilities and comforts of lovemaking were provided. Yet adultery was socially condemned more passionately in Spain than in most other European countries.

"Shall I ring for a taxi, Señor?"

"Please." He gave the man a generous tip and the steward led him to a side door when the taxi arrived in the private courtyard.

He went to a barber's shop where a bootblack shined his shoes while he was shaved. He closed his eyes and listened to the talk around him. The Socialist Trade Union and the Anarchist-Syndicalist Trade Union were in violent political disagreement. Last night they had turned out into the streets in force. There had been bloody skirmishes near the Plaza del Sol: three men killed, five men and two women in the hospital, seriously injured.

Emil Serra stepped out into the gray, April street and a cold gust of wind swirled up the dust. He hurried on to the Café del Sol, ordered coffee and croissants and asked for the morning newspaper. But he was smoking and drumming his fingertips impatiently long before the man he awaited arrived.

Emil Serra did little talking. He nodded his head from time to time while the other man spoke. Presently, Serra drew an envelope from his pocket. The man tucked it away without opening it and left.

Serra's next stop was at a newly built office block. He labored up the stairs to the first floor and entered the offices of the Polish Consulate General. A dark-eyed Spanish youth at the reception desk nodded bleakly. Serra walked along a corridor and unlocked the office reserved for his infrequent visits. He locked it behind him, took paper from his desk drawer and fed it into the typewriter. He balanced his cigar on the edge of an ashtray, thought for a few moments and then began typing. He paused frequently to recall precise details and facts.

He wrote:

April 1936

Spain's political stability has decreased greatly. Even here in the capital there is serious unrest. The supporters of the People's Front Government quarrel violently among themselves. Their opponents use every means to foment riots and disorder. Street shootings take place daily.

A few days ago, a bomb was found in the house of the Socialist minister, Largo Caballero. It is believed it was planted by the Falangists as a protest against their leader José Antonio being arrested without trial.

The government has sent General Goded to Majorca and General Franco to the Canary Islands where they will be less dangerous.

I have learned that a military group, including General Mola and General Sanjurjo, is preparing to overthrow the government. The rising is to take place simultaneously all over Spain; in Spanish Morocco, the Canary Islands and Majorca. Local groups of rebels and army officers will seize public buildings and communication centers, and General Sanjurjo will fly in from Lisbon as soon as the balloon goes up. It's scheduled for the end of April.

Throughout the country the peasants are confiscating enormous estates owned by rich absentee landlords and dividing them up among themselves into small farms. This is illegal without government authorization. But since agrarian reform is government policy, the government hastily authorizes what the peasants have done. But not before bloody clashes have taken place between the peasants and the Civil Guard.

General Sanjurjo has been assured of military aid from Germany if he revolts. You can judge for yourself how that might affect Germany's pressure on Poland!

I *will* know when the rising will take place. You will receive my prearranged coded cable.

Emil Znadlon Serra read through the report and placed it in a thick envelope. He sealed the envelope with the oddly designed charm he carried on his watch-chain. It was of metal, hexagonal in shape, and bearing the letters SRR curiously entwined.

He rolled more paper into the typewriter, wrote a box number at the top and addressed it to: The Mayor, Escoleras, Costa Brava.

DEAR SIR,
My name is Emil Znadlon Serra, of Polish nationality. I am of Spanish extraction, my forebears having fled the Inquisition. I wish to trace my Spanish ancestry and I have learned the name Serra is known in your village. If this is so, I shall be grateful if you can tell me if this family is related to José Serra Organata, known to be resident in Madrid in 1854.

Thanking you in anticipation of your kind reply,

Emil Serra signed the letter and sealed it. Then he walked along the corridor to the private office of the consular general. He knocked and a testy voice answered.

Serra closed the door behind him and the consular general eyed him without enthusiasm.

Serra pushed the sealed envelope across the desk. "The diplomatic bag."

Padowsky held the letter with his fingertips as though it might soil him. It rankled that he was kept in ignorance of Serra's work. It implied he couldn't be trusted with information possessed by a man who was nominally a consulate clerk. He said gruffly: "I'll see it goes."

"There's this too," added Serra. He pushed a petty-cash chit across the desk. Padowsky glared at it. He had his own lavish expense account, but he was obliged to show *how* he spent the money, whereas Serra was privileged to spend freely. Nearly always, as on this occasion, the amount requisitioned was considerable.

Padowsky sighed and scribbled a memo to the accountant. As he gave it to Serra, he asked cuttingly: "Are you through for the day?"

Serra smiled. He took a mild delight in annoying Padowsky. "That's right. In a week's time I'll be ready for another half an hour's typing."

Padowsky glowered. "I suppose they know back home what they're doing," he grumbled in a voice that doubted it.

"They have to take care of an important man like me," Serra assured him.

The funeral cortege wound slowly up the hill to the cemetery. Although the official mourners were few, it was a long procession. The Falangists had turned out in force to demonstrate their resentment of the Republican government, and they marched with Germanic precision behind the bier, holding themselves stiffly and shouting slogans.

The man they honored was unknown to most of them. He had died quickly: an officer of the Civil Guard who had drawn his revolver as President Azaña had passed. Some swore he was a good and honest officer preparing to give his life to save his president. Others maintained he had aimed carefully at President Azaña and would have surely killed him if sharp-eyed, loyal Assault Guards had not first shot him dead.

Emil Serra sat beside the driver of a car that crawled along behind the procession. He inhaled his cigar. The driver was a reporter. "You're sure I'll get a story?" he doubted. "It's pretty quiet so far."

"It'll happen at the cemetery gates." Serra glanced at the crowded sidewalks. "Got your camera ready?"

"Right here." The reporter tapped the glove compartment.

"If you're not scared, we'll do better up front."

The reporter nodded, rammed his foot down on the accelerator and overtook the procession. He roared up to the cemetery gates, braked violently, slewed around and switched off his engine. They waited for the funeral cortege to reach them.

It happened as Serra predicted. Left-wing observers were strategically posted and signaling information. At the precise moment the last of the mourners had entered the cemetery gates, there was a great howl of fury and a body of young Socialists flooded out from a side street and hurled themselves upon the Falangists.

Serra watched the battle with interest while the reporter aimed his camera. Bystanders fled and the streets emptied; the combatants punched, threw rocks, wielded clubs and flourished knives.

A youth stumbled across to the car, his eyes glazed and his cheek slashed from cheekbone to jaw. The edges of the wound gaped, his molars glinting like white rocks in a red sea. He fell across the hood of the car and blood spattered on it.

The Falangists scattered and took refuge inside the cemetery as shots rang out. Not far away two youths sniped at each other from behind wall buttresses.

"That would make a fine picture," said the reporter. His white face shone with sweat.

"Go get it!"

"Are you crazy? They're too far apart to frame. I'd have to be looking over their shoulders."

"Give me the camera," said Emil Serra. He circled around the youth sprawled across the car and strolled to a vantage point to take the photographs. Bullets whined as they ricocheted.

"Come back!" the reporter shouted. "You'll be killed!" He ducked low as a deflected bullet screamed overhead.

Emil Serra leisurely focused the camera and took a number of photographs before he returned to the car. "I've used all the roll," he said.

In the distance sirens wailed as police cars sped to quell the rioting.

"Let's get out of here," panted the reporter.

Emil Serra dragged the injured youth to the pavement, set him down, wadded his handkerchief and pressed it over the wound. Ash from Serra's cigar fell on the youth's blood-soaked jacket. From inside the cemetery more shots rang out and the reporter gestured urgently. "Hurry. The police will call an ambulance for the boy."

The car leaped forward before Serra could close the door. It didn't stop until they were a good distance from the cemetery. The puddle of blood on the hood had been whipped up by the wind and sprayed over the windshield. The reporter grimaced as he wiped it clean with his handkerchief.

"Did I put you onto a hot story, or didn't I?" asked Serra with satisfaction.

"It was *hot!*" confirmed the reporter as he started up the car. He turned right at the next block. "But you're crazy, man. You could have been killed!"

"There was a certain . . . *thrill* . . . which was rewarding." Serra's eyes glittered with amusement.

"Who tipped you off?"

"I have friends in the UGT and the CNT." Serra gestured with his cigar. "I pay handsomely for information." He drew deeply on his cigar and said bluntly. "You, too, are a good friend and a member of the Catholic Political Party. I will pay handsomely for anything you tell me about Gil Robles and his plans."

"I cannot be a traitor to my party!"

"I know that. Anything you tell me is in confidence."

"You'll never tell our political enemies anything you learn from me?"

"I always keep my word."

They were now driving along the Grand Via. "The Catholic Political Party is not happy with Gil Robles's leadership," said the reporter. "Our members talk of uniting with the Falangists."

"I have heard rumors. Do you think it will happen?"

"Our youth leader is in favor and he's got a big following."

"What's the fellow's name?"

"Ramon Serrana Suñer."

"He is a friend of José Antonio, isn't he?"

The reporter smiled smugly. "Also he is brother-in-law to General Franco."

Emil Serra pushed open the wicket gate set in the courtyard door. He crossed the patio to a marble staircase and went up one flight to where a polished brass plate announced:

DOCTOR BOLENSKI

A maid showed him into the waiting room. "Have you an appointment, Señor?"

He glanced at his wristwatch. "I'm dead on time."

"I'll announce you, Señor."

"How are you, Emil?" greeted Doctor Bolenski warmly.

They talked for a while in Polish until the doctor said: "I suppose we'd better get down to business." He crossed to the filing cabinet and from a large envelope drew out two X-ray plates which he placed side by side in a frame. He switched on a light behind them. Serra's vertebra from the base of his neck down to between his shoulder blades showed clearly. Both plates also showed the sharp splinter of shell-shrapnel lodged in the spinal cartilage.

Serra inspected the left-hand plate taken six months earlier and compared it with the more recent plate. "What's the verdict?"

"What do *you* think?" countered the doctor.

"It's moved, hasn't it?"

The doctor nodded. "Very slightly."

"But . . . it's moved the wrong way."

"I'm afraid so."

Serra ran his fleshy fingers through his sandy hair. "How long does it give me?"

"You mustn't be pessimistic. I once had a patient who broke off the tip of a needle in her right hand. During the years that followed, she felt pricking sensations in all parts of her body. Finally, it worked its way out through the skin on the back of her hand. Her *left* hand! It had traveled all around her body."

"But in my case it hasn't got so far to travel!"

"It's moved imperceptibly toward the spinal cord," admitted the doctor reluctantly. "It might move away again."

"But you don't think it will?"

"There's always hope, Emil."

"When shall I call for another checkup?"

"Say . . . two months."

"I haven't got much longer then? Last time it was six months."

"It's a precaution."

"And in two months' time? If it's much closer?"

"I can save you if I operate now."

"With the certainty I'll be paralyzed for life?"

"That's the risk," Doctor Bolenski stroked his beard sadly.

"I'd sooner have the lights go out than lie around helpless."

"We'll face that bridge when we get to it, Emil."

"I'm out of stimulants."

Doctor Bolenski was astonished. "So soon!"

"I've been a busy man."

The doctor walked to his desk and frowned down at it. Then he shrugged his shoulders and reached for his prescription pad. "I'm not happy about this, Emil. These tablets are intended to be used . . . with discretion."

Emil Serra laughed mirthlessly. "Whose discretion? Yours? Or mine?"

"They're chemical bombs. They speed up human metabolism and draw deeply on the body's reserves of strength."

"Is that bad?"

"You'll burn yourself up. Your body's like an overcoat. Look after it and it will last for years. Give it hard wear and in no time, you need another. At the rate you're swallowing these pills you're taking years off your life."

"Should that worry *me?* Spain is the most wonderful country in the world for a bachelor with money."

Doctor Bolenski flushed uncomfortably. "Go easy on them, Emil." He signed the prescription.

"I'm privileged," said Serra, tucking away the prescription. "Knowing I have only a few months gives me complete freedom. I fear no one nor anything. I can be truly unbiased, Bolenski. I can even sympathize with those crazy Anarchists, flaunting their red and black scarves and demanding liberty. Because I have attained liberty. I am free as few men are ever free. I obey no man and no government. I can live as Anarchists yearn to live: without fear, tyranny or shame."

"It's hard to believe any good of them when you hear their bombs exploding around the city."

"That's the trouble with Anarchists, Bolenski. They're anarchistic! Blowing up the headquarters of the Falangists was for some Anarchists a sanctified deed."

"They're mad. Mad! The city is full of fanatics."

"Idealists always threaten peace, Bolenski. They're so convinced their view is correct they're intolerant of all others. The Anarchist's beautiful ideal of equal rights for all men without distinction of sex, race or class is destroyed by his willingness to kill me if I do not share his point of view."

VARIETY HALL was spelled out in dimly glowing electric light bulbs across the front of the theater. In the vestibule were glossy photographs of showgirls and life-size cardboard cutouts of the stars.

Puffing clouds of blue smoke from his Havana, Emil Serra placed a currency note on the ticket office sill. "Box number one," he said.

The ticket vendor winked conspiratorially when he gave him the ticket.

Serra strode through the vestibule and a tired-eyed flower-seller sprang to life. "This way, Señor," she said eagerly. She parted drab velvet drapes and led him up worn carpeted stairs to the upper balcony.

Box numbers one and twelve differed from the other boxes. They both had curtained-off recesses.

The flower-seller took Serra's coat and seated him. Then she went into the curtained recess and checked that the bidet was clean and the couch sheet had been changed. She placed a pedestal ashtray beside Serra's chair. "What do you fancy, tonight, Señor?"

Serra took a wad of notes from his pocket and fanned them out like cards. He played them. "That's for you. This is for a bouquet of flowers. A large one. This for a couple of bottles of champagne. Now. Get one of the girls up here."

"One of the stars, Señor?"

"All right."

"Juana?"

"I don't mind."

"At your service, Señor."

The flower-seller hurried away. Serra leaned over the balustrade and looked down on the audience. The stall seats had broad armrests to hold glasses. It was an intermission and waiters bustled busily along the rows, serving drinks. The theater was old and its once gaudy trappings were drab and faded. The audience was working-class, and the sprinkling of women present were nearly all middle-aged, accompanying their husbands.

The flower-seller returned with champagne in an ice bucket, and Juana arrived immediately afterward. She was a tall, dark, sturdy girl, wearing a flamenco dress with a long, trailing skirt. Her eyelids were painted vivid blue, her cheeks rouged and her mouth coated with flaking lipstick. Her oily black hair flowed down her back to her waist. Her slumberous eyes were her best feature.

"*Ola, guapa!*" he greeted.

"Hello, handsome." She stooped, pressed her cheek against his, and ruffled his hair. She kicked her long, trailing skirt to one side, sat beside him and held his hand.

The flower-seller poured champagne. Juana toasted him. "To good times!"

He drained his glass. "You're more beautiful every time I see you, Juana."

"Anything else, Señor?" asked the flower-seller.

"I'll ring if I need you."

When she closed the door he took a glass vial from his pocket and shook out a large, ash-colored lozenge. Juana watched disapprovingly as he dropped it into his glass, poured more champagne and stirred it around with his finger. The lozenge turned soggy.

"Do you *have* to take that?" she asked.

"Do you object, my love?"

"It worries me."

"Why?"

"It makes you go on all night. It's not natural . . . for a man."

"But great fun!" He chuckled.

"It's dangerously exhausting!"

"A wonderful way to die," he said solemnly.

"I want you around to take care of my old age."

He prodded the lozenge with his forefinger. It was soft enough and he drank it down.

"Does it taste awful?"

"It's like swallowing an oyster."

"Why do you abuse your body?"

"No, my love. *You*'ll do that."

"Are you ready now?"

He nodded.

She glanced toward the curtained recess.

"No," he said. "Out here."

"Like the last time?" She touched him.

"Not your hand."

She pushed her chair back.

"Not that way."

Her eyebrows arched.

"Sit on my lap."

She stared in disbelief. "Out here?"

"That's right."

"But everyone will see!"

He chuckled. "A new experience."

She was distraught. "I couldn't. I *couldn't!*"

"Don't worry, darling. Any of the other girls will."

"None of them will."

"You're wrong. I'll pay double. No . . . treble!"

"Don't you care what you spend?"

"Not a bit. What about it, Juana?"

"I hate you."

"I'll get one of the other girls. Don't upset yourself."

"You're so smug!"

"I'll be generous. I'll pay four times the usual."

"You're set on this?"

"Determined!"

"All right!" she said savagely. She sat on his lap with her back toward him, rested one arm on the balustrade and raised her skirt with the hand out of sight of the audience.

He ran the tips of his fingers down her neck, gathered up her long hair and wrapped it around her throat.

"People are looking," she protested.

"Of course. They can see you're sitting on my lap and are curious."

"They're sniggering."

"You're taking a long time."

"It's awkward. Why don't you help?"

He stubbed out his Havana in the ashtray.

A little later the orchestra filed in and the footlights were turned on. The auditorium lights were never switched off, and more light was thrown on the balcony boxes.

"You're a swine to make me do this."

He chuckled. "Of course."

The stage curtains swept back and a voluptuous girl wearing a blond wig smilingly received the applause that greeted her. Behind her stood a row of naked showgirls wearing headdresses of gaily colored ostrich plumes and high-heeled silver shoes. The nipples of their breasts were painted crimson, and stardust was sprinkled on their pubic hairs.

The blond girl's crimson, sequin-covered frock fitted her like a sheath from armpits to knees where it flared out in a froth of ruffles. Her tight bodice pushed her breasts high, and its deep cleavage all but exposed them. Her off-key voice was strident and unmelodious as she sang, but her ribald words brought gusts of laughter from the audience.

"How long before you are on, Juana?"

"Soon."

"Hurry then. Show some life!"

"They're looking at us and not at the stage," she wailed.

"What do you expect?"

"If I move they'll *know!*"

"Nobody thinks you're up here to drink champagne."

"You want to shame me publicly?"

"You stand on the stage and flaunt your sex. Why feel shame now?"

"*This* is different! I've never felt so ashamed."

"Do you want the money or don't you?"

"Yes, damn you."

"Then . . . be lively."

She cupped her cheeks in her hands to screen her flushed face from the upturned eyes.

"There! You see, Juana. You can do it when you want!"

There were guffaws and loud comments from below when Juana returned to her chair.

Serra said conversationally. "Talk to the other girls, Juana. I want to take three or four home with me tonight."

She eyed him warily. "Anything . . . *special?*"

He smiled. "I want to watch them . . . do things."

"How about me?"

"You'll come too, of course."

"Tell *me*. What will we have to do?"

"*You* won't do anything. *You'll* be my guest."

She scowled.

"Don't be jealous, darling. I like variety." He held his glass to her lips to drink. "How about that sexy military character who's always running around with the girls?"

"That colonel from the Montana Barracks?"

"That's the fellow."

"He's going steady with Alicia. He waits for her every night. He wants to set her up in an apartment."

"Bring them along tonight."

"They might not want to come."

"They will if you tell the colonel we're going to have an orgy!"

There was a knock on the door and the flower-seller called agitatedly: "Hurry, Juana. Hurry. You're on."

Juana hurried away.

Emil Serra had time to pour another glass of champagne and light a cigar before the curtains swept back to show Juana on stage. She was poised in the classical flamenco stance, arched wrists and curved fingers holding *castañuelas,* arms reaching high, head thrown back and spine arched. Juana took her dancing seriously and was usually greeted by a dramatic silence which the orchestra shattered with a flamenco knife chord. But tonight Juana was greeted with tumultuous applause.

Juana remained artistically poised, swaying slightly as she strained to maintain her balance.

The applause continued.

The orchestra conductor signaled the first clarinet notes of *Falla,* but the instrument was drowned by increasing applause and he rapped his baton for silence.

The applause was loud and prolonged, until Juana couldn't keep her balance. She acknowledged the applause with a low curtsy.

Her audience stood, clapped and cheered.

Juana curtsied again. Her lips smiled but there was fury in her eyes as she glanced up toward the balcony box where Serra was sitting.

He smiled down serenely at all the upturned eyes and smiling faces.

4

July 14, 1936

Baudillo Ledesma's private office was behind his residence and adjoining the warehouse where the family wine was stored in great barrels. The walls were of natural rock and very thick. The interior was cool in summer and warm in winter.

Baudillo Ledesma sat at his desk. He had closed the window shutters so the hot July sun would not pour into his office, and he worked by electric light.

Most of the furniture had been in the family for more than two hundred years. The grandfather clock with its heavy brass weights ticked ponderously. The glass-fronted bookcases contained volumes with hand-tooled leather covers, and around the walls hung India-ink maps of the many Ledesma farms and estates. The massive typewriter was still functioning after forty years of service.

From this office Baudillo Ledesma controlled his family's affairs and kept records of all that happened to the family's property and employees. His files recorded his livestock and their breeding, showed how many acres of wheat were sown on each of his farms and listed the annual crop prices for the last twenty years.

It was here that tenant farmers came to discuss their problems with Baudillo or to ask for his help. It was rare they came to pay their rent.

The first caller was Marcel Prada. He hadn't shaved for days and oozed the musty smell of long-slept-in blankets.

Baudillo reached for a cigar and offered one to his visitor. He struck a match and when both cigars were alight he asked gruffly: "What is it this time?"

"I need a loan, Señor Baudillo."

Baudillo's chair legs rasped loudly as he pushed it back. He crossed to a filing cabinet, took out a folder and carried it to his desk. He opened it, ran his finger down a column of figures and read loudly: "Three loans in April. Three in May. Four in June. Two this month already." He snapped shut the folder and smoothed the cover flat as though symbolically closing it forever. "How long do you expect this to go on?"

Marcel Prada's eyes glittered. "I've got a family to keep." He paused, then added significantly. "Rosalia's a handful after what's happened. I never know what she'll do next. She's wild and headstrong. I need a loan to help me over the next few months."

Baudillo glared and without taking his eyes off Prada, opened his desk drawer and took out his checkbook. He wrote in large, sprawling handwriting, ripped out the check and flipped it across the desk contemptuously. "That's it, Prada. That's the finish. Not one peseta more. Don't come again. From now on do what you want. Tell the judge: tell the mayor: tell the Civil Guard. Tell the whole wide world. That's the lot. Do I make myself clear?"

Prada snatched up the check and folded it with eager fingers. "Don't worry, Señor Baudillo. I won't make trouble. I'll protect your interests as I would my own." He rose to his feet, anxious to reach the village bank.

"One more thing, Prada," Baudillo called and Prada turned back with his hand on the door knob.

"What's that, Señor Baudillo?"

"My vineyards. You've paid no rent for three years. If you fail again this year, I'll turn you out!"

"Have no fear, Señor Baudillo. I'll pay."

The next caller was José Pla. He and his wife worked hard, had reared a large family, were scrupulously honest, but were dogged by bad luck. The illness of three of their children required frequent visits to Barcelona, specialists' examinations, and treatment.

Pla said anxiously: "Today I was paid for the olive crop gathered in March."

He pushed across the desk a sheaf of well-thumbed papers which detailed in clumsy, penciled figures the number of baskets of olives gathered, their weight, the cost of crushing, the number of liters of oil yielded and the price they brought.

"You husband your crops skillfully," approved Baudillo. "This is an excellent yield."

"But I have a problem," confessed José Pla.

"Tell me. We're here to help one another."

More papers came from Pla's pockets. Doctors' bills, grocers' accounts, invoices for medicines and costs of farmyard repairs.

"When I pay you your share of the oil, Señor Baudillo, I will have enough left to pay these accounts. But not enough to live on until money comes in from the grapes. Therefore, I ask if I may withhold a quarter of my payment to you?"

"One quarter?" said Baudillo sternly.

Pla's eyes were worried. "One fifth then?"

Baudillo glowered. "You are unfair to me."

Pla's eyes filled with misery.

"Are we not good friends, José Pla? Keep the money and pay when you can. When does a friend need to ask for help like a beggar?"

Pla's eyes were moist. "Are you . . . are you sure, Señor Baudillo?"

"Here." Baudillo's voice was gruff. "Smoke one of these." He thrust his cigars across the desk.

The next visitor was Anton Leon, crafty wastrel, despised by the villagers. The smell of stale wine was strong on his breath as he whined: "Help me, Señor Baudillo. I have exhausted my store of alfalfa and straw."

"Order more on credit," said Baudillo curtly.

"I have tried, Señor Baudillo," Anton Leon spread his hands. "Already I owe so much they will give no more." He shook his head. "Times are bad. To work the land is ruinous."

"Why come to me? Go to your bank. Ask your friends."

"I've tried everything, Señor Baudillo. I cannot feed my livestock. The milk fails, the livestock is hungry. I cannot work the farm and soon it will fail."

Baudillo scowled. He wrote out a letter of credit and skimmed it across the desk. "Sign!"

Leon's eyes glittered craftily. "What is this, Señor Baudillo? It is not the usual receipt."

"It is a legal document. It is your solemn promise to pay back one year from today."

"But . . . should some difficulty occur and I cannot pay . . . ?"

"There must be no difficulty!"

"But Señor Baudillo . . . in life many unjust things happen."

"Then great trouble will come upon you," said Baudillo firmly. "This bill will be presented a year from today and if you do not pay before the sun sets, you will be judged bankrupt. You will be turned off my farm and your possessions will be auctioned to pay your debts."

Anton Leon was worried. "And if I do not sign?"

"Then I will not lend you the money."

"You are a hard man, Señor Baudillo."

"Do you want the loan?"

"Give me the pen."

Anton Leon scrawled his name and his lips were bitter with disgust. "You are a hard man, Señor Baudillo. A hard man!"

Baudillo rose to his feet, strode across to the filing cabinet and drew out a folder. He flung it down on his desk. "This file tells the whole story, Leon. When you and your elder brother ran the farm jointly, it was prosperous. But since he emigrated to America, everything's declined. The crops have failed, the livestock has dwindled, the farm is neglected and you're losing money."

"I've been unlucky!"

"Unlucky? You bring disaster down upon yourself. You get drunk and quarrelsome and all your good workmen have left you. In five years you haven't paid me a peseta rent while the farm goes to ruin."

"Be fair, Señor Baudillo," sniveled Leon. "You have so *much,* whereas . . . I have so little!"

"I've got so *much,* you say! Look at these index cards. These record the vineyards, olive groves and farms belonging to my family. Do you know what they bring to me, Leon? Nothing! Everybody's got troubles. If I'm very lucky, I sometimes get a little rent. Is that having so *much,* Leon?" Baudillo's stubby forefinger jabbed fiercely. "I'll give you more facts. I must pay ground rents and taxes on all these properties from my own pocket. I've two sons studying in Barcelona, two daughters and a son in Madrid and this house to support. Do you know how I do it, Leon? I look after one farm and spend every afternoon there until sundown. I supervise the crops, insure the right proportion of fertilizer is used, study the blood stock and fatten the cows to give good milk. I work very hard, Leon.

"I can be tolerant. I haven't pressed you for rent and I've made loans to help you. But your drinking, gambling and whoring I *won't* pay for from my own pocket. I'll give you a year's grace, to work hard and cut out extravagances. The next time you lift a whore's skirts, you pay with *your* money, and not mine!"

The wedding feast for Miguel and Helena was held in the plaza in the shade of the plane trees. The blacksmith had hammered iron supports into the earth and spitted lambs were roasting over beds of red-hot charcoal. While friends and relatives of the couple attended the marriage service, Hernando cooked. A long trestle table covered with a white cloth was set ready for the newlyweds, their families and the mayor. Other tables groaned under the weight of meats and fruits. A great barrel of wine, a gift from Baudillo Ledesma, was chocked up with the bung tap inserted. Two girls were cutting crusty loaves into thick slices.

Hernando had spitted the lambs, slit the flesh in a number of places and inserted pieces of pork fat under the skin. He had greased the inside of the carcasses with lard and as they rotated over the glowing charcoal, he made sure the outer skin crisped and sealed in the juices. Before each spit was an earthenware bowl filled with water and olive oil, to which he had added salt, pepper and garlic, and as the carcasses revolved he dipped a brush of leafy sage stalks into the mixture and basted the meat. The smell of roasting mingled deliciously with the aroma of sage and the heady smell of wine. When the newly married couple and guests arrived, the meat was cooked to a turn. With a lock of silvery hair falling down over his walnut-wrinkled forehead, Hernando grinned and flourished the sage brush baster in welcome.

Miguel Barras smiled shyly, embarrassed at being the center of attention and feeling uncomfortable in his new suit, collar and tie. Helena was radiant and her eyes shone with a child's happiness. Her wedding gown, adapted from the one worn by her grandmother, was of delicate lace and emphasized her slender waist.

But the nervous strain was a drain on her energy, already sapped by her unexpected indisposition. Her normally rosy cheeks were pale.

Her mother asked: "Are you sure you're fit for the journey, my dear?"

"Yes, Mother. Don't worry."

"You wouldn't like to lie down?"

"I can't, Mother. After all, it is *my* wedding."

"Over here, everybody!" roared Paco Barras, his face shining with parental pride. "Where's the happy couple? They must take the place of honor."

Self-consciously, Miguel and Helena sat at the head of the long table. Doctor Aldo, the mayor and his wife, Don Carlos the priest, Baudillo and Cornelia Ledesma, the captain of the Civil Guard and others took their places while Hernando carved great steaming slices of meat that flowed with hot juices. Relays of helpers carried the loaded plates to the tables and bowls of *all-i-oli* were passed around. Soon all who were seated were eating and the other guests lined up behind Hernando with slices of bread. The *porrón* circulated, wine gurgled and hot, dripping cuts of meat were sandwiched.

Later came the toasts to the bride and bridegroom, to their parents and finally to Hernando the cook. Fruit and nuts were served. Willing volunteers made coffee, and liqueurs were poured.

Teresa and her sister, Pepita, sat on the low parapet wall that surrounded the plaza. Teresa had parted from the other girls when she saw Anselmo Ledesma watching her. Presently he strolled over, wiping his hands on a napkin. Teresa told Pepita: "Bring two coffees."

"Coffee isn't made yet."

"It doesn't matter. Line up for it."

"What's the hurry?"

"Be a good girl."

"You want to get rid of me?" accused Pepita.

"You know that green headscarf I bought last week? You liked it. You can have it if you're a good girl."

"All right," said Pepita. She walked away grinning at Anselmo with childish impudence as he sat beside Teresa.

"It's a wonderful day," he said.

"Helena looks radiant," sighed Teresa.

"She's a beautiful bride."

"Are you staying long, Anselmo?"

"I must return tonight. It's the middle of exams."

"You came especially . . . for Miguel's wedding?"

"A friend only marries once."

"You are not so friendly with Miguel, are you, Anselmo?" Her blue eyes stared into his innocently.

He flushed and smoothed down his black hair. "But Miguel's your brother."

She was content. "It's wonderful to have you here."

"After my exams I'll spend the summer here."

"We'll see a lot of each other then, Anselmo?"

"That's what I want."

"It's what I want too."

They looked into each other's eyes for a long time.

Anselmo glanced away first, abruptly self-conscious. "The roast lamb was marvelous!"

"Beautifully cooked," she agreed solemnly.

There was a long silence.

He gulped. "The *all-i-oli* was also good."

"Yes, Anselmo."

He looked down at the ground and scuffed it with his heels. "I'm only a student now."

"Yes?"

"When I'm qualified I'll be able to decide things for myself."

"Of course, Anselmo."

"At present I depend on Father. But soon, when I can stand upon my own feet . . ."

"Yes, Anselmo?"

"You're still young, Teresa."

"Getting on for seventeen. That's not so young."

"I'm not twenty-one."

"You will be in a few months."

Teresa's brother, Isidro, strolled over to join them, his uniform tunic unbuttoned and his hair cropped short. He cheerfully ignored Teresa's angry glare. "You return to Barcelona tonight, Anselmo?"

"I'll catch the last train out."

"Me too. I only have twenty-four hours leave."

Isidro had been conscripted at seventeen and now had a year's service behind him.

"How do you like army life?"

Isidro pulled a face.

"I'm dreading it," confessed Anselmo. "I put off the evil day with postponements for my studies."

"The food's the worst of all," said Isidro. "Not enough of it and what there is turns your stomach."

Teresa sighed because Pepita was returning with two cups of coffee. Now she and Anselmo would not have another chance to talk alone. "Come to dinner tonight, Anselmo," she invited on the spur of the moment. She made a joke of it. "Mother will miss Miguel."

On the far side of the plaza Rosalia was with three friends. Benito Vigon hovered beside them, sweating in a thick serge suit. His boots shone and he had smeared grease on his wiry black hair in a futile effort to sleek it flat. Now it stood up in spikes. The smell of hair oil and damp earth floated around him in an invisible cloud.

The girls talked animatedly, giggling and pointedly ignoring him. Rosalia was the most vivacious.

"Rosalia," ventured Vigon.

She didn't hear him.

"Rosalia," he repeated nervously.

The girls talked on.

"Rosalia," he said loudly.

The girls stopped talking abruptly and looked at him with startled eyes.

He flushed and said doggedly: "I want to ask you something, Rosalia." His jacket was tight under the armpits and constricted his chest.

"What about?"

"It's . . . personal."

"I have no secrets from my friends."

"I'd rather . . . talk to you alone."

"I don't know when I'll be alone, Benito."

The girls giggled.

He flushed. "Will you go walking with me next Sunday, Rosalia?"

She dismissed his request instantly. "Next Sunday I go to visit my aunt."

"The Sunday after?" he persisted.

"That's when Aunt visits us."

"The next Sunday?" he asked desperately.

She pretended to think. "Perhaps."

"Not perhaps, Rosalia. Say yes or no."

"I can't know what I'll be doing in three weeks."

"Say yes, and go walking with me."

"But if I say yes and then can't?"

His eyes were hurt. "That's happened many times, Rosalia. Each time I waited hours. Please don't fail me again." There was such touching sincerity in his voice that now the girls didn't giggle.

Rosalia said slowly: "All right. The third Sunday from now. I'll meet you here."

His eyes shone. "Is five o'clock all right?"

"Be on time, Benito. I won't wait a minute." Then Rosalia turned back to her friends.

El Hombre Largo, the town's odd-job man, sprinkled water on the dry earth of the plaza, and when the feasting was over, the musicians took up their instruments. The clarinet sounded warning notes to alert the dancers and the *Sardanas* began. Nearly everybody danced to the complicated rhythm and wistful melody of the Catalan folk-dances, holding hands and forming small circles inside larger ones.

"Come dance, Doctor," Rosalia urged the doctor, pulling him into one of the circles.

"I'm . . . I'm too tired, my dear." He tugged out his watch. "I *must* hurry."

"You can't be tired *today!*" said Rosalia, firmly overruling his protests.

Dancing heads bobbed rhythmically, skirts swirled, dust floated like a low mist and the smell of damp earth mingled with body-heated fragrances.

Hernando danced like a dervish, leaping high, his brown face laughing and shiny with perspiration. Baudillo Ledesma danced sedately with a Havana jutting jauntily from the corner of his mouth, while Cornelia gave the steps the grace of a gavotte. Teresa danced at Anselmo's side, thrilling when his fingers squeezed hers, squeezing back and laughing up into his face.

Only Helena, Don Carlos the priest, Vigon and a few others sat out.

"Do you not wish to dance, Helena?" inquired Vigon.

She shook her head. "After so much excitement . . . I'm tired."

"I would like to dance," he confessed sadly. "But I am clumsy. My feet will never do what I wish."

Helena was sympathetic. "It is not difficult to learn, Benito. You must ask someone to teach you."

"I asked Rosalia."

"Well, then. Soon you'll be able to dance."

"Rosalia is too busy to teach me."

"I'll find someone to teach you," interjected Don Carlos. His eyes twinkled. "But I can't promise it will be a girl."

Dancing continued through the afternoon. The girls kicked off their *alpargatas* and the young men eagerly followed their lead, discarding shoes and socks and jackets with immense relief. Then the orchestra played ballroom music and only the younger people danced, while the older people watched contentedly. Instinctively the men grouped themselves together, apart from the women.

Miguel Barras was surrounded by friends.

"Not long now, Miguel!"

"Make sure you don't take the wrong turning."

"If you lose your way, send for me."

Miguel was embarrassed and anxious to leave. He tried to catch Helena's eye.

"What a pity it's happened *now!*" Camila Vigon sympathized with Helena.

"It'll be a test of true love," said another girl. "If he truly loves you, he will be tender and understanding during your bad week."

"Miguel will understand," said Helena with conviction.

Those youths who had no official fiancées took the opportunity to invite girls who caught their eye to partner them. Teresa declined all invitations but when the orchestra struck up a tango, she flushed with pleasure when Anselmo made his way over to her. "Don't you know any dance but the tango?" she asked, as he put his arm around her.

"It is the only dance that appeals to me."

He had learned the steps in a Barcelona dancing academy, but Teresa was a natural dancer.

He was very intent. "Try this. We walk two steps, side by side. I place my foot between yours and swing you around. Don't be afraid. I won't let you fall. Try it again. Good. That's it. Go right down. Your back resting on my knee. That's the way George Raft does it in his new film."

Teresa laughed happily, enjoying herself, and was surprised by the clapping. Everyone had stopped dancing to watch them.

"They're a perfect match," Camila Vigon told Helena.

"Anselmo's awfully handsome," said Maria Guitart. She arched an inquisitive eyebrow. "Has he spoken to Teresa?"

Helena shrugged her shoulders. "I don't know."

"She's *your* sister-in-law."

"Teresa is . . . a discreet girl . . . she doesn't talk much."

"You're getting the hang of it," Anselmo told Teresa. He swung her around and down over his knee with the air of an Apache dancer.

"Mind you don't split your pants," Teresa chuckled.

The dancing went on until evening when mothers solicitously rounded up young daughters and hurried them home. Helena and Miguel had already slipped away on their honeymoon.

The musicians played a last *Sardana* and Don Carlos climbed up on their platform to make an announcement.

"As you know, for a long time, I have been awaiting an assistant. I have learned today a young man has been appointed who arrives tomorrow. I am sure you will all give this young man a hearty welcome and make him feel happy in his new home."

The evening sky flushed pink when the setting sun slipped down behind the distant mountains. The trees took on a coppery hue, and the fine down on young girls' arms glistened like spun gold. The wedding guests melted away and the plaza was at peace.

"Helena was radiant," Cornelia Ledesma told her husband contentedly.

Baudillo frowned. "I wonder if Antonia or Pilar will ever marry?"

It was late evening and only one embassy clerk was in the office. Emil Znadlon Serra nodded to him and strolled along the corridor to his private office. He locked it behind him. He whistled tunelessly,

drew a Havana from his pocket and inserted paper in his typewriter.
He smoked furiously as he typed, scenting the room with expensive
smoke. He wrote:

July 1936

Events have moved very quickly these last few days. There was a
gun battle in the east cemetery between the Falangists and the Communists and one who died was a cousin of José Antonio Primo de
Rivera. He was killed by an Assault Guard named José Castillo. A
few days ago, José Castillo was murdered on his doorstep.

Other Assault Guards, possibly acting on their own initiative,
arrested Calvo Sotelo in the middle of the night, took him away in
a storm-troop car and shot him. His body was later delivered to the
mortuary and reported as found in the street. Calvo Sotelo was a
right-wing member of the Cortes. He had scathingly criticized the
government!

So, today the fourteenth of July, there have been two funerals.
Castillo's coffin was draped in a red flag and headed a procession of
Assault Guards, Anarchists and Communists who shouted slogans and
flourished clenched fists. Calvo Sotelo's body was wrapped in a Capu-
chin robe and, as it was lowered into the grave, his followers saluted
him with upraised arms.

General Mola's coup d'etat planned for April was a damp squid.
But now, General Mola has fixed a firm date for a military uprising.
It will begin in Morocco at five o'clock on the afternoon of July
seventeenth. Simultaneously, military garrisons throughout Spain
will revolt.

The outcome of the revolt is in doubt. Everything depends on the
loyalty of army officers, either to their government or to their superior
officers. From reliable sources I have learned that General Mola has
been promised that Hitler and Mussolini will send him troops, weapons and raw materials as soon as the revolt starts.

Emil Serra read through his report, signed it and sealed it in a
diplomatic envelope. Then he drew from his breast pocket a letter
from the mayor of Escoleras.

My Dear Sir,
In this village there is a Vicente Serra. He believes it is possible you
are related. His family originally came from Madrid.

Vicente Serra is not accustomed to writing letters. He states he is a
poor man and while willing to help you, cannot afford to neglect

his labor unless compensated. He points out that correspondence is also costly and hopes you will reimburse him for the postage.

I wish to add a personal note. Neither Serra nor his wife are in good health. She is pregnant and medical attention is expensive.

Yours faithfully,
FEDERICO MORALES
MAYOR

Emil Serra chuckled, threaded paper into his typewriter and wrote briefly:

ESTEEMED KINSMAN SERRA,
I will visit you as soon as possible. Meantime, exercise your memory and greet me as a long-lost relative.

With sincere best wishes,

Emil Serra wrapped the letter around a wad of crisp new currency notes and sealed them in an envelope.

It was a hot summer's evening and he draped his jacket over his arm as he strolled along the Calle de Velasquez.

The street was crowded. Everybody was out of doors in the hot, breathless Madrid night air. Presently he encountered a young woman whom he vaguely recognized walking between a red-haired student and an older woman. He inclined his head and said: *"Buenas noches."* But it was only after he passed that he remembered she had collided with him earlier in a café. He glanced back over his shoulder and saw how intently she looked up at the red-haired youth who talked so animatedly. Serra sighed.

Abruptly, he was very, very lonely.

Antonia Ledesma at once recalled Emil Serra's flabby paunchiness and sandy hair and was embarrassed by his greeting.

Her aunt asked quickly: "Who's that strange-looking man?"

"I stepped on his toe earlier," Antonia smiled.

Jaime suggested: "Shall we have coffee here, Señora?"

"Anywhere that suits you and Antonia," said Aunt Ana agreeably.

They sat under tall trees on a broad asphalt sidewalk and watched the busy life of Madrid flow around them. The night air was sultry and simply walking made people perspire visibly. Antonia's aunt dabbed away a moustache of sweat on her upper lip and fluttered a tortoiseshell fan with black lace edging. They ordered iced coffee.

Antonia and Jaime talked animatedly while their chaperone half-dozed in the heat. Jaime was an idealistic Socialist who loved an argument. Antonia, now near the end of her student days, was down-to-earth, and the two sharpened their minds on one another. Antonia had the Ledesmas' raven-black hair and her mother's high forehead and dignity. When she was intrigued, her brown eyes glowed. She was attractive, but never became more than friendly with the boys she met. Their interest soon flagged. Her aunt privately suspected the twenty-five-year-old girl tried too hard.

The hot air muffled sound and was tainted with city smells. It carried the roar of powerful cars driven at furious speed. People looked up as they thundered along the avenue toward them. The first was an open car and the letters UGT daubed in red paint on its sides showed it belonged to the Socialist Trade Union. It swerved violently to avoid a pedestrian crossing the road, skidded up onto the sidewalk and smashed into a street lamp. Women screamed, the street lamp slowly toppled and sparks flashed from shorted electric cables. The occupants of the car tumbled out and crouched behind it as the second car raced up and skidded to a standstill. Men leaped from it wearing the red and black scarves of Anarchists; guns were drawn and shots rang out.

Bars and cafés emptied like magic as people fled panic-stricken, scattering chairs and tables, and splintering glasses on the pavement. Men shouted and the scuff of running footsteps almost drowned the scream of ricocheting lead.

Even before the second car braked, Jaime knew what would happen and jumped to his feet. He dragged Antonia and Aunt Ana away from the café and into a deeply recessed doorway. In seconds the street was empty and there was only the whine of lead as the opposing political factions settled down to snipe at each other.

Antonia was trembling with excitement but Aunt Ana was shivering with fear. Jaime was exasperated. "We'll never achieve *anything* this way!" he complained bitterly. "Why *can't* the Left cooperate?"

"Save us, gentle Mother of Mercy, save us," prayed Aunt Ana. Her head was bowed and her praying was a fierce whisper.

Jaime peered out from the doorway.

"Careful!" gasped Antonia. "Be careful, Jaime!"

"It's just high spirits," he reported. "I don't think they care if they hit anything, as long as they make plenty of noise."

From behind the Anarchists' car, an arm lobbed a round black object. It curled up and over the road. Jaime ducked back into cover and wrapped his arms around the two women. "Hand grenade," he warned tersely before its shattering blast tore at their ears. Glass splintered, dust eddied and shrapnel spattered the walls and pavements.

Aunt Ana fell down on her knees, pulling Antonia down with her. "Praise be to the Virgin Mary. Oh, Holy Mother of God, save us this day from our sins."

"All noise and smoke but little blast," Jaime comforted her.

". . . Hail, Holy Mother Queen of Mercy, to thee we send our sighs . . ."

The wails of sirens approached.

"Assault Guards," said Jaime.

Storm-troop cars roared up and attacked the Anarchists from the rear and, finding themselves being fired on from two fronts, the Anarchists ran for the sanctuary of the side streets. The UGT men sped them on their way with lead and traded shots with the Assault Guards. But when more storm-troop cars sirened up, the UGT members discreetly fled.

Shooting ceased, the dust settled and Jaime helped Aunt Ana to her feet. She had lost her fan and complained about it querulously.

An Assault Guard thrust the barrel of a tommygun into the doorway and glared suspiciously. "What are you doing here?"

"Taking cover from the shooting."

The guard glowered, reluctant to relinquish an arrest. "All right. Run along. Keep out of trouble."

Jaime hurried Aunt Ana and Antonia through the cordon of armed Assault Guards and past the smashed shop windows, bomb-torn pavements and bullet-ridden cars.

A few streets away he was able to flag down a taxi.

"What is the world coming to?" wailed Aunt Ana as she sank back against the upholstery. Her hands were still shaking.

"It's the inevitable class conflict," said Jaime.

"What does he say?" Aunt Ana asked Antonia.

"He's always talking politics," said Antonia and frowned at Jaime warningly.

But Jaime was proud of his socialism. "We have witnessed one facet of the conflict between those who have and those who have *not*," he said.

After an evening out in Madrid, Rafael Ledesma and his friends drove back through the main street of Toledo. Although it was late, the cafés and bars were well lighted and the sidewalk tables crowded.

Claudio Ferraz abruptly turned off into a side road parallel to the main street.

"Where are you going?" asked Rafael.

Ferraz's eyes gleamed. "Didn't you see who we just passed? Charugin's Red bitch of a daughter!"

"So?"

"She's with her whore of a mother. They walk along here to reach home." He made a vulgar gesture.

Cadet Castro said uneasily: "It's risky."

"Why? We'll let them get in front, drive up, grab the girl and . . . we're away!"

"There'll be a big squawk!" warned Cadet Castro uneasily.

Juan Redondo's eyes gleamed. "If they want free love we'll give it to them!"

Rafael said slowly: "We could give her a beating!"

Ferraz braked the car in the shadows and they crouched down low. Presently the older woman and her daughter passed on the far side of the road and turned off into a narrow side street.

Ferraz started up the car and followed them slowly, curb-crawling with only sidelights burning. The street was deserted and the windows shuttered.

"Ready?" asked Ferraz.

"Ready," breathed Rafael.

Ferraz tramped down on the gas pedal and the car leaped forward. He flicked on the headlights and twin searchlights slashed through the night. The engine thundered and the two startled women on the sidewalk glanced around and were blinded.

Ferraz rocketed the car toward them and braked hard. Doors burst open and the cadets leaped out.

Rafael tore the mother away from her daughter and hurled her against the wall. Castro and Redondo half-lifted, half-dragged the girl into the car. She screamed piercingly.

The mother rushed at them, face contorted. She locked her fingers in Redondo's hair and tugged with all her strength.

Rafael measured coolly and smashed his knuckles into the woman's face. She went down.

They wrestled the girl into the car. Ferraz rammed his foot down on the accelerator, and the car shot off, headlights blazing and the open door swinging dangerously.

Rafael was in front with Ferraz. The girl was still screaming.

"Shut her up," Rafael said.

"You try," panted Castro.

Rafael turned and punched the girl in the face. Her screams choked off as her mouth filled with blood.

"You didn't have to do *that!*" protested Castro.

"That's the way to treat Red scum!" sneered Rafael.

Ferraz slowed at the next corner and as he rounded it, a Civil Guard leaped out from the shadows onto the running board. The gold braid of sergeant's stripes gleamed against the olive green of his uniform.

"Stop, you bastard!" snarled the sergeant. "Stop!"

Ferraz rammed the gas pedal down to the floor and seesawed the steering wheel, swerving the car violently, trying to scrape the sergeant off against the walls of the narrow street.

"Son of a whore!" shouted the sergeant. He drew his pistol and rammed its muzzle against Ferraz's neck. "Stop or I'll blow your head off!"

Ferraz brought the car to a standstill.

The sergeant was breathing heavily.

The girl was moaning.

"Let her go," said the sergeant.

They released her and she groped her way out of the car. Her dress was ripped and blood made an ugly splash upon it. She held her torn clothing to her and fled.

"You stupid bastards!" said the sergeant. He was trembling with fury as he holstered his pistol. "Don't you know who you got hold of?"

Claudio Ferraz said: "She's Charugin's whore of a daughter!"

"And *that's* the trouble!" thundered the sergeant. He looked at each of them in turn. "I know all of you," he warned. "Any more trouble and I'll talk to your commanding officer."

"What's the matter?" asked Rafael. "Have you joined the workers?"

"I'm older than you," said the sergeant. "I can see farther than the end of my nose. This is the *wrong* time to foment trouble. The pot is

simmering, about to boil over. But we don't want them to be prepared. So go quietly for the next few days. Let them think everything
is peaceful."

Rafael asked quickly: "You've got news? You know when it's going
to be?"

"Only that it won't be long. So be patient and . . . be ready!"

"*Arriba Espana!*" said Cadet Castro.

"*Viva* Mola!" said the sergeant.

5

Miguel Barras woke with a start, stared up at the slatted sunlight on
the ceiling and remembered he was in a hotel in Sevilla.

He swung his legs around off the bed and sat gently scratching his
groin. Sweat filmed his skin, the underclothes he wore stuck to him,
and where he had lain the sheet was stained wet.

Sevilla in July! He felt an intense longing for Escoleras, the blue
sea and a fresh breeze blowing across it. He looked at Helena and
knew again a stab of pride that she was willing to have him for her
man. She was sleeping soundly.

He crossed to the window and peered out through a crack in the
shutters. It would be evening soon, and in its coolness they could
sight-see the city.

He filled the washbasin with water and plunged his head into it.
Even he was weary of traveling, so it wasn't surprising Helena was
fatigued. They had spent the first night in Barcelona, then had a
long, tiring train journey to Valencia, and another long ride to Sevilla.

The hotel was modest and their room had no shower. He stood on
a towel and sponged himself. Soon Helena awoke. She eyed him
shyly. Respecting her modesty, he turned his shoulders so she could
slip out from under the bedsheet and hurry to the curtained bidet
and the privacy she needed. She joined him a little later. Her night-

dress was wet with perspiration and the hollow of her throat gleamed as though smeared with glycerin. "I can't stand much more of this heat, husband."

"It'll be dark soon. Then it will be cooler."

She rested her head on his shoulder and he put his arm around her. "I think it's going to be all right tonight," she whispered.

"Don't worry about it. The only important thing is being with you. Just being with you."

"I feel terrible about it, husband. You must be . . . tormented!"

"We've waited a long time, wife. Waiting a little longer won't matter."

"I'm less patient than you, husband. I want it to happen soon. I want to be *truly* your wife."

He kissed her and she clung to him fiercely until the sweat on their bodies mingled. Then she pulled away. "I'm being cruel."

"Wife. Wife!" he soothed. "Listen to me. I will sit with my back to you while you wash. You'll put on your prettiest dress and we'll stroll around Sevilla, find a good restaurant, have a good meal . . . and perhaps drink a little too much. How's that?"

Her eyes danced. "Wonderful."

He sat with his back to her and listened to the cool sound of running water.

He was thinking of the sea. "I'd love to swim now."

"Husband. I'm *sure* it's going to be all right tonight."

"Good."

"Which dress shall I wear: the yellow or the white?"

"White is always cooler."

"You'll wear your white trousers?"

"They got creased in the suitcase."

"It won't matter."

While she dressed he rolled a cigarette. "How about visiting Perez's sister-in-law?" he asked.

"Is it far?"

"About fifty kilometers."

"How do we get there?"

"By bus."

"Must we go? Bumping all that way over bad roads in this heat?"

Miguel shrugged. "Perez hasn't seen his sister-in-law for fifteen years. If we're passing, he'd like us to call and give her his best wishes."

"Perhaps later, then."

"When it snows," he chuckled.

Miguel dressed while Helena finished her toilette. At once a wet patch stained his shirt between the shoulder blades.

"Are you ready, husband?" she asked gaily.

"Ready, wife!"

"Let's go, husband."

The hotel was strangely quiet when they descended the marble steps to the vestibule. There was nobody in the cool patio and the street outside was deserted.

"It's siesta time," guessed Helena. "It's so hot, nobody goes out."

But when they reached the plaza at the top of the road, they came upon a gang of men wearing Anarchists' black and red scarves, prying up flagstones, digging shallow trenches, filling sacks with earth and building barricades. Two men stopped working and crossed over to Miguel and Helena. Their faces were dirt-streaked and shining with sweat. "We need your help, comrade," they told Miguel. "It is better that your wife goes home."

Miguel's eyes widened. "What's it all about?"

One man glowered. "You ought to know!"

"We only arrived today. We're honeymooners."

Miguel expected sly grins, but the men nodded understandingly. One said: "The generals have revolted and ordered out the troops. But the workers are fighting back. Listen." He held up his hand and when they listened, they could hear a distant crackling. "Small-arms fire," said the man. "We're holding out in the Hotel Inglaterra."

"How long will the trouble last?" asked Miguel anxiously.

"Who knows, comrade? The radio announced it's the futile plot of a few officers. Perhaps tomorrow it will be over."

"You speak with a Catalan accent?" said the second man.

"We come from the province of Gerona. What is the news of Barcelona?"

"All is quiet there. It is only here that the accursed sons of capitalist whores have ordered out the artillery to fire on their brothers."

The men working on the barricades shouted angrily:

"Shameless lazy ones; there's much work to be done."

"Are you deserting your comrades?"

"Pepe, help us lift this flagstone."

Pepe tugged at his companion's arm. "We must go."

The other man smiled at Helena, his teeth white against his tanned face. "Continue your honeymoon, comrade. If you wish to help, return when you can." He flourished his clenched fist. *"No pasaran!"*

As Miguel and Helena strolled on across the plaza, an open truck rumbled past full of shirt-sleeved men. Some carried guns and other wielded shovels. But apart from the barricade hastily being erected and the distant crackle of shooting, the city seemed very quiet.

"Everything happens to us," said Miguel gloomily. "Shall we return to the hotel? We'll take a bus out of here in the morning."

"I want to see more of Sevilla." Helena's eyes gleamed excitedly. "I'm hungry too."

They walked on through deserted streets until they came upon another group of men throwing up a barricade. Then startlingly, there was a flurry of shots. For a long second everybody froze before they dropped tools and scattered.

"Snipers," panted a man, tearing past Miguel and Helena. "Take cover!"

Miguel grasped Helena's hand and ran.

More shots rang out as they neared the sanctuary of the side streets. Helena's pace flagged and Miguel dragged her along with him until she tripped and fell.

Miguel pulled her to her feet. "Hurry!"

Helena stumbled two paces and fell again.

"Run," he shouted, tugging at her.

"Miguel," she whispered. Her eyes rolled up to him imploringly: "Husband . . . !"

He tried to lift her. "Hurry!"

"Ayeee!" she shrilled thinly, and it was then he saw the crimson on her white frock.

"Wife!" he screamed, half-crazed by shock. "Helena!" He looped her arm around his neck and half-pulled, half-carried her. Ricocheting bullets screamed over him, but he was unaware of them. She was a dead weight, her limpness defeating him so that she was slipping through his grasp. He renewed his grip and struggled on and a man leaped out from a doorway, grasped Helena and helped him run with her to a side street.

They propped her up against the wall and she pressed her hands upon her abdomen over the wet stain.

"Wife!" he choked. "Wife!"

"I'm sorry, husband . . . it's all a mess now." Her cheeks were bloodless.

He looked around desperately. "A doctor?" he panted. "A hospital."

His helper said: "The hospital is too far to carry her." He scowled in the direction of the shots. *"Me cago en la madre que te pario!"* he shouted fiercely, shaking his fist at an unseen marksman. "I shit upon the mother who gave you birth, you son of a Fascist whore!"

"Between us we can carry her," panted Miguel.

"No, comrade. Stay with her until I return."

He hurried away and Miguel wiped the sweat beads from her forehead. Her face was shrunken and her eyes deep-set.

"Wife!" he choked and tears rolled down his cheeks.

Her eyes caressed his face. "Don't weep, husband. This is a little thing."

"What can I do, wife? How can I help you?"

"Just hold my hand."

A bakery truck tore along the street and squealed to a standstill beside them. The helper jumped out and opened the back doors. They lifted Helena tenderly and placed her on a mattress of flour sacks. Miguel sat beside her and the driver hurtled off at reckless speed, blasting a way with the hooter like an ambulance siren.

They braked abruptly at a hospital casualty station, crowded with wounded men and women. Young medical students with earnest faces, nurses in bloodstained uniforms and pale-faced nuns in flowing black robes worked feverishly.

The bakery driver plunged into the midst of the crowd and came back with a student doctor. "Let me see her," the youth barked impatiently and, as Miguel made way for him, Helena moaned softly.

"Where are you hurt?" the doctor asked.

"Here," she whispered.

He rolled back her skirt and probed.

"Ayeeee!" screamed Helena.

"Here?"

"Ayeee!"

He flipped down her skirt and wiped his hand on a bloodstained swab. "One for the operating room," he said crisply and hurried away.

Helena whispered: "Hold my hand, husband."

"Don't worry, wife," he comforted. "They'll look after you."

Porters came, lifted her onto a stretcher and wheeled her away. He would have gone with her but a nurse stopped him. "Please stay in the waiting room. Our hands are full. We can't have people hindering us."

"It's my wife. We're only just married and . . ."

"Don't worry. We'll take care of her."

The man who had helped Miguel took his arm.

"Come with me, comrade," he persuaded. "I will wait with you."

The waiting room was a vast hall. At one end was a bar for refreshments. They sat down and ordered brandies.

The bakery driver took a tobacco pouch from his pocket and rolled a cigarette. "Your name, comrade?"

"Miguel."

"I'm Hugo. You wish to smoke, Miguel?"

"No, thank you."

"You are Catalan?"

"From the province of Gerona."

"I have heard about it. The weather there is very bad."

Miguel's eyes were haunted. "Will they give her an anesthetic?"

"Do not worry, Miguel. Our Spanish doctors are the best in the world. They will take care of her."

A burly, cropped-headed man wearing coveralls unbuttoned to the waist, sat down at the table. He drank deeply from a glass of beer and scratched his sweat-moist chest. "*Ola*, Hugo," he greeted.

"What is new, Carlos?"

Carlos wiped his wet hand on his coveralls. "General Queipo de Llano drove into Sevilla in his Hispana Suiza, and I shit upon his car and upon all cars of all the sons of whores of all the Fascists of Spain and outside Spain."

"That Queipo de Llano!" said Hugo disgustedly. "He is always drunk, that one."

Carlos wiped sweat from his forehead with a soiled rag. "This Queipo de Llano with only three men walked into garrison head-quarters and placed its officers under arrest. The swine submitted meekly. Then the whore's son went to the infantry barracks and relieved the colonel of his command. Then with only fifteen Falangists, he went to the artillery barracks where the sons of whores obeyed his orders to turn out the artillery and surround the civil governor's office. The governor surrendered at once, and I shit upon all traitors who abuse the people's faith."

Carlos stopped for breath and above the buzz of conversation, they could hear the distant thunder of artillery.

"The Assault Guards remained loyal," said Carlos sadly. "But they didn't have a chance."

In the vast waiting room every sound was magnified. The smell of stale coffee, tobacco smoke and disinfectant hung heavily like a damp, invisible fog.

"What have you been doing, Carlos?"

"A comrade brought the news to the factory and we turned out and marched to union headquarters where our arms are stored. We held a meeting in the street and voted for rifles to be issued. But we haven't enough, Hugo. Only one man in twenty has a gun. And all day people have been streaming in from the suburbs and villages asking for arms. Queipo de Llano and those sons of bitches of traitor officers may have seized control of the center of the city; but it will do them no good. We'll surround them in their garrisons. So long as they sit tight, they'll be safe. But if one man steps out from behind the barrack walls for just one second . . . !" Carlos made a gruesome slashing gesture with an invisible knife.

Miguel said anxiously: "Shouldn't they have operated by now?"

Hugo glanced at the wall clock. "Too soon."

Carlos eyed Miguel inquiringly. "You have trouble, comrade?"

"The Fascist sons of whores sniped his wife."

"I shit upon all the sons of Fascist whores who shoot from rooftops!" swore Carlos and pounded his fist on the table. "Two of the swine were concealed on a rooftop near the church of the Sacred Heart and sniped for an hour before we drove them out. My brother-in-law, Tomas, was wounded in the thigh. I brought him here and now I wait to take him home."

"He is all right?"

"He has a hole in his leg and a hatred for the Fascist swine that will serve him well."

"Can we not inquire?" Miguel asked anxiously.

"*Bueno,*" agreed Hugo.

They stopped a harassed nurse who said she would inquire for them. Half an hour later when they found her again, she had forgotten them completely. In desperation Miguel seized the arm of a passing doctor, who took pity on him. He summoned a nurse to make inquiries.

She returned and reported that the girl wounded in the abdomen would soon go into the operating theater.

Miguel, Hugo and Carlos paced the hall.

"Then we set fire to the soap factory," said Carlos proudly, his black-rimmed nails rasping loudly on his bare chest. "You should have seen those cauldrons of oil blazing high! The smoke was like a warship's funnel. There were delivery trucks in the yard and the comrades drove them into the heart of the flames so they would also burn."

"It was well done!" said Hugo, nodding approvingly.

"I shit upon capitalists who own factories, pay little to their workers and give money to Falangists to snipe at the people from rooftops!"

"It was well done," repeated Hugo. "Let us have another drink."

"I must go soon," said Carlos as they sipped their brandy. "I have rested enough. Tomas is a big man and could only walk with great pain. We were together at the church of the Sacred Heart and I shit upon the whore's son priest of that church. He preaches against our People's Front Government. When we arrived at his church he'd locked the doors. He was brave and stood outside at the top of the church steps. He mocked us, called us Red rabble, said we defiled the purity of God. We shouted that a believer in Christ will oppose poverty and preach against the capitalists. But he said we were Red scum with no spiritual faith and only greed for material things.

"Then sniping started and some of our comrades fell while we ran to shelter in doorways. Comrades with rifles came running from the nearest barricades and shot back at the snipers. But the priest still stood upon the steps of the church with his arms folded, and when a comrade fell, he laughed aloud.

" 'Let us shelter inside the church,' a man shouted.

" 'Nobody invites rats into a temple,' shouted the priest.

" 'Are those who snipe from rooftops God's disciples?'

" 'They will willingly give their lives for the dear love of the Holy Queen Mother of Mercy,' he answered.

" 'Son of a whore,' the comrades shouted and gestured threateningly.

" 'Listen to me,' said one comrade who has a fluent tongue.

" 'I will not listen to scum,' shouted the priest.

"Then someone cried out that a comrade wounded by a sniper had died and there was a great roar of anger, and the comrades raced up the steps and seized the priest.

" 'So! You will not listen!' shouted one comrade.

"The priest's face was gray and he was shaking but he held his head high. 'I shut my ears to the devil!'

" 'But not for long,' said another comrade. He drew his knife and cut off first the left ear of the priest and then the other. The priest screamed like a woman, his eyes rolled wildly, and when he was released, he ran down the steps with his hands outstretched before him as though he could not see. The crowd parted for him and, as he ran along the street, everybody laughed until their sides ached because a cassock is not meant for running and his flashing white calves were very comical.

"Then the man who had cut off the ears held them high and strutted like a bullfighter after a good corrida and tossed them to the comrades who scrambled for them; and after that we broke down the door of the church."

"We have waited a long time," said Miguel agitatedly.

"The nurse promised to tell us when you can see your wife, comrade," said Hugo. He turned to Carlos. "Is it difficult to burn a church?"

"We did not burn the church. It will be useful for storage or a garage. But we burned the hypocritical symbols, the Bibles, the crucifixes and the altar. We built a great mountain in the middle of the church of pews and confessional boxes, carpets and choirboy robes, and we soaked it in gasoline. The flames leaped so high they licked the roof beams and burned away the paintings around the dome. It grew so hot we could not stay. The flames lit up the stained-glass windows and they shattered with the heat. Then the sniping started from the rooftops again, and Tomas fell and I brought him here."

"It is good to destroy the churches," said Hugo solemnly. "They are symbols of reaction. Priests teach that man shall live by the sweat of his brow. They do not explain why rich capitalists live in luxury, without working!"

"They surely have operated by now," said Miguel.

"I must go," said Carlos. He gave Miguel his great moist hand. "Take heart, comrade. All will be well. Will you come, Hugo?"

"I'll stay with our comrade," said Hugo. "He is a stranger and needs a friend at his side."

"*No pasaran,*" said Carlos, saluting with his clenched fist.

They found the nurse bandaging a woman's arm. It had been

ripped open by a stray bullet. They waited until she finished and
went upstairs with her to make inquiries.

"She's in the operating room now," she reported. "In half an
hour's time you can see her."

"How is she?" asked Miguel anxiously.

"As well as can be expected. Don't worry. She'll have all the care
we can give her."

Miguel and Hugo paced the waiting hall.

"I'm grateful for your help," said Miguel.

"It is nothing, comrade. I see by your hands you are a worker, too.
We are brothers and must help each other."

The nurse returned with a smiling face. "You can see her now, but
don't encourage her to talk. It will tire her."

They went upstairs. Beds had been improvised and the wards were
filled to overflowing.

"There she is," pointed the nurse.

Miguel crossed to the cot and stared down at a stranger.

"But . . ." said Miguel. "This isn't my wife!"

The nurse was surprised. "Not your wife? But wasn't she operated
on for an abdominal wound?"

"Yes."

"This is the girl who had the stomach wound."

"But she isn't my wife!"

The nurse frowned, took them outside and pointed to a wooden
bench. "Wait here, please. I'll find out what's happened." She hurried away.

Hugo rolled a cigarette and gave it to Miguel. The sickly smell of
ether hung heavily in the hot air. Hospital porters wheeled along
trolleys bearing patients wrapped in blankets; doctors in bloodstained operating gowns hurried in and out of wards, and nurses scurried up and down the corridors. From one ward somebody called re-
peatedly, "Water, nurse, water!"

Time passed.

The nurse came back, her forehead puckered. When she was still
some distance away she beckoned to Hugo. Miguel got to his feet too,
but the nurse motioned to him to remain seated. The nurse talked to
Hugo tersely and then hurried away. Hugo came back slowly to Miguel. His face was grave.

"What's happened?" choked Miguel. "What happened?"

"She's dead," said Hugo bleakly. "She died just after we left her. They took her straight to the mortuary."

Andalusia

Captain Acosta of the Civil Guard was expecting the seventeen Falangists when they came to his barracks. He broke open his armory and the Falangists, led by José Valdes, son of the biggest landowner in the district, armed themselves with carbines and tommyguns. Then the captain ordered out the entire force of Civil Guards and marched them to the town hall.

It was a big, two-story building in the center of the village, overlooking the plaza. The lower half was the school and on the first floor were the administrative offices.

Captain Acosta commandeered the building and the children were locked up in a classroom together with the teachers, the porter and a municipal clerk.

José Valdes took a list of names from his pocket. "These are the dangerous ones," he told Captain Acosta.

The captain was seated at the mayor's desk. "Sergeant Corbera!"

"*Mi Capitan?*"

Captain Acosta gave him the list. "Arrest these men. Señor Valdes will assist you. The mayor first."

Mayor Alava was breakfasting with his wife and two daughters in the living room behind his pharmacy shop when Sergeant Corbera and two Falangists arrived. Mayor Alava got to his feet, wiping his lips with his napkin, annoyed that the sergeant had walked straight through his shop without knocking.

"Señor. It is necessary you come at once to the town hall."

"At once?" Mayor Alava frowned.

"At once. It is an order."

"Who gives such orders?"

A Falangist drew his pistol. "I do."

The mayor's wife gasped.

The mayor stared at the pistol disbelievingly. "*Que pasa?* What's happening?"

"Captain Acosta will explain. Hurry."

The mayor smiled reassuringly at his wife. "I'll find out what it's about, Maria. I'll be back soon."

"*Everybody* comes," said the Falangist.

The mayor was a short man but he drew himself up proudly. "How *dare* you show discourtesy to my wife and daughters!"

But Maria was already on her feet, urging her daughters to get up. "Don't argue, Jaime. We'll *all* go."

The Civil Guard and the Falangists flanked them as they crossed the plaza. The morning sun was already hot and beat down upon the mosaic tiles until they scorched underfoot. But within the arched vestibule of the town hall it was pleasantly cool.

Two Civil Guards with tommyguns stood on guard outside the classroom the mayor and his family were herded into. The doctor, the secretary of the Socialist Party, the chairman of the FAI and others with their families had already been detained. More families were brought in every few minutes, and by midday the room was crowded and the guards had been increased to four. The prisoners' pleas for water were ignored and as the temperature soared, they had to break the glass of the barred windows to let in fresh air.

But not everyone on the list was arrested. As news of the uprising spread, many men fled from their homes taking their families with them.

After lunch, José Valdes and Captain Acosta stood at the opened door of the classroom and made a formal declaration.

"This village is now under martial law. The People's Front Government in Madrid has failed. All of you are known to favor the deposed regime, so for the present you will remain prisoners."

Angry shouts answered him and men who had allowed themselves to be arrested peacefully surged forward angrily.

The guards leveled their tommyguns and looked at Captain Acosta expectantly.

"Lock them in," he ordered.

Captain Acosta telephoned to General Quiepo de Llano in Sevilla. "This is Captain Acosta reporting complete success in our village."

"Excellent, Captain." The general's voice was mellow as though he had lunched well. "I will announce your name and your victory in my next broadcast."

"That is kind of you, sir," said Captain Acosta delightedly. "What are my orders now?"

"Dig in. Defend your position. Reinforcements are being flown over from Morocco. Stand firm. *Arriba Espana!*"

Captain Acosta gave orders for the town hall to be sandbagged and barricaded. But the constant crying of the children locked up in the classroom drove a Civil Guard to report: "The children are thirsty and hungry, Captain."

The captain discussed the problem with José Valdes who went to the mother superior of a convent close to the village and persuaded her to care for the children.

"We will need milk, bread and meat," said the mother superior.

"The village is under martial law, Mother. You can take what you want. I will send men with you to the shops to collect what you need."

The day wore on. The prisoners in the classroom begged for water, but their pleas were ignored.

Some of the villagers who had hidden behind shuttered windows finally ventured out and volunteered for service under Captain Acosta's command. Their political views were tested by the Falangists, and the village priest reported about their church attendance. If it was thought they would be loyal to the new regime, they were given a carbine, a cartridge belt and a Falangist armband.

Captain Acosta listened to the radio and heard himself and José Valdes called the heroic saviors of the village. But there was a setback for the captain the following morning. Two of his men were sniped at; one was killed and the other badly wounded. He quickly withdrew his small force into the barricaded town hall and was soon besieged by Trade Unionists and Anarchists who had fled the village, found arms and were determined to retake the village.

All through that long, hot day bullets peppered the besieged rebels from rooftops and street corners, while the prisoners hammered on the door and clamored for food and water. But Captain Acosta had no time to spare for his prisoners' comfort. Two more of his men were wounded, the town hall water supply had been turned off and he had forgotten to stock up with provisions. He could easily be starved out. Surprisingly, the telephone had not yet been cut, so Captain Acosta rang Sevilla. The general wasn't available, but he spoke to a sympathetic army officer who said: "We're besieged too. Stand firm until help arrives," he encouraged.

"When will that be?"

"How long can you hold out?"

"Perhaps until tomorrow. Perhaps only until midday."

"I'll see what I can do."

The army garrisons in Sevilla were strongly manned and could easily hold out against attacks by lightly armed workmen. It was the widely scattered and weakly held pockets of revolt in the small villages that sorely needed reinforcements. The army officer studied maps, consulted superior officers and made long-distance calls.

Lieutenant Renato Maroto came to relieve Captain Acosta the following day. He arrived in a private car leading three army trucks full of Moroccan soldiers whose green turbans and glowering dark faces gave them a fearsome aspect. At the entrance to the village, they met with some resistance from a few men armed with rifles, shotguns and pitchforks, but a disciplined volley from trained soldiers, who leaped from the trucks and aimed carefully, killed some and put the rest to flight. Lieutenant Maroto triumphantly drove on to the town hall and the defenders gave a loud cheer and unbarred the door.

"Captain Acosta?" asked Renato Maroto, stepping down from his car.

"At your service, Lieutenant."

The lieutenant shook hands solemnly and his black eyes traveled on to José Valdes and observed his Falangist armband.

"Senor José Valdes," introduced Captain Acosta.

"We have friends in common," said Lieutenant Maroto, shaking José Valdes's hand. "My uncle is married to the sister of the Marquesa de Obrera."

"I know the Marquesa well," replied José Valdes warmly.

Captain Acosta explained all that had happened, mentioned the children he had sent to the convent, the prisoners in the classroom, the villagers who had escaped arrest, and gave the name of the leader of the armed peasants who had besieged him.

The lieutenant listened quietly, nodding as though he had heard it all before. He was a young man, thirty years old, tall and unusually thin. He had a long, dark face and piercing eyes. While he listened he clenched his fists and rubbed his knuckles together. When the captain had finished speaking he said quietly: "You have done well, Captain."

Captain Acosta flushed happily. "I did my duty," he said modestly.

Lieutenant Maroto's black eyes pierced him. "Can I rely on the cooperation of you and your men for what must come next?"

"But of course, Lieutenant."

"And you too, José?"

José Valdes nodded proudly. "We will finish what we have begun."

"Do you understand military strategy?"

José Valdes nodded slowly. "I think you are about to say, Lieutenant, that from a military point of view this village will be difficult to hold?"

Lieutenant Maroto nodded solemnly. "We have struck hard and gained great advantages. But the Red government will soon gather its strength and hit back. You and your men must be prepared to retreat from the village and take your families with you beyond reach of reprisals."

"I understand," said José Valdes quietly.

Lieutenant Maroto smiled faintly. He leaned forward, his hunched shoulders and long neck, crooked slightly to one side, made him look strangely like a vulture. He took a deep breath and said as though reciting from order sheets: "When our troops occupy a village that has shown resistance, the leaders must be punished so severely they will never dare resist again. If the ringleaders escape, their families must suffer. Ruthless punishment must drive home the lesson that all who resist will suffer. Civilian panic can cripple our enemy's troop movements, and the accidental destruction of hospitals and ambulances has a profoundly demoralizing effect upon soldiers in action." The lieutenant paused to take a breath. "My orders are that when we meet with civilian opposition, the streets shall be placed under fire. No quarter is to be given, and since the Marxist swine fight side by side with their women, no distinction is to be made between the sexes."

Captain Acosta smiled uneasily. "I'm only a policeman, but I'll do my duty."

The prisoners were allowed out of the classroom a family at a time, and water pitchers were given them.

Mayor Alava and his family passed into the vestibule and found themselves before Captain Acosta, José Valdes and Lieutenant Maroto, who sat behind a desk draped with the old Spanish flag. Armed Civil Guards flanked them.

"Mayor Alava," stated Captain Acosta. "Elected mayor by the Socialists."

Jaime Alava asked: "Have I ever behaved unfairly to you, Captain Acosta?" and the captain wriggled uncomfortably, remembering how three nights ago they had played chess like old friends.

Lieutenant Maroto looked the mayor over and then his eyes flicked to the mayor's wife.

"His wife is Catalan," said Captain Acosta unhappily. "She studied in Barcelona University to be a pharmacist."

Lieutenant Maroto's glance passed on to the eldest daughter, a sturdy girl of seventeen whose black eyes glowed defiantly. "Most Catalans are Marxists," commented Lieutenant Maroto. "How about the daughter? What of her?"

"Her name is Catalina. I do not know if she has political opinions."

Maroto looked at the second daughter. "And this one?"

"Constancia is fifteen, little more than a child. She has no political opinions."

"She looks older."

"She is a well-built girl," agreed Captain Acosta.

Lieutenant Maroto gestured. "Return the girls to the room."

Civil Guards ushered the two girls back into the classroom while the mayor and his wife were escorted out of the town hall and down the steps. The sun blazed hotly on two big, army trucks drawn up in the plaza. They were surrounded by grim-faced Moroccan soldiers holding rifles with fixed bayonets. A wooden box was placed below the tailboard of each truck and the mayor was made to climb into one truck with the men, and his wife into the other with the women.

"What's happening, Señor Mayor?" asked the doctor and gave a nervous laugh.

Mayor Alava shrugged his shoulders. "The threat of a military uprising has been in the air a long time. We should have been ready for it. A People's Front Government representing half a dozen different groups can't be strong enough to govern. It should have sacked the old right-wing brass hats and replaced them with healthy young blood."

"Where are they taking us?" asked somebody.

The mayor sighed sadly. "Prison, I suppose." He smiled wryly. "Lenin also went to prison."

"Our wives too?"

"There are women's prisons."

"But . . . we've committed no crime, Señor Alava."

"We have. We oppose the Falangists."

Before another hour had passed, nearly all those who had been imprisoned in the town hall had been interviewed by Lieutenant Maroto and ushered into the trucks.

The lieutenant, Captain Acosta, José Valdes and Sergeant Corbera climbed into the lieutenant's staff car. It drove off and the Moroccan soldiers fastened the tailboards of the trucks and followed the staff car. A confiscated village truck followed behind with armed Moors watching for attempted escapes.

The procession drove to the outskirts of the village where the trucks stopped and the bewildered prisoners were butted with rifles and made to climb out. They stood in the dusty roadway, tired, un-washed and despondent.

Lieutenant Maroto issued crisp orders in Arabic, and the Moroc-can soldiers prodded the prisoners with rifle butts until they formed two long lines facing the ditches, women on one side of the road and men on the other.

"Hands clasped behind and chins on chest," ordered Lieutenant Maroto.

The Moroccan soldiers patrolled the lines, clubbing brutally with gun butts when the lieutenant's orders were not obeyed.

The prisoners were kept standing in the hot sun for long minutes. Some swayed with weakness and a woman fainted.

Moroccan soldiers with tommyguns lined up along the center of the road facing the prisoners' backs.

"Fire!" ordered Lieutenant Maroto unemotionally, and Captain Acosta looked away quickly.

José Valdes squared his shoulders and held his head high, deter-mined to face his duty.

The tommyguns blasted deafeningly. Some of the prisoners were only wounded and leaped to escape, others fell and then crawled, while others writhed and screamed in pain. Two men who jumped the ditch were cut down by concentrated fire. Then the Moors used their bayonets to finish off anyone who showed signs of life. Their black faces under the green turbans shone with sweat and savage fury, and blood spattered their boots.

"They're . . . they're butchers," choked Captain Acosta.

"The best soldiers for the job," said Lieutenant Maroto tonelessly. "They fought us bravely for many years."

"They don't have to do . . . *that!*" whispered Captain Acosta, and his face was sheet-white.

"*That,*" said Lieutenant Maroto, "is their symbolic victory over the white man. They fight for us but instinctively hate us. Mutilation symbolically strips the white man of his manhood and the white woman of her purity."

The butchered corpses were rolled into the ditches, the trucks drove back to the village, and as they rumbled through the narrow streets to the plaza, Moorish soldiers leaned out from the trucks and lobbed hand grenades through cottage windows.

Captain Acosta was shocked. "Can't you stop them?"

"They are obeying my orders," said Lieutenant Maroto tonelessly.

Captain Acosta saw a woman staggering amidst the cloud of smoke that bellied from the door of her cottage. Her fingers clawed the air as though she was blind, blood streamed from her forehead and she fell to her knees. A Moor dropped down from the tailboard of the truck and walked back to her. His bayonet flashed.

"They've gone berserk," choked Captain Acosta. "They'll kill *everyone!*"

Lieutenant Maroto said stonily: "Resistance must be punished ruthlessly and spectacularly. The Reds must be taught an unforgettable lesson."

"I fear we have been thoughtless," said Valdes unhappily. "They should have had a priest to confess them."

"Marxists are anti-God. They have no religion."

"But if they wished to repent, they should have been allowed the last sacraments."

Lieutenant Maroto smothered a yawn. "I will remember to allow them to confess in the future." He glanced at his wristwatch. "It will soon be time for dinner. Good wine, Havanas and a well-earned rest. We will need it for our work tomorrow."

"What work is that, Lieutenant?"

"We will be forced to retreat," said Lieutenant Maroto grimly. "But we will leave behind such terrible evidence of our just anger that all who see and hear about it will walk in fear and never again dare threaten our way of life."

It was midmorning when the Moors came for the girls.

There were five girls, and since they had been separated from their parents, they had remained locked in a classroom without food and water and had slept on the stone floor.

They took Catalina first; she looked very small between the two tall, turbaned soldiers. They led her out from the town hall into the bright sunlight, down the stone steps and across the plaza. They passed Captain Acosta talking to a group of men and she wanted to call out to him, but when he saw her he turned his back.

Captain Acosta was issuing orders to village volunteers wearing the Falangist armband. It had been a hot night, and the morning sun had accelerated the decomposition of the bodies lying in the ditches on the outskirts of the village. The stench was spreading and José Valdes had suggested burning the corpses with gasoline. But Lieutenant Maroto gave orders that Captain Acosta and volunteers anxious to prove their loyalty to the new regime should load vats of olive oil onto a truck and drive out to the execution scene. The lieutenant wanted to preserve the horror of the butchery from decomposition as long as possible.

When they reached the scene the smell of putrefying flesh was so strong they tied handkerchiefs over their noses while they worked. The corpses were swollen with internal gases, and some had burst. Maggots seethed in exposed entrails and blow flies buzzed angrily and settled on rotting flesh like a crawling cancer. The ashen-faced volunteers soaked the corpses in olive oil while Captain Acosta looked on, sickened by his sense of guilt. He had known well many of the dead. The last body to be soaked with oil was Mayor Alava's. He had died instantly and fallen on his face, but a Moor had turned him over to mutilate him. As oil cascaded over the black-coated face, flies flew up in an angry, humming cloud and the mayor's open eyes stared accusingly at Captain Acosta.

The captain turned away quickly, remembering how just a short while ago he had also turned away from Catalina.

"Anything more, Captain?" croaked a volunteer, his eyes tormented above the handkerchief.

"That's all," choked the captain. He was remembering Catalina being led across the plaza by two Moors.

The Moorish soldiers led Catalina across the plaza to the Socialist club house. It was the largest public building in the village, built with funds donated by the Anarchist and Socialist organizations. Meetings were held there, social events and dances. It had a billiard room and a bar, and was the center of the community life of the village. When Catalina was ushered through the bamboo-curtained doorway, she saw the barroom had been converted into a soldiers' billet. Cots lined the walls and Moors sat around cleaning weapons, talking or playing dice. The air was fetid with their strong man-smell mingled with the odor of stale coffee, saddle leather and hair oil. An election picture of President Azaña had been defaced and Falangist slogans were daubed on the walls in black paint.

The Moors gripped her elbows and all but carried her across to the bar where Lieutenant Maroto was seated on a high stool. His long, dark face was expressionless, and his piercing eyes stared at her un-blinkingly over the rim of his glass.

The two Moors stood stiffly at attention.

Lieutenant Maroto inspected Catalina. Her white cotton dress was soiled. She felt shamed by this smart officer with his well-combed hair, soft white hands, smart uniform and clean-shaven jaw. She saw his lip curl in disgust and lowered her eyes. "You filthy daughter of a Red whore," he said softly.

She gasped and turned scarlet.

The Moors pressed closely around her, their faces shining as they savored her humiliation. She stood with downcast eyes while Lieu-tenant Maroto berated her. At last he ceased, sipped delicately from his glass, replaced it on the counter and dabbed his lips with a white handkerchief he drew from his sleeve. He ordered quietly:

"Lick this soldier's boots."

She stared at him wide-eyed.

"Didn't you hear me?"

"I can't . . . I *couldn't!*"

He said evenly. "If you want to leave this room *alive,* do as I say, Red whore!"

Panic boiled high inside her.

"Now!" said the lieutenant.

Her legs trembled as she dropped to her knees.

"Lick, you Red whore. Lick."

She lowered her mouth to the soldier's dust-caked boot and touched it with her saliva-tipped tongue. The wet stain stood out clearly.

"Lick it, I said. Lick it clean. Make it glisten!" The lieutenant's eyes terrified her; she bent her head and worked saliva into her mouth that soon clogged with dust and became paste.

"That's not clean. Look at the heel! Lick it thoroughly. D'you hear me? Lick it clean!"

There came a time when her mouth and tongue were quite dry. "I can do no more," she whimpered.

The lieutenant spoke sharply in Arabic, and a Moor behind her grabbed the neckline of her dress and ripped. Buttons pulled free all down her back and after another tug her dress imprisoned her upper arms. Strong fingers locked in her hair and dragged her to her feet. Another tug, and her clothing was down around her waist. She whimpered fearfully when her breasts sprang free. They swung her off her feet and peeled her clean, holding her by her arms and stripping clothing down to her ankles as though skinning a rabbit. Her limbs turned rigid with shock. They took her at a run across the room to an iron cot stripped of its mattress. They flung her down upon the bare wire springs with her shoulders on the wooden frame and her head hanging down over the end of the bed. Cords passed over her shoulders and under her armpits lashed her securely, and more cords around her ankles parted her legs.

Her head, hanging down over the end of the cot, filled with pulsing blood. She strained to raise her head. The Moors thronged around her and she saw them upside down, hostile Arab faces and hate-filled eyes.

The sullen black faces parted to make way for Lieutenant Maroto. He stared down unemotionally. "Learn what happens to traitorous whores!"

One Moor clamped her head under his arm while another held her hair. Metal skidded across her scalp. With horror she saw the lieutenant waving a long, black braid that was her hair. She screamed and tore at them with her fingernails until they tied her wrists to the sides of the cot. Then scissors snipped again, and the lieutenant flourished a second braid. He lashed her face lightly with the braids and then tossed them to his soldiers as a trophy. The scissors snipped busily and hair fell like black snowflakes.

"Ayeee!" she wailed.

They cropped her hair and razor-shaved it to the skull. When they released her head it dropped back weakly, the underside of her jaw showing the stretched slenderness of her throat. Her tears trickled down to her forehead.

The lieutenant lit a cigarette. "Listen. We brand whores with their guilt and cleanse their filthy bodies!"

She strained her head high then, and saw he held a large bottle of iodine and a pad of surgical gauze. Her neck ached, but with an awful fascination she watched him pour iodine onto the gauze, soaking it until the antiseptic ran freely over his hand.

"The shame of the whore," he said and swabbed her skull, painting her naked head until the skin was brown.

"Scum of a Marxist whore," he said, pouring more iodine until the gauze was soggy. "We cleanse the filth," he said and iodine dripped upon her belly, as his face slipped down away from her vision.

He swabbed brutally. She cried out when his merciless fingers ruptured the hymen, but that pain was soon overwhelmed as the antiseptic gauze lodged at the core of her, ate into sensitive membranes like corrosive acid. Its fiery sting became an unbearable flame that convulsed her until she arched high, almost snapping her bonds before her senses fled.

Her next vague awareness was of the ache of her neck blending with the throbbing inner fire. Her mouth was shriveled dry by the flame within her.

She saw another hanging head on the cot next to her, the bald skull iodine-painted. And on the next cot another head; then another and another! *Little sister Constancia,* she thought. *Please God, not Constancia. I want to die. Please God, make me die.*

Time passed in a haze which presently Lieutenant Maroto penetrated. "Only well-bred young ladies may faint," he said, "not Communist whores." He drifted away from her vision, and she tensed when she felt his fingers at her. Body heat had dried the swab until it adhered to sensitive membranes. When the lieutenant tore it away, she fainted again.

Her next awareness was of a Moorish soldier's weight, while his comrade supported her head. The Moor's eyes glittered as he twisted her breasts until she moaned. Then he spat into her open mouth. He probed her rawness until she swam in a red pain mist.

The Moors were relentless. Smoking and watching; brooding as they waited. Once she pleaded: "Water, water." Two of them stood over her and their hands went to their trousers. Jets of urine beat upon her cheeks, scalded her eyes, and forced her lips apart.

Please God, make me die, she prayed, as thrusting rhythm drove fiery pain ever deeper within her.

The radio blared military music interspersed with propaganda slogans, and once, through the mist of misery she vaguely heard General Quiepo de Llano's ranting: *"Our brave legionaries are showing Marxist cowards what it means to be a man! The Red wives are learning it, too. Communists preach free love and now their women are having a taste of it and learning how men who are truly men make love. Kicking their legs and struggling won't save them from their lessons!"*

She was conscious when the cords were cut from her ankles and wrists, but her head lolled as though her neck was broken when they dragged her out to the plaza. They propped her up against the fountain parapet, and sat her on an Anarchist banner alongside other girls with iodine-painted skulls and dried blood between their thighs. There was the smell of burning, and smoke smudged the sky behind Lieutenant Maroto who towered over them. He unstoppered a large jar of castor oil.

A Moorish soldier brought a jerry-can half full of gasoline and the lieutenant filled it up with the castor oil. He gestured, and a Moor grasped Catalina's head. A wedge of wood was rammed between her jaws, a funnel thrust into her mouth, and her lips held clamped around it. At first the liquid soothed her parched mouth, although it took her breath. They held her nose and pummeled her belly until she swallowed. The fumes scorched her lungs as the liquid ran down her throat. Her mind swam as she fought for breath, knowing she would surely die. But when her mouth was filled again, she swallowed quickly because it was futile to resist.

When she had drunk as much as she could hold, they released her and she fell sideways and lay still, one eye blinded by blood, numbly staring across the mosaic tiles at the army trucks into which the Moors were climbing.

Lieutenant Maroto's riding boots strode away, the loaded army trucks moved off and abruptly the first agonies convulsed her bowels.

A group of armed peasants led by Pablo Villegas had tried to retake the town hall, but had been forced to retreat by Lieutenant Maroto's Moors.

Uprisings had occurred in all of the surrounding villages, and there had been fierce fighting everywhere. Pablo Villegas stormed from village to village, gathering followers and mopping up isolated pockets of Falangist resistance. But some time elapsed before he could return to his own village with six truckloads of armed men.

On the outskirts of the village, the smell of putrefaction was sickeningly sweet, and Pablo Villegas and his men stared at the oil-soaked. butchered corpses simmering in the sun. Strong men vomited.

They drove slowly through the pillaged village. Shredded curtains hung from the shattered window frames of bomb-blasted cottages, and smoke drifted out from others. The bodies of men and women who had been cut down and butchered as they fled from the Moors lay decomposing in the narrow streets. They saw no sign of any life until they reached the plaza where the flames from the town hall leaped high. Thick clouds of smoke rolled over the village, and by the public fountain tormented victims of the Moors writhed convulsively in the filth that defiled an Anarchist banner.

Pablo Villegas and his men looked upon them and the tide of rage within them boiled over.

Lieutenant Maroto's brutality aroused a thirst for vengeance that could not be quenched.

Emil Serra typed furiously:

The revolution began in Melilla, Spanish Morocco, on July seventeenth. The officers in the military garrison ordered out their troops and quietly occupied all the public buildings, declared a state of war and arrested all the left-wing leaders they could find. All the working-class organizations were crushed and their headquarters occupied. By nightfall all Spanish Morocco was in the hands of the rebels, martial law had been imposed and General Franco had broadcast from the Canary Islands promising a new and just regime.

It seems now that nobody in the government took the revolt seriously, and the public was kept in ignorance about it, until the following day, the eighteenth of July. But by this time, risings had taken place in Andalusia.

If the government had at once issued arms to the working-class organizations, it is possible the revolt would have been quelled within a few hours. But the government allowed the decisive moment to slip away.

The risings in Barcelona and Madrid occurred on the nineteeth of July, but were abortive. Fighting goes on elsewhere in Spain.

It is vitally important to General Mola that his Spanish legionaries and Moorish troops be transported quickly from North Africa to spearhead the attack up through Andalusia to Madrid. But the government controls the fleet, which has remained loyal, and dominates the Straits. However, Hitler has supplied Franco with a great fleet of transport planes which is ferrying troops to the mainland.

In Madrid the working-men's organizations have seized power. The Spanish government has almost no authority. The Rebel generals control some areas and the Anarchists and Trade Unionists control others. Nevertheless, there is every indication that the people will support its government if it stands firm. But the government has lost a great deal of ground.

General Sanjurjo took off from Portugal in a small plane, destination Burgos, to meet General Mola. But his plane crashed on takeoff and he was killed. Some say this accident was planned by Franco, who is ambitious to become Spain's dictator.

Consul Padowsky glowered when Serra dropped the sealed letter on his desk. "The diplomatic bag will *not* go out today," he said with savage satisfaction. "There are no flights and trains have been canceled. The unsettled state of the country threatens the safety of my courier and his messages and I don't propose to send the bag until I can be reasonably sure it will reach Poland."

"I'm in no hurry," said Serra and smiled. The caverns of his eyes were dark blue and a jumping muscle below his left eye made it twitch convulsively. He took a petty-cash chit from his pocket and flipped it across the desk. "My expenses."

Padowsky scowled as he signed. "What can you spend money on in a city in a state of war?" he asked bitterly.

"There's always wine, women and song."

Padowsky was pale with suppressed anger. "Keep in touch with the office in case there are unexpected developments," was all he could trust himself to say.

6

Anselmo Ledesma was undisturbed by the hysterical radio announcements that punctuated the playing of military marches.

"We ask the people of Spain to keep tuned in. Do not turn off your radio. The government has the situation well in hand, but lying rumors are being circulated by traitors which are intended to create panic. Keep tuned in and learn the truth."

Manolo, who was just fifteen, watched his brother Anselmo comb his long, black hair and sleek it flat with a soft hairbrush. "Why can't I come with you?"

"Another time. Tonight I go with Diego."

"What shall I do?"

"Read and then go to bed."

"I'm not tired."

"Ask Carmen to play cards." Carmen was housekeeper at the Ledesmas' Barcelona flat.

Manolo pouted. "She never learns. I win every time. It's boring!"

Anselmo chuckled.

"Can't I go with you?"

Anselmo carefully straightened his tie. "Not tonight, Manolo. It's . . . it's a night for grown-ups."

Manolo nodded glumly and eyed him resignedly. "Girls?"

Anselmo gave him a playful tap on the jaw. "When you're older you'll have Saturday nights, too."

The Ledesma flat was in the Via Montaner, a fashionable district of Barcelona and only a short walk from the university and the café where Diego Munez awaited him. The two friends greeted each other and Anselmo ordered *carajillo*.

"What do you think of the news?" asked Diego.

Anselmo waved a deprecating hand. "A few generals have revolted in Morocco. A handful of disgruntled brass hats giving orders to disciplined men who don't know what it's all about; and who wouldn't care if they did."

Diego shook his head slowly. "It's not that simple. The radio asks everyone to keep tuned in, but the government says nothing. I suspect the government can't cope with what's happening."

Diego Munez was an architect by profession and a student of politics.

"It'll be all over by tomorrow," prophesied Anselmo. "Everybody's too interested in the Olympics to worry about anything else."

The waiter served Anselmo, who poured the brandy into his black coffee, added sugar and stirred.

"Holding the official Olympics in Germany is a glorification of the Nazis," Anselmo said. "Holding rival Olympics here in Barcelona is the only way to keep sport clean."

Diego shrugged his shoulders. "So we have right-wing Olympics and left-wing Olympics!" He took two cheroots from his pocket and gave one to Anselmo. "And our Anarchist comrades have snarled up everything. Five thousand international athletes just arriving in Barcelona and the Anarchists have declared a transport strike! They're supposed to be housed in the schools at the Plaza de Espana, but there aren't even enough beds for them! The army is coming to the rescue with cots which will have to be delivered with its own transport trucks."

"You see, Diego. The army is cooperative!"

"I wonder," said Diego.

"Look around," urged Anselmo. "It's a beautiful summer evening. Everybody's happy. Tomorrow everybody will be off to the coast to picnic and swim."

"I hope you're right."

"You should know us Spaniards. Put twenty of us together and you won't find two who agree. How could we organize a revolution?"

"Not everybody thinks like you." Diego clapped his hands for the waiter and paid. "Let's go."

They strolled along Calle Pelayo to the Plaza de Cataluña and stood on the outskirts of a great crowd listening to an orator. He was a stocky man with dark and earnest eyes who spoke slowly and simply. His workman's language expressed his thoughts with startling clarity.

"The generals in North Africa have ordered out their soldiers and taken over the garrison towns."

The crowd roared its anger.

"What happened in North Africa can happen here!"

Loud shouts of agreement.

"Our government is weak. It is afraid to take stern measures against the generals."

"Down with the generals!"

Anselmo looked around at the concerned faces of the crowd.

"A government is strong only when it has the army behind it. When the generals revolt it means tyranny . . . or civil war."

"Down with tyranny!"

"Down with fascism!"

The speaker held up his hands for silence. When he could be heard he said slowly: "The generals have revolted against the elected government and the people. They are traitors. But now, only the people can fight military tyranny."

The crowd gave a wild roar.

The man wiped his hand across his sweating forehead and gave a long look around him. He demanded ringingly: "Why won't the government arm the workers? Can we fight the enemy with bricks and stones and our bare hands?"

The crowd began to chant:

"We want arms!"

"We want arms!"

"We want arms!"

Diego tugged Anselmo's sleeve. "Let's go to the president's palace."

In front of the presidential palace a great crowd filled the plaza, bearing the white banners of the CNT. The men wore their working clothes or overalls and disputed fiercely among themselves as they milled around. A large group chanted monotonously:

"Arm the workers!"

"Arm the workers!"

"I wanted you to see this," said Diego grimly.

"They're just hot-heads letting off steam. Shouting slogans makes them happy."

They made their way back to the Ramblas and strolled toward the harbor.

It was midnight but the Ramblas were as crowded as at noon. Shops, bars and cafés were full, bookstalls festooned with gaudy-covered magazines were doing a brisk business and the long lines of hire-chairs were occupied by the old and young, sitting out in the breathless air while peanut vendors, bootblacks and pastry cooks with large baskets on their arms peddled their wares. When the two young men were midway along the Ramblas, people jumped up from their seats and ran to line the roadway to watch a procession of men in overalls marching with military precision, flourishing clenched fists and displaying the banners of the CNT, FAI and the UGT.

The watching crowds shouted encouragement, and Anselmo, on the outskirts of the crowd, asked: "What's happening? Where are they going?"

A man in front of him turned an excited face. "They're going to the arms depot. The government won't issue arms, so they're going to break open the armory."

"This we should see," said Diego.

Anselmo didn't agree. "They'll stand around and shout their heads off; but they won't do a thing."

Diego shrugged his shoulders.

They walked on along the Ramblas until down a side street they could see the glowing charcoal fire outside the Caracoles Restaurant where spitted chickens roasted in the open air. They crossed to the opposite side of the Ramblas to a stone arch over a narrow alley that led into the disreputable Chinatown area. Under the arch stood a stall and the white-aproned barman set up tumblers half-filled with raisins and filled them up with anis.

The two youths took the tumblers, faced each other and clicked heels.

"To a trip . . ." toasted Diego.

". . . around hell," concluded Anselmo. They threw back their heads and drank anis and raisins at a gulp. The empty tumblers banged on the counter.

"Another," ordered Anselmo. "This time a little more anis."

Again they faced each other but Anselmo toasted first. "To hell . . ." said Anselmo.

". . . and its denizens," concluded Diego.

They walked on under the arch and along the narrow, cobbled streets smelling of garbage and stale sewage. On Saturday nights the district was always full of men and youths up from the suburbs. They shouldered their way along crowded streets, pushed through swinging doors and along a narrow passage into a large hall where benches, upholstered with worn wine-colored velvet, were set out in rows facing a raised platform. Men of all ages were already seated, and as Diego and Anselmo settled down, curtains parted and a young girl, garishly made up, stepped out onto the platform. A blond waitress took Diego's order while the girl on the platform primped and arched her eyebrows at her audience. She writhed her hips and made suggestive movements with her mouth and tongue, then unbuttoned her blouse and displayed one breast on the palm of her hand. She tucked it away coyly as though concealing a great treasure. She turned her back, bent low, flounced her skirt high to show her bare buttocks and flashed an inviting smile over her shoulder before she minced back behind the curtains. She paused a moment to point to a card with number 19 upon it, being held up by a plump woman in a black lace dress. A man got up and gave the plump woman money. She gave him a key and pointed to a doorway. As he went through it, another girl came out from the curtains and minced across the raised platform.

Half an hour later when Anselmo and Diego were leaving, the blond waitress asked: "Didn't you see anything you liked?"

"Nothing that took our fancy."

"I've got a young sister who works at home. You'll like her."

"Why doesn't she work here?" asked Diego.

"She's underage!"

"Give me the address. We might take a look at her."

They went to Maria's. Girls in every stage of undress sat posed provocatively on benches and high stools while men wandered in and out continually, laughing with the girls and making lewd comments. Afterward they visited dives with sawdust floors and walls age-stained the color of tobacco juice. They finally wound up in the cheapest *casa* in the area, where the large room was suffocatingly hot and the air was pungent with sweat and cheap perfume. The women's faces were raddled and witchlike, their eyes hard and glittering. The room was thronged with men and the women thrust in among them, exposed themselves, and touched the men to arouse their desire. The two youths stayed only a short time, then went back to the stone arch and ordered anis and raisins.

"To our next trip . . ." said Diego.

". . . through hell!" concluded Anselmo.

"Those girls any good?" asked the barman sociably, refilling their tumblers.

"Not so far," said Diego.

"We're working up an appetite," explained Anselmo.

"We're students of human nature," said Diego.

Anselmo raised his glass. "And now. A toast to our journey . . ."

". . . to paradise," concluded Diego.

They experimented with a highly recommended house in Balmes that had recently opened. An old crone garbed in black crouched on the pavement outside, hugging a tray of matches and lottery tickets. She whined as they drew level with her, and Anselmo dropped a coin into her outstretched hand. "Keep the ticket," he told her. "It may bring you luck."

A pretty maid wearing a white cap and apron showed them into a luxurious waiting room. At once the madam joined them and while they sipped brandy, the girls of the house came in one at a time and pirouetted gracefully to show their charms. They were all young, charming, ladylike and modishly dressed. They smiled and said, "Good evening," politely when the madam introduced them by name.

The madam asked, "Did you see any girls you liked?"

"The small dark one," said Anselmo. "Maria-Carmen."

"She's *very* experienced. I'm sure you'll enjoy her."

"The one in the green dress," said Diego. "Lolita."

"A hundred pesetas," said the madam.

Diego at once rose to his feet. "Too much."

"But since there's two of you, we'll reduce it to seventy-five," said the madam hastily.

"Tricks?" asked Diego.

"Anything you want," said the madam. "What shall I tell the girls?" She discussed varieties of love-play with the air of a headwaiter booking a four-course dinner.

Barcelona
July 18, 1936

Isidro Barras's year of military service made him aware something very unusual was happening. At midnight the entire garrison was alerted and turned out on parade. After a long but cordial inspection by their officers, they had been dismissed to the barrack room where a large barrel of brandy had been tapped. Now the conscripts were queuing up with mugs for a generous ration. The brandy was strong and those who drew a second ration began to grin foolishly. Meanwhile the colonel and the officers sat around a large table at the extreme end of the barrack room and talked in low voices. Their faces were serious.

Isidro Barras drank only a little brandy. The monotonous soldier's diet of bread and beans had upset his stomach. The brandy made his bowels stir uneasily. He went out to the toilet and in the corridor came face to face with Captain Garon. He drew himself up and saluted smartly.

Captain Garon nodded at him broodingly. "Your name is Barras, isn't it?"

"Yes, sir."

The captain was a tall, dark man of thirty. He was well-liked by the men. He said thoughtfully, "I hope you're sensible, Barras. Can you be discreet?"

"I'll try, sir."

"Tell me. How do the men feel about the People's Government?"

"We don't discuss politics, sir. We're not interested."

"Would the men revolt against the government?"

Isidro's eyes widened. "We've never talked about anything like that, sir. What happens in Morocco is not our business."

"These are bad times, Barras. It may become necessary very soon for you conscripts to make a serious decision."

"I'm . . . I'm not sure I understand, sir."

Captain Garon stared at him hard. "Revolt, Barras. There's talk the army might revolt against the government. Be discreet, Barras. Discuss it with the other men. Find out how they feel about it."

"I'll do what I can, sir," said Isidro unhappily. He eyed the captain warily. "May I ask, sir. What do *you* feel about it?"

Captain Garon's face turned to stone. "A soldier should not have political opinions. His duty is to his government."

Isidro Barras was thoughtful when he returned to the barrack room and soon he spoke to Jorge Vidal who was a natural leader among the men. "What's going on with the officers, Vidal?"

Vidal scowled toward the far end of the room. "I think the rumors are true about the revolt in Morocco. They're not giving us free brandy because they love us."

"What will happen, d'you think?"

"We're just pawns, Barras." Vidal glared at the officers. "They give the orders and we obey."

"But is it right to revolt against our government?" Isidro was worried.

"D'you want to get shot for disobeying orders?"

Another soldier who had been listening butted in: "My father was elected mayor of our village. Everybody voted for the People's Front. So why should we revolt against the government?"

"Suppose we're *ordered* to do it?" said Isidro. The thought shook him. "Suppose we're ordered to take over the presidential palace . . . by force!"

"The officers daren't do it."

"They might."

Vidal turned to another soldier. "What do you think?"

Soon little discussion groups formed and soldiers argued heatedly among themselves.

Presently all the officers stood up. One of them pounded his pistol butt on the wooden table for silence.

The colonel, a short stiff-backed man with iron-gray hair, an imperious manner and a metallic voice, said sharply: "I expect you are all wondering why you've been alerted. There's a very good reason." He glanced at his wristwatch. "In a few minutes you will march to the Plaza de Cataluña. The FAI staged a strike today and the government has learned the Anarchists will attempt to overthrow the government by force. It is our duty to defend our country. We hope a show of arms will discourage the FAI. But if it becomes necessary, I know you will do your duty as loyal Spaniards." He nodded and, surrounded by his officers, marched stiffly out of the barrack room.

At once the sergeants began to shout orders. Isidro Barras and his companions soon found themselves marching six abreast through the night streets of Barcelona. An officer in a sidecar drove ahead of the troops, and the colonel, flanked by his officers, led the column on horseback.

The men's tongues had been loosened by the brandy and they talked excitedly. Opinions differed widely and were hotly upheld. Furious arguments broke out along the length of the column.

"Why should we fight the FAI?"

"The Anarchists want power. They're against all other forms of government!"

"Our duty is to protect the government, although we may sympathize with the Anarchists."

"How do we know the colonel's telling the truth?"

"They're trying to make murderers of us! They want us to shoot down our fellow workers!"

The mounted officers busily rode up and down the column, trying to quell the disorderly arguments, and when Captain Garon drew level with Isidro Barras, he walked his horse. His lean face was dark and somber and he spoke from the corner of his mouth. "How goes it, Barras?"

"Is it true we're going to the Plaza de Cataluña?"

"Quite true."

"The men are uneasy, sir. They're afraid they're being misled. Is it true the Anarchists are revolting?"

"Untrue." Captain Garon spoke clearly and the men within earshot listened intently. "The colonel plans to unite with platoons from other barracks. It's all part of a military plot to take over the city." Captain Garon spurred his horse and trotted to the head of the column where he took his place among the other officers.

Behind him raged fierce controversy.

"We're being misled by our officers."

"But which officers!"

"If we fight the FAI we won't be defending the government . . . we'll be attacking it!"

Jorge Vidal shouted angrily. "We've just had elections and voted the government we want."

Suspicion and doubt spread rapidly through the ranks. Arguments raged so fiercely that some men came to blows as they straggled along, out of step, the lines ragged. Their worried officers rode up and down the columns, trying to voice-whip discipline into men who responded sullenly.

When the marching column had drawn near to the university, the motorcycle officer, who had scouted ahead, roared back. The column was halted and the officers conferred. Presently the colonel rode back halfway along the column and held up his hand for silence.

"Ahead of us a large force of armed Anarchists is barring our entrance into the Plaza de Cataluña. We hope these hotheads will yield to law and order. Otherwise . . . we will have to do our duty."

Officers rode up and down the column giving orders.

"Load rifles."

"Fix bayonets."

Isidro Barras's hands trembled as he fixed his bayonet to the barrel of his rifle. He couldn't imagine himself plunging his bayonet into living flesh.

Orders rang out and disciplined men obeyed woodenly. They formed up across the road in parade-ground rows, shoulder to shoulder.

"Bayonets at the ready."

Their bayonets were a bristling line of sharp steel, poised to impale living flesh.

Officers told the men in the front ranks: "If we give the order to fire, first rank will kneel to shoot. The second rank will remain standing. Is that clear?"

The men listened with wide eyes.

"Bayonets at the ready. Forward . . . march!"

The men advanced in straggly lines, their hands sweating on the butts of their rifles. The officers rode slightly ahead of them, their mounts' iron shoes clattering on the cobbled road. The night air was breathlessly hot and heavy with the odors of summer. Even the usually spruce and cool-looking officers were sweating and anxious.

There was no more talking; there was only a grim foreboding as the men advanced slowly in battle formation, nervous, uneasy and bewildered.

Soon they saw their enemy, a great crowd that solidly blocked the road, an undisciplined, unruly, slogan-chanting mob. A few of the men in the front line had rifles and those behind flourished FAI banners.

The soldiers advanced steadily and as they drew closer, they saw there were women too, flaunting the black and red scarves of the Anarchists and some with cartridge bandoliers slung across their shoulders.

Isidro Barras's mouth was dry and his rifle slippery. In front of him an officer's horse walked sedately. The officer drew his sword and rode with it held upright as though on the parade ground. Isidro wondered if the officers intended to march the men straight at the crowd, herding it back with bayonet points. But when they were only twenty yards from the crowd, an order rang out.

"Squad . . . halt!"

They came to a standstill, their bayonet points a bristling threat.

"Front rank kneel."

There was the creak of leather, grunts and the thud of rifle butts hitting the roadway.

"Front rank take aim."

"Second rank take aim."

The great crowd blocking the road fearlessly faced the rifles. And now the crowd grew strangely silent.

They can't do it, thought Isidro Barras. *They can't order us to shoot down our own people!* But he saw the officers conferring with the colonel and the colonel was gesturing, and in a terrible moment of illumination, he knew that they *would!*

The crowd knew it too. Suddenly it burst apart like a breaking dam, swamping toward them. Those with rifles flourished them above their heads to show they would not use them. Others shouted appealingly, their voices ringing with sincerity.

"Don't shoot us down like dogs, brothers!"

"You are workers and so are we."

"We are your brothers. You cannot fire on us."

Men ran straight at the bristling line of steel bayonets and their eyes shone with the fervor of their belief.

"Front rank . . . fire!" rang out the crisp order.

But the front-rank soldiers were too startled and bewildered to obey.

Jorge Vidal was in the front rank and a pale-faced man wearing a grease-stained overall ran straight up to him and thrust out his callused and workstained hands. "Look, brother. I'm a worker." His cheeks were gaunt with tuberculosis. "You are a worker too, brother! All workers are brothers!" He tore open his overalls and exposed his bony chest to the glittering steel. "Will you kill me, brother?" He thrust closer to the bayonet point. "Will you butcher me, comrade?"

"Front rank . . . FIRE!" screamed an officer.

Jorge Vidal rose to his feet and threw down his rifle. "Fire yourself into the milk of the mother who gave you birth!" he shouted at the officer, overcome by a deeply moving emotion that brought tears to his eyes.

The officer wheeled his horse around and galloped at Vidal with upraised sword.

Vidal stood defiantly, bracing himself to avoid the slashing sword. But a soldier's bayonet swiveled and the officer's mount ran straight onto it and reared up, screaming. Its plunging scattered men, and in the confusion, the officer was unseated and trampled underfoot.

One after another, the soldiers threw down their rifles and shouted joyfully as the spirit of revolt swept through them. The shocking order to fire no longer had to be obeyed, and they laughed with relief. The crowd mingled in their ranks and workmen hugged soldiers as though meeting after a long parting. A white-haired man with a wrinkled face and a bandolier over his patched shirt flung his arms around Isidro Barras. "Barcelona is saved for the workers," he choked fervently. Unashamed tears ran down his worn cheeks. "We *knew* you would not fire upon your fellow workers."

Isidro Barras had a lump in his throat. "Of course we would not," he said and wondered how he could ever have thought he might.

In the confusion, the officers tried to slip away. But they were seen and with angry shouts were seized and made prisoners. A tall man with a bloodstained bandage around his head and carrying a tommy-gun seemed to be a leader and when the captured officers were about to be taken away by an Anarchist guard, Jorge Vidal protested: "Captain Garon is one of us!"

"Which is Captain Garon?" asked the leader.

"That one."

The Anarchist leader said warmly: "So you remained loyal, comrade?"

Captain Garon's face was expressionless. "I'm a soldier. My duty is to be loyal to my government."

The colonel and his fellow officers glowered at him. One spat contemptuously.

"Take command of your troops then, Captain! The Captaincy General in Paseo de Colon is held by revolting officers. We should put it under siege."

"I will assume temporary command only until I receive orders from a superior officer who is loyal to the government," said Captain Garon.

"That is all we ask of you, comrade."

Captain Garon said quietly: "I have no political opinions. I simply do my duty."

"Do your duty, officer. We will not obstruct you."

Captain Garon glanced around and his eyes rested on Vidal thoughtfully. "Do you know a sergeant's duties?"

"Yes, sir."

"Good. You're promoted. Get the men lined up and ready to march."

It was nearly dawn when Anselmo and Diego left the house in Balmes. The old match-seller slept against the wall like a bundle of dusty black rags, but the door's shutting aroused her and her thin voice whined. Diego dropped a coin in her tray, and they walked on toward the Ramblas. Presently Diego stopped and cocked his head on one side. "Listen!"

Anselmo listened. "It's a kid running a stick along railings."

"Machine-gun fire!" said Diego.

Anselmo chuckled. "You're imagining things!"

Not far away a volley of shots rang out. Spasmodic firing continued and at the next corner they came on half a dozen Civil Guards huddled behind a wall buttress. Stray bullets smashed windows and ricocheted off the cobbled roadway.

A Civil Guard spun around and covered Anselmo and Diego with a pistol. "Hands up."

Grinning foolishly the two youths stood still while they were searched for weapons.

"You can drop your hands." The guard rasped the back of his hand across his unshaven chin. "Have you tobacco?"

Diego produced a packet of cigarettes and they lit up.

"What's happening?" asked Diego.

"The bastards have got a machine gun up on the roof. They shoot anything that moves. All we can do is snipe back!"

In the distance sounded the rattle of machine-gun fire.

"What's that?"

"The Plaza de Cataluña. They've taken over the telephone exchange."

"Who's taken it over?"

"The military. Rebel officers ordered out the troops and occupied it before anyone realized what was happening. It's not serious. The army rank-and-file is loyal. They've mostly turned on their officers and made them prisoners!"

Another Civil Guard joined them and gratefully accepted a cigarette.

"Then the revolt's fizzled out?" said Diego.

"Here in Barcelona. We've only got to mop up these Falangist rooftop snipers and a handful of troops in the Atarzanos Barracks. That's the lot!" The guard drew on his cigarette until its red glow reflected on his cheek. "It might be different elsewhere," he said cautiously.

A siren wailed, a police car sped toward them and skidded to a standstill with a scream of brakes. Steel-helmeted Assault Guards tumbled out, armed with tommyguns. An officer said crisply: "We'll put up a barrage to keep their heads under cover. You others, into the building and drive them out." He glared at Anselmo and Diego. "Who are you?"

"We were on our way home."

"Get moving." The officer thumbed. "We've enough trouble without civilians getting shot."

Anselmo and Diego turned around and walked the long way home.

"I was right," said Anselmo. "It's nothing. Just hotheads playing with fireworks."

7

Madrid's evening air was hot and sultry. From the bars and cafés, radios blared out the news that Casares had resigned and was being replaced by Martinez Barrio who was forming a new government.

"Keep tuned in," urged the announcer excitedly. "People of Spain, keep tuned in. Beware of lying rumors and traitors."

The two students strolled toward the Puerto del Sol and when they reached the Gran Via, the road was lined with people watching a marching group of shirt-sleeved workers, all bearing some kind of weapon. The excited crowd flowed after them and Jaime and Guillermo willingly drifted along too, caught up by the restlessness that permeated the city.

"*Que pasa?*" Jaime asked a man with a rifle slung over his shoulder.

"We're going to attack the Montana Barracks, comrade. The government has finally handed out rifles. But the bolts are safeguarded in the Montana Barracks."

"Has the Montana Garrison revolted then?"

"They tried. But we were expecting it. We've got them besieged."

The great crowd marched on chanting slogans until it reached the public gardens in the Calle de Ferraz. Then, spontaneously, the crowd began to run, swamping over the grounds to join the thousands already besieging the grim, gray fortress.

But there was little the attackers could do except snipe at the fortress. Its strong walls were unassailable. From time to time machine guns inside the barracks clattered angrily and scythed the grounds with lead. The attackers roared with anger and shot back with redoubled fury.

Jaime and Guillermo found themselves hunched down behind a concrete parapet beside a streetcar conductor who had lost his cap and who was cautiously sniping at the fortress walls with a shotgun.

It was an old rusted gun with worn hammers. The conductor broke it open and inserted two cartridges. When he closed the breech with a snap that jarred the hammers, they fell and both barrels discharged simultaneously.

The man swore furiously at the great furrow scored in the ground only inches from his foot. The crown of his head, usually covered by his uniform cap, was startlingly white in contrast to his tanned face. He said disgustedly: "Twenty years old! Now it fires itself!"

He took two more cartridges from his pocket and loaded the gun gingerly. One of the machine guns in the fortress chattered angrily.

The conductor aimed carefully, and the jolt of the first barrel firing made the hammer fall on the second cartridge. Blue smoke writhed as the man lowered the gun and glared at it reproachfully.

"What are you shooting at?" asked Guillermo.

"The machine guns at the windows."

"You can't hit them with scatter-shot," said Jaime.

The man glared and fumbled in his pocket for more cartridges. He said nothing.

"The shot won't reach halfway," said Guillermo.

The man's jaw jutted as he inserted cartridges in the gun. He aimed carefully.

"You're wasting ammunition," said Jaime.

The man scowled. "What else can I do?" he demanded angrily. "Throw stones at the sons of whores!"

Another conductor scampered across to them and threw himself down as machine-gun fire raked the grass behind him. "Let me take over here, comrade," he panted.

"Why?"

"I've got a rifle with a bolt!"

The man with the shotgun reluctantly allowed the other to take his place. His eyes gleamed. "You'll let me have a shot at them?"

"Allow me a few bangs at the bastards first!" The conductor took careful aim and fired. He went on shooting steadily and with patience. Nearby, a man cried out and a woman ripped the hem off her underskirt and bandaged his arm.

"They think they're safe," complained the shotgun man. Then he narrowed his eyes. "But when they come out . . . we'll be here waiting for them!"

Emil Znadlon Serra puffed smoke furiously and with detached interest watched nuns driven down the church steps. They submitted meekly to rough handling, bowed their heads, fingered their rosaries and muttered fervent prayers. The watching crowd was incensed by this show of religious faith and surged forward, shouting abuse and tearing the rosaries from their hands.

An Anarchist with a smoke-grimed face, laughing eyes and a black stubble of beard gave them a low, mocking bow. "Will one of you ladies dance?" he invited. "We will dance like angels upon the point of a needle."

The crowd howled its delight. Encouraged, the Anarchist seized the nearest nun by the waist and waltzed her around, laughing at her tearful protests. Workmen seized other nuns and the onlookers laughed until tears rolled down their cheeks as the men waltzed their unwilling partners and clumsily imitated the delicate postures of ballet dancers.

"Give me a kiss, darling," demanded one man and arched a nun back over his knee.

The crowd shouted advice.

"Give it to her, comrade."

"We'll hold her for you, Juan."

"Show us her ass, comrade."

"Stuff her full of rosary beads."

When the men tired of their elephantine waltzing, they spun the nuns into the arms of the crowd. A few nuns broke blindly through the angry mob; but others were beaten to their knees and stripped of their robes. They crawled to the refuge of doorways or side streets, streaming blood.

Emil Serra saw angry men tear off a nun's cowl and expose her shaven head. She was very young, only twenty-two or so, and her delicate white skin emphasized her purity. She did not struggle. She simply closed her eyes and offered herself up to God, submitting her physical being to mob violence. A man slapped her cheek and the imprint of his fingers stood out like a vivid birthmark.

"Whore!" he shouted. "Are you one who marched out to vote against us in the election?"

She seemed not to hear the question and her mouth moved in silent prayer. Another powerful slap split her lips, but in a moment she was praying again.

"Whore! Do you pray to God to overthrow the People's Government?"

Each question was punctuated by a blow. She would have fallen if angry hands had not held her erect. Her prayers intensified.

"Who allowed Fascist snipers to use the church towers?"

"Was your brother priest one of the firing squad that shot the Asturian miners?"

Blows rained upon the nun, angry fists threatened and faces contorted with hate.

"Crucify the whore!"

"Strip her!"

The crowd swamped over her; fierce shouts and men and women kicking and stamping. An Anarchist danced away, triumphantly flourishing a black gown. He pulled it on over his shoulders and somebody fitted a white, starched nun's cowl on his head. The crowd screamed as he minced around at the foot of the church steps, exaggeratedly twitching his buttocks in grotesque imitation of a streetwalker.

There was another gust of laughter when an Anarchist garbed in the round felt hat and long black cassock of a priest ran down the church steps to join him. They waltzed together in an obscene parody of the sex act.

Then the mob stripped the church. Jerry-cans of gasoline were hand-chained to the church steps and poured over the priests' bodies and sacred relics. One man had found the communal wine and swayed drunkenly. He drew matches from his pocket and prematurely lit one.

With a great *whoosh* the gasoline ignited. Those nearest had their faces seared and the drunken man became a blazing torch and ran blindly amidst the scattering crowd.

Emil Serra knocked ash from his cigar. In the night sky was the glow of a dozen other blazing churches and not far away was the staccato chatter of machine guns.

A man hurried past, his voice excited. "We've got a young nun in a house over there . . ."

Emil Serra nodded and strode on toward another part of the tormented city. Perhaps he should have watched what they did to the young nun, he reflected.

There was disciplined calm within the Montana Barracks. All through the long night, the vast besieging crowd had waited patiently. The summer stars had shone brightly and the burning churches had loaned the night a ruddy glow. At dawn, the loyal government troops set up a mortar and at regular intervals the *cruuumph* of exploding shells shook the garrison. Then artillery was brought up and shells began to burst around the garrison's great doors.

Water, electricity, and the telephone had been cut off. But from the upper story of the garrison the defenders could see across rooftops to a neighboring barracks. With binoculars and flags they exchanged messages. They learned they could expect no help from the neighboring fortress which was held by only a handful of men. A conference was called, facts were faced and the officers resolved to fight to the death. A generous ration of brandy was issued to the ranks to hearten them after their long and tiring night.

Captain Dalfeu was only twenty-eight, but his religious convictions enabled him to inspire his men. After the officers' conference, he returned to the barrack room he commanded. Machine guns were set up at sandbagged windows and riflemen sniped at anything moving.

"At ease," said Captain Dalfeu. He smiled. "How about it, corporal. Is there a tot of brandy for me too?"

Brandy was poured and he stood astride, gently slapping his polished boot with his cane. "A toast to Spain, our country!" he said. *"Arriba Espana!"*

"Arriba Espana," his men echoed dutifully after a slight pause.

Captain Dalfeu took out a gold cigarette case, carefully selected a cigarette, snapped his lighter into flame and lit up.

His men watched in expectant silence.

"We've had an officers' conference," he said quietly. "Our position is critical. We may not be able to hold out until we are relieved."

Cruuumph! The building shook and plaster fell from the ceiling.

"We are soldiers and Spain is our motherland. We will not desert her."

The men listened respectfully. Many were still in their teens.

"Spain shall not die!" thundered Captain Dalfeu. "Spain will be saved from Communist violence which is spreading like a cancerous disease." Captain Dalfeu was impassioned. "God and the Virgin Mary will help us," he declared. He looked upward to heaven and slowly and devoutly made the sign of the cross.

His men crossed themselves sheepishly.

Captain Dalfeu pointed a long arm, his forefinger trembling. "Last night priests were murdered, nuns were raped and all the Christian values we hold dear were violated. Man must love his fellowman and respect the laws of God. But a madness has come upon us. A handful of evil men have hoodwinked the good and simple people and poisoned their minds against Christianity."

The captain took out his handkerchief and wiped his moist forehead. "God has called upon *us* to defend the right," he said quietly. "Is there any among you who will not give his life for God, Spain and justice?"

The men shouted:

"Arriba Espana!"

"God is right!"

"Todo para la Patria!"

Captain Dalfeu's eyes were suspiciously moist as he looked around him. "Then let us pray to God for His help." He sank down onto his knees, closed his eyes, clasped his hands and led his men in prayer.

Cruuuumph!

The explosion shook the barrack room but the captain's voice did not falter. Artillery shells battered the fortress doors.

A machine-gunner called excitedly: "Captain! Come quickly, sir!"

Captain Dalfeu ran to the window in time to see the besiegers flood out from cover and swamp over the exposed forecourt toward the fortress; thousands of excited men and women flourished weapons and waved banners, impervious to their danger.

"Hold your fire," said the captain. "Wait for my order. Aim low and take your time."

The great crowd rushed on, screaming triumphantly.

"Are you ready?" said the captain. "Fire . . . !"

Machine guns blasted and rifles fired from fortress windows. The attackers went down like puppets, legs scythed from under them, bodies twisted and faces contorted with shock and agony. The mob faltered in its suicidal charge, then with a great yell of outraged fury fled, panic-stricken, leaving the area before the fortress strewn with dead and wounded.

"Well done," said Captain Dalfeu.

"Knocked them over like rabbits, sir."

"They asked for it."

From the corridor outside there was angry shouting and then pistol shots.

"Remain alert," ordered Captain Dalfeu. He opened the door and

stepped into the corridor. A fellow officer stood at the door of the
next room, holding a smoking pistol. Inside the room three soldiers
lay dead. Their companions stared down at them with shocked, white
faces.

"What's the trouble, Captain Garcia?"

Garcia scowled at his men. He said wearily: "Back to your posts."

They returned to the sandbagged windows and he reholstered his
pistol. He turned to Captain Dalfeu. "I was only away five minutes.
While my back was turned, they tried to surrender. They were waving a white cloth out of the window."

Captain Dalfeu remembered the suicidally charging mob and its
scream of fury when it was fired upon.

Captain Garcia read his thoughts. "We can't be responsible for
traitors' actions."

"How's the fortress door?"

Captain Garcia glanced at his men to make sure they couldn't hear
him. He spread his hands in a gesture of hopelessness. "It'll go any
time now!"

When the fortress doors were finally blasted open by artillery
shells, Captain Dalfeu knew it, because he saw the attackers rise up
and race forward to storm the breach in the garrison's defense. Men
seemed to erupt from the very earth, a great mob howling its rage and
triumph.

The defenders' machine guns fired until the barrels were red-hot
and the guns jammed. By this time the attackers were inside the fortress. The stone corridors rang with howls of rage and the cries of the
injured.

Captain Dalfeu drew his pistol and addressed his men. "For God
and Spain!" he said. *"Arriba Espana!"*

"Arriba Espana!"

He led his men out and along the corridor. The garrison was three
stories high with a large, inner patio. Iron staircases ran from the
galleries to the ground floor. The attackers who had swarmed into the
garrison were fighting their way up the staircases and along the galleries. As Captain Dalfeu and his men emerged from the corridor
onto a gallery they walked straight into the sights of a dozen kneeling
workmen whose rifles rang out simultaneously, scattering the soldiers
like ninepins.

Captain Dalfeu's leg crumpled beneath him, and as he fell he lost his grip on his pistol. His head received a glancing blow against the iron railings and blood ran from his temple as he groped dazedly for his gun. A giant worker towered over him, and growled as he reached for the captain. Fingers gouged into Captain Dalfeu's arm and leg, and he was swung high off the ground and held aloft triumphantly.

The giant paced to the gallery rail, gave a shout of warning and as those below looked up, he launched his victim into space.

A split second later Captain Dalfeu's skull split like a pumpkin, splattering men who had leaped wildly for safety. Among them were Jaime and Guillermo, sickened by the slaughter going on around them.

A man shouted: "This way, comrades. I've found the arms depot!"

There was a stampede to the armory. The doors were broken open and the men inside handed out rectangular black boxes. Jaime and Guillermo claimed one each and found they contained regulation army pistols: 9 caliber Astros.

Close by them a wounded Rebel officer had been taken prisoner. One of his captors loaded his Astra pistol, stooped over the sitting officer, placed the barrel of his pistol behind the man's ear and pulled the trigger. He watched the result with wide-eyed, childish curiosity.

Within fifteen minutes, the fighting was over. Armed workmen were prowling among the bodies of the defenders, finishing off any who still lived.

"Let's get out of here," said Guillermo. He was very pale.

Jaime sighed. "It had to happen," he said sadly. "So much pentup hatred had to end in violence."

When the revolt broke out, most of the artillery cadets stationed in the Arab fortress of Alcazar were on vacation. Among the handful of cadets in the garrison were Ferraz, Castro, Redondo and Rafael Ledesma. They were playing poker when they heard that Colonel Moscardo had arrived in Toledo and had publicly declared that Spain's sacred crusade had begun. He had called on all true Spaniards to do their duty.

Fighting started that same evening when a squad of militiamen wearing blue overalls and carrying rifles issued by the FAI marched into Toledo to take over the Civil Guard headquarters. The Civil Guard resisted, there was spasmodic shooting in the streets and Falangists sniped from the rooftops. At once, Colonel Moscardo ordered the officers and men in the Alcazar fortress to relieve the hard-pressed

Civil Guards and Falangists. The resulting action was short and effective and left Colonel Moscardo in undisputed control of Toledo.

But the victory was short-lived. The government was finding its strength. A long column of militiamen marched out from Madrid and attacked with such vigor that after four days of battle Colonel Moscardo retreated into the Alcazar fortress. He realized that the revolt was going badly and he prepared for a siege. He had many mouths to feed. Nearly two hundred cadets, a hundred officers, eight hundred Civil Guards and two hundred Falangists. He had also taken with him into the Alcazar, two hundred and fifty women and fifty children, many of them the families of militiamen they had captured in a daring raid. At gun-point they were herded into the basement cellars. Among them was the daughter of the Socialist leader, Charugin.

When the government troops arrived in Toledo, General Riquelme, who commanded them, spoke to Colonel Moscardo on the telephone still connected to the Alcazar.

"Your position is hopeless, Colonel. You are surrounded by overwhelming forces. To surrender is not dishonor and will save lives."

Colonel Moscardo was icily formal. "You underestimate the position, General. We have arms, ammunition and food to last a year."

General Riquelme sighed. "This is the twentieth century, Colonel. How long can your old Arab fortress stand against modern weapons?"

"We will not surrender."

"If you oblige me to take the Alcazar by force, you condemn many of your men to death!"

There was a pause, and then Colonel Moscardo said quietly: "Tell *your* men we will care for their women and children as best we can."

Colonel Moscardo hung up.

The next day a commander of the Toledo militia telephoned Colonel Moscardo.

"Colonel. We are willing to allow all the women and children to leave the Alcazar."

"They refuse to leave the garrison. It is the only place they feel safe from Red violence."

"You realize, Colonel, that if anything happens to them it is your responsibility."

"Our country is Spain and our strength is in God."

"You force me to be ruthless, Colonel. Your son, Luis, is my prisoner. He is standing at my side now."

Colonel Moscardo fell silent.

"If you make us barter with lives, Colonel, let us start with your son. Do you want him to live? If so, surrender."

There was a long pause.

"You are lying," said the colonel.

"Hold on, Colonel. I'll pass the telephone to your son."

"Father," said Luis Moscardo.

"You are a prisoner, Luis?"

"Yes, Father."

"What do they say, my boy?"

"That you must surrender. Otherwise, they will shoot me."

"Are you afraid to die, my boy?"

"I do not want to die, Father. But you will do what is right."

"Listen, my son. We must *both* do what is right. We can gain nothing by surrender. My men will be summarily tried and executed if they are not shot down in the act of surrender. So, commend your soul to God, Luis. Die like a true patriot. At the end shout 'Long live Christ the King' and 'Long live Spain.' "

"I will do as you say, Father; and I embrace you with all my heart." There was a tremble in the boy's voice.

"Go with God, my son."

The commander came back on the line. "You have ten minutes to surrender, Colonel."

"Do not delay, Commander. Shoot my son at once if such is your duty, because the Alcazar will *never* surrender!"

Strict discipline was maintained within the Alcazar. Provisions were rationed, guards were changed frequently and the fortress was alert day and night. The women and children were confined in the fortress basement for protection from government planes that bombed the fortress ceaselessly.

When off duty, Rafael Ledesma and his three friends often played poker.

"How long will this siege go on?" asked Claudio Ferraz, as he waited for the others to discard.

"Until we're bombed out," said Cadet Redondo philosophically.

"I hope it's soon," yawned Castro. "I'm bored."

Rafael Ledesma's black eyes gleamed. "But we're heroes," he said proudly. "The whole world knows about us. We're the heroic defenders of Alcazar, a bulwark against the Red menace and a bastion against Marxism."

"You can have the glory," grinned Castro. "I'll take the Charugin girl."

"You're a sex maniac," said Cadet Redondo.

"I can't forget her," admitted Castro. "I had my hand on her in the car. All hot and mushy." His cheeks gleamed moistly. "I can't stop thinking about her!"

Claudio Ferraz grinned. "You'd better not try anything. The colonel will have you shot."

Cadet Redondo discarded. "Give me three."

"I throw in," said Rafael.

"Two cards," said Castro.

Claudio Ferraz took one card and squinted at it, debating if he should raise the bet.

"Suppose that Red bitch was to escape," said Rafael Ledesma thoughtfully.

"What Red bitch?" asked Redondo.

"How *could* she escape?" asked Castro practically.

"At night," said Rafael. "We could drop her over the wall afterward."

"Without the guards knowing?" objected Ferraz.

"They'll help. They can have her, too," said Castro.

"She'll crawl away with her flesh in shreds!" said Rafael. His high white forehead gleamed.

His friends were embarrassed by his vehemence. "I've got three of a kind," said Ferraz uncomfortably.

"That beats me," said Castro and threw down his cards.

"Me too," said Redondo.

"Let's go look at the girl," urged Rafael.

The others exchanged questioning glances.

"We won't start anything until we've made plans," he urged. "We'll just look at her!"

"All right," said Castro and got to his feet.

They walked out into the heat of the inner courtyard. Dead horses killed by bombing planes had been dragged into a corner where they had swollen up in the sun. The cadets' boot heels rang out on the hot concrete as they paced across it and they were immensely relieved to reach the cool shade of the fortress arch. Above them they heard the ominous drone of yet another bombing plane and the government artillery stationed on the Alicares Hill opened up a barrage which hammered the sturdy walls of the fortress.

The two armed guards at the head of the steps saluted the four cadets as they descended into the basement. The cellars were spacious with high vaulted stone ceilings. Straw mattresses were laid out in neat lines on the flagstones and drably dressed women clustered around cooking pots simmering on charcoal braziers. Children played quietly and looked up in frightened wonder at the young men in smart uniforms.

The dejected atmosphere suddenly became charged with tension as bombs fell. The fortress guns opened up against the bombing plane, the building shuddered with the explosions and mothers snatched up their children and cowered over them.

The hostage families of the militiamen were separated from the families of the garrison's defenders. They were at the extreme end of the basement.

The four cadets strolled along to them and stared at them with arrogant contempt. The women scowled back sullenly, bitterness glittering in their eyes.

"There she is," said Castro, pointing at Isabel Charugin. She did not recognize them. It had been dark the night they had seized her; but as their eyes undressed her, she knew again the horror of it. She shrank back, hiding herself behind the other women, and long after they had left the cellar, she was still trembling.

Father Delbos was young to have his own church. It was a very small church in the poor quarter of Barcelona. He considered himself a worldly man. He read widely and believed the Church was lagging sadly in a quickly changing world. He believed communism was an ever-growing menace and regretted that only Hitler and Mussolini stood firm against the rising flood of materialism.

He had welcomed the revolt and was dismayed by its failure. There had been a little fighting that was quickly quelled and now the city had turned mad. Armed militiamen rampaged through the streets, shouting slogans and firing in the air triumphantly, while women screamed shrill encouragement. Now it was night, the sky glowed blood-red, and Father Delbos waited for them to come to his church.

He was quite alone. He barred and bolted the church doors and then knelt in prayer and meditation, remembering how Christ had died for mankind. His eyes filled with tears as he thought of his Saviour suffering the torment of crucifixion with blood running from his side and staining the earth.

Father Delbos prayed for strength and presently a calmness came upon him. He knew he was not of the fiber of martyrs. His cowardice was as much a part of him as the large wart on his left temple. But God knew he was afraid and would protect him. Father Delbos prayed until he heard the menacing rumble of the mob's voice and marching feet.

He sprang to his feet. Sweat stood out on his forehead and his hands trembled. The tramping feet became thunder mingled with screams of rage. Now the mob was all around the church, hammering at the doors and throwing rocks that shattered the stained-glass windows.

Father Delbos shook with fear.

The shouts became enraged with frustration. More windows smashed and the pounding on the doors redoubled.

Slowly Father Delbos walked up the aisle, resolved to throw open the doors, fearlessly confront the howling mob and bless it with the love of God. But when the moment came, he had not the courage. He stared at the massive entrance doors and saw they were strong enough to resist until the end of time. The mob pounded them with fists, rocks and rifle butts, but they were unyielding. He knew then this was his salvation. The mob would grow weary of hammering and go away.

Father Delbos drew himself up bravely and prayed aloud. "I beg you, Holy Father, to forgive these misguided people. They know not what they do and . . ."

He broke off suddenly, cocking his ear. There were sudden shouts of triumph and the rush of many feet. Horror froze him as he divined what was happening. Not far away was a plaza, where a public bench stood under a palm tree. The bench was a solid length of timber and the mob was uprooting it!

The mob smashed its battering ram at the main doors, the hinges screeched and the door frame groaned.

Father Delbos shook with fear. Again and again the battering ram thudded against the doors and the priest forced himself to face the awful reality of death by violence.

The door shuddered under another blow and the iron rivets that secured the locking bar tore free from the wood. The priest knew it could not hold for long. He resolved again to face them fearlessly and shame them with the love of God. He held his head high and clenched his hands at his sides.

The battering ram smashed again and the door all but gave way. Once more and the mob would pour in like a human torrent of hate, tearing, clawing and biting. He would make the sign of the cross and bless them.

The priest wiped the sweat from his forehead. Only seconds now. He could picture the battering ram poised, now swinging forward massively, and . . .

. . . and Father Delbos turned and fled.

He ran blindly, terrified for his life. His black skirts flipped high and his shoes swish-swished like handfuls of sand cast along a stone floor. He raced down the aisle, behind the altar and flung himself into the choirboys' robing room.

He leaned against the lockless door, chilled with horror as the triumphant mob stormed over the church threshold. Women screamed shrilly, men roared and the great vault of the church rang with their rage and hatred. The mob was drunk with power. Confessional boxes were overturned and smashed, the gilt pedestal on which the Bible rested crashed down while axes chopped at God's sacred relics. The mob was everywhere, shouting, screaming and destroying and there was no escape from its fury.

Yet while Father Delbos trembled, he ripped off his cassock and his collar, and tore the buttons off his shirt. He smeared his face with dirt from the floor and searched in the lockers until he found a beret that covered his tonsured head. He cowered in the dark robing room hoping he would not be found, but soon there came the tramp of feet and yellow candlelight exposed him to the man who threw open the door.

The priest stared at him, terrified.

The man gave him only a glance. "Found anything in here, comrade?"

Before Father Delbos could answer, the man saw the hanging surplices. He shouted his find to others and they swarmed into the room, snatching down church robes and dressing up. Father Delbos was swept along with them as they danced out into the church aisle.

Women were holding candles so men could see to do their destructive work. One man was chopping away the support of the pulpit which already leaned over at a perilous angle and others levered with crowbars to pry the altar away from the wall.

"Help me, comrade. Hey, *you!* Help me!"

Father Delbos spun around. A man was breaking a life-size image of Christ upon the cross away from the wall. He paused to wipe sweat from his face and nodded at the priest. "Give a hand, comrade."

Numbly, Father Delbos added his weight to the crowbar. The wall rivets tore free from the cement and the cross slowly leaned forward until it broke away and fell. The plaster face of Christ smashed against the stone floor.

"Now the benches, comrade. They'll make a fine blaze."

Father Delbos labored in a daze, his soft hands moist with cold sweat. He was sick with fear as he tore down crucifixes, desecrated sacred images and dragged holy relics outside to the bonfire pile. He stood back with the others, watched fuel sloshed over it and a match lighted. Flames leaped high and their heat seared Father Delbos with his own guilt.

The mob chanted slogans, the bonfire blazed and militiamen dressed as choirboys danced grotesquely. When he could, Father Delbos slipped away into the night.

He took refuge with one of his congregation named Charon. They sat behind barred doors and bolted shutters and talked in hushed voices. Charon was openly a member of the UGT, but secretly a Falangist.

"They've gone mad," said Charon. "You're lucky to be alive, Father. They're murdering all priests and raping the nuns. Anybody who owns money is in peril. It's mob vengeance."

The priest's hands still trembled. "I must escape," he whispered hoarsely. "I *must* get away!"

"Don't let them catch you alive. One priest had a crucifix thrust down his throat until he suffocated."

Father Delbos pleaded. "Help me. Think of something."

"If you escape from Barcelona, have you anywhere you can take refuge?"

"I've a distant cousin who's a priest. He *can't* refuse to help me."

"He might need help himself."

"He's far away. A little fishing village called Escoleras."

"You must go to him."

"How will I get there?"

"Travel by night. They'll have patrols out but at night they are careless."

"Can I go by train?"

"Fatal. They're watching all the stations. Anyone wanting to travel is instantly suspect. You must walk by night and hide during the day."

"It'll take days to get there!"

"Would you rather lose your head than blister your feet?" Charon drew his forefinger across his throat and the priest shuddered.

"I'll give you a UGT membership card that'll help if you're questioned. You'll have to shave your head completely, because if they take off your hat they'll know you're a priest."

Father Delbos slipped away from Charon's house the following night.

8

Saturday the eighteenth of July, the first day of the revolt, was no different in Escoleras from any other Saturday. In the afternoon an orchestra from Figueras played *Sardanas* in the plaza and afterward introduced the new popular dance hit "The Music Goes Round and Round." The cinema that night showed the American gangster film, *On The Spot.*

The fishing fleet did not go out on Sundays, but by then everybody knew there was political upheaval, and farm workers and fishermen, wearing their Sunday best, argued in the narrow streets or gathered outside the bars and cafés listening to radio announcers feverishly calling upon the people to stay tuned in for up-to-the-minute news.

Juan Morales, the mayor; Don Carlos the priest; Doctor Juan Aldo and other councillors held an emergency meeting in the town hall. They wanted to keep abreast of events, but didn't know how. They had telephoned the mayor of Figueras for news, but he was as ignorant as they about what was happening. Communication with Barcelona was impossible.

Paco Barras climbed the steep stairs to the two dingy offices of the town hall and thrust his silvery-blond head in the door. *"Que pasa?"*

The mayor shrugged his shoulders, spread his pudgy hands and puffed out his fat cheeks. "An emergency council meeting."

"But nobody knows anything," said Don Carlos. He smiled benignly and rested his hands upon his comfortable belly.

Barras nodded as though the reply was exactly what he had expected. "Politics!" he said scathingly as he stepped into the office. "Politics always causes trouble." He was barefooted and he ran his big toe down his brown calf, rubbing away seawater salt.

The young people of the village were quite unconcerned about what was happening far away in Barcelona or in Madrid, and in the late afternoon Teresa, her sister Pepita, friends and some of the older women went to the beach to swim.

On the way Teresa met Rosalia. "We're going swimming," she invited.

Rosalia shook her head regretfully. "I've too much to do."

"But you haven't swum all summer!

Rosalia smiled wryly. "I will when I can."

The group hurried on. The first strip of beach was where the men swam. When they saw the women approaching, their shouting, laughter and splashing was redoubled. The girls giggled and blushed at some of their comments and skirted around the men, pretending to ignore them. They walked on at least a hundred yards before they spread their towels on the sand and pulled off their dresses under which they wore their bathing suits.

The water was crystal-clear and cold. Some of the girls raced out to a piece of floating cork, others dived between legs, some splash-fought and many filtered the sand at the water's edge for limpets. When they tired, they lay in the sun until dry and swam again.

"Isn't that Rosalia?" asked Pepita.

Teresa glanced along the beach where a hundred yards away a white bathing cap bobbed in the water. "It looks like her," said Teresa slowly.

"Have you quarreled with her, Teresa?"

"Of course not, silly."

"Why does she swim alone?"

"Why don't you ask her," said Teresa.

They watched the swimmer wade out from the sea and when she took off her cap and shook out her hair with a familiar gesture, Teresa jumped to her feet and walked along the water's edge toward her. Rosalia watched her approaching a long time before she waved her hand in recognition.

Teresa waved back.

Rosalia stooped, picked up her dress and quickly pulled it on over her bathing suit. When Teresa reached her, she was combing out her long, black hair.

"You said you were busy," said Teresa

"I don't want to swim with the others. They're too noisy."

"If you want to be alone, I'll leave."

"No. Please don't go," Rosalia said quickly. Her eyes pleaded. "Sit down with me."

Teresa sat beside her. "Aren't you going to sunbathe?"

Rosalia's dress clung to her. Her breasts, belly and pelvis were wet-stained as though daubed by an artist portraying woman. "I can't be bothered."

"You used to enjoy sunbathing."

Rosalia shrugged her shoulders disinterestedly.

"Aren't you going to swim again?"

Rosalia shook her head. "I must go soon."

"Why are you so busy, Rosalia? You haven't swum all season."

"I've been helping Father with the allotment." Rosalia folded her towel and presently the two girls walked back along the beach.

"Have you heard from Anselmo?" asked Rosalia.

"I had a letter yesterday. He and Manolo arrive at the end of the month for their holidays. Pilar and Antonia are coming down from Madrid, too."

"Any news of . . . Rafael?"

"The family doesn't want to talk about him. I think there's been some kind of trouble. But I don't ask. It's better not to probe into private affairs." Teresa gave her friend a shrewd glance. "Don't tell me you're still in love with him?"

Rosalia nodded slowly and smiled.

"Did you see him the last time he was here?"

"Just once. When I was working in our olive grove."

"What happened?"

Rosalia shrugged her shoulders. "I was angry. You told me what he'd said about us and I resented it and . . ."

". . . and?"

"We quarreled. He left without saying good-bye."

"You haven't heard from him since?"

"Not a word."

"But you still . . . want him?"

Rosalia's cool, gray-green eyes smoked. "Yes. Despite all that's happened I still want him."

"I shouldn't criticize. I feel the same about Anselmo. He's got his faults but he's just right for me!"

"You'll marry him," said Rosalia confidently.

"You think so?" asked Teresa happily.

"His father likes you, his mother thinks you're right for him so . . . what else do you need?"

"Anselmo has to want me too."

"You *know* he does. He spends all his time with you and writes regularly when he's away. What more can you want?"

"But he's never spoken."

"Do you want a sworn oath?"

"If only he'd say he loves me . . . or something! Then I'd know for certain he does."

They reached Teresa's group of friends and after chatting with them, Rosalia went on home alone. She skirted the group of village youths who stared at her boldly. Then because she was alone and her wet dress outlined her figure, they whistled after her and called out suggestively.

Rosalia walked on proudly with her head held high, but her full lips smiled her pleasure.

Later that evening, Narcissus Coruna arrived back from Barcelona. No trains were running but he had had the luck to thumb a lift on a fruit truck from Valencia heading for the French border. He had been dropped at Figueras and a mule cart had brought him to Escoleras.

A crowd swiftly gathered around him while he tried to answer the questions hurled at him. He was a pudgy youth with a plump face and a thin, reedy voice. He was easygoing, mild and placid. He was embarrassed by being the center of attention and wanted to hurry home. But he had been in Barcelona during the last few vital hours and everyone was avid for news.

"There was fighting," he told the mayor.

"What kind of fighting?"

Narcissus Coruna smiled weakly. "Rifles were being fired."

"Where?" demanded Doctor Aldo.

"In the Plaza de Cataluña. Somebody said the soldiers were marched out from the barracks; but when the Anarchists met them, the soldiers cheered and shouted: 'Down with Fascism!' "

"Did you see my son Isidro?" asked Barras.

"I saw nobody I knew. There were a few dead horses in the street. I went to the station but there were no trains. Two machine-gunners had climbed to the top of Christopher Columbus's column and were sniping. The Civil Guard made me detour through the fruit market."

"Who were the machine-gunners?"

"Falangists, I think. There was some shooting too at the Atarzanos Barracks. But as I passed the fruit market, I saw this fruit truck and offered the driver the train fare and . . ."

"Narcissus," interrupted the mayor sternly. "Could you get any clear idea of what's happening? Is the government about to fall?"

Narcissus Coruna smiled vaguely. "I didn't really think about it. All I wanted was to get home."

Doctor Aldo raised his eyes to heaven. "Narcissus!" he chided. "Perhaps history is being made. And all you thought of was getting home!" He took out his watch and looked at it. "I must hurry," he muttered.

"Any trouble on the road, my son?" asked Don Carlos.

"It was a good journey," said Narcissus. "Little traffic and a good driver. On the outskirts of Gerona we stopped at an inn. Grilled ribs of lamb. Everything was calm."

Mayor Morales smiled happily and spread his hands. "We've nothing to worry about, friends. A few political hotheads caused a disturbance; but nothing serious."

"But we should keep listening to the radio for news," advised Don Carlos solemnly and everyone laughed because all day the radio had announced nothing of importance.

At dawn the fishing fleet sailed out as usual. The rhythmic thuds of powerful, single-pistoned engines were muffled by a thin mist that hovered over the still water.

High-wheeled carts with canvas hoods swayed and lurched along the dusty, potholed roads out of Escoleras, carrying families to work in their vineyards and olive groves.

Doctor Aldo hurried homeward, eager for a cup of black coffee after a sleepless night. Serra's wife had given birth to a skinny baby girl.

Paco Barras's son Miguel was away on honeymoon; and because he could not fish alone, Teresa helped her father. She braced her bare feet against the sun-bleached floorboards and sent the little boat skimming across the calm sea to the *almadraba*. Arrow-headed ripples spread behind her to the beach where Paco Barras waited knee-deep in water. Teresa shipped her oars, peered down through the glass-bottomed *mirafondas* and saw the silvery glint of fish trapped in the net. She signaled her father who smiled contentedly as she rowed back to the beach.

In the café the radios blared reassuringly: "Attention. The People's Government reviews the military situation. The rebellion against the People's Front Government was initiated by traitorous generals in Morocco. The Moorish troops were misled by lies and obeyed orders to revolt against the people's elected government. Some Moorish soldiers have been flown to the mainland but are being rounded up by loyal government troops. Isolated garrisons in other districts of Spain have also revolted. In Madrid all traitorous officers have been taken prisoner. In Barcelona a few officers rebelled but order was soon restored. In Burgos, Saragossa, Pamplona and Valladolid our loyal troops are swiftly quelling all disturbances. In Sevilla the workers' militia is attacking an outpost of Fascist officers and Falangist traitors who have tried to occupy the town."

This report was repeated continually while Paco Barras played cards in a café after lunch. When he went home he was thoughtful. He shouted for his wife as he entered his cottage. She was plucking a chicken and came to the door of the kitchen with feathers sticking to her wet hands.

"How long do Miguel and Helena intend to stay in Sevilla?"

"Three or four days. Why?"

Paco Barras scratched his head. "I hope those political hotheads don't spoil their honeymoon."

A group of men wearing blue overalls stopped the baker's truck on the outskirts of Sevilla.

The driver leaned out of his window and gave the clenched-fist salute, but the rifles still pointed menacingly. The men's leader gestured until Hugo sighed, opened the door and climbed out into the roadway.

"Identification?" demanded the militia leader.

"Don't be officious, comrade." Hugo scowled as he took out his union card, his UGT card and his driving license.

The militiaman studied them carefully.

"I shit on the Virgin Mary!" swore Hugo disgustedly. "Look at my clothes. Do I look like a capitalist spy?"

The militiaman was unimpressed. "Where are you heading, comrade? The fight for workers' freedom is in the city."

"What you say is true, comrade. But I am on a mercy mission." He thumbed at the closed doors of the truck. "A great tragedy. A comrade from Cataluña was honeymooning in Sevilla; but his bride was killed by a Fascist sniper. I am helping him. He is alone, in a strange district, and must take her back to his village. So I drive my van while he keeps the customary vigil at her side."

"You say he is in *your* van, you lying reactionary? How can a worker own a van?"

Hugo spat upon the roadway. "I shit upon the capitalist baker who employs me and upon his truck which I have confiscated."

The militiamen laughed and nodded approvingly but they were still suspicious. "We must see inside. How do we know you are not a Fascist traitor carrying dynamite to blow up bridges and destroy communications?"

Hugo shrugged. "As you wish."

The militiamen gathered at the back of the truck while he opened the double doors. They stared in with hushed respect at the cold, still figure lying on the floor of the van. The white hands were folded on the breast, the face was marble-white and the dark, wine-red stains on the white dress told the story.

Miguel sat hunched on a wooden box, his shocked eyes staring blindly.

The militiaman closed the door. "You are engaged on a work of great humanity, comrade," he said.

"Our Catalan comrade has suffered deeply."

"You have money for the journey?"

"He gave me what he had. It will be enough."

"Good luck and a good journey, comrade."

The militiamen shook Hugo's hand, slapped him on the shoulder and encouraged him with the clenched-fist salute as he drove off.

Half an hour later he was stopped by a patrol of Anarchists who wouldn't let him pass until they had seen inside the van. After that he was stopped every twenty or thirty miles. That afternoon, Hugo drew up in the forecourt of an inn. The sun beat down mercilessly and the metalwork of the van seared at a touch. Its interior was an oven.

He wiped sweat off his face and opened the back of the truck. "How about something to eat?"

Miguel shook his head.

"You *must* eat, comrade."

"I won't leave her. I'll keep vigil until she's home."

Hugo nodded understandingly. "I'll bring you an iced beer."

He left the doors of the truck open so the stuffy air inside could escape. He ate, swallowed two cups of black coffee and carried back two bottles of iced beer for Miguel.

The heat of the sun bounced off the tarred road in a shimmering haze and as he wiped the sweat from his forehead and closed the van doors, he noticed a sweetish smell. He looked around for flowers, but saw only sagebrush and cactus, withering in the dry roadside soil.

The truck was stopped seven more times before it reached Madrid and on the outskirts of the city, a patrol of militiamen put them under arrest. They were detained until the following morning. Hugo was locked in a cell in Civil Guard barracks. Miguel was allowed to remain in the bakery truck in the barracks forecourt with a guard mounted over it.

It was almost noon the following day before they were allowed to leave. They would have been delayed much longer except that Hugo shouted, stormed and blasphemed until somebody brought an FAI committeeman.

The committeeman was weary of his men's officiousness. "I am sorry for the delay, comrade. My men wished to protect our security. You have our permission to go."

"I shit upon your permission!" shouted Hugo wrathfully.

"Be reasonable, comrade. We must be alert for Fascist traitors."

"I shit upon Fascist traitors. But I also shit upon your permission!"

"And I shit upon the mother who gave you birth!" shouted the committeeman, losing his temper.

The two men glared at each other, angered to the point of blows. And then by common accord, they burst into laughter.

"It is a great kindness you do your comrade," said the committeeman.

"But the great whoresons of militiamen stop me every kilometer. I spend more time showing identity papers than driving."

"I will give you a paper to help you, comrade."

The committeeman prepared a carefully worded note which he endorsed with the stamps and seals of the UGT, FAI and CNT.

"This paper will help you, comrade."

"I shit upon delay, therefore I thank you," said Hugo solemnly.

The two men walked to the forecourt where the van waited.

"I wish you a successful trip, comrade."

Hugo placed the paper in his breast pocket. "With your help, comrade."

The committee member wrinkled his nostrils in distaste. "A sewage pipe . . ." he began.

"I shit upon delays," shouted Hugo furiously and sprang up into the driving seat.

Hugo drove hard and his precious paper passed him swiftly through suspicious patrols. It was early evening before he stopped to eat and when he opened the door of the van, he stepped back quickly. He almost vomited as the hot, sweetly sickening stench of putrefying flesh washed out over him.

Miguel sat grimly hunched beside his betrothed, his red-rimmed eyes overbright with strain and fatigue. His face was cadaverous. The smell of death was in his nostrils, had tainted his clothes and clogged the pores of his skin.

Hugo held his handkerchief over his mouth. "Can I get you something to eat?"

Miguel shook his head, clasped his hands and bowed his head until it rested upon his knuckles. He stayed that way without moving while Hugo ate, rested and closed the truck doors again.

They reached Barcelona that same night, drove through it and stopped on the outskirts. Hugo was exhausted. He fell asleep at the roadside below a pine tree some distance from the truck. He slept until the morning sun upon his face awakened him. He avoided opening the truck doors to speak to Miguel and drove hard to Escoleras, where he arrived just before noon.

He drove through the village and brought the truck to a standstill in the plaza. Curious villagers quickly gathered around him as he got down stiffly from the driving seat.

"I am looking for the family Barras," he said.

A stocky man with silvery-blond hair was quickly summoned from his cottage.

"You are asking for me, Señor," said Paco Barras, wrinkling his nostrils against the stench from the van.

"You have a son Miguel?"

"That is so, Señor." Paco Barras's clear blue eyes narrowed warily. "You have news of Miguel?"

Hugo nodded slowly. "Bad news."

Paco Barras clenched his hands. "My son has been . . . hurt?"

"Your son is unharmed, Señor. But his bride . . . she is dead!"

The swiftly growing crowd heard the words and shouted them aloud, spreading the news.

"The bride of Miguel Barras is dead!"

"Helena Medina is dead!"

"Dead . . . !"

Women threw their black aprons up over their faces and wailed.

Hugo went to the back of the truck and opened it and the crowd pressing around him rolled back as the stench flooded out, poisoning the air.

Hugo spoke through his handkerchief. "Your journey is over, comrade. You are home."

Stiffly Miguel climbed out. The smell of death clung to him like a shroud and his hollow cheeks made a stranger of him. "Send for the parents of Helena," he choked. "Send for the priest."

Paco Barras hugged him. "Miguel. My son!" he choked.

Miguel grasped his father's arm and rested his brow upon his father's chest. Then for the first time since Helena had died, great sobs shook him.

"Ayee! Ayee! Ayee!" wailed the women.

Presently Escoleras's church bell began to toll for its first villager to die in Spain's Civil War.

Juan Morales, the mayor's eldest son, tinkered with the old and battered Ford until he got it running. The car was so ancient it was only used for towing or for local deliveries. But the bus from Figueras had broken down and he needed a spare part for a fishing boat engine. Ten men's livelihood depended upon the engine's working again quickly. As he drove out of the village, he pulled over to the side of the road to allow Helena Medina's funeral procession to pass. The black hearse drawn by two gray carthorses, which on other days were harnessed to the dust cart, drew level with him. Respectfully, he took off his greasy mechanic's cap and held it against his chest.

The singing choirboys paced slowly past, their surplices startlingly white in contrast to their dusty black robes. Don Carlos solemnly followed some paces behind them, eyes lowered and hands clasped reverently under his paunch. The new assistant priest, Ramon Sirval, walked behind him with his pale blue eyes staring fixedly as though he could see paradise. His forehead was a pasty white, but his cheeks were rosy. He looked very young and very pure.

Then followed all the men of the village. Juan saw Paco Barras with his head held high and his silvery hair gleaming in the sun. Beside him shambled a dark-skinned grief-stricken man whom Juan stared at a long time before he recognized Miguel Barras.

When the procession had passed, Juan drove out of the village through a green tunnel of plane trees. He was gloomy, remembering how radiant Helena had been on her wedding day. And he thought of Miguel Barras and his haunted eyes, lined face and shrunken cheeks. What he had suffered could drive a man mad. They had had to cover the body with lime as soon as it was in the coffin!

Crickets chirruped loudly in the trees above the throb of the old car's engine, and the sun gold-speckled the oily blackness of the tarred road. The alfalfa in the fields was ripe and tender-green, growing healthily in the rich red-brown soil. A shepherd herded his flock across the road and while he waited for it to pass, Juan shouted good-natured insults at the man. He crossed a long, low bridge over a dried-up riverbed, saw that grass grew thickly on its banks and noted it would make good grazing for cattle. By the time he saw the rooftops of Figueras below him in a saucerlike depression, he had quite forgotten the tragedy of Helena Medina.

He parked the Ford in the shade of the trees in the Ramblas, purchased groceries for his mother, but was unable to buy the spare part he wanted. It had to be ordered from Barcelona.

The town looked as usual. Men sat in the sidewalk cafés discussing politics, people crowded the pavements and window-shopped, and farmers whipped their high-wheeled carts through the cobbled streets. Juan Morales was about to drive home when he bumped into a second cousin.

"Where are you going, Juan?"

"I'm going home."

"Come to our meeting."

Juan was curious. "What meeting?"

"The Anti-Fascist Militia Committee. A delegation has arrived from Barcelona to tell us what's happening."

"Isn't everything quiet in Barcelona?"

"The officer's revolt is over. But the workers' militia and the Anarchists control Barcelona now."

"I don't understand . . ." said Juan Morales, bewildered.

"Come with me and you soon will." His cousin took him firmly by the elbow.

The meeting hall was crowded to standing room only. UGT, CNT and FAI banners were displayed on the walls and at the back of the speaker's rostrum was a red flag emblazoned with a hammer and sickle. Most of the audience was armed with bandoliers of cartridges slung over their shoulders, rifles and pistols.

The first speaker was Daniel Frero, the stocky, dark, curly-headed man Anselmo and Diego had listened to in the Plaza de Cataluña. He wore blue coveralls that gaped open to the waist and around his neck a black and red Anarchist scarf. A pistol was holstered at his side. He had arrived from Barcelona that morning.

He spoke simply but passionately. "The Fascist officers in Barcelona lied to their troops and ordered them to take over the garrisons. But the workers were prepared for treachery. The government refused us arms to defend the state, but we had weapons secreted in our homes. We turned out on the streets to defend our city from the Fascist tyrants." His voice rang. "We won the fight for freedom but at the price of many, many comrades' lives. Among them was our beloved comrade Ascaso, who died fearlessly, leading an attack upon the Atarzanos Barracks."

A great sigh of sorrow swept the hall.

After a respectful pause Daniel Frero continued: "Barcelona is in the hands of the workers. They have asked President Companys to carry on."

Overwhelming applause.

"The workers have formed an Anti-Fascist Militia Committee, composed of representatives of all workers' organizations."

More applause and shouts of approval.

"Freedom is ours and the will of the people will prevail," said Frero. "The towns and villages will follow the lead of the big cities." His voice was impassioned. *"Arise, you starvlings, from your slumbers, Arise, you criminals of want.* The means of production will be taken over by the workers."

Tumultuous cheers and applause.

"We will establish justice, freedom and equality. Nobody will starve while the rich wallow in luxury. Nature does not recognize the boundaries of hedges and ditches. Neither will we. The land is for *all* men!"

Tumultuous applause.

Frero's face was suddenly serious.

"We must be ever wary for the traitors to our cause, the snipers from the rooftops and disloyal officers. Especially must we guard against the petticoated perverters of young and tender minds, who preach that the workingman must stay humble while the collecting plates are weighed down by the wealthy. Comrades: Spain is for the workers. Freedom is ours!"

The audience clapped, shouted, stamped and cheered; flourished clenched fists, jumped up on chairs, shouted slogans and tried to make speeches. The hall became a riot of noise and movement.

Daniel Frero smiled faintly and sat down. Three men began addressing the assembly simultaneously from different parts of the hall and another half a dozen were on their feet, waiting for them to finish.

Juan Morales was bewildered by the impassioned voices, the chanted slogans and the feverish excitement. He was relieved when the meeting broke up and everyone shuffled out into the hot sunlight. He had lost his cousin and had no wish to meet him again. He hurried to his battered Ford and tinkered with the engine to get it started. While he worked a large empty truck drove into the space beside him and parked. The driver took out his delivery book and wrote in it.

A black-bearded man led a group of thirty along the Ramblas. His trousers were worn and patched, his blue shirt sun-bleached and his dusty, canvas-topped boots were split open across the toes. Two cartridge belts crisscrossed his chest, a rifle was slung upon his back and the black butt of a pistol jutted from a stiffly new holster. The men who followed him were also heavily armed and when they reached the truck, they gathered around it. The driver looked at them in surprise and hastily clambered down from his cabin when they gestured.

"We're confiscating your truck," said Blackbeard.

The driver gaped. "I've only just arrived," he explained. "I'm to pick up seed and deliver it to . . ." he referred to his delivery book.

"Not now, comrade. The truck is no longer yours."

The driver scowled sullenly. "Who says so?"

"We say so," said Blackbeard. He grinned and sweepingly gestured to his unshaven, poorly dressed and sharp-eyed followers. Juan Morales saw among them a bootblack who worked the Ramblas cafés, a gasoline pump attendant and a street cleaner.

"Who are you?" demanded the driver.

"We're the Committee, comrade."

The driver watched unhappily. "What do I tell my boss?"

Blackbeard laughed. "Forever!" He gestured and his men lowered the tailboard and began to climb up into the truck.

The driver watched unhappily. "What do I tell my boss?"

"Tell him the workers are using his truck to fight fascism."

Juan Morales listened open-mouthed.

The driver said in desperation. "Give me a paper or something to show you've confiscated it."

Blackbeard's face wreathed in smiles. "Have you a pen and paper, comrade?"

The driver showed his delivery book.

"Then write this." Blackbeard dictated slowly. "We, the Committee of Escoleras, have confiscated truck number whatever it is. Signed. Ricardo Escudo. Have you done it? Good. Give it to me to sign."

Escudo signed slowly, the tip of his tongue protruding from his thick red lips, and his shoulders hunched in a way that showed he was not accustomed to writing.

The driver stared at the signature dismally. "This isn't much good. It's not very official. Haven't you got a rubber stamp or something?"

Ricardo Escudo waved a disdainful hand. "That is all you need, comrade. The workers take what they need. We have no time for bureaucratic bills of sale or capitalist notions of private ownership."

All of his men had by now climbed into the truck and one was behind the steering wheel. "Ready to roll, comrade?" he called.

"What happens to me?" wailed the driver. "What do I do?"

"Join us," said Escudo enthusiastically. "Be a militiaman. Come with us to Escoleras."

"What's the pay?"

Escudo waved a disdainful hand. "Do not worry. We take what we need."

"I have a wife and children to think about."

"The family is your personal problem," sighed Escudo. He reached for the handrail and hauled himself up into the cabin alongside the driver. The truck engine burst into life and the gears grated.

Juan Morales got his Ford going and followed the truck. The truck driver, left behind in the Ramblas, stood forlornly watching them drive away, shaking his head sadly.

The new truck driver often crashed the gears and swerved violently. The vehicle lost and gained speed in fits and starts. Prudently,

Juan Morales followed it at a safe distance. Swaying perilously, the truck almost sideswiped a small bakery truck on the bridge over the dried-up riverbed. As the truck passed Morales, he recognized it as the one which had brought Miguel Barras and his dead wife to Escoleras.

After attending Helena's funeral, receiving everyone's grateful thanks and firmly refusing all hospitality, Hugo started for home. He was anxious to rejoin his comrades in Sevilla. He gave his address to Paco Barras, shook hands with Miguel and set off.

Thirty miles out of Barcelona he was stopped on the coast road by yet one more Anarchist patrol. The sun was bright, his eyes ached and tiredness nibbled at the edges of his mind.

"Identification," demanded a militiaman.

Wearily Hugo felt in his pocket for his precious papers. They weren't there. Frantically he felt in all his pockets and then realized what had happened. He had shown the papers to the last patrol that had stopped him, twenty miles back. They had asked questions, offered him tobacco, smoked with him and then sent him on his way. He was tired and he had forgotten to get back his identity papers. He explained all this, but saw by their wooden faces that they didn't believe him.

"Return with me," he suggested. "I cannot continue on my way without papers."

They returned with him. Ten miles back along the road, they met a patrol but not the one that had stopped Hugo.

"It was another patrol, farther back," insisted Hugo.

They wouldn't believe him.

Slowly and in great detail Hugo explained how he had spent the last few days. But he was tired and confused and he contradicted himself and mixed up dates. Finally two militiamen guarded him while the others walked a little way off and discussed him.

"He's lying."

"He contradicted himself."

"He is not a worker. His hands are soft and smooth like a woman."

"Be just, comrades. A breadmaker's hands will be soft from kneading the dough."

"That is true. But the hands of a Fascist sniper who does not work are also soft."

"It could be true that he drove here from Sevilla . . ."

"He has a truck. It is useful to have a truck."

"But how can it be true when Quiepo de Llano has taken Sevilla? The workers are still fighting in the suburbs of Sevilla."

"Then less reason why he should be here. He is Andaluz and should be in Sevilla, behind the barricades."

"We'll never agree, so let's vote."

A vote was taken.

They went back to Hugo, who eyed them warily. One of the Anarchists pulled out a wallet of tobacco makings and they all lit up.

"You like Cataluña?" asked a militiaman politely.

Hugo puffed smoke and grinned wryly. "The little I've seen of it."

"It is more beautiful than Andalusia?"

Hugo hesitated. "I would not say that."

"Come over here, comrade." They led him off the road to the cliff edge. "Where else can you see such a view as this?" The militiaman gestured proudly, his arm displaying the blue Mediterranean below, the distant gleam of yellow beaches and the cool, pine-studded slopes leading down to them. His eyes were soft with the pleasure of nature's beauty.

"This is the Costa Brava," said the Catalan proudly. "It is a beautiful memory to take away with you, is it not?"

Hugo nodded, seeing the silvery sparkle of the sun on the blue sea, smelling the pine cones and sage bushes, but not noticing the man behind him who had drawn a pistol, not even knowing when reality became extinction, nor of the bullet that tore through the bone behind his ear.

They pulled his shirt up over his head and held him by ankles and wrists. They swung him back and forth. One . . . two . . . three . . . and the corpse arced out over the cliff edge. They watched it fall, scraping against the cliff side, hitting an outcropping rock, bouncing from it like a falling boulder and finally smashing on the rocks below where it was half-floated away by the next wave that frothed in over them.

When they tired of watching the body swirl back and forth in the surging foam they walked back to the road.

"The end of another Fascist traitor," said one militiaman and spat.

"They should all be executed."

"I agree, comrades. All I have said is that *if* this man is telling the truth . . ."

Another militiaman grinned slyly. "Why argue? What difference does it make *now?*"

"The truck will be very useful," said the man who had shot Hugo.

Escudo's confiscated truck swerved into the plaza at Escoleras and squealed to a standstill. The men jumped from it while startled villagers gathered around and stared in astonishment at their weapons.

Ricardo Escudo wiped a hairy forearm across his shining forehead and asked: "Where's the town hall, comrades?"

Half a dozen villagers tried to tell him at the same time, pointing and walking with him as he strode toward it.

Mayor Morales was in the office talking to the town hall's only employee, who combined the duties of dust-collector, town crier and odd-job man. He was a tall, thin and lugubrious man and wore a faded gray uniform with a peaked cap. Everybody called him El Hombre Largo, the long man.

The mayor was giving El Hombre Largo a list of villagers from whom he should collect long-overdue rates and he looked up in astonishment when Ricardo Escudo strode in with two companions. Abruptly the small room was filled with the smell of sweat, garlic and worn leather.

"Are you the Comrade *Alcalde?* The mayor?"

Mayor Morales puffed out his fat cheeks and nodded. He stared at the armed men as though in a trance.

"We are the Committee," stated Escudo.

"The Committee?"

"Haven't you heard, comrade? There's to be a Committee in every town and village to represent the workers?"

"I . . . I didn't know . . . we hadn't heard . . ."

"Can we depend upon the local authorities in Escoleras to cooperate with us?"

Mayor Morales gulped. "Of course. Of course." He fluttered his pudgy hands nervously. "I was elected mayor because the people know me, you understand?" He puffed out his fat cheeks. "You have credentials to show your authority?"

Ricardo Escudo laughed. His teeth were very white against the blackness of his beard. "Credentials, comrade? All of Spain in turmoil and you ask for bureaucratic documents? Are you against the workers?"

"Of course not," panted the mayor hastily.

"You know of the treachery of the generals and the sniping Falangists?"

"Er . . . yes. Yes."

"You understand we are here to defend our elected People's Front Government?"

"Yes . . . yes! Of course!"

Escudo looped his thumbs in his cartridge belt. "What accommodation is there for my men?"

"Your men?"

"They're in the plaza. We total thirty."

Mayor Morales couldn't conceal his consternation. "I daresay we can find room for them with the villagers."

"We must keep together. We need a big building."

"There's the schoolhouse."

Escudo shook his head. "What would the children do?"

"There's the community hall. We use it for dances and showing films . . ."

"We're not going to stop dances and film shows. What else?"

"There's . . . there's only the big house."

"How big?"

The mayor puffed out his fat cheeks and spread his hands. "Very big. Twelve bedrooms but privately owned."

"Privately owned?"

"Wealthy people from Barcelona who spend the summer here. But I don't think they'll rent."

"Rent!" exploded Escudo and laughed loudly. "Let's talk to these wealthy house-owners."

"They've . . . they've not started their holiday season yet."

"Then we'll look at the house."

The mayor frowned unhappily. "It's a waste of time. I'm sure they won't rent."

"Comrado Mayor," said Escudo softly. "I demand your cooperation. I *want* to see the house."

Mayor Morales stared unhappily at the three armed men and saw a glitter of distrust growing in their eyes. He got to his feet quickly. "Wait for me," he told El Hombre Largo.

"You come with us, comrade," countermanded Escudo.

"Yes, come along," said Mayor Morales.

Mayor Morales led the way and Escudo paced at his side. When they reached the plaza, Escudo gestured to his men and they straggled behind him, smoking and talking, their rifles bristling from their shoulders. Many of the villagers followed too, so that when they reached the residence of Marcel del Puente, a large crowd walked up the winding gravel path and climbed the steps to the terrace.

Escudo rested his hands on his hips, and approvingly surveyed the facade of the house with its many brightly painted, shuttered windows.

"No caretaker?" he asked.

"There is a man in the village who looks in twice a week . . ."

Escudo nodded disinterestedly. He drew his revolver, stepped close to the door and with a sharp blow smashed a stained-glass panel. He thrust his hand into the hole and drew back the door bolt.

The mayor was speechless as Escudo flung open the door and stepped across the threshold. Then he spluttered: "You *can't!* It's against the law!"

Escudo threw back his head and laughed. "What law, comrade? Capitalist law?"

"This . . . this is private property."

"Then we confiscate it in the name of the people!" thundered Escudo. He gestured to his men. "Open the shutters, comrades. This is our new home!"

His men flooded into the house, flung open shutters, stripped dust sheets off the furniture, searched cupboards and drawers to see what they contained and plundered the wine stock.

Mayor Morales watched unhappily as Escudo settled comfortably in an upholstered armchair. His bare toes peeped through the broken tops of his canvas shoes and his toenails were rimmed with black.

"I must say . . ." began the mayor.

"Sit down," Escudo said.

"We could telephone to Barcelona and . . ."

"Sit down!" thundered Escudo. He pounded his fist on the arm of the chair and his face flushed angrily.

Mayor Morales sat down.

"You too, comrade."

El Hombre Largo gingerly seated himself on the edge of a chair.

Escudo said slowly: "By their treacherous revolt the Fascists have proved themselves murderers and assassins. Our duty is to protect the people. It is your duty to help us, comrade."

Mayor Morales waved his plump hands nervously. "I will do what is right," he said. "But we must respect the law."

A stock of cigars had been found in a cupboard and a box was given to Escudo. He opened it, selected a cigar, sniffed it approvingly and lit up. "This is a small village. You know *everyone*."

The mayor nodded.

"You know who are Falangists and Lliga members!"

The mayor hesitated.

"Answer."

"There are one or two," said the mayor warily.

"Their names?"

"They are not active."

"It does not matter. Their names?"

The mayor was apprehensive. "Why do you ask?"

Escudo glared. "Comrade Mayor. In Barcelona the Falangists sniped from rooftops. They killed innocent men and women simply to create panic. This must not happen here."

"The men I know would not shoot their friends. They are sincere men like you, and work for the good of everyone."

"Do you support the Fascists, comrade?"

"I'm a Republican," said the mayor. "I *know* these men and they are *good* men."

Escudo's eyes glittered. "Will you swear none of them conspired against the government? Will you stake your life on them, Comrade Mayor?"

"I'm sure they would not."

"You are with us or against us, Comrade Mayor. If any of these men act traitorously against the people, it will be with *your* encouragement."

Mayor Morales stared at him unhappily.

"I do not think you are a traitor, Comrade Mayor. But you surely cannot answer for *everyone* in the village."

Mayor Morales moistened his dry lips. "I do not accuse anyone, you understand."

"Make a list of names, comrade," Escudo told the Long Man. "Add names yourself, especially those who are staunch churchgoers." He puffed cigar smoke at Mayor Morales. "The names, comrade. The names."

When the list was ready, Escudo asked the Long Man: "You know where these men live?"

The Long Man nodded lugubriously.

Escudo gave orders. "Round up these suspects. Lock them up in the town hall."

Mayor Morales turned pale. "Lock them up?"

"Until tomorrow when we can deal with them."

The mayor was stunned. "More than forty men to be locked up all night in two small rooms. It's . . . inhuman."

"Should they be given luxury hotel accommodation?"

"I thought . . . you only wanted to talk to them."

"I will. But not now, comrade."

"Tomorrow?"

Ricardo Escudo puffed cigar smoke and his white teeth gleamed. "Probably."

"Meantime they're to be locked up like animals!" The mayor was so indignant he spluttered.

"And why not? It is time the workers are waited on."

"But Don Carlos is an old man."

"Don Carlos is the priest?"

"He is a good man."

"A priest has no problems. He prays to God who fixes everything."

"But why must they be locked up?"

"To prevent any treachery before their trial."

"Their trial?" The mayor's eyes popped.

Escudo's white teeth gleamed. "Not a military court held in camera with Fascist judges. Instead, a democratic tribunal held in public."

The mayor stared in astonishment.

"*You* will be one of the judges, Comrade Mayor."

"But . . . what are they accused of?"

"That we shall decide tomorrow, Comrade Mayor."

9

The Long Man polished his battered bugle, took it to the plaza and blew upon it three loud, discordant notes. The villagers came hurrying to hear him. The Long Man waited until a crowd had gathered and then read from a paper in a loud, husky voice.

"At six o'clock this evening, the Workers' Committee of Escoleras will hold a tribunal. They call on everyone to attend to give guidance and information about the accused. That is all."

The Long Man tucked his bugle under his arm and walked ponderously to the public fountain to repeat the announcement, leaving behind him the villagers talking and speculating excitedly.

That afternoon a long trestle table was set up under the trees and covered with red bunting. High-backed chairs were placed behind it for the judges. Long before time, the plaza was full of villagers, most standing. Fishermen came straight to the plaza when their boats docked, their clothes damp with brine and flaked with fish scales. Land workers came with hands stained by soil and carrying farm tools.

The judges solemnly seated themselves and the prisoners were brought from the town hall at rifle point and made to sit on the ground on one side of the tribunal bench. Escudo had appointed himself a judge, together with four of his men and Mayor Morales. He rose and stared with hard black eyes at the villagers.

"Comrades. The task of our Workers' Committee is to defend the people and its government. Traitorous officers, Fascists, Falangists and lick-spittles of the capitalists threaten our security and our peace. We want no snipers' bullets killing women and children, as happened in Madrid and Barcelona. We must defend ourselves. We must uproot the traitors before they act against us!" He paused as though expecting applause.

The villagers stared silently, their faces sullen.

Escudo pointed. "Your own Mayor is one of your judges."

Mayor Morales's face turned a shade paler.

"If you wish others to sit among the judges, you may nominate them."

The villagers stared stolidly, their silence resentful.

Escudo showed his white teeth in a smile. "Very well; we'll proceed." He glanced at the list in his hand and with difficulty read the first name aloud. "Jaime Turro."

Rifle butts prodded Jaime Turro to his feet and across to the solitary chair placed in front of the judges' bench.

Turro was twenty-six, a dreamy-eyed youth who loved hunting and training dogs. Most days he worked in the fields with his father, but whenever possible he slipped away with a shotgun or borrowed a boat to go fishing. He had been locked up without food for more than twenty-four hours and his belly groaned with hunger.

Escudo glowered at him. "Are you a member of the Catholic Party?"

"I am a Catholic," agreed Turro. His voice was husky with nervousness.

"You are against the People's Government?"

Turro was bewildered. "I am for the Church."

"The Church is against the government," stated Escudo flatly.

"Perhaps it is."

"You do not deny it?"

Turro grinned ruefully.

"You oppose agrarian reform?"

"You mean splitting up big farms into lots of little farms?"

"That's right."

"It might be a good thing. But those who want it are jealous of those who have more land than them."

"Then you are opposed to agrarian reform?"

"I don't see why lazy farmers should benefit by doing nothing."

After a few more questions Escudo conferred with his fellow judges. "What is your opinion, Gomez? Is he against us?"

Four judges thought Turro was against the government.

"I don't have to ask *you*," Escudo told Morales. "We have a majority opinion."

Turro was led away under guard.

"Who's next?" Escudo asked Morales.

"Be merciful," pleaded the mayor. "Don Carlos is an old man and these long hours of waiting have tired him greatly."

"Don Carlos," shouted Escudo.

Don Carlos was exhausted and guards had to support him as he hobbled to the chair. He had mislaid his round black hat and the cotton wool fringe of his tonsured head made him look frail and weary. But as soon as he was seated, he drew the dusty skirts of his cassock around him and proudly faced his judges with his hands resting on his full belly.

"You are a priest?"

"Do I look like a fisherman?"

"You are against the People's Government?"

Don Carlos glared. "What nonsense you talk, man. What do I know of governments?" He gestured angrily. "Governments are man-made and man-destroyed."

"Do you deny you feed the masses the opium of religion? You preach contentment with their lot in this world and promise they will live better in the next?"

Don Carlos scowled. "Young man," he said sternly. "You have never been to my church. How can you know what I preach?" His tone was of a schoolteacher, rebuking a naughty schoolboy, and brought smiles to many faces.

Escudo too was amazed by the old man. "You support a church that favors fascism?"

"I *don't* support the Church," snapped Don Carlos. "I quarrel with it constantly. It does many things that are wrong and wicked. But it also does many things that are very good."

"You approve of fascism?"

"Do you approve of red hair, young man?"

Escudo smiled tolerantly. "What's red hair got to do with it?"

"The color of a man's hair is part of a man's personality. So are his ideals. You don't approve of them or otherwise . . . you simply accept them."

"What about *your* ideals, Don Carlos? Are you a Fascist?"

"I'm a humble man who wants to do good." The priest's eyes gleamed. "But without a pistol on my hip and a gang of armed ruffians behind me."

Escudo's men laughed delightedly and slapped their thighs. Escudo threw back his head and roared loudly. The villagers smiled and relaxed and were proud of their priest.

"We defend the people, Don Carlos," explained Escudo. "But you transform us into the agents of the Devil."

"With your men's looks it would be hard to transform them into angels!" said the priest tartly.

The relieved villagers laughed.

Escudo said quickly: "My men are armed to protect the workers. This interrogation is to search out enemies of the people."

"I shit upon whoreson Fascists," swore one of the judges.

Don Carlos was an old man with a bowel disorder and being locked up so long had made him uncomfortable and irritable.

"And I shit upon your interrogation!" he said fiercely.

A great gust of laughter came from the listeners and Don Carlos adjusted his cassock and smiled benignly.

When the laughter had died down, Hernando pushed through the villagers and walked up to the tribunal bench. A guard pointed a rifle at Hernando's belly, but Hernando gestured it away contemptuously. "Don't point that at me!"

"Let him speak," said Escudo.

Hernando stood astride, his bare legs as brown as hickory and his often-patched shirt and pants a sun-bleached patchwork. He looped his thumbs in his black sash and glared at Escudo challengingly. His silvery goatee jutted aggressively. "I speak in the name of the people," he said fiercely. His moustache bristled and his silvery hair was stirred by a sudden breeze. "This tribunal is a parody of justice!" he thundered. "We demand that you leave us in peace . . . as you found us!" He pointed at Don Carlos. "Are you so blind you cannot see this old man is good-intentioned?"

"Are you too a good Catholic?" asked Escudo slyly.

Hernando was scornful. "I shit upon God, I shit upon the Virgin Mary and I shit upon the Church." He took a deep breath. "And I shit upon this tribunal." Again his outstretched finger pointed at the priest. "But this old man of the Church intends only good to *all* men."

"He is your friend?"

"He is *not!*" thundered Hernando. He glowered. "We argue bitterly!"

Don Carlos smiled benignly.

Paco Barras stepped forward from the front ranks of the villagers. "I too say Don Carlos is a good man. He does not demand gifts from the people as do many priests. Also he often gives to those in need, from his own pocket."

"The church bell is cracked and some villagers made a collection to buy a new bell," shouted José Guitart. "But Don Carlos gave the money to the poor. He said when it needed a bell to summon the people to the cinema he would buy a church bell."

One after the other, the villagers stepped forward to praise the priest.

The Committee listened quietly. Finally, Escudo said: "The people think highly of you, Don Carlos."

"Then I am happy," said the old man simply.

"The Church is a menace to Spain's peace. But you may remain in the village, Don Carlos. But *not* as a priest. You will not wear your cassock, give sermons, preach or follow your calling."

"Is this freedom? Is this democracy? Have you held elections to outlaw religion?"

"These are emergency measures," said Escudo dryly. He gestured at his followers and grinned. "My armed gangsters insist upon this precaution, Don Carlos."

The priest spread his hands and smiled wryly. "Who am I to be a martyr?"

The villagers chuckled.

Don Carlos said seriously: "My young assistant is a good boy. He will do as I tell him."

"Where is he?"

Ramon Sirval stepped forward and stood beside Don Carlos.

"Do you understand you are not to wear priest's robes or hold services?"

Sirval looked at Don Carlos questioningly.

"They have not asked you to renounce your belief in God, my son. They only ask you to stop thrusting God down other people's throats."

"I will do whatever Don Carlos says," answered Ramon Sirval.

"Very well," Escudo flashed his teeth in a smile and waved the two priests away. "Off home to your bed, old man. Take your assistant with you." He looked at Mayor Morales. "Who's next?"

"José Miaja," said the mayor.

Don Carlos hobbled away, helped by Ramon Sirval, and José Miaja took his place. He was a handsome youth, the son of wealthy parents. His father was a notary, at present away on business.

"You are a member of the Lliga?"

José Miaja was proud of it. "I am."

"Did you attempt to panic the village when the rising began in North Africa?"

"I knew nothing of the revolt."

"If you had, you would have sniped at women and children from the rooftops?"

"What nonsense. Everyone knows I would never do that." José glared at his accusers. "It is a lie to accuse Lliga members of murder." His lip curled in scorn. "Lliga men are not armed ruffians."

"Are the following also members of the Lliga?" Escudo nodded at Morales who read aloud a list of names.

José Miaja nodded.

"You are not many, are you?" commented Escudo.

"We are not a mass movement," retorted José Miaja proudly. "We seek a higher level of life for people through efficient administration."

"You don't deny having Fascist sympathies?"

"Would you believe me if I did?"

The tribunal continued its hearing, accusing instead of interrogating, listening to opinions instead of proven facts. Many of those publicly examined were the wealthier people of the village and many were religious idealists who affirmed their Catholic faith with passion. There were women as well as men, youths and old men, poor workmen and middle-class tradespeople, and it was dark before they had all appeared before the tribunal and then been taken away under armed guard to be locked up once more in the town hall offices.

"Comrades," announced Escudo solemnly. "The hearing of the tribunal is concluded. Those we have detained are self-confessed enemies of the People's Government. We will consider what must be done with them."

The villagers slipped away to their homes and cafés to discuss and argue this injustice. When Don Carlos had been put at liberty, it had all seemed an amusing affair. But now the villagers were angry and the relatives of those who were locked up were incensed. A small village is a large family and resentment against Escudo flamed high.

Leaning heavily on Ramon Sirval, Don Carlos limped home and sank down with relief in his favorite armchair. His housekeeper fussed anxiously. "You're exhausted, Father. I'll make you some soup and then straight to bed. What wicked, terrible people! The world is going mad!"

Don Carlos held up his hand soothingly. "Thank you, Ana. Please hurry."

Ramon Sirval stared at the floor in worried silence.

"What's ailing you, my son?"

Ramon Sirval's pale blue eyes looked straight at him and his cheeks flushed crimson. "I have no wish to deny my Church," he said simply.

"We must do what our conscience dictates," agreed Don Carlos. "God's work is helping man spiritually. Can you do this best by becoming a martyr?"

"Tell me, Don Carlos. Do I deny God if I deny his Church?"

"We have not denied the Church. We have only agreed not to administrate . . . for a time."

The young man wanted more reassurance, but Ana burst in. "Father, there is a man who *insists* he must see you. He says it's a matter of life and death."

Don Carlos sighed and his eyelids fluttered wearily. "Very well. Show him in."

The man was wild-eyed, dirty and unshaven. His filthy clothing stank of the cowsheds in which he had hidden. He said hoarsely: "Sanctuary. I beg of you to give me refuge, Ramon."

Don Carlos stared.

Ramon Sirval widened his eyes in startled recognition. "Father Delbos!"

"You must help me. I've come from Barcelona. The mob is killing priests and raping nuns."

Don Carlos's moon-round face was weary with strain. "How can *we* help you, brother?"

"Hide me," pleaded Father Delbos. "Hide me." He bowed his head and tears ran down his cheeks. "I don't want to die," he whispered. "Please don't let me die."

Don Carlos shook his head sadly and Ramon Sirval looked away, ashamed of his kinsman's emotions.

Ana came into the room bearing a large, steaming dish and the appetizing smell of onion soup filled the air.

"Set a place for our visitor," said Don Carlos.

Ana stared. Then she frowned. "If you say so, Father," she said disapprovingly.

"And prepare a room for our guest."

"Prepare a room!" Ana was scandalized.

"Father Delbos is hungry and tired, Ana."

"Forgive me, Father. I'll see to it at once."

"Remember this, Ana. Nobody must know we have a guest. Is that quite clear?"

Ana looked at Father Delbos with new understanding and sympathy. "Trust me," she said. "I won't give him away."

After the tribunal, Mayor Morales was obliged to return to Escudo's headquarters for dinner. He sat unhappily on the terrace of Marcel del Puento's residence while committeemen roasted a freshly killed young kid over a charcoal fire. It was well garnished with garlic and sage and its smell was delicious. But Mayor Morales lost all desire to eat as he listened to the committeemen.

They were idealistic madmen. They were fanatics so blinded by their belief in goodness that they saw issues only in black and white. The heat of the charcoal fire cracked the terrace mosaic tiles and a committeeman broke a window by carelessly leaning his rifle against it.

"You must be careful of other people's property," remonstrated the mayor.

The committeeman grinned. "Private property!" He took a rifle and smashed another window. Everybody chuckled as shattered glass tinkled on the tiles.

The mayor gulped. "That's . . . vandalism!" he objected.

"It's freedom," corrected Escudo. "Freedom from material values. By smashing that window, Comrade Gomez showed his contempt for luxury and wealth. We have no need of material things. It's the greed of individuals, the Church and the Fascists that prolongs the troubles of the world."

When they ate, each man carved off a hunk of steaming meat and held it in his hands. And while they ate, Escudo told the mayor what would be done with the prisoners.

The mayor stared at him disbelievingly, his fat face pale. "You're . . . mad!" he whispered.

The committeemen chuckled. Escudo roared with laughter.

"But why?" choked the mayor. "WHY?"

Escudo's white teeth sank into hot meat and tore at it. Meat juice dripped from his black beard. "The People's Government must be wise. Never again shall treachery menace freedom. The weeds that check healthy growth must be uprooted."

It was after midnight when some of the committeemen, led by Gomez, drove off in their confiscated truck. A little later, the Mercedes saloon car they had confiscated from the Ledesma family rolled smoothly up the gravel drive.

"Let's go, Comrade Mayor," said Escudo, narrowing his eyes.

Unhappily Morales climbed into the car with Escudo and other committeemen. It started up and sped down the gravel path; Morales bent forward to bury his face in his hands.

When they returned much later, the mayor was in a state of shock.

"Take care of him," ordered Escudo.

Committeemen took him to a bedroom, lifted him onto a soft mattress and took off his shoes.

Mayor Morales lay quite still, staring up at the ceiling. Tears ran from the corners of his eyes.

Escudo came to see him, studied him for a time then, shrugged his shoulders. "Better get some sleep," he told his companions. He yawned and the cavity of his mouth was a warm pink contrast to his black beard.

Marcel Prada made the discovery the following morning when he took the mountain road to his olive grove. At first he thought discarded clothing had been scattered along the verge of the road, but later, when he had shaken off the numbness of shock he counted thirty-eight men and women. Not all had died at once. Some had writhed in agony until a merciful pistol shot behind the ear ended their suffering. He knew them all well. José Miaja, Jaime Turro, Señora Piero, and others who had appeared before the tribunal.

Marcel Prada turned his cart around and lashed his mule with the loose end of the reins, racing to spread the news that civil war had come to Escoleras!

BOOK II

1

Marcel Prada lashed unmercifully and the startled mule cantered to escape the cut of the whip. The canvas-hooded cart rocked perilously as it tore down the steep track and on the bends the mule's worn shoes struck sparks. Marcel Prada's eyes were wild and he began shouting his news when he reached the outskirts of the village without checking his mad pace. Wheel rims rang on the cobbles and scattered pails of refuse left out for the dust cart.

"Murder!" shouted Prada hoarsely. "Mass murder!"

The villagers rushed to their doors, garbage pails clanged, iron-shoes clattered and Prada's cart scraped itself to a standstill against the whitewashed wall of Guitart's cottage.

"Mass murder!" choked Prada. He sawed the bit in the mule's mouth to pull its head around, lashed and rattled on to the plaza.

The villagers ran from their houses and followed him through the narrow streets. In the plaza a crowd gathered while Prada stammered out his story.

"Mass murder I tell you. Shot dead. Lying there like rag dolls."

The news spread swiftly, but nobody believed it until Jesus Guitart ran into the town hall and found the rooms empty that the victims had occupied.

Children were sent to bring their fathers in from the fields. Doctor Aldo was aroused from his bed, Don Carlos was summoned and Baudillo Ledesma was awakened. The villagers yoked up mules, horses and donkeys and a long procession wound up into the foothills. The men were grim-faced and their women wailed. Hardly a family was unaffected by the death of a relative. A long time later the procession returned, the men bareheaded and grimly silent, their women distraught with grief. The carts were loaded.

Escudo had posted armed committeemen at the entrance to the village. They had set up a machine gun on a tripod and were prepared for trouble. But Baudillo Ledesma and Doctor Aldo, at the head of the returning procession, walked past the committeemen without looking at them. The villagers followed their example, although some of the bereaved women spat and with taloned fingers gave the evil sign of vengeance. Don Carlos, unfamiliar in civilian clothes, rode in Juan Morales's old car and when the bodies were laid out in two rows in the cemetery, in defiance of watching committeemen, took out a Bible and read the burial service. Then he called upon the villagers to kneel and led them in prayer.

As soon as the service was over, Baudillo Ledesma strode away purposefully. Doctor Aldo ran after him and grasped his arm. "Where are you going?"

"I must talk to Escudo."

"Baudillo. Don't do anything crazy!"

"I know what I'm doing."

"I'll go with you."

"You're busy, Juan. I'll handle this."

"I'm *not* busy, Baudillo. I can't do anything for people when they're . . . dead!"

"Come then if you wish."

The two men strode on to Escudo's headquarters and two armed committeemen hurried after them: "Where are you going?"

"To talk to your chief."

"We'll go with you." They followed the two men to Marcel del Puento's residence and up the winding drive to the terrace steps.

Escudo was seated at a period mahogany desk that had been dragged out on the terrace. He was studying a list of rates the town hall had assessed the villagers.

He looked up at the scrunch of gravel and rose slowly to face Ledesma and Doctor Aldo.

"Are you responsible for these mass murders?" demanded Baudillo fiercely. His jaw jutted aggressively.

Escudo's eyes narrowed. "There has been a mass execution," he said carefully. He gestured politely. "Won't you sit down?"

"I don't sit with murderers," said Baudillo. He was trembling.

Doctor Aldo placed a soothing hand upon his arm. "Gently, Baudillo. Gently."

Escudo's eyes glinted. "What was done was justified."

"Murder cannot be justified."

Escudo took a cigar from his breast pocket and bit off the end. "Spain's government was elected by the will of the people. But Fascist officers rebelled against the government. They were assisted by Falangists, who sniped and murdered from rooftops while the churches gave over their church towers to Fascists with machine guns." Escudo put the cigar in his mouth, struck another match and drew on the Havana with unconcealed pleasure. "Spain cannot live with traitors in her midst. Those who were executed freely confessed to being our enemies."

"You must be *quite* mad," said Baudillo. His voice was shocked. "You'll have to massacre a whole nation to get rid of those who don't share your opinion."

"It's not merely *my* opinion. We must destroy all who organize against us. But we are reasonable. Don Carlos was said to be a good man and we gave him his freedom. But nothing was said in defense of the others."

"Nobody dreamed a madman planned murder!"

Escudo's eyes glinted. "Careful with your words, comrade."

"The entire village calls you a murderer."

Escudo shrugged his shoulders.

"Such a terrible crime must be avenged," said Baudillo. He pointed an accusing forefinger. "I'll not rest until justice is done."

Escudo's teeth gleamed against his black beard. "Report my actions to whom you wish."

"Moreover," threatened Baudillo, "not another villager must be harmed."

"The People's Committee will take all action necessary to protect the People's Government," said Escudo coldly. He turned his shoulders on them to end the interview.

Baudillo Ledesma and the doctor walked slowly back to the plaza where the shocked villagers gathered around them. The doctor gave a brief résumé of their talk with Escudo.

"My friends," promised Baudillo Ledesma. "Everything possible will be done. I'll have this shocking crime investigated and the murderers punished. Meantime, we must all remain calm. There is great tension throughout all Spain and we must not incite more violence. Those who have lost loved ones want vengeance. But we must seek not vengeance, but . . . justice!"

Juan Morales tinkered with his old Ford until the engine started and drove Baudillo Ledesma into Figueras.

At the town hall, at the judges' court and at the Civil Guard headquarters, Ledesma was turned away by armed militiamen who directed him to the building the FAI had commandeered and made their Committee headquarters. He asked to see the Committee secretary and waited two hours in a stuffy waiting room crowded by people with questions or complaints, or needing travel permits.

Baudillo paced the waiting room like a caged lion, his jaw jutting as he puffed hard on his cigar and his bushy eyebrows meeting in a black line of anger. When he was finally shown into the secretary's office he was sweating and irascible.

The secretary was also busy; impatient and harassed. He waved a hand at the chair opposite him. "Sit down, comrade. Speak up quickly."

Baudillo didn't sit down. He placed his hands on the secretary's desk and leaned across it with his cigar jutting aggressively. He asked fiercely. "Where do I go to lay a charge of murder?"

The secretary sat back in his chair, stared at Ledesma's cigar and wrinkled his nostrils fastidiously. "Murder's a serious charge," he said. He looked up at Ledesma coldly. He had observed the well-cut quality of his clothes and resented his aggressive manner.

"I live in Escoleras," said Baudillo Ledesma. "A ruffian named Escudo, claiming to be in authority, has murdered thirty-eight villagers. In the name of justice I demand he be arrested and brought to trial."

The secretary knew Escudo. "Were those people Falangists? Were they traitors to Spain?"

"I know nothing of their politics."

The secretary eyed him sharply. "Are *you* a Falangist?"

Baudillo glowered. "I have no politics. And now I speak of justice, not of politics."

"Is it justice you go well clothed while others wear rags?"

Baudillo's jaw jutted. "I work much harder than most men to dress the way I choose."

The secretary smiled wryly and scratched the wet sweat patch beneath his armpit. "As you wish. I will make a report that Comrade Escudo shot thirty-eight traitors."

"That's not enough," stormed Baudillo. He smashed his fist upon the desk. "Are assassins to go free?"

The secretary flushed. "We are doing our best. But we've many problems. The workers are fighting for their lives. We must deal with our secret enemies, too."

"I demand an investigation of this mass murder. As a loyal Spaniard I insist upon a proper judicial inquiry."

The secretary sighed. "Such an investigation will take weeks. Probably months!"

"I don't care if it takes years. I demand justice."

"If you insist," sighed the secretary. He reached for his note pad. "You accuse Comrade Escudo of murdering thirty-eight inhabitants of Escoleras?"

Baudillo Ledesma nodded.

The secretary asked questions and wrote. Finally he threw down his pen and leaned back in his chair. "That's all," he said wearily. "Your charges against Comrade Escudo will be thoroughly investigated. If they are proved he will be found guilty. If your accusations are false, you will answer for them."

"I'll repeat my accusations *and* prove them!"

"Very well, comrade." The secretary shouted and an armed militiaman leaning against the wall in the corridor outside, entered. "This man is to be detained," said the secretary.

Baudillo stared. "Detained? Why?"

"You have made serious accusations. If they are untrue you are guilty of obstructing the People's Government."

"You're blackmailing me into withdrawing my charge!"

"If you *do* withdraw it, you'll clearly be guilty of false accusations."

"And that murderer Escudo . . . is he to be detained?"

"I will send for him," said the secretary wearily. "Then we shall decide."

Baudillo was taken to Figueras prison. The contents of his pockets were put into a little canvas sack and tied up with a tag bearing his name. He was given a receipt for it and then taken across a patio to a steel wicket door set in a stout frame of iron bars. It opened onto an inner patio lined with cells. The cells were small but the doors stood open so the prisoners could circulate. The prison had never been so crowded. That night, when the prisoners were herded into the cells, Baudillo Ledesma found himself with nine other men in a space originally intended for one man. The solitary iron cot cemented into the wall was occupied by the first three men to reach it. The others slept on the floor, shoulder to shoulder, backs against the wall and legs overlapping.

The man who slept next to Baudillo Ledesma was a mental defective. He drooled from lips that were festering sores, and he had almost no control over his bowels which he discharged into an iron bucket.

The next day when Baudillo Ledesma demanded to see his lawyer, his jailers smiled and nodded. But his lawyer never came.

Ricardo Escudo was drowsy after his lunchtime wine. He strolled out into the cool shade of the terrace, bit off the end of a Havana and struck a match. He revolved the cigar end in the flame, placed the cigar in his mouth, lit another match and inhaled with relish.

By this time, the avenger had him lined up in his sights. Two shots were fired in quick succession. The first bullet hit Escudo below the nostrils, smashed through his teeth into the cavern of his mouth and tore out through his neck. The second bullet hit his temple, was deflected and ripped away a piece of his skull just above his ear. Escudo fell like a stone. His head hit the mosaic tiles solidly and his smoking Havana rolled across the terrace.

Committeemen drew their pistols and ran to hunt the assassin, while others gathered around their leader.

Escudo choked on the blood that filled his mouth. They turned his head to one side. His chest heaved and his eyes stared glassily.

"Get the doctor!" ordered Javiar Gomez, and three committeemen hurried away to scour the village.

Doctor Aldo was brought in the Ledesma Mercedes. He set down his battered medical bag, knelt beside the wounded man and examined him. Then he looked up at the ring of anxious faces and asked tiredly. "What do you want *me* to do?"

"You're a doctor, aren't you?"

"But not a miracle man." The doctor pulled out his watch and glanced at it hurriedly. "There's nothing I can do."

Their faces were shocked.

"If we take him to a hospital . . . ?" said Gomez.

"You certainly can." Doctor Aldo stood up and brushed dust from his trousers.

"It's all right to move him, then?"

"He's dying. Move him and he'll die a little sooner."

Their eyes showed their misery. It was strange, reflected the doctor; they could cold-bloodedly butcher men and women, yet feel so deeply for a personal friend.

"He was a good comrade," choked Gomez. "He always did what was right."

Doctor Aldo gave him a hard stare.

"Can't you do *something* for him, Doctor?"

"Is he in pain?" asked another anxiously.

Escudo's breathing was faint now and his glazed eyes stared more fixedly. The cushion below his head was soggy with blood.

"I can inject morphine, but there's no point," said Doctor Aldo. He passed his hand across Escudo's staring eyes. There wasn't a tremor. The doctor pulled out his watch and glanced at it. "Nothing I can do."

"How much longer, Doctor?"

"Very soon."

"Stay with us until the end, Doctor. We may have need of you."

Doctor Aldo shrugged his shoulders. "Very well."

"He was a loyal comrade," said Gomez and there was a catch in his throat.

The other committeemen nodded agreement.

"He was clever," said another man. "He couldn't read much but he memorized lectures. He knew a lot about history; and philosophy, too."

Another man said wryly: "D'you remember the talk he gave us about Karl Marx? I thought it'd be about revolutions; but it was all economics. I couldn't understand a word. But Comrade Escudo knew it all. What a head he had!"

"He was a *true* comrade!"

Escudo's eyelids fluttered. His jaw sagged and his breathing was so faint they couldn't hear it.

Doctor Aldo held his pulse for a few moments, then closed the eyes. He stood up, took out his watch, glanced at it and said quietly: "That's all."

There was shocked silence.

One man swallowed with difficulty.

Another knuckled the corner of his eye.

Doctor Aldo frowned down at the dead man's ragged, sun-bleached shirt, worn trousers and broken shoes that showed his black-rimmed toenails. "What did he do?" he asked.

"He was an Anarchist," said Javiar Gomez simply.

"I mean . . . what did he do for a living?"

"He was a road-mender."

Javiar Gomez and three committeemen at once reported to FAI headquarters in Figueras.

"We've had trouble in Escoleras, Comrade Secretary. Escudo has been murdered. The villagers are restless."

"A complaint has already been lodged against Comrade Escudo," said the secretary.

"We rounded up the Fascists and executed them. Murdering Comrade Escudo was an act of vengeance. We'll need more arms and men to maintain order."

"We can supply the arms, comrade. We've opened up the fortress armory. But we can't spare any men."

"Where is everyone?"

The Anarchist secretary shrugged harassed shoulders. "Everyone is doing what they know best. Some are taking over the factories, others are rounding up Fascist reactionaries and others have gone to the front. Sevilla's still in the hands of Quiepo de Llano. It'll mean a big battle to win it back."

"I *must* have more men to maintain order, comrade."

"Get them where you can. Hire them. We'll pay from party funds. Try the poor district at the back of the town. Plenty of men are ready to carry a gun for food and tobacco."

"But are they the type of men we want, comrade?"

"We're at war, Javiar. General Mola's using trained Moors against us. We can't be too scrupulous, comrade."

Javiar Gomez and his comrades enlisted thirty unemployed men who had no political convictions and who bargained craftily about pay before they were taken to FAI headquarters and issued rifles, pistols, ammunition and hand grenades.

The natural leader of these men was a stocky, thick-necked man named Varela. He had artful, twinkling gray eyes and a barrel chest. He was thirty years of age and permanently lamed by a horse that had rolled on him. His head had been shaved to the bone and growing hair covered his scalp with a fine, black fuzz. Before they reached Escoleras the incompatibility of his men with the Anarchists had become obvious and they instinctively separated into two groups. The newcomers invaded the Committee headquarters, delightedly ransacked the residence, made up bundles of personal loot to take home to Figueras and glowered sullenly when Gomez restricted their wine ration. They spat on the floor, filthied the bathrooms and bred lice into the furniture upholstery.

Gomez promptly commandeered a smaller house alongside and

moved his men into it, leaving Varela and his companions in possession of the Marcel del Puente residence.

The villagers stayed behind shut doors when Escudo was buried.
Not one villager showed in the cobbled streets as the committeemen
carried him to the cemetery, sadly slid his stiffened body into a wall
niche and watched the Long Man seal it with cement.

The Long Man was more lugubrious than usual. He had worked
hard already, burying Escudo's victims. And as soon as Escudo was
buried, Gomez gave the Long Man another task.

Sadly the Long Man went home for his battered bugle and
sounded it at all the public places. He read aloud in mournful tones
the message Javiar Gomez had written:

> "If the murderer of Comrade Ricardo Escudo does not surrender
> to stand trial by midnight, two villagers will be arrested and held
> as hostages."

With the Long Man seated beside him, Javiar Gomez went
through the council records and made a long list of names. He had
already posted armed men at strategic points in the village and was
confident this show of force would maintain order for his collectors.

When they called on Paco Barras he was sitting on the beach in
front of his cottage, baiting *palangre* hooks with sliced octopus. The
evening sun tinted his arms golden and the sky was so blue that the
mountains behind the village stood out cleanly like cardboard cutouts. The smell of burning sugar came from inside the cottage where
Elisa Barras was making cream caramel. Teresa and Rosalia sat with
their lace-making pillows gripped between their knees and their bobbins flicking musically through their fingers.

Miguel sat apart on a low chair, staring out to sea with unseeing
eyes. Lines of bitterness engraved his face and aged him greatly. His
sideburns had become cotton-wool tufts. His family were tactful.
When he spoke, which was seldom, they answered him; but otherwise
they respected his wish to be left alone.

"Time is the greatest healer," said Doctor Aldo. "Give him time."

The two collectors were young and idealistic. One was barefooted
and the other wore *alpagartas*. Their shirts were torn and their trousers work-stained. But their rifles were well oiled, their ammunition
belts glittered with brass-capped cartridges and their leather pistol
holsters were new and stiff.

"*Salud,* comrade," they greeted Paco Barras.

He looked up at them slowly, his blue eyes widening a fraction of an inch. Very deliberately he placed his work to one side, climbed to his feet and stood with legs astride and thumbs looped in the waistband of his trousers. *"Bon día,"* he said in Catalan.

"We are collecting, comrade." The speaker was from Murcia and spoke in Spanish.

Paco's blue eyes stared at him levelly.

"How much will you contribute, comrade?"

"For *what?*"

"To help the People's Front Government."

Elisa Barras had come to the door of the cottage and was standing in the shadows listening. The clicking of the lace-making bobbins faltered.

For a long time Paco Barras stared at them, his widespread toes digging into the sand. Then, without a word he turned and went into his cottage. A few moments later he came out with a coin and gave it to them solemnly.

The collector held the coin on the palm of his hand and smiled down at it. "Please, comrade. This is a serious matter."

"You asked for a contribution. I have made one."

The man put the coin in his pocket. "It's not enough," he said flatly. "We need much more. We committeemen must eat while we protect the village."

"We didn't need protection until you arrived."

"If we weren't here, *anything* might happen!"

Paco Barras glared. "Innocent men and women have been murdered by you."

"It was a necessary precaution, comrade. If the Fascists were to have their way here, you'd soon know the difference. In Andalusia, Moorish troops are set loose in working-class suburbs to massacre everyone. The streets run with blood!"

"You were there?"

Paco Barras's sarcasm glanced off them. "Comrade. You can hear about it on the radio. La Pasionaria tells it in detail. We need your contribution, comrade."

Barras looked at their rifles and holstered pistols and spread his hands. "What do you want from me? I'm a poor fisherman."

"The cause needs all you can spare. Give generously, comrade. Do not fear that the wealthy will escape. They will contribute . . . *magnificently!*"

Paco Barras went into the cottage and came out with another coin.

"Comrade!" they remonstrated.

"That is all the money I have," he said flatly.

"You must have more, comrade?"

"Why?"

"This is so little!"

He gestured. "I fish. I have wine in the house. Meat, bread and vegetables I pay for with my catches. I need little money."

"Leave him be," said the other collector. "He is clearly an Anarchist and without respect for money."

His companion glowered. "If there are many such, how will we eat?"

"Leave this one in peace, comrade. The wealthy will supply our needs."

Later the collectors called upon Cornelia Ledesma.

She received them in her husband's office and kept them standing.

"Money is needed to maintain the Committee in Escoleras, Comrade Ledesma. This is the amount you should contribute." The man slid a signed paper across the desk. "A proper record will be made of your contribution, comrade. This is your receipt."

Cornelia Ledesma's face darkened and she skimmed the receipt back across the desk. "You're out of your minds!"

The collector firmly replaced the receipt on the desk. "This is the contribution we require," he stated flatly.

"You have already robbed us of our car."

"It is not stolen. It has been commandeered for the period of the present emergency."

"Stolen!" insisted Cornelia Ledesma.

The collector shrugged his shoulders.

"Our car was my husband's livelihood," said Cornelia. "He needed it to visit his farms and control his tenants. He does all their thinking for them. Now the farms will fail."

"Your husband has little faith in his fellowmen," said one committeeman critically.

"He has little faith in anyone except me."

"Nevertheless, we need your contribution," they insisted gently.

Cornelia stared coldly. "What happens if I refuse to pay?"

"It will show you are opposed to us."

"Would that surprise you? After you've imprisoned my husband . . . without trial?"

"Those who refuse to help us are opposed to us."

"So you'd murder me too. Is that it?"

"We would consider your attitude, comrade. Then we would vote to decide what action to take."

Cornelia Ledesma opened the drawer of her husband's desk, snatched up a ledger and threw it at them. "If you can read, you can check my bank balance."

Triumphantly the collectors pointed to the red ink total.

"That's what I *owe* the bank," she told them.

They were mystified. "How can this be, comrade? The council records show you are wealthy landowners."

Cornelia sniffed. "We *are* large landowners. But other men farm our land, pay very little rent and borrow money when they are in difficulties."

"Nevertheless, comrade, we *must* have your contribution."

Cornelia smiled icily. "Take some of the land?"

They considered the offer seriously. "We cannot eat land."

She shrugged her shoulders. "Well then?"

"You have wine in your storehouse, Comrade Ledesma?" they asked.

She eyed them steadily. "You know of it?"

"We have been told of it."

"Then why ask?"

"We will take two barrels," said one. "It will be your contribution."

"Also a side of salt pork," said the other.

Maria Dedijerra operated the tiny Escoleras telephone exchange in her small shop in the main street. When a red light flickered, indicating a trunk call from Barcelona, she excused herself to Señora Medina, who was buying darning wool, and sat at the switchboard.

"Barcelona calling Escoleras eight," said the operator crisply.

"I'm putting you through," said Maria. She cranked the dynamo vigorously, summoning Cornelia Ledesma to the telephone. "Barcelona for you, Señora," she said and unashamedly kept the key pressed forward to listen.

"This is Anselmo, Mother."

"How are you, son?"

"Bad news, Mother. I won't be coming down."

"What's happened?"

"I have to report to barracks; *tomorrow!*"

"But . . . what about your postponement until after your exams?"

"That's all suspended. There's a state of emergency."

Cornelia sighed deeply. "I was so longing to have you home, son."

"Even if I left Barcelona now, I couldn't get back by tomorrow. Everybody's overexcited here. If I was late back, they might even shoot me as a deserter."

"Don't take any foolish risks, son," said Cornelia anxiously. "How are things in Barcelona?"

"Pretty quiet, now. The fighting's over, the rooftop snipers have been mopped up and life is back to normal. But the city's policed by militiamen, and two columns of militiamen have marched off to relieve Saragossa. Otherwise everything's quiet."

"And Manolo?"

"He's fine, Mother. Shall I send him down by himself next weekend?"

"No," said Cornelia slowly. "For the present, it is better he remains in Barcelona."

"How are things with all of you, Mother?"

She hesitated. "Everything's fine, Anselmo. Everything's fine."

"And how is Father?"

Again Cornelia hesitated. "He's very busy with the farms."

"Give him my love, Mother. Tell him I'm sorry I couldn't come, but I'll get leave as soon as I can."

"I'll tell him, son."

"And . . . Mother?"

"Yes?"

"If you see Teresa . . . ?"

"Yes, Anselmo?"

"Give her . . . give her my love!"

"Of course. Now don't do anything stupid and *don't* get mixed up in politics."

"I won't, Mother."

Maria Dedijerra disconnected the line and went back to her customer. "They say everything's quiet again in Barcelona," she said conversationally.

Señora Medina's face was pale and her eyes sunken. The death of Helena had shocked her deeply. She wore a long black dress and headscarf that made her look like an old woman. She said bleakly: "It's too late now. Too . . . late!"

"Do you want this packet of needles? Shall I wrap it?"

"It doesn't matter," said Señora Medina. She dropped a coin on the counter. "Nothing matters now."

She shuffled out into the strangely quiet streets. The bars were empty, the street corners deserted, and everywhere was an ominous air of suspense.

Nobody had confessed to killing Escudo and two hostages had been taken at random. One was a young married woman with a two-year-old child and the other was the father of a family of five. They were prisoners under guard in the town hall.

The villagers feared what would happen to them.

2

Emil Serra stabbed furiously at the typewriter keys. He wrote:

> The officers' revolt, opposed by a spontaneous uprising of working-men's organizations, is settling down into a civil war. The legally elected government, supported by left-wing organizations, is now warring against a large proportion of the army, including Moorish soldiers. The mutineers have a firm hold on the mainland.
>
> The Spanish government has asked Britain and France to sell them arms. Both countries refuse, claiming they wish to maintain neutrality.
>
> France has one hundred and forty thousand pounds sterling of Spanish gold in her bank vaults which Spain has sent against weapons to be supplied. The French government has publicly refused the Spanish request for arms. But secretly it has arranged to send the arms through Mexico. Thus do Britain and France avoid angering Hitler and Mussolini.

Mussolini makes no secret of Italy's intervention in Spain. He declares openly that Italy will not tolerate a Communist state in Spain. Italian transport aircraft, armaments and troops are flowing into Spanish Morocco.

Hitler is solidly behind the Falangists. I am informed that two German trading companies have been formed: the HISMA and ROWAK. These companies control a fleet of ships that insure speedy delivery of war materials. German volunteers, together with their commanders and tanks, are already fighting on Spanish soil.

The United States has passed a "Neutrality Act" which forbids the sale of arms to foreign belligerents!

So, while the mutineers are supplied arms by the Fascist dictators, the elected government of Spain is refused them by democratic countries!

Even Stalin follows a cautious policy. Russia's economic plan to build up her basic industries will be jeopardized if Russia is involved in war, so officially Russia won't sell arms to the Spanish government. But international Communists have started a fund to help the Spanish people and Russia has already contributed a thousand million francs.

Spain's Civil War might develop into a struggle between communism and fascism; with Russia, Italy and Germany providing the finance and armaments, while the Spaniards contribute the blood that will be shed. The supply of armaments will enable this Civil War to go on very much longer than otherwise.

Spaniards are not being led by the nose, however. Passions flame high and idealists are willing to die for their cause. The spirit of self-sacrifice is contagious. Even boys only fifteen or sixteen, armed with bottles of gasoline and a slow match, throw themselves under the wheels of Falangist armored cars, giving their lives. The Anarchists are capable of any sacrifice. And so are the Falangists.

General Mola controls the northern half of Spain, while the government controls the south. There is now a military breathing spell with little action. Two columns of militiamen that left Barcelona to liberate Saragossa have been held within sight of the town, and the Alcazar in Toledo is still holding out against militiamen. Colonel Moscardo claims the women and children in the Alcazar are seeking refuge from Red tyranny. Militiamen say their wives and children are being held there as hostages.

Desultory fighting goes on all along a loosely held front. Both sides hold villages or towns and in between are undefended sectors which can easily be penetrated by either side.

The rapid advance through Spain of the African army, commanded by General Franco, dealt a serious military blow to the government. At times the African army advanced at the rate of fifty kilometers a day. The only town that gave serious resistance was Badajoz, the frontier town linking the government with Portugal. But its five thousand defenders were overwhelmed in a day. Legionaries and Moors stormed the broken city walls with bayonets and knives, and vicious hand-to-hand fighting ensued.

By night Badajoz was a town of corpses. The legionaries and Moors gave no quarter. Those who surrendered were herded through the streets to the bullring and mown down by machine guns. The executions went on for many days. Now that Badajoz is in General Mola's hands, he will drive on toward Madrid.

The anarchistic militiamen who try to stand against the African army are quite undisciplined. They resent taking orders, frequently hold a vote to decide if an officer shall be obeyed and often attack when they should stand firm; or attack when they should retreat.

The inefficiency of the Spanish government is very evident within the capital. A dozen or more left-wing groups in the government argue violently among themselves. Already there is an acute shortage of food in the city. But there is no stinting of the food sent to the men at the front who for the moment have such a surplus that great mounds of it are rotting in the hot sun.

All revolting officers who were made prisoners have been found guilty by a military tribunal and have been executed. These trials and executions were held by rank-and-file militiamen who have no government authority.

About the time we received news of the massacre in Badajoz, the political prisoners in the Model Prison started a fire, attacked their guards and tried to break out. Militiamen home on leave raced to join the angry crowds who were storming the prison, seeking vengeance. Falangist prisoners were dragged out and shot and their bodies paraded in front of the other prisoners to put the fear of death into them. About eighty prisoners were killed by the mob before the CNT leaders arrived. They pleaded for restraint and prevented the rest being massacred.

There is no functioning justice in the city. Nearly all the lawyers and judges are right-wingers and they have gone into hiding. Inexperienced and inefficient government supporters have been appointed to replace them. But pure justice is completely outweighed by political bias and anyone accused of being a Falangist or a member of the Catholic Party is automatically found guilty and usually executed.

Madrid is a city of fear and death. Armed men roam the streets at night, knock on the doors of suspected traitors and take them off to the outskirts of the town to shoot them. Yet Madrid is still a lively city. The cafés stay open, the number of whores has doubled, and there is dancing and champagne. There is even plenty to eat if you have the money to buy and are willing to risk being interrupted by a militiaman's bullet.

Emil Serra read his report, sealed it in an envelope and put it on one side to take to his consulate in the morning.

He glanced at his wristwatch. It was after midnight and the three girls he had brought back to his apartment were awaiting him.

Their faces brightened when he joined them. An enormous mattress was on the floor, covered with silken drapes and pillows in Oriental style. The three girls lay upon it languidly, their soft skins scented with rare perfumes Serra had supplied. One girl had high cheekbones, almond eyes and lemon-tinted skin. Her inscrutable, Oriental beauty was strangely delicate.

Serra threw off his dressing gown and they entwined their limbs with his, caressing him with sensitive fingers and wooing him with their voices. The Chinese girl raised a penciled eyebrow and asked: "Are you ready?"

"Go ahead."

She lit the spirit stove that stood beside the bed, opened a screw-capped jar and thrust a knitting needle into its tarry contents. She twirled the needle deftly, winding onto it a daub of the black substance. She held it in the flame of the spirit lamp, her eyes glittering with concentration. The others watched, fascinated, as she wafted the black daub in and out of the flame with a skill that needed the instinct of centuries to acquire.

"It is almost ready," she told Serra.

He grunted and stretched out, resting his head on the lap of one girl who stroked his forehead and abandoning himself to the caresses of the other.

The Chinese girl now took up the pipe and with great care held the opium over the flame until it frizzled and spat. She transferred the black daub to the bowl of the pipe just above the orifice of the stem and handed the pipe to Serra.

He inhaled deeply.

"It is good?" asked the girl.

He nodded. "Very good." He inhaled deeply three times more and then the Chinese girl took the pipe from him.

"Yes?" she asked in her tinkling voice.

"Yes. It is very good now." He closed his eyes and the sweat gleamed on his fleshy face. He lay quite still for some minutes and then made a slight gesture.

"You can start," he whispered huskily.

Anselmo Ledesma reported to the barracks in Barcelona. A steel-helmeted guard lounged in the shade of the arched entrance. He gave a cursory glance at Anselmo's call-up card and thumbed over his shoulder. "Across the forecourt and the second drill hall on the left."

The drill hall had a corrugated iron roof and the morning sun beating down upon it baked the air inside. Anselmo was one of the first to report and he and others talked and smoked while a hundred or more conscripts straggled in.

Presently the sergeant stood them shoulder to shoulder in four rows while a tired-eyed, neatly uniformed officer addressed them. "You men are conscripted to serve your country at a critical moment in its history. We urgently need men at the front and you will receive only a basic training before you go into action." He added wryly: "You won't have a chance to grumble about parade-ground drill." He walked along the rows of young men, eyeing them with disapproval. "Has *none* of you had military training?" he asked despairingly.

Heads shook.

The officer sighed. "All right. Any questions?"

"Do we have a choice about what we do?" asked Anselmo.

"No choice. You're all infantry. Any more questions?"

Heads shook.

"Very well."

The officer walked down the line studying each recruit and from time to time asking, "What's your name?"

"Pedro Gonzalez."

"Make a note of it, Sergeant."

"Yes, sir."

Anselmo's name too was recorded.

The officer finished his inspection and ordered: "Read the names listed, Sergeant. When a man's name is called, he will raise his hand."

The sergeant read the list of names and Anselmo and a few others raised their hands.

"You men are promoted to corporals," announced the officer tiredly. "Now, Sergeant, take these men over to Medical for their outfits."

The medical examination was cursory. As each man came naked and damp from the shower with his head cropped to the scalp and his body hair shaved off, the doctor looked him up and down quickly, glanced at his teeth and waved him on to the store.

The range of uniform sizes was limited but Anselmo, who was slightly more than medium height, was lucky. His khaki shirt and trousers fitted him and his boots were the right size. Even his forage cap fitted. But very tall men and very short men looked like music-hall comedians with trousers hitched up under their armpits or reaching only halfway down their calves.

"Can't something be done?" they wailed.

"When you get to the front, you'll meet plenty of men with wrong-size clothes who'll be pleased to swap," said the sergeant. He grinned. "What are you worried about? You don't have to kill the enemy with your looks!"

They were lined up in the forecourt and inspected by an unsmiling officer who stared fixedly at their cropped heads. "Anybody want an hour's leave to see his girl friend?" he asked, and the men glowered sullenly. One youth who had had a luxuriant head of wavy hair surreptitiously flicked a tear from the corner of his eye.

"The sergeant will give you rudimentary drill instruction. You will be issued with arms and basic food rations and will leave Barcelona this evening." The officer nodded and paced away.

"*Peloton . . . firme!*" roared the sergeant.

Although they drilled perfunctorily, it was tiring marching in the hot sun. Soon their khaki shirts and pants were stained with sweat and those whose boots were too small limped painfully. A bugle summoned them to lunch in the mess hall. Tin plates were heaped high with beans ladled from steaming copper cauldrons and they were given a hunk of bread and diluted wine. After they had eaten, each man was issued a Mauser rifle and bayonet, a bandolier of cartridges, two hand grenades, a blanket and a pack of iron rations. They were lectured on the care of weapons, shown how to load and fire their rifles and told how to use their hand grenades. The same evening, they were ordered out to the parade ground, lined up four abreast and marched to the railway station.

It was a hot evening and, laden with the unaccustomed weight of their equipment, they were soon sweating again. But as they marched through the busy streets, the crowds on the pavements cheered and shouted encouragement, armed Anarchists and militiamen off duty saluted them with clenched fists and pretty girls threw flowers and ran along at their sides. They felt they were marching off to save mankind from a terrible fate and were proud and pleased, until they reached the station and were crammed into a waiting troop train. They sat or stood squashed together in narrow compartments, the air fetid with their breath and sweat. Then, as the slow huffing of the engine replaced the enthusiastic cheers of the encouraging crowd, gloom and misery settled upon them.

"Has anyone got a cigarette?" asked one man.

They shared cigarette paper and black tobacco as the suburbs of Barcelona slowly slipped away behind them into the dusk.

Anselmo sighed and looked around at his companions. "You're a blue-looking bunch!" Only one man laughed. The compartment bulbs were painted blue so the train would be less of a target for strafing planes. Anselmo smoothed his hair back behind his ears and grinned ruefully when his fingers slid over his cropped head. "Has anybody got a comb?" he asked. Now some men laughed halfheartedly; shared misfortunes lose their sting.

"Anybody know where we're going?" asked a youth in steel-rimmed glasses.

"We're heading north toward Madrid," said a baker's apprentice. "I know this line well."

"Then we're going to Saragossa," said Anselmo.

A moody, depressing silence settled upon everybody.

After a long pause a white-faced youth with thick-lensed spectacles asked: "Has anybody ever been in action?"

Nobody spoke.

"I've read that when a man goes into battle for the first time he soils his pants."

"Just a minute," said Anselmo. He fumbled in his pocket. "I'll lend you my diapers."

The chuckles were polite but unenthusiastic.

"Have any of you made a will?" asked the youth with glasses.

There was shocked silence as the question brought everyone face to face with the reality of death.

After a pause a man said: "I haven't anything to leave, anyway."

"But you should make a will," said the spectacled youth seriously, as though he had given the matter a lot of thought. "Your parents will be consoled if they know your last thought was for them."

"Jesus Christ. I'm not dead yet!"

"What do you want to do, scare the shit out of me?"

"We've plenty of time. We haven't even reached the front yet."

"How hard-pressed are they at the front?" asked the youth with glasses. His white face was very intense. "We might march straight into action!"

"We won't die yet," said Anselmo confidently. "Life's only just getting interesting."

The train rolled on through the darkness, the young men sweated in the fetid air and pencils passed from hand to hand as notes were scribbled and tucked away.

"What's your name, amigo?" asked Anselmo.

"Perez. Elio Perez," said the youth with glasses. "I'm a student, studying to be a lawyer." Elio Perez smiled sadly. "That's why I thought about my will, I suppose."

"I've had my studies interrupted, too."

Elio sighed unhappily. "I'm a pacifist." He gestured helplessly. "But in Spain they won't let you be a pacifist. You join the army or they shoot you." His face was so tragic the others laughed.

Elio Perez blinked around reprovingly. "It's not funny. They've given me a rifle and showed me how to use it. But I don't want to kill anybody. I'd just as soon shoot the officer who gives me orders as the man I'm supposed to point the gun at."

The carriage rocked with laughter.

Perez stared around miserably. "I don't want to kill anybody. I don't even know what the war is about. If we had any sense we'd all drop our weapons and go back to Barcelona."

"Careful, Perez. Careful!" warned somebody.

"Is it wrong to speak the truth?"

"We don't all think like you, Perez. Some of us are provoked by injustice. So watch your tongue, amigo. Those not with us are against us!"

"I'm not for or against anything except peace!"

"If we're truthful," said Anselmo, "we probably all think like Perez. What's in this for us, anyway? If we're killed we'll be called heroes. It's fine being a hero; but it's not much fun if you're dead."

There were gloomy grunts of agreement and the train clack-clacked on into the night. The stuffy compartment made them drowsy and they slept fitfully as the train rolled on slowly, stopping often at junctions to allow other trains to pass, but always heading steadily north.

When the gray light of dawn was edging into the sky, the train came to a standstill at a level-crossing where troop transports were waiting and took the conscripts to a small village close to the front that stretched from Saragossa to Huesca. The whitewashed cottages they passed looked deserted. But the villagers were cowering in their houses, peering furtively from darkened doorways at the newly arrived troops.

The trucks stopped in the plaza in front of the village church, which had been turned into a billet. It had been stripped of its sacred relics which were piled up outside to provide fuel for the field kitchens the cooks had set up in the plaza. Soon the inevitable beans were simmering and loaves were being sliced into thick hunks. Weariness and lack of sleep had dulled the men's appetites, but when the smell of cooking pervaded the morning air, their hunger was aroused. They clustered around the cooking pots, devoured thick slices of dry bread and clamored to be served even before the beans were soft. There was no lack of beans and the cooks' ladles filled plates so high that even the hungriest man was satisfied.

Afterward they spread their blankets on the church floor and slept.

They awoke at noon and most of the men stripped to the waist to sluice themselves clean at the fountain. Some of the men used the church chalice to shave in. Then they were lectured about the care of weapons and each man had to load and unload his rifle under the critical eye of his sergeant. Bayonets had to be sharpened and rubbed clean. The sergeants were professional soldiers who had no patience with raw recruits. The officers were overworked and had little contact with the men. They spent most of their time poring over maps or making radio reports. The men were confined strictly to the church and its plaza and were ordered to bed down at ten o'clock.

It was after midnight when the sergeants goaded the corporals into wakefulness and charged them with arousing the men and getting them on parade. They were going into action.

Despite the heat during the day, the nights in this part of Spain were unusually cold. The men shivered in their thin shirts and trousers, as they climbed into the transport trucks. For two hours the trucks bumped and rattled along dirt roads without headlights and only starlight to guide them. They set down the men at the base of a steep hill.

Sergeants led the way then on foot. The conscripts complained bitterly as the straps of their rifles chafed their shoulders. Their equipment weighed them down, their ill-fitting boots blistered their feet and the steepness of the paths sapped their strength. All through the long night, the sergeants urged them on along stony paths until the breath rasped in their lungs and their legs were leaden. There were halts for rest, but the men groaned with the effort needed to rise to their feet again.

When dawn broke, they were at the summit of a steep mountain and they were allowed a longer rest while wineskins, dry bread and preserved sausage were passed around.

From then on, the going was downhill and easier. They were a thousand meters above sea level and looked out over an enormous patchwork plateau of multicolored fields.

Anselmo had been checking their position from the stars and knew they had spent the entire night circling around a mountain range. Now they were descending on a village nestling in a valley on its far side. The village looked small at a distance, but as they drew closer they saw it was a walled town with outer ramparts nearly twenty meters high, as stoutly prepared to defend its citizens from attack as it had been more than a hundred years earlier when Napoleon's army besieged it.

The slopes surrounding the town were frugally cultivated. Long rows of grapevines were ruled neatly across the reddish-brown earth and olive trees were symmetrically planted. The paths down were winding and treacherous and they had to walk in single file. One man slipped and had to be left behind with a broken ankle.

Nearer to the town the men were brought to a standstill and after an officers' conference, they were divided into two sections. One section was marched on to encircle the town and attack it from the rear.

Anselmo and others presently found themselves posted in a shady olive grove where they could look down on the town walls not much more than half a mile away.

"We attack at three o'clock," a sergeant told them. "That's siesta hour and they won't be expecting it."

The men took out tobacco makings, smoked and waited. The sun blazed down and they were grateful for the shade of the olive trees. They squatted on the sandy soil and talked in low voices. The sweat stains spread darkly over their khaki shirts, insects hummed and the hot air prickled until their skin itched. The smell of sage and dry earth mingled with the acrid tang of their black tobacco.

They heard the engine hum of a bombing plane long before it came into sight. They shielded their eyes, peered up into the blue sky and saw its silver glint. It flew around a number of times as though making sure of its prey before it headed away, its engine throb slowly diminishing to silence. Then it came back on its bombing run, a silver streak in the bright sun that was strangely remote from the dark plumes of smoke it sowed. The explosions were the faint *ploffs* of bursting paper bags. The bombing plane ran in three times over the town to drop all its bombs. Then it turned lazily and coasted back toward Madrid.

The sergeant glanced at his wristwatch, rose to his feet and ordered: "Three o'clock, boys. Let's go."

They started walking toward the town. Black smoke spiraled up over its high walls and they could hear the boom of artillery. When they drew closer they heard a sound like sand scattered along a stone corridor. Somebody said it was small-arms fire. They left the worn paths, slithered down steep slopes and plodded across vineyards and olive groves, spreading out widely and often losing sight of each other. Anselmo rested behind a mound of large stones in the corner of a vineyard. He wiped sweat off his forehead and lit a cigarette. At the far end of the vineyard a comrade was squatting under the shade of a tree. Anselmo waved to him and the man waved back. Far over on his other flank he glimpsed the top of a man's head as he relieved himself behind a bush.

Time passed.

They saw nobody and received no orders. Earlier there had been a rumor that a column of Anarchists would also attack the town; but shelling had long since ceased and small-arms fire was desultory now. The sun blazed down, beating through the slender, silvery leaves of the olive trees and Anselmo tucked his handkerchief under his forage cap so it hung down over his face, leaned back against the pile of stones and dozed uneasily. The fierce chattering of sparrows awoke him and he looked around guiltily. Then he relaxed because the man on his right was still sleeping under an olive tree. He couldn't see the man to his left, but when he whistled, the bushes parted and the man flourished his clenched fist. There were no sounds of battle, so Anselmo strolled over to him, offered the man a cigarette and they both lit up.

"*Que pasa?*" asked Anselmo.

The man shrugged his shoulders.

"Do we still have to attack?"

"I hope not." The man pointed. "Those walls are high. We'd be shot down like rabbits." They talked for a while and then Anselmo walked across to the man on his other flank. He had awakened, had removed his boots and was sadly contemplating his blistered feet.

"What's happening?" asked Anselmo.

The man shrugged. "Maybe they've forgotten about us."

"Have you seen the sergeant?"

"Not for a couple of hours."

"What about the man on your flank?"

The soldier grinned lazily. "We've lost touch."

"Perhaps the sergeant gave orders we don't know about."

"It could be." The man smiled complacently.

Now a group of seven men appeared and tramped toward them across the loose soil of the vineyard. As soon as they could be heard one cupped his lips and shouted: "What's happening?"

"We don't know. We're waiting for orders."

They joined Anselmo. "Have you seen any officers?"

"We don't even know what's happened to our sergeant."

"Perhaps the attack's been called off," said one man contentedly. They all sat down under an olive tree and smoked. There were still no sounds of battle and after an hour they decided to retrace their steps and find an officer. They started off in single file but they lost their bearings and argued fiercely. And then, when they were crossing a vineyard, shots sounded and bullets hissed overhead. They dropped flat, burrowed into the troughs between the vines and shouted warningly: "Don't shoot, comrades. We're on your side."

The firing continued.

"We're friends," they shouted. "Down with fascism."

The shooting ceased.

"Don't kill your own comrades," they called, keeping their heads low. Anselmo tied a white handkerchief to the barrel of his Mauser, cautiously raised it and waved it from side to side.

A voice ordered: "Drop your weapons and stand up with your hands above your heads." Apprehensively they rose to their feet, fearing they would be scythed down by a machine gun.

"Advance slowly. Keep your hands above your heads."

They stumbled across the vineyard toward a patrol of militiamen. "What are you men doing over here?" their officer demanded.

Everybody tried to explain. The officer listened, his face lined with worry. He spread his map on the ground and they gathered around him, all trying to point out where they had been. "You shouldn't be here," frowned the officer. "You should be over here." His forefinger pointed to the other side of the map.

"Shall we go there now?" asked Anselmo.

The officer put away his map. "Everything's balled up. The shelling was to start *after* we were in position. But it started before we got here; and was directed against the side opposite to us."

"Will we still attack, Señor?"

"Not now. You men had better find your way back to your transport trucks." The officer indicated prominent landmarks for their bearings and they made their way back over steep mountain slopes, sweating and slipping while hunger gnawed at them. Many hours later they found a truck waiting to pick up stragglers. Most of the men and officers had long since moved off.

They climbed up over the tailboard and braced themselves against the jolts as the driver lurched along the potholed road, and it was after midnight when they arrived back at their church billet. They were so tired they rolled themselves in their blankets and instantly fell asleep.

Five men were lost that night. They failed to answer roll-call the next morning and were never seen again.

For the next few days the men were confined to the church and the plaza, forbidden to go beyond these limits without special permission. The robing room of the church was turned into a latrine, but was quite inadequate for so many men. Soon the arches and dark corners of the church were used, and the stench of excretion began to mingle with the smell of sweat and simmering beans. The public fountain ran dry and water had to be carried in buckets from an almost dried-up stream on the outskirts of the village. There was barely enough for drinking and none for washing. Food platters had to be licked clean and the unvarying diet of beans had its inevitable effect on the men's bowels. So, it was almost with relief that they received orders to move out again and they clambered up eagerly into the transport trucks. Hours later they lurched through the narrow streets of a shell-shattered village. On the far side of it a patrol of militiamen cheered them on with clenched fists and shouts of "Down with fascism!"

The trucks dropped them at the foot of a steep hill and they scaled it, using narrow and dangerous goat tracks until they found themselves on a summit plateau no more than an acre in size. They relieved a unit of POUM and some Anarchists who had dug in on the hilltop when the first attack had been launched against this front. There were shallow trenches with dugouts, sandbagged parapets and machine-gun nests. The living conditions were miserable. Every drop of water had to be brought up steep paths in barrels tied to the backs of donkeys. Firewood had to be gathered, tied in bundles and carried up on men's shoulders. There were more men arriving than being relieved and there was not enough room for them all in the dugouts and trenches. They had to get to work at once, extending the trenches and dugouts and filling sandbags for the parapets. The sanitary conditions were appalling. Excretion was trodden in everywhere until the stench was inescapable. When the sun was at its highest, men breathed through their handkerchiefs.

A tall flagpost was erected in the center of the plateau with a red flag flying. When Anselmo looked over the sandbagged parapet and out across meadowlands where untended crops were rotting, he saw a Nationalist's flag flying on a hilltop some eight hundred yards away.

The cooks set up their food kitchens and poured the inevitable beans into cooking pots. Anselmo squatted on his heels to avoid sitting on the soiled earth, pulled out a pack of cigarettes and handed it around. Everyone lit up and one man said disgustedly: "Do they issue gas masks?"

The sun beat down, the hot air stewed and sweat sprang out on their skin with every movement. Anselmo scratched himself and took from his pocket a stubby pencil and an old envelope. After thinking, he wrote:

MY DEAREST TERESA,
I am deeply disappointed I will not spend my holiday in Escoleras, nor have the opportunity to see you . . .

A man brushed against him, his shirt open to his waist and his chest wet with sweat. He almost knocked the paper from Anselmo's hand. "Sorry, comrade," he apologized gruffly.

Anselmo smoothed the paper upon his knees. What should he write, he wondered? That he was in the front line? That the smell was unbearable? That his bowels revolted against the diet of beans? That the biggest danger he faced was infection?

"War is not noble," he wrote. "It is a stupid, filthy business."

He gnawed the end of his pencil: "I am in the front line for a few days . . ."

It was three and a half months before he was relieved.

Every day, Antonia, her sister Pilar, and their aunt rolled bandages and packed first aid kits. The Madrid hospitals were overflowing and the trainloads of wounded streaming in from the front increased the chaos. There were not nearly enough doctors, nurses nor medical equipment, and many wounded men died of neglect.

There was little political upheaval in the city. A moratorium of debts had been declared and some restaurants had been commandeered by the trade unions. The trade union trucks that brought food into the city supplied it only to these restaurants. The workmen in nationalized factories were given food vouchers instead of money and could exchange them in these restaurants for limited quantities of cooked rice, potatoes and meat. The factories taken over by the trade unions were kept running by workers' committees that replaced the original board of directors and shareholders.

Pilar and Antonia were worried about their brother Rafael. They knew he was with Colonel Moscardo in the besieged Alcazar, but strict news censorship prevented them learning more. Traveling was restricted too, so all they could do was roll bandages, prepare splints and hope the war would be over soon.

One morning, on the way to the Red Cross, they met Ricardo Pieno, a student friend of Guillermo and Jaime. He was wearing the militiamen's uniform of blue overalls with the letters CNT stitched on the breast. His arm was in a sling.

He dismissed his wound as a mere scratch, although his forearm had been shattered by a bullet. When Pilar asked for news of Guillermo he avoided her gaze. "Guillermo?" he said as though he couldn't recall the name.

"You all marched off together, didn't you?"

"Yes!" he remembered unwillingly. "Yes. Guillermo was there too."

"How is he?" asked Pilar anxiously.

"During the fighting . . . there was much confusion. I was wounded and taken to a base so I was out of touch."

"Then you have no news of Guillermo?"

"There *is* news of Jaime," he told Antonia. "Have you not heard? He was wounded; not too badly. We were brought back in the same ambulance train but were sent to different hospitals."

Antonia's face was shocked. "Jaime's wounded?"

"Not badly. His leg."

"Nobody told me," Antonia said agitatedly. "What hospital?" She looked around for a taxi, forgetting they had been commandeered.

"Don't worry, Antonia," he soothed. "It's not serious."

"I must go to him." She clutched at Pilar. "Come with me?"

"Of course."

"I'm due to report for an X-ray." Pieno excused himself.

"We understand, Ricardo. We'll see you later."

Pieno waited until they were some yards away and then called back Antonia. "I couldn't tell Pilar," he confessed.

"It's about Guillermo?" guessed Antonia. "He's . . . badly wounded?"

"He's . . . poor Guillermo was killed."

"Holy Mother of Mercy. How can I comfort Pilar?"

"I'm sorry," he said. "Guillermo was one of my best friends."

Pilar started walking back to them and Antonia hurried to meet her. "I'm coming," she called. "I'm coming."

"What were you talking about?" demanded Pilar.

"Ricardo wanted me to tell you something."

Pilar stopped dead, grasped her sister's arm and stared at her with blazing eyes. "About Guillermo?"

Antonia's eyes filled with tears.

"He's been killed, hasn't he? That's what Ricardo told you?"

Antonia bowed her head.

"I knew it would happen," said Pilar quietly. She held her head higher. "Ever since he went off, so proud and idealistic, I knew it would happen."

"He was so young," choked Antonia.

"I knew it would happen. I *KNEW!*"

"You must be brave, Pilar."

"I'm prepared for it, Antonia. All the time I've known this would happen. I loved Guillermo . . . he was right for me. But I was *too* happy. I knew it *couldn't* last!"

"Don't bottle it up, Pilar."

"I did all my crying the day he went away. I've no tears left."

The hospital staff was overworked and resentful of visitors. The two girls were rudely ordered to wait.

They sat on a long, crowded, wooden bench in a stone corridor for more than an hour before a nurse in a bloodstained smock led them to a ward upstairs.

Jaime was stupid with drugs, his shock of red hair a vivid splash against the white pillow, his bloodless cheeks so pale his flesh was waxy. He rolled his head feverishly from one side to the other, his brow puckered with pain, and he gave a dry sob from time to time. When they spoke to him, he looked up with pinpointed pupils devoid of recognition.

"Jaime!" choked Antonia.

His fingers clenched and unclenched convulsively.

"I warned you," said the nurse sternly. "It's a waste of time seeing him today. He doesn't know you."

From his waist down the bedclothes were spread over a wire cage.

"Is he badly hurt?" asked Pilar.

The nurse nodded. "Bad enough."

"It's his leg?"

"It's been amputated."

Antonia choked.

The nurse put her arm comfortingly around Antonia's shoulders. "You're not doing yourself or him any good," she said, leading Antonia toward the ward door. "Come back tomorrow."

Crying silently, Antonia allowed herself to be led away.

From a tower in the Alcazar overlooking the south facade, a Civil Guard saw a militiaman duck low and run across a narrow alley between houses. The guard aimed carefully, waited patiently and when a second militiaman dashed across the street at the same spot, he pulled the trigger. The militiaman leaped into cover like a kangaroo, either hit or badly startled.

As though the shot had been a signal, a machine gun opened up and the Civil Guard ducked as lead spattered the stone wall below him. Now machine guns inside the Alcazar began chattering and men snatched up rifles and ran to the walls to resist a mass attack. Presently the besieger's 10.5 cm. guns opened fire as they usually did about this time each day, and shells exploded against the sturdy fortress walls with as much effect as a schoolboy's catapult. There were no visible targets. Tiring of the shooting, everybody stopped firing at once. The sudden silence after such an ear-splitting racket was so unexpected that everybody laughed.

Rafael was on duty in the tower with the Civil Guard who had started the shooting. "Did you get him?" he asked hopefully.

"I don't know. He was in my sights only a split second."

"The Red bastard!" said Rafael.

In the town below a field loudspeaker concealed in one of the houses was turned up to full power. A brass band played revolutionary songs and these were followed by a recording of one of La Pasionaria's most moving speeches. The defenders of the Alcazar had no choice but to listen. Some of the men grinned, others yawned disinterestedly and some scowled.

"I'd like to have my hands on that Red bitch for five minutes," growled Rafael.

"So would a lot of us."

"I'd shove a hammer up one end and a sickle up the other!"

La Pasionaria's speech came to an end, but the revolutionary chorus that followed was cut short. Now somebody talked to them through a microphone.

"Comrades of the Alcazar. Listen! Comrades of the Alcazar."

Rafael picked up his rifle, ran to the parapet and squinted along the barrel through a gap in the sandbags. "If I could see the bastard I'd shoot his teeth down his throat!"

The microphone voice talked on. "We appeal to you, comrades. Surrender the garrison and hand over your traitorous officers to stand fair trial. Deliver up your women and children prisoners to prove you believe in truth, liberty and justice."

"It might be that house with the green balcony," said Rafael. "Spray the roof. I'll watch for a chance to snipe."

The loudspeaker was switched off as soon as firing broke out. Most of the town's rooftops had been sandbagged and gave cover for marksmen who returned the fire. Shooting went on a long time. One determined militiaman sniped persistently at the fortress tower, his bullets hitting it and screaming as they ricocheted away.

After a time all was quiet again. The day's excitement was over.

Time hung heavily on the hands of the defenders and some grew lazy with inaction. But Rafael was proud of his cadet uniform, kept it well brushed and his linen spotlessly clean. He was disgusted with the many Civil Guards who used the siege as an excuse for disheveled uniforms, unbuttoned shirts and tunics, unshaven chins and dirty boots. He tried to shame them by example. He strolled the fortress courtyards with stiff military precision, holding himself erect and ignoring the enemy shells which exploded against the fortress walls or whined overhead to burst on the plateau beyond. When their duty turns permitted it, Rafael's friends, Cadets Castro, Redondo and Ferraz, strolled the forecourt with him in the shade thrown by the high walls.

"How long will this go on?" asked Castro one day.

"It won't be long now before General Mola relieves us. And then . . . heaven help the Red scum!" said Rafael. His black eyes gleamed maliciously.

"Face facts," urged Claudio Ferraz. "They can starve us out."

"The water cisterns hold a year's supply," argued Rafael. "The riding-school horses give all the fresh meat we need and the storehouse is loaded with provisions. Long before the Red swine starve us out, General Mola will attack them from the rear."

"A concentrated bombing attack can flatten us," argued Redondo. "Or they can bring up heavy artillery and smash the walls."

"They won't do that," said Rafael, grinning slyly. "Their own Red bitches and spawn would be killed, too."

"Colonel Moscardo's got the *wrong* idea," said Ferraz. "I wouldn't keep them in the basement away from danger. I'd line the walls with them. We could shoot over their shoulders and the Reds wouldn't dare fire back."

As they talked about the women prisoners they glanced across the courtyard at the arched doorway that led to the underground vaults. A young Civil Guard sat dozing in the shade, his chin on his chest and his rifle propped up against the wall beside him.

Rafael pointed. "See that example of our Spanish efficiency! The Germans are a great nation because they don't tolerate that kind of slovenliness."

"We may not be disciplined," defended Ferraz. "But any Spaniard is worth ten Germans. They can have their spit and polish and mechanical efficiency. But a handful of barefooted Spanish soldiers with clasp-knives would take a hill defended by a hundred Germans with modern arms."

The young men had drawn level with the wash yard where the women were allowed up three at a time to wash their linen. A young girl crept up the stairway from the basement, padded barefooted past the sleeping guard and ran across to the wash house. She didn't see the cadets.

The young men exchanged quick glances and followed her. The morning's washing was hanging in the late afternoon shadow, and the girl was pressing the linen against her cheek to see if it was dry. The four cadets startled her. She spun around and faced them uneasily. "I've come for the washing," she explained.

They nodded and circled around her, their smiles sinister. The girl backed away, her eyes suddenly filled with fear.

The guard was asleep and the courtyard deserted.

"The riding stables," said Redondo crisply and his words were a signal. They leaped upon her. She tried to scream, but Ferraz clamped his hand over her mouth while they pulled her skirt up over her head to muffle her cries. They dragged her to the stables at a run, her brown, bare heels trailing on the flagstones. They flung her down on the straw and Ferraz knelt on her upper arms, half-sitting on her head.

"Strip the bitch. Strip her!" chocked Castro, trembling with excitement.

Rafael slashed with his cane and red-wealed her belly; but Redondo grasped his upswinging arm and clung to it grimly. "Hold it, Rafael. We're not going to *kill* her!"

Ferraz said fastidiously: "She's probably full of syph!"

"I'll chance it," grinned Castro. "Afterward, I'll stuff her full of horse shit. Make her eat it too. Then we'll send her back to them, a bride of the Red Christ."

"You can turn her ass red, Rafael," grinned Redondo.

"Look," gloated Castro. "I bet she's virgin!"

An authoritative voice whiplashed: "Release that girl."

They spun around guiltily and were relieved it was only a Civil Guard captain. He wore no cap and his tunic was unbuttoned to the waist. Castro grinned. "You can be first."

The captain's face was pale. "Release her."

"We're having a little fun, Captain."

"Release her!"

They were cadet officers and contemptuous of a mere policeman. "Please yourself, Captain. If you want you can watch."

The captain drew his pistol. "I'll tell you just once more; release her."

They knew he couldn't be serious. "Watch this, Captain," said Redondo. "See how she reacts when I do . . . this!"

The captain fired. The sound of the shot shook them. They stared from his grim face to Redondo, who clutched his arm disbelievingly. Blood dripped from his fingertips. "You shot me!" he whispered incredulously. "You *shot* me!"

The girl tore free, pulled down her skirts and fled. The captain gestured with his pistol. "Turn around and start walking. If you think I won't shoot again, try me."

Dazedly they were herded across the courtyard to their commander's office. Redondo's arm was numbed. He hadn't yet begun to feel the pain.

Their commanding officer supported the Civil Guard captain. "Prisoners are to be treated with every consideration," he said sternly. "Especially the young women. The eyes of the world are upon us. I won't have it said we do not behave as good soldiers and . . . as gentlemen!"

Redondo was taken to the hospital. The bullet had broken his arm and it had to be set. Rafael, Ferraz and Castro were sent to the punishment cells in solitary confinement.

Javiar Gomez, who had taken over after Escudo's death, became increasingly worried about Varela and his followers. He regretted he had recruited them.

Since the two hostages had been arrested, there had been no more trouble in the village. The committeemen were resented but there was no more violence. Gomez felt sure that in time the villagers would understand that what Escudo had done was a moral necessity. But Varela's men were lazy, dirty and power-drunk. They swaggered through the streets, pushed villagers off the pavements and provoked angry comments which they silenced with a drawn pistol or rifle butt.

Gomez and his Anarchists were numerically weak and Varela craftily insisted on voting upon all major issues and always gained the majority decision. Javiar Gomez took the two hostages to Figueras, intending to recruit more genuine Anarchists. But at FAI headquarters all his plans were changed.

"I've tried to get in touch with you, Comrade Gomez. The party needs you badly." The secretary's eyes gleamed with enthusiasm. Men hurried in and out of his office busily.

"My loyalty is to the party, comrade," said Gomez.

"Good. Things are moving quickly. The officers' revolt has sparked off *our* revolution. The workers were forced out into the streets to fight fascism, but now they're in control. In Madrid and Barcelona we've taken over the factories and the basic means of production. This is the end of capitalism. A new era of equality is beginning."

"Do we have a worker's government in Barcelona, Comrade Secretary?" There was wonder in Gomez's voice.

"We have united with President Companys. In these early days of crisis we must cooperate with those whose aim may not be quite the same as ours."

"I have not heard on the radio that we have a workers' state!"

"Madrid will declare it, comrade. Already the peasants are dividing up the great farms. In Madrid the big factories are operated by workers' committees. That's why *we* need *you*, Comrade Gomez. You are an experienced electrician. Yesterday we took over the Gerona Electricity Generating Company. The director and shareholders have been dismissed. It's essential we have comrades on the workers' committee who understand the business."

"When do you need me?"

"At once, comrade. I'm leaving now for the factory meeting. You must come with me."

Gomez hesitated. "I have brought two hostages."

"I'll send them to the garrison prison."

"And . . . Escoleras?"

"We must concentrate on the big issues, comrade. The small ones will take care of themselves."

Javiar Gomez called in the two men who had accompanied him. "These are two good comrades and friends."

The secretary understood. "They shall come with us. As many as possible shall be present at the birth of our new regime."

Baudillo Ledesma's confiscated car waited outside the FAI headquarters and Gomez spoke to the driver.

"Then you will not be returning to Escoleras, Comrade Gomez?"

"This other task is more important."

"But . . . what am I to do, comrade?"

"Explain what has happened."

"But . . ." the driver's face was worried. "What shall *we* do?"

"Just . . . carry on!"

"And . . . *who* will give the orders, Comrade Gomez?"

Gomez hesitated before he answered. "The comrades must elect another spokesman," he said gruffly and turned away quickly to escape his comrade's accusing eyes.

That same night, by an overwhelming vote, Varela was elected leader of the Escoleras Committee.

3

The Committee became the hub of Escoleras's existence. Its members bristled with weapons as they patroled the streets. In the name of the People's Government they exercised despotic power, confiscated what caught their fancy and destroyed things like children yielding to a destructive impulse.

Their leader Varela displayed subtle cunning and ruled with an iron hand, but disguised his actions as benevolent and democratic deeds.

Pedro Turro was taken to Committee headquarters when he flatly refused to make any contribution to the support of Varela and his men. He declared his son had been murdered and he wouldn't lift a finger to help his son's assassins.

Varela listened to Turro's protests sympathetically, nodding his cropped head and rubbing his hand over its black fuzz as though smoothing it flat. Finally he shrugged his broad shoulders and said quietly: "Señor Turro, we have asked you for a donation. You have refused. That is a decision *you* have made and not us!" Pedro Turro was then allowed to leave and tell his friends what had transpired.

But in the early hours of the morning Turro's neighbors were awakened by rifle butts smashing down his door. They peered out apprehensively from their darkened windows and watched Turro bundled into a waiting car. A shepherd found his body two days later, fifty yards off the road and riddled with bullets.

After that committeemen laughingly asked villagers if they wanted to be taken for a ride. When they made their collecting rounds, there were none who refused to donate.

Mayor Morales had been a sick man since the massacre. He sat at home, haggard-eyed and twitching nervously. He could never talk about watching those villagers, who were his friends, shot dead, and he never smiled. His fat shriveled and his skin hung in loose folds that made an old man of him.

The villagers learned to suffer the ruffians who ruled them in sullen silence. They learned patience and discretion and avoided arousing their anger. And life in the village went on.

Teresa and Rosalia sat together every afternoon lace-making. They talked of the war and of the letters Teresa received from Anselmo, of Benito Vigon who fawned on Rosalia like a faithful spaniel, and about Rafael Ledesma who was besieged in the Alcazar. Rosalia was thrilled because the Nationalist radio called the defenders the "Heroes of Alcazar."

Paco Barras was always grimly silent when he and Miguel landed their catches. Armed committeemen were usually waiting to confiscate part of it. The People's Front radio assured everyone there was political liberty and freedom, but the villagers lived under the iron heel of a merciless aggressor.

One morning, Jesus the baker was escorted to headquarters by two committeemen. Varela scratched himself and smoothed flat the black fuzz of his cropped hair while Jesus eyed him apprehensively.

"What have *you* done for the cause of freedom?" demanded Varela.

"Every day your men take away the bread I bake," panted Jesus.

"Call me comrade," said Varela, his small gray eyes twinkling.

"Comrade," hastily added Jesus.

"But we also need *money*," said Varela, reaching for a cigar.

"I have no money. I am a working man."

"Comrade," smiled Varela.

"Comrade," choked Jesus.

"You are a master baker. Where do you hide your money? Your comrades have need of it." A cloud of blue smoke huffed into Jesus's face.

Jesus coughed. "It is not true. I have no money."

Varela snapped his fingers. Two committeemen brought in a man from a neighboring village. Jesus had once employed him for two days and had sacked him because he had stolen.

"I have seen him counting his money," said the man maliciously. "He keeps it in a wooden box like this." With his hands he demonstrated the size of the box. "Where he hides it I do not know. But in the box there is much money. Much, much money!"

"What do you say to that, Master Baker?"

"He is a liar. Never have I owned such a box. Or money to put in it."

"Then we will search."

Jesus sweated. "I have no hidden money," he insisted.

The committeemen searched his house thoroughly. They dug in the cellar and probed under the eaves of the attic. And they finally found a large sealed earthenware pitcher with a slot cut in it. The pitcher was so heavy one man could hardly carry it.

Varela held the pitcher between his hairy hands while his small gray eyes watched the sweating Jesus unblinkingly. Then Varela dropped the pitcher. It smashed on the stone floor and coins rolled, rang and glittered.

"You lied," accused Varela solemnly.

"I swear I did not. My house is two hundred years old. A forebear must have hidden the pitcher. I did not know about it," whispered Jesus faintly.

"You were saving this money to help the Fascists?"

Jesus's face was sheet- white. "No," he whispered.

"How shall we punish him?" Varela asked his companions.

They shrugged disinterestedly. One suggested he should be shot.

A nephew of Jesus had slipped through the guard around the house and was listening. When he heard this suggestion, he hurried back to the village. Jesus's brother-in-law seized a pitchfork and ran out into the street. "We must stop them," he shouted. "They're going to murder Jesus."

When the villagers saw the brother-in-law fearlessly brandishing his pitchfork, his anger and indignation became contagious. Men and women snatched up scythes, rakes and wooden staffs and ran out into the streets. They marched through the village, their numbers swelling with every step until they were an enraged mob led by Don Carlos, Doctor Aldo, Hernando, Paco Barras and Jesus's brother-in-law. They advanced vengefully upon Committee headquarters.

The committeemen heard them coming and grouped defensively.

But when they saw the size of the angry crowd, they looked at Varela fearfully, wondering if they should shoot and run, or run without shooting.

Varela proved his qualities of leadership. Without hesitation, he stepped forward to meet the approaching mob. He thrust out his jaw and his cropped head looked as hard as a rock. He faced the mob so challengingly it came to a standstill some yards from him.

"What is this?" demanded Varela.

"You have arrested Jesus, my brother-in-law."

"He's not arrested. He's answering questions."

"You have threatened to shoot him."

Varela chuckled. "What nonsense!" He gestured disdainfully. "He is not even detained. He can leave with you."

The anger of the mob melted like butter in the hot sun. Jesus flung his arms around his brother-in-law's neck and tears of joy ran down their cheeks. They hurried away home and the villagers followed them, smiling sheepishly and carrying their farm implements awkwardly as though ashamed of having brandished them aggressively.

That same night rifle butts broke down the door of Jesus's brother-in-law. Six other villagers were taken from their homes at random. The volley of shots from the execution squad echoed through the narrow streets of the village and the next morning the bodies were displayed in the plaza under a placard:

WARNING
These men and women defied
the People's Committee.

For the first few days he was in Escoleras, Father Delbos was content to remain within the sanctuary of his room. He rested and slowly recovered from the fears that had gripped him. He no longer trembled when a fisherman in the street called to another or when something fell.

As time passed he recovered not only his courage but also his faith in the Falangist cause. Often he tried to lure Don Carlos into his room to talk politics, but that astute man adroitly evaded him, recognizing a duty to help a fellow priest, but unable to pretend a liking for the young fanatic.

But Ramon Sirval had a very young man's respect for an older priest, and was often inveigled into Father Delbos's room where he fidgeted uneasily on his chair while Father Delbos talked on and on.

Ramon Sirval had a deep and sincere belief in the goodness of God, but no political opinions. He was bewildered by Father Delbos's passionate justification of General Mola, the Moorish soldiers and the African army under General Franco.

"I love my fellowmen," Ramon Sirval ventured timidly.

"You must learn to hate too, brother," urged Father Delbos. His small black eyes glowed. "The Reds are anti-Christ. Ours is a sacred crusade against the disciples of the Devil. The greatness and the very roots of our Church are threatened by the Red anti-Gods. We are fighting to save the world from perdition."

"I am not convinced that shedding blood . . ." began Ramon Sirval.

"Blood *must* be shed! Jesus Christ shed his blood for the love of mankind. We *must* shed blood too! The agents of the Devil must be destroyed. Yes. Even a priest can take up a weapon in defense of God, the Church and our Holy Mother of Mercy."

When he had no one to talk to, Father Delbos crouched beside his radio listening to all the stations he could find on short and long waves and making notes of what he understood of the foreign news broadcasts. With a hand-drawn map of Spain he studied the progress of the Civil War and was overjoyed when the African army of Moors and legionaries swept northward toward Madrid.

It was not safe for Father Delbos to show his face in the streets where a stranger would at once be noticed. But although the church had been boarded up, there was still access to it through Don Carlos's house. Father Delbos exercised in the church, walking up and down the aisles in the cool, colorful light that filtered in through the stained-glass windows. He liked best of all to climb the narrow, winding staircase to the bell tower and from its narrow slits look out over the entire village.

The bell tower provided a dominating view of the port. He could see the long, wide scimitar of yellow beach stretching away along the bay, and in the evening he could watch the fishing boats chugging back to the tiny harbor.

Father Delbos stared out over the wide bay to the left where not far away was France. And then to the right where the steep cliffs of the Costa Brava stretched to Barcelona. And then, as the priest thought of the Falangist victories he had heard reported, the importance of Escoleras as a port dawned upon him. When the revolt had begun, the rank-and-file of the fleet had remained loyal to the government. They had killed their officers and taken over the ships. But a few battleships had gone over to General Mola and General Franco. Father Delbos saw how easy it would be for General Mola's warships to sail into Escoleras and disembark troops. An effective bridgehead could be made in Cataluña and in the same way that the legionaries and Moors had advanced on Madrid, so they would be able to sweep up the Costa Brava and capture Barcelona, Spain's greatest industrial city.

The idea burned in Father Delbos's brain. It could be Spain's salvation. He drew maps of the village and the port and marked where troops could be landed. Little by little he worked out an entire invasion plan. When it was finished he wrote a covering letter to a trusted Falangist friend in Barcelona, sealed it all in a large envelope and asked Ramon Sirval to post it.

It was a week before the letter reached Barcelona and was delivered to the concierge of a block of flats in the Calle Muntañer.

The bulky letter was addressed to a man the police had arrested some days earlier. The concierge was an Anarchist and a staunch supporter of the Worker's Militia Committee. He weighed the letter in his hand thoughtfully, studied the precise and educated handwriting and then took the letter to the police.

The police chief read Father Delbos's letter and because he was a cautious man, took it personally to military headquarters. If Spain was to be invaded in the northeast as well as in the south, he wanted to take all precautions. He showed the letter to a high-ranking officer. Other officers were summoned and they stood around a large-scale map of the Escoleras area, considered Father Delbos's plans and drew their conclusions.

"This map has been prepared by an ignorant amateur," summed up a lieutenant colonel. "No troops can disembark where indicated because the water is too shallow for troop-carrying craft. Moreover, General Mola has only a few warships. We know where they are and will be advised if they take troops aboard. Long before any invasion could mature, we'd have a warm reception prepared."

"These plans then are not dangerous?" asked the police chief.

"Not at all."

"You will give me a paper confirming you have seen this letter?"

"My adjutant will prepare it for you."

"Will I leave the letter with you?"

"I do not need it," said the lieutenant colonel. He arched one quiz-
zical eyebrow. "It will be useful to know who wished to pass on such
information to an avowed Falangist?"

"I will inquire about it," said the police chief grimly.

After the police chief left, the lieutenant colonel turned to his fellow officers thoughtfully: "That invasion plan is hopeless. But until
now we have concentrated on blocking the enemy's advance. Perhaps
we should also consider coastal defense in the Mediterranean."

The police chief sent Father Delbos's letter, together with its map
and plans, to Figueras. The Figueras Anarchist Committee was absorbed in the task of transforming profit-making factories into workers' cooperatives and issuing food barter vouchers instead of wages.
The routine of investigating a Fascist traitor was turned over to a
youth not yet sixteen.

The youth's name was Julio Marin. He had pleaded to join the
FAI because he wanted a shiny new pistol. Now he wore a leather
cartridge belt with the pride of a god wearing a crown.

Marin's dark skin, raven hair and large, white-toothed smile betrayed his gypsy ancestry. He went barefooted and his ragged trousers
reached only halfway down his calves. He could not read or write but
was alert and intelligent. He took the paper Father Delbos had written on to a printer in Figueras and asked: "Can you tell me who uses
this notepaper in Escoleras?"

The printer examined the paper and said unhesitatingly: "This
was cut in Figueras by Barea."

Printer Barea said he had been supplying the same notepaper for
fifteen years. "It's the notepaper of Don Carlos, the Escoleras priest."

Julio Marin gave a large-mouthed, toothy smile.

On the outskirts of Figueras he squatted at the roadside in the
shade of a plane tree and waited patiently. Traffic was scarce and he
rolled and smoked four cigarettes before a commercial truck came in
sight. Julio stepped out into the road, held up his hand authorita-
tively and drew his pistol. He was proud of the letters FAI stitched to
his worn shirt, proud of the power they gave him.

The driver was a nervous man with a UGT permit to deliver vegetables to Escoleras. He eyed the pistol warily and quickly opened the
door for the boy to sit beside him.

In Escoleras Julio found his way to Committee headquarters and
talked to Varela. "These are invasion plans and a letter prepared by a

traitor in your village, comrade," Julio said importantly. He placed the documents on the desk in front of Varela.

Varela scratched his cropped head as he glanced through the papers. Then he called to one of his men. "Find out who uses this notepaper," he ordered.

"It is the notepaper of Don Carlos, the priest," said Julio Marin smugly. He drew his pistol from the holster and polished the butt. "I discovered that in Figueras."

Varela scowled. "So what?"

Julio shrugged his shoulders. "I am to give you these documents, comrade. You are to handle the rest."

Varela called loudly: "A couple of you go and bring in that whoreson priest!"

Julio's eyes gleamed. "Shall I help, comrade?"

Varela glowered. Then he grinned. "Of course, comrade. Bring in the priest at pistol-point!"

The stunned villagers watched sullenly as Don Carlos and Ramon Sirval were herded along the main street at pistol-point. But the old priest smiled benignly, chattered amiably to his guards and rested his hand affectionately on the shoulder of Julio Marin who flourished his big pistol proudly. Ramon Sirval's pale blue eyes stared straight ahead of him and his rosy cheeks were flushed, making his aquiline nose and high forehead seem quite bloodless.

"*Salud,* Don Carlos," Varela greeted the priest formally and ran his hand over his head, smoothing down the black fuzz that had grown into a stubble.

"*Buenos días,*" said Don Carlos cheerfully. "Have you sent for me to pray for your wretched soul?"

Varela scowled. "The villagers respected you, Don Carlos. They vouched for your honesty. But you have abused their faith."

Don Carlos frowned. "I don't understand."

Varela opened his desk drawer and took out Father Delbos's letter and plans. "Perhaps this will remind you, Don Carlos."

The priest recognized his notepaper and as he read the letter he understood instantly the stupidity of Father Delbos. *You fool, Delbos,* he thought as he read on. *You worthless fool!*

"You are a surprisingly slow reader, Don Carlos."

The old priest looked Varela straight in the eyes. He said tonelessly. "What do you want of me?"

"You admit you wrote this letter?"

"No."

"Now you lie, you son of a whore!" roared Varela. "It's your note-paper! How can you deny you wrote it?"

"I neither admit nor deny writing it."

Varela's eyes twinkled. "You prefer to sit on the fence, eh?"

"I do what is right and good."

Varela jutted his jaw and pounded his fist on the desk. "You priests are scum! You preach brotherly love while you sharpen the traitor's knife."

"Surely, knifing is more your speciality," said Don Carlos bitterly.

Varela gestured to one of his men. "Get the car."

Don Carlos knew then he was to die and he stiffened, his eyes flicking sideways to his assistant's white face. "Listen, Varela," he said clearly. "I accept the blame for *everything*. My assistant knows *nothing. Nothing!*"

"The only difference between you two is that you are older and more cunning!"

"You intend to kill us?"

"You'll rot in the Figueras jail while you await trial as traitors."

"Ramon Sirval has no part in this. It's injustice to punish an innocent man."

Varela's grin showed ugly, yellow teeth. "The People's Front Government must be protected."

The car arrived and the two priests sat squashed in the back between two armed guards. Varela and another man rode beside the driver and two guards stood on the running boards. Julio Marin tried to climb aboard, but was cuffed away. Like a monkey he sprang at the spare wheel bolted to the back of the car as it drove off and clung to it. The car's springs creaked alarmingly under the weight of its passengers and it lurched dangerously on the bends. It built up speed slowly but when it was only a little way out of Escoleras, Varela gave orders to the driver and the car turned off the road to Figueras and followed a secondary road up into the mountain foothills.

Don Carlos's face became grim and he leaned forward to speak into Varela's ear. "I swear before God that boy knows nothing about this business!"

Varela drew two cigars from his breast pocket and passed one back to the priest. "Try one. They're good." He chuckled. "The best Marcel del Puento could buy!"

Don Carlos slumped back against the upholstery, the cigar clutched unheeded in his pudgy fingers and misery in his eyes.

"Let me light it for you, Father," offered one of the guards.

"Comrade!" the other guard corrected.

Don Carlos puffed the cigar to life and looked slyly at Ramon Sirval. The youth hadn't spoken a word. His rosy cheeks were pink and his blue eyes were unafraid.

"Do you *understand* what has happened?" Don Carlos asked him carefully.

Ramon nodded. "Yes, brother. It is the will of God!"

"I am an old man and to die a little sooner does not matter. But you are young and with many years before you to do God's work. It would not be wrong for you to come to terms with these men."

Ramon Sirval's blue eyes blazed fanatically. "Jesus Christ died for mankind. If I die too, I will be serving God and my fellowmen."

Don Carlos sighed.

The guards chuckled. "Listen to Jesus Christ!"

"Do him a favor, friends. He *wants* to die!"

They roared with laughter.

Don Carlos drew hard on his cigar, surprised he could still enjoy the flavor of a good cigar. "Be sensible, Ramon," he urged. "You're a man first, and a priest afterward."

But Ramon Sirval ignored the older man's plea and stared ahead of him as though seeing God. "I have no fear, brother. I forgive them because they know not what they do. My blood will wash away their sins and I am content to die for God the Father, the Son and the Holy Ghost."

"He's mad!"

"Next thing he'll be pleading to be crucified!"

The guards grew hoarse with laughing.

But Don Carlos was plunged into misery. His round, usually smiling face was sullen.

Ramon Sirval startled them all by suddenly singing, "Sing praises to our Lord and Christ in sin." His voice was girlishly high-pitched.

The guards made expressive faces to each other, tapped their temples with their forefingers and shrugged their shoulders.

Presently the car drew over to the shoulder of the road and braked to a standstill under the shade of trees growing in an olive grove. The guards dropped off the running boards, the doors were opened and the priests climbed out.

Don Carlos looked around slowly; at the blue sky and a fleeting cloud like a puff of cotton wool; at the distant green-brown mountains silhouetted against the horizon, the silvery-green leaves of olive trees and the rich brown soil. He took a deep breath, relishing the scent of pine trees and mountain sage. Then he looked at Varela. "Have you no mercy for the boy?"

Varela shook his head.

Don Carlos shrugged his shoulders, drew long and hard on his cigar, exhaled, smiled and tossed the cigar butt away. "Where is it to happen?"

Varela pointed.

"You will allow us to pray?"

"If it is your wish."

Don Carlos's old legs were stiff and his large belly overbalanced him, but the guards helped him to kneel. He thanked them solemnly. Ramon Sirval knelt beside him and they bowed their bare heads and clasped their hands in prayer. Don Carlos murmured indistinctly but the young priest prayed in a ringing voice.

The committeemen stood around, embarrassed and impatient. Julio Marin, who had snatched up Don Carlos's cigar butt and was puffing it enthusiastically, smiled toothily.

After some minutes when there was no sign of the prayers abating, Varela stepped up closely behind the old priest, pressed his pistol against the bone behind the ear and fired. The impact of the bullet lifted the old priest slightly and he seemed to hover before he crumpled forward on his face.

When the shot rang out Ramon Sirval leaped to his feet. He looked down at Don Carlos and his face was radiant. "Let me die for you, O God. Let me be crucified. Let my blood wash away the sins of these ignorant men who know not what they do!"

The guards eyed him in amused astonishment.

The young priest beat his chest with his fists. "Scourge me," he cried, his eyes blazing with fanatical zeal. "Scourge me as you scourged our Lord. Strip me. Bring me a crown of thorns. Where is the crucifix?"

"The crazy bastard."

"Listen to the whoreson."

"Crucify me!" he screamed, his eyes blazing. "Are you afraid. Crucify me!"

"All right. If that's what you want, you mad bastard!"

Jeering at him, they dragged him to a tree, looped cords around his wrists and drew him up until his feet swung clear of the ground. He was in pain but his face was radiant. "Scourge me so I suffer for you and for God," he pleaded.

"He's really asking for it!"

They tore off his clothes and whipped him with nettles until an angry rash mottled his white skin. But the young priest was immune to pain. He sang hymns, his face glowed with a divine light and he ceaselessly prayed for them to shed his blood that he might suffer for their sins.

They made a crown of thorns which bloodied his forehead and he thanked them. They hit him and he blessed them.

They finally became enraged because they could not hurt him and he had no fear of death. One of the guards drew a sharp knife. "You ponce," he shouted. "How do you like *this?*" The blade slashed the flesh below the priest's ribs, opening it like a mouth. From the bloody lips spilled a thin, red trickle.

Ramon Sirval looked down upon the man and said fervently: "Bless you, brother. You have sinned and my blood will wash away your guilt."

The priest's complacency goaded the guard to frenzy. "You've asked for it, *maricon!* Since you beg to suffer I'll make you truly a *maricon!*" His companions watched curiously, wondering how the priest would react. The pain of the savage amputation jolted the priest out of his state of religious ecstasy. He screamed terribly as his life's blood ran down his legs.

The guard stepped back and wiped his hands on his trousers. "Now suffer for us, you bastard!"

They walked to the shade of a distant tree, smoked and passed around a wineskin. Almost an hour elapsed before Julio Marin ran over to them with his white teeth flashing against the dark skin of his face. "Finished," he declared and drew his forefinger across his throat.

"Get a can of gasoline from the car," ordered Varela.

They drenched the hanging body and the clothing placed below it, stood back and tossed a lighted match upon it. The gasoline exploded into a sheet of flame that scorched their faces. The hanging figure, bathed in a shimmering blue flame, startlingly came to life, convulsed and writhed, and for brief seconds a thin wail of agony whined amongst the crackling of burning leaves and branches. Then the figure stiffened as it twisted, its blackened hair blazing and the brains sizzling in the skull.

When Don Carlos and Ramon Sirval did not return that day, the alarmed villagers searched for them.

And found them.

"The Committee say they were traitors and smuggled information to the Falangists," Ana told Father Delbos tearfully. "But it's a lie. Don Carlos was a good and honest man."

Father Delbos's knees trembled and his hands shook. "Nobody . . . nobody knows I'm here?"

"Nobody," she said. "You have nothing to fear. After this, none of the villagers will ever betray you. Never!"

Miguel Barras lived in a bitter and melancholy world of his own. Nothing touched him, neither his family's wish to comfort him nor the atrocities inflicted upon the villagers. He cared not that his family and others were slowly stripped of their possessions by the avaricious Committee.

Then one day he came alive. He came down from his bedroom with a few personal possessions tied up in a bundle and announced: "I'm going."

Elisa's eyes filled with tears as she looked into her son's tormented face.

Teresa pleaded. "Don't go, Miguel. Stay with us. We *need* you."

Paco Barras asked: "Where are you going, son?"

Miguel's black hair which had once clustered his forehead in ringlets now hung lifeless, his cheeks were hollow and his eyes haunted. "I don't know, Father. But I cannot stay here. I must find myself . . . or lose myself entirely."

Barras sighed.

"There is no other way, Father. I am as though dead inside."

"Go then, if you must, Miguel. But remember this is always your home."

"Thank you, Father."

Pepita pleaded: "Bring me a talking doll when you come back."

Miguel ruffled her hair and for the first time since Helena's death the ghost of a smile touched his lips.

He went by train to Barcelona and straight to the recruiting barracks. After waiting more than an hour, a soldier led him to an office where a solemn-faced officer with a five-pointed star on his sleeve eyed him keenly and pointed to a chair on the opposite side of his desk. "Sit down."

Miguel sat.

"Documents?"

Miguel slid his identity card and fisherman's permit across the desk and the officer scrutinized them carefully, turning them over and examining them closely to make sure they weren't fakes. Satisfied, he leaned back in his chair. "So you want to volunteer, comrade?"

Miguel nodded.

"Your age group will be called soon. Why don't you await call-up?"

"I want to fight now. I don't care where. The more danger the better!"

The officer's eyes were wise. "You seek danger?"

"Yes."

"You're not afraid to die?"

"No!"

"Perhaps . . . perhaps you *want* to die?"

"Perhaps."

"You are willing to obey suicidal orders?"

"I will do what is necessary."

The officer took a pack of cigarettes and offered them to Miguel. As they lit up, he asked: "Why have you lost the desire to live?"

Miguel's face set grimly. "It is a personal matter."

"Sometimes it helps to talk about . . . sad things."

Miguel said tonelessly: "I was on my honeymoon in Sevilla the day war broke out. My wife was killed by a sniper."

"By a Fascist bullet!" said the officer.

Miguel looked at him sharply. "How do you know?"

"The Falangists sniped at men, women and children to spread panic."

Miguel's black eyes were fathomless.

"The workers of Sevilla resisted to the death," said the officer. "But they hadn't enough weapons. The Moors butchered them. Then they brought up artillery and shelled the workers' houses into rubble."

Miguel stared steadily.

"You want revenge against those Fascist swine?"

Miguel nodded.

"Then find the courage to live. Do not die merely to avenge your bride's death. Die bravely, freeing the civilized world from fascism."

Miguel still stared.

"Join one of our Steel Corps. They're fearless men who are trained to die for freedom."

Miguel nodded.

The officer wrote on Miguel's card: *"For Military and Political Training."*

Miguel asked: "The Falangists sniped from the rooftops and killed people?"

"They killed hundreds!"

"They deliberately murdered innocent . . . ?"

"The Fascists *are* murderers," stated the officer. He pressed a button on his desk and when a soldier appeared said: "Take this man to Medical."

Miguel stripped and showered. His hair was cropped, the doctor ran an approving eye over his fine physique, and he was issued a uniform. He slept in the barrack room with conscripts, and for a few days drilled with them on the parade ground. Then he was ordered to report for special training.

He sat in a classroom with two dozen other men, some as young as Miguel, some middle-aged and some in their fifties. Most of them had the callused hands of workers; but there were those too with the clean appearance of better living.

Their lecturer was an officer about thirty-five. He wore pince-nez and a five-pointed star on his tunic sleeve. He said conversationally: "These talks, comrades, will give us a clear picture of what we are fighting against." He paused to insure they were all listening and said slowly: "Never forget we are fighting fascism!" He took off his pince-nez and rubbed them on his sleeve. "Fascism is the ultimate weapon of capitalism. It maintains capitalism by violence. The time for change has come. The workers are ready to take over the means of production and insure prosperity and equality for all. But the capitalists will not allow this without a struggle. So . . . we have fascism. Hitler and his Fascist thugs reign supreme in Germany, bolstered by the wealthy capitalist bosses, while the workers live in misery."

The lecturer replaced his pince-nez carefully and then continued: "The capitalist bosses in Spain have subsidized the Fascists . . . the Falangists! These paid hirelings and murderers snipe from the safety of rooftops and explode bombs in children's classrooms. They will do *anything* to smash the workers."

Miguel leaned forward, eyes gleaming intently.

"The priests are the lick-spittles of the capitalists and are in league with the Fascists. The Falangists and the Catholic Party took up arms against the people and from the church towers Fascists fired on humble people."

The lecturer didn't teach. He explained. And as Miguel listened, he saw everything much more clearly. At the end of the lecture he asked simple questions. And at the end of the week, the lecturer noted on Miguel's enlistment card that he was an excellent political student and good party material.

A guard in one of Alcazar's towers gave the alarm when he saw the fuel tanker being brought up. High-powered hoses were soon spraying the walls of the fort with gasoline.

All morning the hoses poured out thousands of gallons of the inflammable liquid until fumes penetrated even the cellars where the hostages huddled miserably. The smell tainted their food, hampered breathing, clung to hair and clothing and caused sore throats. In the hot sun the vaporized gasoline made the air shimmer and the senses swam tipsily.

Apprehension increased in the fort, until one man became hysterical and screamed he didn't want to be burned alive. But when exploding gasoline bombs were thrown against the fortress walls to ignite the fuel, very little was achieved. The fuel blazed and the sturdy stone walls were bathed in flames. But when the blaze died, the defenders had suffered not at all.

Rafael and his friends in their punishment cells heard the derisive shouts of their comrades mocking the attackers.

Every day government bombing planes dropped bombs on the fortress without causing much damage and a steady artillery barrage was kept up, hammering the strong walls and trying to make a breach in them through which militiamen could attack.

One day a truce was called. There was a ceasefire and a government emissary with bandaged eyes entered the fort and was taken to the commander. The emissary offered surrender terms which were instantly rejected. The emissary then suggested a prolongation of the truce while women, children and the wounded left the fortress. This offer, too, Colonel Moscardo curtly rejected. He and his men would defend the fort to the death, even if all had to die; the women and children as well as the men.

The emissary sadly left to report failure, the ceasefire terminated, and the government sent miners and explosive experts to Toledo. Sappers began to tunnel under the fortress walls.

Sound vibrations travel a long way through earth and for those inside the fortress began a long period of nagging fear. The underground thud of miners' picks grew steadily louder as the tunnel lengthened. Sound spread and magnified until it seemed all the solid ground below the defenders was excavated and that the entire fortress would be swallowed up in a great yawning hole.

The defenders located two tunnels that burrowed under the outer walls of the fortress. When the thud of miners' picks ceased, they knew dynamite was being tightly packed into the cavities beneath them. All day and all through the long night the defenders sweated in apprehension, knowing that if enough explosives were used they would be blown apart.

Then at dawn a heavy artillery barrage began and every government gun available opened up and battered at the walls. It was the prelude to a determined assault and Rafael and his companions were released, the women and children were battened down in the subterranean vaults, and the defenders grimly checked their weapons and waited.

The first mine exploded with a tremendous earthshaking concussion. The fortress's east tower lifted skyward before it crumbled and fell and a few seconds later the second mine exploded, dissolving part of the outer wall into a great cloud of dust and gasses.

Within the fortress, officers coolly issued orders. The inner walls of the fortress were still intact and from behind their cover the defenders leveled their rifles and waited.

The militiamen attacked through the dust and smoke, shouting gleefully, not aware as they scrambled over broken masonry that only the outer parapet of the fort's defenses had been breached.

But they were soon made aware of it. Rifles volleyed and machine-gun bullets cut them down. One determined group of militiamen, their overalls white with dust, valiantly scrambled to the summit of the heap of rubble that had once been a tower and triumphantly planted a red flag.

An officer shouted an order. Small-arms fire drowned his voice but Rafael saw his arms waving and understood. With others he leaped down from the fire-step into the courtyard and followed the officer at a run to the ruined tower, firing as he went.

The militiamen stared in astonishment before they hastily knelt and returned the fire.

Rafael had lost his rifle when he leaped from the parapet, but he had drawn his pistol. He paused, aimed carefully and fired. The man he shot at threw up his hands, arched backward, hovered for a split second and then fell. It was the first man Rafael had killed and he felt exalted. But death was too final and the next time he aimed low and laughed when the militiaman went down clutching his groin, his cry of agony drowned by the sounds of battle.

The militiamen were untrained workers whose ragged, inaccurate shooting was quite ineffective. They were picked off with such ease by disciplined soldiers that they were suddenly overcome with panic. They fled blindly, leaving their red flag undefended. Only one man tried to help a wounded comrade and Rafael brought him down with a bullet in his spine. The officer who had led the charge snatched up the red flag, flourished it derisively and shouted insults after the fleeing militiamen.

Elsewhere too the attack had failed and the militiamen retreated with their morale badly shaken while within the fortress all were jubilant.

But a week later another tunnel had been dug and dynamite charges placed under the northeast tower. Only the fear of injuring the hostages restrained the sappers from using enough explosives to destroy the entire fortress.

Again the defenders prepared to make a last stand. Sadly this time, because by a bitter whim of fate help was so near. General Franco's African army was on the outskirts of Toledo and about to cut the road to Madrid.

Once again the defenders withstood a heavy artillery barrage at dawn and then came the earthshaking concussion of an enormous explosion. A great part of the mined tower leaped high in the air and fell in a smoking mound of rubble. But once again the sappers had failed. The ruins of the tower were almost as easy for the defenders to man as the wall itself, and the courageous but foolhardy attack of the militiamen was easily beaten back.

There was no time left to sap under the fortress again. The next day the militiamen saw the African army flowing down from the heights commanding Toledo, and driving around to cut the road to Madrid. Unhesitatingly they marched out to do battle although hopelessly outnumbered. Relentlessly they were beaten back until they had to yield Toledo.

Street fighting in Toledo went on all day and the long-besieged defenders of the Alcazar joined their rescuers in an orgy of reprisals which went on for another three days.

While green-turbaned Moors stormed through the town, tossing hand grenades into doorways and windows, Rafael and his friends rampaged through the field hospitals, finishing off militiamen too severely wounded to be moved. Afterward they returned to the Alcazar to release the women and children hostages.

Among them . . . the daughter of Charugin!

The two planes could not be seen against the bright blaze of the sun but their engines could be heard clearly, throbbing loudly when they were overhead and then diminishing as they sped away, only to return again.

Teresa's eyes were sharp and she was the first to see them. She pointed. "There they are. Directly above the harbor."

They were two silvery minnows swimming in the great blue bowl of the heavens, wheeling slowly, the loud throb of their engines quite out of proportion to their size.

Varela and the committeemen set up a telescope on its tripod in the plaza but didn't know how to focus it. They could see nothing at all.

"Whose planes are they?" asked Doctor Aldo.

A young fisherman with eyes accustomed to scanning great and empty distances said wryly: "They glitter in the sun and I cannot see the markings."

Doctor Aldo drew out his watch and glanced at it. "They're government planes," he decided. "They must be."

Paco Barras smoothed his blond hair back behind his ears, grinned and shrugged his shoulders. "As long as they don't bother me, I won't bother them."

A black speck fell from one of the planes but was quickly lost to sight. Then everyone stared in amazement as a great spout of rock and dirt geysered upward from a hill slope half a mile beyond the village. Black smoke billowed lazily toward the sky. The sound of the explosion reached them seconds later and was terrifying. It cracked the air apart, the earth shook and the echoes went rolling out over the sea in never-diminishing thunder.

"They're overhead!" screamed an old crone and everybody ran.
Parents snatched up children and cowered with them in their whitewashed cottages, Committeemen crouched in doorways and futilely
fired at the sky and some villagers simply kept running, terror-
stricken. Everyone heard the whistle of the next bomb. It landed on
the beach at the water's edge, shattering cottage windows and spatter-
ing stone walls with shrapnel.

The planes dropped six more bombs before they flew away. Two
fell inside the harbor and sank a moored fishing boat and two made
craters in the road at the entrance to the village. One fell harmlessly
on a vegetable patch and another destroyed a fisherman's cottage. A
family of six were buried in the ruins and only a badly injured little
girl survived.

The planes returned again before dusk, destroyed two more houses
and killed and injured more villagers.

A meeting was held in the plaza and it was decided the women and
children must be sent to villages in the mountains for safety. Varela
and the Committee were asked to supply transport and committeemen went to Figueras to borrow trucks—without success.

The planes returned again the following morning but although
the bombs fell off target, killing a goat tethered in an olive grove, the
tension in the village was so great that Varela went personally to Figueras and returned with four large army trucks. Most of the women
and children left the village, among them Elisa Barras and Pepita.

"Don't worry," Teresa assured her mother. "I'll cook and take care
of Papa."

"And when the bombs fall, you'll shelter where the wall is strongest?"

"Don't worry about us, Mother. You look after Pepita."

The trucks lumbered off, women and children fluttering white
handkerchiefs, some smiling sadly, many weeping. The trucks drove
up into the mountains through green valleys and over high hills.
They passed many villages and at the biggest ones billeted as many
women and children as could be accommodated. Some families were
driven fifty miles off and months passed before their loved ones could
visit them.

Escoleras was strangely silent without the mothers and children.
Like most of the older women, Elisa was self-effacing and hovered
quietly in the background at home. But her absence was noticed. Her
happy humming while she washed and laundered and her cheerful

clattering of crockery was missed. The kitchen was oppressively quiet. Teresa sang, cooked new dishes and tried to make up for her mother's absence, but it was a long time before she or her father became accustomed to it.

The planes didn't return again for some weeks. Then, when it was being proposed that the children and wives should be brought back, there was another raid. But there was little damage and the villagers had learned how to shelter under strong kitchen tables that would protect them if their cottage collapsed around them. Soon they grew accustomed to the spasmodic raids and the first villager to hear a plane's engine ran to sound the siren fixed to the roof of the fish market.

One day Paco Barras's brother arrived in Escoleras. He had lived in Barcelona for twenty years. The two brothers sat on the beach in front of the white-walled cottage talking about their youth and friends and relatives while Teresa fried fresh-caught baby squid which the two men found so tasty she was obliged to keep serving.

But at last Federico stated the purpose of his visit. Food was scarce in Barcelona and the price of fish was rocketing. He proposed Paco Barras should buy all the fish landed in Escoleras and send it to Barcelona.

Paco was at once hostile to the suggestion. "How would I send fish to Barcelona, Federico?" he scoffed. "I have no transport."

"Transport is arranged," said Federico. He drew a paper from his pocket. "This is a permit from the UGT. A truck will leave Escoleras every morning for Barcelona."

"Federico! Why ask me to do this? I am a fisherman."

"You are also my brother."

"Surely there are many others who will do this for you?"

"But I cannot trust them as I trust you."

Paco Barras spread his hands in a gesture of helplessness. "Why me? Why?"

Federico smiled wisely. "You will earn a great deal of money, Paco."

"What need have I for money? We have fish and we have wine." He smiled wryly. "The Committee takes everything else; money, sheets, blankets, cutlery, everything!"

"It is not justice, Paco. The government is against such robbery. This is the kind of tyranny that *must* be stamped out."

"It is unwise to stamp on men who bristle with weapons."

"When I return to Barcelona I will talk with influential friends."
Paco's blue eyes were bitter. "The dead cannot live again."

"Terrible things have happened everywhere, Paco. We Spanish are passionate and hot-headed. We can be very kind and good. But we can also be very wicked and cruel."

"Life is often hard to bear, Federico. It is a pity men make it even harder."

"You will do it, Paco?"

"Do what?"

"You will buy fish and send it to Barcelona?"

"I have no money to buy fish and I know nothing of prices. What I catch myself I barter for my simple needs."

"My employers will arrange adequate credit for you at the fish market. Money will be deposited in a bank in Barcelona so you can buy fish to a limit of thirty thousand pesetas."

Paco Barras's eyes widened. "That is a fortune!"

"Fish buying is big business."

"I know nothing of prices."

"It does not matter. You must buy as cheaply as you can. Later, when you have learned, your commission will increase as your buying improves. We know the market values in Barcelona and will know whether you buy well or poorly."

"Federico!" Paco Barras pleaded. "Find some other man."

"Paco. I beg of you because I am your brother. Do this thing for me."

"Why me? Why me, Federico?"

"I have eight children and the oldest is still in school. In Barcelona there is an acute food shortage. Also there is unemployment. I am liked by my employers but if they have no fish to sell, their business will fail. Then what will I do?"

Paco sighed sadly.

"You will do this, brother?"

Paco spread his hands and smiled wryly. "You have eight children. And because you have worked so hard with your wife in this way, now I must become a buyer of fish."

"If a man cannot call upon his brother for help, he can call upon no one."

"Teresa!" shouted Paco Barras. "Bring more of these delicious squid." He took the *porrón,* tilted back his head and the rich black wine jetted into his mouth.

"You agree then, Paco?" asked Federico anxiously.

Paco Barras drank deeply and his throat muscles moved rhythmically as he swallowed. He nodded his head.

Federico returned to Barcelona and the next day Paco Barras started to buy fish. The fishing boats returned to the harbor at any time of day or night and their catch was at once carried into the fish market and sold by auction.

Paco had little notion of the value of fish. He knew he could exchange a small squid for a loaf of bread, that a sole was worth a bottle of good-quality wine and that a basket of sardines could be traded for a leg of lamb. But he had no idea what a ten-kilo case of *merluza* could cost in pesetas. So at first he studied the buying, and his keen fisherman's eyes accurately calculated the weight and the quality of the fish while he remembered the prices paid.

Before the Civil War the only fish-buyers in Escoleras were fishmongers from the surrounding villages. But now these men couldn't pay the prices, Paco Barras noted. There were one or two buyers from Barcelona who bought everything between them while they smoked long, thin cheroots and hurled bantering remarks at each other.

When Paco Barras tried to bid, the big city buyers scooped him. He studied fish prices for many days before he made his first successful bid for twenty cases of *merluza*. Then the Barcelona buyers united and overbid so he couldn't buy again that day.

He loaded the twenty cases of *merluza* onto the truck, tacked a stenciled destination card on each case and the next day received an encouraging telegram from his brother:

KEEP BIDDING STOP BUY EXPENSIVE BUT BUY, BUY, BUY.

The following day he surprised himself and everyone by jumping in split seconds before the other buyers, anticipating them and bidding recklessly, so that most of the fish was bought by him. He was pleased with himself. He enjoyed pitting his wits, knowledge and fisherman's judgment against the sleek, city-suited men who now glowered at him over their cheroots, instead of smiling with a superior air.

In a few weeks Paco Barras had whittled fish-buying down to its essentials. All his life he had handled fish and at a single glance could accurately calculate its weight. This gave him an advantage over men who rarely touched fish with their hands.

At the end of the month he was the biggest fish-buyer in Escoleras and rarely made mistakes. Other men might estimate wrongly and buy fish that weighed less than they calculated. But never Paco Barras.

At the end of the month, Federico sent him a note of the commission he had earned. Paco had never dreamed so much money could be earned so easily. Federico urged: "Buy all the fish you can, Paco. We never have enough. Buy as much as you can, as cheaply as you can."

That same day Paco Barras made a great decision. He told Teresa: "Roll up a mattress and two blankets."

She stared in astonishment.

"I do not go far. I will sleep at nights outside the fish market."

"Why, Father? What's happened?"

"More fish is sold at night than by day. When I am asleep I do not know when a fishing boat arrives to unload its catch. But if I sleep outside the fish market I shall be alerted and ready to bid."

She was dismayed. "You will leave me to sleep alone in the house, Father?"

"You are a grown girl, Teresa. And it is only a hundred paces to the fish market."

"Why do you want to do this, Father?"

He looked at her slyly and it was the first time she had ever seen him look sly. "It is profitable."

She was surprised. "You have need of money?"

He shook his head.

"Well then?"

He smoothed his blond hair back behind his ears and smiled gently. "It's not for me. It will be for you, Pepita, Isidro and Miguel."

"Don't do it for me, Father. I prefer you to sleep comfortably at home."

He sighed. "Also it is for Federico who has eight children."

"You must do as you wish, Father," she snapped and angrily banged around in the kitchen.

But later when he went off to the fish market she had prepared a roll of his mattress, two blankets and a pillow. As he walked away along the beach she came to the door and scolded: "And don't get those blankets smelling fishy!"

In the early hours of the morning he ran home and excitedly shook her awake.

"Come quickly, Teresa. Help me. Come quickly."

She blinked sleep from her eyes.

"Quickly. Come with me. At once!"

He hurried away and she climbed out of bed, pulled on her work frock and ran after him. He was in the market hall with a mountain of sardines he had bought. A truck was waiting to transport them to Barcelona but first they had to be packed.

They worked quickly, boxing the slippery fish in long, straight rows and spreading chopped ice over each layer. The fine fins cut their hands and fish scales coated their arms to the elbow. When they had finished, there were forty-five cases.

"Thank you, daughter," said Paco Barras. "Go home now and pre-pare breakfast. I'll come along shortly."

"Will we do this every morning, Father?"

"This is not work for you, daughter. I called you because there was nobody else. But in the future, I will have a man I can call upon if there is need."

Teresa walked tiredly back along the village street, her bare feet coated with dust, her frock clinging damply to her thighs, and fish scales flaking from her arms. When she neared her home, she was delighted to see Pilar Ledesma coming toward her and ran to give Anselmo's sister a friendly greeting. But Pilar glanced away quickly as though she had not seen her.

Teresa flushed and her heart missed a beat.

Pilar walked straight past her, head held high, deliberately ignor-ing her. Teresa ran on home, fighting to hold back her tears. She was more hurt than angry, knowing Pilar had a hint of Rafael's false pride in her makeup.

4

After cooking lunch and washing the dishes, Teresa combed her hair and plaited it in two braids. She put on a white blouse with a fine lace edging and a black skirt. Her long, slim legs made her look very young and coltish as she walked to the Ledesma house. Two commit-teemen called after her, but she tossed her head disdainfully.

Pilar greeted her as an old friend, as though they had not met earlier, and they sat in the cool of the patio with Señora Ledesma and talked. Pilar avoided talking about Guillermo's death.

"And Antonia?" asked Teresa.

"She stayed in Madrid to be near Jaime. He can't bear knowing he's a cripple for life. Antonia sits with him day and night, but he hasn't the will to get better."

"This terrible war!" choked Señora Ledesma. She was thinking of Baudillo, still in Figueras jail.

"Any news of Rafael?" asked Teresa.

"Not a word. He was in the Alcazar, but now it's been relieved he'll be with his regiment. It's dreadful that while we're bombed in Madrid, Rafael is helping those who are trying to kill his own family. But he can't help himself, I suppose. He has to do what he's told, doesn't he? That's the army, isn't it?"

Teresa nodded.

"It's Anselmo you really want to know about, isn't it, Teresa?" Señora Ledesma smiled.

"You have news of him?" asked Teresa quickly.

"A letter came today." Señora Ledesma put aside her crocheting and took the letter from the pocket of her gown. It was hastily scrawled, assuring his mother he had plenty to eat and that he was far from the fighting. At the end he had written a separate paragraph:

> Please tell Teresa I'm well and receiving her letters. I am too busy to write much but I think about her a great deal. Give her my love.

Teresa's eyes shone moistly when she handed back the letter. "Anselmo doesn't mention Señor Ledesma."

Señora Ledesma concentrated on her crocheting. "I haven't told Anselmo. I don't want to worry him."

"And . . . how is Señor Ledesma? Have you seen him recently?"

"I was allowed a short visit. He's cheerful and scolded me for worrying about him. He expects to be released soon. But he's so thin! His clothes hang on him! And the conditions are appalling. Poor Baudillo has always been so fastidious and it's misery for him to live like that!"

"Can't the lawyers do anything, Señora Ledesma?" asked Teresa.

The older woman raised a delicate hand to finger the pearls Baudillo had given her on their wedding anniversary. Her voice was husky. "They're doing what they can; but there's terrible disorder. So many judges and lawyers were shot as Fascists at the start of the

trouble! They're trying to get the courts functioning again. But
meanwhile, everyone has to wait. Also Anton Leon, who owes Baudillo a great deal of money, has sworn poor Baudillo has many Falangist friends."

"Meanwhile poor Papa has to stay in prison!" said Pilar bitterly.

"We must all have patience," sighed Señora Ledesma resignedly.
"Our men must wait for an end to the fighting and we women . . .
we must wait for our men." She looked up at Teresa. "Patience is
our only consolation, my dear."

After fourteen weeks Anselmo's company was relieved. There was
no moon, and all through the long night they stumbled through the
darkness, legs aching and rifle straps cutting into their shoulders.
Thorns and brambles tore at their trousers, their feet bled in their
broken boots and they often fell. But the nightmare journey ended
weeks of inactivity on the hilltop.

Soon after dawn they arrived back at the small village where the
church was their billet. But by mistake other troops had been moved
up and the officers could do little to ease the congestion. Every nook
and cranny of the church was occupied by tired men sleeping off
hours of exhausting marching, and the newcomers had to sleep in the
plaza which was already so full it was difficult to find room to stretch
out.

Anselmo Ledesma sat with his back braced against a tree and
looked around with red-rimmed eyes. A newly arrived militiaman
squatted down beside him. He was no more than sixteen but his eyes
burned with idealistic fervor. "Did you kill many Fascist swine, comrade?"

Anselmo laughed bitterly. "Are you looking for glory, boy!"

The youth's eyes shone. "We're holding the lines. *No pasaran!* We
fight for freedom against the menace of fascism!"

Anselmo's stiff fingers went to the breast pocket of his filthy shirt
and drew out tobacco makings. They both lit up. "Do you want to
hear about the fighting?" he asked.

The boy leaned forward with gleaming eyes.

"We were on one hilltop and about nine hundred meters away the
Fascists occupied another hilltop."

The boy held his breath.

"We were dug in and they were dug in. For miles and miles it's the

same ragged front, with some hilltops commanded by them and some
by us."

"Yes?" encouraged the youth.

Anselmo drew deeply at his cigarette and exhaled slowly. "And
. . . that's it! Sometimes they sent out a night patrol and we fired at
noises we heard in the dark. Sometimes it was them firing at us."

"And . . . the fighting?"

"Sometimes we shot at each other during the day; but it's a waste of
ammunition. We're too far apart."

"But . . . wasn't there fighting?"

"Plenty," said Anselmo. "We fought the fleas and pubic lice; the
stench of human excretion, the monotony of beans and our sense of
futility!"

The boy scowled. "Futility!"

"How else can you describe months of privations on a hilltop? War
can bring out a man's courage; but not his nobility." Anselmo drew
hard on his cigarette, exhaled and stubbed it out. He closed his tired
eyes for a moment and was instantly asleep.

He slept on while officers telephoned and dispatched messengers.
Transport trucks arrived, soldiers were driven away and when Anselmo awoke only his company occupied the church. The cooks built
fires under pots of beans and freshly baked loaves were brought up. A
barrel of wine was tapped and tin mugs placed under it. Then after
eating their fill the men clustered around the fountain, stripped
naked and washed delightedly. Scissors snipped busily as they
trimmed their hair and shaved off their beards. Their clothes still
stank, their feet were bleeding again and the lice foraged anew; but
they felt like men once more.

But somewhere, somebody had blundered again. At first too many
troops had been brought up to relieve the men in the front line.
Now, more troops had been sent away than should have been. After
only twenty-four hours at base, Anselmo's company was ordered back
to the front line. Other troops would relieve them almost at once,
they were told. But pressure on the Madrid front increased, reinforcements were hastily dispatched to the north and Anselmo and his
company sat it out on another hilltop.

It was a dark night and the sentry was nervous. He nudged his
companion into wakefulness. "Perez, there's somebody out there. I
heard the clink of a rifle against stone."

"I shit upon the whoreson who disturbs my sleep," growled Perez, but he too listened and presently they heard the sound of stealthy movements.

"Halt! Who goes there?" challenged the sentry, sweating with excitement.

From lower down the hillside a frightened voice called: "Don't shoot. I'm a friend."

"Give the password."

There was a long silence.

"The password!"

"Don't shoot. Please don't shoot. I don't know the password. I want to surrender."

"It's a trick," breathed Perez.

"Get the captain," said the sentry. But already men were gathering, awakened by the sentry's challenge. Commissar Rosen was among them. He was a small man, his eyes almond-shaped and his skin yellowish. He spoke perfect Castilian Spanish.

"I'll take over," he said quietly. He called down into the darkness. "Listen. If this is a trick, you will be shot. Throw away your weapons, stand erect and walk up here slowly with your hands above your head. Do you understand?"

"I understand," called the man.

The men leveled their weapons and waited tensely.

"Start walking," ordered the commissar.

The man's boots scraped on a stone as he stood up. The commissar gestured and a powerful flashlight beam stabbed out and found the soldier. He was blinded as he stumbled uphill toward them with his hands above his head.

The man came on, reached the parapet and climbed over it. The torch was switched off and the blackness became intense.

Commissar Rosen asked grimly: "So you want to surrender?" He was only a blurred silhouette in the darkness of night.

"Yes," panted the man. "Take me prisoner. I've had enough. The cold, not enough to eat, the lice, not enough sleep . . . !"

"How about your cause?" asked the commissar.

The man spat. "I shit upon the cause!"

"How long have you been out there?" asked the commissar.

"Hours," said the man. "I lost my way."

"You certainly did," agreed the commissar grimly. "You've deserted back to your own side!"

There was a long, stunned silence. The man gulped. "Who . . . who are you?"

Somebody switched on the flashlight and the deserter looked around him despairingly, his eyes widening when he saw Commissar Rosen's leveled pistol. "I couldn't stand it any more, Commissar!" he choked. "Look!" He held out arms as thin as broomsticks. "I've been at the front for months without leave."

"You were ready to betray your comrades?"

"Not betray them, Commissar. I just wanted to get away . . . from all this."

"There's another way to get away from it all, traitor!" said the commissar, pulling the trigger. "Like *this,* and *this,* and *this!*"

Emil Serra had bought a new streamlined typewriter upon which even his pudgy fingers could type swiftly.

> Madrid is a besieged city, attacked strongly and defended valiantly. The battle for Madrid will be long and bitter.

> Madrid is a hotbed of foreign intrigue and unofficial representatives of all nations try to arrange armaments' deals. Corruption is rife. Russian arms are flowing into Spain. One large consignment of old-fashioned Lewis machine guns for which there is no ammunition was recently delivered. It had been lying in a Russian warehouse since 1914!

> The Communist Party is small, but its few members make their presence felt. The Communists control distribution of the Russian weapons and call the tune. There is a battle for power between unorganized Anarchists who are trying to take over the factories, and the few Communist Party members who wield enormous influence on the government. The government is preventing the factories being socialized by the workers. It seems that social revolution is acceptable to the Communists *only* when they initiate it!

There was a knock and Emil crossed to the door.

A sallow-faced man smiled ingratiatingly. "Will you be long, Emil? They're waiting."

"Is everything set up?"

"Ready when you are."

"I'd better come."

Emil Serra locked the door of his study and padded barefooted along the corridor to his lounge. He wore only cotton underpants and

his flabby paunch rolled over its waistband like melted fat. He ran
stubby fingers through his sandy hair and smiled sheepishly at his
guests. "I shan't be long. Make yourselves at home. Cigars, drinks,
food. Help yourselves. Do anything you like!"

His guests chuckled.

"If you'll just look things over . . ." suggested the sallow-faced
man.

Emil glanced at the projector and the silver screen pinned to the
wall. There were three cans of films that would run for two hours.
Large, comfortably upholstered chairs faced the screen and the male
guests were already seated. Some were high-ranking officers and
others were diplomats. One man was a professional double spy, passing from the government to the Nationalist side frequently and with
little apparent difficulty.

The girls were young and the prettiest to be found in Madrid.
They were charmingly available in tantalizing underwear as they
offered around trays of choice foods, caviar, pâté de foie gras, oysters,
champagne and lobsters. One girl sat astride a colonel's thigh and
tempted him to bite the stuffed olive she held between her white
teeth. Another poured champagne and giggled encouragingly as an
ambassador's secretary ran his hand up her leg.

"Just a few minutes, friends," Emil told his guests. He hurried
back along the corridor and as he left the room, the red star-scar
splashed across his shoulders aroused curious comment.

Emil Serra locked the door, and sat at his typewriter:

> There are no official records of casualties, but they must be high. It
> is sad that the best types, the thinkers, idealists and those who be-
> lieve in goodness and justice, are being killed off so quickly. They
> rush to the front to fight for what they believe in. The cunning ones
> hang back.
>
> But at last, firm steps are being taken to stop the terrorism of self-
> appointed judges and executioners. The public is warned by radio
> not to answer knocks on the door after eleven at night and militia-
> men have been warned it is a serious crime to arrest anyone without
> a government order. The bands of roving bandits who kill and plun-
> der while pretending political authority are steadily being rounded
> up.
>
> The government should have stopped this terrorism earlier. Through-
> out Spain people have been tyrannized by illegal committees, and a
> great hatred of the government has developed because of them.

The bulk of Spain's national gold reserve is now in Russia. It is being held against payment for the armaments Spain is receiving. Foreign volunteers are swarming in over the Pyrenees. Many are political refugees from Hitler and many are idealists like George Orwell and André Malraux. These eager volunteers boost the morale of conscripted Spaniards.

President Azaña was startled by the sound of gunfire and departed rapidly for Barcelona without even warning his ministers. He steadfastly refuses to return to the capital and speaks to his ministers by telephone.

The Germans offered General Franco more arms and men on the condition that German officers command their own forces! General Franco accepted and already German pilots and aircraft are flying into Spain. I am informed that a total of 6,500 men, fifty bombing planes, fifty fighter planes, antiaircraft and antitank guns, as well as forty tanks are scheduled for early delivery from Germany.

Four hundred thousand Russian soldiers are reported on their way. They've been coming a very long time, yet they never arrive. In fact, the only Russians in Spain are a couple of technicians who have been strictly forbidden to go to the front line.

Emil Serra sealed his report, locked it away in his private safe and joined his guests. Champagne had mellowed everyone and most of the guests were by now in a state of undress. The colonel, who had news for Emil about an error in the amount of the gold sent to Russia, was laughing up at a tall brunette who stooped over him. She had dipped her breast into champagne and a great glistening tear of the amber liquid fell from her hard nipple.

A Scandinavian attaché was maudlin drunk. "Feed me an olive," he told the blonde curled up on his lap. She placed it between her ripe-red lips for him to bite.

"No," he said tipsily. "Not that way. Make it warm first."

"You're so *wicked!*" she giggled.

Another guest was a middle-aged woman reporter from Nebraska who wore mannish skirts, a shirt and tie and smoked cheroots. The dainty brunette sitting on her lap with eyes dreamily closed seemed to be enjoying herself more than anyone.

"Ready when you are, Emil," said Sallow-face.

"Everybody ready?" Serra called.

There was a chorus of approval.

The lights snapped off and rays from the projector hit the screen. A man gasped, a girl giggled, and soft, romantic music floated on the air as the title appeared:

FOUR MEN AND A GIRL

"They're in color," said Sallow-face. "It's so much better than black and white."

A long line of troop trucks rumbled into Escoleras, coated with white dust. They came to a standstill in the plaza and khaki-uniformed soldiers stiffly climbed down, stretched themselves gratefully, unloaded their weapons and equipment and lined up at the drinking fountain.

Committeemen ran to headquarters and returned with a glowering Varela. Flanked by his men, he limped up to the tall dark officer who was giving orders and said fiercely: "*Saludos,* comrade."

Captain Garon turned slowly and studied Varela solemnly. "*Salud!*" he said, weary of this eternal fraternal greeting.

"You intend to stay long, Captain?"

Captain Garon looked at the committeemen's worn clothing and weapons and his brooding eyes hardened. "By what authority do you question me?"

"We're the local Committee."

Captain Garon's orders had been precise. He was to defend Escoleras against any naval attack, stamp out terrorism and inspire confidence in the villagers. "Escoleras is now a garrison town," he stated. "I wish to cooperate with the local authorities. I want to see the mayor, the judge and the doctor."

Varela's eyes narrowed. "The mayor is sick and the doctor is busy. The Committee handles all the village affairs."

"And the priest?"

Varela laughed and ran his hand over his recently shaved head. "You should know better, Captain."

"You killed the priest?"

"He was a traitor who smuggled invasion plans to the Fascists."

Captain Garon nodded somberly. "Why wasn't he arrested and sent for trial?"

Varela shrugged his shoulders and grinned. "We had to shoot him when he tried to escape."

"That's all, thank you," said Captain Garon in cold dismissal.

"How long will you stay, Captain?"

"Probably for the duration."

Varela scowled. "It is not necessary. The Committee will maintain order."

The captain's eyes were icy. "I have my orders."

"And where will you billet your men?"

"Here in the plaza. We have bell-tents. As many men as possible will be billeted with villagers."

Varela could feel his power slipping away. "Call on me for any help you need, Captain."

"If I need it."

The villagers welcomed the soldiers, relieved that they were only young conscripts.

Captain Garon visited Mayor Morales who was still a very sick man. Afterward he talked with Doctor Aldo and others. He was taken to the cemetery and then up into the mountains to see the shallow graves of the villagers who had been executed.

Captain Garon returned to his company, turned out a squad of thirty men, ordered them to fix bayonets and marched at their head to Varela's headquarters.

When Captain Garon arrived, Varela was awaiting him on the tiled terrace. "What's the trouble, Captain?" he asked softly.

Captain Garon's voice was toneless. "When the local authorities are inefficient, it is my duty to impose martial law."

Varela said softly: "The Committee *is* efficient."

"Who is the head of the Committee?"

"I am," said Varela. He jutted his jaw.

The captain demanded. "Show me an order endorsed by the FAI or any similar organization confirming your appointment."

"Such a document is not necessary."

"I demand proof of your authority."

"I do not choose to show it."

"Then you and your men must leave Escoleras at once."

Varela smiled dangerously. "And if we refuse?"

"I will hand you over to the civil authorities in Gerona."

Varela chuckled. "These are revolutionary times, Captain. A new order is emerging from the old. The Committee is part of it."

Captain Garon glanced at his watch. "I'll give you ten minutes. We'll escort you to the outskirts of the village."

Varela squinted one eye. "Cooperation between us could ease many of life's problems, Captain. We could grow rich."

"One minute has elapsed."

Varela glared. "Do you think I can be pushed around by a bunch of toy soldiers? Look at the windows behind me, Captain. A dozen rifles are trained on you. Go away while you're safe, Captain. Then return with a sensible compromise."

"Eight minutes left," said Captain Garon. He unbuttoned his holster flap. "You must make the decision, not me," he said emotionlessly. "I have no choice. I simply do my duty."

"Do you want to die, Captain?"

"Few men want to die."

"If you make an aggressive move, Captain, you will certainly die."

The captain shrugged his shoulders. "Shoot me and my men will open fire. Perhaps you can kill them too. Then the rest of my company will come running. I doubt if you can kill them all. But if you do, military headquarters in Barcelona will be alerted and those of your men who still survive will be hunted down. Whatever you decide, Varela, the outcome will be that you leave Escoleras."

Varela sighed. "Put up your guns," he ordered his men over his shoulder. "Get your equipment. We're moving out."

Committeemen stumbled down the steps of the residence, bowed under the weight of their arms and plunder. They spat at the soldiers' feet. Then with Varela leading them and Captain Garon's men following them with fixed bayonets, they walked to the outskirts of the village.

Varela sneered. "Thank you for the escort, comrade. Tomorrow we'll be back with our official authority!" His men laughed uproariously.

Captain Garon stared after him impassively. He waited until Varela's men were out of sight before he marched his men back to the plaza.

Varela and his men straggled on lightheartedly, passing around a goatskin heavy with black wine. They drank freely, laughed and jested coarsely. Some four miles from Escoleras they turned off onto a broken road leading to the distant mountains. Varela's foresight had insured against failure with Captain Garon. In a field not far from the road they had hidden three trucks loaded with the silverware, blankets, food, jewelry, and everything else they had confiscated.

Varela's men clambered onto the trucks and clung like limpets as they lurched along dusty roads. Varela had studied a map and decided upon Perallera, a village of only four hundred inhabitants. The trucks pulled up in the plaza in front of the church and as the startled villagers gathered around, Varela announced: "We are the Worker's Committee for the defense of Spain. Who is the mayor?"

Having established their new headquarters, Varela and his men drove the trucks into Figueras the next market day. Their plunder was sold for a good price with which Varela bought gold. Then he and his men drove back to Perallera to plunder anew.

Teresa fanned the charcoal to white-heat, the beefsteak on the grill sizzled and spat and the aroma of roasting meat filled the kitchen.

Paco Barras had hurried home from the fish market to snatch a quick meal and when there was a knock on the door, he called to his daughter: "I'll get it."

He was surprised to find himself staring into the dark eyes and somber face of Captain Garon. "Señor Barras?"

Paco Barras nodded coldly. The Committee's reign of terror was still sharp in the memory of the villagers.

"Your son is Isidro Barras, Señor?"

Paco's blue eyes narrowed. He smoothed his blond hair back behind his ears and nodded.

"Your son is my friend, Señor Barras. He gave me this letter of introduction." Paco Barras recognized his son's handwriting and widened the door. "Come in," he invited. "Please come in."

"Thank you." The captain stood politely, glancing around the simply furnished living room.

"Sit down," urged Paco Barras. He shouted into the kitchen. "Teresa. We have a visitor. Bring wine."

The captain sat down while Paco Barras read his son's letter. Teresa entered with a decanter of wine and the captain rose to his feet.

"My daughter," introduced Paco Barras. "This is Captain Garon who was Isidro's officer in Barcelona. Isidro asked him to call upon us."

"I am delighted, Señorita," said the captain. He clicked his heels, took Teresa's hand and touched the backs of her fingers with his lips.

Teresa flushed and her eyes sparkled. "Welcome to our home, Captain. Have you eaten?"

"Thank you. I eat with my men and . . ."

"I am cooking lunch now. We'll be delighted to have you with us."

"No argument," interjected Paco Barras firmly. "Sit down, Captain. I insist. You are my son's friend and his home is your home."

Captain Garon smiled at Teresa. "If you are quite sure . . . Señorita?"

"It will be a pleasure, Captain."

While Teresa cooked she studied him secretly. He was much older than she was, thirty or thirty-five; almost old enough to be her father. But his dark handsome face and brooding eyes were strangely fascinating. And he looked very smart in his uniform.

Captain Garon told Paco Barras about the early days of the revolt in Barcelona, how he had talked to Isidro and other men in his regiment and how they had decided to remain loyal. As he talked, he watched Teresa. Isidro had not mentioned he had a sister. He saw she was very young, perhaps fifteen, her figure thin and angular and not yet softened by the curves of maturity. But her manner was grown-up and her blue eyes friendly and understanding. He had never seen anyone so fair. Her two braids gleamed like silver. He noted with surprise that her long slim legs were those of a young woman and not an adolescent. With a start he realized Paco Barras had asked a question. "I beg your pardon?" he said apologetically.

"How long will you stay in Escoleras?"

"For the duration, I expect."

"And have you recent news of Isidro?"

"He's being trained as a dispatch rider. He'll have a motorbike and he'll be taught to be a mechanic."

Teresa brought the food to the table and served it.

"Delicious," said Captain Garon. His knife cut easily into the tender meat, and rich, red gravy flowed abundantly.

Teresa and her father drank from the *porrón* but Captain Garon preferred a wineglass. They talked about the war, the captain mentioned what he planned for Escoleras and while Teresa brewed coffee and the men lit cigars, he brought up the purpose of his visit. "I hope the villagers won't mind my soldiers being billeted on them. They are good boys. But if they behave badly, they must be reported. I'll have them disciplined."

Paco Barras smoothed his blond hair back behind his ears and shrugged his shoulders. "It is war and we must bear with many things," he said philosophically.

"The government will pay billeting costs."

The corners of Paco Barras's eyes crinkled. "When? And with what?"

"Every day things are better organized."

"You wish to billet a soldier with me?" asked Paco Barras shrewdly.

There was a pause and the captain looked down at his hands. "When billeting was arranged, I gave instructions you were not to be approached because you are Isidro's father."

"Ah!" said Paco Barras. He wondered if he was supposed to be grateful. Teresa brought in the coffee, scalding hot and very black. The captain inhaled its aroma with evident pleasure.

"Sugar?" she asked.

"Two please."

"Bring the liqueur brandy," said her father. Teresa poured the amber liquid into two small glasses and the captain held his glass by the stem, twirled it beneath his nostrils and nodded approvingly.

"I knew you'd like it," said Paco Barras contentedly.

The captain sipped, nodded his pleasure and carefully replaced the glass on the table. Then he said with studied casualness: "I have not yet selected a billet for myself."

Paco Barras smiled and nodded, hearing the words but not understanding their intent until he saw the hint of disappointment in the somber, dark eyes. He leaned forward quickly. "Captain, I insist you stay with us. You shall have Miguel's room."

Teresa gasped.

"Are you sure . . . ?" doubted the captain.

"We won't permit you to stay anywhere else. You are Isidro's friend and you must stay in his home."

"But . . . Father . . . !" interjected Teresa. He looked at her and she frowned.

"I will disturb you very little, Señor," promised the captain. "From early morning I will be with my men and I will eat at our camp. But I do need a good night's sleep."

"You shall dine here too," insisted Paco Barras. "Home cooking is important for a man."

"You are very kind, Señor Barras."

"Miguel's room will be ideal," said Paco Barras enthusiastically. "You will be very comfortable."

"Then if you do not object . . . ?"

"To have you as our guest will be an honor and a pleasure, Captain," said Paco Barras and scowled at Teresa's frantic facial messages.

"It will be a privilege to be your guest," said Captain Garon.

Teresa gathered up dirty crockery and stormed into the kitchen. She washed up, clattering the dishes angrily. The men talked, smoked and drank liqueur brandy and Teresa had to wait until Captain Garon had again kissed her hand and departed before she could voice her protests.

"What can you be thinking of, Papa! He can't stay *here!*"

"And why not, my girl? He's a friend of Isidro's and an officer, too."

"But you're not here all the time, Papa."

"He won't be here much either."

"But at night, Papa! He'll be sleeping in the house with you away at the fish market. The two of us . . . alone in the house!"

Paco Barras scowled. "What nonsense is this? You're a mere child."

"It's not nonsense, Papa. I'm sixteen!"

"And I can't trust my own daughter?" He flushed with embarrassment.

"Of course you can, Papa."

"Is not Captain Garon clearly a gentleman?"

"It's the neighbors, Papa. People talk. You *know* how they gossip."

Paco Barras smashed his fist down on the table. "Are our lives to be ruled by a gaggle of clucking, slander-tongued old hags?"

"Mother wouldn't like it."

Paco Barras spread his hands in defeat. "All right, Teresa. I'll make my excuses to Captain Garon."

She saw he disliked to go back on his word. "Will most of the other houses have soldiers?"

He nodded.

"We'll try it for a while, Father, if you wish," she agreed reluctantly, to his immense relief. "But you'll have to spend more time at home."

Captain Garon was an ideal guest. He arrived for dinner each evening, displayed perfect manners and soon retired to his room. He was courteous and thoughtful and often brought cigars for Paco Barras or sweets for Teresa. Every morning he was up early and away. He worked very hard. Under his supervision technicians prepared a large-scale map of the area and started driving a road across a headland to link up coastal batteries. He built concrete pillboxes at the entrance to the harbor and began work on concrete gun-emplacements on the mountains overlooking the village. He commandeered a large fishing boat with a ninety horsepower engine, installed machine guns in the bow and stern, and appointed Jesus Guitart, who had some naval experience, as captain. The boat patrolled the coast, vigilant for any attempted invasion by the Nationalists.

Escoleras hummed with activity and the villagers, freed from fear of committeemen, were grateful and willingly helped the military when called upon.

Captain Garon was so much an officer and a gentleman that the malicious tongues did not wag and Paco Barras soon began to spend most of his time at the fish market again.

One day a bombing plane smashed the water pipes and escaping water turned the narrow alleyways between the houses into ankle-deep mud. The mains were turned off and the villagers had to draw water at the public wash-house.

Teresa lined up at the fountain with the other housewives and was embarrassed to find herself behind Josefina Aubel, the village whore, who lived in a large, comfortable cottage on the outskirts of town. The village prudes had often demanded she should be expelled from the village. But Don Carlos had been tolerant and had obliquely defended Josefina with comments about people who threw stones. All the young men of the village knew Josefina and any married man seen late at night at Josefina's end of the village was tongue-lashed by his wife when the scandal reached her.

Josefina was a lusty, dark-eyed brunette of thirty. She laughed easily and had no shame. Since the troops had been billeted in Escoleras, two girls from Figueras had come to help Josefina. Teresa and the other women eyed the newcomers curiously as they chatted with Josefina.

"Hurry along, girls," called Josefina impatiently. "Keep that water running."

"Are you *so* busy, Josefina?" chuckled Constancia Guitart.

"She is," jested another woman. "Do you know why? She's got your Jesus waiting in her sitting room."

Washerwomen with arms lathered to the elbows slapped wet clothes on washtub sills and chuckled.

"I've no time for my old friends now," smiled Josefina. "Too many soldiers!"

"Is it true you report to barracks before lights-out, Josefina?"

The lighthearted bantering went on while Josefina's pitcher was filled. Then, while she waited for her two companions, she looked at Teresa with a friendly smile.

Teresa flushed and wanted to look away, but politeness made her return the smile.

"You're growing up, Teresa," said Josefina, looking her up and down. "How old are you now? Fifteen?"

"Sixteen," said Teresa. She flushed even more because everybody was listening.

"You have beautiful legs," said Josefina.

Teresa wanted the ground to swallow her up.

"I'd give everything to be *your* age with my knowledge," said Josefina wistfully. She stooped to her pitcher and her scoop-necked blouse showed her breasts hanging heavy and ripe. She swung her pitcher up onto her shoulder and balanced it easily, bare feet astride, one hand on her hip and her skirt pressing against her thighs. Her dark eyes inspected Teresa critically. "You should do something about your breasts."

"Teresa's still young," said the woman behind Teresa.

"Not every girl's overloaded like you, Josefina," said another.

Josefina thrust out her breasts proudly. "I used to be flat like Teresa."

The washerwomen squealed with laughter.

"It's true," insisted Josefina seriously. "I was as flat as a board. Now I'm as round as oranges."

"As melons!" shouted Constancia Guitart and Josefina laughed louder than anyone.

"You must do something," Josefina told Teresa.

Teresa looked away. Her cheeks were burning.

"Don't be shy, Teresa," coaxed Josefina. "We're women together talking women's talk. You need massage."

The washerwomen listened intently.

"Why do you think I'm so well developed?" asked Josefina.

"Massage?" repeated Teresa and was confused by the washerwomen's laughter.

"Massage is very important," said Josefina. "But it has to be done properly." The corners of Josefina's mouth twitched.

"How . . . what do you do?" ventured Teresa.

"*You* can't do it," said Josefina and there was a tense and expectant silence.

"Then . . . ?"

"It has to be done for you," said Josefina and Teresa's cheeks flamed as the women laughed explosively.

"You find someone to do it for you," advised Josefina.

Above the laughter an older woman called out: "Enough, Josefina! You're embarrassing the girl."

"It's good advice. If she doesn't want to be as flat as a board she'd better get them played with quickly!"

Josefina's two girls swung their pitchers up onto their shoulders and walked away, their skirts twitching provocatively. Josefina followed them, her hips broad and firm. When they were out of earshot the women who had laughed with Josefina tore her to pieces.

"Did you see that blouse? Indecent!"

"Not a stitch on underneath. She might as well go naked."

"She doesn't know what it means to feel shame."

"Don't take any notice of her," a woman advised Teresa. "She talks dirty."

"It's true what she said," defended another woman. "I used to be small, but as soon as my man started, I was astonished how quickly they developed."

"It's an old woman's tale."

"Look at me," invited another. "I've got three children and a husband with four hands and I'm *still* small."

"But you're *not* flat-chested. You've got . . . *something!*"

Teresa's pitcher was full. She swung it up onto her shoulder and shyly muttered, *"Adiós."* She hurried away, happy to escape from older women whose knowledge and shameful talk disturbed her deeply.

When the north wind blew down from the ice-covered Pyrenees, it was too cold to shower, and one evening Teresa boiled water over the kitchen range and sluiced herself down, standing in an enamel bowl. She cupped water in her hands and ran it over herself, rinsing away the lather, and on impulse gathered up her breasts. She ached with chagrin. She was like a boy, except that her nipples were large.

She pinched up her boyish rolls of flesh and moved them gently. Would massage really help, she wondered? She was still wondering when Captain Garon opened the cottage door and stepped inside. He had closed the door behind him before he saw her.

Teresa was so confident she had locked the door that she stood rigid with shock for long seconds before she moved. Her clothing was on the other side of the room. With a gasp she sped to the stairs and skimmed up them, tore open her bedroom door and locked it behind her.

Captain Garon was as surprised as she was. But he smiled as he pictured her again, standing slightly crouched and then fleeing like a frightened deer, her white buttocks lean. He went into the kitchen, picked up the bowl and poured the water down the sink.

It had been a slack day and he had come back earlier than usual. He went to the sideboard, poured a Cinzano, diluted it with soda water and read the newspaper.

Time passed. Teresa didn't come down. Her clothes were draped over a chair. He took them upstairs and knocked on her bedroom door. "I've brought your clothes, Teresa. I'll leave them outside."

He went downstairs and waited a long time before he went up to her room again. He knocked on her door, but there was only silence. "Teresa," he said softly. "Listen to me carefully. It is not a shameful thing that has happened, Teresa. For a fleeting moment I saw you as a woman. But for a man to see a woman is not shameful. Only old gossips make these things shameful. I saw you, Teresa, and you are beautiful. There is no shame in beauty. A man looks upon a woman to find beauty, not to find shame."

He imagined her listening with beating heart.

"Are you listening, Teresa? Tell me that you understand."

Teresa whispered: "I can hear you, but I cannot face you."

"Your shame is false. I did not see you with disgust. I felt reverence for your beauty."

"You have many words, Captain," she choked.

"Listen, Teresa. It is time for dinner. We will both forget this. Presently you will come down and cook and we will dine as though it never happened."

"I'll try," she whispered.

He waited downstairs and when he heard her steps upon the staircase he did not look up from his newspaper. She hurried into the kitchen and as she fanned the glowing charcoal and set the table, his naturalness reassured her until she could even sit opposite him to eat.

He cut bread and passed it to her. She poured wine into his glass. He made a casual comment and she replied and was astonished she could. Then as he drank his brandy, he said: "All forgotten, Teresa?"

"I felt such a fool," she confessed.

"It must be momentous for a girl the first time a man sees her unclothed."

Teresa averted her face from him as she gathered up the dirty crockery. "Please don't talk about it," she pleaded. "I thought I'd locked the door."

"You are beautiful to look upon, Teresa."

"You say that to please me."

"But you *are* beautiful," he protested.

"You know I'm not!"

"I do not deny you are flat-chested," he said, and she flushed violently. "But you are young and have the sweetness of innocence."

She kept her face turned from him.

"Your beauty is of a rosebud in the spring, about to bloom."

"Please stop," she pleaded.

"Does it anger you that I talk of your beauty?"

"It . . . it is not seemly."

"Not seemly? Is it wrong to say you are sweet and young? That you are innocence budding into full bloom?"

"A man may speak thus to his betrothed."

He chuckled. "Must I marry to tell a girl she is beautiful?"

"You should not speak in such a way."

He was astonished. "Why not?"

She said flatly: "It is not seemly. That is all."

He nodded sadly. "You are so young, Teresa. Yet already you think like the old scandal-makers of the village."

"It is the way of life in a village."

"It is the way of life for old crones who were robbed of their own joy of living and who in their bitterness want to deprive others as they were deprived."

"I have all I need, Captain," she said.

"Because you do not know what you lack. Spain is fifty years behind Europe. Courting couples are chaperoned, a girl may kiss only when betrothed and sex is indecent."

Her voice was sharp. "I don't wish to speak of these things."

"You are intelligent, Teresa," he said and she thrilled. "You think for yourself and must see that the old-fashioned ideas will go."

"We have to live according to laws," she said.

"But the laws must be sensible. Is it wrong for a man to touch a woman's hand?"

"No."

"To touch her arm or rest his fingers upon her shoulder?"

"It depends . . . how he does it."

"But is it evil?"

"I suppose not."

"Is it evil to place his fingers upon her lips? Or place his lips to her hand when he greets her?"

She could see where the argument was leading and fought it. "It depends upon the thought behind the action."

"But the simple act: lips against fingers. Is that bad?"

Reluctantly she shook her head.

"Then when a man places his lips upon a woman's lips, is that evil?"

"Not if they are betrothed or if she is his wife."

"And if she is neither?"

"Then . . . it is improper."

"But *why,* Teresa? Tell me why it is bad . . . or evil?"

She searched for an answer. "It is not the act of kissing that is important. It is the thought behind the kissing."

"And what is that thought?"

"Love," she said simply.

"And is love bad?"

"I mean . . . lust!"

"And is lust evil?" he asked gently.

She was startled by his question. "Lust . . . lust is uncontrolled passion."

He smiled blandly. "Is it evil for a man to be overwhelmed by his passion for a woman?"

"It's not evil . . . if they are married!"

"Do you believe trees will not grow without a golden ring around them? Do you believe lambs frisk in the fields only when a priest marries the ewe and the ram? Do you say a man cannot feel overwhelming desire for a woman until they have been mated in church?"

She was confused. "I do not think about these things. But lust is an evil thing that destroys."

"Lust *is* wonderful. I am a man and I lust after women, beauty, sweetness and innocence." He paused and then added deliberately: "I lust after you and your sweet, immature beauty, Teresa."

She turned pale and shivered as though he had called her a whore. "You're disgusting," she choked. "While you are in this house, never speak to me again so indecently." She flung down her drying cloth, and ran upstairs to her bedroom.

Later, lying on her bed, she listened to his footsteps ascending and her heart hammered when it seemed he would knock on her door. But he passed on to his own room and a little later she heard the metallic sag of bedsprings.

She lay awake long into the night, reliving their conversation.

When he came home the following evening, he was stiffly polite and addressed her as Señorita Teresa. When she served the food he stood formally waiting for her to be seated.

They ate in silence. Presently she said softly: "Thank you, Captain."

"For what, Señorita Teresa?"

"For taking such pains not to offend me."

"It is your house, Señorita Teresa. I am your guest."

"I do not mean to be unfriendly, Captain."

"I must respect your wishes, Señorita Teresa."

"I want you to feel welcome. All I ask is that you do not speak . . . indecently."

There were devilish glints in his brooding eyes. "I have a fault. I speak my feelings aloud. I often surprise myself by what I say."

"You surprised yourself yesterday, Captain?"

He shook his head slowly. "No. I have known a long time that I lust after you."

She flushed angrily. "You're doing it again!" But the devilment in his eyes betrayed him and she smiled. "You said that to tease me."

"Is to be lusted after so unpleasant?" he asked.

"Please, Captain. Let us be good friends. Do not talk this way."

"Why not, Teresa? We're intelligent people."

"Only a man and his wife or his betrothed talk of such things."

He looked at her steadily. "Teresa. Will you marry me?"

She gasped.

"Don't answer now," he said. "Think it over."

Her heart beat so fast she felt faint. She arose and ran upstairs and as her bedroom door slammed, he smiled wryly and reached for the brandy bottle.

A little later she came downstairs and seated herself at the table. She was quiet and composed and without looking at him, asked: "You were not joking?"

"No," he said solemnly.

"Such a joke would be cruel and you are not cruel, Captain."

"I mean it, Teresa. I want you to marry me."

"It is very special for a girl when a man proposes."

He nodded. "I know."

"I still can't believe you mean it after knowing me so little."

"But I know you well, Teresa. Much better than you know yourself!"

"But you don't know about Anselmo. He's my age. We're ideally matched in every way."

"I'm sorry. I didn't know you were betrothed." His voice was husky.

"He hasn't spoken. But he will."

"Then . . . your answer is no?"

"But you have paid me a great compliment, Captain."

He smiled wryly. "So now I must lust after you in vain?"

The phrase no longer sounded indecent. Teresa chuckled.

The next night at dinner Captain Garon held her chair and when she was seated, slipped his arms around her.

She gasped and tugged at his wrists. "Let me go!"

"As you wish," he said and instantly released her. He circled around the table, sat opposite her and eyed her angry face with amusement.

"*Never* do that again," she flared. "*Never!*"

He arched one mocking eyebrow. "Did I harm you?"

"You . . . insulted me."

"It is natural for a man to fondle a beautiful object."

"I don't *want* to be touched."

"You are selfish, Teresa. I may mean nothing to you; but it is selfish to deny me the pleasure of taking you in my arms for a few fleeting moments."

"Such embraces are for man and wife."

He sighed. "I resign myself to misery." But after dinner when he got up to get a cigar, he again caught her by surprise when he passed behind her chair. His arms encircled her and his hands rested firmly on her breasts. She wanted to push him away, but controlled herself and sat stiffly erect with her hands linked limply in her lap.

He chuckled in her ear. "Where is the evil in this? I do not even touch the *real* you, only your dress."

"Tell me when you're finished," she said, and she thought of Josefina stooping for her pitcher.

"It is not a pleasure for you?"

"No."

He took his hands away but she relaxed too soon. His hand came back again, sliding down inside her frock. His palm was warm and the tips of his fingers rested lightly on her ribs. It was so unexpected her detaining hand could only touch his through her dress.

"This is what I have long desired; to hold you like this."

"Please leave me alone."

His hand moved, finger and thumb teasing her nipple until it swelled and hardened, the pleasure of it racing through to her very core. In alarm she grasped his wrist. "No," she panted. *"Por favor!* No!"

"Do I hurt you?"

"Please . . . stop."

"Are you unmoved by my touch?"

She confessed. "I have strange feelings."

"Pleasurable sensations?"

"They frighten me."

At once he released her, strolled back to his side of the table, lit a cigar and blew smoke at the ceiling. She sat quietly, marveling at the sensations he had aroused.

After a time he said quietly: "You no longer deny it is a pleasure to be touched?"

"It . . . it is improper."

"You amaze me, Teresa. You are intelligent but obstinately cling to primitive ideas. I caress you and you receive pleasure. Where is the evil in this?"

"It . . . it might lead to bad things."

"But if it goes no further, if I merely caress you and give you pleasure, is that evil?"

"It must not happen again."

He smiled. "Why not?"

"Because I'm not sure of myself."

"Do not be frightened, *chiquita*."

"Please, Captain. I beg of you. Do not do it again."

He looked at her steadily and then nodded solemnly. "It shall be as you wish."

She lay awake a long time that night, thinking of Josefina's ripeness, her own flat breasts and the strangely exciting emotions. She rolled her nipple between forefinger and thumb, but could not evoke the same sensations. She wondered if it would happen only when a man touched her. She thought about it so much that the following evening she was almost ready for Captain Garon to embrace her again.

He was charming to her and a delightful conversationalist, but was careful not even to brush against her in passing.

For two more nights the captain displayed exemplary manners and she realized he intended to respect her wishes. Paradoxically, she wanted his touch. After dinner she made coffee and placed it before the captain. "Two sugars?" she asked.

He smiled lazily. "Yes, please." His hand rested on the table and impulsively she took it and turned it palm upward. Then looking at him steadily, she raised his hand to her lips and kissed first his thumb and then his forefinger. He at once pulled her down upon his lap. "You are truly beautiful, *chiquita*."

"I'm . . . I am all confused," she confessed.

"Do you want . . . shall I caress you?"

"I think . . . I think I am afraid of it."

"You have nothing to fear, *chiquita*." His eyes were sincere. "I will care for you, because I love you. Nothing will happen that . . . *you do not wish!*"

"I am still afraid," she confessed.

He unbuttoned her dress and eased it off her shoulder. She wore no slip and she stiffened when he looked at her. "You are truly beautiful," he said reverently. "So young, so innocent and so fresh." She trembled when he touched her.

"You're not still afraid, *chiquita?*"

"Only a little. Tell me, Captain. Is it true that this makes a girl . . . mature?"

"It is often said; but I do not know if it is true."

"Is it because I am small that you call me 'little one'?"

"I call you *chiquita* because you are my little girl."

"Captain. I will not grow lopsided?"

She abandoned herself to the pleasure his touch aroused. But an ache grew within her that with the rhythm of his fingers became more and more urgent. His hand ran swiftly down her dress, sliding over the curve of her belly until his palm rested on her triangular mound, his fingers curling over it and pressing tightly. Her hands sought desperately to prevent him, but exquisite pressure exploded within her and her senses swam until she cried out. He held her tenderly while the pounding of her heart eased and her breathing calmed.

"How was it, *chiquita?*"

"I almost fainted."

"It was something special, *chiquita?*"

Her eyes were wide with wonder. "I . . . it was like floating on a cloud. Never have I known such a feeling."

"This is the pleasure a man gives to woman."

"But you touched me where only a husband may touch his wife."

"I touch your hands and I touch your breasts, *chiquita*. It is natural . . . it is not evil. When I touch you elsewhere . . . where is the evil in that?"

"Now you have touched me, will it spoil me for my husband?"

He chuckled at her fears. "How can it spoil you?"

"Is there not a sign, a bleeding that tells a husband his bride is pure?"

"Only a foolish man looks for this sign, *chiquita*. And only very few ever find it. A girl who is energetic, climbs mountains, rides a horse or rows a boat often breaks this sensitive membrane without knowing."

She nodded. "I have heard of this. I row and work hard and am very energetic."

"Then assuredly you will be unable to give your husband a sign."

"Nevertheless, Captain, it is not seemly a girl should abandon herself so completely to anyone."

"You can trust me." He stared into her eyes compellingly. "With me you can let yourself go completely, because I will never do anything you do not wish."

She looked up into his dark eyes and nodded slowly. "It is true, Captain. I *can* trust you."

He smiled. "Then make me coffee, *chiquita.*"

The following day, while she cleaned and cooked, Teresa resolved she must end the intimacy. But the memory of his touch and the sweet weakness that had swept through her dissolved her willpower.

She anticipated dinner with a nervousness that made her tremble and after they had eaten, she sighed involuntarily when he held her close to him. "You are beautiful, *chiquita*. I cannot resist you."

She ran her fingers through his sleek black hair. "All day I have been thinking of you, *mi Capitan*."

He rose to his feet and took her hand.

"What is it, *mi Capitan?*"

"Let us go to your room where you can relax."

She held back. "I trust you, *mi Capitan*. But . . . I want to go pure to my husband. I want . . ."

"I understand, *chiquita*."

She looked into his eyes and was reassured and it was she who led the way upstairs. She sat upon the bed, but he pulled her gently to her feet and his fingers went to the buttons of her dress. He thrust it down over her shoulders and admired her. "You're beautiful," he said in a hushed voice. Then his hands went to her other clothing and her instinctive protest was overcome by her trust in him and her delight at his admiration.

"Lie back, *chiquita*." He sat on the edge of the bed beside her. "Close your eyes."

He kissed her cheeks, her lips and her breasts. Then he caressed her from shoulder to knee, arousing her rhythmically while aeons of time passed. His fingers rejoiced in the response of young flesh, and he caressed onward until shuddering gasps greeted the avalanching climax. Then slow contractions and a low sobbing that was also a deep sigh.

"You are very patient with me, Captain. Very . . . tender and gentle."

"It is my pleasure, *chiquita*, to give you pleasure."

"Is it possible for you to have such pleasure, *mi Capitan?*"

There was a pause. "It is."

"Do you wish such pleasure, *mi Capitan?*"

"It is not important what I want. Do *you* wish to give me pleasure?"

"I am selfish, *mi Capitan*. I receive everything and you . . . nothing."

"I do not complain."

"Can I caress *you, mi Capitan?*"

"If *you* want me to have pleasure," he insisted. "Not because I wish it."

After a pause she said softly: "*Mi Capitan*. You . . . you will have to show me what I must do." He smiled down at her for some moments before he stood up and unbuckled his belt.

5

They lay side by side in the quietness of the night. She ran her fingers up across his moist skin to the black curling hairs on his chest and tugged them teasingly. "You have taught me so much in a few days, *mi Capitan*." She sighed happily.

"You are an eager student, *chiquita*."

"It's nice, the aftermath; being at your side and feeling you against me."

"You are not shamed by your nakedness?"

She chuckled.

"Nor that I touch you?"

"I know now that I was very simple then, *mi Capitan*."

"Not simple, *chiquita*. You are very tender and sweet."

They lay quietly enjoying their peace. "Tell me, *mi Capitan*. The things of which you spoke that save unmarried girls from shame? Can they be bought easily?"

He chuckled. "Every barber's shop sells them."

"You can buy them if you wish?"

"I already have them."

"You have?" She sat up and looked at him sharply.

"Many men carry them," he explained.

"Do you mean that whenever you meet a girl . . ."

He laughed away her suspicions. "You are enough for any man, *chiquita*."

She relaxed, mollified. After a pause she asked: "And with these things a girl can . . . ?"

"When they are used a girl does not find herself with child," he said flatly.

"I knew nothing of these things."

"There are many different types. They have been used for centuries."

She rubbed the sole of her foot up and down his shin, flattening the strong hairs and feeling them spring up again.

"*Mi Capitan,* are you rested?"

"You sensuous little devil!"

"Do you have one of those . . . things . . . ?"

"Listen, *chiquita.* I will love you . . . like *this.*"

"*This* . . . is what I want."

"You are forgetting Anselmo, *chiquita.*"

"I have not forgotten him."

"Do you not wish to go intact to your bridal bed?"

"I have thought about it, deeply, *mi Capitan.* To be touched one way . . . or another . . . it makes little difference."

"Understand this, *chiquita.* To a man, this is a fleeting delight. To a virgin it means much more; and also to her husband."

"I have thought long about it, *mi Capitan.*"

"You have trusted me, *chiquita.* I understand that when blood is hot and desire strong . . ."

"I am quite decided. There is no shame with you, *mi Capitan.*"

"It is better not."

She reproved him mockingly. "*Mi Capitan.* Do you scorn me!"

"That I will never do." He kissed her lips, her cheeks and then her breasts.

He was quiet beside her, his skin burning her arm and her thigh. "You are sad?" he said.

"Yes, *mi Capitan.*"

"A woman is always sad the first time."

Woman, she thought, *I am no longer a girl. I am a woman.* "You know more about a woman than is good for a man to know."

"What I know, women have taught me."

"Then you also, were an enthusiastic student," she said with a choke in her voice. He raised his hand and wiped away the tears he could not see.

"And you know about these, too," she choked.

"It is the privilege of a woman to cry the first time."

"I have been remembering, *mi Capitan.* It is but a short time since I ran to my room, ashamed you had seen my nakedness. Then you comforted me and showed me there is no evil in physical pleasure."

"Is it not so, *chiquita?*"

"I now see it is so. But I am still your conquest. I have been seduced. I congratulate you on your victory."

"*Chiquita.* You trusted me and I kept faith."

She gave a harsh laugh. "*Afterward,* I can see everything so clearly. You are a perfect gentleman. When I pleaded Stop, you at once desisted. You whetted my appetite and then drew back. Always you emphasized it was never what *you* wanted. It was only what *I* wanted. Tenderness and patience were all you needed and you have them in abundance."

"You are bitter, *chiquita.*"

"I do not blame you. But I am no longer pure and Anselmo will be hurt."

"Then do not hurt him, *chiquita.*"

"I cannot go to my husband with a lie upon my lips."

"To remain silent is not a lie."

"Not to tell Anselmo is a silent lie."

"Will he be understanding? Many men will not wed a girl who is not pure."

"Anselmo will understand, although he will be hurt."

"Then tell Anselmo; and if he is stupid and does not want you, I will marry you."

She teasingly tugged the curling black hairs on his moist chest. "Tell me, *mi Capitan,* are other women as I am?"

"You are as spontaneous and as lively as a kitten; as a man wants a woman to be. Like any other healthy young animal, your natural impulses bubble over."

"I fear you understand me *too* well, *mi Capitan.*"

"I believe I understood you the moment I first saw you."

"Did you think this . . . would happen between us?"

"I think I knew it."

Her eyes widened. "How?"

"I could smell it on you as I can smell you now."

She raised her arms above her head and stretched deliciously. "You don't care what you say, do you, *mi Capitan?*"

"Do I need to guard my tongue when we understand each other so well?"

"Would you marry a girl who is not pure?"

"*Chiquita.* Will you marry me?"

"I am thinking of Anselmo."

"From what you tell me, he is not stupid. Even if you *tell* him, I fear he will still marry you."

They lay quietly for a while. "Tell me, *mi Capitan*. I have grown bigger, have I not?"

"You are still sweet tenderness, *chiquita*."

"Do you want to kiss them?"

Life in Escoleras under Captain Garon settled down into orderly routine. Fuel for the fishing boats was severely rationed, catches were small and prices soared. But Paco Barras's talent as a buyer gave him an income that compensated handsomely for staying away so long from home.

Building went ahead at full speed, concrete pillboxes sprang up on the beach, coastal guns were installed on the heights and a double carriage road was cut across the spine of the jutting headland. The sporadic bombing raids did little damage.

Most of the young men of the village had been called up: Benito Vigon, Juan Morales and Julio Prada were at the front and Narcissus Coruna had quietly slipped away when his call-up papers arrived. It was rumored he had crossed the frontier into France clandestinely.

The war did not change Hernando's way of life. He fished, collected snails and frogs, shot rabbits and partridges and gathered mushrooms and pine-nuts. He ignored the bombs, the soldiers and the war.

One day Señora Ledesma was summoned to Figueras and two days later a tragic cortege wound its way to the village cemetery. Most of the prisoners crowded together in Figueras jail had been struck down by a mysterious illness. They coughed until they spat blood. Señora Ledesma was not told her husband was seriously ill until the prison governor called her to Figueras. Baudillo was formally released and rushed to the hospital, a specialist from Gerona was brought in, but it was too late. Baudillo Ledesma was comatose. His death shocked the village.

Mayor Morales was still a nervous wreck and shoemaker Corbeta, aided by the Long Man, acted as the village's mayor while the villagers tended their olive groves and vineyards and dug their allotments. But there was food rationing and hunger in the big cities.

Teresa had never felt so happy. She sang as she worked around the house. She loved Anselmo and intended to marry him. But meantime, she was very happy with Captain Garon. The awakening of her

sexual desires had immensely widened her horizon. Reality was a riot
of pleasing colors; even simple foods had became subtly flavored. She
felt pleasure at the velvet touch of a peach and the scratching of her
fingernails across silk was music. She was so happy she feared people
would divine it was caused by physical love.

But no one suspected them. Captain Garon was always formally
polite in public.

"Good afternoon, Señorita Barras."

"Good afternoon, Captain Garon."

And they would pass each other without a second glance.

They had miraculous escapes. Once a neighbor burst in upon them
as they embraced. But the neighbor was looking back over his shoulder and they broke away before he saw anything. Another time Paco
Barras was hungry and came home after midnight. The cottage was in
darkness and he climbed the stairs, pounded on Teresa's door and
asked her to cook. She stumbled from her bedroom, flushed and
sleepy-eyed and with her nightgown rumpled. As he followed her
downstairs, he saw Captain Garon's open door and his unoccupied
bed. "The captain is not home yet?" he asked.

"Sometimes he is very late," said Teresa over her shoulder. "I do
not worry because he has a key."

"I hope he doesn't wake you up," grumbled Paco Barras.

"He is careful not to do that," said Teresa and in the darkness of
her bedroom, Captain Garon relaxed, knowing the danger of discovery had passed.

Captain Garon behaved so correctly that even the black-garbed
crones who watched the smartly uniformed officer arrive at and de-
part his billet, never dreamed the handsome man and the angular
young girl were lovers.

But when they were alone, they lost all restraint. She would seize
his hand and press it against her, often the aggressor, knowing he
responded instantly. And locked in her bedroom they abandoned
themselves recklessly. She teased him with her lips, her tongue and
her body, writhing in his arms, twining her long legs around him,
smothering him with her silvery hair and binding him to her with it,
nibbling and biting and heightening his desire, struggling provocatively and moaning softly until all energy was spent.

Her breasts grew. She worried, remembering the swelling ripeness
of Josefina and fearing people would guess her secret.

"You are naturally small-breasted," the captain reassured her.

She stared down at herself critically.

"Scarcely a handful," he said. "But so tender and sweet."

"Perhaps nature knows best," she said thoughtfully. "If I had more of them, their pleasure might be too much to bear."

"You like your pleasure to be unbearable, *chiquita?*"

"Aaaah, *mi Capitan!* You can never resist a challenge."

"You are more woman than twenty other women together."

"And you are much more man than I can handle!" She teasingly entwined her long, silvery plaits around him. "Now you are my prisoner, *mi Capitan.*"

"Prison is great joy!"

"Pay me ransom, and I will release you."

"How can I pay when I am captive, *chiquita?*"

"You are mine. I will never loose you."

"Marry me, *chiquita.*"

She looked away from him. "It wouldn't work, *mi Capitan.* I love Anselmo."

"Do you think of him when you and I are together . . . like this?"

"I don't. But one day he will come for me and when that day arrives I will not be able to help myself. I will go to him. I have made no secret of this, *mi Capitan.* All *this* that is between us is . . . magic! But what has grown between me and Anselmo since we were children cannot be destroyed."

His dark face was somber and his eyes sad. "Then I must enjoy you while I may."

"Ah yes! Enjoy me, *mi Capitan.* Enjoy me!"

Autumn's warmth blended into the cold of winter. On the distant Pyrenees the snow fell heavily. Deep drifts formed in the valleys and were sealed in by a skin of ice. The wind that tore over them and down to the sea was frosty. The Tramontana lashed the sea into white foam, and spray became fretted patterns of ice as it splashed upon the harbor wall. The gale stripped branches from the trees and ripped away the bark.

Paco Barras sat around the cottage, grumbling about everything and particularly about the storm which had stopped the fishing fleet putting out to sea. Every night they were three for dinner and Teresa went up to bed unhappily, her legs trembling with her desire.

The Tramontana died, the fishing boats sailed out and Paco Barras

carried away his mattress and blankets to sleep again upon the quayside. The first night they were alone, Captain Garon stayed until
morning. But when he saw her later that day, he knew instantly
something had come between them.

"What is it, *chiquita?*"

"Anselmo has written."

His face fell. "Anselmo is well?"

"In a few days he arrives in Escoleras!"

Captain Garon swallowed. "You'll be pleased to see him."

Her eyes shone. "I have longed for this!"

"I am happy for you, *chiquita.*"

"I ask a favor of you. Anselmo does not know his father died. The
news will hurt him deeply. Therefore, I will not tell him yet about
us."

"*Chiquita.* There is no need to tell him . . . ever. Many happily
married women were wise and did not tell."

"*Mi Capitan.* Will you make excuses to my father and stay no
longer in this house. I do not wish Anselmo to see you here. Also, now
that Anselmo is coming, I have lost desire. I do not want to hurt you.
But I cannot pretend what does not exist."

He said bitterly: "You wish me to leave now?"

"It . . . it will be better."

"You do not wish then . . . ?"

"If it is *your* wish, then later today you must take your pleasure."

He shook his head angrily.

"I am sorry, *mi Capitan.*"

After dinner he packed while she washed up. When he came downstairs, she dried her hands and faced him.

"Will I return when Anselmo's leave is over, *chiquita?*"

"It is something I do not know."

"You will tell me later, *chiquita?*"

"I have hurt you deeply, *mi Capitan?*"

"You have, little one. But women always hurt the men who love
them. If they had not the power to do so, they would not be loved."

"Do you . . . hate me?"

"How could I hate you, *chiquita?* Hate would be stupid refusal to
accept facts."

"I hope . . ." she faltered. ". . . I hope you will not be . . .
lonely."

His dark eyes gleamed. "Who do you recommend? Josefina?"

She thought of Josefina's rounded breasts and smiled. "She has no need of you, Captain."

He crossed to the door, opened it and looked back over his shoulder. "But perhaps I *will* have need of her."

When he had closed the door she stood frowning at it. Then she crossed to the sideboard, opened the top drawer, took out Anselmo's letter and sat down to read it yet again. She carried the letter upstairs to bed, holding it against her moist breast, feeling virginal and pure and recalling how Anselmo's honey-brown eyes laughed. She pictured him with a spiritual fervor that was innocent of passion.

Captain Garon receded to the outer fringes of her thoughts.

Even her father noticed her pale purity. "Do you feel well, daughter?"

"I feel *wonderful*, Father! Why do you ask?"

"You are white-faced and dreamy."

"I am happy, Father. Very happy."

"Because Anselmo will soon come home on leave!" he said and wiped his plate clean. "Ah!" He chuckled.

"You're not funny!"

He chuckled again and she spun on her heel and slammed outside. When her temper had cooled, she walked down to the water's edge and pulled in the cords attached to the lobster pots her father had laid earlier.

Her father called from the doorway behind her. "Still fishing, daughter?" His chuckle angered her until she flushed scarlet.

The troop train to Barcelona was packed and Anselmo Ledesma stood all the way, so crushed by other militiamen it was difficult to breathe.

He was weary when he left the station but he had to walk to his apartment because there were no taxis. His uniform was filthy, dirt was ingrained into his skin, he was lice-infested and his unwashed feet showed through his broken boots. He walked north along the Ramblas, his rifle strap chafing a shoulder sore that never healed, and the civilians he met gave him a wide berth. Soldiers on leave, unwashed and bearded, always stank.

Housekeeper Ana opened the door to Anselmo and, despite his filthy state, flung her arms around him and hugged him delightedly. He stripped off his rags, wallowed in a hot bath, shaved, trimmed his hair and disinfected it with surgical alcohol. When he put on a suit and a clean shirt, he felt wholesome for the first time in months.

Brother Manolo had left Barcelona, so after a short walk around the city, which had changed very little, he dined in a restaurant just off the Ramblas and went to bed early.

The next morning he was stopped twice by military police on his way to the station; and before being allowed onto the platform, his travel permit was inspected by three different officials. The train arrived late at Figueras, long after the daily bus to Escoleras had left and he was walking when an army car overtook him and braked. The driver asked: "Want a lift?"

"To Escoleras?" said Anselmo. He saw the somber-faced officer in the back seat and saluted.

"Hop in," said the driver.

"Thank you, sir," Anselmo said to the captain as he climbed in.

"It's a long walk to Escoleras," said the officer.

"The train arrived late, sir."

The captain eyed him curiously. "You are a native of Escoleras?"

"Home on leave after six months at the Saragossa front, sir."

"How is it out there?"

"Not much change, sir."

"Much fighting?"

"Very little, sir. Both sides are sitting it out."

The captain nodded as though he knew it all. "How long are you on leave?"

"Seventeen days more, sir."

"Make the best of them," advised Captain Garon and lapsed into silence.

At Escoleras Anselmo hurried up the drive to his home. Years seemed to have elapsed since he was last here and the cool, shady terrace aroused nostalgic memories as he ran up the steps and into the house.

His mother's hair was much grayer and her black eyes, dulled by inner hurt, warned him at once of tragedy. When he ran to take her in his arms, her poise collapsed. She clung to him with tears running down her cheeks. "My son. My boy! How good to have you home again."

"What has happened, Mother?"

"You must be brave, son. Your father . . . !"

He thought of his father, broad-shouldered and with his cigar jutting aggressively as he stabbed with his forefinger to emphasize a point.

"What . . . how did it happen, Mother?"

Pilar, Antonia and Manolo were home too and the family reunion helped to ease Anselmo's grief. He was now the head of the family and upon him fell the responsibility for its affairs. Anselmo set to work with a will. Madrid was besieged, so he decided Pilar and Antonia must remain in Escoleras. Jaime had died a few weeks after his leg was amputated, and Antonia was willing to forget her grief in work. Anselmo showed her and Pilar how to keep the ledgers and prepare quarterly bills for rents. He made charts of crop rotations so they could supervise the farming.

Anselmo avoided meeting people, for he was bitter over the manner of his father's death. But he saw a great deal of Teresa and confided in her. "I can't go on," he confessed. "A man must have a reason to fight. For months I served at the front, while my father was imprisoned and neglected until he died!"

"His death was a terrible blow to everyone, Anselmo. But so many have suffered! We must try to live with sadness."

"I'm not going back to the front," said Anselmo flatly. "I won't fight for men who murdered my father."

She was worried. "If you desert they'll put you in prison . . . might even shoot you!"

"I've thought it all out, Teresa. I've no convictions for either side. So I'm going to France. I'll be interned but the war won't last forever. As soon as I cross the frontier, I'll send you a message and you must tell my family what I have done."

She said unhappily. "We may not see each other for a long time?"

"Perhaps sooner than you think, dearest. The war can't last long."

She smiled through her tears. "Do what you believe is best but come back safely." Her hand brushed his and he held it tightly.

"I knew *you'd* understand, Teresa."

"I understand you because . . . because I'm so much a part of you, Anselmo."

His eyes were tender. "I'll think of you all the time, dearest one. Call and comfort Mother often and don't let her worry about me."

"I will. Being with her brings you closer to me."

"Tell me, Teresa. Is there anything you need?"

"Only that you come back to me, Anselmo."

They walked on, holding hands and presently they saw Rosalia who smiled and waved from the other side of the road. They waved back. "Have you heard from Rafael?" asked Teresa.

"None of us has had any news of him since the letter he sent after the relief of the Alcazar."

"Rafael's a strange boy," said Teresa.

Anselmo's face was grim. "He's become a stranger to us. Sometimes I feel he hates his family."

When it was time to go, Anselmo packed sandwiches and wine in a knapsack and caught the bus to Figueras. A farmer's delivery truck gave him a lift inland and dropped him in the foothills of the Pyrenees. He had a map and a pocket compass and after binding strips of cloth around his calves to protect them from thorns and brambles, he set off. The terrain was wild, the hilly slopes treacherous, and soon his legs ached. His city shoes were unsuitable for rough walking and his suit chafed his crotch and armpits. He toiled on for hours, climbing steadily toward two distant mountain peaks. By late afternoon he had reached a humid zone where trees grew thickly, and creeper, clinging undergrowth and brambles made the going harder. He forced on, often unable to see his landmarks and by nightfall was tired and ready to sleep. As soon as it was light, he would be able to walk on to the frontier and slip across it the same day.

It was cold. He sat braced against a tree, hunched his shoulders and closed his eyes. Presently he shivered. And then, with a sound like corn scattered across a tiled terrace, the Tramontana whispered through the trees. Within half an hour the north wind had blown itself up into a raging gale. It howled over the icy mountain peaks and turned the earth iron-hard with frost. Anselmo huddled for warmth against the tree trunk but the wind cut into him as though he was naked. He groaned with the ache of his frozen extremities and although the night was so dark he could not see a yard before his nose, he rose to his feet and kept moving. Frost crackled stiffly in his clothes as he bowed his head and blundered on, into the night, stooping low to butt against the wind. He lost all sense of direction. Presently, far below him, he saw yellow pinpoints of light and stumbled toward them. The wind tore at him and his tears froze on his cheeks. He tripped over a rusted barbed-wire strand and was still clutching it when the earth disappeared under him. A sharp barb ripped his flesh and he plunged downward until his outstretched arm was splintered back against his chest. Blackness engulfed him.

The Tramontana died as abruptly as it had begun and the morning sun warmed Anselmo's frozen limbs and revived him. He lay still a long while until his bemused senses told him he had fallen into a rock quarry. He tried to sit up but his left arm collapsed. He looked down at it and then away again quickly. He fumbled in his knapsack with his good hand for the wineskin and drank deeply. The wine warmed him. Congealed blood had closed one eye and he washed it away with wine while he thought what he should do.

There was no hope he could walk on to the frontier. He needed urgent medical attention, yet must be wary finding it, because deserters were shot. He ate a little and when he felt stronger, he climbed to his feet and stumbled on until he came to a path. Here he sank down on a tree stump and rested.

Presently a shepherd came along with his flock. He looked at Anselmo shrewdly. "I know a man who will take you to the nearest village," he offered and helped the injured youth to stumble to a farmhouse. The farmer was loading vegetables into a high-wheeled cart and broke off to brew hot coffee for Anselmo. But he could do nothing for the youth's injuries, so he propped him up in the cart between sacks of potatoes and whipped up his horse. Every time the iron wheels bounced over a pothole, the edges of broken bones grated agonizingly and at times Anselmo lost consciousness. Finally the farmer brought his cart to a standstill. "Do you wish to enter the village?" he asked discreetly.

"I am a deserter," said Anselmo flatly.

"Then it is dangerous to go to the hospital where patients are registered. Last week a deserter was caught and shot not two miles from here."

"I need help," choked Anselmo.

"I will find a barn to hide you. Then I will look for someone to help you."

"You are very kind," said Anselmo and ground his teeth against his pain.

Teresa was washing up after dinner when she heard the scratching at the kitchen door. She opened it, started back and stared with shock at the shadowy figure.

Anselmo whispered: "Teresa. Help me!"

A great wave of compassion overwhelmed her and she was crying as she helped him inside. "What have they done to you?" she wept.

His eyes were bright with fever. "Hide me . . . a doctor!"

"You must go to the hospital."

His fingers gouged into her arm. "They'll shoot me!"

"I'll hide you upstairs." His eyes were glassy and each stair seemed a mountain they would never surmount. Once when he knocked his injured arm, he cried out aloud. He fell upon the bed, his eyes burning, his chest heaving and cheeks and temples wet with an abnormal sweat. She forced brandy between his dry lips and he stared at her in his delirium without knowing her. Teresa ran downstairs, snatched up a shawl and ran out into the street to find Doctor Aldo.

Doctor Aldo slid a needle in under the flesh, pressed home the plunger and dabbed away the pinprick of blood with cotton wool. "Water," he said crisply. "Lots of hot water."

Teresa fanned charcoal desperately to keep it glowing below the cooking pot. When the water was steaming, she put another pot on the fire and carried the hot water upstairs. Doctor Aldo was undressing Anselmo and called a warning. "Wait, girl. I'm putting him to bed."

Teresa walked straight into the room and placed the cooking pot on the washstand. "I'll help you."

The doctor glanced at her anxiously. This was not work for a young girl. Even in hospitals there were male nurses in the men's wards. But the quiet, confident way she worked reassured him.

Anselmo's skin was burning and as dry as sandpaper. "Keep the thermometer under his armpit while I look at his arm." Doctor Aldo washed away congealed blood and studied the ripped flesh. The rusty barb had torn deeply, the edges of the wound were festering and a telltale swelling in the armpit showed poison was in the bloodstream.

Teresa checked the temperature. "He's a hundred and four," she said agitatedly.

Doctor Aldo nodded grimly. "I've got to clean up this arm." He gave her a shrewd sideways glance. "Shall we tell his family?"

"Only if it's absolutely necessary."

"He'll have a better chance in the hospital."

"They'll shoot him," she said flatly.

"He may die without proper attention."

"You must do all you can, Doctor."

"He'll need care and nursing."

"I'll nurse him. He'll be safe hiding here."

"And your father . . . what will he say?"

"Would Papa turn away an injured man?"

Doctor Aldo absentmindedly tugged out his watch and thrust it away without looking at it. "You'll have to help me." He opened his medical bag, took out a case of scalpels, a bottle of ether, rolls of bandage and catgut. He worked deftly, trimming the raw edges of the wound, swabbing up pus and cutting away infected flesh. He left the wound open to drain. Anselmo moved restlessly and mumbled deliriously. Beads of sweat sprang out on his forehead as quickly as Teresa wiped them away.

"This arm's a mess. Broken in three or four places. It won't be easy to set. But first we've got to stop infection. Later on, we'll try splints." The doctor gave Teresa detailed instructions and for the next few days she never left Anselmo's side, catnapping on the floor beside him when tiredness overcame her. She found reserves of strength she never knew she possessed and fought for Anselmo's life as he hovered on the brink of death, delirious, sweating profusely. He had no control of his bowels and she bathed him to keep him cool, washed him, changed the sheets patiently and fed him liquid food through his dry, cracked lips. When she slept, his slightest whimper brought her instantly awake and twice she wrestled with him when in delirium he fought to go out into the street.

Sometimes her father came into the room and stood watching unhappily, knowing there was nothing he could do. Doctor Aldo visited after dark every day and administered more drugs.

Then came the joyous day when Teresa knew instinctively that Anselmo had passed the crisis. His feverish turning and tossing changed into a calm, deep sleep. Sweat beaded him, but his flesh was cool. Yet his black stubble did not hide his sunken cheeks, his limbs were fleshless and his ribs stood out starkly. Doctor Aldo now set the broken bones and put the arm in a plaster cast.

Teresa nursed Anselmo until he regained strength enough to know he had nearly died.

"It must have been beastly . . . the things you had to do for me!" he said shyly.

"It did not worry me. It was necessary."

He looked away from her. "I am a man . . . you are very young, dearest. I would not want you to have seen me . . . thus!"

"There is no shame in it, Anselmo. A man is a man and a woman is a woman. And it is not shameful."

His puzzled eyes met hers. "You speak with worldliness, Teresa. Yet you are so young."

"But I am old too, Anselmo. Much older than you understand."

When he could sit up he did everything for himself. His wound, healing under the plaster, irritated maddeningly where he couldn't scratch. But it was his only discomfort. He was mending rapidly.

One day Captain Garon called at the cottage.

Teresa was upstairs with Anselmo, her lace-making bobbins flying while he read, propped up by pillows.

When the knock came she motioned Anselmo to remain silent and hurried downstairs. Captain Garon's darkly handsome face aroused a stab of pleasure that she instantly suppressed.

"Good afternoon, Señorita Barras." He was icily formal.

"Good afternoon, Captain." She hesitated. "Will you come in?"

He waited for her to sit before he took the chair she indicated.

"Will you have a drink, Captain?"

"No, thank you. I shall detain you only a minute." He drew from his pocket a buff-colored paper, unfolded it slowly and studied it. "You are acquainted with Anselmo Ledesma?"

Her heart thumped. She nodded, not trusting herself to speak.

"Do you know his present whereabouts?"

She shook her head. Her stiff facial muscles made a mask of her face.

"If you see or hear of him, it is your duty to report it at once, Señorita Barras." He folded the buff paper and tucked it away.

Her mouth was dry. "What has Anselmo done, Captain?"

His brooding eyes searched hers. "He has deserted."

"You have spoken to his relatives?"

"They know nothing of him."

She gulped. "They say . . . they say deserters cross the border into France."

He nodded slowly. "He has had the time to cross the border."

"Do you think badly of him, Captain?"

"I do not make judgments. I am a soldier and obey orders."

"Anselmo is not a coward. He is bitter. They killed his father."

"I do not question what a man does, Señorita Barras." Captain Garon leaned forward and spoke in a low voice: "How are you, *chiquita?* You have been hiding. I've tried for a glimpse of you without success. I miss you so much."

She held her breath, thinking of Anselmo upstairs. She said: "Give me time, Captain. Let me find myself in my own way."

His dark eyes glistened. "Only to see you makes me burn with impatience, *chiquita*."

"Do not anticipate, Captain."

He nodded sadly and rose to his feet.

She closed the door and walked slowly upstairs. Anselmo had got up and was sitting in a rocking chair, his plaster arm supported by a silk scarf sling. He saw her face and asked: "Trouble?"

"You're wanted for desertion. They've been to your home, too."

He glanced down at his arm. "As soon as I get rid of this plaster, I'll be on my way."

"What you tried to do was madness, Anselmo. Have you talked to Doctor Aldo?"

He nodded. "I'm waiting for news."

Doctor Aldo had news that same night. "There are many others who want to escape to France, but at this time of year it can't be done without a guide. They know the mountain paths like the palms of their hands. But they won't risk being shot without a good inducement."

"The cost is not important, Doctor."

"You will go in a group of a dozen. From the moment you start, you are under the guide's orders. It will be hard going and anybody who can't keep up will be left behind."

"That's fair."

"You must have warm boots and thick clothing. There is deep snow in the valleys and ice on the upper slopes."

"I'll get you warm clothing," offered Teresa. "And Father has a pair of stout shoes."

"I can't take the cast off for another fortnight," said the doctor, and Teresa sighed with relief.

But the fortnight flashed past and after Doctor Aldo cut away the cast and examined the wasted arm, he nodded with approval. "The bone's lumpy where it hasn't set evenly; but it's not bad for a rough set. Wriggle your fingers."

Anselmo wriggled his fingers.

"Now bend your arm."

Anselmo winced. Doctor Aldo grinned delightedly. "Keep bending your arm," he encouraged. "It'll hurt. Your muscles are lazy."

Anselmo extended his arm and smiled wryly. "It's . . . crooked!"

"It won't show so much when you put on more flesh."

"When do I leave?" asked Anselmo.

"Tonight."

Teresa turned and ran downstairs so they would not see the sudden tears in her eyes.

Teresa prepared sandwiches to last Anselmo through the long journey and they spent their last few minutes sitting quietly together. "Let me know quickly that you are safe, dearest."

"I'll get word through to you somehow."

"And . . . and come back soon."

His honey-brown eyes gleamed. "I promise I'll come back . . . to you!"

Her eyes were radiant. "I'll be waiting!"

"You have done so much for me. You saved my life."

"If I saved your life it was to save my own. I would not want to live without you."

"I care for you deeply, Teresa." He took her hand and squeezed her fingers. "Wait for me, Teresa."

"I will, Anselmo." She leaned toward his lips and he kissed her tenderly.

She clung to him and as their emotions quickened, he held her more tightly until she sensed his manhood stirring. He broke away from her, breathing heavily. "Forgive me," he said hoarsely.

"Forgive you for what, Anselmo?"

"It was wrong to hold you . . . thus!"

"No, Anselmo . . . I care for you."

"I care for you, too, Teresa. But to hold you thus . . . !"

"You have never kissed me before, Anselmo. It was what I wanted."

"These are bad days, Teresa. I cannot now speak as I would wish; but you know what I wish to ask . . . ?"

"I am patient, Anselmo. I will wait."

"And I will come to you," he said with great sincerity and kissed her on the cheek as he would his sisters.

6

Doctor Aldo came for Anselmo after dark to accompany him to the fish market where he climbed into a truck and hid between boxes of fish. A tarpaulin was pulled over him.

The truck delivered to villages in the mountain foothills and in the early hours of the morning Anselmo was dropped off at a barn where he hid for the rest of the day. When it was dark he rendezvoused with the rest of the party, and when they set off, the sky was clear and the weather warm. But bad luck dogged them and some hours later, the unpredictable Tramontana began to blow. The temperature fell sharply the higher they climbed, but they battled on grimly, heads down and leaning into the wind. Their toes and fingers were numb, every step had to be won from the wind and when it began to snow the gale became a blizzard that whipped their cheeks and blinded them. Only the fear of being abandoned kept them moving.

Their guide found a shepherd's refuge built from flat stones. Its roof was low, but it was big enough for them all to huddle inside, squatting on a frozen carpet of sheep droppings.

"We'll exhaust ourselves uselessly against this wind," said the guide. "It is better to rest and sleep if we can."

They ate and drank, their body heat warmed the hut and although snow drifted up against the open doorway, they managed to sleep.

They sheltered in the shepherd's hut for two days. The guide had never known such a blizzard. They dug themselves out into a world thickly carpeted by snow with an iron-hard icy surface—and stumbled along behind the guide whose unflagging strength and unerring sense of direction gave them confidence. They scaled steep, craggy cliffsides, forded torrents so cuttingly cold they sobbed with pain as they waded them, and tramped through forests of tall trees bowed under blankets of snow.

Finally they crested just one more ice-cap and a white, tree-lined slope fell away sharply to a plateau far below. The guide pointed.

"You cannot go wrong. Straight down to the plateau. On its far side another slope descends to meadowlands. From there you will see the church spire of a French village where you can surrender yourselves."

"And you, friend. You will return alone?"

Their guide grinned. "It is difficult to leave Spain . . . but not so difficult to return." He stood on the hill crest and watched them flounder down the slope and when they reached the bottom he shouted a farewell, waved, and slipped back out of sight beyond the ridge.

Now they were in France they forgot their tiredness and within two hours they were sitting side by side on a wooden bench in a police station and grinning happily at a weary sergeant who wrote in a big ledger. A second gendarme brewed coffee in a large pot and a third had gone to buy bread.

The sergeant, who spoke pidgin Spanish, was bored by this routine. He asked sourly: "I suppose none of you remember your names or carry identification papers?"

They grinned and shook their heads.

"The French government will make no official report to the Spanish government," he reassured them. "But it is convenient to have your names."

Again they shook their heads.

The sergeant shrugged. "We'll give you numbers. You're all charged with entering France illegally."

They nodded agreement.

"Later . . . you will be returned to Spain!"

Their faces showed their consternation.

". . . unless you're political refugees."

"We're political refugees," said Anselmo quickly. "If we return to Spain we'll be persecuted for our opinions."

"Therefore," continued the sergeant implacably, "you are invited to join the French Foreign Legion."

Their faces were pale, their eyes worried.

"Or else," continued the sergeant, not keeping them too long in suspense, "you will be detained in a camp for refugees."

Anselmo cleared his throat. "Can't we become citizens and live like Frenchmen?"

The sergeant shrugged his shoulders. "That may be possible . . . later. But first, the internment camp."

A gendarme distributed long loaves of bread still hot from the oven and the Spaniards munched contentedly and gulped black coffee from a canteen they passed from hand to hand.

Outside there was a squeal of brakes and a police driver stamped in, shaking snow off his boots. He eyed the Spaniards cheerfully and thumbed over his shoulder toward his police van. "You'll be cramped, but you haven't far to go." Half an hour later they were being ushered into modern roomy cells at the rear of a newly built police station.

Two weeks later, with blanket rolls over their shoulders, they marched through the double gates of a barbed-wire enclosure and Spanish prisoners already there gave them a welcoming cheer.

For the first few days after Anselmo left, Teresa ran to the door at every step she heard and looked expectantly at anyone who called. But it was a week before Doctor Aldo came with the news that Anselmo had arrived safely in France. Teresa called on Señora Ledesma and told her he was in France where he would remain until Spain was at peace.

After weeks of spending almost every hour at Anselmo's side, Teresa missed him so much she often cried herself to sleep. But as the days passed the pain of Anselmo's absence eased and she kept busy with her lace-making or helped her father tend the vineyard and fish and thought of Anselmo with hopeful anticipation, not sadness.

One day, returning from the country carrying a bundle of olive branches for the kitchen fire, she saw Captain Garon trotting his horse toward her. He had never looked so smart and handsome. She stood to one side for him to pass but he reined in his mount and looked down at her somberly. "It's good to see you after such a long time," he said sadly.

"I've been very busy, Captain."

He nodded. "I am too. Most of the day I'm away from Escoleras, building the fortifications along the coast."

Her bundle of wood cut into her shoulder and she lowered it to the ground. She smiled up at him with her work frock pressing against her thighs and her legs astride. "What news have you, Captain? Will the war last much longer?"

He shrugged his shoulders. "Both sides seem evenly matched." Then in the same tone he added: "You are more beautiful than ever, *chiquita*."

She looked away from him. "Don't say these things, Captain. Let us remain friends."

"Is a friend forbidden to admire you?" His eyes lingered on her breasts. "You are becoming more womanly."

She flushed and was suddenly breathless. She stroked his mount's head to conceal her emotions.

"Leave your bundle at the pathside," he said. "I will send someone to deliver it to your home."

"Thank you, Captain. But I am almost home. Also I am strong."

"Yes, *chiquita*," he said. "You are *very* strong!" His riding breeches were pressed, his boots gleamed. His brass buttons were well polished and his spurs were steely blue. He sat well in the saddle and his breeches strained tight over his muscular thighs. Her heartbeat quickened and her mouth was dry.

"Nothing has changed, *chiquita?*" he pleaded.

She shook her head.

He sighed. "Anselmo must be quite a man!"

"I love him," she said simply and swung the bundle of wood up onto her shoulder.

"I hope you will both be very happy." He sighed and rode away sadly.

For the rest of the day she couldn't stop thinking about the captain.

The following day Paco Barras brought home a double handful of sardines and they were still flapping when he dropped them on the kitchen table. Teresa cleaned and grilled them over the charcoal fire and while her father ate, she said casually: "I have seen Captain Garon."

"I trust you gave him my best wishes."

"Of course, Father. There is no longer need for him to sleep in the encampment. He hinted he would like to be billeted with us again."

"You did not refuse him?"

"I said I would talk with you."

"Tell him he is welcome." Paco Barras reached for the *porrón*, threw back his head and wine squirted into his mouth. "He can have Miguel's room again," he said as he placed the *porrón* on the table.

Captain Garon was away when Teresa called at his headquarters, but she left a message and that same evening his aide brought his luggage and carried it up to his room. Captain Garon arrived a little before dinner, greeted Teresa with shy formality and watched her set the table.

When they were eating he said: "Thank you, *chiquita*. I am very happy to be back."

She kept her eyes lowered. "It's good to have you back, Captain."

He toyed with his food. "I was delighted when I received your message. Does it mean . . . has anything changed, *chiquita?*"

She wouldn't look at him. "I love Anselmo. Nothing can change that."

After a pause he asked: "Did he ask you to marry him?"

"He kissed me."

He nodded. "A gentleman does not kiss a woman unless he intends marriage."

"I have always known we would marry. It . . . it is right we two should marry."

"Will you go to France to join him?"

She stared impassively: "Is he in France?"

He shrugged his shoulders. "Where do you think he is?"

"If he sends for me I will go to him; wherever he is."

"You must be patient," he consoled.

"You are kind, Captain and very understanding."

"It is because I care for you, *chiquita*."

She looked down at her plate. "I also care for *you, mi Capitan*. But not in the way I love Anselmo."

He stared at her for a long time, understanding all that was not said. "I am content, *chiquita*." He sipped coffee and smoked a cigar while she washed up. Then she took off her apron, wiped her hands and looked at him shyly. He rose to his feet, clicked his heels and bowed solemnly. "After you, Señorita."

At the door of her bedroom he swung her up in his arms and carried her across the threshold.

"It's been a long, long time, *mi Capitan*," she said breathlessly as he caressed her.

"A long, long time!" He sighed contentedly.

They lay in each other's arms listening to the beat of their hearts and comforted by the moist touch of each other. He said softly: "Anselmo should be very grateful to you. He owes you his life."

"What are you saying, *mi Capitan?*"

"If you had betrayed him he would have been shot."

She stiffened.

"I am not stupid, *chiquita*. A man was seen injured. He was described. I was notified of Anselmo's desertion. It was not difficult to add two and two. For weeks you never left your cottage. Why did Doctor Aldo visit you so frequently?"

She relaxed. "You knew all the time?"

"I guessed."

"Yet . . . you let him get well and go away."

"It was what *you* wanted."

"You are very generous, *mi Capitan*. Not many men would be so noble."

"I care for you, *chiquita*. I have no wish to *hurt* you."

"You're the kindest man I know. I feel secure with you . . . dependent upon you."

"Stay dependent upon me a long time."

"Are you still tired, *mi Capitan?*"

"It is not possible to remain tired alongside you, *chiquita*."

"Then kiss me . . . there!"

The sandbagged trench around the hilltop was camouflaged by the snow and even the slit-trench, cut horizontally across the hill slope halfway down, was difficult to pick out. Behind the sandbags weary militiamen crouched over small fires they strove to keep burning with little fuel. They huffed on their fingers and slapped their arms against their sides. Most of them wore newspapers wrapped around their limbs under their ragged clothing.

A mile away the walled town of Teruel stood on a low hill and Nationalist bombing planes circled above it, contemptuous of its antiaircraft fire as they bombed it at leisure. Sometimes shells exploded against the walls or within the town, or whistled over it and burst on the churned-up hillside.

A corporal passed along the trench shouting orders, lookout guards were posted and the rest of the men reluctantly left their fires and filed along the trench to the rear of the hill. When they had gathered together, their captain said bleakly: "Men. A comrade is here to talk to you." He tried not to hear their disgruntled growls.

The speaker was a stocky man with raven-black hair, cotton-wool sideburns, swarthy skin and dark eyes. His jaw was long and as he spoke, hands on hips and feet astride, they saw his face was lined beyond his years. He wore a threadbare overcoat that flapped open over blue overalls and he talked to the men as equals. "Comrades. We'll fight fascism better if we know what we're doing. Some weeks ago we attacked and occupied Teruel. We've been holding it despite fierce

Fascist counter-attacks and the pockets of resistance within the town.
We are shelled by superior artillery, we have no fighter planes to send
against the bombers and our troops are greatly outnumbered."

The speaker paused and a soldier asked: "So what do we do, comrade? Sit here on our asses for the next twenty years?"

"We must prepare for a full scale Fascist onslaught in the near future. We must not yield. *No pasaran!*" The speaker's eyes glowed and
spittle flew from his lips. "Comrades, the slavering Fascist beasts are
at our throats. Hitler, Mussolini and Franco intend to enslave mankind. We will stand solidly against them in unity with our brother
workers of the world."

The speaker brandished his clenched fist. "The Fascist traitors
shall perish. An end to the fifth-column snipers lurking on rooftops.
An end to capitalist lick-spittles who conspire to rob the workers of
their labor."

The men suppressed yawns and warmed their frozen hands beneath their armpits. They sighed with relief when the speaker finished with a rousing *"No pasaran!"*

"No pasaran," the men chorused, obediently flourishing clenched
fists before hurrying back to their fires.

Despite the cold, sweat stood out on Miguel Barras's forehead. He
wiped the back of his hand across his wet lips and turned to the captain. The fanatical glow in his eyes died slowly. "Thank you, comrade."

"It is for the cause," said the captain with his tongue in his cheek.
He disliked the intrusion of politics into warfare. It was bad for discipline.

"Be prepared for anything, Captain. If they break through, they'll
besiege Teruel." With a sweeping gesture, Miguel indicated all the
defended hilltops. "This is our front line and this is where they *must*
be stopped. Teruel can be held; but if this defense line breaks,
Teruel will be lost."

"I understand," said the captain and resisted adding: *It would be
evident to a child.*

"No pasaran!" said Miguel.

"No pasaran," echoed the captain bleakly.

Miguel was gloomy as he made his way to the base of the hill where
a military car was waiting to drive him to the next hilltop. He knew
that the tide of the war was going against the people.

It was dark when he arrived back at his billet in Teruel which he

shared with Godo, another trained propaganda agent. They occupied
the attic room in the commandeered mansion that was staff headquarters. Miguel was so weary he fell asleep on his cot before Godo
returned and Godo still hadn't shown up at dawn when the enemy
began a heavy artillery bombardment that continued all day. The
whistle of shells, the blast of explosions, flying shrapnel and collapsing masonry gave the tired defenders no respite as they crouched behind the ramparts, stamping their numbed feet, blowing on their fingers and grimly awaiting the forthcoming attack.

The German bombers circled ominously, the growl of their engines giving warning of the death they dropped. Then German pursuit planes screamed over the town at treetop level, their machine-
gun bullets raking the narrow streets. Meanwhile, Franco's troops
were crossing the Alfambra River and marching south to encircle
Teruel.

When there was a lull in the bombing, Miguel set out to find
Godo. On the outskirts of the town he saw his comrade's car overturned in a ditch where it had been dragged after a direct hit by a
shell. Already it was blanketed in snow but Miguel Barras and his
chauffeur dug at it with bare hands. There were no bodies in the car,
but dried blood stained the seats. "Back to Teruel," ordered Miguel.

A first aid post had been set up under a stone arch and the yellow
flicker of candles threw weird shadows over the injured who lay in
rows on the floor. More wounded were brought in every few minutes,
as they were dug out from bomb rubble. Those who died were laid
out near the entrance, faces covered, awaiting removal to the burial
pits. Miguel inquired and learned that two men found injured at the
roadside had been brought in late the night before. They had been
given first aid and sent on to the hospital.

They found Godo's chauffeur first. The blast had blown him from
his driving seat and he had fractured his skull. He was conscious but
stared glassily at Miguel without recognizing him. The stumps of his
arms were swathed in bandages.

"What happened to his hands?"

The medical orderly scowled. "Frostbite. We had to amputate."

Later they found Godo, his face sheet-white and his pupils pinpoints as he stared up at the ceiling. Only the slight throbbing of a
vein in his neck showed he still lived.

"How is he?" asked Miguel.

The doctor said: "Shrapnel tore away his kneecap. He was lying out in the open a long time. Frostbite got him. We amputated up to here." He ran his finger around his thigh immediately below his hip joint.

"What are his chances?"

"Practically none."

Miguel glowered. "One more murder to chalk up against those Fascist bastards."

The doctor was startled by Miguel's vehemence. "Men get killed in war," he said. "That's what war's about."

"It's not war when Fascists snipe from rooftops," said Miguel fiercely.

The doctor sighed and edged away. "I've a lot of work to do, comrade."

Miguel left the hospital and as he stepped out into the frosty sunlight, a cold shadow flitted across him. He looked up at the German plane that wheeled overhead, its engine-throb drowned by the crackle of machine-gun fire from over to his left. He shook his fist angrily at the pilot circling the bombing area.

Back at headquarters, Miguel joined the officers grouped around a map of the surrounding countryside. Black arrows showed how advancing enemy troops were circling the town to cut the supply road from Valencia. Red flags showed the position of government reserve forces. Several International Brigade battalions were only a few kilometers away and a few Steel Corps units were standing ready to strengthen any weakness in the defense line.

Miguel called the political commissar to one side. "I wish to rejoin my Steel Corps unit, comrade."

The commissar frowned. "It is not necessary, comrade."

"We must use every effort to defeat fascism."

"True, comrade," agreed the commissar. "But not all men have your strong convictions. They need to be encouraged and inspired. Your work is as important as is the ammunition for our weapons."

"It's essential to halt the enemy before Teruel is besieged. It is easier to lead from the front than encourage from behind."

The political commissar flushed; but there was no criticism of him in Miguel's eyes, only the glow of his fervent faith.

"Be careful, Miguel," he warned. "Lead the fight against fascism if you must, but take no risks. We cannot afford to lose you."

Miguel hung four hand grenades from his belt, put two more in his overcoat and filled the pockets of his coveralls with ammunition for his pistol. He slung a bandolier of rifle cartridges over one shoulder and crisscrossed it with another bandolier. His rifle was an old Mauser with a worn strap and a battered stock. But it was well-cared-for, its mechanism worked smoothly and its butt nestled familiarly into Miguel's shoulder.

Army transports from Valencia were driving up to the forward lines and Miguel leaped onto a running board and clung grimly as the truck lurched over the frozen potholed track. When it halted to unload ammunition, Miguel walked on. He found his Steel Corps unit dug in behind a low stone wall that stretched cross-country like a hedge.

Miguel grinned a welcome to his comrades, rested his rifle against the parapet, unbuttoned his pistol holster and looked out across snow-covered ground that sloped away gently to a distant hilltop. The gray sky was the horizon and behind the hill crest, the enemy was preparing to attack again.

The cold was intense. Men's breath steamed as it huffed from their lips and turned their beards white with frost. Their clothing was stiff, metal rifle barrels seared the flesh at a touch, and hunger gnawed at them. They had been fighting for Teruel for two months and the strain showed in their haggard faces.

Miguel stared out somberly over snow-covered meadowlands littered with overturned carts, weapons, dead mules, damaged vehicles and men who had fallen. Truck engines often couldn't be started again when switched off in this intense cold and had to be abandoned. The snow-coated muzzles of overturned cannons pointed starkly at the leaden sky, their breeches smashed so the enemy couldn't use them.

A barrel of brandy was broached for the men. Miguel cupped his mug in his hands as though it warmed them, bringing it up to his mouth and sipping slowly, relishing the brandy's fiery bite on his tongue and its scented aroma.

A middle-aged man next to Miguel said he was a miner. He had escaped death many times; but his parents had been killed by bombs, his brothers in action and his wife and sisters by the Moors. His children had disappeared. He hoped they had been found and sent to England or the States by a refugee organization. His name was Leon and because he was bald, he felt the cold cruelly in his head. He wore a knitted Balaclava stuffed with paper and old rags that made his head enormous. Like Miguel, he had had intensive training and as he sipped his brandy, he stared unblinkingly over the parapet, eager for action.

"How was the attack this morning?" asked Miguel.

"Hot! The materiel they've got! And men too. Too many. They were falling over each other." Leon grinned delightedly. "But they haven't got warm clothing. We've got the textile factories and I hope the bastards freeze until their *cojones* drop off!"

"Soon they'll be wearing Nazi uniforms, straight from Germany."

"If we win they'll need German passports and nationality . . . those that live!"

A shell screamed overhead and two hundred yards behind them a geyser of snow and earth spurted high. More shells fell fast and furiously.

Leon grinned maliciously. "Get ready, comrade."

The barrage lasted only a few minutes. Leon drew a deep breath. "Here they come." He spat and pressed the butt of his rifle to his shoulder.

The gray tanks advanced at a walking pace and by an acoustical freak their metallic clanking crescendoed to a loud thunder and then abruptly diminished to a clockwork whirr. They came on relentlessly across the snowy fields, machine-gun muzzles jutting viciously like the stinging horns of scorpions.

Defense artillery opened up halfheartedly but couldn't get the range. Then a squadron of Italian Fiat planes screamed over a hill crest and skimmed along the defense lines, spraying lead and distracting the defenders' fire from the approaching tanks. The Fiats were a tempting target, and men fired at them with rifles and machine guns. The nose of a Fiat dipped sharply and it flew into the ground, bursting into flame and cartwheeling. A column of red and yellow smoke poured upward into the frosty air.

The other Fiats wheeled sharply and flew back, spitting angry revenge. Lead tore up the hard earth, and grit spattered like rain. A soldier near Miguel fell to his knees. A bullet had traversed his body diagonally, entering his neck and tearing out through his side above his hip. His lips moved, but he made no sound while his eyes mutely appealed to his comrades. They dragged him into the shelter of the wall and propped him up against it.

Then the tanks were upon them!

The defenders tore the pins from their hand grenades and recklessly exposed themselves as they lobbed the grenades under the tank tracks. A tank came to a standstill not many yards from Miguel and raked the parapet with a storm of lead. Bullets ricocheted off the wall above Miguel as he threw another grenade. As soon as it exploded, he vaulted the wall, plunged through the smoke and scrambled up onto the tank. Its surprised crew heard his boots scraping on the casing and gasped in astonishment when their turret hatch was flung open. Miguel pulled the pin from a grenade, dropped it inside the tank and leaped to the ground. Another leap took him behind the shelter of the stone wall before the grenade exploded. All along the line, tank crews were learning that fearless men are dangerous and some tanks were already scuttling around and limping back to their own lines.

Then came the cavalry.

The mounted men were gathered on the other side of the hill and now they rode over its crest at a gallop, legionaries and Moors who served in the saddle and who rode as naturally as they walked. They avalanched upon the defenders with pointed lances and swinging sabers. Here and there a rider and his mount fell, but the cavalry had the advantage of surprise. It swept on and jumped the stone wall, wheeled around and charged back at the defenders. Infantry followed close behind the cavalry and the defenders were now attacked from front and rear.

Miguel drew his pistol and stared grimly over the wall at a galloping Moor whose steel-tipped lance pointed straight at him. Unhurriedly, he raised his revolver and fired. The Moor rode on. Miguel fired and missed again, then leaped sideways as the rider jumped the wall. Miguel rolled over and sprang to his feet as the Moor reined around and galloped back. The steel point of his lance extended three feet beyond his mount's muzzle. Miguel fired but his pistol jammed. He ran to one side but the Moor swerved too, his glittering lance-tip steadfastly aimed at Miguel's chest. In desperation, Miguel threw himself at the horse's front hoofs and the horse reared back on its haunches, its shoes slithering on the icy ground. Miguel sprang for the horse's bridle, cruelly tugged its head around, seized the Moor's boot and heaved him out of the saddle.

Miguel triggered his pistol experimentally and the horse screamed and went down, flattening the Moor who was rising to his feet. The whites of the Moor's eyes were yellow-tinged. He groped for his pistol while Miguel took careful aim and fired.

Miguel glanced around breathlessly. The defenders had suffered many casualties, but the cavalry charge had been suicidal. The mounted men were hopelessly outnumbered and although their attack had been spectacular, only a few were still fighting. The rest had been unhorsed and slaughtered.

But now the Fascist infantry was upon the defenders, their steel bayonets glinting. A terrible hand-to-hand battle ensued; men hacking and stabbing wildly, their eyes crazed, their fear forgotten. The defense line bulged inward and broke and the attackers were through, widening the breech, pouring into it and curling it back on both sides.

A bugle sounded and a thin line of reserve troops howled as they charged to reinforce the collapsing defense line. The badly mauled attackers feared a trap and dropped back, firing as they retreated, dragging with them their wounded companions.

They withdrew to the far side of the hill crest. With the sound of battle gone, the defenders heard the moans of the wounded amidst the crackle of flames as tanks flared like torches. The churned-up snow was littered with weapons, wounded and dead, bleeding horses and water canteens.

Lookouts were posted while the dead were laid out and their identity cards collected by an officer. The defense wounded received first aid and were loaded into ambulances. Enemy wounded were dealt with by a political commissar whose pistol barrel became too hot to touch.

Defense losses had been high. A decision was made to drop back to a stronger position on the hill slopes around Teruel. Army trucks moved up and the retreat began. The Steel Corps manned the wall while the retreating troops dug in.

Miguel placed ready on the parapet wall three loaded German pistols he had taken from enemy dead, two Italian rifles and a dozen hand grenades. If the enemy poured over the hill crest again, he wouldn't waste time reloading.

The government troops retreated half a mile, dug in on the slopes before Teruel and set up artillery and machine-gun emplacements. The Steel Corps held the line for five hours before a messenger came with orders for them to fall back. They retreated unhurriedly.

Miguel glanced back and saw one man had ignored the order to withdraw. Miguel approached him and when he drew near Miguel realized the man was a mere youth. He sat on an empty ammunition box behind a Lewis gun on a tripod. A pan of ammunition loaded the gun and another pan was ready in reserve. The youth looked up at Miguel and then glanced away disinterestedly.

"Time to go," said Miguel.

The youth ignored him.

"What's the trouble, comrade?" asked Miguel.

The youth's eyes were hostile. A scar on his cheekbone pulled down the corner of his left eye and made his eyelid droop sinisterly. He stared at Miguel but said nothing.

"We've orders to retreat," said Miguel.

The youth shook his head.

"They'll attack any time now. Is that what you're waiting for?"

The youth nodded.

"You can't handle that gun alone. Where's the rest of the gun crew?"

The youth glanced toward the corpse of a heavily bearded man. The top of his skull was torn off and the gray matter of his brain sparkled with frost. The youth stared back over the parapet and across the snowy slope where soon the enemy would advance to occupy the position vacated by the defenders. There was something odd about the boy, Miguel noticed. The texture of his cropped hair was soft and grew too low on his neck. The hands that held the machine gun were small and the wrists were long and narrow. He wore a thick overcoat over blue coveralls and the legs of his trousers were tucked into rubber boots.

"Listen, comrade," Miguel said sincerely. "None of us is afraid to die. But we'll help our cause most by selling our lives dearly. We've abandoned this line to the enemy. But when they try to occupy our new positions, we'll scythe them down like wheat."

The youth's drooping eyelid gave him a sinister sneer. He gestured to the machine gun as though to say: *I can't leave this to the enemy!*

"We've got better guns," said Miguel.

The youth shook his head obstinately and Miguel was ashamed, remembering that weapons were scarce. The youth pointed over the parapet as dark figures showed against the snow on the distant hilltop. The Lewis stuttered, the youth's hands vibrated and the dark figures leaped for cover.

The smell of burnt cordite hovered on the frosty air and Miguel scowled disgustedly. "You should have waited until they were out in the open."

The youth shrugged his shoulders wryly.

"You've warned them we're here. We'll have to move."

The youth shook his head.

"I don't care that you want to die," shouted Miguel angrily. "But we'll make the enemy pay a high price." He stooped, dismounted the gun barrel and swung it up onto his shoulder. He ordered gruffly: "You carry the tripod and ammunition."

The gun barrel weighed on his shoulder with the ache of a blow, and as he stumbled through the snow, he was uneasily aware his back was exposed to the enemy.

"Watch behind," he warned. "Shout if they start coming."

They hurried on, sweating profusely despite the cold. The youth's breath rasped loudly as he bowed under the weight of the tripod. When they reached their new lines, an officer stood up behind a barricade of rocks and shouted: "You two. Dig in on that slope over there alongside that big rock!"

The slope was steep and treacherous, but they scaled it in easy stages, resting frequently, Miguel dragging the gun up after them instead of carrying it. They found a natural hollow as big as a shell crater alongside the rock, and after they had rested, they built a parapet in front of it with large, flat stones.

"You aren't the gunner, are you?" guessed Miguel. "Your comrade was the gunner?"

The boy colored.

"Didn't you get training as a gunner?"

The youth's heavy-lidded, distorted eye made him look crafty. He shrugged his shoulders.

"When we've got the gun set up, I'll give you a lesson."

When the parapet was high enough, Miguel planted the tripod and weighed down its legs with heavy stones. "When overlooking a steep slope, set up the gun so you can swing it freely." Miguel demonstrated. "Make sure outjutting rocks or trees don't obscure your vision. When the enemy is attacking uphill, don't aim at their heads. The bullets might go over them. Aim at their knees. A wounded man causes them more trouble than a dead one."

The youth listened intently.

"Don't fire at isolated men unless they're close enough to threaten you. Men bunched together are the best target. Aim at those in front. If you miss, you may still hit those behind. Understand?"

The youth nodded.

"The rest you can learn in action," said Miguel dryly and took out his cigarette makings. "I lugged that heavy gun up this slope. It's your turn now, comrade. Get some ammunition."

Miguel smoked and cleaned the gun while the youth staggered up and down the slope with ammunition. The effort taxed his strength and presently he sank down, gasping for breath.

"Take a rest, comrade," said Miguel. "I'll forage some grub."

The supply line from Valencia was still open and Miguel returned with three loaves, a goatskin of wine, a hunk of salami, olives and a bottle of olive oil. He had found a piece of canvas used to cover a field gun, and he spread this on the icy ground to sit on while they ate. Miguel cut thick slices of bread and salami and opened the can of olives. The youth dripped olive oil onto the bread and made sandwiches. They ate quietly, enjoying the simple meal as if it was a well-cooked banquet. The youth sighed with satisfaction as he wiped his greasy fingers on the skirt of his overcoat.

"That was good!" said Miguel, licking his fingers. "You sleep; I'll keep first watch."

The youth nodded, stretched out on the canvas sheet and closed his eyes. Miguel yawned, then swore softly and scratched vigorously as body lice burrowed into his flesh.

The youth's eyes opened.

"Bloody lice!" said Miguel. He had unbuttoned his fly. "Eating me alive!" he complained, scratching furiously.

The youth averted his face. "Please, comrade," he said.

Miguel froze. The youth's voice was low and husky but there was no mistaking its feminine intonation. Miguel hastily rebuttoned his fly. "It's all right," he said gruffly. "You can turn around. I . . . I didn't know!"

She kept her eyes averted.

"You should have told me."

"I prefer to be thought a man."

"Get some sleep if you can. I'll give you two hours."

"Thank you, comrade." She closed her eyes and almost at once was asleep.

He frowned down at her in perplexity. Her scarred cheek and drooping eyelid made her ugly; battle-strain had lined her face. But months of fighting in terrible weather had aged even hardened men. Her eyes were dark-ringed, her forehead wrinkled; and deep furrows of exhaustion ran from her nostrils to the corners of her mouth. Yet later he had to scold her because she allowed him to sleep too long. She shrugged her shoulders. "You were tired," she said simply.

"We're comrades. We share the good things and the bad things!"

"It was good to see you sleeping soundly, comrade."

The cold sharpened their hunger and Miguel made another trip for food. He returned with half a kilo of salt ham which they ate ravenously.

The temperature dropped sharply that night. The other men huddled closely together to generate warmth but Miguel's companion hunched herself against the stone parapet.

"We can warm each other," Miguel argued. "I will respect you."

"It is better this way, comrade."

"Listen. I will lie with my back touching you. The night is cold and we need each other's warmth."

"No," she said flatly.

He lay on the canvas. But the cold cut into him like a knife and he could not sleep. She huffed on her numbed fingers and her teeth chattered, but long hours elapsed before she moved onto the canvas beside him. "Don't move, comrade," she pleaded.

He lay still as she pressed against him, her icy hands creeping into his armpits to steal his warmth, her groin against the curve of his buttocks and her knees under his thighs. Her teeth chattered for a long time before she was warm enough to sleep.

The attack came at dawn. During the night reinforcements had been brought up and the Nationalists swung into action gleefully. Long lines of tanks rolled forward remorselessly and behind them came the armored cars and infantry with fixed bayonets.

Six weeks earlier General Franco had publicly declared that the brooch of Teruel was the clasp of the year's victory. Those officers who took Teruel would make Franco's premature boast come true and gain the general's favor. But there was an early setback. The tanks and armored cars were useless when they reached the steeper slopes of the hills they attacked. Engines whined, tank treads spun in churned-up snow and one tank tumbled backward under its own weight. An impetuous officer rashly ordered a frontal attack by the infantry. The attackers shouted: *"Arriba Espana, Viva Franco!"* as they stormed the steep slopes with the eagerness of young puppies, while the defenders watched them in wonder.

The attackers were seasoned warriors who had served in the Moroccan wars. But the steep slopes soon robbed them of their initial impetus and their fast clambering diminished into a slow, uphill climb.

The defenders, lining their barricades with rifles and machine guns, waited patiently.

The slope immediately before Miguel was so steep the attackers did not tackle it. Instead, they bunched close together on an easier slope to the right. Miguel swiveled the barrel of the Lewis gun to cover them.

When the attackers were close to the barricades, a murderous blast of rifle and machine-gun fire spewed one long scything burst. It swept away the attackers like chaff. Yet those who followed stumbled on doggedly into the curtain of steel. Miguel gripped the Lewis gun and slowly wiped the slope clean while the girl steadied the vibrating tripod.

The attackers stormed on into a hell of destroying steel, drunk with enthusiasm, inspired by each other's heroism, climbing over the bodies of their fallen comrades and shouting *"Viva Espana."*

Only one attacker came close enough to the barricades to lob a hand grenade over and presently the few survivors of the heroically senseless attack turned and stumbled back down the slope.

Of the company that had valiantly charged the heavily defended ridge, only a handful of shocked, white-faced men returned to confront an equally pale officer who realized he had made a major blunder.

He knew now the ridge could be taken only after it had been heavily bombed and shelled. The officer wrote a message and dispatched it by runner, avoiding the accusing eyes of the survivors.

Confident another attack would not be launched for some time, Miguel dismantled the Lewis gun and cleaned it. The girl helped. "What is your name, comrade?" she asked.

"Miguel. And yours?"

"Catalina."

"How long have you been fighting, Catalina?"

"I was with a woman's brigade; but I asked to join the Steel Corps. It is not permitted, but I pleaded and they gave way."

"You are a Communist?"

"I am anti-Fascist. All *they* stand for I am against. I'll hate them to the death."

"They have made you suffer?"

"They murdered my family."

Miguel scowled as he greased the gun's mechanism.

The wounded on the slopes cried out their pain. Some tried to drag their torn bodies down the slope while the defenders bowled hand grenades down among them. Catalina said: "Every time a Fascist dies, my heart exalts."

"We never see the true enemy," said Miguel. "He's the one who monopolizes the means of production and sits behind a desk in a bombproof shelter."

"That is politics," she said sharply. "I hate Fascists."

The first aerial attack came an hour later. Six German pursuit planes flew low across the slopes, spraying the defenders with bullets. They flew so fast guns couldn't be brought to bear on them, but the defenders shouted obscenities at them as they died.

Next came the Heinkel 52's with cargoes of two-hundred-and-fifty-pound bombs. It was precision-bombing by German pilots under German command and their objective was total elimination of the hillside defenders. Great geysers of smoke and rubble spurted high and the earth shook. The defenders lived in an insane world of raining earth, steel and blood, until their gibbering, panic-stricken minds cringed and screamed. They were shocked, shattered, deafened and blinded. With bleeding hands they clawed deeper into the earth while screaming steel scooped them up and tossed them high in bloody fragments.

"You bastards!" Miguel choked, shaking his fist at the smoke-darkened sky. "You filthy German bastards." He dragged himself from his foxhole and swiveled the Lewis gun upward. Catalina joined him. "I'll help."

He peered through the clouds of dust and smoke. "I can't see them!"

They saw a man stumbling toward them with hands outstretched, beseechingly. His lower jaw was torn away. He fell to his knees and bowed forward until his forehead touched the ground.

"Here comes one," shouted Miguel, but his voice was drowned by the thunder of explosions and when he fired, the Lewis vibrated soundlessly.

The Lewis jammed. Miguel tinkered with it, but there was grit in the mechanism. "We'll have to strip it down!" swore Miguel. He dismantled the barrel from the tripod and there was a momentary lull in the bombing. The next sound split the air apart and the blast tore them off their feet. A great fist hit Miguel between the eyes and as though in a dream he faintly felt the impact when he hit the ground again. Then came the deeper darkness.

Catalina lay half-dazed for a long time before she could sit up. She was covered with dirt and dust. Blood stained her sleeve and she touched it, feeling for a wound; but her flesh was numb and unresponsive. She saw the overturned Lewis, with its ugly snout pointing skyward, and, with an effort, got to her knees and looked around for Miguel. He was lying beside a large rock where the blast had thrown him and she thought he was dead because his face was a red mask. But his pulse beat strongly. When she wiped his face clean with her coat, she saw shrapnel had torn open his cheek. Through the wound, she could see his teeth gleaming against the bloody mush of his mouth.

She dragged him into their foxhole, lay down beside him and pulled over them the piece of canvas to protect them from the rain of dust and grit. She could now feel the ache of her own wound; her brain reeled from the earth's concussions and her strength drained from her until blackness swallowed her up.

When the Heinkels had dropped their bombs, the pursuit planes came in again, flying low over the upturned earth and firing at anything that still moved. Then the infantry attacked, legionaries and Moors advancing steadily up the steep slopes with fixed bayonets and gaining the barricades without firing a shot. Amidst churned-up foxholes and trenches men, incredibly, still lived; men who screamed with the pain of terrible injuries or stared at their enemy with battle-shocked eyes. The Moors bayoneted them methodically.

An officer saw the overturned Lewis gun on the steep hill slope to his left, ordered his men to search for survivors and then countermanded the order. He could see no signs of life and taking Teruel was much more important. "On to Teruel," he shouted rousingly. "*Viva Espana!*"

When it was dark, Catalina peeled away the canvas. It was heavy with dirt and fallen rock fragments, and lay upon them like a leaden shroud. Miguel was only half-conscious. She helped him to his feet, looped his arm around her neck and took his weight as they walked. She was uncertain where to find the government lines and stumbled blindly through the darkness with Miguel's weight bearing her down. She talked to Miguel encouragingly, but her head was splitting apart. Every pulsing beat of her heart stabbed agony through her arm.

She rested frequently, sipped wine from the goatskin or nibbled bread she carried in her pocket. And always the effort of goading Miguel to his feet again exhausted her. They staggered on, hour after hour, their feet frozen by the icy ground. Gun flashes lit up the horizon and artillery rumbled. It was almost dawn when somebody shouted: "Halt. Who are you?"

"Long live the Republic, comrades," she called. Her voice was so weak she feared it was not heard.

There was a long pause. "Walk forward, you Fascist bastard. Hold your hands high and walk slowly."

"We are two, comrade. We are both wounded."

She heard the sentry calling another and the sharp snicks of rifle bolts. She sensed rifles pointed at her through the darkness. "Do not be afraid, comrades," she called. "We're both wounded. We are coming in. Shoot us if you must."

She stumbled on, bowed under Miguel's weight, and a blinding light flashed out. As she blinked tiredly, men relieved her of Miguel's weight. Her knees were weak and they lifted and carried her. A bottle neck pressed against her teeth and the fiery bite of rum burned her tongue. Then much later a doctor's lined face, yellowed by candle-flame, loomed over her. He ripped away her sleeve, stiff with blood, and she almost fainted when he swabbed the wound with surgical alcohol.

"I can't dig it out," decided the doctor. "It's a hospital job."

"And . . . my comrade?"

"He's going with you. An ambulance is leaving shortly."

She sat beside Miguel in the ambulance, her arm thick with bandages and throbbing painfully. Miguel lay semiconscious on a stretcher, his head swathed in bandages. His skull was fractured. When they reached the hospital, Catalina accompanied Miguel to the ward. "Don't worry, soldier," a doctor reassured her. "He's in safe hands now."

"Can I see him soon?" she asked anxiously.

"After we've operated. Anyway, you've a wound yourself that needs attention."

"I'm worried about him," she said.

The doctor eyed her closely. "Forgive me, Señorita. The uniform deceived me." He gave her an aged, wise smile. "Line up and get that arm looked at. I'll take care of your comrade."

There was a steady flow of casualties and the doctors worked feverishly. Wounded militiamen lay on the operating table in the blood of other men. A white-faced student stripped off Catalina's bandages and probed with soft fingers. "A piece of shrapnel is lodged against the bone."

"It feels like a cannonball," she said wryly.

"If infection sets in you may lose your arm."

She said expressionlessly: "Just patch me up so I can go back to the front."

"I'll give you a local. It'll be painful."

"I'll stand it."

He prepared a probe, pincers, a scalpel and cotton wool. "I'll try to be quick." He thrust a needle in under her skin and anesthetic numbed her arm. But when the probe went deep, scraping the bone, she groaned and her face became a death's head with feverishly glowing eyes. He gave her a gag of wood bound in bandages. "Bite on this." Her teeth grated upon it and her arm was crimson with blood.

"I'll leave in a drip tube for fear of infection," he said.

"It is not necessary. I am strong and healthy."

"Shrapnel wounds are dangerous. You'd better rest here for a while. We'll find a mattress on the floor for you."

"It does not matter," she insisted. "I am strong." But during the night her temperature rose sharply and the next day she was delirious, unaware of the sharp scalpel cutting away the seat of an infection and making new outlets for drip tubes. For days she was gripped by nightmares and a long time elapsed before she recognized the shadowy figure at her bedside. She smiled weakly. "I am pleased you are well again, comrade."

Miguel's fractured skull had knitted well, but from his cheekbone to the point of his jaw ran the red welt of a raw scar. He fingered it tenderly. "Now you know why the doctor calls me handsome."

"You're . . . quite better?"

"Convalescent. How do you feel, Catalina?"

She looked down at her arm. "I've still got it."

"Doctor says you can get up tomorrow."

"How long was I unconscious?"

"Ten days."

"I must have been bad."

"You were. You're much better now."

"I feel fit."

"I . . . you know you saved my life, Catalina?"

"As you once saved mine, Miguel." She laughed grimly. "How goes the fighting?"

"Teruel has fallen. Our troops fought bravely and retreated in order; but we lost a great deal of valuable war materiel."

"Where is the fighting now?"

"Franco's driving a wedge between Cataluña and the rest of Spain."

"When do we go back to the front, Miguel?"

"Soon. The doctors have ordered us a few days for recuperation."

"I'd rather go straight to the front, Miguel."

"It's not important what *we* want, comrade. What is best is what is good for the cause. The doctor says we need a break."

7

Miguel and Catalina were discharged from the hospital with seventy-two-hour passes and tickets to Madrid. They were surprised by the gayness and optimism in the city. Expensive nightclubs were doing excellent business with high-class whores and war profiteers who cheerfully paid extortionate prices for choice beverages. In the better class restaurants the best foods could be ordered—caviar, sturgeon, trout and roast venison—although the majority of Madrileños were lucky to eat a horse steak once every few weeks. Men became rich by catching dogs and cats, and rats too were sold for a good price.

Miguel and Catalina booked into a modest hotel in a humble district of Madrid and ate out. They walked the crowded city streets and window-shopped curiously as though visiting an alien world where everybody was clean and fresh-smelling. Militiamen on leave were commonplace and the two drew no attention to themselves. Catalina trimmed her hair and when she wore her topcoat, few would have suspected she was a woman.

They went to a music hall but were unamused by the trivial jokes. The tinsel and feathers worn by the dancing girls seemed tawdry and tarnished, and the laughter of the audience was like the braying of donkeys. They left before the show finished and walked back slowly through the blacked-out streets to their hotel. Catalina turned the key of her door. "Good night, comrade."

"Good night, Catalina."

Within minutes he was knocking at her door. She opened it and he stepped inside, grinning sheepishly. The raw weal on his cheek stood out like a whiplash. He closed the door and without looking at her said: "I want to talk, Catalina."

"Yes, comrade," she said quietly.

"I respect you as a comrade. But I also respect you as a woman."

She said tonelessly, staring over his shoulder into space: "You want to take me to bed?"

He was embarrassed and looked at the floor.

She sighed. "I am sorry, comrade. I cannot do what you want."

"You are a woman," he said simply. His dark eyes were appealing.

She returned his stare levelly, then turned away, unbuttoned her overalls and took them off. Then the man's shirt and the long woollen underwear. She stood before him, naked and goose-pimpled, her eyes dull and her voice emotionless. "It is better you see for yourself, Miguel. I am no good to you or any man."

Her breasts sagged, limp pouches of flesh. She gathered them up in her hands, displaying the ugly scar tissue that pocked them.

"I had months of draining tubes, Miguel. They wouldn't stop seeping pus. Amputation would have been cleaner. And I am a mess down below." Her fingers traced the great scars on her abdomen. They looked like bayonet slashes.

He stared at her. Pity overwhelmed him and killed his physical urge.

"I don't refuse you, Miguel," she said. "But I have no feelings."

"*Nada,*" he said thickly. He walked to her bed, sat down, took out a cigarette and lit up. "How did it happen, comrade?"

She picked up her woollen underpants, stepped into them and pulled the thick undershirt over her head. "The war." She crossed to him. "Give me a cigarette."

He lit one for her and she sat beside him and smoked.

"My village was taken by the Moors," she said simply.

His face was grim. "Did they . . . ?"

She nodded. "Terrible things. And then . . . I don't know how many they were. I was semiconscious most of the time. So many . . . they destroyed me down below. They twisted and bit my breasts too. Infection set in and then abscesses. They forced me to drink gasoline and castor oil and my bowel burst. I prayed to die. For months I suffered agony, my legs drawn up by pulleys and tubes draining away the poisons.

"I was a hospital casebook, Miguel. I had peritonitis, infected ovaries, an injured womb, syphilis and a burst bladder. I should have died a dozen times."

The raw scar on his cheek throbbed. "They killed my bride!" he choked. "And . . . they did this to you!"

She rested her hand upon his. "We will have vengeance, Miguel. We will return to the front."

"Where do you come from?" he asked.

She told him.

His eyes widened. "Do you know the name Perez?"

"It is a very common name."

"My home is Escoleras and . . ."

"Escoleras! My aunt's mother is named Perez and she lives in Escoleras."

"Then you are Catalina Alava?"

"And you?"

"Miguel Barras. I intended to visit your family but my bride was killed."

"It is a small world," she said.

"It would be a very happy one without the bloody Fascists!" he said fiercely.

Emil Serra dropped a comfortable cushion on his swivel chair and sat at his typewriter.

After two years of battle, General Franco's victory is in sight. German bombing and pursuit planes have given the Nationalists such superiority it is surprising the government still holds out. The capital is besieged, starved, bombed and rationed. But its defenders are tenacious. The Anarchist troops are ill-disciplined and untrained, but indomitable. Their courage is needed, because they are fighting a streamlined, modern, mechanized army. Germany has no interest in a Spanish truce. Hitler has tested new weapons and strategies, using Spanish flesh and blood for targets. German tanks have made deep penetration attacks which have cut into government defenses with startling success. The size of German bombs has been stepped up and now thousand-pound incendiary bombs are used. Mussolini has been shown that his troops have much to learn. Wherever his men have been brought into action, they've been quickly routed by government soldiers.

The socialistic attitude of the government has evaporated. The people have forgotten socialism. After two years of warfare, political idealism has been almost wiped out. In the early days of the war everybody wore overalls, flourished a clenched fist and said *"Salud."* But class-consciousness has asserted itself again. The "haves" distinguish themselves from the "have-nots."

The Anarchists who took over the factories soon found it requires brains, ability and experience to organize industry. Production without an experienced "capitalist" supervisor led to production chaos and breakdown. From sheer necessity industry has been handed back to private control with the government keeping a fatherly eye on it.

The Communist Party has been growing continually stronger and now wields enormous influence over the government. The Communists are so far to the right of the Anarchists, and have such a moderating influence upon the hotheads, that they can count on the support of liberal-minded men.

There's a mystery about the gold Spain sent to Russia. One box of gold seems to have got lost in transit! The gold was deposited against supplies of arms, and no doubt Russia will be delighted to go on supplying war materiel at high prices until this gold reserve has been absorbed. Communist officials here are whispering that Stalin is paranoic. Hence, the purges and executions in Russia. The Russians here cringe at the thought of being recalled to Moscow. A never-ending Spanish war would be paradise for them.

Official Britain sits on the fence and blandly asks for proof of intervention. Britain, it seems, is happy for the war to continue in Spain so long as it doesn't disturb the uneasy peace in Europe.

France is the one country that would like peace in Spain. The unceasing flow of refugees into France has become a serious economic problem. Providing food and accommodation for thousands of virile young Spaniards who have deserted is a severe strain on France's already overstrained economy.

My secret information is that the government is preparing an all-out onslaught against General Franco. The aim is to split the Nationalist forces, roll them back and regain lost territory. It will be a powerful assault against the west bank of the River Ebro!

Emil Serra sealed his report in a diplomatic envelope. He strolled into his bedroom where the three girls were awaiting him. He lay down on the bed and stretched himself comfortably. He gestured at the sweaty paunch that overlapped his pajama cord and said: "See if you can massage it away." Their subtle fingers massaged and kneaded.

Emil closed his eyes and sighed. "Maria," he said quietly.

"Yes, my darling?"

"Roll me a cigarette with black tobacco. Mix hashish with it."

"For you alone, my darling?"

"Make one for yourself, too. The others will help us tread the clouds together."

The assault on the village began at dawn with a heavy artillery barrage. The objective had no strategical value, but the remnants of a badly mauled International Brigade column had occupied it to make a last stand. This pocket of resistance hindered the remorseless steam-roller advance of the Nationalist forces and had to be wiped out.

When most of the whitewashed cottages had been reduced to rubble, the Nationalists moved up, their armored cars leading and infantry with fixed bayonets following them.

Not all the defenders had died and the survivors hastily set up machine guns and turned their fire against the armored cars. Their bullets ricocheted off steel plating, but one burst of lead sprayed through a vision slit, killing the driver and his mate. The vehicle ran wild, exposing the troops behind it.

But the defenders were hopelessly outnumbered. The armored cars rolled on to the plaza and the street-fighting that followed was an inevitable triumph for the Nationalists. They mopped up remorselessly, tossing hand grenades into houses still standing and spraying lead with automatic guns. They advanced until they reached the slaughterhouse on the outskirts of the village.

It was a large building with walls three feet thick, and its high, narrow windows, sandbagged and plugged with mattresses, provided excellent cover for the machine guns of its handful of defenders.

Lieutenant Casas was a young soldier who had risen from the ranks. He had studied Napoleon's campaigns and when his superior officer had ordered him to take the village, he had eagerly accepted the commission. He had advanced methodically with the minimum of losses and now he carefully considered this last hopeless stand of the enemy.

He studied the slaughterhouse through binoculars and saw that rubble and fallen masonry prevented close approach by armored cars. He knew he could call for bombing planes, but that would be wasteful. An artillery barrage could be brought up to pound the slaughterhouse to ruins. But that would take time. Yet to take the slaughterhouse by a frontal attack would be suicidal.

Lieutenant Casas imagined what Napoleon would have done and ordered a truce flag to be shown. One of his men flourished a white handkerchief tied to a bayonet and after a pause, a white handkerchief on a stick was waved from a slaughterhouse window.

Lieutenant Casas took the white handkerchief and stepped out into the open.

"Careful, sir," warned his sergeant. "Don't trust those swine."

But Lieutenant Casas lived by the rules of war. "Only cowards fire upon a flag of truce," he said. "Whatever else they may be, the enemy are not cowards." Unafraid he walked alone to the slaughterhouse, unarmed except for his holstered pistol.

Twenty yards from the slaughterhouse a voice ordered him to stop.

"I am ready to discuss surrender terms," he said calmly.

After a pause the unseen man said tersely: "We fight to the death."

Lieutenant Casas nodded. It was the reply he expected. "The decision is yours," he said. "But my duty obliges me to point out the hopelessness of your position."

"Our position is not hopeless, as you'll find out."

"You will achieve nothing, neither hold up our advance nor assist your comrades. You are surrounded and hopelessly outnumbered. I will not risk one soldier's life attacking you. We will send for a bombing plane."

"We'd rather be bombed than murdered in cold blood."

The lieutenant said coldly: "Soldiers don't murder. They take prisoners."

"How many prisoners have you taken who still live?"

The lieutenant flushed angrily. "Many," he said coldly. "You have listened to your own lying propaganda. At the beginning some prisoners may have been executed. But since then, General Franco himself has issued orders that all prisoners must be treated under the conditions laid down by the League of Nations."

"Since when?" jeered the voice.

"Since months ago." Lieutenant Casas's voice rang with sincerity. "Soldiers are not murderers. When obliged to kill, we kill! You have fought bravely and can achieve nothing by continued resistance. There is no disgrace in defeat and I call upon you to be reasonable and surrender."

There was a long pause. "I am the only Spaniard. My companions are of the International Brigade."

"Their nationality is not important. They will be treated as prisoners of war."

"I will talk with them. Two are badly wounded and another slightly. But they fight like tigers and I do not think they will surrender."

"Talk with them," agreed Lieutenant Casas.

After a few minutes the unseen Spaniard called out again. "Will you give your word the injured will receive proper medical attention and will be treated as prisoners of war?"

"I give my word," said Lieutenant Casas instantly. "It is the word of General Franco!"

"Your dying oath on the blood of your mother?"

"On the life of my mother."

"How do you want us to surrender?"

"Lay down your weapons and come out single file with your hands above your heads."

"The wounded must be carried."

"They may be carried then."

The sturdy oak beams that barred the slaughterhouse doors were removed and the first to emerge was the Spaniard. His eyes were tired and his face lined. Behind him came the International Brigaders, one with a stomach wound, carried between two, another with a smashed knee, carried upon the back of a giant, blond German, and a third wounded man with his arm in a sling made from a scarf.

Lieutenant Casas ordered his men to help carry the injured to the armored cars. Then, after posting a strong patrol in the village, Lieutenant Casas returned to his base.

The officers had lunched well to celebrate their victory of the previous day. A long trestle table was set up between the tents, choice wines had been poured and now cigars were being lighted while coffee and brandy were served.

The general at the head of the table had unbuttoned his belt and jacket and his open shirt showed his flabby flesh. He had drunk too freely and he proposed toast after toast.

"To General Franco."

"To General Franco," chorused his officers.

"*Arriba Espana!*"

"*Arriba Espana!*" they cried, gulping and pouring more wine.

The general sprawled back in his chair, legs parted and a half-empty glass hanging limply in his hand.

"To our sacred crusade!"

"To our sacred crusade!"

Lieutenant Casas discreetly approached the banqueting table and stood behind Captain Ledesma. Lieutenant Casas clicked his heels. "Pardon, *mi Capitan.*"

"What is it, man?" asked Captain Ledesma. He wiped his lips delicately with his napkin.

"The mission is completed, sir. The village is in our hands."

"Excellent, Lieutenant."

"Thank you, *mi Capitan.*"

"Thank you, Lieutenant." Rafael's tone was curt dismissal.

Lieutenant Casas loitered. "About the prisoners, sir."

Rafael stared in astonishment. "Prisoners?"

"We held a truce parley and they surrendered. Seven prisoners, sir. Three are wounded."

"They surrendered?"

"It is their privilege, *mi Capitan.*" There was a hint of reproval in the lieutenant's voice. "General Franco himself has ordered we shall take prisoners."

"That is true," agreed Rafael slowly.

"What shall we do with the prisoners, sir?"

Rafael frowned. Then he rose to his feet. "Will it please the General to excuse me, Señor?"

The general blinked owlishly, his cheeks flushed and his hot eyes melting. "Excused?" he asked throatily.

"If it does not displease the General."

"Nothing displeases me!" declared the general fiercely. He pounded his fist on the table, laughed wheezily and flourished his arm. "More wine," he demanded. He held his glass at arm's length and smiled foolishly as wine flowed into it.

Captain Rafael Ledesma strode away from the table. "Where are they?" he asked over his shoulder.

"Over here, *mi Capitan.*"

"How many did you say?"

"Seven, sir. Six foreigners, one Spaniard."

They stepped into the shadow thrown by the ruins of a bombed barn. The man with the stomach wound lay on a stretcher. The other six sat with their backs resting against the wall of the barn. When Rafael approached the prisoners looked up at him listlessly.

"Which of you is Spanish?" asked Rafael.

The Spaniard got to his feet.

"Stand over there."

The Spaniard moved away a few paces.

Rafael unbuttoned the holster of his pistol.

Lieutenant Casas said: "They are unarmed, sir. They will give no trouble."

Rafael drew his pistol and fired at the prisoner nearest to him. As the man slumped forward, Rafael fired again.

"*Mi Capitan!*" choked Casas.

The third man tried to get to his feet, but Rafael shot him through the chest.

"They are prisoners of war," shouted Lieutenant Casas.

Another shot. The target was the man with his arm in a sling. Rafael swiveled his pistol to fire again at the man with the smashed knee.

"General Franco . . ." choked Lieutenant Casas who was almost crying. "I gave my word . . ."

Rafael fired his last bullet at the man on the stretcher.

The air rang and smelled of cordite.

"What have you done, *mi Capitan?* What have you done?"

Rafael put away his pistol and held out his hand. "Your gun, Lieutenant."

The lieutenant stared at him wildly.

"Your pistol, Lieutenant. It's an order."

"Please, *mi Capitan.* I beg of you . . ."

Rafael's eyes were of steel. "You disobey my order?"

The lieutenant's fingers trembled as he drew his pistol. Rafael took it, aimed carefully and fired two more bullets.

Lieutenant Casas sobbed.

The Spanish prisoner's face was pale and he shook uncontrollably. "You filthy Fascist bastard," he choked. "You murdering son of a whore."

Rafael shot him in the stomach. The Spaniard jackknifed, fell and writhed in agony. Rafael stood over him. "Don't dare insult me."

The anguished eyes of the wounded man turned to him. Rafael leveled his pistol and put a bullet through the Spaniard's head. He blew smoke away from the pistol muzzle and held it out. "Your gun, Lieutenant."

There were tears in the lieutenant's eyes.

"Haven't you learned prisoners are a nuisance, Lieutenant?"

"But General Franco's orders were . . ."

"You misunderstood his orders, Lieutenant. General Franco referred to soldiers who are prisoners of war. He did not refer to the Red scum of Europe."

Rafael wiped his hands on his handkerchief and tucked it away in his sleeve. "Get this mess cleaned up quickly, Lieutenant. I'm going back to finish my coffee. Don't disturb me again."

Anselmo was one of the Spaniards in the French detention camp who volunteered for work. Every day they were marched out to labor in the fields. Although the work was hard, they could earn and buy extras; tobacco, brandy, sweets and clothes. Only rarely did anyone try to escape. It was difficult to remain at liberty and find a job without identification papers and most men were content to while away their days until they could return to a Spain at peace.

The open air, simple food and exercise made Anselmo fit. His face bronzed, his shoulders broadened and his arms grew muscular. After his service in the Spanish army he could make no complaints about the conditions in France.

But after dinner one evening, the camp commander entered the mess hall and addressed the men. "I am sorry to bring you unpleasant news. A ministerial decision has been taken which affects all of you." The camp commander paused and looked around. The men were giving him all their attention.

"The French government can no longer permit Spanish political refugees to remain on French soil. Those of you who wish may apply to join the French Foreign Legion. After five years' service, a volunteer automatically acquires French nationality."

The Spaniards turned down their mouths and grinned wryly.

"Otherwise you must return to Spain. Most of you claim protection from persecution. But you may decide which part of Spain you wish to enter. You may return to the government zone or to General Franco's territory. You have forty-eight hours to decide."

Deep depression overhung the camp as men talked dismally about their future. A handful of men volunteered for the French Foreign Legion. It was a hard and dangerous way of life, but most of them were criminals who had escaped from prison or were wanted for serious crimes in Spain.

But the majority of prisoners had fled from Spain to escape military service. They had little alternative. If they returned to the Spanish government zone, they might be shot. Anselmo and most of the others chose to be repatriated to General Franco's sector.

An entire carriage was allocated to Anselmo's group and coupled to a freight train traveling north. For two days they stayed in it under guard, eating and sleeping and only occasionally stretching their legs at small, wayside stations. They arrived at their destination at night and were led to a large warehouse where they could sleep. The following morning they were given a cup of coffee at the station buffet while they awaited the transport trucks. Anselmo was among the first batch of prisoners to climb up into the back of an open truck.

After the warm south, the chilly air of northern France was depressing, and as the truck wound higher into the mountain toward the frontier, the men huffed on their fingers and swore bitterly. They had eaten only snacks for some days. When they reached the Spanish frontier, they were ravenously hungry.

The truck stopped at the red and white striped barrier post, while a French officer gave the truck a cursory examination. Then he flourished a white-gloved hand, the barrier post lifted and the truck lumbered on across the two hundred yards separating Spain from France. The French officer called: *"Bon voyage."*

The Spaniards smiled sadly. *"Adiós!"* they chorused dolefully.

The truck rolled on, the Spanish frontier post lifted, the truck passed under it and came to a standstill on Spanish soil.

They were at once surrounded by Spanish frontier guards armed with pistols and rifles. But the pistols were holstered and the rifles slung carelessly across their shoulders. The guards smiled cheerfully.

"Welcome back to Spain," they called.

"A toast to General Franco."

As the refugees jumped down from the truck, glasses of brandy were thrust into their hands. A uniformed guard was pouring liberally from a keg and those who wanted could get refills.

"A drink for you too, driver," invited their Spanish officer. His smart uniform was newly tailored.

"Thank you," said the driver. He tossed off his generous tot of brandy and climbed back into his truck. "I've got to hurry," he explained. "Six more batches to bring up."

"Tell them they'll get a welcome," said the officer.

The driver backed around, the frontier post was lifted and the truck drove back to France.

"Cigars," offered the captain.

The refugees lit up and puffed contentedly.

"Why did you take so long to come over to us?" the officer asked casually. He was a plump man, easygoing and good-natured.

"We had to await our moment to make our escape," said Anselmo carefully.

The captain nodded sympathetically. "They made you fight for a cause you did not believe in?"

Anselmo nodded.

"All you could do was desert and escape through France to join General Franco in the north?"

"Exactly," said Anselmo and they all nodded eagerly, content it was explained so easily, knowing now everything was going to be all right.

"Fill up the glasses again," said the captain and when they were ready he proposed: *"Arriba Espana. Viva Franco!"*

"Arriba Espana. Viva Franco!" chorused the refugees solemnly.

Soon a Spanish army truck rolled up for them. *"Buen viaje,"* the captain wished them as they clambered into it.

The truck wound down through a valley to the meadowlands beyond. A military car followed with four poker-faced guards carrying submachine guns slung across their shoulders.

The truck rumbled on. It was warmer in the lowlands and the aroma of good cigars and the glow of brandy in their empty bellies made the men contented. They began to sing. They sang of Pancho Villa and his many strange adventures, each told in a short verse and each verse more outrageously vulgar than its predecessor.

> *"Una para sus maletas,*
> *El otro para sus cojones!"*

they sang lustily and abruptly stopped singing as the truck braked to a standstill before the double doors of a barbed-wire encampment.

Guards jumped out from the military car behind and leveled their submachine guns and a tall, sallow-faced officer stepped forward. "Get down, you Red swine!"

They jumped down from the truck, clustered together and looked unhappily at the stockade of stout wooden posts and coiled barbed wire. A corridor led through this barbed-wire forest into a large compound beyond.

The officer gestured impatiently. "Inside. Single file." The guards held their submachine guns menacingly.

The refugees shambled into the compound and looked around disgustedly.

There must have been two thousand other prisoners. There was no shelter except the ones men had made by digging up large stones with bare fingers, building low walls and roofing them with clothing. There were no cooking facilities. Men who were ill or wounded lay exposed to the elements, dependent upon their comrades' goodwill. The emaciated limbs of the prisoners showed through rents in their filthy uniforms.

Anselmo and his group were instantly besieged by poor wretches who begged or tried to steal their possessions. Touched by their misery the newcomers were generous with their sweets, cigarettes and rations. Anselmo gave his spare pair of socks to a barefooted man and a packet of chocolate to a prisoner with a filthy bandage around the stump of an amputated hand. Great tears rolled down the man's cheeks and Anselmo turned away in embarrassment.

Anselmo's group chose a corner of the compound to entrench themselves, and because they were still healthy and strong they cleaned away the human excretion around them. They resisted the other prisoners' constant begging and not many days passed before most of the group was suffering the pangs of hunger more acutely than the fleshless prisoners, who were accustomed to it. When the guards emptied bins of potato peelings and yellowed cabbage leaves over the barbed wire, they too learned to fight for it, rolling in the filth to gain possession of a scrap of food.

Anselmo met one guard who showed some humanity. He was a middle-aged man who, like most professional soldiers, obeyed orders without feeling hatred for the enemy.

"This is madness," Anselmo told him. "I fought with the Reds from necessity and I escaped to join General Franco's forces. So why am I kept prisoner under conditions which will surely kill us all in time?"

"Many crossed to France," said the guard. "Many, many, many! Spies, agents provocateurs, and deserters! Now they come to General Franco's zone. But . . . can they be trusted?"

Anselmo gulped. "I was conscripted by the Reds. They murdered my father and I am against them. But . . . I could have stayed with the Reds and fared better than this!"

The guard shrugged. "Thus is war."

"Must we stay here and die?" asked Anselmo desperately.

"You will give your name and particulars and they will be investigated. If everything is satisfactory, you will be allowed to join General Franco's troops."

"And those who cannot give a good account of themselves?"

The guard drew his forefinger across his throat significantly.

"Nobody has yet asked my name."

"You must be patient. Sometimes weeks or months elapse before a visit of the Commission."

"Am I then to remain here . . . months?"

"Thus is the war," said the guard and smiled wryly.

"But I have done nothing to justify this!"

The guard shrugged. "Who is innocent? Who decides who is innocent? We have thousands of prisoners; government soldiers captured after a battle, men politically active against General Franco, Germans, Czechs, Poles and Englishmen, foreigners with weapons they used against General Franco's loyal Spaniards. Who is to decide their crimes? And how? There are deserters, cowards, men who simply do not want to fight; and the homosexuals, thieves, Gypsies and vagabonds. Who is to judge them? And how? Are they guilty? Of what are they guilty?"

"Exactly," panted Anselmo. "*Who* is guilty? We're involved with insanity. Everyone is mad!"

The guard shrugged. "Thus is war, my friend."

When he had been in the camp a week, Anselmo had his boots stolen. So, like many others, he cut up cork-tree bark which kindhearted guards tossed over the barbed wire from time to time and bound it to his feet with strips torn from the tail of his shirt.

When he had been in the camp a month, his body was wasted, his limbs emaciated and his clothes hung in tatters. He lacked the strength to fight for scraps of food and spent his days sitting in the warmth of the sun, listlessly searching his body for lice.

Every morning the corpses of those who died the previous night were left at the compound gates by the prisoners. Later, an army truck took them away. There was an average of five deaths a day. At this rate, Anselmo calculated he could live another seven months.

8

Teresa and Rosalia set off early with baskets balanced on their heads and food in a knapsack. When they reached the new road, the one Captain Garon had made, they walked along it. They were accustomed to going barefooted, but the road gravel was sharp and they kept to its grassy edge, walking in single file.

Rosalia walked in front, hips swaying and the hem of her skirt whipping across the backs of her knees. She had lost the top button of her dress, the second was hanging by a thread and the third was missing. Teresa caught an occasional glimpse of her bare back.

Presently they left the road and followed steep paths over mountain slopes where only sage and thistles could drain moisture from the sandy soil. Beyond the hill crest was a valley through which a torrent flowed when it rained. Everything here grew abundantly. The two girls set to work gathering wild strawberries and nuts. Food and fruit were so scarce now that the hard labor was justified. They searched with youthful zest, combing the valley, ranging up and down its slopes, and when they reached its far end at noon, their baskets were half-filled.

"Let us rest in the shade," said Rosalia. Her face was flushed and perspiration beaded her upper lip. Damp sweat patches marked her bodice where her breasts had rested when she stooped.

"Let's carry on into the next valley," suggested Teresa. "Then we can rest at Mas Alba."

The girls toiled up the stony hillside, increasingly aware of the weight of the baskets balanced upon their heads and Teresa saw the faint white lines on Rosalia's back.

On the crest of the hill, Rosalia stopped in the shade of a pine tree. "I'm tired. Let's rest." She swung her heavy basket down off her head and her dress strained tight. Thread snapped, the last button flew and Rosalia's dress opened, exposing her shoulders.

Teresa gasped.

Rosalia straightened up and spun around. Her face was crimson.

Teresa swung her basket down to the earth and eased her aching back. She said quietly: "So *that's* why you wouldn't swim with the rest of us!"

"You . . . you saw?"

"It must have been a terrible beating. Was it your father?"

Rosalia looked away. "No," she said quietly.

With a flash of feminine intuition, Teresa knew. "It was Rafael!"

Rosalia's hot eyes pleaded desperately. "Don't tell anyone, Teresa. Swear you won't tell anyone."

"All right. I swear it."

"Help me with my dress."

Teresa drew in her breath sharply when Rosalia turned her shoulders. "It's . . . it's all down your back!"

"Down to my thighs," said Rosalia.

Teresa was furious. "He should be punished . . . he should have the same thing done to him!"

"Perhaps I was to blame, Teresa. I was furious for what he said about us and I taunted him. I went too far. He lost control of himself and when I laughed at him . . . he turned crazy."

Teresa fastened Rosalia's dress with a safety pin. She trembled with indignation. "He's an animal!"

"Yes," said Rosalia softly. Her eyes were dreamy. "He's put his brand upon me."

"When he did this . . . did he . . . ?"

"No," said Rosalia. Her chest heaved. "But something happened to me, Teresa. I wanted him . . . Teresa . . . ? Have you let a boy touch you . . . or anything?"

"Do you see me with other boys?"

"There's only Anselmo, then?"

"I'm longing for a letter. But it's difficult to get letters through from France."

"Has Anselmo ever kissed you?"

"Just once. Before he went away the last time."

"But . . . nothing else?"

"You should know Anselmo by now. He's a gentleman."

"Then you have never . . . at all?"

Teresa picked up her basket. "We'd better get moving."

Rosalia grunted as she swung her heavy basket up onto her head. "I haven't either," she said. "But I get excited thinking about it. Especially in the mornings when I wake up."

"I don't like talking about these things," said Teresa primly. "When a girl marries it's between her and her man."

"You're too straitlaced, Teresa. I have these feelings. Other girls too. It's not wrong to talk about it."

"I don't say it's wrong. I just don't like to talk about it."

They were walking side by side and Rosalia ran her eyes swiftly over her friend's figure. "You're not as mature as me, Teresa. I feel these things more strongly than you."

"Who else knows what Rafael did to you?" Teresa asked tonelessly.

"My parents, Doctor Aldo, and now you. My father took me to Rafael's parents and told them."

"Rafael's poor mother," sighed Teresa.

They walked on down into the valley and as they approached the deserted Mas Alba farm they saw how it was decaying with neglect. The Alba family had lived in the old mansion for more than two hundred years. It had round towers with arrow slits, large cool terraces and high vaulted rooms. When the war started the family had locked up the mansion and fled, fearing for their lives. During the past two years, the outbuildings had been broken open and farm implements and stores had been stolen. The olive and wine presses had been smashed and the wine storage vault had its double doors hanging from their hinges.

The girls crossed to the well in the forecourt and set down their baskets. The sun blazed fiercely. Teresa sent the well-bucket ringing down into the echoing depths and listened for its faint splash far below. She hauled up the bucket and deftly flipped it up onto the well parapet. They drank their fill and then plunged their faces into the water.

The cool, shady interior of the wine store was inviting.

"Let's eat inside," Teresa suggested.

When they entered the wine store there was a shadowy flicker as though a bird had flown across the sun. The walls of the store were lined with wine casks twice the height of a man. Once, grape juice had fermented inside these enormous barrels, absorbing the wood's matured flavor that made Mas Alba wine famous throughout the region. Now the barrels were thick with dust and the wood so shrunken that many iron hasps had sprung loose.

"D'you think they're all empty?" asked Rosalia.

"Sure to be."

Rosalia walked along the line of casks, tapping them with her knuckles and listening to the hollow echo. As she walked further into the vault, the sunlight retreated and shadows closed in around her. Suddenly she froze. A man was crouched low between two barrels. His eyes were staring.

She turned and ran, screaming in terror. "A man," she choked, communicating her terror to Teresa who backed toward the doorway.

"Run, Teresa. He may be a madman!"

"Wait. Please wait." The voice that wailed after them was reedy and disembodied. "It's me, Rosalia. Don't be afraid. It's Narcissus. Don't be afraid, Teresa."

Their fears dissolved into astonishment. He edged slowly into the sunlight, his hands spread appealingly.

"What are you doing here, Narcissus? We heard you'd crossed to France."

He cast a frightened glance around him. "Don't tell anyone you've seen me."

"Of course not."

"I'm hiding."

"You've been living here all these months, Narcissus?"

He smiled timidly. "Almost two years."

"How do you get food?"

"Father comes once a week with a sack of provisions."

"And nobody has ever found you?"

He grinned craftily.

"But *we* found you," said Teresa.

"That's because I'm not afraid of you. I saw you long before you got here and didn't bother to hide properly."

Rosalia glared at him shrewdly. "Peeping Tom," she accused.

He flushed. Then his eyes gleamed. "Would you like to see my hiding place?"

He led them to the extreme end of the wine store and around to the back of one of the enormous casks. He removed a section from the cask and squeezed through it. His voice rumbled and echoed inside the barrel, almost unrecognizable. "Come through."

He lit an oil lamp and they saw he had a mattress and blankets, books, food, pitchers of water and tools with which he was making a model sailing boat. The smell of wine was overpowering.

"Let's get out of here," choked Rosalia. "I can't breathe."

They clambered out of the barrel and walked back to the sunlight. "Nobody will ever find me," boasted Narcissus.

"Surely you don't *live* in that barrel?" said Teresa.

"I stay outside. But when anyone comes I hide." He chuckled, his laugh high-pitched and girlish. "Once some peasants came to steal farm tools and I had to hide in the barrel all day. It's the longest I've ever stayed inside and I was drunk for days afterward."

"We've brought lunch. Join us," invited Teresa.

While they ate, they talked of the events of the village during the last months. Narcissus was well informed about everything. His father spent several hours with him every week.

Presently the girls arose to leave.

Narcissus gave his weak smile. "You despise me, don't you?"

"Why should we?" said Teresa.

"You think I'm a coward."

Rosalia shrugged. "Nobody knows what the war's all about."

"Then . . . don't tell my father you know. He'll worry."

"All right."

"If you're near here again . . . come and see me."

"It's a long way, Narcissus," said Teresa. "We don't often come this far."

It was a hot, airless night, the impenetrable black velvet of the sky unrelieved by stars or moon. It was a night for bivouacked soldiers to lie naked and sweating upon their blankets, lulled by the monotonous call of cuckoos and the rhythmic croaking of bull frogs.

The long war had become an endurance test and the Nationalist sentries were as casual about their monotonous duty as their officers. They smoked at their listening posts, laughed, told jokes and secretly sipped brandy.

But this midnight on the twenty-fourth of July, 1938, government troops were massing on the other side of the Ebro and men were quietly uncovering boats that had been concealed by day from Nationalist binoculars. They carried them to the riverbank and slipped them into the water without a splash. It was so dark the men's faces were faint white blobs as they climbed into the boats and took up the oars.

Sergeant Benito Vigon sat in the stern of his boat. It was weighed down to the gunwales by men and equipment. Other men stood thigh-deep in water, holding the boat against the gentle tug of the current. Vigon glanced at his watch. It was fifteen minutes after midnight.

An officer walked along the bank, silently signaling orders, and the men who steadied the boats waded into deeper water, pushing the boats ahead of them and giving a final powerful thrust that sent them on their way.

All along the river, between Maquinenza and Fagon, overladen boats crossed swiftly and silently, the boat bows grinding softly on the shore of the far side within seconds of each other. The men waded to the bank, some holding automatic guns, while others carried the heavier Maxims. Surprise was their best weapon and the Nationalists were caught completely offguard.

There were spasmodic flare-ups of fighting at isolated Nationalist outposts, but by two in the morning government troops had driven a wedge three miles deep into enemy territory and established a bridgehead which they rapidly fortified. More weapons and men were ferried over. Pontoon bridges were brought up in army trucks and engineers toiled like ants, joining the spans, securing the bridge ends and cheering excitedly when the first trucks began to roll across to the Nationalist side of the river.

When dawn broke, the men were exalted when they saw the mass of armaments and equipment that had crossed the river. The militia-men advanced to take Gandesa, singing, shouting, and flourishing their weapons triumphantly.

Gandesa came in sight during the heat of the afternoon. The sur-rounding country was flat but studded with small hills. On the crest of one of these hills the Nationalists had built an observation post.

A florid-faced captain who limped from a recently healed wound studied the post through his glasses and decided tersely: "Lieutenant Corba. That observation post must be destroyed. It can direct artil-lery fire against us."

"Si, mi Capitan," said Lieutenant Corba. He turned to Benito Vigon. "Sergeant. Take your men and occupy that observation post."

"Al orden!" said Benito Vigon. He had ten men with automatic guns and he gathered them around him. "We are at a disadvantage, attacking uphill," Vigon warned. "But there are only two or three men and they can't cover all sides of the hill at the same time. We'll surround the hill and then attack. Once that attack starts, keep it going. Use the cover of rocks and boulders but keep moving. Any questions?"

The men grinned eagerly, flushed with the confidence of victory.

"Best of luck, men," the captain said.

"Check your ammunition, comrades," reminded Vigon.

"Lieutenant Corba," said the captain.

"Yes, sir?"

"You go with them."

The lieutenant's eyes widened. *"Me,* sir?"

"It is a great encouragement when an officer leads."

"Sergeant Vigon is very capable, Captain." There was a sheen of sweat on the lieutenant's forehead.

"It is fitting an officer leads this attack."

Lieutenant Corba swallowed. "Very well, Captain." His hands shook as he took an automatic gun from a soldier.

Sergeant Vigon eyed him curiously. "Your orders, Lieutenant?"

"Carry on, Sergeant."

Vigon set off, leading his men toward the hill. When they drew closer they circled around it. Occasional bullets screamed overhead, showing that the men in the observation post were vigilant. They gained the shelter of the boulders at the foot of the hill and Sergeant Vigon realized the job was easier than it looked from a distance. The observation post was on a small plateau and had a dominating view of the surrounding countryside. But the hill was so steep the attackers could reach the edge of the plateau without being seen. It was only the last fifty yards of their attack, across exposed ground, that would be dangerous.

Lieutenant Corba had his shaking hands under control when they reached the summit of the hill. There was a brief pause while the men regained their breath and then without waiting for orders, one gave a fierce yell, jumped up and charged across the plateau toward the observation post. His courage inspired Lieutenant Corba who also shouted and began running, leveling his heavy automatic gun while his men charged with him, yelling fiercely as though in ecstasy.

And then they came under fire from the stone-built observation post. The man in front of Lieutenant Corba was snatched up and tossed to one side, seeming to hover in the air splayed out like a starfish before he fell, sprawling on the earth like a broken doll.

Fear hit Lieutenant Corba, a shocking and overwhelming fear that stampeded reason. Without knowing it he threw away his weapon as he turned and fled.

Sergeant Vigon shouted: "Attack, Lieutenant. Attack!"·

The lieutenant ran blindly, not even seeing Vigon.

Vigon leveled his weapon and pressed the trigger. The burst of lead all but cut the lieutenant in two. Vigon turned and fired at the observation post as he raced toward it. He jumped the body of a fallen comrade and stormed on, firing at the slits in the concrete pill-box, vaguely aware he was screaming with excitement. He and his men blazed with their guns and lobbed hand grenades until only dust and rubble remained.

Three Nationalist soldiers died defending the observation post. Five of Sergeant Vigon's men were wounded and one killed.

They made their way back slowly down hill. Sergeant Vigon carried the body of Lieutenant Corba over his shoulder, heedless of the blood that soaked his khaki shirt.

The captain watched Sergeant Vigon lower the dead lieutenant to the ground and walk over to him to report. "Good work, Sergeant," said the captain. He took cigarettes from his pocket. "Smoke?"

"Thank you." Sergeant Vigon took a cigarette and they lit up.

The captain exhaled smoke through his nostrils. "I watched the action through field glasses, Sergeant. You did what was necessary. Tell me, Sergeant. Would you also shoot *me?*"

Sergeant Vigon glowered. "Do you want me to say I'm prepared to shoot all officers?"

"Yes," agreed the captain thoughtfully. "I suppose that *is* what I want you to say."

"Then I will say it, Captain. We fight for democracy and liberty. We fight against the dictators who crush freedom. We fight for justice. But we fight as men and not as cowards, and our officers must be worthy of us."

"I could arrest you and court-martial you for shooting an officer!"

"It would be unjust, Captain. I am a sergeant and my orders are to shoot any officer who retreats without written orders."

"You take your orders seriously, Sergeant."

"War is a serious business, sir."

"Lieutenant Corba was not a coward, Sergeant. He has fought well in too many battles. The strain became too much for him. I sent him, hoping he would prove himself again."

"He turned and ran at the wrong moment, Captain."

The captain sighed. "When I have time I will write to the lieutenant's wife and give her my sympathy."

"Another comrade was also killed in the attack, Captain."

"Then I will write to his wife also."

"That is the democratic way, Captain," said Sergeant Vigon seriously. He saluted with a clenched fist and turned away to join his men.

9

Day and night the radios blared in homes, streets, bars and cafés; in Madrid and Barcelona; in the villages and in market towns. The joyful news of the government's great counteroffensives against the Fascist troops was being spread.

The Ebro had been crossed, masses of men and equipment had driven deep into enemy territory, the Nationalist forces had been rolled back and were retreating in confusion. The tide of battle had turned, large numbers of enemy soldiers were prisoners and the war was all but over. Democracy, freedom and liberty would triumph over fascism.

People were happy and rejoiced, many because it was victory for the government, but all because the end of the war was in sight.

In the northern sector near Burgos, the official headquarters of General Franco, Captain Rafael Ledesma was recalled from leave by telegram. He reported to his commanding officer.

"Captain Ledesma. You have heard that the situation in Gandesa is ticklish?"

Rafael Ledesma nodded. "The swine have crossed the Ebro!"

His commander frowned. He disliked emotionalism. "We were caught by surprise," he said quietly. "We have lost strategical positions as well as considerable territory. We *must* halt the enemy advance."

"Spain will never submit to the Reds!" declared Rafael.

His commanding officer heard him out. "That is as may be," he said softly. "I am outlining the military situation, Captain Ledesma. Your leave is revoked. I'm sending you to the Gandesa front."

Rafael Ledesma clicked his heels. "At your orders, Commander."

"We are preparing a counteroffensive. The fighting will be fierce."

"That is where I would wish to be, Commander."

"The enemy are using an International Brigade and a brigade of Catalans for an assault on the town. They are well-trained and deter-

mined men. Counterattacking against them will mean heavy losses,
Captain Ledesma."

"A good soldier counts his losses *after* the battle, Commander."

"You are very young, Captain Ledesma. You have distinguished
yourself as one of the heroes of Alcazar. You have a good record and
this action in Gandesa can mean your promotion."

"I am delighted to know it, Commander."

"Think of it as you lead your men into action. It will encourage
you."

In Escoleras, news of the Ebro offensive and the end of the war was
received with undisguised delight. Everywhere were smiling faces
and happy chaffing. Doctor Aldo joked with his patients, gave away
cigars and forgot to pull out his watch and look at it. Father Delbos
went from bar to bar solemnly declaring that everyone should give
thanks to God for bringing peace. Shoemaker Corbeta, the acting
mayor, asked the Long Man to take out the council bunting, and
Señora Ledesma made a pilgrimage with Antonia, Pilar and Manolo
to place a wreath on the tomb of Baudillo Ledesma.

Teresa and Rosalia went to the beach far away from the others and
stretched out in the hot sun. Rosalia lowered her bathing suit and
bared her back. The white weals stood out clearly on her suntanned
skin.

Teresa was lying on her belly. She rolled over on her back and
lowered her suit to expose her small breasts to the sun. "I still don't
know what you see in Rafael."

"He has something I can't help loving. I expect it's the same with
you and Anselmo."

Teresa poured oil into the palm of her hand and massaged it into
her breasts. "Anselmo's not like Rafael."

Rosalia propped herself up on one elbow. "You want to get your
breasts brown?"

"It looks so silly, tanned in some places and white in others."

"What does it matter? You're the only one who sees it."

"I don't want to be piebald."

Rosalia giggled.

"Don't keep looking at me. You embarrass me."

"You shouldn't be embarrassed by another girl. You've not much
to show anyway."

"Mother used to be like me. She didn't grow big until after Miguel was born."

Rosalia nodded wisely. "Marriage makes a difference."

"Some girls are naturally small-breasted," defended Teresa.

"Have you heard that if you've got a boyfriend and he . . . you know . . . he holds you, then you grow bigger more quickly."

"An old woman's tale," said Teresa.

"It might be true," said Rosalia.

"A woman is the way she is made," said Teresa.

"It would be nice though, wouldn't it?" said Rosalia slyly. "When I think of Rafael I think of him . . ."

"Don't, Rosalia," said Teresa.

"If we can't be frank between ourselves . . ."

"I don't want to talk about it, Rosalia . . . It's . . . too personal!"

Rosalia rolled over on her back and lowered her bathing suit. "I'll get brown too, Teresa. When Rafael comes home . . . maybe he'll like a wife who's brown all over."

Teresa closed her eyes against the sun, felt its heat upon her breasts and thought of Anselmo until her nipples hardened. "The war has robbed us of so much," she said bitterly. "Now it's over we can make up for lost time."

Miguel's Steel Corps unit had crossed the River Ebro near Amposta in support of a brigade of Catalan Anarchists. But their attack in this sector was doomed before it started. A government traitor had sold news of the assault to the Nationalists and a formidable ground-force ambushed them.

Again and again the government troops hurled themselves against the impenetrable steel barrier the Nationalists had erected; and again and again they reeled back. For twenty hours the attackers fought on, without food or rest, desperately trying to hold on to a flimsy bridgehead. But the weight of Nationalist artillery brought up against them was overpowering and finally they were forced to retreat.

Miguel and Catalina had set up a Maxim to hold the bridgehead while the government troops retreated. The barrel of the gun grew hot and Catalina's hands were black with grease as she fed it belts of cartridges. The walking wounded and the badly wounded carried by their comrades filed back across the remaining pontoon bridge, foot-sore and hungry. Miguel concentrated fire upon a disabled tank to prevent its bringing its guns to bear on the bridge.

The last of the troops and wounded crossed the bridge and a mine-layer came running back: "Retreat, comrades. It's an order. We're going to blow up the bridge."

Catalina snatched up the ammunition belts and Miguel swung the smoking gun across his shoulder, feeling the burn of it and smelling scorched cloth as he ran.

An armored car opened fire and bullets hummed around them. The tank lowered its gun and a cannon shell exploded fifty yards behind them, sending up a geyser of earth and smoke that screened them.

Their boots slapped loudly as they crossed the bridge and then they were among their comrades. At once a sapper drove down a plunger and detonating charges blew the bridge apart.

Beyond range of enemy fire, a canteen was set up and Miguel and Catalina made their way to it. Their eyes were red-rimmed, their faces smoke-blackened and their lips dry and cracked. They grabbed hunks of bread and dried meat and sank down gratefully in the shade of a tree, leaning against its trunk with their thighs touching.

"We fought a good fight, Catalina," sighed Miguel and bit deeply into the dry bread.

"But we lost many good comrades, Miguel."

A radio had been set up and its volume was turned high. A Madrid radio announcer declared enthusiastically: "The forces of fascism are being steadily rolled back. Franco is defeated. Our victorious fighting comrades do not know the meaning of retreat."

Miguel swore softly.

"Kill that radio," shouted somebody.

Anselmo sat against the compound wall with a ragged trouser leg rolled up over his knee. He frowned at the festering ulcer in his calf. An emaciated man groaned as he lowered himself to the ground beside Anselmo. "You've heard the news from Pepito, the guard?"

Anselmo shook his head disinterestedly. His open sore was eating deeply into his flesh. It wouldn't heal because he lacked vitamins. His nails were brittle and broke easily, his hair was falling out and his teeth were loose in their sockets.

"The government launched a big offensive," said the man worriedly. "This can be the turning point of the war."

Anselmo looked at him with new interest. "The end of the war?"

"You know what will happen to us if the military position gets bad? They won't bother with prisoners? They'll set up machine guns and mow us down!''

Anselmo shrugged his shoulders and looked at his leg. Nothing was important any more. Machine-gunning would be an easy way out for all of them. He was surprised that not only was he resigned to death but that it seemed preferable to his present way of life.

Emil Serra knew he should report that German experts were holding day-and-night conferences at General Franco's headquarters and giving strategic advice about the best way to counterattack the Spanish government's offensive at the River Ebro.

But he had visited his doctor earlier and his X-ray plate showed a pronounced movement of the shell splinter. Life was now only a matter of months, if not weeks. So tonight, he took out the hypodermic he had just bought and gave it to the dark-skinned Moorish girl he had brought home with him.

"You have to inject into a vein," he explained. "Do you understand?"

She nodded.

"Jab the needle in the vein here. Then draw up the plunger a little and draw off blood so it mixes with the liquid in the hypodermic. Then you shoot the whole lot straight into my arm. You understand?"

She nodded doubtfully.

"Listen. I've never done this before. I don't know its effects. You've got to stay and look after me. That's what you're getting paid for."

She nodded obediently.

"It may boost me higher than a kite and you may find yourself alone for a time. On the other hand, I might go crazy for you."

"I will care for you," she said simply.

Emotionlessly she watched him fill the hypodermic with a transparent liquid he drew from a small vial. Then she rested the sharp needle upon the flesh of his arm just above a vein. He blocked the vein with his thumb and it swelled and throbbed. "Don't be afraid," he encouraged.

The needle went in smoothly but the girl was nervous and sucked in her breath, making a slight hissing noise.

"You're doing well," he encouraged. She raised the plunger and red wisps of blood were sucked up into the colorless liquid.

"Pump it up and down," he instructed.

She pumped the plunger until the liquid was rosy pink.

"Okay. Now shoot it home."

She applied steady pressure to the plunger and he bared his teeth as the liquid spurted straight into his bloodstream. Then she withdrew the needle, smeared away the blood spot with the ball of her thumb, sat back and watched him impassively. He lay back on the bed, closing his eyes and relaxing. He breathed deeply and the flabby flesh on his chest and belly shimmered like jelly. "It's got a kick," he whispered. "It's hitting me; it's *really* hitting me."

She sat beside him, the palm of her hand resting gently on the moist skin of his belly. Her dark Moorish face was inscrutable and her large dark eyes were expressionless. He moaned softly and presently he slept, his face working and sweat springing out on his body and running off him to turn the sheets wet.

Close to Gandesa an officer shouted an order. A thin line of brigadiers sprang to their feet, yelled fiercely and charged across the furrowed earth of a vineyard. Rifles cracked, machine guns stuttered and men fell.

The rest charged on, inspired to fearlessness by their idealism. They ran through a withering hail of lead.

Machine guns spat and a man fell to his knees. He supported his weight with his arms but his head hung heavily. He was a docker from the East End of London and he bit his lip to hold back his sobs as the pain within his chest expanded enormously. Weakness overcame him and he sank slowly to the ground, crushing under him the ripening grapes until they bled.

He lay in the hot sun with his eyes closed, a Cockney in a foreign land, shedding his blood for a cause he believed in passionately but without great understanding.

Around him the battle raged on and nobody could come to ease his last suffering.

BOOK III

1

Rain threatened to add to the misery of the ragged soldiers clustered around the blackened cooking pot. Sun-dried cornhusks boiled and bubbled and Isidro Barras ladled the steaming, brownish liquid into enamel mugs held out by grimy hands. The dark mixture had an acrid smell and with imagination a man could pretend it had the taste of coffee.

"They promised us woolen cardigans before the cold weather set in," grumbled a man.

"They'll come, comrade!" said Leon. *"Mañana!"*

"Like the boots we never got."

"And the socks!" The speaker scowled down at the esparto string that tied his boot soles to their uppers.

"What's happened to our textile factories in Sabadel?" demanded another man.

"They were bombed like us, comrade."

"Who wants more coffee?" invited Isidro. He breathed deeply as though inhaling a delicious aroma. "Lovely coffee!"

"Filtered through the sex hairs of a mangy goat," growled a man and spat out cornhusks.

The men laughed.

"When the war is over," said Isidro Barras, "I will burst my gut with good coffee. Coffee from Africa, coffee from Brazil, coffee from the West Indies and Turkish coffee."

"And coffee filtered through the sex hairs of a beautiful blonde," said Leon and everyone chuckled.

"We'll wait a long time," sighed a sad man.

"Don't be defeatist, comrade. We've almost won the war!"

"What! Won the war? Waiting for them to fly over and bomb us?"

Half a dozen men argued eagerly.

"We've made a smashing attack across the Ebro."

"And the enemy are smashing back!"

"We've consolidated our position. This is just a breathing spell."

"If we make one more big effort like that they'll drive us back to the sea," said a wit.

One man scratched his hairy chest. "I don't ask for victories. All I want is a pair of boots and some clothes. Look at these trousers. I haven't had them off in six months. They stand up by themselves!"

"What's that?" asked a soldier and pointed.

Their curious eyes followed the direction of his finger. The ground sloped away from them gently for a kilometer and then climbed steeply to a ridge of low mountains. Now the entire summit of the ridge had sprung into flames. In the dull, gray light of morning, fire rolled along it like a wave of crimson surf.

Billowing smoke drifted lazily and long seconds elapsed before the thunder of artillery reached them. The earth vibrated and a sharp-witted officer ran along the trench parapet, shouting and waving his arms. He broke the spell and men ran for cover as the first shells exploded around them. They burrowed deep into their trenches, digging with bayonets, pocketknives and bare hands until their nails bled. They dug fearfully, then frantically and finally in maddened desperation. They were accustomed to bombing raids that sometimes left deep craters as a grim reminder the war had not ceased; but never had they known such a bombardment as this. So many enemy guns had been brought up overnight that their thunder overlapped. Whistling projectiles fell like steel rain, the air boiled, the ground shook, and day became night as smoke hung like a pall. Earth spurted like fountains, scattering rocks, debris and dust.

Isidro Barras dug frantically with his bayonet, hacking out an over-hang under which he could shelter. He was so deafened by explosions he watched his hands working as though in a silent film. Dust and dirt rained down and his mouth was dry with fear. There was a roaring blast of geysering earth and Leon was flung along the trench at Isidro, knocking him down. Isidro lay dazed, his arm and shoulder numbed and several seconds elapsed before he struggled to his knees.

Through the smoke and whirling dust, the dirt-smeared face of Leon glowed translucently, the skin drawn tightly over cheekbones as his jaws parted in an unheard scream. Blood spurted from his ears, nose and eyes. The flesh of his chest was peeled down, exposing the shining whiteness of splintered ribs, rust-brown pulsing lungs and blue-pink intestines.

"*Madre mia! Madre mia!*" whispered Isidro. He wanted to help his comrade, but horror numbed him. He wanted to escape from such awfulness. If Leon had been an injured animal he would have used his rifle. But this *"thing"* was a *comrade,* a tortured man who screamed for death, yet could not die, who writhed and clawed the air.

Isidro fled along the trench, heedless of whirling shrapnel, and screamed when *"something"* clutched his legs. But it was a comrade only dimly seen in the swirling smoke who swore furiously but did not cease his frenzied efforts to burrow deeper into his foxhole.

Isidro used his rifle bolt to dig beside him. His mind was swamped by the horror of the *"thing"* that lay back there, screaming soundlessly amidst the thunder of the explosions. Then just beyond the rim of the trench two shells exploded, their heat flashes searing his flesh. He blinked his smarting eyes against the swirling dust and his breath rasped painfully. But fear gave him the strength to scrape a hole into which he could huddle as he dug still deeper.

The barrage was murderous. Shells screamed terrifyingly and the government lines were hammered, battered and pounded until it seemed impossible humans could live within that boiling, bubbling cauldron of exploding earth. Yet miraculously men did live. They clung tenaciously to life, earthworming amidst geysering soil that buried them even deeper. They survived the tearing steel and erupting earth. With nostrils, ears and mouths clogged with dust, they burrowed ever deeper and endured the unendurable.

The Nationalist barrage went on for hours. Modern artillery from German factories was being used in a ruthless counterattack to the Ebro crossing. The full fury of countless guns was concentrated on one small sector of the front, turning trenches into man-made hell.

The bombardment ceased as abruptly as it began. The thunder of cannon-fire rolled away into the distance and dwindled to a whisper. Dust and smoke wreathed amidst the rustling, sandpaper sound of thousands of grains of upturned soil falling back to earth.

And then came silence. Long, long seconds passed before anything moved in that churned-up, desecrated wilderness.

Then the earth stirred, rustled in a miniature avalanche, and a skinned and bloody hand searched blindly for the sun. The torn-up ground heaved as grotesque figures broke free from the tomb's embrace; shell-shocked men deafened by the awful silence and stunned by concussion; husks of men, not thinking beings. With animal instinct they clawed free from the grave, hands outstretched to ward off unseen obstacles as they stumbled away from the front line. Many were wounded and staggered only a few paces before they fell. But no man could think of his comrades. These shattered remnants of a company could only obey the instinct of self-preservation. And as they stumbled toward the rear, the Nationalist troops advanced without meeting resistance to occupy the vacated trenches.

Isidro Barras survived. He clawed free from the earth and staggered back toward the Ebro. Blast had ripped away his clothing and his flayed flesh felt scalded. His arm had been hit by a large rock, grit grated between his teeth and there was fear-nausea in his bowels from the agony of a shrapnel-gashed thigh. He staggered on through a world strangely dark to his red-rimmed eyes. All around him other gray ghosts stumbled, swayed and bled their way back to the River Ebro.

Isidro Barras did not see the gulch and plunged into it headfirst, his fingers raking the soil as he rolled into a clump of cactus. He lay exhausted for some time before he stumbled on again, unaware that his hands dripped blood or that cactus thorns bristled in his arms and face.

The command post was an old farmhouse with a roof of moss-covered tiles and stout walls of natural rocks. Coils of barbed wire surrounded the farmhouse, and it could be approached only through a narrow, well-guarded gap. All around, exhausted men slept on the ground where they had dropped when their officers dismissed them. Electricians were running out telephone lines, sandbags were being filled and stacked on the parapets of slit trenches and sappers inside the farmhouse burrowed deep below its stone-cobbled floor.

The command office was below ground and roofed with railway ties shored up by pit props. The earth walls were lined with thin slats from orange crates. A trestle table ran the length of the chamber and maps were spread out and held down by thumb tacks. There were seven telephones, each identified by a daub of colored paint. An adjutant answered them patiently.

Commander Calargo scowled as he studied a large-scale map of his troop positions. His officers gathered closer around him. "They're not using military tactics," grumbled Commander Calargo bitterly. "This is the strategy of capitalism." His jaw jutted and his eyes were fierce under his bristling eyebrows. "They're using two hundred batteries in this bombardment. It's a monopoly war, comrades. We haven't the weapons or the ammunition to fight back and we're being steamrollered! They pound at a sector until all resistance is flattened and then advance, occupy the rubble and fortify it."

"If our aircraft could bomb the batteries . . ." began one officer.

"Hopeless," said Commander Calargo. "Our planes are outnumbered five to one."

"I'm sorry," said the adjutant loudly into the telephone. "Those are Commander Calargo's orders. Resist. A position is not untenable until there are no defenders. Those are your orders. *Resist!*"

"If we dig deep and hold out until the enemy ammunition is exhausted . . ." suggested another officer.

"Their ammunition is inexhaustible," said Commander Calargo flatly. "All of Germany's armament factories are working for them."

"But we have the Soviet Union behind *us,* comrade," said a third officer.

Commander Calargo looked at him sharply, and his gray eyes glinted. "That is true. Comrade Saludo. But always we wait for these supplies of arms that never arrive. Every week they are on the way. Every day they are due . . . *Mañana!* But the day of delivery never dawns. The Catholics may fight with weapons of the spirit, comrade. But we are materialists. We cannot fight with cannons made of Russian dreams or the ammunition of Communist propaganda."

"International difficulties have impeded shipments . . ." began Captain Saludo.

Commander Calargo held up his hand. "Please! Explanations do not help. We must face facts. A wave of counterattacks has been launched by a vastly superior army. The first attack caught us by surprise, our troops retreated and we lost the Heights of Caballs, one of our most strategic positions." Commander Calargo looked at each of his officers in turn. "We must be realists. We must withdraw across the Ebro."

There were startled exclamations.

The commander waited until there was silence. "The enemy's steamroller tactics make it impossible to hold our lines. But the River Ebro is a natural bastion. We can fortify it and hold it against the heaviest attacks."

"To retreat is unthinkable, Comrade Calargo," protested Captain Saludo. "There has been so little fighting Madrid will not agree that we surrender so easily what it has cost so much to gain."

The commander's lip curled. "Our retreat will be disciplined and planned. We will yield only to avoid heavy losses. But the enemy's advance will be costly. The ground we gained in the first two days of our assault across the Ebro will take the enemy a month to recapture." He raised one gray, bristling eyebrow. "Will this dishearten the political bureaucrats languishing behind their desks in Madrid, Comrade Saludo?"

"If we hold out another week Russian supplies are sure to reach us," said the young officer.

"There is always, too, the hope we still might sweep the enemy back to the Atlantic," said the commander dryly. He stooped over the map and stabbed with his forefinger. "These are the sectors we'll hold to the end. These sectors will yield slowly when pressure is brought upon them. We must plan now for our army to cross the Ebro with the minimum loss of manpower and materiel. The enemy will anticipate our withdrawal. There will be bitter fighting when they strive to prevent our troops crossing."

Commander Calargo straightened up. "Some of our troops must cover the crossing."

There was a tense silence.

The commander's sharp eyes narrowed. "I have selected *your* men, comrades, for that honor." The commander paused and then added gently: "With or *without* material help from the Soviet Union."

The adjutant had a respite from his telephones. He sprawled in his chair with a cigarette dangling from his lower lip, his khaki tunic unbuttoned at the throat. The commander opened a bulging leather briefcase and drew out a thick, manila envelope. He opened it and handed each officer papers that bore his name.

"These are your orders. Your maps will make them explicit. If you lose contact, you will still obey these orders." The commander looked at his watch. "Go away and read them carefully. If anything is not clear, see me before you return to your units. If I don't see you again this side of the Ebro, I know you'll prove to the world no soldier is so valiant as a fighting Spaniard." The commander stood at the door and shook hands with each officer as he left.

Captain Saludo was first up the stone steps into the farmhouse kitchen. He screwed up his eyes as he stepped out into the blaze of the sun. Then he strode briskly across to his military truck. His men were relaxed in its shade and they began to climb to their feet when he approached, but he waved aside formality. "Take it easy, comrades."

He sat with his back resting against a wheel of the truck and took a pack of cigarettes from his tunic pocket. Tobacco was scarce and he made a ritual of lighting the cigarette. Then he sighed, exhaled smoke and unfolded the paper his commander had given him.

Sometime later he sighed again. He folded the paper, replaced it in his pocket and got to his feet. He had no questions. His orders were only too clear.

"Sergeant," he said tiredly. "Let's get moving."

"Where to, Captain?" asked Sergeant Benito Vigon.

"Back to our position."

"Yes, Captain."

The truck backed around, Captain Saludo and Sergeant Vigon sat beside the driver and the rest of the men hunched in the back of the truck as it rumbled over the broken roads. Occasionally a bomb crater split the road apart and the driver had to back up until the roadside ditch was shallow enough to cross, and then lurch over fields until he could gain the road again.

"We have new orders, *mi Capitan?*" asked Benito Vigon curiously.

The captain scowled. "Yes."

The truck bumped on.

"We will see action soon, Captain?"

"Yes," snapped Captain Saludo.

After another long pause Vigon ventured. "Have Headquarters made ambitious plans, Captain?"

Captain Saludo said fiercely: "If you must be so bloody curious, Sergeant, I'll tell you. You and me and the rest of the men are about to become heroes."

"Heroes?"

"Precisely," said the captain. He smiled mirthlessly. "But dead ones, Sergeant. Dead ones!"

Winter came early. By the end of October the autumn rains had come and gone and the earth was iron-hard. At dawn the grass was brittle with frost, ice filmed the water buckets and frostbite was added to the miseries of the men in trenches.

They crouched low behind the parapets, the tips of their ears numbed and cold air knifing their lungs. The government troops were more warmly clad than the Nationalists. Catalan factories turned out jerseys and undershirts that sometimes got through to the front lines.

The summer uniforms of the Nationalists were quite inadequate for the extreme climate. But they were well fed. They controlled the

Atlantic ports. And while government troops grumbled at their
meager rations they knew that in Barcelona and Madrid the people
starved.

November came and the nights grew longer, darker and colder. A
strong wind whirled snow down from the high mountains and it lay
like a white carpet on the plains; it drifted up against the gun emplacements, the trench parapets and shell crater perimeters. The
River Ebro flowed sluggishly as though already thickening into ice,
tugging powerfully at the piers of the wooden emergency bridges sappers had thrown across it.

Sergeant Daniel Frero eyed the swirling river unhappily and shivered in the wind: he had hoped that today the current would flow less
strongly. But there had been heavy rain in the mountains during the
night. He broke a branch from a bush, tossed it into the water and
watched it swiftly swirled away.

Flat-bottomed boats lined the bank, skillfully camouflaged with
green-painted canvas and rope netting entwined with vines. But the
bridge could not be camouflaged. It stood out starkly against the river
and today, as every day, Italian Savoia Marchettis came diving down
from the sky with engines thundering.

Men ran to their slit trenches, a machine gun chattered and tracer
bullets smoked up through the frosty air. Riflemen clapped their
weapons to their shoulders and took careful aim, knowing that sometimes a lucky shot can pierce a fuel tank, smash a prop or kill a pilot.

The planes screamed down at the bridge, but now antiaircraft guns
had got the range and great bursts of shrapnel built an arch of splintering steel above the bridge. Shock waves threw the aircraft about
the sky so violently their run-in was disrupted and the bombs fell
wide of the target.

But as the planes climbed and circled away, another Savoia Mar-
chetti came in low and true on target, taking the antiaircraft gunners
by surprise. A truck was feeling its way cautiously across the bridge
and its driver glanced up and saw the bombing plane flying straight
at him. He lost his head, jumped down from the cabin and ran for the
nearest bank. The truck rolled on driverless, smashed through the
bridge rail and landed on its belly with its front wheels spinning over
the swirling flood below.

The bomber flew on through a haze of flame and smoke. Tommyguns and Maxims chattered and rifles spat. But the Italian plane flew

through it all, its nose rising slightly when it dropped its bombs. The ominous black eggs exploded against the riverbed, sent up great spouts of mud and water and drenched men a hundred yards away. They turned the river into a churning flood of brown cream.

One bomb hit the bridge.

The bombing plane climbed desperately. But a thin plume of black smoke trailed from it and expanded into belching flame. The defenders gave loud shouts of triumph, climbed out of their slit trenches and whooped with glee. Some still continued firing at the plane. It flew on, clawing at the air to climb higher while its wake of black smoke obscured it. When it exploded, a sheet of flame ripped the sky apart and filled it with falling debris.

The sappers muttered disgustedly when they inspected the damage to the bridge and set about repairing it. The work was hazardous. They clung like flies to vibrating wooden stays while the river raged around its piers and the wind tore at them. It was the third hit on the bridge and its framework was sorely strained. The truck that had smashed over its parapet could not be lifted back, so the sappers used wooden props to lever it over into the racing flood. All day they labored, hindered by the snow that began to fall. By dusk the bridge piers had been strengthened, crude stays spread the stresses, and the gaping hole torn in it by the bomb was planked over.

When night fell, troops that had been waiting within sheltered valleys slung their rifles across their shoulders, shuffled into line and set off through the night to the river.

Sergeant Daniel Frero and his unit peeled away the snow-covered camouflage netting over their flat-bottomed craft and dragged the craft down to the water's edge. It was more raft than boat, fashioned from two dinghys connected by wooden planks. Fifty or sixty men could stand on the planking, but their weight sank the hulls dangerously low.

A dozen or more of these craft were ready to ferry men across the river under cover of darkness. But the wind and current were so strong oars could not be relied upon. Rope ends were brought across the bridge and lashed to the crude rafts so they could be hauled across the river and drawn back again for the next cargo.

Strict orders had been issued that no lights should be shown. So when the retreating troops reached the Ebro, there was impenetrable darkness. Only one vehicle at a time could cross the creaking bridge and soon there was a long column of waiting trucks, armored cars and wheeled guns. Troops could follow trucks across the bridge on foot only in single file and ten paces apart.

Guided by shouted orders from dimly seen officers, the retreating soldiers stumbled down to the riverbank and gingerly edged out onto the rafts. They huddled close to each other, sensing the instability of the craft.

Sergeant Frero shone his flashlight quickly on the other bank, pushed the raft off from its bank and allowed its tailing rope to run through his hands. Almost at once the rope burned his palms as the current swept the flimsy craft away. Sergeant Frero shouted, his men leaped to help him and the runaway rope was braked at the cost of many skinned hands. In the darkness Sergeant Frero did not know if the strain on the rope was caused by the comrades on the other bank tugging too strongly, or by the strength of the current.

Daniel Frero's raft reached the other bank safely and, relieved of its human cargo, was easily hauled back across the river. Despite the snow and darkness, Frero's men regained confidence. But now the enemy began to shell the bridge. Gun flashes lit up the horizon, shells whistled overhead and waiting troops cowered under outcrops of rock, in ditches and under trees. Truck drivers awaiting their turn to cross the bridge watched the gun flashes unhappily. The barrage continued ceaselessly. Some shells fell far away but others exploded in the river or on its banks.

When the walking wounded arrived, they were given preference to cross the bridge on foot. But there were far more than could cross during the night. So the rest were helped down the ramp of the bank to embark on the rafts. Their bandages were filthy, some hobbled, aided by tree-branch crutches, some were blind and had to be led, and many were dumb with pain. They were helped onto the rafts and huddled closely in the darkness, hunching their shoulders against gusts of snow-laden wind.

An officer came running along the bank. "Sergeant Frero. Sergeant Frero. Cross over with the next raft. Find out what those fools are doing on the other side. We're not getting the men across quickly enough."

"It's the river, Captain. The current's so strong that . . ."

"I know that. Do something about it. Hitch on stronger ropes; use more men."

"Yes, Captain."

Sergeant Frero's raft was ready to leave. He gave swift orders to his corporal, climbed aboard and shouted: "Cast off!"

As soon as the raft left the bank, he sensed the fury of the river vibrating the planks he stood upon. The fierce wind snatched at the raft and rushed it downstream. The wounded huddled closer and the man next to Frero moaned.

"Courage, comrade," comforted Sergeant Frero. "When we're across the river your wound will be dressed."

"Holy Mother of Mercy," moaned the man.

When the raft was midstream the current fought the straining muscles of the men on the far bank. The river roared, water foamed and white-crested waves rocked the craft dangerously. Distant gun flashes reflected on the water and through the whirling snowflakes Frero glimpsed other rafts bobbing like corks, their restraining ropes stretched taut. The whimpers of the wounded were a ghostly wail sighing on the wind.

Frero's raft rocked dangerously. Now it was being towed upriver, butting into wavelets until spray drenched the passengers.

Upriver a shell scored a direct hit on a team of men hauling in a loaded raft. The released tow rope smoked through its block-and-tackle and the raft swirled wildly as it hurtled downstream. It was pulled up with a jerk by its tailing rope which was instantly ripped from the grasp of the men holding it, and the raft raced on downriver. It snagged on the next tow rope, slid along it and smashed into the next raft. Tow ropes snapped and men spilled into the raging torrent.

Daniel Frero heard shouts of alarm above the shriek of the wind and glanced up to see a great churning mass of wreckage hurtling toward him. It swirled past, rolling over and over, missing them by scant yards. But a split second later a shocking jolt tumbled the wounded men like playing cards. The wreckage had fouled the raft's tailing rope and snapped it. Miraculously the towing rope held. But the raft tipped perilously, taking water over the dinghy gunwales. The panic-stricken wounded men surged to the other side of the raft and it lurched violently and wallowed. Daniel Frero could feel it settling as the overladen hulls filled. He groped for the broken end of the tailing rope, hauled it in and thrust it through the darkness at the man beside him. "Tie this around your waist."

The man cried out. Sergeant Frero had nudged his shattered arm. And at the same moment, one of the dinghys sank. The raft keeled over, spilling men into the water like a handful of rice.

Sergeant Frero clung to the rope as his world overturned and the next moment was in icy water that numbed his lungs. The rope snapped taut with a jolt that all but tore his arms from their sockets. He sensed men being swept away, helpless in the black flood. He passed the rope around his chest and managed to knot it. The rope cut into his chest and armpits but now he could use his fast failing strength to keep his face above water. Before him was the dark mass of the waterlogged raft that the current was sweeping across the river.

The raft crashed into the far bank and Sergeant Frero tried to stand but couldn't find bottom. He clawed at the crumbling, sandy bank. Then he heard voices and he shouted. His strangled cry was whipped away by the wind, but men heard him and hauled him up to safety.

He lay vomiting water and shivering violently. After a time he felt stronger and rose to his feet with the help of the men who had saved him. They took him upstream to report to the officer in charge.

The officer swore. "Four rafts lost and all those men swept away! All right, Sergeant. You've done all you could. Stay this side of the river and get warm."

"Yes, Captain," said Daniel Frero. His teeth chattered violently.

A Catalan militiaman led Sergeant Frero to a dugout, helped him strip off his clothing and lent him a blanket. Another soldier brought him a mug of brandy and a cigarette.

Presently the numbness left his limbs. Sergeant Frero complained bitterly in Catalan. "All those wounded comrades . . . lost!"

"We had it bad this side too, Sergeant. We lost thirty men with one shellburst."

"Those Fascist bastards!" said Sergeant Frero.

The man who had loaned him the blanket said: "I've seen you before, comrade."

Sergeant Frero eyed him curiously. "I don't remember . . . ?"

"In Figueras. A couple of years ago, just as the war started. You were speaking at a meeting . . . !"

"I remember Figueras," said Sergeant Frero. He studied the sturdily built man with broad shoulders and a shy smile. "But I don't remember you, comrade."

"I was one of the audience. My name is Juan Morales. My father
. . . my father is mayor of Escoleras."

"You are from Escoleras?"

"I was born there. You are from Figueras?"

"No. I am from Badalona."

"I have relatives in Badalona."

Outside sounded the *whoosh* and concussion of an exploding shell.
Dirt and earth pattered like rain and choking dust swirled in through
the doorway.

"How is it on the other bank, Comrade Sergeant?" asked Juan
Morales.

Sergeant Frero drew deeply on his cigarette. He said carefully:
"We never falter in our resistance to fascism."

"I understand," said Juan Morales quietly. "But . . . *how* are
things on the other bank?"

Sergeant Frero sighed. "Bad," he admitted. "There are many
wounded and the men are disheartened."

In the early hours of the morning the orders came to move out. It
was a quiet night and only occasional shells whistled over as the
troops clawed themselves up out of their foxholes.

They were wasted ghosts: exhausted, starved, and shell-shocked.
They stumbled glassy-eyed away from the lines they had held so tenaciously.

Down the slopes to the waiting army trucks staggered the remnants
of the company that had covered the retreat of the government forces
over the Ebro.

Captain Saludo wore a bloody bandage holding in place a large flap
of flesh. Shrapnel had all but scalped him and exposed the naked
bone of his skull. He suffered terrible headaches, spells of blindness
and at times his mind wandered. He depended increasingly upon Sergeant Vigon, who walked beside him. Vigon's cheeks were gaunt and
his eyes were sunken. But he cared for Captain Saludo and steered
him around shell craters into which he would have fallen.

Empty ammunition boxes were placed under the truck tailboards
and the badly wounded were helped up first. The other men
clambered into the remaining trucks and huddled together, swaying
as the trucks lurched over the potholed roads.

The trucks rolled on toward the Ebro, groping down winding

roads, using only blue-painted side-lights. The throb of their engines radiated outward through the darkness and dominated the night. Finally the line of trucks squealed to a standstill at a bridge and there was the inevitable waiting as they crossed one at a time.

Sergeant Benito Vigon was in the last truck and as it slowly moved up to the bridge an officer appeared at the tailboard.

"Who's in charge here?"

"Captain Saludo," said Sergeant Vigon.

"I wish to speak to him."

"A head injury, sir. His mind's wandering."

"Who's relieved him?"

"I've taken charge, sir. There's nobody else."

"What's your name?"

"Sergeant Vigon."

"Who is behind you, Sergeant?"

"We're at the rear of our company, sir."

"Then there's nobody else behind you?"

"I don't know about other brigades, *mi Capitan*."

"They've all crossed. Yours is the last."

The truck jolted, and moved up as another truck groped its way across the shaking bridge.

"Jump down, Sergeant."

Wearily Benito Vigon dropped over the tailboard.

"We'll walk down to the bridge, Sergeant."

"At your orders, Captain."

They paced slowly along the line of waiting trucks. Benito Vigon limped.

"It was tough back there, Sergeant?"

"Very tough, Captain."

"Cigarette?"

Benito Vigon took the cigarette gratefully. The officer held a match for him and he sucked the acrid smoke down into his lungs with relish. Through the darkness, somebody shouted. *"Coño!* Put that bloody light out!"

"Tired?" asked the officer sympathetically.

"We haven't slept for days."

"Try this, Sergeant. It will pep you up."

Vigon took the hip flask and tilted it against his lips. He drank only a little.

"Take a good gulp, man. Drink it all. I can draw more."

Vigon drank greedily. The warm sting of the brandy was heavenly. He handed back the almost empty hip-flask with a sigh of contentment and wiped the back of his hand across his lips.

"What's the mood of the men, Sergeant? Are they despondent?"

"They're exhausted, Captain. They've been through hell. Continuous shelling, no food, no sleep, no medical attention . . ."

"You and your men will go to the rear. You'll get leave and adequate rations."

"The men deserve it, Captain."

"Another cigarette, Sergeant?"

"Thank you, Captain."

The officer carefully cupped the match in his hand. "Three or four days' rest and they'll be fit again, Sergeant?"

"Three or four days isn't long enough, Captain."

"We may have to recall them quickly."

"Men are flesh and blood, Captain."

"They'll resent being recalled so soon?"

"It's a matter of endurance, Captain. Can they not be given a fortnight's leave?"

"We'll need every man, Sergeant."

Surprise was in Vigon's voice. "Another big battle, Captain?"

The officer sighed. "Our retreat has heartened the Nationalists. They'll launch a large-scale attack across the Ebro before we've time to dig in."

"But . . . during these weeks of fighting there's been plenty of time to dig in, Captain."

The officer scowled. "You know we Spanish leave everything until *mañana!*"

At the approach to the bridge was the entrance to a dugout cut into the sloping bank that lined the road. The officer urged Vigon through the sack-clothed doorway into a large earth chamber roofed with planking. It smelled of fuel, tar and damp earth.

Vigon blinked until his eyes were accustomed to the kerosene lamp. He saw a trestle table with maps and telephones, cases of supplies stacked around the walls and a charcoal brazier. A uniformed clerk half rose but resumed writing when the officer gestured to him.

Vigon saw now that the officer was slim and young, no more than twenty-three or four. His eyes were pale blue and he had a mischievous grin. He crossed to a crate, levered off its top with a screech of nails and drew out two bottles of brandy. He gave them to Vigon. "Take these when you go, Sergeant. Give the men a bracer."

"Thank you, *mi Capitan*."

"Take these too." The officer opened another crate and took out two boxes of cigars.

Sergeant Vigon was embarrassed. "This will mean a lot to the men, sir."

The officer chuckled. "Don't thank me. Thank the Nationalists. We captured these stores when we first attacked across the river."

"Thank you, sir. I'll take these to the men at once and . . ."

"No hurry, Sergeant. A long time yet before your truck crosses the bridge."

"My comrades will be grateful for the brandy and . . ."

"Relax, Sergeant. Relax. Sit on that packing case."

Sergeant Vigon sank down and sighed gratefully. The brandy in his empty belly was spreading a comforting glow.

An orderly entered and saluted. "Captain Sagon."

"What is it?"

"You sent for the commander of the Steel Corps, sir?"

"That's right."

"He's outside, Captain."

"Send him in."

Two men entered, their worn khaki uniforms bearing the insignia of the Steel Corps. One was broad-shouldered and stocky, with raven-black hair. His companion was younger and slimly built.

Captain Sagon said briskly. "This convoy is the last. As soon as it's on the other bank we'll blow the bridge. When the last truck crosses, fall back across the river and report to me so I can give demolition orders to the sappers."

The stocky man glowered. "As you say, comrade." His voice raised a pitch. "This is only a technical retreat, comrade. We will hold the Ebro against the Fascist swine."

"Yes, of course, comrade," soothed Captain Sagon.

Sergeant Vigon stared at the stocky man. He vaguely recognized him despite the raised, red welt that scarred the man's cheek from eyebrow to jaw. Then the voice struck a cord of memory. "Miguel!" he said delightedly. "Miguel Barras!"

Miguel's swarthy skin had yellowed and his face was aged. He scowled into Vigon's red-rimmed eyes and slowly recognition came to him, too. "Comrade Vigon!" he said. But there was no warmth in his voice.

"You two know each other?" said Captain Sagon.

"We are from the same village, Captain."

"Then you'll have things to talk about while I check with the sappers." The captain left the dugout.

The two men stared at each other curiously.

"I didn't know you, Miguel, because of the scar."

"A scar is of no importance, comrade."

"What news have you of home?" Vigon asked. "For two months I have received no letters."

Miguel said tautly. "For me there is only the front line and the fight against fascism."

The slim youth tugged at Miguel's arm. "Soon we must fall back so they can blow the bridge." The youth's left eyelid drooped, pulled down at its corner by a livid scar.

Miguel shook himself. "We must go, comrade," he told Vigon. His left fist came up in the clenched fist salute. *"No pasaran!"*

"No pasaran, Miguel," said Vigon sadly. He watched them file out of the dugout and sighed.

The uniformed clerk glanced up. "So you know him?"

"I thought I did."

"They're wonderful fighters; completely fearless."

"He didn't even offer to shake hands," sighed Vigon.

"Anti-Fascists can't be sentimentalists."

Benito Vigon said slowly: "I'm against the Fascists. I hate them. But I like to shake the hand of an old friend. Is that bad?"

The clerk scowled. "Don't expect me to criticize a party man." He buried his nose in his ledger.

Captain Sagon did not return. After a while Vigon went outside and saw his truck was soon to cross the bridge. He climbed up over the tailboard and passed the bottles of brandy around. Then the cherry-red glowworms of cigars warmed the darkness.

The truck moved up, crossed the swaying bridge, bumped down onto firm ground and speeded to catch up with the convoy.

The brandy had revived the men and presently one began to sing quietly. Another joined him. Then another. Soon they were all singing and Benito Vigon fought back his tears that men so battleworn should have so much courage.

Half an hour after the last truck crossed the bridge Captain Sagon

gave the demolition order. The plunger was rammed home and the
bridge disintegrated. As the echoes of the explosion died away, Captain Sagon's aide said consolingly: "It's taken them weeks to win back
what we gained in a few days."

"But we've lost more men and materiel in these last few weeks than
is believable."

"But we fought well, *mi Capitan.*"

"Too well," said Captain Sagon bitterly. He stared out across the
swiftly flowing river. "Some of us reached this side of the Ebro," he
said grimly. "But the best of our army lies on the other side, where
the sun dies."

2

In the Nationalist prison camp, Anselmo Ledesma had lost all sense
of time. He responded only to the goad of hunger and pain.

The cold was the worst. It bit through his summer clothing, turned
his flesh mauve and numbed his senses. The prisoners survived icy
nights only by huddling like pigs and sharing their bodily warmth. In
the mornings their clothing was frozen stiff and ice matted their
moustaches and beards. Nearly always somebody died during the
night.

Anselmo Ledesma knew he was close to death.

His limbs were sticks and his ribs stood out starkly. He was tormented by the lice in his hair and beard, and the crab lice that burrowed into his groin. His abdomen was raw from the frenzied scratching of his dirt-rimmed nails.

The worst of all was his leg ulcer. It grew malignantly as though
thriving on its own festering pus. It had eaten a hole in his leg the size
of his fist. He covered it with a filthy rag but it still smelled abominably. Nobody in the camp received medical treatment, but a fellow
prisoner who had been a hospital orderly said his leg wouldn't heal
until he was physically fit. Like the other prisoners he was dying
slowly of starvation. Some prisoners, those who had been dying the
longest, had even eaten the excretion of others.

Anselmo Ledesma did not want to die. But he wanted to face death bravely and not drag out existence. So, every day he considered running to the barbed-wire stockade and climbing it swiftly while the guards threw up their rifles and squeezed their triggers. He had seen dozens die like that. One man's clothing had snagged on the barbs and the guards had left him hanging there as a warning.

The guards were a mixed bunch. Some of the older ones felt sorry for their prisoners. A one-armed, gray-haired guard sometimes dropped scraps of food on the ground close to the barbed wire and turned his back so he would not see Anselmo's arm stretch out for it.

But some of the younger guards were political fanatics and took pleasure in their prisoners' suffering. They ate in front of their victims, threw down scraps of food and when hungry hands reached out, used rifle butts to mash fingers against the ice-hard ground.

One sadistic officer paraded the prisoners and asked for twelve volunteers. Nobody stepped forward. The officer insulted them as cowards until first one prisoner and then another stepped forward.

The twelve volunteers were led out of the stockade and the other prisoners watched enviously when they were given cigarettes. Then they were lined up and marched off. Ten minutes later there was the stutter of a machine gun. When the volunteers did not return, their fellow prisoners realized that they had volunteered . . . to be shot by a firing squad!

One day a group of officials toured the camp. The guards entered the prisoners' compound and herded them back with tommyguns until the officials could stand in a space cleared for them. They stared around bleakly. They were an investigating committee appointed by the Nationalists to prepare a report on conditions in prison camps which would be submitted to the International Red Cross.

The emaciated, ragged and vermin-infested prisoners pressed forward curiously. The committee members stared back.

Anselmo forced aside other prisoners until he was in the front rank. A guard eyed him warningly and menaced him with his tommygun.

Among the committee members was a man Anselmo recognized as a friend of his father's; a chemist who had cooperated with Baudillo Ledesma in analyzing the farm's soil. It had been many years ago and the chemist had moved to San Sebastian long before the war. But Anselmo had not forgotten the man's high, craggy forehead and determined jaw.

"Señor Chiminez," he called. His voice was weak and reedy, lost in the vastness of the open air.

The committee was turning away and the guard jabbed his tommygun menacingly. "Get back there. Stand back!"

Anselmo's throat muscles seemed knotted. He screamed the name but it came out like a strangled groan. "Señor Chiminez!"

"Silence," snarled the guard. "Back up!"

But miraculously the chemist heard his name called. He turned, ear cocked and eyes alert.

Anselmo waved his thin sticks of arms. "Señor Chiminez," he choked and flinched as the guard drew back his tommygun as though to lunge.

The chemist peered at Anselmo shortsightedly, his curiosity aroused. "How do you know my name?"

The guard grudgingly allowed Anselmo to answer. "I am Anselmo Ledesma from Escoleras," he panted. "You were a friend of my father. You visited our house many times."

Señor Chiminez stared at the bearded, vermin-infested prisoner coldly, shrugged his shoulders and turned away.

"Señor Chiminez!" The desperate entreaty forced him to turn back.

"My father was your friend, Señor Chiminez. The Reds killed him! I escaped, but I've been a prisoner here for months. Help me. Please help me!"

"What do you expect me to do?"

"Talk to somebody in authority. Get my case heard. I'm not a Red."

The other officials had reached the compound gate and were waiting for Chiminez. He nodded curtly. "I'll see what I can do." He turned away.

Hope buoyed up Anselmo then, but as the days passed, his despair returned. Anselmo had quite forgotten Chiminez when two guards entered the compound and called his name. He limped across to them painfully, holding his trousers up around his wasted hips.

"You're Anselmo Ledesma?"

He nodded.

"Where are you from?"

"Escoleras."

"Follow us."

They took him out of the compound and across the forecourt to a shed. "Strip and shower," they ordered.

He stripped and stepped under a shower. Icy needles sloughed away his top coat of filth. There was no towel and he was shivering when he pulled on the clean pants and shirt they gave him. They marched him to an interrogation room where a bleak-faced officer seated at a wooden table kept him waiting for almost an hour before he pointed to a hard-backed chair facing him. "Sit," he ordered.

For a long time he stared at a filing card, reading it over. Finally he asked, "You're Anselmo Ledesma?"

"*Sí*, Señor."

"From Escoleras?"

"*Sí*, Señor."

"You were in the Red sector?"

"I was conscripted in Barcelona."

"How did you get to France?"

"I deserted after the Reds—killed my father."

The bleak eyes of the interrogator stared stonily. "How do I know you're not a spy planning sabotage?"

Anselmo gulped. "It's difficult to prove a negative."

The eyes turned hostile. "How do I know you deserted? How do I know you didn't plot to desert to our side and betray us?"

Anselmo could not answer.

The officer shrugged his shoulders and glanced back at the filing card. "Anything else you can tell me?"

Anselmo leaned forward, his eyes burning. "They killed my father! No man will fight for those who've murdered his flesh and blood."

The officer's voice was dull and disinterested. "How do I know they killed your father?"

"It can be proved in Escoleras."

"But not here!" The chair creaked as the officer moved and Anselmo knew he had achieved nothing. He said desperately: "I have a brother on this side who will vouch for me."

The officer paused in the act of returning the filing card to its box. His gray eyes stared curiously.

"My brother, Rafael, was a cadet in the Alcazar when the war started. He must have received the news of our father's death."

"How?" The officer's voice was steely. "Do you allege there is communication between our side and the Reds?"

"Mother wrote to Rafael to tell him about father. She sent the letter to Switzerland through friends. The message may . . . may have got through."

The officer sighed and wrote on the index card. "All right. That's all."

The guards took Anselmo to the infirmary. There were bars across the window and armed guards patrolled the building. Some of the patients were recovering from wounds, but most of them were ill from malnutrition.

A watery soup of boiled vegetables with sometimes a piece of meat floating in it was served three times a day. A ration of black bread made from crushed maize was issued every morning. On this meager diet Anselmo grew stronger and even put on flesh. A doctor examined his ulcer, soaked cotton wool with surgical alcohol and swabbed the raw wound clean. He plugged the open sore with a crystalline powder. Anselmo lay bathed in sweat, so weak that the sharp sting of antiseptic brought him close to fainting. But the ulcer quickly responded to treatment and within days was drying up.

The patients talked little about themselves. They were uncomfortably conscious of their guards and the bars at the windows, and chose their words carefully, as though on probation. Some had been delivered to the Nationalist frontier by French guards, some had crossed the frontier clandestinely and others had surrendered in battle. One man, who had been shot by a Nationalist sentry, claimed he had deliberately led his patrol into captivity. All of the patients loudly praised the Nationalist army and General Franco and bitterly indicted the government. They all prayed fervently when the priest visited the ward to hold a service.

Finally, Anselmo was taken for interrogation. He sat opposite the officer and looked nervously into the man's cold gray eyes.

"We have received a report from your brother. He confirms your father died while imprisoned by the Reds. It has been decided you can enlist with the Nationalist forces, Ledesma."

Anselmo gulped. "That means . . . I'll be released."

"You'll leave here with others who are enlisting."

"I understand, Señor."

"You will take an oath to be loyal to General Franco."

"*Sí*, Señor."

"I must warn you we are filing your dossier."

"I understand, Señor."

"Do your duty as a soldier, be true to God and the Virgin Mary and you have nothing to fear."

"I have no fears, Señor."

"But . . . if you neglect your duties . . . your record will count against you. Your allegiance to General Franco will become suspect."

"I'm not a traitor, Señor."

The officer sighed. "I certainly hope not."

Twenty-four hours later Anselmo Ledesma swore allegiance to General Franco, was issued a uniform and went with many others to the station to await the troop train that would take them to the front.

A torrential downpour filled the mountain streams with racing, muddy water. The heavy rain awakened Hernando. He lit a kerosene lamp, drank from his goatskin bottle and rolled a cigarette while he watched the drumming curtain turn the sand into a moat around his stone hut. When the rain finally stopped, he rolled up his trousers and took a flashlight and a potato sack to the river. It was dawn when Hernando returned to his cottage. He built a fire and filled a cooking pot with water. He dropped into it peeled potatoes, onions, tomatoes. and sage from the mountain. A branch of dried *guindilla* hung on the wall and he broke off a pod, cut it into small pieces and sprinkled the hot pepper into the water while he stirred.

Doctor Aldo was tiredly plodding homeward along the beach. He stopped to talk to Hernando who sat crosslegged on a straw mat before an old fish box which served as a table. *"Bon día,"* said the doctor. He stooped, and rested his battered medical bag on the sand.

"Bon día, Juan," said Hernando. He smiled up at the doctor and offered him the goatskin wine bottle.

"Thank you, no," refused the doctor. He wiped his forehead with his handkerchief. "I have drunk too much coffee. I dislike coffee. It spoils the palate. But it wards off sleep."

"You were called out?" guessed Hernando without curiosity. He wiped a large knife and placed it on one side of his table. "It is a privilege to be of service to one's fellowman," he said solemnly. "But a man should also have time to attend to his personal affairs."

The doctor sighed. "The Hippocratic oath is a serious liability, Hernando." Then he smiled and his face lit up. "Wars come and wars go, but life goes on. José Guitart tonight became the father of twins. Both girls, and as pretty as buds in spring."

"It is good to hear of new life in these days of death," said Hernando soberly. "José Guitart will be very proud." He paused and then added: "When he hears the news!"

"You too have worked tonight," said Doctor Aldo, nodding at the half-filled sack which rippled with movement.

"The rain brought its abundance." Hernando untied the mouth of the sack and reached inside. "It will be an honor if you will eat with me, Juan."

"It will be *my* honor," said the doctor. He watched Hernando draw out a green-skinned frog as large as his fist and hold it down firmly on the fish-box table. "It is a big one, Hernando."

"They are all this size, Juan. The small ones I left in the long grass to grow fat." He picked up his big knife.

"We are lucky, Hernando," said the doctor. "We in the villages do not starve. There is always fish to be caught, a potato or a turnip in a farmer's barn, a new-laid egg or a newborn lamb. You have your endless larder, Hernando; rabbits, partridges, snails, frogs . . . how about squirrels, Hernando? Is squirrel good to eat?"

Hernando held the frog still, and with one firm stroke cut it in two through its middle. He pushed the head and forelegs to one side and they hopped across the table trailing bloody entrails until they fell off the edge and writhed in the sand. Hernando skillfully skinned the haunches and back legs and tossed them, still twitching, into the sim-mering pot. "Squirrel should be eaten with rice," he said. "But it must be spiced. Squirrel flesh is tough and tasteless. Now a hedgehog . . . that is different. Baked hedgehog is delicious!" His brown hand groped for another frog. "I have never eaten snake," he said as his knife cut deep. He deftly peeled skin from the quivering haunches. "Man is repelled by snakes," he said thoughtfully. "This repugnance I do not understand, Juan, because an eel is a water snake and an eel I will eat with relish."

"It is all in the mind," said the doctor. "Anything that nourishes is good to eat. Snake meat can be as easily dissolved by human digestive juices as lamb, pork, chicken or beef. They say there are no cats, dogs nor donkeys in Madrid or Barcelona because all have been eaten. Even sewer rats are hunted. When the belly is full, it is easy to be squeamish. But hunger can make even snake meat change its taste!"

"This war!" said Hernando, shaking his head and cutting busily. "Are we all mad, Juan? Nobody wants war. Yet we are in the midst of suffering and killing that nobody wants!"

"The world *is* mad," confirmed Doctor Aldo laconically. "War is madness. But it is not lasting. Otherwise mankind would soon destroy itself."

Hernando chuckled. "Perhaps that would be a good thing for the other species, eh, Doctor?"

"I do not think the war can last much longer, Hernando."

"I hope what you say is true, Juan." Hernando eyed the bubbling pot with satisfaction. "I do not read newspapers and know little of the lies that are circulated."

"The government has retreated across the Ebro and the Nationalists attack with increasing fury. Every day the fighting draws closer, Hernando. It may even come to our village."

"If we are sensible, we will cross the mountains into France before that day comes," said Hernando.

"You have used *guindilla*, Hernando?"

"Naturally. Hot pepper brings out the subtle flavor of frogs' legs."

"How many pods, Hernando?"

"One."

The doctor was scandalized. "Only one!"

"My *guindillas* are dynamite, Juan."

"But in a pot so big you need at least two."

"In a pot so small, two *guindillas* would burn the skin off your lips."

"You invite me to eat with you, yet deny me spice!"

"I will compromise, Juan," surrendered Hernando. "I will add another half *guindilla*."

"This talk makes me hungry, Hernando. How long before it is ready?"

"Return in an hour or so, Juan."

"What will you do with these?" The doctor nudged the quivering mountain of frogs' forelegs with his toe.

"They make good fish bait."

"Have you remembered salt for the pot?"

"I have remembered the salt, Juan. Do not fear. The gravy will be seasoned and the frogs' legs will be as toothsome as the breast of a spring chicken."

Doctor Aldo consulted his watch. "I must hurry." He sighed, picked up his battered medical bag and tiredly trudged away across the wet sand.

In the plaza he came upon Father Delbos talking with two widows. The priest hurried across the road to meet him. "Good morning,

Doctor. I know you are a busy man, but I beg a few minutes of your precious time."

Doctor Aldo disliked the priest's fawning insincerity. He said dryly: "I can spare a few minutes."

"This coming Sunday I will hold a service in the village church. You have heard how the will of God has asserted itself."

"I am aware religious worship is no longer suppressed," said the doctor dryly.

Father Delbos smiled uncertainly. "I want my first service to be a success, Doctor. I expect the cooperation of everyone. I look to you, Doctor, to give me every assistance and spread the word. A crowded church will demonstrate, as never before, the resentment people feel for their oppressors."

"If it pleases you to hold a service on Sunday, Father Delbos, I am content. But I hope you will pray for peace and not the victory of one side only."

Father Delbos flushed. "I am not ashamed of my faith, Doctor. We suffer under the reign of Anti-Christ but must hold true to God and the Virgin Mary. The forces of evil will be conquered and men will live again through their love of God and of what is right."

"If God brings this bloody war to a swift conclusion, I'll ask no more of him," said the doctor quietly.

"I am sure your prayers will be answered," said Father Delbos devoutly. He smiled silkily. "I insist, Doctor. It is your moral duty to urge your patients to attend church next Sunday."

Doctor Aldo bit back an angry retort. "Good day, Father Delbos."

"Go with God, Doctor Aldo."

The doctor smoldered with suppressed fury. He was agnostic. But as a doctor, he knew the spiritual comfort religion can give to simple, uncomplicated minds. He did not arouse doubts in the minds of those who benefited from prayer and meditation. But it angered him that the simple faith of ordinary people was used by men like Father Delbos as a political weapon.

Doctor Aldo was still brooding about Father Delbos when he saw villagers hurrying down the sloping, cobbled street toward the harbor. A boy went past at a run and the doctor grasped him by the arm. "What is it, Pepe? What's happening?"

"A warship's coming into the harbor!"

Doctor Aldo turned and hurried after the villagers. When he

reached the quay he shielded his eyes against the sun and stared out across the misty water at a thick plume of smoke on the horizon.

The gunboat was some miles off shore and ranged up and down, broadside to the village, like a terrier searching out a rat.

Some said it was a British warship policing foreign intervention, some said it was a government destroyer and one man swore it was a Russian gunboat. Those who owned telescopes focused them on the sinister, gray hull. But the warship flew no flag and there was much excited speculation before Jesus Guitart, who that very morning had become a grandfather, warned tersely as he gazed through a powerful telescope, "They're breaking out the flag now."

The villagers waited in silence.

There was a sharp intake of breath from Jesus Guitart. "It's a Nationalist gunboat!"

"A Nationalist gunboat," a man shouted loudly.

"A Franco gunboat. But what's it doing . . . *here?*"

"Perhaps it means the end of the war."

"It wants to surrender?"

"It's some kind of trick."

A man shouted: "The military must be told. Run and tell the soldiers!"

But Captain Garon had long since been alerted and a few minutes later he galloped along the beach and spurred his mount through the river and up the steep path to the gun emplacement on the heights behind the village.

Soldiers strolled down to the harbor and watched idly with their rifles slung over their shoulders and cigarettes drooping from their mouths.

"You're right, Guitart," said a man with a telescope. "I can see the Nationalist flag clearly."

"What are they up to?"

"Do they know about it in Barcelona? They could send a bombing plane. One egg would send it to the bottom!"

Jesus Guitart closed his telescope and packed it away in its leather container. He wore a black patch over the eye he had lost in a shooting accident and walked with a marked limp. Years ago he had been stung by a water spider. Blood infection followed, surgeons removed a piece of bone from his shin and one leg was now shorter than the other. Guitart was a democrat and he had been given command of a small fishing boat armed with machine guns to patrol this section of the coast. "No bombing plane will get within accurate bombing range of *that* gunboat," he stated knowledgeably. "It can put up an antiaircraft barrage that'll knock any plane out of the sky!"

Nobody was worried about the Nationalist gunboat. The young soldiers strolled away and the villagers were drifting homeward when they heard a thin, high-pitched whistle that might have been a distant train or a factory siren. While everyone looked around in surprise, the whistle became deafening, and a shell exploded on the slopes close to the summit of the mountain behind the village. There was a yellow flash and a great spreading cloud of smoke and dust. Afterward came the sound of the explosion, a terrifying thunderclap. The shock waves made the earth shake. There was another shrill whistling and those who looked toward the warship saw the stab of flame as a third shell was fired.

Women screamed, men shouted, and abruptly there was panic. Soldiers, men and women fled wildly, seeking shelter like rabbits running to their burrow. They huddled under tables in their stone-built houses, cowered beneath carts in their barns and quaked in underground cellars. But the shelling was harmlessly directed at the mountain behind the village and presently a few men left their refuges to watch the shells bursting.

When Captain Garon arrived at the concrete gun emplacements, he slid down off his sweating mount, snatched the binoculars an orderly gave him, focused them on the distant gunboat and asked crisply: "Have you got the range?"

"They're beyond range, Captain."

Captain Garon thought for a moment. "Start firing anyhow. Six rounds each gun."

Orders rang out and the coastal guns fired.

The guns were high above the village and their thunder shocked the cottages to their foundations. But those villagers who were watching saw that the white plumes of water from the exploding shells were nearer to the shore than to the gunboat.

Presently the shore guns fell silent. Only an occasional shell now exploded upon the mountains behind the village.

More and more people came out of their houses to watch the occasional eruptions of smoke and ravaged earth.

And then one shell fell short!

It exploded on the outskirts of the village, destroying two cottages and a stable, killing two elderly women and a man, and all their livestock. Neighbors were seriously injured.

Villagers plunged back into their refuges.

But Jesus Guitart flew into a terrible rage. He shook his fist at the gunboat and his black beard bristled fiercely. He shouted passionately, as though he could be heard: "You bastards! You wicked, black bastards! I shit upon the mother who gave you birth." His good eye flashed fiercely as he limped from house to house, battering at doors, shouting insults and goading men into action.

"Juan Costa, don't skulk!" He roared, kicking open the man's door. "I shit upon the coward's milk that weaned you!"

He raged through the village, his impassioned fury inspiring his followers. The wilder his oaths the greater his following.

"I shit upon the breast of the Virgin Mary and of cowards who do not fight back!"

"I shit upon the sea and on God!"

"I shit upon the *coño* of the Virgin Mary and all the sons of prostitutes on that Franco warship!"

Another shell whined overhead. It fell outside the village, but much closer than the villagers liked. There was a howl of rage from the men following Jesus Guitart and he no longer needed to urge them on. Now they ran on ahead of him and reached the coastal patrol boat before he did. The diesel engine fired and the men on deck cheered as powerful pistoning vibrated the deck. Jesus Guitart limped to the wheelhouse, shaking his fist at the distant gunboat. "Cast off," he roared and as the bow swung away from the dock he pushed the buzzer to the engine room for full speed ahead. The propeller churned and white wash arrowed out behind the converted fishing boat.

Jesus Guitart steered straight toward the Nationalist gunboat, beckoned a man to take over the helm and stumped to the bow of the craft where two Maxim machine guns were mounted on fixed tripods.

"I shit on the Italian and German navy," Guitart stormed. "Get that gun swiveling loosely. Make sure it won't jam. I shit upon the sea and *maricones*. Never before have I seen such *maricones*. These are machine guns, not powderpuffs. They are to tear men apart with leaden teeth, not to sweeten a donkey's ass with honeyed caresses!"

The machine guns swiveled, their crews sweated, the ammunition boxes were placed ready and Jesus Guitart stumped to the engine-room hatchway. With reckless disregard of personal safety, he slid down the metal ladder.

The engine cylinder was taller than he and twice his girth. It sat solidly on massive engine bearers and every time its piston drove down, it shook the vessel from stern to stem. As Guitart faced his engineer the flooring jogged them with the rhythm of the pounding piston.

"We need more speed, Manolo," said Guitart.

"The fuel cocks are wide open. She's doing the maximum."

"I shit upon the sea and your fuel cocks. Listen, *maricon;* one who is content with such slowness is not fit even to suck the ass of a donkey. We need more speed. We *must* have more speed or the Fascist sons of whoring nuns will escape us."

"You are mad, Jesus. How can an engine work faster than its maximum?"

"When does a cow give better milk? When does a horse work harder?"

"That's different," said Manolo. "It's a question of feed. When you give a horse oats instead of straw . . ."

"An engine is a horse, *maricon!* A metal horse! Change its diet. Give it food that will make it run faster! Even if you make it drunk it doesn't matter. Speed is essential!"

"Do you want me to blow up the boat, you crazy one-eyed maniac?"

"You have gasoline?"

"A ten-gallon drum."

"Pour it into the fuel tank," ordered Jesus Guitart and dragged his short leg across to the ladder and climbed up on deck.

The gunboat was far ahead, a low-lying, ominous gray silhouette, and as Guitart looked at it, he saw a pinpoint of yellow flame as another shell whistled toward the coast.

"You whoring black bastard," he panted, stumping toward the bow and shaking his fist, his black beard bristling and his one eye glittering furiously. The machine-gun crews hunched down behind their weapons, their faces drawn and grim. "Give them a burst. Give the bastards hell!" roared Jesus Guitart and the machine guns chattered.

From the gun emplacement, high above the village, Captain Garon saw the fishing vessel set off.

"The crazy fools!" he said aloud. "They must be out of their minds." But there was a prickling at the back of the eyes which made him blink furiously.

The gunboat's funnel belched black smoke as it zigzagged in toward the coast. Its behavior was so curious that many villagers suppressed their fear and gathered on the harbor wall to watch Jesus Guitart's tiny patrol vessel heading toward the grim, gray silhouette.

"That Jesus Guitart!" said one man. "He's . . ." He broke off searching for the right word and found it with surprise. "He's . . . he's a hero!"

"He's mad. They haven't a chance!"

"What does it matter?" said the first speaker. "To be a man is the important thing. To be a man and unafraid."

Jesus Guitart ordered that the machine guns be warmed up again; their sharp staccato chatter carried across the water to the harbor and the watching villagers gave a cheer.

But Jesus Guitart's wife clapped her hands to her cheeks and rocked from side to side. "Oh, the woe of me! Ah . . . that crazy man of mine! Oh dearest, kindest Holy Mary, I pray thee to save him. He's a coarse man with his rough ways and bad words but he is not a wicked man. Holy Mary, Mother of Christ, save him from his wicked pride and sinfulness."

"Be quiet, woman," complained her brother-in-law. "Would you rob a man of his finest moment?"

"Ayeee!" wailed Constancia Guitart.

"That Jesus. He's crazy, that one!" said Marcel Prada enviously.

Paco Barras had been counting cases of fish being unloaded from a sardine boat when the first shells whistled overhead. His first thought was for Teresa and he ran to his cottage, his wooden clogs impeding him until he kicked them off to run barefooted. He met her running along the beach to find him. He hurried her back to their cottage and they sheltered there, listening to the whine of shells and waiting for the thunder of their explosions.

"Will there be a battle, Father?" asked Teresa anxiously. She had seen Captain Garon gallop along the beach and up the steep path to the coastal batteries. Her heart had thrilled because he had looked so handsome and dashing.

"The Nationalists are testing our shore defenses," said Paco Barras. His blue eyes were ice-chips. "Men are mad to do these things to their own kind!"

Another shell whistled overhead, much closer this time, and he held Teresa comfortingly as they waited for its explosion.

"Are you afraid, Father?"

"Only for you, daughter."

When the shelling eased they ventured out and Teresa surprised
her father by her indifference to danger. They watched Jesus Guitart
set off, and it wasn't until Constancia Guitart began to wail that Teresa became worried. "Isn't there some way to stop them, Father? It's
madness. They haven't a chance."

Paco Barras sighed sadly. "Thus is life. Men try to accomplish the
impossible while their women weep for their foolhardiness." The
chatter of Jesus Guitart's machine guns carried to them and the courage of the men aboard the tiny vessel brought lumps to many throats.

The Nationalist warship zigzagged toward the harbor at full speed.
Then abruptly the bow fell off and the warship swung around in a
great curving arc until its stern was toward Escoleras. It increased
speed and steamed away toward the horizon.

Jesus Guitart howled with rage, shook his fist and shouted at his
machine gunners who were firing frantically at an enemy they could
never have got within range of.

On the dockside the watching villagers gave a great, ringing cheer.
"It's seen them!" shouted someone and for a moment it did almost
seem as though the gunboat had sighted the furious Jesus Guitart and
his men and turned to escape.

But in the gun emplacement, Captain Garon swore softly as the
warship circled and headed away.

"Six more rounds," he ordered and through his binoculars watched
the shells explode in the sea. Grudgingly he admired the enemy warship's captain's daring and skill. The vessel had come within a hundred yards of the range of the coastal guns before mockingly sweeping
around and speeding away.

The villagers dug out the injured from the ruins of cottages and
Doctor Aldo attended them. He washed dirt from wounds, stitched
torn flesh, splinted fractured bones and soothed with his gentle voice.
Vaguely he was aware of Father Delbos hovering over the dead and
dying, his face glowing with divine zeal as he prayed devoutly.

Doctor Aldo supervised the loading of the badly injured into the
army truck which would take them to the hospital in Figueras and
then attended to the less seriously injured. Then he washed away his
tiredness with two cups of hot coffee and set off to eat with Hernando.

He was the last of the guests to arrive at Hernando's hut. The
others were Mayor Morales, Marcel Prada, Paco Barras, Jesus Gui-

tart, Pedro Bastico, shopkeeper Coruna and several other villagers. They seated themselves on upturned fish boxes and Hernando ladled the steaming stew into enamel plates.

Marcel Prada was the first served.

"How is it, friend?" asked Hernando anxiously.

Prada sucked flesh from a frog's leg and ground the soft bone into paste between his teeth. "Delicious! There is only one fault." He reached for the wineskin and drank deeply.

"What is the fault, friend?" asked Hernando anxiously.

"It is too hot. It is the *guindilla*. You have used it not wisely, but too well."

Hernando's blue eyes twinkled at the doctor. "How about that, Juan?"

Doctor Aldo dipped his spoon and tasted. Unluckily he scooped up a *guindilla* seed and it split open between his teeth. At once his mouth was aflame. He put down his plate and delicately spat to one side while the others chuckled.

"How is it, Juan?" persisted Hernando. His blue eyes pleaded for an honest answer.

Doctor Aldo dabbed his watering eyes. "You were right, Hernando. It is spiced too highly."

"We enjoy it nevertheless," said Paco Barras, eating contentedly.

"Of course," said Doctor Aldo.

"Life is to be lived; and to live we must eat," said Hernando, spitting out a *guindilla* seed.

"And to live is human and to have human failings," said Doctor Aldo.

Hernando glanced up as Vicente Serra trudged along the beach to join the group. Serra's face was gaunt and he was pitifully thin. Everyone knew he and his wife starved themselves while hoarding olives, salted sardines and wine to sell at famine prices.

Hernando said: "Get a plate from inside and help yourself, Vicente."

"*Gracias*, Hernando. *Gracias*," said Serra. He stepped into the hut and hunted until he found a large mug. He helped himself from the pot. The mug held much more than the plates and he filled it to the brim, scraping the spoon around the pot, filtering the liquid and retaining the solids. He ate noisily, wolfing the delicate white meat so quickly he could not taste it. The others were embarrassed that a man should be so hungry when his house was stocked with food.

Serra was the last to be served but was the first to finish. His sharp eyes hunted around hungrily and Hernando, who had traded half a pail of snails for two loaves of bread that morning, nodded to the door of his cottage. "There's another loaf inside."

Jesus Guitart tilted back his head and squirted wine into his mouth. His good eye gleamed contentedly. "Excellent, Hernando," he praised. "A delicious meal."

Hernando smiled and picked his teeth with a sliver of wood cut from the edge of the fish box.

"And how is your wife, Vicente?" Doctor Aldo asked Serra.

"She is well, Doctor."

"She still has that cough?"

"It's a habit, Doctor. Cough, cough, cough all day!"

"I should give her an examination."

At once Serra was on the defensive, fearing a doctor's fee. "There's nothing wrong with her, Doctor. If there was, I'd call you at once."

Doctor Aldo bit back an angry reply and inquired quietly. "And the child? She is well?"

"She's fit and well, Doctor."

"When I saw her the other day, Vicente," said the doctor slowly, "she wore only a torn cotton slip and no shoes! This is winter, man! Some days are bitterly cold. A child shouldn't go barefooted in this weather."

"We put shoes on her, but she tears them off," said Serra defensively.

"The child shouldn't be here at all," lectured the doctor. "You should have sent her and your wife into the mountains and safety."

Serra glared. "What about the expense?"

The doctor lost his temper. "To the devil with expense. What kind of man are you, Serra? Does money mean more than the welfare of your wife and child?"

Serra flushed. "Maria wouldn't go."

Doctor Aldo sighed because this was true. Maria would risk death from air raids to avoid spending.

"Don't worry," said Coruna. "Everything will improve when the war ends."

Hernando arched one eyebrow. "What will change except that men will kill fewer of one another?"

"Our way of life will change. We'll be happy again."

Hernando widened his eyes. "I see little that can change. I live beside the sea. It lulls me to sleep at night when there is calm; and when it storms I sit entranced and watch its fury. I have food in abundance. There are rabbits and partridges in the mountains and when it rains there are frogs and snails. There are wild nuts and fruit and those who have vineyards and olive trees invite me to help myself. The sea is bountiful and I exchange my catches for wine and good bread. I have no master and work only when I wish. I am a simple but happy man and now we are at war the only change in my life is that I am sad men are so violent."

"What's a man to do about clothing, Hernando?" asked José Vigon. He was a short-breathed man and his chest heaved as though he had run a long distance. His fleshy neck was thick and bulged out over his buttoned shirt collar.

Hernando's blue eyes twinkled. "While amigo Vicente Serra is obsessed by money, our amigo José Vigon loves clothes. On Sundays he walks to the café in new and squeaky shoes and sits uncomfortably still, to preserve the crease in his trousers. You, Manuel Coruna, have a landlord's love of property and have bought the cottages on both sides of your shop." Hernando gave a twist to his bristling moustache and his blue eyes twinkled a challenge. "None of you is free," he said. "I am the only free man." He glanced down at his patched trousers, black sash and mended shirt. "I have no wish to strut like a turkey cock," he chuckled. "Clothing is to warm my body, not my vanity. When linen tears it is quickly mended. A man who can sew can make trousers last a decade and a well-patched shirt a lifetime."

Doctor Aldo took out his watch and glanced at it. "You are a truly happy man, Hernando." He stuffed his watch back into his pocket and picked up his battered medical bag. "You are a *pure* Anarchist, Hernando."

Hernando shook his head. "I am not an Anarchist, Doctor Aldo. I am *me*."

"In a strange way," said the doctor slowly, "I think you are the spirit of Cataluña."

Hernando's beard jutted. "I am not Cataluña, nor an Anarchist, nor a spirit. I am me!" His fist pounded the fish-box table. "I am my own man. I am . . . *free!*"

"Precisely," agreed the doctor, nodding vigorously. "In some strange way, you *are* the spirit of Cataluña." He muttered a farewell and hurried away.

Hernando glared after him indignantly.

"Hernando," wheedled Vicente Serra, "Would you have another crust of bread?"

"All I have is a haunch of rabbit which I boiled yesterday and is now cold in its own jelly."

"I will not say no to it," said Serra.

Hernando brought him the cooked rabbit he had set aside for his supper.

"Father Delbos wants everyone to go to church next Sunday," commented Manuel Coruna lazily. He drew deeply on his cigarette and watched the smoke dribble out from his lips. Then with a sly glance at Hernando, he asked: "Will we see you in the front pew, Hernando?"

Everyone laughed.

3

The aged waiter led Emil Serra up the darkened stairs at the back of the bar and opened the door of a small office. The empty drawers of the filing cabinet yawned open, the strong-box door was swung back against the wall and the floor was strewn with papers.

"Will this do?" asked the waiter. His watery eyes stared away into space. Now the proprietor had fled to France, he came to the bar every day from habit.

"This will do fine," said Serra. He startled the old man by thrusting a handful of currency notes into his hand. "This is for you. Now leave me in peace." He thrust the bewildered old man outside and shut the office door.

There was a desk by the window scarred with cigar burns. A heavy, old-fashioned typewriter stood upon it. Serra lit one of his last cigars, inhaled with relish, and then studied his stubby fingers curiously. He held them spread out as though about to play a tremendous chord, wriggled the fingers of his right hand and watched the way they moved with interest. Then he looked at his left hand and again wriggled his fingers. Finally he flicked both hands as though shaking water off them.

He searched through drawers and cupboards until he found envelopes and paper, sat down at the typewriter and fed paper into the machine.

He typed slowly because the machine was old and the keys jammed.

The end of the war is in sight. The swift collapse of the government forces surprised even the pessimists. In a few weeks, the Nationalists have swept through Cataluña.

General Franco's big attack began on Christmas Eve. There was a vague suggestion the Pope wanted a truce for this hallowed anniversary. But there was to be none of this spiritual nonsense. A heavy assault by Spanish and Italian troops across the River Ebro caught the government troops by surprise.

At the beginning of January a significant battle took place in Borgas Blancas. The town was of no great military importance, but its capture seemed to break the spirit of the government's troops. From then on, it was a rout with almost no fighting as the Nationalist troops swept on through Cataluña.

I left Madrid with the government and was in Barcelona when the Nationalist troops made their breakthrough. There was widespread panic. Those in the towns and villages around Barcelona flocked to the city for refuge. Those already there fled to the country. Everybody wanted to *"escape."* Nobody worked. Public transport failed, government officials and civil servants deserted their posts, the municipal workers disappeared and the streets stank of the rotting garbage. The city was without water.

The government hastily shifted its headquarters to Gerona and this increased public alarm. Meanwhile, the Falangists who had remained underground in Barcelona once again sniped from rooftops and spread terror.

I bribed a high-ranking army officer to place a commandeered truck at my disposal. Despite this, getting out of Barcelona was a problem. The air raids had been stepped up, the port was constantly bombed and the roads were so blocked that without a motorcycle escort to clear the way, I would never have got through.

I followed the government's retreat to Figueras where Negrin and other members of the Cortes are now working out the terms under which they will surrender. But they know this offer is a waste of time. None of them believes General Franco will accept any terms other than unconditional surrender. The Nationalists have won the war and Negrin's peace offer can be no more than an attempt to secure safeguards for those who surrender. But General Franco will promise nothing and there is no confidence on the government's side that he will be merciful to the vanquished.

There are three or four routes from Figueras to the French frontier and they are all blocked with refugees and retreating government troops. This flood of refugees is a big headache for the French. At first, the frontier guards refused to let them through while the French government hastily tried to arrange for a neutral zone in Spain under international control where refugees could take sanctuary. But the Spanish Nationalists wanted "unconditional surrender" of *all* Spanish soil. So the French government permitted civilian refugees and wounded men to enter.

I have today learned that the French government is now permitting the entire government army to take refuge in France on condition that all arms are surrendered at the frontier. When a thin line of French frontier guards was confronted by a large army of desperate men fleeing from an army that pressed them hard in the rear, the French, diplomatic as always, decided that if the retreating Spanish government army was going to flood over the border anyway, it would be better for it to do so *without* its weapons.

Emil Serra got to his feet, strode across to a cracked mirror and stared intently at his reflection. He stuck out his jaw and rasped his fingers across its three-day stubble. He glowered at his image, sighed and went back to his chair to resume typing.

This is almost certainly the last report I shall send you. In Madrid, Doctor Bolinski confirmed the inevitable. The shrapnel moves remorselessly; paralysis and death are now quite near. Already my hands and feet tingle and are losing sensation. As I type this letter I see my finger hit the keys but feel only a vague, cotton-woolish contact.

I do not intend to leave Spain. I have so little time left I could not reach Poland even if I had the wish. But since I have lived in Spain I have grown increasingly wedded to it. I feel at home here. My ancestors came from Spain many years ago and I have traced a distant kinsman who lives near here. So, my dear superior, instead of joining the great procession of refugees winding up the mountain roads toward the frontier, I will make my way to Escoleras and seek out my distant relatives.

Emil Serra sealed his report with his watch charm and addressed it to the Polish Consulate, Paris.

Downstairs the bar was empty except for the aged waiter who sat in a cane chair watching the straggling refugees passing in an endless column. He got to his feet.

"A brandy," said Serra and as the old man poured he said: "Make it a large one."

"Yes, sir."

Serra lit another cigar. "Where is the nearest whorehouse?"

"There's two, Señor. One in the poor quarter on the main road to the frontier. The other's on the road to Olot. It's expensive, Señor. But I'm told the girls are excellent." The old man shrugged his shoulders. "Perhaps with all this trouble they've closed."

Serra found the place with ease, a well-built villa in a high-walled garden. He walked up the sweeping drive, drawing hard on his cigar and humming to himself. A maid in a swishy black taffeta dress, white cap and apron opened the door and eyed him doubtfully.

"May I come in?" he asked.

She looked him up and down dubiously.

He understood her distrust and with a chuckle plunged his hand into his pocket and withdrew a handful of crumpled currency notes.

The sight of the money was enough. She widened the door.

She left him in a comfortably furnished waiting room with leather upholstered chairs. A tall, severe-faced woman with iron-gray hair entered and asked with dignity: "Can I help you, Señor?"

"How are the girls?"

"Would you like to see them . . . ?" She stepped toward the door.

He held up his hand. "Just a minute. Let's talk. How many have you?"

"Seven, Señor. They are *all* very young and very attractive."

"How are things? Are you busy?"

The madam smiled wryly. "This isn't the best of times."

"How about the maid? She looks pretty."

The madam was doubtful. "If you are very interested, something can be arranged. But I don't recommend her. She's not experienced and hasn't the talent for it."

"All the girls live in?"

"Each girl has her room. They're all spotlessly clean."

"Lock all the doors and throw away the key," he decided. "We'll have an orgy."

She frowned disapprovingly. "I wouldn't dream of it. I have my regular clients and . . ."

"Get in all the food you can buy on the black market." He began to take money from his pockets. "I don't care what I pay," he said.

She smiled. "Who could refuse you?"

They went into the sitting room where the girls were playing cards or sewing and he joked with them, shouted for champagne and proposed a toast. "To the great gift of sensation!" he said and laughed a little wildly.

"Hurry, girls," he invited. "Strip off."

They stared at him.

"Let's all enjoy one another," he said. He poured more champagne. "What are you waiting for?"

The girls looked at the madam and when she nodded, they undressed.

"You too," he told the maid.

She was opening another bottle of champagne. She looked at the madam in surprise.

"Do what he wants, Rosa. It will be well worthwhile."

The maid took off her cap and apron and flushed as she pulled the hem of her taffeta skirt up over her head.

"You too," said Emil Serra, grinning at the madam.

The madam drew herself up sternly. "I'm afraid I couldn't . . ."

Serra plunged his hand into his pocket, pulled out a thick wad of notes and scattered them on the table. The girls stared at the money with wide, disbelieving eyes. The madam smiled thinly. "Señor, you make it impossible to resist you." Her fingers went to the buttons of her dress.

Emil took a glass vial from his pocket, dropped three lozenges into a glass of champagne, swirled them around until they were soggy and gulped them down. He beckoned to the nearest girl. "Come here, beautiful. Help me undress."

They all clustered around him, pretending to admire him. They took off his shirt and jacket and pulled off his trousers. He stared into the mirror, despising the sickly whiteness of his skin, the flabby rolls of fat. He was amazed the girls could conceal their repugnance. He reached out to the nearest girl with his forefinger and stroked her nipple.

The girl giggled and thrust her breast closer.

"You like that?" he asked curiously.

"I *love* it!"

He watched his finger with interest as it circled the halo. "You feel that?" he asked.

"Of course," she said. "It's delicious!"

"Well I don't." He held his forefinger up close to his face and stared at it intently, and the girls laughed uncertainly when he flicked both hands vigorously as though to shake water drops from them.

For a week Teresa saw little of Captain Garon. He arrived late at night, his face drawn and his eyes tired. He was away again before dawn, creeping out so as not to awaken her.

There was now no doubt the war was lost. The roads to the frontier were flooded with refugees and fleeing troops, and even the radio reports were dispirited.

For three days, on Captain Garon's orders, none of the fishing boats had been allowed to leave port. Now the fishermen stood on the dock and watched with bitter eyes as soldiers rowed from one moored fishing boat to another. In the bilge of each fishing boat they placed a charge of explosive with a time fuse. It usually blew out the bottom of one boat before they had rowed to the next. Many of the fishermen had tears running down their cheeks as they watched their vessels and their livelihood destroyed.

Teresa on her own initiative had gone to Captain Garon's command post and persuaded his sergeant to interrupt him.

The sergeant had come back flushed from a tongue-lashing. "The captain's very busy, but he will spare you five minutes."

She had been escorted to the bell tent that served as his office. A trestle table was littered with maps and papers and he had looked up at her with eyes that were infinitely tired. "Please be quick, *chiquita*. I have much to do."

"It's about the fishermen," she had begun. "Is there no way their boats can be saved . . . ?"

"No!" he had snapped. "Don't waste time discussing it. My orders are clear. No shipping is to fall into the hands of the enemy."

"But it's . . . it's vandalism."

He said tonelessly. "The war goes on. Madrid still fights. Our government has moved to Valencia. Because Cataluña is falling does not mean the war has ended."

"To fight the war is one thing, *mi Capitan*. But to destroy the fishermen's boats is to rob them of their means to live. It is not war . . . it's . . ."

His face set hard. "War is a resort to primitive brutality. Those who use brutality most efficiently have more chance of being the victor."

"You have no sympathy for these poor fishermen, *mi Capitan?*"

He had sighed. *"Chiquita. Chiquita!* Of course I feel for them. I am human, am I not? If I had full command, no soldier would be placed in danger and no weapon discharged. But I do not command. Nobody commands. All of us, even the generals, must obey."

Her eyes were sad. "There's nothing you can do?"

He shook his head. "Nothing."

"Then . . . then what will happen now?"

"The war will be directed from Valencia. If we keep the men together and escape to France, we can embark for Valencia in troopships."

"Then you are leaving Escoleras?"

He looked at her steadily. "This I must talk to you about, *chiquita*. I will come to you tonight. Expect me."

Throughout the rest of the day there was feverish activity. Nothing was left behind that would benefit the advancing enemy. When the last fishing boat had been sunk, truckloads of stores of explosives were driven to the end of the harbor wall and tipped into the sea.

There was now no fish to be bought and Paco Barras slept at home. His heavy snoring was reassuring to Teresa when her bedroom door opened silently and Captain Garon came to her. It was a cold night and she shivered as he threw back the bed sheets. His skin burned and when she rested her palm upon his forehead it was feverishly wet.

"You are ill," she whispered. "You've worked too hard."

He held her tightly, his thighs hot against hers. Since the great retreat had begun, he had not come to her; he was dead to physical desire. She held him in her arms, content simply to have him at her side.

"We move out tomorrow," he whispered.

She nodded.

"I do not wish to leave you, *chiquita*."

At once she was planning. "I know a place I can hide you. There is a suit that belongs to my brother and we will burn your uniform."

"No," he said flatly. "I cannot desert my men. I must lead them to

France." He held her tightly, drawing her cheek down upon his chest and pushing her hair away from her ear so he could circle his fingertip around it. He whispered: "I beg of you. Come with me, *chiquita*. In France we can be married. Or perhaps we will return at once to Valencia and be married there."

She lay quite still.

"*Chiquita!*" he pleaded. "I need you . . . I love you!"

Desire stirred inside her. But she was unmoved by his words. It was Anselmo she wanted for her husband.

"It is no good, *mi Capitan*," she whispered. "You have taught me to be a realist and now we must both be realists. It is Anselmo I love. That is not something I have decided. It has been decided for me. All of me yearns for him. It is only with Anselmo I can be truly happy."

"Have you not been happy with me, *chiquita?*"

"Yes indeed," she said softly. "But it is a different happiness. A physical happiness. Did you not teach me that to feel desire is human? Did you not teach me that physical love is beautiful and pleasurable . . . *for its own sake?*"

He sighed. "Then you will not come with me tomorrow, *chiquita?*"

"I cannot. I must wait for Anselmo."

"If I write, will you reply, *chiquita?*"

"Perhaps."

"You are not sad that we may not meet again?"

"It saddens me greatly. But this terrible war has taught us to endure sadness."

He rested his hand on her breast. "Shall I make love to you?" He had no desire. He wanted only to give her pleasure. She pressed her hand over his until it was still.

"It is enough to lie quietly with you, *mi Capitan*."

He was exhausted and fell asleep in her arms. She dared not move for fear of waking him and lay for a long time, listening to his quiet breathing. The bed springs creaked in the other room as her father turned over and she tensed until his snoring started again. She aroused the captain by pulling gently on the lobe of his ear. "You must go, my love. I am afraid my father will awaken."

He kissed her breasts and her lips tenderly and crept away.

She slept soundly and awakened late. She prepared breakfast for herself and her father, and after she had washed up she hurried to the artillery camp.

She stared with shock at the empty plaza.

Nearby Father Delbos was talking loudly to a group of villagers. "Now the soldiers have gone we must appoint responsible villagers to represent us," said Father Delbos.

Teresa turned and walked back toward her cottage as though dazed. She had not expected to feel the captain's absence so deeply. *What's the matter with me?* she thought, blinking back her tears. *Am I in love with him after all?*

The narrow, winding road snaked up the steep mountainside and overhung a precipitous drop into a ravine. The road had been hacked out of solid rock. Its surface was a layer of loose shale in which the truck tires often spun without gripping as the drivers coaxed their vehicles around the sharply banked bends.

Some trucks towed field guns, some were loaded with weapons and ammunition and others were packed with troops. Conditions were so cramped that many men preferred to walk.

One transport truck crawled up a steep section of the road at a snail's pace, making alarming metallic sounds. The sweating driver pressed hard on the accelerator and double-clutched into low gear. But although he was quick the truck had slowed to a standstill and began to run backward before he let up the clutch pedal. He let it up too quickly, the truck jerked and its engine cut out. The driver swore, put on the handbrake, pressed down the clutch pedal and switched on the engine. The hot engine started up at once, but the hand brake couldn't hold the heavy truck. It began to run backward downhill more and more swiftly.

The driver revved up the engine and slipped the clutch, braking the truck but filling the cab with the smoke of scorching clutch leather. The truck began to inch forward.

And then it happened.

There was a metallic clang and the truck began to run backward again. The engine roared as the driver accelerated frantically without at first realizing that the connection between wheels and engine had snapped.

"Put the brake on, you fool!" someone shouted.

The driver craned his head out of the cab as the runaway truck gathered speed. He was perilously close to the crumbling road-edge that overhung the abyss and knowing so many lives depended on him brought the driver close to panic. The steering responded stiffly and the truck swerved wildly as it ran backward with smoking brake-linings. And as its runaway speed increased, the driver realized he would be unable to steer around the next sharp bend. Deliberately he ran the truck in toward the mountain wall. The back wheel jolted down into the rain gulley, the truck scraped and slithered along the rock face and metal screamed. An overhang in the rock wall splintered one side of the truck and men spilled out of it.

The driver jumped down from his cab. He was trembling. A man's arm had been gashed and a comrade tore his shirt sleeve to bind the wound. Tired men gathered around the truck and watched the driver and another crawl under it and lie looking up at its underside. They crawled out again, their hands greasy and oil smudges on their faces. "Nothing we can do, sir," they reported. "It's a welding job."

The gray-faced officer swore and pulled his peaked cap farther down over his forehead. At this height the air was thin and the cold cut like a knife.

Behind them was the roar of another truck. It labored uphill towing a field gun. The gunners walked behind the truck, pushing to ease the strain on the engine. Brakes squealed when the driver brought the truck to a standstill and a red-faced artillery officer strode up, shaking his fist angrily. "Why are you blocking the road? Get moving, will you!" He caught sight of his fellow officer and flipped his hand in a token salute. "It's dangerous to stop and lose momentum on these steep slopes."

"The crankshaft snapped. We ran backward," explained the officer tersely. "We can't move."

"Then get your men to give my truck a push." The artillery officer gestured to his driver, but the man shook his head.

The artillery officer strode across to him. "Do I have to shout. Get going!"

The driver scowled. "Not enough room to pass, Señor."

"There's plenty of room. I'll guide you."

The driver shook his head obstinately. "Too risky, Señor. The road's crumbling at the edge."

"I'll decide if it's risky," roared the officer. "Get going!"

The driver was tired and his nerves were frayed. He swore under his breath as he edged the truck forward at a snail's pace. The engine roared wildly as he slipped his clutch and black smoke belched from the exhaust pipe, enveloping those who pushed behind.

The artillery officer stood in front of the truck, beckoning it forward with guiding hands. Presently it became apparent there was not room for the truck to pass, and that its wheels overhung a very treacherous section of the road.

"Brake!" the artillery officer called in a ringing voice. "Stop!"

The driver applied the brakes and thrust his head out of the cabin. "What's the matter, sir?" he sneered triumphantly.

"Don't try it, driver," the artillery officer said with infuriating calm. "You'll never make it." He turned to his fellow officer. "We'll have to move *your* truck out of the way. It's holding up the entire convoy."

"We'll push it onto the shoulder of the road, if your men will help."

The artillery officer walked to the edge of the road and stood staring down into the ravine. "We'll tip it over," he suggested. "Why leave it behind for . . . them!"

Men gathered behind the truck and pushed while the driver stood on the step of his cabin and steered. The gunners helped rock it back and forth, and with a united heave they finally got it moving. It rolled slowly across the road and just before the front wheels reached the edge of the precipice, the driver jumped. The front wheels hovered on the edge, shale and loose stones spurted and then the wheels leaped forward into space. With a thud the underside of the truck came down heavily on the broken edge of the road. The front wheels of the truck spun slowly and the artillery officer scowled. Now the road was completely blocked.

Behind them the convoy was piling up. Officers and men came hurrying to learn what caused the holdup. Everybody shouted advice to everyone. Then the men tried to push the truck over the edge by brute force. They borrowed jacks from other trucks, raised the back axle and built small mountains of stones under the back wheels until the truck balanced precariously on the lip of the precipice. A dozen men levering with crowbars got it seesawing, until finally, with a loud screech, it slid downward. The back wheels hit the edge of the precipice and the truck bounded outward into space, turning over slowly in mid-air. It hit the rock slope far below and bounced outward like a toy. Its spare wheel broke free.

The second time the truck hit the slope, it burst into flames.

"That's it, men. Start moving," shouted the officer and wryly his men realized that now they had to walk.

Miguel Barras had been riding in the jettisoned truck and now, as he stood staring out across the ravine, Catalina gripped his arm. "What is it, comrade?"

"*Nada*," he said. But his dark eyes were brooding and his swarthy face was pale.

Catalina followed his gaze to where the valley ran between two distant hillocks and met the sea. The sea was a misty blue and beside it clustered the white specks of a village.

"Is that a village?" she asked.

He nodded and color came back to his cheeks.

"Is it . . . *your* village? Your home?"

He turned away quickly. "I have no home. That village is but the geographical position I occupied when I was born." He walked on, his hands thrust deeply into his trouser pockets. She hurried after him, her heavy man's boots scrunching on the loose shale, the metal canteen hanging from her belt clinking against her rifle like a cowbell. She grasped Miguel's arm. "Listen, comrade. It is your home. Now you are so close, you should go there."

He strode on, his face set. "They are simple people. They do not understand the fundamentals of the class war."

"But your family, Miguel! Do you not wish to see them . . . even for a short time?"

He shook his head.

They walked on, their shoulders brushing. He said: "I have grown apart from my family. I see now that I lived among them without true understanding of life. There is nothing there for me any longer. It is a part of my life that is dead!"

"You still love your family, Miguel."

He laughed hoarsely. "Comrade. I have no time for sentiment."

"If you wish it, Miguel, I will go with you down into the valley and to your village."

For a moment his pride faltered and he half-turned toward her. Then his face hardened and he strode on. "Our fight for freedom never ceases."

"As you wish, comrade," Catalina said tiredly.

She dropped behind him, unable to keep pace with his angry stride.

The convoy toiled slowly on toward the frontier.

4

The village seemed deserted without the soldiers. The fishermen stood in sullen groups, bitterly lamenting the sinking of their boats. There was an air of brooding uncertainty. Even Father Delbos, who had not concealed his delight at the soldiers' flight, was cautious. The tide of war might turn and fill the village with government troops again.

Rumor ran rife. The Nationalist troops had occupied Gerona. Señor Negrin and the Cortes had fled from Figueras to France. Russian troops were disembarking in Valencia. England and France had decided to give military help to the legally elected Spanish government. Nobody knew how the rumors started nor how much faith could be placed in them. The villagers were resentful of the military regime that had governed them for two years yet apprehensive of the arrival of Nationalist troops.

Rosalia's ailing mother was ill again and after breakfast Teresa walked alone to the inland village of Pilsa, eight miles to the north of Escoleras. She took with her a bag of squid her father had caught the night previously. The squid were fresh and Teresa soon found a farmer's wife who at once killed and skinned two rabbits in exchange for them.

Teresa ate at the farm and returned to Escoleras by a cross-country detour which took her through an abandoned farm. She hoped to find wild mushrooms sprouting in its neglected kitchen garden. She strode effortlessly along the troughs of loose earth between the rows of grapevines, climbed a terraced hillside where grapes had once grown abundantly and dropped down the other side into the valley of Adal. The Adal farmhouse stood forlornly deserted, its windows smashed, shutters hanging open and barn doors gaping. But as she approached the outbuildings, she thought she saw a flicker of movement.

There were no mushrooms. She searched diligently, but the kitchen garden yielded only two onions. She dropped them into the sack with the rabbits and slung it across her shoulder.

As she was leaving she again saw a flicker of movement inside one of the outbuildings. It could have been a farmhouse fowl that had escaped slaughter. Teresa crossed to the building and stared into its shadowy interior. There were empty wine barrels, discarded farm implements, an old cart with broken shafts and a mound of moldering sacks. At the far end was dusty, discarded furniture with mildewed stuffing leaking from the upholstery. White fungus coated the woodwork. Again she sensed movement and walked into the shadow, peering into the gloom hopefully.

It wasn't until she was within his reach that she saw the soldier. He was pressed flat against the wall and stood quite motionless. The whites of his eyes gleamed and he held his breath. The unexpectedness of seeing him made her scream. He reached out a detaining hand and she turned and fled.

She ran toward the open doors but from the deeper darkness between two storage bins another figure appeared and sprang upon her. Strong arms encircled her, lifted her off her feet and threw her down.

The two of them held her firmly until her screams died away into sobs of apprehension. One of them had a low, deep voice and he talked soothingly until her heart ceased its frantic thumping. His cheeks bristled with black stubble and his ragged uniform was filthy. His tunic gaped open and showed a pale-skinned chest encrusted with dirt and curling black hairs. The other man was younger, unshaven and fair. The golden stubble on his chin had a reddish tinge. His uniform too was filthy.

The older man soothed: "Don't be afraid, girl. We won't harm you. Please don't scream."

"Let me go!" she said angrily, trying to twist free.

"Promise you won't run away?"

"Let me go!"

Warily they allowed her to sit up. She looked at them searchingly, her fears evaporating when she saw they were only tired and hungry men.

"How dare you!" she stormed. "Have you no shame? Are you men without respect?"

The older man apologized awkwardly. "You screamed and frightened us, Señorita."

"You are grown men . . . and soldiers! Yet a girl frightens you with a scream!"

The older man flashed a worried glance at the open door of the outhouse. "They've broken through. They can be anywhere."

"Who?" she asked, although she guessed.

"The Nationalists. They've cut through Cataluña like a knife through butter."

"I thought . . ." she began. "I thought the government forces had retreated to France."

The older soldier scowled. "They were the lucky ones. But they caught up with our company near Figueras. We held them for a time and then scattered."

"Are the Nationalists in Figueras?" she asked eagerly, thinking of Anselmo.

"They're all around us, girl."

"I haven't seen them."

"Watch her, Juan," warned the older man. He crossed to the door and peered out.

Juan's blue eyes smiled uncertainly. She was surprised how boyish he looked. His chin was weak and his lips were like a girl's. She couldn't imagine him killing and facing death. He said apologetically: "I am sorry we angered you, Señorita."

The older man strode back, his forehead furrowed. "We must stay out of sight until dark. Then we can move on."

"Where will you go?" she asked.

"We'll cross the frontier into France."

"Do you know the way?"

He nodded doubtfully.

"There are a number of roads," she said, wanting to help them.

"Roads are out," snapped the older man. "The Nationalists are so close they'll reach the frontier before we do."

Teresa said slowly: "You wish to cross the frontier clandestinely?"

"It's the only way."

"It's very difficult. The mountains are treacherous, the passes are few and the paths are easily lost."

"What do *you* know of it?" he sneered.

"Many men from our village crossed the mountains into France," she said simply. "Thus I know it is not easy." She arched one eyebrow. "The war is ended and you are both Spanish. Why do you not surrender and become prisoners?"

The older man sighed. "What must we do to surrender?"

"You put down your weapons and go to meet them with your hands above your head."

Juan said bitterly: "Tell her, Ernesto."

The older man said tonelessly: "Some of our comrades did that, Señorita. They held their hands above their heads and walked toward the enemy to surrender."

"And . . . ?" asked Teresa.

Ernesto raised an invisible tommygun and squinted along its barrel. His tongue clicked, imitating the staccato chatter of bullets.

Juan sounded slightly hysterical. "They won't *let* us surrender!"

"I will draw you a map," she offered.

Ernesto had a stub of pencil and they used yellowed paper that had lined the drawers of a broken-legged table. While Juan kept watch at the door of the outhouse, Teresa drew a map and gave Ernesto instructions.

"You must go in a straight line north toward this mountain with a round tower upon its summit. Five kilometers from here you will come to a river. After the rains, it will be deep and the current strong. You will have to swim it."

Ernesto's bearded face was tense with concentration.

"At the foot of this mountain you come to a main road. You must then face northwest and seek two mountain peaks. They are five kilometers away. In the 'V' made by these peaks, you will see the tip of another mountain. That is far away and is in France. You approach it between the two peaks, but the path is steep and slippery. It will be very cold and you will have snow and ice. Sometimes the path dwindles away and you will have to make your own way up the mountainside and this is hard because the slopes are thick with undergrowth and brambles."

Ernesto's eyes gleamed. "If the undergrowth is dense we will not be detected."

"But between here and the first mountain there are only olive groves and vineyards. You can be easily seen at a distance. So you must keep to the hedges."

"Juan," he called to the youth at the door.

There was no answer.

Ernesto rose to his feet. Juan had fallen asleep against the doorpost. Ernesto looked down at him and shook his head sadly. "Let him sleep," he said wearily. "Let him sleep. We've had no rest in forty-eight hours."

"You will need two days or perhaps three, to reach the frontier," she warned.

"In an hour it will be dark," he said. "Tonight we will rest and at dawn be on our way."

A motherly compassion swelled up inside her. "When did you last eat?"

"Eat?" he said and laughed. "So long ago I cannot remember."

Her sack of food lay in the shadows where it had fallen when they sprang upon her. After a moment's hesitation she said: "You've got to eat. You'll need all your strength to reach the frontier. I've got food."

"Where?" His eyes glowed.

"I'll cook for you. Don't get excited."

"Where is it?"

She pointed to the sack. He upended it and snatched up the mauve, skinned rabbits. "Juan!" he shouted. "Look! Food!"

Juan went on sleeping, dead to the world.

Ernesto snapped at a rabbit, his white teeth tearing the raw flesh. But Teresa snatched it away from him. She scolded angrily: "Be a man . . . not an animal! Wait until I cook it."

He said craftily. "Make smoke and they'll know we're here."

"Charcoal doesn't smoke," she said. She thrust the rabbit back into the sack and walked away from the outbuilding to the farmhouse. Ernesto followed her after stirring Juan to wakefulness with the toe of his boot. The younger soldier stumbled after them, drugged with sleep.

The farmhouse kitchen was coated with dust. Vandals had smashed the furniture and windows. But the bell-shaped chimney above the fireplace was big enough to roast a spitted pig. A wooden box beside it was half-filled with charcoal.

Teresa soon had the charcoal glowing redly. "Have you got a knife?" she asked. She cut one rabbit through the middle and then quartered it. She placed each quarter on the glowing embers and gave the fan to Ernesto. "Keep it glowing," she ordered.

In a cupboard she found a jar of salt that had turned hard. She powdered it between her fingers and sprinkled it over the roasting flesh. In a cruet she found olive oil dregs and the few drops served to give the browning meat a flavor. She wrapped the two onions in a poultice of wet earth and placed them on the red embers. Soon they were simmering in their own juice and giving off an appetizing savor.

The soldiers crouched around the fire impatiently. When she

finally yielded to their entreaties before the meat was properly cooked, they ate ravenously, burning their fingers and lips, sucking the bones clean of flesh and crunching them to powder. In minutes they had devoured the rabbit and then stared at her with hungry eyes.

With a sigh, Teresa took out the other rabbit and quartered it.

The sharp edge of their hunger had been eased and now they were willing to wait until the meat was cooked. The onions too were ready and they ate them slowly, relishing each layer they peeled off and placed upon their tongues, as though it was a priceless delicacy.

Teresa ate a little of the rabbit before they finished every last scrap of it.

Juan took out a packet of black cigarettes and offered one to Teresa. She shook her head. Ernesto took one and the two men lit up.

"What I'd love now," dreamed Ernesto, "is a cup of rich black coffee."

"I'd like a liqueur," said Juan. His eyelids fluttered with fatigue. "A Terry cognac or a Mono anis."

It was dark now and their only illumination was the red glow from the fireplace. Teresa said: "I must be going."

Ernesto got to his feet. "Where?"

"Home. My father awaits me."

"Perhaps the Nationalist soldiers have occupied your village!"

She shrugged her shoulders. "So what?"

"They might ask where you've been. What you've seen."

"What if they do? What do I care for soldiers?"

"You'd tell them about us!" he said flatly.

"I won't tell anyone about you," she said quietly. "If you leave at dawn, by noon you'll be far away."

"You might tell the Nationalists."

She was surprised. "Have I not drawn you a map and cooked for you?"

"You say you will not talk. But nevertheless it is what happens. Questions are asked and although it is not intended, answers are given. Then more questions and more answers and finally men die."

"Do not fear," she said, moving toward the door. "I will not talk."

But he stood before her, looming over her. "You will stay with us, *chica*," he said quietly. "When it is time for us to go, you too can leave."

"It's impossible. My father will worry."

"When you explain he will understand."

"No," she said flatly. "I must go." She pushed past him.

His fingers gripped her arm. "You will stay." He twisted her wrist until she sank to her knees.

"I tried to help you," she choked.

"I am sorry, *chica,*" he said. "We are not ungrateful. But we can take no risks."

She looked at Juan and his cheeks were red in the charcoal glow. His eyes met hers and looked away guiltily.

"I hope you both starve," she said bitterly. "I hope you lose your way and your boots crumble until you're barefooted. I hope the Nationalists capture you!"

They stared at her unhappily. "Do not think badly of us, Señorita," pleaded Juan. "Try to understand. Our lives are in danger."

She became aloof and hostile. "You are animals," she said flatly. "You don't deserve to be treated like human beings."

Ernesto sighed. "What do you want?"

"To go home so my father does not worry for me."

"We are sad your father will worry. But he will worry for only one night. Whereas, if the Nationalist troops make you talk, we shall die and stay dead forever!"

They placed logs on the fire to burn slowly and keep them warm. Juan fell asleep with his back against the farmhouse wall and when Teresa saw Ernesto nodding she rose softly to her feet and moved to the door.

A sixth sense aroused Ernesto and he was upon her as she stepped out into the darkness. He spun her back into the kitchen and her cry of indignation awoke Juan, who bleared around sleepy-eyed.

"She won't let us rest," said Ernesto grimly. "Find some cord, Juan."

Juan found a length of baling cord and although Teresa struggled furiously, she was no match for both of them. They bound her wrists behind her.

"We've got to sleep, Juan," urged Ernesto. "Our lives may depend on it."

They gathered old sacks and made a mattress of them beside the fireplace. They made Teresa lie down and ran a cord from her bound wrists to a shutter hasp cemented into the wall. They lay on either side of her and Ernesto loosely tied her ankle to his.

"Pigs!" she said bitterly.

They pulled sacks over them to keep out the cold and almost at once the men were asleep. Teresa was uncomfortable and changed her position often. The sacks were mildewed and musty and the stale sweat smell of the men's unwashed bodies was nauseating. She didn't think she would sleep, but did so without knowing it.

It was still dark when she was aroused by the movements of Juan. He was pressing against her, sleepily conscious she was a woman. She lay with her limbs rigid. But he pressed against her more vigorously, his aroused manhood asserting itself. When she moved away from him he firmly sandwiched her against Ernesto.

Juan felt for her and she shuddered when his hot hand invaded her bodice. She steeled herself to his touch, hoping he would be shamed by her lack of response. But he pressed against her with a physical desire as urgent as his hunger had been.

Her defensive movements awoke Ernesto and abruptly she was between the probes of their individual desires. Ernesto caressed her with rhythmic understanding.

She whispered pleadingly: *"Por favor. Por favor!"*

But they sought to inflame her desires, and Juan's fumbling caresses grew bolder until he encountered Ernesto's more knowledgeable hand.

"Shall I go away?" choked Juan.

"We're comrades," said Ernesto. "Haven't we shared everything?" He ruthlessly bared her. "What are you waiting for?" he said gruffly. "Go ahead."

"In the name of God, I beg of you!" she choked.

But Juan rolled his weight over upon her. "Do I hurt you?" he whispered.

"Please don't make me with child," she whimpered. The dread of it made her senses swim. "Ah, God! Don't do it!"

She braced herself and screamed "NO!" with the first full thrust of his manhood.

"Aayee!" she moaned as he moved with feverish, youthful vigor. "Pig. Don't make me with child. Ah, don't! *Ah, don't!*" Yet without wanting it, her body moved with his rhythm.

"Rape!" she whimpered, without conviction, as her loins responded. "Oh, God; let me be!"

When Juan was spent and his full weight bore down upon her, she was startled to hear herself shout: "You bastard!"

"Listen to the whore," scorned Ernesto. "No decent girl talks that way." He loomed over her, grinning through the darkness, his muscles tensed and his desire burning against her.

"Please," she whispered. "I beg of you. Please don't make me with child."

"I will see to it," he promised insincerely and the breath went out of her with his first, firm thrust. His loins poised to synchronize with her movements.

"Please. Don't!" she sobbed.

"Aaah . . . !" he whispered. "You're made for it!"

"For mercy!" she choked. "Don't make me with child." Yet her knees drew themselves up and compliantly parted.

"Let yourself go," he panted, his words hypnotic, driving up into her with his rhythm while she responded helplessly. And only after he had lain quiet a long time did she herself become calm and know that it was done.

He sat up and the sweat and wetness upon her turned icy in the morning air.

Already the first faint gray of dawn was in the sky and they quickly gathered up their things, guilty and anxious to be away. But as they hurried to the door she pleaded: "Untie me!"

"You'll get free," said Ernesto gruffly and pushed Juan out of the door ahead of him.

She lay for a long time with tears on her cheeks.

Then came fear.

Their seed was buried deep at the core of her. And Anselmo . . . ! She was anguished by the thought she might need to tell him she was with child.

She was shivering in the cold morning air. She rolled over and sat up. Her thighs ached as though bruised. She got to her knees and then stood up. The movement sharpened her awareness of their seed, and her fears intensified. She pulled the cord taut and frayed it against brickwork until it parted. She sat, passed her bound wrists under her buttocks and under her feet. When her tethered hands were before her, she worried the cord loose with her teeth.

When she stepped out into the gray light of morning the grass was white with frost. Beside the well was a half-filled horse trough. Her breath steamed as she broke the ice, and she felt their seed glowing within her like a hot coal. She kicked off her shoes and climbed up into the trough. The water reached her knees and its icy bite made her gasp. When she pulled off her dress and slip, her naked body looked very pale and ethereal. She sat down quickly, catching her breath at the icy agony. Her breasts shrank, hardened and turned blue, and her teeth chattered violently. But she forced herself to remain seated until she had lost all sensation in her limbs. She climbed out of the trough stiffly. Her flesh was a bluey-pink as though she had been thoroughly beaten. She pulled on her slip, smoothed it against her wet thighs and belly and stumbled back inside the farmhouse. She shivered violently as she huddled herself among the sacks with her wet garment clinging to her like an icy shroud. Her teeth wouldn't stop chattering and she wondered if she had killed herself. There was an unbearable ache at the nape of her neck and a bar of ice pressed hard against her forehead causing intense pain to her eyes and nose. Presently, she felt strangely lethargic.

When she awoke she was still shivering. But the sun had dispelled the morning frost. She arose stiffly, put on her torn knickers and was grateful for their extra warmth. But tears sprang to her eyes again. "Pigs," she said aloud.

She felt purged now, as though she had passed through a purifying flame; but her limbs ached and she was as weak as an old woman when she stepped out into the sun and pulled on her dress.

As she made her way home she invented a story to tell her father. She had been set upon by two soldiers. They had snatched the sack containing the rabbits and as they had gloated over their loot she had run away, hiding in the deserted Adal farmhouse and not daring to venture out until morning.

She was turning over the story in her mind as she trudged across a vineyard when not far away she heard a subdued metallic chattering. She picked her way slowly across the loose soil, mildly startled by a soft *swish, swish, swish.* She heard someone calling and saw a soldier gesturing to her fiercely from the gulley that ran all around the vineyard. "Down into the ditch!" he shouted.

She stared at him bleakly and walked on.

Swish, swish, swish.

"Into the ditch!" shouted the soldier. "They're shooting!"

She felt no fear and was only vaguely surprised the swishing was caused by bullets. Nobody had reason to kill *her*, she thought numbly as she reached the edge of the vineyard and jumped down into the gulley.

The soldier crouched low and ran to meet her. His face was dark with anger. "Are you out of your mind?"

She said tonelessly: "What's it to you?"

"You want to get yourself killed? Don't you know there's a war?"

"Yes," she said bitterly. "There's a war. And when there's a war . . . *anything* is justified!"

He looked at her perplexed. "Crouch low," he ordered. "I'll take you to the lieutenant."

"I won't see your lieutenant," she said tiredly. "I'm going home."

"You'll come with me," he insisted.

"I *won't!*" she flared. But she had noticed a difference in his uniform. "What army are you?"

"The only army that is an army." He grinned reassuringly. "You've no more worries, Señorita. The Reds are beaten."

He took her to an olive grove in a hillside hollow where many young soldiers were resting. They looked tired but triumphant, and eyed her curiously as her escort ushered her past them. The soldier led her across to a group of men who rose to their feet at their approach. The soldier saluted sharply. "I saw this prisoner walking across a vineyard under fire from the enemy," he reported.

A sallow-faced officer stared at her stonily. He raised his right arm with fingers fully extended and said crisply: *"Arriba Espana!"*

Teresa complained. "Why have I been brought here?"

The officer clicked his heels, his arm still rigid in the Fascist salute. *"Arriba Espana! Viva Franco!"*

She looked at him as she might a tiresome child. "What do you expect of me? That I do this?" She raised both arms in a mocking imitation of his salute. *"Arriba Espana. Arriba* anything you want!" She sighed. "Does it make any difference?"

The officer lowered his arm and scowled. "You'd better be careful."

"What must I be afraid of?" she asked listlessly.

"Explain yourself," he rapped. "What are you doing here?"

It was easy to tell the story she had prepared for her father. "And I remained in hiding all night," she concluded.

His forehead furrowed. He paced away from her, spun around and strode back. "Describe these men."

She shrugged her shoulders. "They were soldiers wearing dirty uniforms." She wrinkled her nose. "They smelled . . . terrible!"

"What else?"

"One was young," she said. "About twenty. The other was older."

Again he paced up and down with his hands clasped behind him.

He swung around and stabbed his finger at her. "They were Reds?"

She nodded. "I suppose so."

"Our men would not steal," he stated.

She shrugged her shoulders.

"Such men are criminals, not soldiers," he stormed. "They are the scum we're driving out of Spain."

She asked: "Please may I go? My father will be worried."

"First come with me," he said shortly. He strapped on a Sam Browne belt, holstered a pistol and adjusted his peaked cap at a rakish angle. "Follow me." He set off, walking quickly. The soldier who had captured her trod closely on her heels.

At the extreme end of the olive grove a group of Nationalist soldiers were seated around a stone-built hut. They sprang to attention when the officer arrived, and Teresa drew in a quick breath when she saw their prisoners. Both men were stripped to the waist; and barbed wire was twisted around their wrists. Juan's face was greenish and his eyes were glazed. He was kneeling and holding himself as though he had received a powerful kick in the belly. Blood oozed from his ear, and he had vomited over himself.

Ernesto stood beside him with his head hanging. His face was bruised and swollen beyond recognition.

"Have they talked?" asked the officer.

A sergeant with rolled-up sleeves and bleeding knuckles said: "They swear they threw away their weapons and intended to surrender."

"Take a good look at these men, Señorita."

Ernesto's suffering eyes met hers, then looked away guiltily. They pulled Juan's head back by his hair so she could look into his battered face. He moaned and blood frothed on his lips.

"Take a good look, Señorita. Are these the men?"

There was hope in Ernesto's eyes. He gulped and his bound hands moved slightly as though mutely imploring her mercy. Then remembering he had violated all claim to compassion, his shoulders slumped dejectedly and he looked away.

"Are these the men, Señorita?"

"No," she said quietly.

"You're quite sure?"

"These are not the men."

The officer led her away. "I should keep you prisoner," he said.

She was astonished. "Me a prisoner? Why?"

"How do I know you're not a spy? How do I know you won't give information that'll lead my men into a trap?"

She looked at him unhappily, having no answer.

"What is your village?"

"Escoleras."

"It's in that direction?" He pointed.

"You can see it when you get to the top of the next hill," she confirmed.

He looked her up and down. "How old are you?"

"Eighteen."

"What's the matter with you Catalans? Don't you wash?"

She flushed. "Of course we do."

"Why don't you wash your hair? It's matted with filth."

She ran her fingers through her hair and they came away smeared brown. She remembered how Ernesto had thrown her to the ground. She dropped her gaze, shamed by the distaste in the officer's cold eyes.

"All right, Señorita. You may go home. Go straight there. If you try to circle back around us, you'll be shot. Do you understand?"

"I'll go straight home," she promised. She hesitated timidly.

"What is it?" he rasped.

"Your two prisoners . . . what . . . what will you do with them?"

His eyes were icy. "You'd better be off quick; unless you want to join them!"

She hurried away. Her head was aching and shivers ran up and down her spine. She feared she had caught a cold.

5

That same afternoon the Nationalist troops entered Escoleras. An armored car cautiously approached the village outskirts, its machine-gunner alert. But the villagers showed no hostility, and the armored car drove on to the plaza followed by six other armored cars, a staff car bearing smartly uniformed officers and transport trucks carrying Spanish and Moorish troops.

Father Delbos had found Don Carlos's black cassock, had brushed it and now wore it proudly as he headed the welcoming committee he had quickly formed. It was made up of shopkeepers and included the reluctant Doctor Aldo.

As soon as the officers stepped out of their staff car, Father Delbos flung up his arm with the palm pressed outward. His voice rang around the plaza. *"Arriba Espana. Viva Franco!"*

The officers briskly returned his salute and looked expectantly at the other members of the welcoming committee. One or two sheepishly raised their arms.

"Welcome to Escoleras, gentlemen," said Father Delbos. "Tonight I'll hold a special service of thanksgiving. When the Reds retreated, I and other responsible villagers assumed temporary authority while awaiting liberation . . ."

The officers solemnly shook hands with everyone. But after weeks of campaigning, they were bored by the trivialities of civilians.

"I need to billet my men," the captain said. "Afterward we must set up a field kitchen."

"We've already arranged for it, Captain," said Father Delbos smoothly. "Your men can be comfortably billeted in the village social hall. We've cleared out the seats. Also a large warehouse has been generously offered by Señor Medas. At the other end of the village, there's a large field that will be ideal for your kitchen."

"You've been very helpful," said the captain. Now that the enemy was in full flight, he wanted his men to snatch a badly needed rest and eat cooked food.

Guards were posted and the soldiers were dispersed to their billets. The villagers were slightly reassured when they saw the soldiers were well disciplined.

Father Delbos presented himself at the officers' headquarters and asked for an interview.

"Tell him to call tomorrow," said Captain Rota tiredly.

But Father Delbos would not be denied. "It is a matter of great importance. It concerns the safety of the State," he told a corporal.

Wearily Captain Rota agreed to see him. The priest produced a list of names. "For two and a half years, I have watched and observed. I know those who fear God and those who deny him. These are the traitors, Captain Rota. These are the Reds and their supporters who have almost destroyed our Church and our country. I have made notes against each name!"

Captain Rota stared down at the list unhappily. He sighed. "I will deal with this tomorrow."

The priest drew himself up. "It is a matter of great urgency!"

The captain said coldly: "If you've waited two and a half years, another day won't make much difference!"

"These men are Reds and associates of Reds. They are anti-Christ and anti-Church."

"I will deal with it," said Captain Rota.

"When, *mi Capitan?*" insisted the priest.

"Mañana."

The priest shook his head. "Captain, I respectfullȳ suggest you have a moral obligation to deal with this matter *at once!* The Red troops are fleeing to the French border. But they have left saboteurs in our midst, men who are traitors to Spain and who will destroy our ammunition dumps, attack us in the rear and rob us of the military advantages we have gained so dearly."

Captain Rota's mouth turned down as he studied the list of names. "These people are going to do *all* this between now and tomorrow morning?"

"I am only a simple man of God," said Father Delbos. "Military matters are *your* affair." His blue eyes were guileless. "With your experience, *mi Capitan,* you will know how much importance to place on this information. You are doubtless right that there is no immediate danger from traitors. But hasty judgment can sometimes result in a serious error."

Captain Rota stared hard at the priest.

The priest stared back, his blue eyes very solemn. "I have seen the Red terror," he said quietly. "Have you, Captain? Have you seen nuns raped by the mob and then sat upright on pointed stakes? Have you seen priests with genitals hacked off? Have you seen the flames shoot high and God's sacred relics burned in the inferno of the Communist hell?" The priest breathed hard. "Have you seen Christ on the cross torn down and trampled underfoot, the Holy Chalice besmirched by pigs or heard blasphemy pour like excretion from the lips of beasts?"

"You have the advantage on me," said Captain Rota coldly. "I am a soldier and have seen only how men die on the fields of battle."

Father Delbos leaned forward, his weak jaw jutting and his soft, white forefinger stabbing forcefully. "The names on that list, Captain, are men of evil. You must purge the village. *Now!* Tomorrow may be too late. The Red poison spreads swiftly." He paused and then added very clearly: "It will be terrible, Captain, if because of neglect, men die by sabotage."

Captain Rota sighed. "Very well, Father Delbos. Tell me more about these people. Who is this Federico Morales?"

The priest moved closer and lowered his voice. "Federico Morales was mayor when the Civil War started. He worked hand-in-glove with the Communist Committee. He was mayor when sixty loyal villagers and Falangists were cold-bloodedly murdered. He is a criminal whose hands are stained with the blood of patriots."

"And this man, Pedro Bastico? What have you against him?"

"Pedro Bastico is an artisan who makes cartwheels. Often men meet and talk in his workshed. They speak disparagingly of General Franco and today when your troops arrived, I saw him turn his back and walk away. He is anti-Christ. Recently I asked him to come to *Misa,* but he laughed at me! *'Why should I go to church?'* he asked. *'To be closer to God.'* I told him. He laughed again and made a vulgar gesture. *'If God is in your church,'* he said, *'he is not the kind of man I want to meet.'* That is the way he spoke, Captain. He blasphemed. He took the name of the Lord in vain!"

"What other villainy has Pedro Bastico committed?"

"He is a friend of Morales."

The captain scowled at the long list of names.

"You must act," urged the priest. "These men are dangerous."

The captain sighed. "I'll have these men brought here and I'll talk to them. It will be helpful, Father, if you will make precise charges."

At once Father Delbos was moving to the door, bobbing his tonsured head in farewell. "I cannot be an instrument of vengeance, *mi Capitan.* I can give guidance to those who uphold the law. But as a man of God, I may not enter the arena of battle except as a servant of God."

Captain Rota glowered blackly at the list of names. Then he summoned his adjutant. "I've been given a list of suspects."

The adjutant nodded. "Shall I arrest them, Señor?"

"Bring in the first two. I'll talk to them and see how it goes."

A sergeant and two green-turbaned Moorish soldiers brought in Morales and Bastico. The two men sat nervously on the edges of their chairs while the captain and the adjutant eyed them. Then Captain Rota glanced down at the handwritten notes Father Delbos had given him and asked: "Which of you is Federico Morales?"

Morales's face was pale and his wide eyes betrayed his fear. "I am Morales," he croaked. His hands rubbed the tightly stretched serge of his trousers, drying his sweaty palms.

"You were present when sixty villagers were murdered by the Communist Committee?"

For a moment he thought Morales would faint. "It was forty!"

Captain Rota's cold eyes studied him. "Do you think the lesser the number of victims, the smaller the crime?"

"It was terrible!" choked Morales. His eyes were haunted. "Everyone was deeply shocked."

"You were mayor and condoned this mass murder? You were present at the shooting?"

"I was against it. But the committeemen were armed . . . They were wicked, desperate men . . ."

"What did you do to prevent this mass killing?"

"I . . . I protested . . . I called them murderers . . ."

"Your efforts were not very effective!"

"I was alone . . . and in their power."

"But you weren't *always* a prisoner. What did you do afterward? Did you denounce these criminals, arouse the antagonism of the villagers against these killers?"

Morales's hands were trembling. He stared at Captain Rota, and the tip of his tongue moistened his colorless lips. "I . . . I was ill afterward," he said hoarsely. "I was . . . ill!"

"Ah!" said Captain Rota. "You were ill!" He glanced down at his notes again. "You are Pedro Bastico?"

Bastico was a heavily built man in his late forties. His hair was thick and black, but with silvery sideburns. His gray eyes were wary. "I'm Bastico," he confirmed challengingly.

"You are a member of the Communist Party?"

"No."

"You were once a member of the Communist Party?"

"No."

"You are a Red or have Red sympathies?"

Bastico leaned forward, his elbows resting on his knees and his broad hands hanging down between them. "I'm not Red and I'm not black. My color is the same as most other Spaniards. Communist sympathies? Tell me things about communism, then ask me if I sympathize with them."

"You're anti-God?"

Bastico sighed. "I'm not anti-anything."

"You do not go to church?"

Bastico smiled slowly. "Few villagers have gone to church these last two years." He shrugged his shoulders. "Even so, not all men worship God in church."

Captain Rota read Father Delbos's notes. "Do you deny you have denounced religion?"

Bastico said nothing.

"Did you hear me? Do you deny you have denounced religion, spoken in favor of socialism and praised La Pasionaria?"

Bastico clamped his lips shut and scowled.

Captain Rota's voice was a whiplash. "Do you hear me? Answer!"

Bastico's eyes flashed. "To accuse is easy."

"I do not accuse. I ask you to deny or confirm my statements."

"I deny everything!" said Bastico.

Captain Rota stared at him thoughtfully.

Bastico glared back.

The captain shrugged his shoulders. "Take them away. Keep them under lock and key."

They were walked to the old Civil Guard headquarters.

"It'll be the same all over again, Morales," said Bastico bitterly. He spoke Catalan so the guards would not understand. "Another reign of terror!"

"I was forced to witness the shooting. It made me ill . . . nervous strain. There are people who will swear to it . . . the doctor . . ."

Bastico said quietly: "Face reality, Morales. We won't have a trial. In all the towns and villages they've captured, they've always shot . . . somebody!"

Morales's hands were trembling. "You think . . . they're going to shoot us?"

"Not if I can help it," said Bastico grimly. His eyes narrowed. "Will you wait for them to shoot you? Or will you try to escape?"

"Please Holy God, save me," Morales whispered. "Please Holy Mother of Christ."

"Make up your mind, quickly," said Bastico. "We've only got seconds."

"I don't want to die," moaned Morales. "Please Holy God, don't make me die."

"We've only one chance," said Bastico grimly. "Listen carefully. When we get near to Ibarra's house we must walk more slowly and drop back a little behind the guards. When we are level with the Ibarro doorway, we must spring inside it. The door has an iron bar. It will hold them while we climb the stairs to the roof. There are many rooftops we can cross and many ways to escape through the houses of friends."

"They will shoot us," quavered Morales.

"Walk more slowly," said Bastico, dropping back. "Decide quickly, Morales. I do this with you or alone."

"Please Holy Mother of God, help me," wailed Morales. But he walked more slowly and a muscle in his cheek twitched violently as Ibarro's house drew nearer.

"Are you ready, Morales?"

"Bastico. I beg of you! *Por favor.*"

"What is it, man?"

"I am afraid. I am *afraid,* I tell you!"

"Who is not afraid, fool?" Bastico's forehead gleamed. "Walk slower, man. Walk slower!"

They were slightly behind their guards and as they drew level with Ibarro's house, Bastico hurled himself at the nearest guard. His strong arms wrapped around the man's waist and hurled him sideways against his companion. The two collided with startled grunts and swiftly unslung their rifles. But Bastico had already plunged through the open doorway after Morales. The heavy wooden door slammed shut and the iron bar dropped into its socket. The guards reached the door a split second later, pounding their rifle butts against it. One guard pointed his rifle at the sky and fired. Startled villagers drew back from windows and doorways, and other soldiers came running.

Morales ran up the steep, stone stairway. Sweat poured down his pale cheeks. Bastico was behind him, thrusting hard at his buttocks. "Quickly, man. Hurry. May I shit upon the breasts of the Virgin Mary if you do not hurry."

They stumbled out onto the flat roof and Bastico ran to the nearest parapet and swung his leg over it. "Hurry," he urged. The sound of rifle butts splintering the door below goaded Morales to unexpected efforts.

They reached a rooftop seven houses away. Bastico ran to the roof door, but it swung open and a woman warned: "Not here. They're in this street and searching the houses."

Bastico turned away, tugging Morales by the arm. They reached another parapet but an alleyway separated it from the next rooftop. Bastico jumped it easily. Morales stood on the parapet, his legs trembling and his eyes wide with terror. "Bastico!" he croaked. "Help me!"

"Jump, man! It's no distance."

"I can't."

Bastico reached out. "Hold my hand and jump. I won't let you fall."

A Moorish soldier in the street saw them and fired excitedly. His bullet smashed Morales's shin. The mayor whined with agony as he fell. His wail of pain trailed after him until his skull smashed against the cobbles.

A bullet chipped stone close to Bastico's foot. He raced on across the rooftops, his underclothing wet with the sweat of fear. Behind him, hoarse voices shouted to him to stop.

He edged around a chimney stack, vaulted a parapet, dropped six feet to a lower roof and ran across to a doorway. From the corner of his eye he sensed movement and shot a startled glance at the soldier on the parapet of the house next door. The man had a tommygun and grinned viciously.

Bastico skidded to a standstill. He flung a quick glance over his shoulder at other soldiers rooftops away, gave a despairing glance toward the door leading to the street below. Then, with a sigh of resignation, he shrugged his shoulders and grinned wry surrender at the soldier with the tommygun.

The soldier's smile expanded to show his teeth, his finger tightened on the trigger and explosive fire tore Bastico apart.

Captain Rota told his sergeant to show in Doctor Aldo.

"I am very tired, Doctor," he said as soon as he entered. "I have many things to do and want to snatch a little sleep. However . . . Do sit down."

"I prefer to stand," said Doctor Aldo crisply. He was angry. "Are we about to suffer another reign of terror?"

Captain Rota flushed. "Of what do you complain, Doctor?"

"Two men have been murdered! Another eight have been arrested by your orders. Will they also be murdered, Captain?"

"Murdered?" Captain Rota scowled. "I must remind you we are at war. Military law prevails. Prisoners who escape risk being shot." He shrugged his shoulders. "My men did their duty."

Doctor Aldo glared.

Captain Rota stared back levelly.

"Juan Morales suffered more under the Communist Committee than anyone can imagine," said the doctor grimly. "Bastico never harmed anyone by a thought or an action in all his life."

"I regret what happened, Doctor. But this is war."

"How about the other villagers you have arrested, Captain? They're men of good repute. We know of no reason why they should be prisoners."

"I know nothing against them, either. But they have been denounced, Doctor Aldo!"

The doctor was startled. "I do not understand, Captain. I can think of nothing for which they could be denounced."

"All are accused of being Reds; of being anti-God; of being capable of conspiring with the enemy, engaging in sabotage and acting as spies."

"I find it hard to believe anyone could denounce them on such absurd charges."

"Nevertheless, they have been denounced!"

Doctor Aldo eyed the captain steadily. "In confidence, can I know who has denounced them?"

"I am not permitted to tell."

"It could not have been a responsible person."

The captain examined his fingernails. "It *is* a responsible person."

Doctor Aldo's eyes glowed. "Father Delbos!"

"Is a priest not a responsible person?"

"The man's a religious fanatic; so biased he's unbalanced."

The captain said quietly, "Father Delbos supports our crusade, Doctor." There was a warning note in his voice.

Doctor Aldo retorted flatly: "Any fanatic is unbalanced!"

"It may be as you say, Doctor Aldo," said the captain stiffly. "Nevertheless, I cannot ignore information given by those who serve our sacred cause."

"You've even got Hernando in prison!" said Doctor Aldo bitterly. "What could anyone say against Hernando?"

"Quite a lot is said against him," said the captain wearily. "He is an Anarchist, he never goes to church, he associates with Reds, he leads an improper and immoral life."

Doctor Aldo raised his eyes despairingly toward the heavens. "Hernando led the villagers against the Communist Committee. He criticized them violently to their faces. Hernando's love for his fellowman is fuller, richer and truer than most of those who spend hours on their knees before an altar. Hernando lives irregularly because he is an irregular man. He never takes, but always gives. If he is immoral because he visits the village whorehouse, then he is as immoral as the rest of the men of the village."

"All you say may be true, Doctor. But these men have been denounced and my duty is to act."

"These men are all innocent," said Doctor Aldo quietly.

"I hope they are," said Captain Rota. "I will not set up my own military court. I will send the prisoners to Gerona where they will be properly charged and held for trial."

Doctor Aldo was furious. "Without any proof? Without even knowing who has denounced them? They'll be imprisoned for months! Is this your Nationalist justice, Captain?"

"It is military justice." The captain smiled thinly. "As commander of forces occupying hostile territory, I could have them shot at once as denounced saboteurs. Consider yourself at liberty to call upon me again if you have problems, Doctor."

Doctor Aldo stooped, snatched up his worn medical bag and stalked to the door. He paused to look back over his shoulder. "You'd better put me on the list, too, Captain. I don't go to church, I associate with Reds like Hernando and I think Father Delbos is a hypocrite."

"Do you wish to denounce him?" asked the captain somberly.

"I denounce my ass!" said the doctor and slammed the door.

6

The madam's gardener led Emil Serra out of the patio to a dirt path between stone-built cottages. Drab-garbed women sat lace-making in their open doorways.

Although the gardener was more than twice Serra's age, he walked so fast it was difficult for Serra to keep pace with him. They threaded through a vegetable plot, climbed a stone wall into a vineyard and followed along the ditch that separated it from a neighboring olive grove.

The old man often waited for Serra to get his wind, and each time they stopped, Serra drank deeply from a brandy bottle. He was drinking to blend the numbness of his extremities with the tingling that alcohol produced. His feet dragged leadenly, the world around him swayed and his thoughts seemed clogged. He stumbled along with his gaze fixed on the heels of the old man's worn, rope-soled *alpargatas*. Presently the old man stopped.

"You see a mountain to your left that has a cluster of pine trees growing on the slope almost to the summit? Now look to your right. You see a ruined farmhouse two kilometers away? Now, midway between the two, do you see a tall eucalyptus tree?"

Emil Serra strained his eyes at the blurred horizon. "I see it," he said uncertainly.

"Head for that tree. It stands beside a cart track that leads into Escoleras. From here you can find your way alone and I wish you the best of luck."

Emil Serra pulled out his wallet and counted out so many notes the old man was alarmed and stopped him. "Please, Señor, that is enough. It is more than enough! No more! *Please,* no more!"

Emil replaced his wallet.

"That eucalyptus tree," the old man repeated.

"I see it," said Emil. He screwed up his eyes but the horizon shimmered.

He stumbled on, not clearly realizing the old man was no longer with him. When the brandy bottle was empty he threw it away, listening to it thud on the earth and stupidly watching it glittering in the sun. He flicked his hands and they were numb to the wrists. He laughed and stumbled on again. But the last gulp of brandy was too much even for his alcohol-hardened system, and abruptly his abused stomach revolted. Ripped apart by nausea he fell to his knees and vomited violently. He tore off a piece of his shirt, wiped his face clean and after he had regained some strength, climbed to his feet and went on.

His brain was clearer now and he saw that the eucalyptus tree was far off to his left. He altered direction and stumbled toward it. There was a damp smell to the soil and even in the meadowlands the breeze carried on it the sage-scent of the mountains. The colors were strong; the upturned earth was sometimes blood-red or as black as velvet. There was the silvery green of the olive trees and the warmer greens of the heath. His senses seemed suddenly acute; and all they sensed was familiar. The country around him was so familiar and comforting, it was . . . like coming home! He stooped for a handful of soil and sucked it to know its taste. He picked a leaf from a bush and chewed it. He ran his tongue along the mossy underside of a large rock and thought, *This is home. I have come home.*

Abruptly he felt a great urgency to reach Escoleras before it was too late. He hurried on, forcing his numbed feet into a shuffling run and watching the ground to make sure he placed them correctly. He heard a shout and when he looked over his shoulder, a uniformed man gestured to him from a clump of trees. But time was more important now than it had ever been. "I can't wait," he shouted breathlessly. "I've no time to wait for a bus."

He ran on, ignoring the shouts until there was the crack of a rifle. Simultaneously, a sharp blow in his thigh knocked him to the ground. With an effort he rose to his feet, ran a few more paces until his leg collapsed, then pitched forward on his face.

Sergeant Leon was bitter. His best friend, and also his brother-in-law, who had campaigned with him throughout the war, had been killed the day before.

The manner of his dying grieved Sergeant Leon even more. They had come unscathed through many battles. But with the enemy in full flight and the war as good as over, death had come ingloriously, like a traitor. Somewhere on the slopes of a distant rock-strewn mountain, a sniper had taken careful aim and pressed the trigger. Sergeant Leon and his brother-in-law were walking side by side. Sergeant Leon heard the fleshy *phut* as the bullet entered his brother-in-law's back and a split second later heard the crack of the rifle. But there was no telltale smoke to show where the sniper was hidden.

His brother-in-law fell to his knees. His eyes glazed and at once he coughed blood. He did not die quickly, and Sergeant Leon stayed at his side, weeping with misery and frustration as his friend's lungs slowly filled with blood and drowned him. Afterward he searched the mountain slopes, combing every gulley and ravine where a sniper could lurk. But the killer had slipped away.

So, as Sergeant Leon led a small patrol to the inland village he had been ordered to occupy, his mood was grim. Knowing it, his men discreetly kept their distance from him.

One of his men who was in the lead shouted, "Halt." He shouted again. And again.

Sergeant Leon ran forward as the soldier raised his rifle and fired. The soldier lowered his gun and the sergeant knew he had brought the man down.

"I winged him, sir," the soldier said dourly.

They approached the wounded man warily but it was evident he was not armed. He was sitting up and staring thoughtfully at the spreading red stain on his fleshy thigh. His eye sockets were cavernous and his wildly glowing eyes were unutterably weary. "It doesn't hurt," he said. There was a note of surprise in his voice.

"It often doesn't at first," said the man who had shot him.

Sergeant Leon asked sharply: "Why didn't you stop?"

Emil Serra bleared up at him. "I'm . . . I'm going to Escoleras," he said as though it explained everything.

"I'll ask you again," said the sergeant dangerously. "Why didn't you stop?"

"I must get there quickly. I haven't much time. I can't wait for the bus."

Emil's voice had lost its strength. But Sergeant Leon heard the lilting intonation in the man's voice and accused sharply: "You're not Spanish!"

"But I am," said Serra and smiled strangely. "I'm a Spaniard a hundred years old. I know the taste of the soil."

"He's crazy," said a soldier.

Sergeant Leon's eyes narrowed. "Papers?"

Emil stared at him dazedly. "Papers . . . I can't remember."

"You're lying," accused Sergeant Leon. He was listening intently and now the foreign accent clearly betrayed itself. "You're *not* Spanish!"

"I'm Polish," said Emil. All of his leg was numb but he found he could stand if he didn't place too much weight on it. "The Polish Embassy," he said. He looked at the ring of grim eyes. "Diplomatic immunity." Clarity of thought approached and receded like waves of pain and the need to reach Escoleras before it was too late was compulsive. These men were obstructing him and he said resentfully: "Leave me alone. Take your hands off me."

"Why are you dressed in civilian clothes?" demanded Sergeant Leon. His voice rose angrily. "You're a spy for the International Brigade! Why are you here on Spanish soil . . . killing Spaniards?"

A black wave rolled in over Emil Serra and he said loudly: "No time to wait in line." He tried to stride away but as the men closed in his leg collapsed again. He found himself lying on the ground.

"Tell the truth. Who are you?" demanded Sergeant Leon. He stood over Serra with his legs apart and his rifle gripped tightly.

"I've got to go now," panted Serra. His eyes burned. "No time. No time now at all."

"Answer my questions!"

The black wave receded and Serra found himself staring up at an angry-eyed man. The dull throb in his thigh reminded him he had been shot and he hurled at the sergeant the most terrible insult he could think of in Spanish. "Leave me alone, you son of a whore!"

Sergeant Leon's face turned black, the skin stretched taut across his cheekbones and he was aware of the startled faces of his men. He didn't think. He raised his rifle and smashed it down. The butt hit Emil Serra's outstretched fingers with the force of a sledgehammer. Blood spurted and the shocked soldiers stared down at a raw mess of flesh and bone.

Sergeant Leon was instantly appalled by what he had done and unnerved by Serra who looked down at his smashed fingers, looked back at the sergeant and then . . . chuckled.

"You big black, Fascist bastard," said Emil and held up his mangled, dripping fingers.

The soldiers were ashamed. One man pulled out a filthy handkerchief and wrapped it around the injured hand.

"That's a lesson for you," said Sergeant Leon grimly. "This is war.

Now. Do you deny you're a member of the International Brigade?"

But another black wave was enveloping Serra as he struggled to answer the persistent questions. Yes. He was Polish. Yes, there were lots of Polish volunteers in the International Brigade. He knew because he had met some of them. The questions nagged maddeningly, making him wait in line and he said: "Yes. The International Brigade."

They lifted him to his feet and helped him hobble. He went with them in a cloud of misunderstanding, every step strangely pleasing because it brought him closer to Escoleras and as the black wave receded, he saw they had reached a stone-built farmhouse. They stood him against the wall and a soldier made a crude crutch of a broken branch to help him stand. Then they faced him, raising their rifles, and with sudden clarity he knew he would now never reach Escoleras.

There was no sensation at all in his hands or feet and the prickling at the back of his neck was more intense. It made his thoughts wander. He wanted to warn them to hurry or they might be too late. The toy soldiers leveling their rifles were suddenly so ridiculous he laughed loudly.

Sergeant Leon waited until he had finished laughing, and Emil Serra, seeing the sergeant's glaring eyes, remembered a taunting phrase. *"No pasaran!* They shall not pass!" he shouted just before the rifles volleyed.

"Communist bastard," spat Sergeant Leon. "He might be the one who murdered Juan yesterday."

"Sergeant. Over here, please," called one of his men. At the back of the house was a well. A dropped stone fell for a long time before they heard the faint splatter of water. "That's better than digging a grave, Sergeant?"

"All right."

"No identification. All he had in his pockets was this." It was the well-filled wallet and a watch and chain with an oddly designed hexagonal charm bearing the letters SRR curiously entwined.

"Probably stolen," said Sergeant Leon. He counted the money.

There was a loud splash from the well.

"We don't know who he is or where he came from," said the sergeant slowly.

His men looked at him expectantly.

"There's no next of kin we can notify. We might as well split this lot among us."

The men gathered around him eagerly.

"Nobody had better talk about this," he warned.

"Sergeant. Give me the empty wallet and I'll throw it in after him."

A soldier examined the watch charm. "It's some kind of hard metal." He looked around. "Does anybody else want it?"

The others were too busy counting to answer him.

"All right, men," said Sergeant Leon presently, buttoning his pocket flap. "Let's go."

7

One night the village was shaken by a terrible explosion. Wreckage and debris were scattered over a large area, and a dozen small fires started. The startled villagers jumped from their beds and ran out into the streets. To alarm and confusion was added fear as angry soldiers herded the villagers into the plaza at bayonet-point. One man who resented being bullied struck out and was shot in the leg. Another was treated for a bayonet wound. A third who tried to escape when challenged was brought down by a fusillade of shots before he had run twenty yards.

The Nationalist ammunition stores had exploded. Thirteen soldiers had been killed and another twenty were badly injured. It was probably sabotage. So, while the fires were fought the soldiers stormed into every house and rounded up all the villagers.

Captain Rota sent for Doctor Aldo, Father Delbos and other representatives of the villagers and asked them to identify the man who had been shot while escaping.

Doctor Aldo knew him by sight. He was from an inland village and had no right to be in Escoleras. Doctor Aldo stared down at him and said he did not know him. The other villagers followed Doctor Aldo's lead and the dead man became *"the unknown."*

Many of the villagers had not been given time to put on more than a topcoat over their nightclothes. They shivered in the freezing night air, shut their ears to insults, and suffered the cold and the soldiers' blows in submissive silence. It was dawn before they were allowed to return to their homes.

Doctor Aldo helped the military surgeon, amputating, stitching deep wounds and splinting broken bones. It was early morning when he went home to snatch a few hours sleep and midday when he arose again. He had a quick meal before he set off on his rounds.

The village brooded with suppressed terror. Only the Administrative Office set up by Captain Rota to deal with village affairs showed signs of life. Here a long line of women patiently waited in the street. They were applying, as they did every day, for a permit to travel to Gerona. They were the wives of men sent to Gerona and awaiting trial.

Doctor Aldo sighed and hurried on to the Barras's cottage. He shouted when he pushed open the door and Paco Barras called to him to come up.

He climbed the stairs to where Teresa lay in bed. Her cheeks were flushed, her eyes overly bright and her silver hair was lifeless as it splayed across her pillow, looking as if it might come away in handfuls. Paco Barras sat beside her, tired-eyed and worried.

"How is she today?" asked Doctor Aldo as he put down his medical bag.

"About the same," sighed Paco.

Teresa coughed, a harsh coughing that shook her violently. Doctor Aldo noticed she had lost more weight. The coughing made her retch and she leaned over the side of the bed. Rust-colored sputum dribbled into an earthenware bowl. She lay back weakly on her pillow and closed her eyes. Her breath rasped.

Doctor Aldo placed a thermometer under her armpit although he knew by touching her dry skin that she was still running a high fever.

"She doesn't get any better," choked Paco.

"Every illness must run its course," soothed Doctor Aldo. He was angry at his impotence to heal her. Good vaccines could give a patient quick relief. But in the turmoil and confusion of war, he had been unable to obtain adequate medical supplies.

"She's still got a temperature," he told Paco Barras as though it was of little importance. "In a day or two now, she'll be over the crisis. Cheer up, Teresa. It won't be long now."

Her eyelids fluttered as she made a weak attempt to smile.

"She's . . . she's complained of a pain in her side," said Paco.

"That's not unusual," said Doctor Aldo. "Don't worry about it."

But his inner anger increased. This was what he feared: the development of pleurisy. If the attack was bad, her lung could collapse. That would mean surgery.

"Sometimes it gives her great pain," said Paco.

"If it gets any worse we'll do something about it," soothed the doctor. "Meantime we'll tape her. That usually eases the pain."

"Isn't there anything else we can do, Juan?" pleaded Paco Barras.

"Patience, Paco. Patience cures most illnesses. All we doctors can do is help nature's healing powers. You should bring her mother home as soon as possible. Women are better nurses than men."

"Aren't there any medicines . . . ?" asked Paco anxiously.

"Stick to the pills she's already taking. There are none better available." The doctor smiled sadly. The sugar pills he had provided for Teresa were to soothe her father's anxiety. "I'll call in again tonight." He waved cheerfully as he left.

He finished his rounds and on his way to his surgery again passed the waiting line outside the Administrative Office. The sad line of women had their black shawls pulled tightly around their shoulders and their frozen fingers under their armpits. Inside the office, two sergeants were smoking and chatting and making it obvious they were intentionally keeping the line waiting. Crude, hand-printed notices hanging on the office walls warned: *"It is forbidden to speak or write Catalan."*

An armed soldier was waiting for the doctor outside his house. He saluted smartly and handed the doctor a letter.

"You'd better wait," said the doctor. He opened the letter and read it.

DOCTOR ALDO:
Two more of my men died during the night. I hold the village responsible for their murder. If any other incident occurs, I will make reprisals.

CAPTAIN ROTA

Doctor Aldo sighed. "There's no reply," he said and wearily entered his house.

During the next few days tension increased when yet another soldier died from his injuries. The Moorish and Spanish troops became provocative. They stopped villagers, insulted them, demanded to see their papers and manhandled them. Whoever was heard speaking Catalan received a severe beating. Marcel Prada incautiously called across the street to a fisherman friend, asking if he had fish for sale, and was knocked down by two Moorish soldiers and kicked unconscious.

The line of villagers seeking travel permits daily grew longer. It often waited four or five hours before the door opened, and the door was firmly closed again within half an hour. Those in the line who hadn't been dealt with had to return the following day. A sullen, resentful silence welded the villagers together in a passive hostility toward the soldiers. And the soldiers made no secret of their dislike and distrust of Catalans.

Pablo Biquito was stone deaf. He carefully tied his pick and shovel to the iron rack of his ancient bicycle and tested the pressure of his worn tires with a callused thumb. His wife hurried downstairs, panting with the effort of catching him before he set off. "Pablo!"

He swung his leg over the saddle.

"Pablo!" she panted, running after him as he pushed off. Her plump fingers grasped his arm. He looked around quickly and braked, balancing himself on one foot.

"Pablo. Bring back some firewood. Do you understand? Firewood?"

He watched her lips intently.

She mouthed again, loudly and slowly. "Firewood."

His face lit up. He grinned and mimed striking a match, applying it to a fire and warming his hands.

She nodded contentedly. "That's right, Pablo. As much as you can bring."

He nodded, pressed down on his pedal, wobbled and rode away along the cobbled street toward the outskirts of the village.

It was just after dawn and the morning air was chilly. There were many soldiers patrolling in pairs, and the first couple he met made him pull up. One covered him with a rifle while the second examined his identity card. The soldier flung it on the ground so that Pablo Biquito had to dismount from his bicycle to retrieve it. As he did so, the soldier spat, his spittle narrowly missing the deaf man's outstretched hand.

With an expressionless face, Pablo Biquito tucked away his papers, mounted his machine and rode on.

Twice more he was stopped within the space of seventy yards by soldiers who had watched him present his papers to others. But Pablo

Biquito was placid. He showed his papers meekly, ignored the sol-diers' insults, which he read on their lips, and rode on impassively.

When he reached the end of the village, he passed a bomb-destroyed shop. The roof had caved in and two soldiers sheltered in its doorway from the cold wind. They saw Pablo Biquito cycle past and called to him. He rode on.

The soldiers ran into the street and shouted. When he didn't stop, one of them fired his rifle into the air.

Pablo Biquito still cycled on.

"The son of a Red whore!" Both soldiers aimed their rifles and fired simultaneously.

Pablo Biquito jolted forward as though a giant fist had punched him between the shoulderblades. His cycle swerved and keeled over. Pablo Biquito pitched forward on his face and lay still. When the soldiers reached him he was quite dead.

Another incident occurred that same night. Doctor Aldo was calm-ing the fears of the hysterical wife of Jesus Guitart.

"I beg of you, Doctor. You must do something for Jesus," pleaded Constancia Guitart. Her eyes were sore with weeping and for weeks she had slept only fitfully.

"Be patient, Constancia," soothed the doctor. "Jesus is not the only man who's been arrested. There are dozens in prison and as innocent as your husband."

"Is his innocence important?" she panted. "Maria Molino who had a permit to visit her daughter in the hospital in Figueras says she was told seventeen men were shot in Gerona last week."

"Don't listen to rumors and wild stories, Constancia. Jesus has a dozen good friends with him, Hernando and Vigon and many others. If they intended shooting them, they would have done so long ago. Don't worry, Constancia. He'll come up before court, prove his inno-cence and return home."

The doctor's confidence was reassuring. She asked hopefully: "Can't you help us to see our men, Doctor Aldo? Every day we line up for travel permits and after hours of waiting we are told to return '*mañana.*' "

"I will see what I can do," he said, knowing he could do nothing.

"There's my son, too," Constancia whimpered. "Who knows where he is now!"

"Constancia, I shall be angry with you. All Spain is in confusion.

That is why you have not heard from José. Be patient. When trains and buses are running again you will have news."

It was then that the girl from the brothel came to call him away.

He gave Constancia tablets. "Take these. They'll make you sleep. And . . . *don't* worry!"

She smiled through her tears. "Thank you, Doctor."

The brothel girl hurried ahead of Doctor Aldo along the narrow streets. She took him in through the back entrance. Josefina was writhing on her bed with blood running from her bitten lips. Her private parts were red; raw and swollen.

Doctor Aldo quickly opened his battered leather medical bag and took out a hypodermic. "What caused it?"

"*Guindilla*," said one of the girls.

"Hold her still," said the doctor, filling the hypodermic. He stood over Josefina, glaring sternly. "Don't move, girl. This will hurt at first, but it will ease the pain."

Her cheeks and breasts ran with sweat. "Do what you must, Doctor. Anything. *Anything!* Please stop the pain. Dear Virgin Mary, Mother of God, please stop the pain."

When he put the hypodermic away he demanded grimly: "How did it happen?"

All the girls told him at the same time and he pieced together the story.

Two soldiers had called and Josefina had refused to admit them. She was bitter because of the killing of Pablo Biquito who was a cousin of her uncle. The soldiers returned later with half a dozen companions and forced their way inside. At first, they had cajoled, but Josefina was adamant and called them murderers. The men became angry, insults flew backward and forward. Then one soldier said: "If you won't with us, you won't with anybody." They sprang upon Josefina, rubbed crushed *guindilla* pods into her and held her down so she couldn't remove them.

"It's like acid eating into you," whispered Josefina. "Doctor, will there be permanent injury?"

"You've a very severe irritation of sensitive membranes," he said. "You're inflamed and swollen. But in a few days the swelling will ease and afterward there'll be a swift improvement." He looked around at the girls. "Why didn't you run for help?"

"They wouldn't let us out."

Doctor Aldo's eyes glittered. "Was anybody else hurt?"

A girl showed him a bruised wrist. "One of them held me and said he wouldn't release me until I loved him. But he let me go finally."

"I'll report this," said Doctor Aldo grimly.

Josefina sat up and her eyes narrowed anxiously. "Don't make more trouble for us, Doctor. I don't want the rest of my girls getting the same treatment."

"Will you recognize the men again?"

Josefina eyed him cautiously. "Perhaps."

"What they did was abominable, woman," flared the doctor. "They must be punished."

Her eyes slitted. "Infect me with syphilis, Doctor, and there's nothing I'd love better than to pass it on to all of them." She shrugged her shoulders. "But we have to be realists, Doctor."

"How does it feel now?"

"It's just . . . all numb."

"No pain?"

"No . . . just the numbness."

"Here are some pills that will make you sleep. Take them and stay in bed. Try to sleep before the numbness wears off. If it's painful again keep bathing with warm water, inside and out. There's no more I can do for you."

As he was leaving, somebody who entered through the unlocked back door tried to draw back, but was too late to avoid meeting the doctor face to face. The doctor stared past him expressionlessly, but Father Delbos reached out a detaining hand. "Someone is ill, Doctor?" he asked uneasily.

"It's one of the girls," said the doctor. "I've given her treatment. It's nothing to worry about."

The priest cleared his throat. "I expect . . ." he said huskily. He cleared his throat again. "You're surprised to see me here, Doctor?"

"Nothing surprises me, Father Delbos," said Doctor Aldo coldly. He pulled out his watch and glanced at it. "I must hurry."

"I've called to give a little spiritual guidance to these . . . sinners," said Father Delbos. His face was yellow and very shiny.

"I hope you'll be able to help them in their need, Father Delbos," said Doctor Aldo acidly. He strode off.

It was late, but Captain Rota received Doctor Aldo, standing stiffly, his face set in hard lines.

"We must have an understanding, Captain," said the doctor grimly. "Are you imposing martial law; or are you giving your men full license to behave like wild beasts?"

"I have already stated in writing that what happened this morning was a regrettable accident. My men did their duty. Those who ignore a sentry's challenge must take the consequences. It is regrettable the man was deaf; but it places no blame upon the men who challenged him."

"There are many other guards who heard the warning shot and could have stopped him," said the doctor bitterly. "If you shoot old men who are deaf, will you also shoot children too young to understand the challenge to halt?"

"You exaggerate, Doctor."

"I do not exaggerate about the injuries to the girl I have just visited." In a few terse sentences, the doctor told what had happened to Josefina. "Your men behaved like animals," concluded the doctor. "Will you conceal their guilt under the cloak of military necessity?"

Captain Rota flushed. "If the facts are as you say, the men responsible will be severely punished." He took a deep breath. "When will the"—he paused —"the young lady be well enough to attend a parade and identify the men?"

"She should be fit enough tomorrow."

"Tomorrow evening then, Doctor? I'll arrange for my men to be assembled."

"I will accompany her here."

"Don't worry, Doctor. The culprits will be severely punished."

"It is better that such incidents do not occur at all."

Captain Rota shrugged his shoulders. "In these difficult days we must be prepared for anything!"

Doctor Aldo nodded and walked to the door. But when he reached it, he paused and looked back. "If it is within your power, Captain, will you help someone in the village?"

The captain sighed. "What do you want of me?"

"She is a young girl attacked by pneumonia. I cannot get supplies of a vaccine that may prevent her illness turning into pleurisy."

The captain reached for a pencil. "What is the name of the vaccine?"

The doctor told him.

"I'll telephone Madrid and ask for it to be rushed to me," promised the captain.

"Thank you," said the doctor quietly. Then he said again, "Thank you, Captain!"

When Josefina's girls awoke the following morning, they found a basket of food and an envelope containing money on the doorstep. There was also a note written in pencil on cheap notepaper:

> We are sorry. You angered us and we lost our tempers.
> Please forgive us.

When Doctor Aldo called to escort Josefina to military headquarters, she refused. She said she was afraid of reprisals. But Doctor Aldo was insistent and because her establishment depended upon the toleration of the mayor, the doctor and others, she agreed. She dressed soberly in a severe gray frock with a white collar and cuffs and covered her hair with a black scarf tied under her chin.

Captain Rota received them and listened with a serious face while Josefina told what had happened. When she had concluded he said gravely: "These are very serious charges you're making."

She nodded.

"Under civil law, sexual assault means a long prison sentence for the culprit."

"Yes," she whispered.

"Military law is more severe than civil law."

"This is what I have been told."

"Very well, then. How many men attacked you?"

"Eight."

"You can recognize them?"

For a moment Josefina hesitated. Her eyes narrowed. "I *couldn't* forget them after what they did!"

"Please wait for a few minutes while the men are assembled."

The men were paraded at attention. Josefina, preceded by the captain and followed by Doctor Aldo, walked slowly along the lines of men, looking into each man's face searchingly. Moving caused her some pain and she walked with a slight limp to ease it. Dozens of eyes watched her furtively.

Josefina walked every row and looked into the face of every soldier.

"Well?" asked Captain Rota.

"No," said Josefina. "They are not here."

Doctor Aldo stared at her disbelievingly.

"I don't recognize any of the men here as those who attacked me last night," said Josefina firmly.

"Are you *quite* sure?" asked the captain.

"They might have been soldiers from another company," suggested Josefina.

"That is most unlikely," said Captain Rota, frowning. "Unless they came from Figueras."

"Are you sure all your men are on parade?" asked Doctor Aldo.

"All of them," confirmed the captain. "I suspended all other duties."

Doctor Aldo walked Josefina home. "Why did you lie?"

"Why did I do *what,* Doctor?"

"Don't talk back at me, woman. Answer my question."

Her face was sad. "Isn't there already too much misery in our world, Doctor? Why make it worse?"

"Their punishment would have been a warning to others."

"But forgiving might be even better, don't you think, Doctor?"

"Josefina," he sighed. "For a sinner you have an ungodly amount of goodness inside you."

He would have left her at the door of her house, but she urged: "You must come in."

He took out his watch and glanced at it. "I've no time."

Her eyes danced. "Some friends sent some presents this morning. Among them was a bottle of genuine French brandy. I'll be honored if you'll be the first to sample it, Doctor."

"*Genuine* French brandy?"

"Martell. Three Star."

Doctor Aldo glanced at his watch again. He said crisply: "I can spare five minutes."

The vaccine Captain Rota asked a friend in Madrid to dispatch urgently was placed on a plane destined for Barcelona. But the plane turned back with engine trouble and was not in service again for five days. Meanwhile, the forgotten vaccine remained in the cargo hold. When the plane was finally unloaded in Barcelona, the vaccine was mistakenly sent with another consignment to Lerida. Thus seventeen days elapsed before Doctor Aldo received it.

By then Teresa's pneumonia had run its course and the hard swelling in her side confirmed the doctor's fears that pleurisy would develop.

8

The camp was a barbed-wire stockade beside the sea; three high walls of stout timber posts and a moat of barbed wire through which not even a rabbit could wriggle. The fourth side of the camp was the sea.

Inside the camp was misery.

Without adequate clothing, shelter, food or hope, the exhausted government troops had been turned loose into a compound of barren sand and left to solve the problem of living.

These were the cold months when icy winds blew down from the Pyrenees and the temperature dropped below freezing at night. To protect themselves from the rain and snow, despairing men scraped shallow trenches in the sand and huddled in them.

Every few days French guards issued a sadly inadequate ration of bread, and cooks appointed by the prisoners were given a miserable supply of beans and potatoes to brew a watery soup.

Between the barbed-wire jaws of the stockade, which bit into the sea to the depth of a man's waist, hungry men raked the sand with their fingers, hoping to find limpets, a crab or some form of marine life. Other men fished with infinite patience with lines made from threads picked from their clothing, the hooks fashioned from clam shells. When a fish was caught the lucky fisherman devoured it at once, the scales, head, bones and raw flesh swiftly chewed and swallowed to appease the ache of hunger.

During the day, the French guards were ever alert for prisoners who tried to swim out to sea and along the coast where they could wade in to land again beyond the camp's confines. More than a score of men had made the attempt. Swimming was strictly forbidden and as soon as a prisoner's feet could no longer touch the sea floor, the guards opened fire.

At night, powerful searchlights blazed across the strip of beach that lined the surf. This was forbidden territory after dark. The French guards were as vigilant at night as by day.

395

The name of the camp was Saint Juan. It was a day's march from the Spanish frontier and Miguel Barras was one of its prisoners.

Miguel chose a strip of beach away from the other prisoners and squatted on his heels, staring into the sea with painful intensity. For many hours Miguel had squatted at the water's edge with his eyes riveted on the shard of broken crockery he had found and partly embedded in the sea floor at knee depth. He combined knowledge with patience, and finally was rewarded. He remained quite still, giving no sign of the upsurge of excitement within him when he saw the octopus.

He watched its vaguely shimmering shape through the transparent water as it approached the gleaming porcelain shard with the delicate curiosity of a marine ballet-dancer. First the tip of one tentacle lightly touched the white lure; and then another; and another.

Miguel tensed himself and waited until the octopus was drawing the fragment of broken crockery into its maw before he sprang.

He launched himself bodily through the air, eyes straining to see his prey, his mind calculating the deflection of the water so that when the icy shock of it engulfed him, his outstretched fingers clawed into the writhing, jelly-substance like hooks.

The octopus throbbed and pulsated madly, its formlessness oozing frantically between his fingers. A lashing tentacle struck his wrist and curled around it, suckers greedily adhering to his flesh.

He lurched to his feet, standing knee-deep in water, and watched a second and third tentacle writhe around his forearm. It was not a big octopus but when he ripped away the tentacles, red blotches had already formed on his skin and the sharp beak that could nip out a solid wedge of flesh was probing at the back of his hand. He worked one finger under the thin layer of flesh that hooded the head of the octopus, and it went mad, lashing with its tentacles frantically. Swiftly he worked the fingers of both hands under the hood and peeled it back, almost, it seemed, turning the octopus inside out. And when this was done, the octopus was dead, although the tentacles which clamped on Miguel's arm still sucked greedily.

Miguel thrust the octopus into his trouser pocket and crammed it deep with his fist. He waded out of the water and shook himself like a dog. His eyes ran along the line of surf to the French guard at the seaward end of the camp wall. The guard had rested his rifle barrel on the parapet and leveled it. When he saw Miguel looking at him he lowered his rifle, grinned cheerfully and gestured as though to say: *You might have tried to escape.*

Miguel trudged up the yielding sand to the higher levels of the beach. Catalina lay listlessly in a shallow trench no deeper than a coffin. Driftwood that Miguel had gathered, tied together and covered with a piece of sacking, protected her face from the rain and sun. She lay upon her side, her fevered black eyes staring numbly at the loose sand wall of the trench. She scratched it with her little finger and watched it crumble, dissolving away as her private world had long since disintegrated. Miguel's shadow fell across her, but she did not glance up.

"How are you feeling?" he asked.

She didn't answer. She scratched at the trench wall and another sandy trickle of hopes and dreams added themselves to the growing mound of disillusion.

"Hungry?"

No answer.

"I've caught an octopus. We can eat."

"Leave me alone," she said wearily. She shivered.

Miguel stared down at her unhappily. "I'll be back soon."

He walked to one of the cooking fires and on the way picked up a thin, pointed stick. There were many men around the fire, and when he squatted on his haunches, they drew close to him.

He watched them warily as he drew the octopus from his pocket; but they were too weak to try to wrest it from him.

He drove the pointed end of the stick into the rubbery flesh and twirled it, winding the octopus on to it like spaghetti. Then he held the stick over the fire. The watching men moved closer, but drew back again when he snarled.

Patiently he roasted the flesh, and when it was cooked, he pulled it off the stick and made his way back to Catalina. As he walked, he bit pieces from it, chewing with a controlled slowness that enabled him to savor its flavor.

Catalina hadn't moved. But she pushed herself up on her elbows when Miguel stood over her and said quietly: "I'm sorry for my rudeness, Miguel."

"*Nada,*" he said. "Everyone can get moody." He squatted and gave her half of the octopus. "Sink your teeth into this."

Her eyes gleamed. "What about you, comrade?"

"I've eaten my share."

"You share everything with me."

"That's because I'm a Communist." The thought amused him and he laughed. And as her sharp teeth tore the octopus apart, she realized it was the first time she had heard him laugh.

He placed his hand upon her forehead. "You still have a fever."

"It is influenza," she said. Under her worn battle tunic, her thin body was shivering.

"You must leave with the others," he suggested.

The camp commander had told the refugee troops the Nationalist government would allow them to return to Spain. Some thirty thousand men had already accepted the offer and every morning a new line waited at the compound gates to be marched to the frontier.

"And you, comrade? What will you do?"

Miguel's eyes glowed. "Those fools who go back put their heads into a noose. They return to the prisons and the firing squads."

"You would have me return to this, comrade?" she mocked.

"You are a woman and a Spaniard is always noble with a woman."

"Always?" she grated and he remembered the vile things they had done to her.

"If you return in woman's clothing as a refugee they will not harm you."

"And what will you do, comrade?"

He glowered darkly. "I'll carry on the fight against fascism."

"You'll carry on the war from South America?"

The Spanish government, now in exile, was transporting refugee Spaniards to Mexico and the Argentine.

Miguel shook his head. "No," he said emphatically. "The war against fascism must be waged in Europe! Far away, across the seas, I can be only a spectator and not a man of action."

She watched his lips and his glowing eyes. "What you say is good, comrade. But if we stay here, we'll starve."

"Nothing is static," he said. "History is in a constant state of change. Remember Marxian philosophy, comrade."

"How do you apply dialectics now, Miguel?"

"I only know that I must stay. But . . . you . . . you can return to Spain and escape this living hell."

She shook her head. "No, comrade. I stay with you."

On the other side of the concentration camp, Commissar Rosen crouched in the shallow hollow he had scraped in the side of a sand dune to protect himself from the wind. He scowled at the green-gray Mediterranean, scuffed into white-crested waves by the wind. The ache of hunger was a nauseating lump in his belly. He had lost all his fat in a few weeks. And to hunger was added the misery of loneliness. The men shunned him. When he joined a group, it split up and scattered.

He understood why.

They thought he had abused his power. But he had never done anything for selfish reasons. Everything he did had been for the cause. The Party came first and should always come first.

But not all the men were good Communists. They didn't understand the necessity for cold reason. They were emotional. He had encouraged them, telling them Stalin was sending troops and arms. It was good political tactics to strengthen their will to go on fighting. But when they were finally forced to retreat, they were resentful of *him* because the promised Russian reinforcements never arrived.

Commissar Rosen was brooding bleakly when he saw a soldier wearily stumbling through the deep sand. The man blew on his fingers and held them under his armpits to warm them. When he drew level with the commissar he complained:

"*Que frio!* So cold, Commissar Rosen."

The commissar was pleasantly surprised to be greeted.

"Cold enough to freeze them off," he said delightedly, blending vulgarity into the conversation because the working classes like earthy talk.

The man swung his arms vigorously and slapped them against his sides. "It's the Tramontana," he complained. "It's the curse of this region. In the winter it brings ice and snow and the old folk die and the young ones are sick with influenza and pneumonia."

"Ah. You are Catalan. You know this district?"

"And you are from Bilbao, are you not, Commissar?"

"That's right, comrade." The commissar wished he had a cigarette to offer this young soldier. "The other men won't talk to me," he confessed sadly. "I don't know what they think I've done to them."

"Some men have strange ideas."

"Everything I did was for the cause," said the commissar. His almond eyes peered anxiously into the young man's face, seeking his sympathy.

"The war's over anyway," said the young man philosophically. He slapped his hands under his armpits, blew on his fingers and thrust them deep into his trouser pockets. "One of our guards found a sheep that strayed out onto the road and was killed. The guard threw it over the barbed wire and now we've got it cooking nicely. Won't you join us?"

The commissar's mouth watered at the mere thought of roasting meat. But he held back. "What about the others?"

The young soldier nodded encouragingly. "Some of the men harbored a grudge. But you can't nurse a grudge all your life." He thumbed cheerfully. "Follow me, Commissar. We've had it spitted over the fire for more than two hours. It should be just right!"

He trudged off slowly, glancing over his shoulder from time to time to make sure the puffing commissar could keep up with him.

"Is it much farther, comrade?" panted the commissar.

"Not now. See that group of men? That's it." The young soldier held his head high and gently sniffed the air. "Can you smell it, Commissar? The wind's blowing the wrong way, but I can just catch a whiff of it."

Commissar Rosen stood still and sniffed. At first he could smell nothing. Then just momentarily, he caught a snatch of the roasting fragrance before the wind tore it away, the delicious mouthwatering aroma of roasting meat.

"It must be done to a turn," said the soldier and quickened his pace. The commissar stumbled along behind him, head down, his breathing labored.

The soldier led him straight up to the group of men and they parted and let him through. It wasn't until their ranks had closed again behind them that the commissar sensed the strained atmosphere.

There was no warming fire, no roasting meat. Only a long, deep trench lined with slats of orange crates to prevent the sides caving in.

The commissar looked around slowly at the ring of sullen faces. He saw Gallo, whom he had ordered to shoot a traitor who came from the same village; Vilatenim, the friend of a deserter he had executed, and other men whom he had denounced for lack of discipline. There was Corbero, too, whom he had had to club with his pistol because he had been afraid to take out a patrol. The hostility in their eyes made his flesh crawl. He said reasonably: "Don't look at me this way, comrades. Everything I did was for the cause."

Their eyes were filled with hate.

"We are comrades," he panted. "We fought shoulder to shoulder, faced the same risks, ate the same rations and shared the same misfortunes." He gulped. "I'm a refugee prisoner like the rest of you."

"Only because you didn't reach Barcelona in time to ship out with the other rats!"

The commissar flushed, remembering angrily how the others had panicked and sailed without him. But it was a fleeting thought. He looked around for the young soldier who had brought him and pleaded: "You know me, don't you, comrade? You understand I had to do what I did, don't you? It was all for the cause. You understand. Tell them you understand."

The young soldier's voice was toneless. "Do you remember a very young soldier who was afraid? He was crying in the trench and refusing to go over the top?"

The commissar licked his lips. "There were a number," he whispered.

"You shot him in the leg?"

"He was a coward. An example has to be made of cowards, otherwise fear spreads like contagion."

"You could have shot him in the calf; but you shot him in the knee. You shattered it. His leg had to be amputated."

Despite the cold there was sweat on the commissar's forehead. "Many hasty things happen in the heat of battle," he murmured. He ran his finger around his collar which was suddenly very tight. "Do you think I *wanted* to shoot him? Comrades! I *had* to do it. For the cause!"

"He was my brother," said the young soldier tonelessly.

The commissar turned his almond eyes away from the young man's face. "I'm sorry," he said. He added defensively: "He was a coward. A coward!"

"He was fifteen years of age," said the young soldier. "He was a child with a child's fears and he cried like a child. And you, Commissar. You *shot* him! In the *knee!*"

They sprang upon him so suddenly that they had ripped open his tunic and peeled it down his arms before he realized it. They tore his shirt and used it to bind his hands behind him, stripped down his riding breeches and strapped his feet together with his belt.

"What are you doing, comrades?" he panted fearfully.

They swung him off his feet, carried him to the deep trench and dropped him into it. He lay at the bottom moaning with pain, one of his arms splintered up behind his back. He looked up and they were a ring of white faces and hostile eyes around a rectangle of gray-blue sky. "Listen to me, comrades," he pleaded tearfully. "I must have a doctor. You can't . . ."

But they weren't listening. They were moving one of the wooden slats that lined the trench. Sand dribbled, slid and then avalanched, aided by their thrusting feet. He knew then their terrible purpose and began to scream.

Sand caved in, ran down over his legs and feet and filled up the trench around him. He screamed like a madman and his eyes rolled wildly.

They removed more wooden slats. The sand moved slowly at first and then flowed into the trench like water finding its own level, surging as though troubled and then growing calm and finally still, until it was a shallow depression.

Quietly the men walked away from the unmarked grave.

The Tramontana howled across the compound, stirring up storm clouds of driving sand that flayed the skin. But as the days passed the wind died to a gentle breeze, the warmth of the sun could be felt and the prisoners bared their wasted bodies to its rays. More soldiers elected to return to Spain and were marched away, and the first boat-load of refugees destined for Mexico left the camp.

As the number of prisoners decreased the conditions improved. Food was not adequate, but men no longer starved. There was an issue of warm clothing and corrugated iron, nails and pit props were supplied to build shelters. The French government announced there was local work available for those who applied. Miguel put down his name and after some days was summoned to the compound office. He took Catalina with him.

A bored French official glanced up at Miguel, then consulted the paper before him.

"You are Miguel Gonzalez?" He spoke Spanish well, but with a marked accent.

"*Sí,* Señor."

"You have papers to prove your identity?"

"They are all lost, Señor."

The immigration officer sighed. "Any identity tags, army papers?" He didn't expect a truthful answer. Those who feared to return to

Spain wanted to start a new life in a new country with their slate wiped clean.

Miguel shook his head.

"Nothing to prove your identity? No letters, visiting cards, club membership?"

"Nothing at all, Señor."

The official sat back in his chair and looked at Miguel, seeing a typical Spaniard with gray-streaked black, curling hair, swarthy skin and dark brooding eyes. A red welt scarred his face from his cheekbone to the point of his jaw. Doubtless a battle scar. The man looked strong and vigorous. "You have applied for work in this area?"

"*Sí*, Señor."

"You know the Spanish government *will* allow Spanish subjects to return to Spain?"

"It is an offer I do not wish to accept, Señor. I do not want to be imprisoned or shot."

The official studied him thoughtfully. "We have no reports that repatriated Spaniards have been badly treated."

"Details of reprisals are not shouted from the housetops, Señor."

The official shrugged. "How about the Argentine? Or Mexico?"

"Thank you, Señor. The Mediterranean is my home. The sea and mountains are part of me."

"Do you wish to become a French citizen with French nationality?"

"*Sí*, Señor. Until I can return to my own country."

To return to their own country was the dream of so many of them, reflected the official boredly. "You understand you may be liable for military service in the French army?"

"*Sí*, Señor. I understand that."

"You also know that if you are allowed to work, you must report to the police every week. If you fail to do so, you become liable to arrest."

"I will obey the law, Señor."

"You have little choice of work. It is hard and badly paid."

"I am not afraid of hard work. But there is an additional matter, Señor." Miguel glanced over his shoulder at Catalina, who edged forward. The official saw a thin, weakly youth whose soft features were marred by an ugly facial scar. One eyelid drooped heavily, giving him a sinister appearance.

"I can't promise not to split you up," he said flatly, anticipating the request.

Miguel drew a deep breath. "It is important we are together, Señor."

"It cuts right across our policy," said the official sharply.

Miguel stared at him for long seconds. Then he said quietly: "Señor. These are unusual circumstances. This companion is . . . my wife."

"What!" The official was shocked. He looked at the youth keenly and then realized that Miguel spoke the truth.

"She's here against all regulations. No women are allowed in the men's compound. She should have declared her sex on arrival."

Miguel and Catalina listened submissively.

"I'd better find something for you quickly," he grumbled. He picked up a pen. "Name?" he asked testily.

Catalina hesitated only a moment before she said: "Catalina Gonzalez."

The next day a guard escorted them to their new work. The French farmer who employed them owned enormous tracts of sandy, inhospitable land that stretched for kilometers. Crops could be grown in only a few places. Much of the land was low-lying and when the sea rose with an on-shore wind, the soil turned marshy. The farmer owned a great herd of goats, and Catalina and Miguel were to shepherd this great flock to the mountain foothills and fatten them up on the sparse vegetation of the upper mountain slopes.

They lived in a stone hut on a mountain slope. It had one, large, all-purpose room, an open chimney, a bed of straw, a few cooking implements and a barrel of wine. Every few days a team of donkeys climbed the broken paths to their hut to take away the filled churns of milk.

Good grazing areas were hard to find and were widely scattered. Every day they walked many miles, climbing steep mountain slopes, in search of new feeding places. Their efforts were rewarded. The flock grew sleek and fat and without becoming aware of it, Catalina and Miguel became bronzed and fit. They toughened with the healthy open-air life and their muscles grew springy and resilient. Day after day they roamed the mountains and learned to know them thoroughly, and always they were in sight of the valleys that led through the Pyrenees into their own country.

They ate well. The supplies sent up by donkey were adequate, but

Miguel supplemented them. He gathered mushrooms and knew which of the giant toadstools were edible. He gathered berries and nuts and often brought back a hedgehog to bake. He was adept at catching rabbits with snares and even learned to catch them with his bare hands. He moved stealthily with his grazing flock, while his keen eyes searched the gorse where rabbits made beds of dried grass and curled up within them. Once he came upon a hare so large he thought it must be a sleeping fox. He approached it stealthily and dealt it a blow on the head that killed it instantly.

They were paid a pitiful sum for their labors but had little need of money. They had a roof and food and the farmer gave them warm clothing. They spent their wages on brandy, tobacco, newspapers and a French-Spanish dictionary with which they translated the headlines. Thus they learned that Europe had forgotten Spain, but was very concerned about the eloquent Fascist dictator of Germany.

9

As soon as he could, Anselmo obtained leave and made his way home, cadging lifts in military trucks. Traveling used up most of his precious seven days of liberty and restricted his stay in Escoleras to forty-eight hours.

He wept when he greeted his mother and sisters, because there had been many times when he had thought he would never see them again. It was a happy homecoming, although he felt uneasy, almost guilty in his Nationalist uniform. But freedom from war and the fear of bombing was all that most people asked.

He visited Teresa and was shocked she was so pale and frail. She sat in a rocking chair on the beach in front of her cottage with a warm blanket over her knees. Rosalia sat beside her.

The two girls were talking when Teresa saw Anselmo approaching, and her face lit up like the sun coming out from behind a dark cloud. If she had not been so weak, she would have run to meet him. Instead, her eyes shone mistily as he took her hands in his.

He looked down at her for long moments and then gently raised her fingers to his lips.

Teresa would not talk about her illness. It was Rosalia who told him of the long weeks with a rubber tube in her side draining away fluid and then the long weeks of slow recovery.

"I'm rapidly getting better, Anselmo," Teresa told him. "I'm over the illness. All I have to do now is regain my strength. You'll see. In a few weeks I'll be as fit as ever!"

They had so much to talk about that Rosalia discreetly slipped away. But soon she was back again, unable to suppress the question burning within her.

"What of Rafael, Anselmo? He is well? Have you seen him?"

Anselmo's eyelids hooded his honey-brown pupils and the crinkles of laughter at the corners of his eyes disappeared. "Yes," he said slowly. "I have seen Rafael."

"What is it?" asked Rosalia anxiously. "He is not wounded?"

Anselmo shook his head. "No." He looked away from them and into the distance. "Rafael . . . he is not like a brother. He is not like any of us. He . . . our mother is terribly hurt."

"What is it, Anselmo?" Teresa asked. "What has he done?"

"He says we turned him out and . . . that he has no need of any of us."

"But his mother, Anselmo! Does he deny his own mother?" Teresa was shocked.

"He's changed unbelievably. It's . . . it's something I can't explain. He's . . . evil."

"Why don't you reason with him?" Rosalia's voice was accusing.

Anselmo's honey-colored eyes met hers. "You still hope he might marry you?"

Rosalia flushed. Then she held her head high. "And why not?"

"Forget him, Rosalia," he advised quietly. "He'll never return to Escoleras."

"What did he say about me?"

"Leave it be, Rosalia," he said gently.

"Did he give you a message for me?"

"It is better you forget him."

"Did he give you a message? Did he? *Did he?*"

"It was not a message," said Anselmo. "It was an insult."

"What did he say?" Rosalia's voice was close to hysteria.

Teresa looked at Anselmo. "Tell her. Whatever it is, she must *know!*"

Anselmo took a deep breath. "Rafael said if you go to him on your knees to beg his forgiveness, he'll strip the skin from your back again."

Rosalia turned pale. There was compassion in Anselmo's eyes. "How *can* you love him?"

"I'm not sure I do love him," she said slowly.

"Then . . . forget him!"

Her eyes became very large. "Who will want me now? I bear Rafael's brand." She turned and ran along the beach, her shoulders shaking.

Anselmo made as if to follow her.

"You cannot help her," said Teresa. "She can only help herself."

Teresa's parents and her younger sister, Pepita, arrived home then with vegetables they had searched for in the neglected fields. It was almost three years since Anselmo had seen them, and he was pleasantly surprised to see Pepita had grown into a vivacious, dark-eyed girl with auburn hair and rich red lips.

"How beautiful you've grown, Pepita," he admired. "You're a young woman, all grown up. Are you courting?"

She was delighted at the thought of it. "No, Anselmo. But soon. Soon!"

"The boys won't leave you alone for long, I'm sure."

"Don't flatter her, Anselmo," said Elisa happily.

Paco Barras brought a table out into the sun and placed on it a *porrón* of wine, salted anchovies and a hunk of black maize bread.

"Have you enough food?" asked Anselmo when they urged him to eat.

"In the villages people manage to live," Paco Barras told him. He chuckled. "You don't see fat people any more. But in the villages there's always something." He shrugged. "The land and the sea are our larder; so eat, Anselmo."

The bread was hard and dry but with a little olive oil poured over it and sprinkled with salt, it was not unpleasant.

Presently, Hernando came striding along the beach, balancing a wicker basket on his shoulder. When he reached them he set it down and they saw it was full of live sea-urchins, their long, black spines glistening wetly in the sun.

Anselmo and Hernando embraced each other, chest to chest, slapping each other's shoulders. Then Hernando stepped back a pace and looked Anselmo up and down with wicked humor glinting in his eyes. "The sooner you get out of those clothes the more you'll enjoy life." He twirled the waxed ends of his bristling moustache.

"I'm hoping for a quick discharge, Hernando."

"How do you like being a soldier?"

"It's hell." Anselmo shrugged his shoulders. "They give you a uniform and a gun and threaten to shoot you if you don't obey orders."

"Ah, yes! And it isn't pleasant being shot, Anselmo?"

Anselmo eyed him critically. "You haven't changed at all, Hernando. Except you're not very sunburned."

The ageless old man chuckled. "I've been in prison."

Anselmo was startled. "In prison! Why send *you* to prison?"

Hernando gently tugged his beard. "I wasn't alone. I had good company. Lots of friends from Escoleras. Listen. Let's open these *garrotas*. I want to see the color come back to Teresa's cheeks."

Doctor Aldo had urged sea-urchins as part of Teresa's diet and Hernando had spent all morning in his fishing boat prying them loose from the rocks with a long cane split open at one end. Now, with knives and scissors they gingerly cut them in half, drained them and placed the shells on the table with their pink and yellowy meat exposed to the sun. There was enough for everyone and they used spoons to scoop up the pulpy flesh. As they ate, they talked.

"I do not understand, Hernando. Why did they send you to prison?" Doctor Aldo asked.

Hernando shrugged his shoulders. "Because men hate and are suspicious and are convinced there is only good and bad." Hernando ate the contents of a *garrota* and reached for another. "Men fear that those not with them are against them. Therefore the silent man becomes an enemy."

Anselmo asked quietly: "Who denounced you, Hernando?"

The old man shrugged his shoulders. "Who can know?"

"Did you fare badly, Hernando?"

"How can I fare badly? They took me away and I was grateful for the journey because I travel so little. In twenty-five years I have not visited Figueras. They gave me a cell to live in, a cot and a blanket. They gave me food too. Not as much as I would have wished, it is true. But one cannot have everything. At night I slept without worries and by day I talked with other prisoners. Sometimes there was a little wine somebody brought in and always some tobacco . . ."

"You didn't mind being in prison?"

Hernando chuckled. "It was an experience and all experiences are interesting."

"And finally they set you free?"

"Yes," said Hernando, and his face became serious. "But not all of us." He frowned.

"Are many men still awaiting trial?"

"Three from our village have been released. Before that, five villagers were found guilty of vexatious activity and were sent to prison. Jesus Guitart appeared before a military court just before I was released. No one yet knows the findings of the court."

"This injustice is the hysteria of victory," said Anselmo. "But soon the bitterness of war will be forgotten and the reprisals will cease."

"The sooner the war is forgotten the better," agreed Paco Barras.

"Eat up, Teresa," urged Hernando. "Eat all you can. Doctor Aldo said you must eat dozens!"

Teresa's pale cheeks flushed prettily. She caught Anselmo watching her and smiled happily.

Anselmo came again the following day and found Teresa alone. He drew up a chair and sat beside her. The sun was warm and the sea calm. The ring of hammers against iron chain echoed across the bay. The fishermen had borrowed two barges from Barcelona and were winching up their scuttled fishing boats and beaching them for repairs. It was exhausting work but they had successfully beached two boats. While some cut timber to patch the great holes blasted in the vessels' bilges, others stripped down the engines, eased and greased the rusted pistons in their cylinders and made them serviceable again. From time to time there was a muffled explosion.

"Is that distant cannon fire?" asked Anselmo.

"It's a new way of fishing," said Teresa. "The soldiers row out in little boats and drop hand grenades into the water. The explosion kills fish and they float to the surface. The soldiers scoop them up with fishing nets and sell them."

"Do they catch a lot of fish?"

"Too many."

"Why don't the village fishermen do it?"

"Nobody is allowed weapons or explosives."

"Are the fishermen resentful?"

Teresa nodded. "And angry too. For every dead fish that floats to the surface a dozen sink and rot. The fishing grounds are being destroyed. The fishermen have protested, but it's useless."

"Perhaps I should speak to somebody," said Anselmo slowly.

"It won't help. *They* are the conquerors and we are the vanquished. Who will forbid the Nationalist troops to eat fish?"

"Your father still fishes?"

"He and Hernando sometimes put down nets. But there is a strict control. All catches are inspected, the fisherman is allowed some for his personal needs and the rest is bought by the authorities. They pay almost nothing; but we cannot argue because it's supposed to be sent to areas where people are starving. Anyway, Father has little chance to fish. Every day soldiers come to borrow his boat and of course, he can't refuse them."

He nodded slowly. "We're having hard times, Teresa. But now the war is over, things will get better."

He turned to her, his face serious. "Soon we can start living again, Teresa."

"Yes." Her eyes were shining.

"I mean . . . you and me, Teresa. We can start living. It's always been us, hasn't it? If it hadn't been for this accursed war . . . !"

Her face was radiant.

"Will you marry me, Teresa. Will you be my wife?"

"Of course. Of course, Anselmo!" She gave her hands to him. His honey-brown eyes looked into hers tenderly. "I owe you so much, even my life!"

He gripped her fingers tightly and she rested her cheek upon his hand. "I love you so much, Anselmo," she said and was crying with happiness.

"The next time I come I'll speak to your father. As soon as I am discharged we can be married."

"That is everything I want," she said quietly. "I think I might have died of my illness had it not been for you, Anselmo. Thinking of you gave me the strength to hang on for just another day. And then one more day after that. And yet another!"

"I must tell you I haven't been an angel, Teresa." He looked away from her shyly. "There have been other women. Not all were whores. There was a woman in Barcelona. I lived with her almost three months."

"It doesn't matter, my love. It doesn't matter at all."

"You can trust me, Teresa. There'll be no one else from now on. And I'll come to you clean. Our children will be strong and healthy. You'll be proud of them, Teresa. So terribly proud of them!"

She knew then she must tell him.

"Do you remember Captain Garon who was here, Anselmo?"

He frowned, puzzled by the switch in the conversation.

"He was military commmander in Escoleras, Anselmo. He was billeted in our cottage."

Anselmo vaguely remembered a lean-faced officer with dark, brooding eyes who had given him a lift in his staff car.

"He was billeted here," repeated Teresa. Then she added quietly: "We became very friendly."

Anselmo looked at her curiously.

"Captain Garon was lonely; he had many responsibilities and was grateful for my friendship."

"Why do you tell me this, Teresa?"

"There should be no secrets between us, my love."

"What happened, Teresa?"

"He asked me to marry him. I told him it was impossible, that I loved you and *only* you. That all my life it had been only you, Anselmo."

"You told him about me?"

"He is a good man, Anselmo. When you deserted and I hid you and cared for you, he knew about it. But he didn't arrest you. He gave you the chance to escape to France."

"He was very fond of you?"

"He was. When the Nationalists were near he asked me to leave with him. I didn't give it a thought, Anselmo. You are the only man I can be happy with."

"You weren't in love with him?"

"Never. What was between us was only physical."

"Physical?"

"He was very gentle and very understanding and we were thrown together and when it happened, it was before I realized it."

He stared at her.

"It didn't mean anything. It was purely physical. But I had to tell you, Anselmo."

He was sitting quite still. His face was stiff as though his facial

muscles had all drawn taut. He said in a strange voice. "It was . . .
physical?"

At that moment came the explosion!

It was so loud it was terrifying. The earth shook, sound waves
cracked the ear and the echoes went rolling like thunder over the sea.
Almost instantaneously there was another tremendous explosion, and
another!

They stared in shocked alarm at the end of the harbor wall which
had disappeared in the midst of a great cloud of spray and churning
sea. Then, when the white mist rolled away they saw the end of the
harbor wall was missing and the next section was tilting crazily as
though about to topple into the sea. One of the salvaged fishing vessels moored to it was listing and sinking. The sea was littered with
floating debris and bobbing heads. Already the fish-market siren was
wailing and villagers were running.

Dust, grit and water fell like rain on the village and Anselmo
choked: "People have been hurt. I must help." He ran off along the
beach without another glance at Teresa, his heavy army boots leaving
deep impressions in the wet sand at the water's edge.

Teresa watched him all the way to where the beach merged into
the concrete approach to the harbor, and then he was lost among
other hurrying figures. The siren wailed mournfully, troop trucks
raced to the quay and little boats skimmed out across the water toward the bobbing heads. One lone fisherman was struggling to haul a
limp figure into his boat.

Teresa was still very weak. There was nothing she could do except
sit and watch. Villagers scurried around the dock, soldiers moved purposefully and a troop truck reversed and raced away, driving recklessly through the village, taking the injured to the hospital in
Figueras.

Her father came home much later. His eyes were tired, there was
dried blood on his shirt and he walked heavily. "What was it, Father?" she asked breathlessly. "What happened?"

He sank down wearily onto the sand. She saw his bare foot was
spattered with dried blood.

"What happened, Father?"

He spread his hands and looked down at them. He turned them
over and stared at their palms as though expecting to read something

written upon them. He said huskily: "The three boys who borrowed my boat . . . blown to pieces."

She recalled them instantly; three young soldiers, swaggering boyishly in their conqueror's uniforms as they formally asked permission to borrow the boat. Then laughing at the discomfort of their companion who inexpertly pushed the boat off from the beach and filled his boots with water.

"Our boat, Father?"

"The boat is not important. We can save and buy another. But they were just three boys; not as old as Miguel!"

"What happened, Father?"

"They were fishing with hand grenades at the end of the harbor wall." With his brown forearm, Paco Barras wiped the sheen away from his forehead. "Do you remember when the Reds left they ran trucks to the end of the harbor and tipped explosives into the sea?"

"But doesn't water . . . ?"

"They must have been well packed. The whole lot went up. The end of the harbor's disappeared. We don't know yet how many have been killed because there were many small boats. There were soldiers on the harbor wall, too, unloading fish. Ramon Coll was with them and there's no trace of him; and Pedro Puig . . . his leg's a mess. It'll have to be amputated!"

"Father. Did you see Anselmo?"

"Everybody was helping. There was a young soldier with a deep gash in his arm. He was bleeding like a pig and I kept my thumb on the artery. There were so many others badly hurt it was a long time before they could get around to him. I didn't see Anselmo, but he was sure to have been helping."

"But you have come home, Father."

"The badly injured have been sent to Figueras and the less seriously injured are taken care of. There's only the . . . the cleaning up."

"Then what can Anselmo be doing?"

He looked at her sharply. "You're waiting for him?"

It was on the tip of her tongue to blurt out: "He wants to marry me," but she held back the words. "His leave expires soon," she said.

Anselmo did not return.

Her mother and Pepita came back from foraging in the fields and prepared vegetables for a stew. The sun sank below the horizon and presently Marcel Prada came striding along the beach.

"Good evening," he said.

Paco, Pepita and Teresa replied politely: "Good evening."

"A terrible accident; a terrible accident!" said Marcel Prada, shaking his head.

"Shocking," agreed Paco Barras, as though saying "Amen."

"We nourish the seeds of our own destruction," said Paco Barras. He took out a package of cheroots and offered them. "Smoke?"

"Thank you, friend," said Prada.

Both men lit up.

"How is your family?" asked Paco Barras politely.

"All are well. But Rosalia . . . all men know daughters are trouble."

Paco Barras chuckled. "You do not need to tell me, amigo. I have two!"

"I have a message for you," said Marcel Prada. He drew deeply on his *caliqueño*. Then he said tonelessly: "Anselmo had to leave Escoleras quickly. He asked me to convey to the Barras family his regret he was not able to call personally and bid you farewell."

There was an awkward silence.

"Thank you for bringing us the message," said Paco Barras and looked at Teresa.

She asked quickly: "You saw Anselmo?"

"He was hurrying, Señorita Teresa. A truck was taking the injured to Figueras and it was convenient for him to catch the evening train to Barcelona. He caught me by the arm and said: 'Marcel Prada. I beg of you, go to the house of the Barras family and explain I must seize this opportunity to leave Escoleras.'"

"You are very kind, Señor Prada," Teresa said quietly. "I am grateful to you." But within her was anguish.

Tragedy struck again that same night.

The village streets were quiet, except for the measured tread of patrolling soldiers. Abruptly lights went on in a cottage and a woman ran screaming into the street.

Constancia Guitart ran along the street barefooted, clad only in a flannel nightgown. She wailed hysterically. Neighbors clustered around her and tried to comfort her as she sobbed despairingly.

"Send for Doctor Aldo," cried Maria Turro.

"Ah, Holy Virgin Mary, save me from my agony!" wailed Constancia Guitart. She tore at her hair, flung herself down on the cobbles and hammered them until her fists bled.

Her neighbors could do nothing with her.

"Aaayeee!" she wailed. "The pain in my heart. The agony. Holy Virgin Mary, save me. Oh, Jesus, beloved husband. Why have they done this to you?"

Doctor Aldo came quickly, buttoning his trousers as he strode along the street.

"Aaayee, Doctor," she wailed. "The murderers! They've killed him. Ah, Holy Beloved Virgin. My Jesus. My dear Jesus. They have shot him!"

"Quiet woman, *quiet!*" stormed Doctor Aldo, his voice instantly having effect. "Why are you making a spectacle of yourself?"

The tears ran freely down her cheeks. "He's dead. They've killed my Jesus. They've killed him!"

"You're out of your mind, Constancia. You don't know what you're saying."

"I dreamed it, Doctor. It's happened. They've killed him!"

Doctor Aldo took her firmly by the arm. "Come. This is no time to be waking everyone. It's four o'clock in the morning. Back to bed."

He led her upstairs to her bedroom, followed by many neighbors who soon made the room smell of garlic and bad breath.

"Now go to sleep," urged Doctor Aldo, helping her into bed. "Take this pill." He called over his shoulder. "A glass of water."

Neighbors stampeded to the kitchen.

"Take this, Constancia."

She swallowed the tablet and lay back. He said gently: "Relax, Constancia. All this is imagination and nothing else. Constancia, do you hear me?"

"Yes, Doctor." Her face was haggard and her eyes deeply sunken but she was calmer. Presently she closed her eyes.

Doctor Aldo gestured to the neighbors and they melted away.

"Sleep. Sleep," soothed Doctor Aldo. "Sleep."

But Constancia was already asleep.

It was almost dawn before Doctor Aldo got to bed and it seemed only a few seconds elapsed before there was hammering at his door. Pulling on his dressing gown he opened it and a uniformed soldier saluted him. "Captain Rota will be pleased if you will call as soon as possible."

"Very well," yawned Doctor Aldo. He put water on the stove to boil while he dressed. He awakened himself with strong, black coffee and it was not quite nine o'clock when he called on Captain Rota.

Captain Rota rose to his feet and stood stiffly erect when the doctor entered.

"You asked me to call, Captain?"

"Yes, Doctor." Captain Rota stood with feet astride and linked his hands behind his back. "I have received a communication from headquarters in Gerona. I pass it on to you as a representative of the villagers."

"Unpleasant information, Captain?" sighed the doctor.

"I am afraid so."

"We're accustomed to bad news," said Doctor Aldo bitterly.

"I have a report from the military court that heard the charges against Jesus Guitart."

Doctor Aldo sighed. "I assume he was found guilty?"

The captain's face was grim. "He was found guilty and sentenced to death."

Doctor Aldo's voice was shaky. "He will appeal?"

"An appeal is impossible."

"Every man has the right of appeal . . ." began Doctor Aldo.

Captain Rota overtalked him. "To appeal is *impossible!*"

Slowly the doctor's eyes filled with dread understanding.

Captain Rota said: "Jesus Guitart was shot this morning."

There was a choking lump in the doctor's throat. He pictured the boisterous Jesus Guitart, roaring good-humoredly as he stumped along the street with a pirate's patch over one eye and his black beard bristling. He asked tonelessly: "At what time was he executed?"

"At four o'clock this morning," said the captain and then stared in astonishment at Doctor Aldo.

The doctor was looking down at his watch and shaking his head. "Four o'clock!" he said bitterly. *"Four o'clock!"*

On her way home from working in the vineyard, Rosalia often met a young soldier. He had first spoken to her soon after the Nationalists arrived in Escoleras. He had been lounging with companions on a street corner and they had encouraged him.

"Ola, guapa," he had called.

She had walked past with her head high.

The next time they had met he had only one companion. He had spoken to her as she passed, but she had ignored him.

Next day she had met him on the footpath she always used on her way home. He had grinned and blocked her path.

She looked through him and stepped to one side.

But he side-stepped in front of her so she almost bumped into him. She side-stepped again and once more he barred her way.

She stood quite still then, and stared impassively over his shoulder, waiting for him to let her pass.

His cheeks were flushed and he stammered shyly. He was lonely, he said, and attracted to her. He wanted to go walking with her. She ignored him.

Her icy indifference finally discomfited him and he stepped aside. Rosalia walked on without giving him a glance.

He learned his lesson and never again attempted to speak to her. Now, whenever she met him, he stepped aside and watched sadly as she swept on. But he often followed her at a distance. When he was off duty he came to the olive grove where she was working and sat not far off, watching her. Once, when she had believed herself to be alone and had relieved herself, she later caught a glimpse of him hiding in a distant thicket.

On her way home one day, she saw him coming toward her. His manner was casual as he pretended this was an accidental meeting. Rosalia was moody and depressed. She was twenty and lonely. Most girls her age already had boys, although most of them were in the army or in France. So, as the blond soldier drew closer, she studied him thoughtfully and when he stepped aside for her, she gravely inclined her head.

His face lit up.

She walked on.

His footsteps followed her. She half-turned and glanced over her shoulder.

It was enough.

"Señorita. Forgive me, Señorita."

She paused, her black eyes pensive.

"Señorita!" He was crimson-faced and tongue-tied.

"Do you want something?" she asked tonelessly.

"Señorita. May I walk with you a little way?"

She said gracelessly: "I can't stop you."

He matched her pace. "May I know your name, Señorita?"

"Rosalia Prada."

"Don't you want to know *my* name?"

"You can tell me if you want."

"I am Juan Gonzalez."

"A very distinctive name," she said tartly and his hot eyes showed his hurt.

"I beg you to forgive me, Señorita. I must have angered you greatly when I first spoke to you in the street. It must have seemed an insult."

"I ignored it," said Rosalia.

"Will you forgive me?"

She shrugged her shoulders. "If it gives you pleasure I'll forgive you."

"It is improper to call after a girl."

"Then do not do it."

He sighed. "It is difficult to talk with you, Rosalia. I want to be your friend, but you are hostile. Do you dislike people?"

"I do not dislike people, Juan Gonzalez. But I suspect their motives. Do you think I am impressed by a conscripted soldier, far from home, who wants to have his fun with a local girl?"

He said fiercely: "That's not true!"

"Is it not?"

"Do you not understand how I feel for you, Rosalia?" he said quietly. "There are always girls. But when I saw you . . . it was different."

Despite herself she was flattered. But she asked bluntly: "What do you want of me? Speak plainly."

"I want your friendship, Rosalia. I want to walk at your side, listen to your voice, see your eyes and watch the way your hair tumbles over your shoulders. I want to . . ."

"Go away with your fancy words. What do you think they'll get you?"

He asked sadly: "Why are you so hard?"

"This is as far as you should walk with me. My father will be angry if he sees you."

"May I see you again, Rosalia?"

"Do you want to?"

It was a question that clinched his answer. "I think I shall die if I don't," he said and she almost laughed at his solemnity.

"We will meet somewhere. The village is small," she said.

"Will you go to the olive grove tomorrow?"

"Perhaps."

"May I talk with you there or help you with your work?"

"We will see," she conceded and wondered again if he had often spied on her and flushed, wondering what he may have seen.

He came as often as he could and helped her work.

"Where do you come from?" she asked.

His gray eyes were solemn. "From . . . from Pamplona. And you. Have you always lived here?"

"I want to know about *you*," she insisted.

He shrugged his shoulders. "There is so little to tell. I went to college but the war interrupted my studies."

"What is your ambition, Juan?"

"Perhaps to be an engineer; to build canals, bridges and waterways. My father wants me to go into his business, of course. I am the only son and one day it will be mine, so there is reason in what he says."

"And what is your father's business?"

"He has a bull farm. Not ordinary bulls . . . the fighting bulls."

She was impressed. Everyone knew the bulls bred for the bull-ring were very valuable. With a shock she realized his father was probably very wealthy.

"It is a big farm?"

He shrugged disinterestedly. "About four thousand hectares, I believe."

"So big!" Her eyes were wide with wonder.

"It is necessary with four thousand head of stock," he explained. "Remember, only one bull in a hundred is worthy of the Plaza."

She was silent, trying to calculate what four thousand head of stock might be worth. "Have you ever fought bulls, Juan?" There was a new respect in the way she looked at him.

"Only the young ones," he laughed. "Those with short, soft horns. They butt, bruise and trample but rarely kill."

"It must be exciting," she breathed.

"It bores me," he said honestly. "I prefer car racing."

"You drive racing cars?"

"At home I have three. Two for the track, stripped down to save weight and with souped-up engines. I've got a two-seater sports car to run around. Father hates it and calls it a fire engine because it's red." He smiled ruefully. "I wish I had it now; we could have some fine trips together."

"You must be well-known in Pamplona," she said.

"My father is well-known."

"I've heard so much about Pamplona but I've never been there," she said wistfully.

"I'll take you," he offered.

"You will?" she asked delightedly.

"The very first opportunity." Then his face dropped. "What about your parents?"

"Don't worry," she said confidently. "I'll talk them around. Tell me more about the bulls."

Sometimes he could spend all day with her and then he brought meat and wine from the cookhouse. They picnicked beside a stream and afterward rested in the shade of the olive trees, during the midday heat. He never attempted to embrace her but she sensed his longing and respected him for his restraint.

One day she sent him to get water from the stream. When he returned she was stooped over the fire, and the top button on the back of her dress was open. Instinctively he stooped and she shuddered as his hot lips touched the back of her neck. "Please," she whispered and was surprised by her breathlessness.

"You are lovely, Rosalia," he said. "You are beautiful."

"Beautiful?" she said. "Can you not see my scars?"

"I see, my love," he said gently. There was no horror in his voice, only tenderness. "Who did this shocking thing?"

She was so relieved he did not recoil from her, she hardly knew what she replied. "It was my grandfather, when I was a child. He beat me and afterward my father almost killed him."

"My poor Rosalia," His strong hands held her shoulders while he kissed her gently, running his lips along the white weals.

She couldn't believe it. "You're not . . . revolted?"

"I'm shocked by cruelty," he said seriously. "But you are still beautiful."

"It's not only my neck." She dared to tell all. "I was beaten from shoulder to thighs."

He turned her around and stared at her intently. "Nothing can alter my feelings for you, Rosalia."

She was unbelievably happy. "You care about me, Juan! You really care!"

"I love you," he said simply and as though sealing an oath, he solemnly kissed her on the lips.

She quickly turned her mouth aside so his lips were upon her cheek.

"Let me kiss you, my love."

"To kiss . . . it is only permissible between those who are betrothed."

"Do you refuse me then, Rosalia?"

"Refuse you?" She was confused and afraid of her own passions.

"Marry me, Rosalia."

"Oh, Juan. Juan!"

"Say you'll marry me, Rosalia," he pleaded. "*Say* it. Promise me."

"Oh, Juan! I can't refuse. I can't."

It seemed natural when he pulled her dress down her upper arms. She made a half-hearted attempt to stop him and then his arms were around her and his lips were between her breasts.

"Oh, Juan. Juan!" she whispered and stroked his hair.

"Come," he said breathlessly. "There is a soft grass in the shade of the tree."

"*Por favor*," she whispered, holding back. But her longing matched his and all too soon she was looking up at the green fretwork of foliage against the blue sky, feeling sad and spent, yet happy too. He lay thrusting against her, his hand resting upon her possessively.

"I love you, Rosalia. I love you," he whispered.

She pressed his cheek firmly upon her breasts. "I love you, too, Juan," she said and realized with a shock it was true. A great wave of affection swept over her.

"Was it as good for you as it was for me?" he asked.

"I am afraid, Juan," she confessed. She ran her finger around his ear. "Are you sure I will not be with child?"

"This is your first time?"

"You must know, Juan. Were there not signs?"

"A woman never conceives the first time."

"Are you sure, Juan?"

He hesitated. "I have always believed it so. But it is of no importance if you are my wife."

She pressed his head so hard against her breasts it hurt. "When will it be, Juan? Must we wait long?"

He pulled away and propped himself up so he could look into her eyes. "Soon, my love."

"When will you talk to my parents?"

He smiled lazily. "Soon," he said. "Soon." His eyes gleamed excitedly. "I have a plan. We will keep our love a secret. When I go home on leave to Pamplona I will arrange the wedding. I will return with my car and take you and your parents to Pamplona where we will be married. It will be a surprise for them."

"That is wonderful," said Rosalia. "How long must we wait?"

"Only a few weeks. Already I have applied for leave."

"Will you not speak to my parents beforehand?"

He was disappointed. "If it is your wish I will talk with them to-day. But I had thought to please them with this surprise."

"Perhaps your way *is* best, darling," she yielded.

"You are beautiful," he whispered.

"And quite shameless, I fear," she sighed.

"I love you," he said and his breath was hot upon her breasts and his lips searching.

She sighed and her fingers gripped his hair. "I love you, darling. Aaayee! How I love you!"

Every day he found time to see her. Sometimes they could talk for only fleeting minutes, but other days they could spend many leisure hours together.

One day as she lay within Juan's embrace with the sun pleasantly hot upon her thighs and belly, she asked: "How long before you get your leave, Juan?"

"This coming week."

"That is good. The sooner we marry the better. There is a reason."

"Yes?" His voice was wondering.

She took his hand and moved it higher, pressing his palm upon her belly. "It is under your hand."

"You are sure, my love?"

"Quite sure."

"You have visited a doctor?"

"It is not necessary. It is a woman's affair; something she knows with her mind and body."

"You cannot be certain until you see a doctor."

"Have you not noticed how my breasts have swollen?" He saw then how her body had subtly adapted to creation.

"The sooner we marry the better, Juan. It will stop people talking."

"Do you care what people say?"

She made a disdainful gesture. "I do not care a fig for people's talk. But I worry for my parents."

"They say a woman enjoys lovemaking most when she is with child," he said. "Is it true?"

"It is always good with you, Juan."

He was given leave the following week. He gave her his address in Pamplona and promised to send a telegram when he arrived. She became anxious when she did not hear from him and haunted the telegraph office for days. Then she realized there had been a misunderstanding and wrote to him. She waited many more days and then her letter was returned marked: *Address unknown.*

The fear that had been growing inside her overcame her pride. She dressed in her best clothes and went to see the military commander.

Captain Rota received her politely, listened with a frown and when she had finished, thrust a cigarette between his lips and lit it angrily. "Señorita, why do you come to me?"

Her eyes were wide. "I need your help."

He arose and strode up and down the room. "What can I do, Señorita? You meet a soldier named Juan Gonzalez. There are thousands of Juan Gonzalezes in the army, Señorita. You say he comes from Pamplona and that his father breeds bulls. If he had been American his father would have owned oil wells in Texas. If he had been English, his father would have been a lord!"

"But he was one of your own men, Captain. You must know something of him!"

He threw up his hands and then let them drop to his sides despairingly. "One hundred and fifty men left here last week for Malaga, to be demobilized. By now, most of these men are already home. However, Señorita, if you can tell me *which* of them called himself Juan Gonzalez, perhaps I can obtain his address."

She stared at him helplessly and her lips trembled. "Perhaps . . . I could write to them . . . ?"

"What, all of them!"

She nodded helplessly.

There was compassion in his eyes. "Would it help you, Señorita? If he wants to reply to a letter, he would have written long before this."

"What can I do?" she wailed. "What *can* I do?"

"Have you no friends? Nobody you can confide in?"

"Nobody that can help me."

He sat down at his desk and picked up his pen. "Give me your name, Señorita. I will make inquiries. Perhaps there truly is a Juan Gonzalez whose father has a bull farm."

But some weeks later there was still no news of Juan Gonzalez and Marcel Prada came home to find his wife screaming at Rosalia.

"What is it? What's happening?" he demanded.

"Your whore of a daughter. She's with child. Look at her belly. Look at her breasts!"

Marcel Prada flushed darkly. "He'll marry her," he vowed. "Whoever it is, he'll marry her."

"The girl's a fool," Rosalia's mother shrieked. "She doesn't even know his name. One of those soldiers told her a cock-and-bull story!"

Marcel Prada's eyes narrowed. "A whore," he said bitterly. "Going with a man she doesn't even know. A whore!"

Rosalia's eyes flashed. "He promised and I thought he loved me . . ."

"Don't answer your father back."

"You're a whore," said her father. He stepped forward and jutted his chin. "Whore," he spat. He looked slyly at his wife. "What will the doctor say?"

She understood his question and shook her head. "Doctor Aldo won't do anything like *that*."

"Some man's brat dumped on her and *we* have to keep it."

"I won't ask *you* for charity," said Rosalia.

"The disgrace!" wailed her mother.

"She's a whore," said Marcel Prada. "We must send her away."

His wife's eyes gleamed with hope. "There's cousin Flora in Barcelona. She could give her a room. Nobody would know and she could say her husband was killed in the war."

"Whore!" said her father.

"The sooner you go the better," urged her mother. "Before anyone notices."

Rosalia faced them with resolve and anger. "I'll go tonight," she said proudly.

"Don't think we're being unkind, dear," sobbed her mother.

"I'll catch the night train to Barcelona," said Rosalia tonelessly.

But it was many, many days before she could obtain a travel permit and by then everyone in the village knew why she was turned out of her home.

10

Benito Vigon was with the rearguard forces that made a stand at Borjas Blancas for several days in the attempt to hold the National-ist's final assault across the River Ebro. Sergeant Vigon's company was orderly in its retreat, and when the army convoy began its winding climb up the steep roads to the mountain frontier, Vigon realized the entire army was going into exile.

Because of his rank, Sergeant Vigon rode in the crowded cabin of the truck instead of in the back with his men. As they drew closer to the frontier he recognized familiar landmarks and presently he saw the outline of a low-lying mountain and knew that if he stood upon its crest, on a clear day he would be able to see the glittering white speck of Escoleras against the soft blue of the sea.

He wondered who tended his olive trees and vineyards, longed to see the cobbled streets and harbor and wondered if Rosalia Prada was still as vivacious and attractive. He swallowed the lump in his throat, looked either side at the tired faces of his officers, cleared his throat and asked: "Must we go into France? Is it dishonorable to sur-render?"

They looked at him wearily. "There will be reprisals, on-the-spot executions. They will accept no peace terms, only surrender."

"It is impossible to shoot an entire army," argued Vigon.

"Impossible? It's a day's work for a company of machine-gunners."

The truck drove on and Benito Vigon slumped in moody silence. When they reached a steeply sloping hairpin-turn the convoy crawled.

"I'll walk and stretch my legs," said Sergeant Vigon.

He paced along beside the truck and when it speeded up, he made no effort to keep level with it. When he looked out over the valley he could still see the familiar outline of the mountain crest. He stopped, took out a cigarette and lit up. A sweating truck driver swore at him as he edged past. "Keep the road clear, you great *coño!*"

Sergeant Vigon stepped off the road verge and slithered a little way down the steep slope into the valley. Another truck rumbled past. A red-faced officer leaned out from the cabin and roared: "Where are you going, Sergeant?"

"To piss!" shouted Benito Vigon, suddenly angry. "To piss, *mi Capitan!*" He waited until the officer was beyond earshot and shouted: "To piss upon officers and the Nationalists, the government, the army and the war!" He looked up at the sky and shouted. "I piss upon all Spaniards and their madness; upon our dreams and our illusions; our vanity and our pride!"

Another truck passed and the men in it jeered at him.

"Listen to that crazy man talking to himself!"

"Who're you shouting orders at, Sergeant?"

Vigon glared after them furiously. "I piss upon all of you. The army, its officers and the war."

"And I shit upon you!" a soldier shouted back. "I shit upon all sergeants and the mothers that gave them birth."

Sergeant Vigon slid down the slope a few meters. His feet were thinking for him. He looked up the steep slope toward the road, and faces stared down at him curiously from the passing trucks. He stooped as though to do up a bootlace and the rifle slung across his shoulder slipped down his arm and its barrel clinked on the stony soil. He slid down the slope to a thick clump of undergrowth and concealed himself in it ostentatiously with the air of a man about to relieve himself. But under cover of the bushes he quickly slid down the steep slope into the valley, the soles of his boots rasping over the sharp stones; brambles and thorny vines tearing his face and hands. A half a mile deeper down the valley there was a fold of land and once around this he was out of sight of the road and could walk upright.

He was astonished. He had become a deserter! But he strode on with confidence and realized he was going to visit Felipe. Then in a flash of self-illumination he knew he had planned this since he first saw familiar landmarks from the truck.

Felipe's farm was huddled in the mountains between Escoleras and the Pyrenees. It was far from any other dwelling; there were no roads, electricity or telephone and only well water. Felipe and his sons rode into Escoleras every few months with mules laden with farm produce which they bartered for stores. It was a long journey to Felipe's farm from Escoleras and he seldom had visitors. But Vigon and friends had occasionally stayed with Felipe overnight when they had been hunting wild boar. Felipe's remote farm was an ideal refuge for a deserter.

It was many miles of tramping, across deep ravines and perilous mountain slopes, to reach the farm. Dark was on him before he realized it, and he made camp, knowing the dangers of blundering blindly through the starless night.

He made a fire, huddled beside it and nibbled a piece of dry bread he had in his pocket. He dozed off and the fire dwindled to ashes without the cold awaking him. The sun on his face aroused him. He yawned, stretched, searched his pockets and found a few bread crumbs which he let dissolve on his tongue. Then he took his bearings and set off again. At noon he toiled up just one more steep hill, crossed its summit and stared down into the valley at Felipe's farm, nestling between the pigsty and a large barn. He shouted and walked toward it.

The echo of hoofbeats was carried to him. He looked around and saw a horse galloping across from the far side of the valley. He slowed his pace. When the rider drew close he recognized Felipe's daughter, Violante. Her mount was large, heavy-boned and graceless, but Violante handled it expertly, bringing it to a plunging standstill alongside Vigon.

"Good day, Violante," greeted Vigon. "Is your father at home?"

She stared down at him with dull brown eyes. She had twisted a length of straw rope around the horse's muzzle as a bridle and she rode bareback and astride. Her tucked-up skirt showed unwashed bare thighs and a woolen underskirt, gray with wear. The soles of her bare feet were as black and hard as leather.

"Father is looking at the crops. He'll be back soon."

She was only twenty-five but the hard, mountain life made her look ten years older. She had a Mongolian-shaped face, a snub nose and a receding chin. Her dirt-matted hair fell loosely over her shoulders and was streaked with gray.

"I wish to stay with you for a while," he said.

Her brown eyes were disinterested. "Talk to Father when he comes." She nodded toward the farmhouse.

"Thank you, Violante."

"It is nothing."

She rode on ahead of him to the farmhouse, slid from the horse and loosed it to crop the sparse grass that grew around the house. When

Vigon arrived chickens screeched and flapped their wings, dogs barked fiercely, goats in the corral bleated and the stench from the pigsty engulfed him.

"You want a drink?" asked Violante. She took down a worn wine-skin hanging from a peg outside the door and tossed it to him.

He unscrewed the cap and drank deeply. The wine was very strong and had the bitter tang of the goat. He growled his satisfaction and recapped the wineskin. "I am hungry," he said simply.

"Come and eat." She led him into the farmhouse which smelled as strongly as the pigsty alongside. It was one large room with a large, bell-shaped chimney in one corner. It was filthy. Straw thrown on the floor and covered with sacking served as beds, the rough-hewn wooden table was littered with dirty crockery and scraps of food, and the walls were so smoke-blackened soot could be removed from them with the stroke of a finger.

"Bread," she said, finding a hard crust among the scraps on the table. "An onion."

Vigon was too hungry to be fastidious. He peeled the raw onion of its outer skin and ate it slowly.

She watched him expressionlessly. Nature had not been kind to Violante. She was solidly built and ungainly, her big hands were rough and her shoulders as broad as a man's.

"How is your father?" he asked politely.

"Well."

"And your brothers?"

"They are also well." She had three; Tomas, Virgil and Zacarias.

"They did not go to the war?"

She shrugged her shoulders. "Only Father has been going to the village."

The three·sons were of military age, but nobody would make the long, tiring trip into the mountains to serve the call-up papers, even assuming the births of the sons had been registered.

"Has there been fighting here in the mountains? Soldiers?"

When she shook her head, he could see the lice on it. Since her mother had died many years before the family had slipped steadily. They ate their food raw and in the coldest weather brought the animals into the house and shared their body warmth.

Felipe returned soon, riding a surefooted mule and followed by his sons mounted on frisky donkeys. Felipe was a powerfully built man of fifty-five with a peasant's heavy, blunt features. His three tall sons had the same flat, Mongolian features as their sister and their dull, black eyes greeted Vigon without enthusiasm.

"It is a long time since you've visited us," said Felipe. He shook Vigon's hand with a grip that threatened to crush bones.

"I've been away at war."

Felipe nodded. "It is better to stay away from war." He spread his hands, embracing the mountains. "It is better to farm as we do. All this is ours!"

"Can I work here for a time?" asked Vigon.

Felipe eyed him shrewdly. "You want wages?"

"Money is not important."

Felipe looked at his uniform. "You are no longer a soldier?"

"The war is over."

"If you wish you can stay. But the work is hard."

"I'm not afraid of work."

"That is good."

"It is better . . ." said Vigon tentatively, ". . . it is better nobody knows I am here."

"Do not fear. We will not carry tales."

Felipe's land was hard to farm and unrewarding. Its yield was so poor that only by laboring ceaselessly could they squeeze a living from it. Every day everyone worked from morning until night. There were the farm animals to be fed, the cows to be milked, the horses, pigs, goats and chickens to be tended. There were far-flung fields of crops to be weeded, farm tools to be repaired and fences to be made. Vigon returned to the farmhouse at night almost too tired to eat and fell quickly asleep despite the lice, the tolling of cowbells and the squeals of the pigs next door.

Sunday was the day they ate meat. Felipe brought a squealing kid back to the house. Virgil held it by its back legs with its head hanging down and Tomas deftly slit its throat. Violante caught its blood in a bowl and while Zacarias and Virgil skinned the small carcass, the bowl was passed around so all could gulp the warm salty blood. Violante was the last and licked the bowl clean.

They built a fire in the open and spitted the kid over it between two forked sticks. The flames leaped high, crisping the outer flesh and heating the meat but not truly cooking it. When the outer skin was burned black, Felipe said solemnly: "It is Sunday."

They all knelt around the fire. It was a ritual that had begun many years ago when Felipe had first brought a wife to his home. After her death Felipe had continued the ritual in her memory.

Vigon knelt embarrassedly. When he glanced either side, he was surprised the others had closed their eyes reverently.

After a few minutes, Felipe intoned uncertainly: "O Lord . . . give us bread."

"Give us bread," echoed the others.

"O Lord . . . make us good."

"Make us good," they chorused.

"O God . . ." stammered Felipe and then broke off. "Can't remember any more," he said apologetically.

Tomas said quietly: "It's in the Bible, Father."

"Fool! I can't read!"

"Benito Vigon has been to school."

Felipe's eyes lighted up. "Will you read the Bible for us, Benito?" He got to his feet and hurried into the house.

The Bible was wrapped in rags and buried in the straw they used for a mattress. It had belonged to Felipe's wife and he treasured it. He unwrapped it with trembling hands.

Benito was crimson with embarrassment. "What do you want me to read?"

"The part Maria used to read. The part where God gives us bread."

Vigon turned to the Lord's Prayer. He took a deep breath. "Our Father which art in Heaven . . ." he began.

They were down on their knees again, hands clasped tightly, eyes closed and their heads bowed until their chins touched their chests. Vigon sighed and read the prayer slowly. Never in any church had he seen such devout worshippers.

"Amen," he concluded.

"Amen," they chorused.

They rose to their feet and Felipe said sadly: "There used to be singing, but I can't remember the words. I've forgotten the music, too."

"If you want to sing, the words don't matter. It's singing together that's important," said Vigon.

"We haven't sung for a long time," said Felipe. "Turn the meat, Tomas."

Zacarias fed the fire with wood chips, Tomas turned the spit and

Virgil thrust a knife into the flesh to test if it was tender. Violante stood to one side with her back toward them, feet apart and abdomen thrust forward. She lifted her skirts and urinated in front of her like a man.

"This morning I raised a hare down in the valley by the broken pine tree," said Felipe. "Tomorrow I'll take my gun and the dogs and see if I can raise him again."

"Today's a holiday. Let's try to raise him this afternoon."

Felipe shook his head. "He won't return so soon."

The drumming of urine died away and Violante shook down her skirts and turned back to them.

"Are we going to eat hot vegetables today?" asked Virgil.

Felipe looked at Violante. "Have we potatoes?"

"I'll look." She went into the house and brought out a cooking pot of water. She dropped unpeeled potatoes into the pot just as they had been dug up.

"With you reading the Bible every Sunday, Benito, we'll soon remember that prayer again."

"Any time you want I'll read it to you, Felipe."

"Then there's the laws," said Felipe thoughtfully. "Stealing is a sin, isn't it? And blasphemy? And killing?"

"The Ten Commandments," said Vigon.

"It's also a sin for a girl to be with child without a husband."

"I'm not sure about that," said Benito.

"It *is* a sin," asserted Felipe triumphantly. "Maria was very insistent about it. 'Our sons must not sin,' she said many times. 'But neither must our daughter.' "

Virgil cut a long, thin strip of meat and gave it to his father. "It's hot."

Felipe blew on it and chewed it. Virgil cut another strip of meat and Tomas and Zacarias also drew their knives. They ate standing around the fire, cutting off strips of flesh and tearing at it with their teeth. It was partly charred, partly crisped and partly raw. The potatoes floated in a broth of scummy water. They speared them with their knives, eating them half-cooked and washing them down with large draughts of wine. They had prodigious appetites and the digestions of goats. They ate all the potatoes, drank the broth in the pot, stripped all the meat from the carcass and ground the bones between their teeth.

Because there was so much to do, time did not lag for Vigon. After the day's work there were always a dozen jobs around the house, drawing water, pitchforking fresh straw, chopping wood or repairing fences. Vigon adapted himself to their way of life although they were puzzled he washed so frequently and that he boiled vegetables until they were soft and soggy instead of eating them crisp and juicy. They were amused that lice made red blotches on his soft skin and at times crazed him with irritation.

Then one day Felipe said: "This Saturday I will go to the village."

Benito Vigon said quietly: "I will accompany you, Felipe, if I may."

"It will be my pleasure," said Felipe formally.

They set off before dawn, Felipe on horseback and Benito mounted on a donkey, his feet in the panniers. Three more donkeys followed them in single file, legs bowed under their loads of root vegetables.

At midday they stopped to eat and in the early evening they were within sight of Escoleras.

Vigon slipped down off his mount. "I'll leave you here, Felipe."

"May you have good fortune, Benito."

"Thank you for your hospitality, Felipe. I am very grateful."

"Visit us again, Benito, and read the Bible. I fear I am already forgetting the Lord's Prayer. *Adiós,* amigo."

"*Adiós.*"

Felipe rode on into the village along a well-worn path. Benito left the path, walked across country, dawdled in the fields until it was dark and then stealthily entered the village. He slipped into his house just as his family were sitting down to eat.

"Benito!" choked his mother and tears of joy ran down her cheeks.

"Glad to have you home, son," said his father, blinking his eyes furiously and chewing hard on his black cheroot so he wouldn't betray emotion.

His sisters, Camila and Edita, rushed to embrace him but he warded them off. "I'm so dirty. Let me wash and put on clean clothes." He was pleasantly surprised that Camila had grown into a young and attractive woman.

He stripped and washed, using hot water for the first time in many months. His ragged uniform was thrown into the garbage bin and he put on a clean serge suit. The trousers flapped loosely around his legs and his leather belt drew in three notches more. The war and living rough had whittled him down to hard flesh, muscle and bone.

His family waited dinner until he joined them and as he ate hungrily, relishing squid fried in butter, he mentioned briefly his adventures and heard the news of the village.

"Have there been many reprisals, Father?" he asked, wiping the gravy from his plate with a hunk of black bread.

"Many terrible things have happened, son. But the war is over and although the hate and suspicion are still with us, the passions are cooling."

"What will happen if I am caught, Father?"

"You must avoid it, son. Many who should know better still seek vengeance. A conscript government soldier may be set free, or might be sent to prison. Those known to be Communists have been sentenced to life imprisonment or shot. Take care not to be denounced or accused of being anti-Christ. To be against the Church is to be against Franco."

"Did you kill anyone, Benito?" asked Edita, her eyes large and round.

Vigon laughed bitterly. "I was too busy trying to avoid being killed myself." He quickly changed the conversation. "How you've changed, Edita. When I went away you were a child. Now look at you! You're beautiful."

"Don't tease her," smiled his mother.

"Why can't I be beautiful, Mother?" demanded Edita indignantly. "I'm thirteen!"

"And you, Camila? You have not yet a *novio* to marry you?"

"With all the young men away at the war," she scoffed.

Vigon then asked the question he was longing to ask.

"How about Rosalia?" he said and quickly took the black cheroot his father offered him and struck a match, pretending to be intent on puffing it into a cherry glow.

There was an awkward silence.

After a pause Camila said tonelessly: "Rosalia?"

He stared at her anxiously through a haze of smoke. "Yes. Rosalia."

"Rosalia Prada?"

"Is there another Rosalia?"

"No," said Camila. She got up and began to clear the table.

Vigon looked at his mother, his father, and then at Edita. He scowled. "What's happened?" he asked. Then he was alarmed. "She wasn't killed, was she?" He half-rose to his feet. "Nothing's happened to her?"

"Don't worry," said his mother. "It's nothing like that."

"Tell me," he insisted.

"You tell him, Father."

"Rosalia's going to have a baby," chanted Edita, no longer able to contain herself.

Maria Vigon slapped her face. "Out into the kitchen if you can't control your tongue."

Vigon's face was pale. "I didn't . . . I didn't know she was married."

"She isn't!" sang out Edita triumphantly. She adroitly dodged her mother's slap and ran into the kitchen chanting: "Going to have a baby without a father."

"Is it true?" asked Vigon.

"It happens," said Camila defensively.

"Won't the man marry her?"

"First she's got to find him."

Vigon was shocked.

"A soldier told her a fine story and then disappeared."

Benito said slowly: "The man must be mad. Rosalia will make a fine wife for any man."

"But not every man who promises wants a wife," said his mother grimly.

"I'll talk to her," said Benito.

"You'll have to be quick," said his father. "She's been turned out of home. Today she received her travel permit and tomorrow she goes to Barcelona."

Benito ran upstairs, shaved off his beard, combed his hair and slicked it flat.

He went downstairs, but his father stopped him at the door. "Where are you going, son?"

"To see Rosalia."

"It is better to stay in the house. I will tell her you are here."

"She has pride, Father. She will not come to me. I must go to her."

"And if you are stopped and they ask for your papers?"

"It is a risk I must take, Father."

"You're a fool," sighed the older man.

Benito stepped out into the narrow street and made his way quickly to Rosalia's house. On the way he saw people he knew who at first were surprised, but then smiled and said *"Bon día"* as naturally as though he had never left the village. But just before he reached Rosalia's house he came face to face with Father Delbos. The priest paced majestically along the street, occupying all the pavement. His face was pale beneath his round black hat and his black skirts rustled importantly. The priest approached imperiously and Benito stepped out into the cobbled street. "Good evening, Father," he said respectfully.

Father Delbos stared at him hard and his footsteps slowed. "Are you from the village?" he demanded, his eyes suspicious.

"Of course, Father," said Benito. He hurried on.

The priest stared after him.

Marcel Prada opened the door to Benito's knocking. His face was flushed as though he had been drinking.

"May I visit you?" asked Vigon.

Marcel stepped back, holding the door open so that Benito could enter the flagstoned kitchen. Isabel Prada looked up from her ironing. "So you're back at last, Benito," she said without friendliness. "Have you news of my son Julio?"

"Where was he fighting, Señora?"

"Who can tell? He never had time to write."

"Very many retreated to France, Señora."

Isabel thumped her iron angrily as she smoothed flat her husband's shirt. "Men make wars but women pay for them with sorrow."

Benito glanced around him. "Is Rosalia at home?"

Her father said flatly. "She's upstairs. She's not fit to mix with decent folk."

"Keep your temper, Marcel," soothed his wife. "Don't start again."

"I . . . do you think I could talk to her?" asked Benito.

"You know what she's done?" asked Isabel Prada, thumping the iron loudly.

"Yes. I'm told she is to leave tomorrow?"

"She'd leave tonight if there was a bus," said her father.

"May I talk to her?"

"She doesn't deserve to speak to decent folk."

"I . . . I'd still like to talk to her."

Marcel Prada narrowed his eyes. "Why?"

"Perhaps . . ." stammered Vigon. He flushed violently. "Perhaps . . . she will marry me."

Isabel Prada froze, her iron scorching a bedsheet. She stared at him with widening eyes.

Marcel Prada drew a deep breath. "What did you say?"

"I want to marry Rosalia."

Marcel Prada exchanged glances with his wife. Then he paced to the foot of the stairs and called up in an authoritative voice: "You up there, whore. You hear me? Come down."

There was no reply.

Marcel Prada roared angrily. "I'll shit upon all the saints before I'll allow a whore of a daughter to defy me. Come down or I'll get my strap."

There was silence for a few moments. Then the upstairs door opened. The smell of scorched linen pervaded the kitchen and Isabel Prada scolded herself bitterly.

Rosalia slowly descended the stairs, holding her head high.

"*Bonne nuit,* Rosalia," said Vigon.

She was unashamed of her swollen abdomen. "How are you, Benito? You look thinner but stronger." The ghost of a smile glowed in her eyes. "Have you lost weight chasing after the girls?"

Vigon was breathless. Rosalia's impact upon him was deeply disturbing. "I want to see you," he choked.

She was strangely self-possessed. "You may, Benito. Take a good look at a fallen woman."

Benito looked at her unhappily.

Marcel Prada said abruptly: "Vigon wants to marry you. If he is such a great fool, take advantage of it."

An unexpected softness came into Rosalia's eyes. "Thank you, Benito," she said wistfully. "It is kind of you."

"Don't waste time," said Marcel. "It must be as soon as possible."

"*What* must be as soon as possible, Father?" asked Rosalia.

"I'll talk to Father Delbos and you can wed this week."

"No," said Rosalia. "I'm not going to marry."

Her parents stared in amazement.

"I'm not ashamed of anything I've done. I want neither pity nor charity."

"You must be out of your mind, girl. You'll never get another chance like this," said her mother.

"Rosalia," pleaded Vigon. "I *want* you. I've always wanted you and you've always known it. I don't care what people say or what you've done. It is *you* who matters!"

She studied him thoughtfully, beginning now to think seriously of his offer.

Her mother sensed it. "Be sensible, Rosalia. Sit down with Benito and talk things over."

But at that moment there was the thud of a rifle butt against the door; it swung inward and two soldiers stepped into the kitchen. They leveled their rifles at Benito and one held out his hand. "Papers," he demanded.

Benito stared at him in dismay. "I . . . er . . ." he stammered. His eyes went to Rosalia.

"Papers?" demanded the soldier.

Vigon gulped. "Rosalia . . . wait for me?" he pleaded.

"No papers?" said the soldier grimly. "All right. Come along."

Vigon stood staring at Rosalia until they seized him by the arms and hurried him outside. "Rosalia," he called over his shoulder. "Wait for me. I'll be back. Wait for me!"

It was easier to handle Vigon outside in the street. A rifle butt slammed against the base of his spine arched him in agony and he made no resistance when they marched him to the barracks where Father Delbos was waiting.

"Can he give an account of himself?" he asked the soldiers.

"He has no papers, Father."

"I was right, you see," said Father Delbos contentedly. "I was right!"

Vigon was handcuffed and put in a stone cell for the night. The following morning a military truck took him to Figueras. From there he was transferred to Gerona. Most of his fellow prisoners were soldiers who had been waiting months to stand trial.

11

Rosalia left her home with all her worldly possessions tied up in a blanket.

She closed the door upon her parents and walked through the village streets, braving the dozens of eyes that watched from behind drawn curtains.

The old bus was half-empty when it lurched into movement. Vicente Serra sat behind Rosalia and she could feel his hot breath on the back of her neck. "Going to Figueras?" he asked into her ear.

She was tempted to ignore him. She gave a slight nod.

"I'm going there on business," he said importantly.

She made no comment.

"Can you hear me, girl?"

She nodded.

"Listen," he whispered conspiratorially. "I know a lot of soldiers in Figueras. Get yourself a room, don't overcharge, and I'll keep you busy. I won't want much either."

Rosalia rose to her feet and walked along the lurching bus to another seat. Everybody looked at her and then looked away again quickly.

"Whore!" said Serra in a low but penetrating voice. "She's nothing but a whore!"

Teresa received a letter Anselmo must have mailed as soon as he arrived in Barcelona.

> TERESA,
> I am shocked you do not understand my attitude toward family life. The essence of matrimony is loyalty. Any girl who is loose before marriage will go with *anyone* after marriage.
>
> A. L.

She wrote him a thoughtful, reasoned letter. She said she could understand that in anger he had written a letter which he must regret. She looked forward to his next leave when they could talk over everything. She reaffirmed that she loved him and would be a devoted wife and mother.

Anselmo returned the letter without opening it.

Teresa sighed when she received it. Anselmo was going to be tiresome, but she was sure she could convince him. So sure there was a spring in her step and a sparkle in her eyes.

Señora Ledesma rarely left the house. The last few years and the death of Baudillo had aged her greatly. She spent most of her days seated in the warmth of the sun in the patio, reading or crocheting.

But one day she felt the urge to visit the church and on the way home she met Teresa.

"*Bon día,* Señora Ledesma."

"*Bon día,* Teresa. You're looking so much better. Doctor Aldo told me you were very, very ill."

"Thank you for the flowers you sent, Señora."

"It was nothing, child. I wanted to call to see you but I had a bad attack of rheumatism and couldn't move."

They talked about the shortage of food and then the older woman asked abruptly: "What has happened between you and Anselmo, my dear?"

Teresa smiled wryly: "We quarreled; but it is nothing serious."

The older woman's eyes were sharp. "You *are* in love with him aren't you?"

"I am, Señora."

"Then . . . why do you quarrel?"

"All lovers have their tiffs. And it is so nice to make up afterward."

"Then it's nothing serious, my child?"

"Anselmo is being a little . . . difficult."

"I was worried," admitted Señora Ledesma. "While he's been stationed in Barcelona, he's been seeing a great deal of a young woman he met recently."

Teresa's heart thumped.

"So . . . I wondered . . . ?"

"Anselmo wrote to you about her, Señora?"

"He writes me a long letter every week."

"He wanted you to tell me, so I would be jealous," said Teresa confidently.

But doubts undermined her confidence and when she went to bed she lay awake, tortured by nagging fears. Her fears grew every day. She wrote many letters to Anselmo but he ignored them. She became nervous and bad-tempered and lost weight.

Then Anselmo's sister wrote to her from Barcelona.

My dear Teresa,

Because of your close friendship with our family, I'm writing to let you know that on the twenty-seventh of next month, Anselmo will marry Silvana Rodrigues. She's from a very good family whose finances suffered disastrously during the war. The wedding will be in Barcelona and all the family will be present, including Mother, who will spend the week here.

I know this news may be a shock, Teresa. But it would have been wrong to let you learn about it from another source. With sincere best wishes to you and your family.

Ever your friend,
Pilar

Teresa read the letter and stood as though turned to stone. Then she made her way upstairs to her bedroom and locked herself in.

She remained in her room for three days. She refused to eat and asked only to be left alone.

On the fourth day when her father had decided to break down the door, she came downstairs. She was quiet and composed and looked normal. But her face had hardened and her eyes were dead. She said tonelessly: "Don't worry about me. I was being temperamental."

"What's happened, my dear?" asked her mother anxiously.

Teresa said as though it was of no importance: "Anselmo is to marry in Barcelona on the twenty-seventh of next month."

That afternoon Teresa spent a long time brushing her long hair and braiding it. She put on her best frock of black velvet trimmed with crisp white lace, and *alpargatas*. She walked along the cobbled street to Manuel Coruna's grocer's store. Narcissus was at the back of the shop scooping dried beans from a sack and weighing them out into kilo packets. Teresa crossed to him. He looked up in mild surprise.

"*Ola,* Narcissus," she said.

"*Bon día,* Teresa," and he straightened up, smiling sheepishly, his plump face very pale.

She studied him objectively. She saw his weak jaw, his soft, spaniel eyes, his rounded shoulders and his flabby hands. She sighed.

"What is it, Teresa?" he asked anxiously. His voice was reedy.

"I was thinking that you work too hard. You hardly ever go out, Narcissus."

"There's . . . there's not much to do if I go out, is there?"

She looked at him steadily. "I don't know, because you've never asked me to go with you."

He gaped. "Do you mean . . . ? Will you go walking with me this evening, Teresa?"

"I'd like it very much, Narcissus."

They went walking every evening for a week.

They strolled along the harbor wall to its end where the cracked concrete tilted crazily, half-submerged in the swirling sea. Here they sat and talked as young people should, alone but in full view of the gossips who could see that nothing improper was happening. The music of the sea was around them.

"Do you like to be here with me, Narcissus?" she asked.

"I am always happy to be at your side."

She sat with her skirt discreetly tucked under her, dabbling her feet in the water. She looked up at him. "Do you wish me to be your *novia?*"

He hadn't dared suggest it so soon. "Oh . . . it is what I want more than anything, Teresa!"

"Your parents will not mind?"

"I am sure they will be very happy."

"When will you come to speak to my father?"

She saw the nervousness in his eyes and added reassuringly: "I will be with you when you ask him, Narcissus."

He was visibly relieved. "Perhaps . . . you will prepare him for my visit?"

"Come tomorrow, Narcissus. I will prepare him."

"As you say, Teresa."

She looked at him steadily. "There is another thing, Narcissus. We are not strangers. Life is fleeting. Let us not waste it. Let us be wed soon."

He was disturbed. He had vaguely thought of an engagement lasting two or three years.

"We have known each other a long time, Narcissus. It is only custom that requires a long courtship."

Her eagerness stimulated him. "Why not?" he said and was pleasantly astonished at his own recklessness. "Let's get married soon. When shall it be?"

Again she shocked him. "Next month."

"Next month!" he echoed. His mind was busy with all the problems; time off from the shop, a new suit, a list of wedding guests, the honeymoon and a hundred other details. The worry of it all overwhelmed him.

"Don't you want to marry me, Narcissus?"

"Of course. It's . . . it's just that it's so soon."

"It isn't, Narcissus. There's plenty of time to arrange everything . . . if it's *really* what you want."

"Of course I want it. You *know* I do."

"Well, then?"

"We'll marry next month," he stated firmly.

In a faraway voice she said. "Make it the twenty-eighth."

Narcissus plunged into the preparations for the wedding. He visited Father Delbos, the day was fixed, marriage papers were prepared, the wedding luncheon arranged and travel permits obtained for their honeymoon in Madrid. Narcissus suffered violent attacks of indigestion and couldn't sleep.

The days passed swiftly. No bridal gown could be bought because the textile factories had been bombed, but Teresa adapted her mother's wedding gown.

Time flew and before Teresa was fully prepared for it, the day was the twenty-seventh; the day of Anselmo's wedding. Teresa remained in her room all day but came down in the early evening. Narcissus was awaiting her. "Teresa," he ventured timidly. "This is our last day as *novios*. Will you . . . will you walk with me?"

They walked through the village and out to the end of the harbor wall. Teresa didn't speak a word.

Narcissus took out his handkerchief and spread it for her to sit on.

"Forgive me, Narcissus," she said tonelessly. "Today I feel despondent."

He sighed, not knowing how to comfort her, and they sat in silence for a long time.

"Teresa," he ventured.

"Yes?"

"We will marry tomorrow?"

"It has been arranged."

"I want to tell you this, Teresa. I asked a friend of mine in Barcelona . . . He telephoned. Anselmo was married at midday."

She sat quite still for a long time. Then she turned to him. "You know about Anselmo?"

"It is Anselmo you love, isn't it?"

"Is it so evident, Narcissus? Does everybody know?"

"No," he said quietly. "I know because I love you. I watch you and know how you feel before you know it yourself." His spaniel eyes were shining moistly. "Is that love, Teresa?"

"I think it must be."

He took a deep breath. "If you still want to marry me tomorrow, Teresa, I shall be very happy."

She pressed his hand. "We will marry, Narcissus."

Their marriage, the wedding luncheon and the drink-befuddled wishes of their guests were unexciting for Teresa. The long journey to Madrid in a slow train, the modest hotel, and the "sights" of Madrid were boring routine. Narcissus was an eager but inept lover, with limited stamina. He was all that Teresa had anticipated; but she knew how to make him contented.

Coruna's grocery store had a large apartment above it where the family lived. A double bedroom was given to Teresa and Narcissus. She now began a new way of life, helping in the store. She still found time to help her father too, rowing out in their little boat to lay the fishing lines.

Two months later Anselmo brought his wife to Escoleras and soon after, they met Teresa face to face in the plaza. Anselmo stared at her wooden-faced, but Teresa was composed. She said, as though greeting an old friend, "Congratulations, Anselmo." Then she smiled at Anselmo's bride. Although she had braced herself for this moment, it was difficult. The girl was delicately attractive and graceful. Such a sweetly feminine creature would have a tremendous impact on any man.

Anselmo said coldly: "Teresa, I'd like you to meet my wife, Silvana." He paused. "My dear, Teresa is a very, very old friend."

"I hope all Anselmo's friends will be my friends, too," smiled Silvana.

"Anselmo is well-liked," said Teresa. "You'll have many new friends."

"Anselmo's told me so much about Escoleras and how beautiful it is. I'm so happy to be here."

"It's not only the village that is beautiful," said Teresa. "There are the mountains and the valleys and then there is our coastline. The rugged coastline so typical of us Catalans."

"What I love about the Costa Brava," thrilled Silvana, "is that it is so savage, so primitive!"

"If you wish," offered Teresa, "I will borrow my father's boat and we can row out along the coast and fish."

"I'd *love* it!"

Anselmo said coldly: "I'm sorry, Teresa. I can't allow it."

"But you'll come too, Anselmo," said Teresa. "We'll make a day of it. We'll fish and cook our catch on a beach."

"It cannot be, Teresa," said Anselmo. He looked at Silvana with a tenderness that made Teresa drive her nails deeply into her palms. "Silvana must take great care. She mustn't be energetic or get excited."

There was a great swelling in Teresa's chest. "Why?"

"She is with child," said Anselmo contentedly.

"You . . . you are doubly blessed, Anselmo," choked Teresa. She turned and hurried from them, blinking furiously.

Narcissus closed the accounts book of the store, yawned, rose to his feet and stretched himself. He took down a long sausage of dried salami hanging from a roof joist, cut slices from it and ate them. He looked at the old pendulum clock in the far corner of the store. It was after midnight and his parents had long ago gone to bed.

But not Teresa!

He took off his smock, hung it up and went out through the back door onto the beach.

Teresa was standing barefooted on the silver sand, staring up at the moon. The sea surfed gently along the beach, tinting it with phosphorescence. He stood behind her and rested his hands on her shoulders.

"The day's work is done, Narcissus?"

"Of what are you thinking, *querida?*"

"Of life."

"Or of love?"

"Of life," she sighed. "Always I think of life. And now I will give life. Imagine Narcissus, I am carrying our child!"

"I love you," he said sincerely. His lips moved along her shoulder and her neck. "I love you so much!"

"You are kind and good, Narcissus."

BOOK IV

1

The watchman limped along the darkened cobbled streets knocking on doors and waiting for sleepy answers growled from upstairs bedrooms. As the first gray light of day peeked over the distant mountains, the sleepy fishermen launched their dinghys and rowed out to the moored fishing boats.

The sea was still and the oars spread silver ripples. Seagulls wheeled overhead and screeched mournfully as the engines started, their piston thuds echoing across the water. Heavy anchor chains rattled across the wooden decks and out through the hawses.

The fishing fleet headed out to sea as the village came to life. Housewives and fish-buyers gathered on the dock to meet the small-boat fishermen who had spent the night with baited lines. Bidding for the catches was cautious; everybody needed food but few had money. Fuel oil was rationed and fishing boats went out only one day a week. In the towns and cities the people were starving.

Isidro Barras shipped his oars and leaped nimbly onto the dock. His bare, brown foot warded the bow of his boat away before it rasped against the concrete. At once he was surrounded by villagers who shouldered each other to see his catch. It was small. For months the sea had denied its abundance, the breeding spoiled by those who had fished with sticks of dynamite.

Isidro had two squid, an octopus, five scorpions and a sole; but the bargaining crowd fell silent as three Civil Guards approached with tommyguns slung across their shoulders.

"Name?" demanded one guard crisply, eyes sizing up Isidro's catch.

"Barras." Isidro scowled.

"You live here?"

"I was born here."

"Papers!"

Isidro sighed and reached into his hip pocket.

"*Nada*. It doesn't matter. I've seen you around." The guard pointed at the boat. "Any contraband?"

Isidro smiled wryly. "No contraband, *Cabo*."

"Do we need to search? Shall we take up the floorboards?"

Isidro's face was stiff. "I've nothing at all but . . . fish." He swallowed. "If you . . . ?"

"*Gracias*," said the *Cabo* instantly. "Which do you want, Juan?" he asked his companion.

"I'd like the sole."

"A couple of scorpions will do me," said the third Civil Guard.

"I'll take a squid," said the *Cabo*.

Isidro stepped down into his boat and handed up the fish.

"Haven't you anything to wrap it with?"

Isidro found a piece of rag and wrapped the fish.

"*Gracias*," said the *Cabo*. He eased the strap of his tommygun, the crowd parted, and the Civil Guards strode away.

Isidro scowled.

"You're lucky," said a villager. "Yesterday when they picked on Coll they took *all* his catch except an octopus."

Isidro sighed. "When there is no wine we must drink water." He raised his voice. "How much for these scorpion fish?"

Isidro sold his fish quickly, keeping his eye on Ines Brunet who was walking along the dock. He hurried to meet her and she scolded him. "What will people think, the way you pay me attention!"

"Is it not polite to greet a neighbor?"

"Very well, neighbor. Good morning."

He walked beside her.

"See how everyone is watching us," she protested.

"What of it? Can I not talk to you and walk with you at the same time?"

"Not without gossip."

"Why are you up so early?"

"Papa's fishing boat docked last night and all its catch was bought by a Barcelona merchant. Papa is packing the fish in ice and I'm taking him his breakfast." She held up a rafia bag containing black bread, a slice of salami, and a bottle of wine.

"Why do you not wear shoes?" he criticized.

"Because I do not choose."

"It is not seemly that a young lady should go barefooted."

She giggled. "A 'young lady,' " she mocked.

Isidro frowned. "You do not make the best of yourself. Your father is a skilled carpenter who employs men. Also he owns a fishing boat.

It is not necessary to demean yourself by going barefooted like a peasant."

Her black eyes danced. "How many times have I seen your own sister, Teresa, barefooted and working like a man, drawing in the fishing nets and wading in the sea."

"Teresa is different. Everybody knows she is as strong-willed as a man. She will work with the men or sew with the women. She will argue her opinion against the schoolmaster and will even go into a bar unescorted. But you are different, Ines. You are *entirely* feminine. You should be more . . . reserved."

"What is it to you, the way I am?" she teased.

"I like to see you at your best."

"He who bids the musicians play should make known his wishes." She looked away shyly.

"Ines," he said breathlessly. "Will you go walking with me Sunday evening?"

She shrugged her shoulders. "If you wish I will meet you in the plaza next Sunday. We will walk there if you want it."

"I *do* want it," he said fervently.

"But there must be no nonsense about barefootedness!"

"I do not mind how you come . . . as long as you come, Ines."

"I will wear shoes," she said. Her eyes shone. "Black shoes with high heels!"

"Walk with me a little now," he urged.

"Impossible. My father awaits me." She quickened her pace. "It is better you leave me now. I will see you Sunday."

He nodded obediently, watching her walk along the quayside to the fish market; then he sighed and went home.

Nobody was awake at this early hour and he crept up to his bedroom, stripped off his damp clothes and shivered as he snuggled between cold sheets. He quickly fell asleep and it was midday before he awoke and went downstairs to find Doctor Aldo attending his father.

A week earlier, Paco Barras had upset a pan of boiling water over himself and now he sat with his outstretched leg resting on a chair while Doctor Aldo removed strips of dead, gray skin with tweezers. The leg was swollen and as the skin came away, the raw quick was exposed. Elisa Barras hovered anxiously, giving her husband comfort. Pepita held an enamel kidney bowl into which the doctor dropped the slivers of skin.

Paco looked up. "How was the fishing, son?"

"It was not bad, Father. But the Civil Guard are hungry men."

Doctor Aldo said angrily. "Their appetites are more than fishermen can satisfy."

"Did you protest, son?"

"To protest is dangerous."

"I am pleased you were wise."

"But I am also angry."

"Do not worry. Soon my leg will heal and we will fish together. We will have enough for all of us."

Doctor Aldo removed a long sliver of skin and, as Paco Barras gritted his teeth, the doctor asked: "Have you no news of Miguel?"

There were beads of perspiration on Paco's forehead. He said slowly: "Miguel wrote that he has been released from the French concentration camp and is working for a farmer."

The doctor shook the tweezers. "Will Miguel not return to Spain?"

"I fear we have lost a son," said Paco Barras sadly. "The boy is obsessed by the murder of his bride. Those who have seen him tell me he is filled with hate. He is our flesh and blood but he is cold toward us and wishes to live apart. And now that France is at war with Germany, we do not even receive letters from him."

Pepita asked: "If I volunteer as a nurse, can I go to France and heal the wounded? Then I can find Miguel."

"Have we not had enough of war that you must cross the border to find another?" growled Paco Barras.

"She's young," her mother excused. "She has a woman's urge to comfort the sick."

"Then why doesn't she pour me brandy instead of toying with that enamel dish!" roared Paco, his eyes bright with pain.

"I will get it for you, husband," soothed Elisa. She took down the brandy bottle.

Doctor Aldo dropped the tweezers into the kidney bowl and took cotton and alcohol from his bag. "Drink up quickly, Paco. I'm going to clean it now and it will . . . hurt!"

Paco Barras clenched his hands. "Go ahead, Juan."

Isidro said quietly: "Many Spaniards now in France have new hope. They believe the Allies will fight fascism; not only in Germany but also in Spain!"

"Listen to him," choked Paco Barras. He was white with pain as Doctor Aldo sponged. "Three years of misery and now he wants it to start all over again!"

"I do not want war, Father. I only repeat what everybody is saying."

"What everybody says is nonsense!" roared Paco.

"Don't shout so," soothed Elisa.

"I *will* shout!" he roared. Then he glared at Doctor Aldo. "Why don't you cut my leg off and have done with it!"

The doctor dropped a cotton swab into the kidney bowl. "All finished, Paco. Now a soothing ointment and in a week or so it will be healed."

"The entire government army took refuge in France, Father," said Isidro. "They'll fight against Hitler."

Doctor Aldo bandaged deftly and said: "France doesn't want to fight Hitler, only to pacify him. The French are afraid of communism. They suppress left-wing hotheads more vigorously than the Fascists do."

Paco Barras's pain had been soothed by the ointment. "We have no need of politics in Escoleras. Leave us in peace and we live contentedly."

Doctor Aldo finished bandaging and rose to his feet. "You have heard about our new neighbors?"

Paco Barras's eyebrows arched in curiosity. "I know only that a family of Gypsies with many children has occupied a bombed cottage."

"They've come from Jaen, walking every step of the journey with all those children. It took them three years and two more children were born on the road. They've got only the clothes they stand up in. They've been begging. The mayor offered them work but they don't want it. They sit in the sun and sing and dance flamenco. Some of the children are very good. Afterward they pass a hat. There've been a few fowl missing and washing has mysteriously disappeared from the clotheslines." Doctor Aldo chuckled.

"Where are they heading?"

"They may stay in Escoleras," said Doctor Aldo. "Nobody charges them rent. They're patching the hole in the roof with corrugated iron, begging bits and pieces of furniture and setting up a home."

"Who owns the cottage?"

Doctor Aldo sighed. "It belongs to the Plana family. But they were all killed and no relatives have claimed the property."

"It's better the Gypsies should have it than the state should take it over," said Paco Barras.

Doctor Aldo knocked on the door of Serra's cottage, opened it and stepped into the gloom of the stone-floored living room. Maria Serra sat on the floor on a piece of sacking and used her bare toes to draw taut the fishing net she was repairing. She glanced up at the doctor and looked away quickly. "Good morning, Doctor." Her fingers flew as she patched. She was paid by the piece and wouldn't waste a second.

Doctor Aldo drew back the sackcloth curtain at the window and crossed to the cot in the corner. It was made from two fish boxes, and the child sleeping in it was pale and sickly.

"She's sleeping," said Maria. "Don't wake her."

Doctor Aldo stared down at the child. "She's not strong, Maria. How old is she now? Three years? She should be full of life and playing with other children." His eyes glinted. "You should be ashamed of yourself, woman. You neglect this child."

She glared. "What more can we do? We give her *everything!*"

"Feed the child," he said flatly. "Give her good food that makes bones and puts flesh on her."

"We do what we can. But food's expensive. She eats more than we do."

It was true. Maria's pinched cheeks, shrunken breasts and skinny arms showed she ate barely enough to keep herself alive. Vicente Serra was equally frugal.

"If you and Vicente devote your lives to saving money, it is your privilege," said Doctor Aldo sternly. "But you have a responsibility to your daughter. Her health is in danger."

"Last night we had boiled potatoes and half of them went on *her* plate."

"Potatoes!" he stormed. "She needs food . . . *not* stuffing! Give her chicken, beefsteak and lots of fish!"

Maria's eyes were black buttons gleaming in the dark hollows of her eye sockets. "Such food is *impossible,* Doctor. It costs a fortune!"

"So what, woman! Spend a fortune. Make your child healthy!"

Her lips trembled and her eyes were shocked. "We can't, Doctor. We *can't* spend the money."

"You and Vicente have been saving for years. You've a small fortune stored away."

"We can't touch our savings, Doctor. It's there in case we ever have need of it."

"I shit upon your meanness," stormed the doctor. "Unless better care is taken of that child I'll report you both!"

His next call was upon Teresa Coruna. Manuel Coruna was weighing out dried beans for a customer and Narcissus was balanced on a high ladder, stacking rope-soled *alpargatas* on the top shelf. Teresa was setting out boxes of salted herrings on the display counter.

Doctor Aldo greeted them crisply, took out his watch and said: "Let's see how it's going, shall we, Teresa?"

Emilia Coruna was preparing lunch in the tiny kitchen behind the shop when Teresa led the doctor through it and upstairs to the bedroom.

"How do you feel?" he asked, motioning her to lie down.

"I've never felt better."

"Good." He examined her.

"Excellent," he reported briskly. "Excellent!" He washed his hands in the bowl of water on the washstand. Teresa stood up and shook down her skirts.

He turned to face her, drying his hands on a towel. "Excellent," he said again. "You're as sound as a bell, Teresa. Everything is as it should be."

"How about my need to keep running to the toilet?"

"That's quite natural. Your bladder's compressed. Everything has to give way a little. The baby makes everything move over to give it room. How's your appetite? Are you eating well? Any yearnings?"

"I'm always as hungry as a horse."

He studied her, seeing her as a man and not as a doctor. She had blossomed and was beautiful in a comfortable, matronly way. Her skin was clear and glowing and her eyes wise and peaceful. She was nineteen, he recalled, but looked younger. The pronounced swell of her pregnancy above her coltish legs was incongruous.

"There's no way to tell if it will be a boy or a girl?"

He shook his head. "What would you like?"

"A girl," she said at once.

"Narcissus would like a boy?"

"A father always wants a son."

"You're both young. You've plenty of time to have lots of both kinds."

She nodded and he saw a hint of resignation in her eyes.

He thought of Anselmo's wife and said: "It'll be a race between the

Ledesmas and the Corunas." He had spoken thoughtlessly, and was relieved when Teresa looked at him with untroubled eyes.

"How is Silvana?" she asked.

"She is well. Quite well." He frowned, thinking of the two women's attitudes to childbirth. Teresa was busy helping her husband, whereas Silvana made the household revolve around her while she lay in bed.

"Is . . . is Anselmo happy?" asked Teresa.

He looked at her steadily and because he knew how devoted she had been to Anselmo, he replied honestly. "Yes, Teresa. Anselmo is very happy. He wanted a wife to bear him children and now a child is on the way."

"I am pleased if Anselmo is happy," she said quietly.

The doctor pulled out his watch and glanced at it. "Have you news of Rosalia?" he asked.

"She hasn't written for a long time. She lost the baby. You knew about that, didn't you, Doctor?"

"Yes." He sighed. "I must get along."

He had only one more patient to visit when he reached the outskirts of the village, so he loitered to talk to Hernando.

Hernando had a cooking pot simmering on a bed of white-hot charcoal. He took off the lid, dropped in a handful of wild mushrooms and a delightful odor wafted to the doctor's nostrils. "It smells delicious!"

"A wild hare I shot this morning," said Hernando proudly. "One head of garlic, three bay leaves, one *guindilla,* half a liter of wine, some pepper and now the mushrooms."

"It makes my mouth water."

"Come back in two hours and it will be ready," said Hernando. He twirled his waxed moustache. "But now tell me what news you have of the city."

Doctor Aldo shook his head. "Things go from bad to worse. There is no confidence in the government. Everywhere there is fear and suspicion. Industry is at a standstill and without capital. Spain is dead, Hernando. Only the secret police, the Civil Guard and the judges are active. The prisons are overcrowded with men who've been denounced. Those who are suspected of being Socialists get long terms of imprisonment. Those believed to be Communists are executed.

But what makes everything worse, Hernando, is the war between the Allies and Germany. All the frontiers are closed. Spain is isolated. Our problems are ignored by other countries which have too many problems of their own."

Hernando stirred the simmering pot with a wooden spoon. Steam wafted up with an appetizing aroma. "The government that governs best is the one that governs least of all," Hernando said philosophically. He looked up then as Father Delbos approached. His blue eyes gave no smile of welcome.

"Good morning, Doctor. Good morning, Hernando," said the priest. He spoke in Spanish but Hernando replied in Catalan.

"*Bon dia,*" said Hernando.

"It is possible we shall have a shower toward evening," said Doctor Aldo.

Father Delbos's nostrils quivered. "Your stew smells delicious!" He still spoke in Spanish.

Hernando restrained an impulse to invite the priest to eat with him. Instead he said in Catalan, "Send someone with a dish and it will be my pleasure to send you a sample of my cooking."

"It is kind of you, Hernando. I will send my woman." The priest frowned. "You have noticed I always speak in Spanish. It is best we forget we are Catalans and weld ourselves into the Spanish nation and grow strong."

Hernando hooked his thumbs into his black sash. "I can't change what I am, Father Delbos. Catalan is my mother tongue and I always speak it, but I understand Spanish and will speak it to those who are not Catalan."

"Hernando, by keeping the Catalan language alive you drive a wedge between the peoples of Spain."

"I am driving no wedge," said Hernando. "There are some people who are very good and some who are very bad. But what they are does not depend on the language they speak."

"It is forbidden to speak Catalan," said Father Delbos flatly. "That is the law."

Hernando stared at him unblinkingly. "You are Catalan. Will you denounce me for speaking Catalan?"

Father Delbos flushed. "Of course not."

Doctor Aldo took out his watch and glanced at it. "I must hurry." He nodded briefly at the priest and spoke to Hernando in Catalan. "I will see you soon." He strode away.

Hernando took out a worn leather pouch and rolled a cigarette. "Smoke?" he asked the priest.

The priest lit up and coughed at the acrid bite of the black tobacco. "Where do you get your tobacco?" he asked curiously.

Hernando twirled his moustache and nodded toward the mountains. "I grow it secretly." He chuckled. "It tastes better without government tax."

The priest frowned. "Tell me, Hernando. Why do you never come to church? Everyone says you are a good man. But you never worship God."

Hernando laughed. "What has the Church to do with God? In church, you burn incense, chant in a strange tongue, sing sad songs and stand up and kneel down many, many times. I don't know God but if all this pleases him, he must be a man of very simple tastes."

The priest exhaled smoke through his nostrils. "You are intelligent, Hernando. You can understand that the simple people have need of symbols to help them focus their faith."

"The churches wanted war," said Hernando slowly. "They declared General Franco's rebellion a sacred crusade."

"And so it was. Would you want the Red scum of Moscow making us slaves?"

"I prefer that there is no slavery, either to Moscow or to the Church."

Father Delbos's eyes narrowed. "You presume to criticize, Hernando? Can you not see that mankind is on the threshold of greatness? Hitler is gathering his strength and the Vatican and Mussolini are behind him. The Red scourge will be stamped out. The forces of God's crusade will turn to the east and confront the twin evils of Judaism and Marxism."

Hernando said briskly: "Excuse me. I have an important job." He disappeared inside his hut and pulled the sackcloth curtain across the doorway behind him.

Father Delbos stood frowning at the simmering pot for some minutes. Then he sighed and made his way along the beach to the quay. He stood watching the fish being unloaded and presently was given a rafia bag of fish. It was the custom.

2

Madrid was crowded with Nationalist soldiers. There were victory parades, the sidewalk bars were crowded and there was a surge of gaiety as though everyone was determined to forget the sad past and build a happy future.

Antonia Ledesma was on her way home from the university when she saw a group of officers standing under the gaily-striped awning of a hotel that had been commandeered by the military. The familiar posture of one of the officers caught her attention and she ran across the road. She went up to him excitedly: "Rafael. It's me, Antonia!"

He had changed greatly during the last three years. He was taller, his forehead seemed higher because his hair had receded, and the skin of his face was drawn drum-tight over his facial bones.

He turned to her lazily, black eyes glittering and eyelids narrowing. He said coldly: "How are you, Antonia? I wondered if you were in Madrid." His manner was so distant it killed her impulse to embrace him.

"We've been worried about you, Rafael. You haven't written." Her voice trailed off because the other officers were eyeing her curiously.

"Señores," said Rafael stiffly. "I present my sister, Antonia!"

The officers gravely raised her hand to their lips. They were all very young and the smartness of their uniforms with ribbons and medals made her aware that Rafael too had gained distinctions.

"We must have a drink," said Rafael.

The other officers tactfully excused themselves and Rafael urged Antonia into the hotel bar. They sat at an isolated table.

"It's been a long time, Rafael. Three years and not a word from you in all that time!"

He crossed his legs and his spurs jingled. He placed his riding crop on the table and grinned sardonically. "I no longer belong to the family. I was turned out!"

"You . . . you heard about Father dying?"

457

He glowered. "Murdered by the Reds!"

"I don't know what happened between you and Father, Rafael. But he loved you. He would want you to come back to the family."

His face was an expressionless mask. "I had all this talk when I last saw Anselmo. I don't need the family. I prefer to make my own way." He grinned mockingly. "Anselmo can be a father to you all."

"You're breaking Mother's heart!"

"She has two sons and daughters to fill the gap I leave."

"You *will* come home, won't you, Rafael? Promise me."

He shook his head arrogantly. "The family and I are too far apart. Nothing can bridge the gap."

"I do not know why you quarrelled with Father, but it is wrong to allow it to cut so deeply."

He shrugged his shoulders. "Does it matter?" He slashed the table-top lightly with his crop. "We must be realists and accept things for what they are and *not* for what we want them to be." He glanced at his wristwatch. "I must leave in a few minutes. I've been summoned to headquarters."

"When will I see you again, Rafael?"

"That depends on what I am doing."

"How can I get in touch with you?"

He grinned mockingly. "I move around a great deal."

"Perhaps we may have need of you, Rafael," she said gently.

He studied her coldly. "You're twenty-eight, aren't you? You'd better watch it or you'll get left on the shelf, and don't think I'll saddle myself with a spinster sister!"

She drew back as though he had slapped her face. "That's a cruel thing to say, Rafael."

"I'm a cruel person."

She picked up her handbag and rose to her feet. He stood up at once, outwardly polite and gentlemanly. "Allow me to call you a taxi."

"I haven't taxi money. I walk."

"It will be my privilege to pay."

"Your privilege is to hurt those who love you."

He turned away and called the waiter over to pay the bill. Then he escorted Antonia to the hotel foyer, his spurs jingling, his crop flicking his polished riding boots and the tunic of his uniform bright with medals.

He signaled to the door porter, who called up a taxi reserved for officers. Rafael spoke to the driver and gave him a currency note. The man saluted.

Rafael turned back to Antonia. "He'll take you home."

She looked at him steadily. "When will we meet again, Rafael?"

He shrugged his shoulders. "Is a brother-and-sister bond important? Would we bother about each other if we hadn't shared the same parentage?"

She stared at him for a long time. "Something terrible has happened to you, Rafael. You're not . . . not quite human."

"That might be the best way to adapt to the world in which we live," he said sardonically. He opened the taxi door, held her elbow as she climbed into the taxi and saluted her gravely.

Rafael took a following taxi and drove to his appointment at general headquarters.

The general was a gray-haired man with tired brown eyes. He gestured wearily. "Sit down, Ledesma."

Rafael sat stiffly on the edge of his chair while the general glanced through the dossier he had before him. He raised his eyes to Rafael. "Your record is clean, Ledesma. You're very loyal to the regime."

"It is my honor to be loyal to my country, General."

"The loyalty of Spain's true sons is to be rewarded."

Rafael lowered his eyes. "I do not seek reward, only to do my duty."

"These are critical times," said the general. "We have won the war. Now we must win the peace. Spain must be rebuilt. But we must guard against the Red enemy still in our midst."

Rafael nodded.

"There are still many who oppose us, Ledesma."

Rafael narrowed his eyes. "The lower classes are traitors ever ready to sell Spain to Moscow."

"It is General Franco's wish that all who have been influenced by Red propaganda shall undergo corrective training."

Rafael's eyes were sharp with interest.

"Such men cannot be allowed liberty to preach dangerous philosophies. For their own good they must be reeducated before they can take their place in society again."

Rafael nodded.

"You are young, Ledesma," said the general. "But I believe I can trust you with the responsibility of setting up these disciplinary camps."

All day Teresa had endured the warning pains in silence. But at seven in the evening, a pain seized her so fiercely that she knew her time had come.

She crouched over the counter, gripping her hands together until they were bloodless. Her eyes glazed and she said faintly: "It is my time, Narcissus. Get Doctor Aldo and the taxi."

Narcissus fled as his mother took Teresa's arm and helped her to a chair. "Is it a big pain?" she asked.

"The first big one."

"Why did you not speak sooner, silly girl?"

Doctor Aldo hurried in with his worn leather bag. "How long between pains?" He took out his watch to check for himself. "You should have spoken sooner," he scolded. "It's a long way to Gerona and the roads are bad."

The taxi was old but was kept moving by the mechanical genius of Juan Morales. The old car wheezed, rattled and bumped over the potholed road with Juan Morales torn between the necessity for speed and the comfort of his passenger.

Every time a pain came, Teresa braced back against the upholstery and gripped Narcissus's arm with such intensity that he turned pale.

Doctor Aldo timed the intervals. "I think we'll be all right," he said doubtfully.

Teresa summoned up a smile. "Suppose our child is born in the taxi, Narcissus."

Juan Morales blushed and stamped down hard on the accelerator. "You'll be all right," said the doctor.

"And . . . and Silvana, Doctor?" panted Teresa. "What news of Silvana?"

Five days earlier Silvana Ledesma had felt her first pains. Doctor Aldo had been aroused in the middle of the night to accompany her to Gerona. But the pains had been imaginary and, after staying with her all night and most of the following day, he had finally left the clinic to care for his other patients.

"Anselmo telephoned," he told Teresa. "She's having more pains. This time it could be the real thing."

"You said it would be a race between us!" Teresa broke off and braced her shoulders against the upholstery. Her body arched and the muscles of her face tightened and pulled down the corners of her mouth. Her nose was thin, prominent and waxlike.

"It's a big pain now," the doctor told Narcissus.

It was dark when they reached the clinic. Two nuns took Teresa upstairs to a labor ward and helped her undress. Doctor Aldo left Narcissus in a waiting room and went to see the hospital doctor.

"Another maternity, Pedro," he greeted. "This one held out as long as she could. I don't think she'll be more than an hour. How's the Ledesma woman?"

The doctor raised his eyes to heaven. "More trouble than a dozen others. Screams every time she has a twinge. If she wasn't allergic to anesthetics, I'd have quietened her long ago. She's just going to the theater."

Teresa was being helped into a hospital cot when she first heard Silvana, who had a private room alongside the public ward. Its door was open and a trolley was wheeled in to take Silvana to the operating theater. A pain started and her screams rang out along the ward. The screaming dwindled to a whimpering and the hospital orderlies swiftly transferred Silvana to the trolley.

"She's been doing that all day," said the woman in the cot next to Teresa.

"Some people are more sensitive to pain than others," said Teresa.

"And some like to draw attention to themselves!" snapped the woman.

Teresa had to lie back then because another pain racked her. When it was over she propped herself up on her elbow. Silvana began screaming again. Teresa saw Silvana's trolley rolling along the corridor and a man walking behind it. At first she didn't recognize the weary figure with bowed shoulders as Anselmo.

Narcissus came up to the ward and he and Doctor Aldo sat with Teresa for a time. Soon Doctor Aldo was called away. Narcissus held her hand. Presently screens were placed around her and a nurse pulled long woolen stockings on her legs. There were only short intervals now between pains and she sensed the urgency of the orderlies as they lifted her onto a trolley. Narcissus walked beside her, holding her hand until they reached the door of the operating theater. He kissed her lightly and she was wheeled into the smell of ether and antiseptics. She was lifted off the trolley onto the operating table and masked faces loomed over her.

"You lost the race, Teresa. Silvana won."

"What . . . ?" asked Teresa faintly.

"A girl," said Doctor Aldo. "A beautiful little girl. On the small side but healthy and screaming lustily."

There were metal stirrups to support the weight of Teresa's drawn-up legs. The hospital doctor made an examination. "It won't be long," he said. He looked hard at Teresa. "It'll be a tight one."

Teresa had another pain coming. Doctor Aldo went to the foot of the table and braced the soles of her feet against his shoulders. "Bear down," he said.

"Ahhh! That's good," she said huskily. Her lips writhed back away from her teeth and her eyes bulged as the pain gripped her.

"Strain," urged Doctor Aldo. "Push down."

It was a fine exhausting pain and her cheeks were wet with sweat when it eased. She glanced at the inspection window and smiled encouragingly at Narcissus who was watching her with worried eyes.

"Tell him to go away," she told Doctor Aldo. "It hurts him to see me."

"He won't," said Doctor Aldo. "He insists on staying."

Another long pain began and when it was over, the hospital doctor scolded angrily: "Scream, woman. Don't bottle it up. It's not natural!"

Teresa's eyes flicked to the window and she smiled weakly at Narcissus. "I'm all right."

"I can give you a whiff of something to make it easier. This is a tight one."

"No," she said quickly. "I want my baby to be healthy."

"It is better if you can do without it," sighed the doctor.

"Will it . . . will it be long?" asked Teresa.

"Any time. But it won't be easy, young woman. The baby's gone full term and is big."

The baby was born fifteen minutes later.

Narcissus saw the hospital doctor hunched down between Teresa's parted thighs. The doctor straightened up and handed a lump of bloody pinkness to a nurse, who took it deftly and dangled it by its feet like a skinned rabbit. The nurse slapped, the wizened little face screwed up and the mouth opened enormously to cry. But no sound reached Narcissus on his side of the inspection window. The nurse swaddled the baby in a towel, placed it on one side and turned back to the operating table.

Narcissus's heart thumped painfully. An emergency? He stood on tiptoe to see over the shoulders of the doctors but could see nothing.

He studied Teresa's pale face. Her nose was pinched and waxen and her face bore the shadow of pain it had worn since her labor began. He clenched his hands tightly and there were tears on his face. "Please God, don't let her die," he prayed aloud.

The gowned figures straightened up and pulled their masks off their mouths. With relief, Narcissus saw sheets being tucked around Teresa. A bell rang somewhere and hospital orderlies entered the theater, lifted her onto a trolley and wheeled her away.

Narcissus looked at the baby. He saw the bloodstained toweling move slightly, but no one took any notice of it. The doctors were talking, the nurses were dropping used instruments into trays and gathering up used swabs. He wanted to hammer on the glass and shout: *"The baby! What about the baby!"*

At that moment, Doctor Aldo turned and smiled at Narcissus. He nodded encouragingly and spoke to one of the nurses. She hurried across to the door of the operating room and called: "You can come in." There was a splash of blood on her white gown and the sharp tang of antiseptic stung his nostrils.

"Congratulations, Narcissus," said Doctor Aldo. "It's a boy."

Narcissus stared at the moving bundle anxiously. "Why don't they do something for him?"

"Don't worry," soothed Doctor Aldo. "We give him a few minutes to adapt himself to his new environment. There. You see. Nurse is going to clean him up now."

The nurse unwrapped the towel. The baby's wide-open eyes seemed to search for Narcissus and then stared straight at him. He thought: *It's my son and he knows it. Look at the way the little devil's staring at me. He knows I'm his father.*

The wizened features screwed themselves up, the eyes became slits and the mouth gaped. The baby cried lustily. But Narcissus was worried by the great mauve stain that discolored its shoulders and buttocks. "Is that a birthmark?" he faltered.

Doctor Aldo chuckled. "Bruises. He'll lose them in no time. Imagine how you'd look if you'd been cramped up for weeks like this little chap."

"Teresa?"

"She's fine, Narcissus. She's strong and healthy. She'll be sore for a time but you can see for yourself what a big head your son's got. Lots of stitches. But she'll soon be fit again."

A week later Teresa was back in the shop and working as hard as ever, breaking off only to breast-feed her son.

Silvana stayed weeks more in the hospital. She returned to Escoleras in an expensive limousine hired for the journey. She had had new dresses made for herself while she was in the hospital, clothes for the baby, crisp linen uniforms for the baby's nurse and costumes for the young woman who was to be her companion-helper. For the christening, more than two hundred expensively printed luncheon invitations were sent out.

Narcissus and Teresa were invited but shortly before they were due to set off for the Ledesma house, Teresa had a headache. Narcissus stayed at home to keep her company.

The night was so silent that Miguel heard the men approaching through the valley when they were more than a kilometer away. He waited patiently, as still as the mountains around him. When they were so close that he could hear their heavy breathing, the swish of the undergrowth, the scrape of iron-shod hooves on the pebbles and the metallic clink of weapons, one of them whistled a signal.

He whistled back and they grunted happily and hurried toward him, disturbing the night with their voices and heavy boots. Presently they reached him, a single file of armed men leading laden donkeys.

"It is you, Miguel?" the first asked softly into the darkness.

"It *is*, Comrade Munez," snapped Miguel. "But I could easily have been a French gendarme or a German patrol. They'd have had plenty of time to prepare an ambush, warned by the noise you were making!"

"We did not use caution because we trust you, comrade," said Munez. "You have the ears of a hound and I swear you see in the dark. You would have warned us if there had been danger."

"That may be so," grumbled Miguel.

"You will lead the way, comrade?"

"Follow silently because in these mountains sounds carry swiftly from one hill crest to another."

He led them for almost an hour, picking his way through the darkness with uncanny ease and walking with the surefootedness of a goat. He halted at a belt of dwarf pines growing so closely together they seemed impenetrable.

"Keep close together," he ordered.

He forced his way in among the trees, bending back branches to scrape through. Soon he reached a cleared path where the pines had been uprooted to leave a passage a yard wide. This led on for a hundred yards to the rock face of a mountain. Miguel used a flashlight, knowing the thick canopy of pine needles above them effectively screened the light. At the rock face, Miguel pulled aside uprooted trees he had placed across the entrance to a natural cave. He stepped inside and lit the oil lamp standing on a ledge just inside the entrance. The yellow light revealed an enormous cavern with a roof so high that the light of the lamp did not reach it.

The donkeys were led into the cavern and their panniers unloaded. Boxes of ammunition were stacked high and covered with rubber ground-sheets. Tommyguns were greased and swathed in oily rags, explosives and hand grenades were wrapped in waterproof paper.

Miguel surveyed the stock of ammunition with grim satisfaction. Week by week he had watched it grow until there was enough to wage a minor battle.

The men sat down to eat and rest before their long journey back. Some were Spanish refugees with bitter memories and others were French patriots awaiting the day they could strike at the Germans who occupied their country. There was one among them whom Miguel did not know. Munez introduced him. "Comrade Miguel, this is Comrade Jean-Luis, second in command of our Resistance Corps. He has heard of you."

Jean-Luis was a man of Miguel's age, dark, serious-eyed and with a high, prominent forehead. His handclasp was powerful and there were calluses on his fingers.

"Congratulations, comrade," he said. "You've found us a perfect arms dump. When the time comes, we will have all the arms we need."

"How long must we wait, comrade?"

Jean-Luis shrugged his shoulders and his dark eyes studied Miguel's impassive face. "We must await the right moment. America will come into the war, Britain will launch an invasion and on that day all French patriots will arise."

"To fight blindly is not enough," said Miguel. "There must be organization. We must hit the enemy where it hurts. We must harry him and destroy him with sabotage."

Jean-Luis lowered his eyes. "I'm told you are an indomitable fighter against fascism."

"To destroy fascism is our only hope," said Miguel. "Britain and

France betrayed us. They watched Italy and Germany turn Spain into a testing ground for war. But now *they* know the menace of Fascist aggression. This is Spain's last chance to escape Franco's dictatorship."

Jean-Luis said quietly: "I need men like you. You're wasted in these mountains. You must work in the towns, in Perpignan or Narbonne, Dijon or Marseilles."

"There are difficulties, comrade," said Miguel. "Who would lead your men to this cave?"

"I will leave a man to study the landmarks." Jean-Luis scowled. "There may not be many more trips. When France surrendered, many of us hid our arms and ammunition. Most of it is stored here. But we have no way to get more unless they are smuggled to us by the Allies."

"There is a matter of documents, too," said Miguel. "I am a Spanish refugee and here in the mountains I am not suspect. But in the towns I will be quickly noticed."

"The French officials will help us," said Jean-Luis. "You will have a French name and papers and a job like other Frenchmen. You will live with a family and keep contact with us for active work."

Miguel's face was expressionless. "I am not alone and I do not wish to leave my wife."

Jean-Luis had been told of Miguel's brooding, silent wife who had been made ugly by a facial disfigurement. "It is better if your wife is at your side. It will help divert suspicion from you."

"Arrange it then, if you will," agreed Miguel.

"I will send someone for you when it is done."

"What work will I do?"

"The factories work day and night. The demands of our German master are insatiable. You can learn quickly to be a machinist or an assembler in an armaments factory."

Miguel glowered. "I will not labor to make armaments for the Germans."

Jean-Luis eyed him steadily. "There are many ways to work for the Germans," he said softly. "There are hand grenades that explode prematurely, shells that are duds, oversized cartridges that jam machine guns and range-finders that fail when needed."

Miguel looked down at his hands. "I will do my best."

After the men had rested Jean-Luis shook Miguel's hand. "I will arrange everything, comrade," he promised.

Three weeks later, a man brought Miguel and Catalina the documents they needed to start their new life in Perpignan.

Teresa heard the baby whimpering in the room behind the shop, quickly finished serving her customer and called to Narcissus: "I must go now."

"All right. Tell Father there's no need to come out unless I call him."

In the back room Emilia Coruna was stooped over the kitchen range, fanning charcoal to a white-hot glow with a rafia fan. Beans were simmering in a blackened pot. Manuel Coruna was weighing out dried lentils into paper bags. He glanced up when Teresa entered. "Good. You heard him. Until now he's been sleeping soundly."

She crossed to the cot and stared down tenderly at her son. She stroked his cheek with her forefinger and felt such a sudden rush of love for him that she picked him up and hugged him. After a few moments he cried in protest.

"You're hungry, Leon," she soothed. "Don't cry, little one. Mama will care for you. Mama will always care for you."

She sat in the rocking chair and unbuttoned her blouse. Her father-in-law turned his back and she eased out her breast with gentle fingers. It was swollen with milk and she smiled, remembering how once she had feared that her breasts would never mature. She pressed the hardened nipple until the milk ran from it and she lowered it to her son's greedy mouth. The touch of his lips made her gasp and she steeled herself to endure his rhythmic sucking. Her nipple was ulcerated and would not heal while she breast-fed.

"He can be weaned," Doctor Aldo had told her. "There are baby-food preparations."

"Will it be bad for him if I don't feed him, Doctor?"

He had sighed. "Spain is so poor that baby preparations are not what they should be."

"Then I'll bear the pain, Doctor."

Teresa endured the pain until it was time to change and then teased her son's greedily pouting lips with her other nipple, chuckling as his face reddened with anger before she lowered herself to him. When her son's hunger was satiated, he fell asleep at once and she tucked him in lovingly. Then she heated water in a pan and bathed her breasts. Her ulcerated nipple was split open and she covered it with a wad of gauze before she eased her breast back inside her blouse.

"Don't go back into the shop yet," said her mother-in-law. "Narcissus will manage. Sit quietly for a while. You tire yourself too much."

"I don't get tired. I'm naturally active, Emilia."

Nevertheless, Teresa sat and watched her father-in-law weigh lentils. The strain of childbearing, washing diapers and working in the shop *was* tiring, she realized. She closed her eyes and dozed. Later, she drowsily acknowledged Anita Braguera, a friend of her mother-in-law who had called, then almost fell asleep again. But abruptly she awakened, aroused by the name "Ledesma" and sat listening with her eyes closed.

". . . absolutely appalling extravagance, costing a fortune and how'll he keep pace with the taxes and everything and the farms not paying and a maid just for the baby and a companion too because she's so weak after it all and doesn't even know how to boil water."

Anita Braguera's daughter was employed by the Ledesmas.

". . . won't feed the baby, frightened to spoil her figure, spending all that money, criminal extravagance I call it. And what for, I ask you? Because, young as she is, she's already big and droopy and my Anna saw her in one of those French nightgowns you can see through and says they hang like a goat's udders. With all those fancy airs and young as she is, she's growing so fat I daresay without moving a finger to help in the house . . ."

Anita Braguera's voice droned on: "And my poor Anna with her hands swollen with chilblains washing in cold water and scrubbing away her smelly stains and the poor Señora Ledesma hardly daring to say a word because whenever there's a row, she starts her shouting and screaming and it's Anselmo who suffers most, poor boy, trying to keep the peace between mother and wife and she's got him right under her thumb because . . ."

Narcissus opened the door, smiled at Teresa and looked at the cot.

"He's had his feed and he's sleeping soundly," said Teresa. She half-rose.

"No, no. No!" insisted Narcissus. "Rest a little. We're not busy and I'll call you if it's necessary." He frowned. "Everybody's gone down to the beach. They say there's been an explosion."

"Explosion?"

Narcissus shrugged his shoulders. "I didn't hear anything myself."

"Neither did I," said Manuel Coruna.

Emilia Coruna said: "I thought I heard a muffled bang a while ago."

"Dynamiting fish," said Manuel Coruna.

"It's not likely," said Teresa. "The penalties are too harsh now it's illegal."

Narcissus said: "Somebody will come in and tell us about it." He went back to the shop.

Teresa closed her eyes and rocked herself gently.

The door burst open and a white-faced, wild-eyed Isidro choked: "It's Pepita. It's Pepita!"

Teresa came up out of her chair, her heart hammering. "What is it? What's happened?"

"It's Pepita. She's hurt badly." Isidro was crying. "Blood all over her." He sobbed. "Our little Pepita."

Nervous tension made Teresa furious. She seized him by the arms and shook him. "Don't stand there crying, you great fool. Tell me . . . what's happened?"

"They were playing on the beach and they found a hand grenade buried in the sand. It . . . it went off!"

Teresa snatched down her shawl. "Where is she?"

"She's . . . they've taken her to Gerona."

"And Mama and Papa?"

"They've all gone in the taxi with Doctor Aldo."

"Why didn't they come for me?" she choked. "Mama and Papa will need me."

"There wasn't room. The Farina boy was hurt and his parents went too."

Teresa stared at Isidro. "Sit down," she said quietly. Isidro sank into a chair weeping.

Narcissus was hovering anxiously in the background. "Pour him a drink," she said, surprised at her calmness. She waited until Isidro had gulped down the brandy before she asked: "How badly is Pepita hurt?"

"I . . . I couldn't see. There were so many people and . . . a lot of blood. Doctor Aldo says she's hurt badly."

Teresa's jaw jutted. "We're going to Gerona," she told Narcissus.

"There's only the one taxi," he said. "It might not return until tomorrow."

"We can't wait. Go to Girales and hire his truck."

Narcissus hesitated.

"Hurry," panted Teresa. She ran to the cot. "We'll have to take Leon."

Narcissus hurried away.

Teresa wrapped the baby in a shawl and turned to Isidro. His lower lip was trembling and his eyes were glazed with misery. "You remain here, Isidro. Someone must look after the house."

He nodded numbly and buried his face in his hands. She poured him more brandy.

The truck was seldom used and half an hour was lost finding fuel for it. It was a slow-moving monster with solid rubber tires, and it jolted violently as it lurched over the potholed road. The bumping soon awoke Leon. Teresa crooned to him and cushioned him against the severest jolts but the journey seemed interminable. Finally they reached the hospital. Teresa thrust Leon into Narcissus's arms, jumped down from the driver's cabin and ran up the steps.

Her parents were seated at the far end of the vestibule. A lump rose in her throat when she saw her mother's red-rimmed eyes. Her father stood up and she suddenly saw that he was old. He took her hand and held it tightly.

"How is she?" panted Teresa. "Where is she?"

Her mother buried her face in her hands and rocked from side to side.

"Mama. Please, Mama," comforted Teresa.

"She's . . . in the operating theater," said Paco Barras.

Teresa knew overwhelming relief. "She's going to be all right!"

Her father looked away. "The Farina boy . . ." His voice was husky. "They did all they could but . . . they couldn't save him."

A black cloud of dread engulfed Teresa as she pictured Pepita, precocious and full of life. Suddenly she felt faint.

Narcissus came up behind her with Leon in his arms. She glanced at the baby to assure herself he was comfortable and turned back to her father. "Papa. How bad is she?"

He stared at the floor and shook his head. "The doctor didn't say."

"How long . . . how long has she been in there?"

"It seems hours."

"Stay with Mama and Papa," she told Narcissus.

A nurse took her up to the operating theater. Doctor Aldo was outside talking with a surgeon. As soon as he saw Teresa he hurried to meet her, took her by the arm and led her along the corridor. His face was serious and his grip on her arm was tight. "It's a terrible thing," he sighed. "A terrible accident."

"How . . . how bad is she, Doctor Aldo?"

"She's being taken up to the ward now."

Teresa's heart leaped. "She's not going to die?"

"No. She's going to be all right." His grip tightened upon her arm. "But she's been badly hurt."

"She'll get better, won't she, Doctor?"

He hesitated. "Yes." But there was such restraint in his voice that she eyed him sharply. "What is it, Doctor Aldo? Tell me the truth."

"Her face," he said sadly.

The world stood still.

Teresa held herself stiffly, and her voice was emotionally detached. "Is she blind, Doctor?"

"No. But one eye was so badly injured it had to be removed."

"She'll be scarred?"

"Scars are not important," he said. "They heal." He frowned down at the floor. "It's her hands too, Teresa. She . . . she must have been holding the grenade when it exploded."

"Poor Pepita," choked Teresa. "Poor little Pepita!"

"There was nothing we could do. There wasn't much left of her hands to save anyway."

"Oh, my God!" Teresa closed her eyes and tears ran down her cheeks.

"She'll get better, Teresa," said Doctor Aldo. "Medicine and nature will heal her injuries. But only her family can help her accept that she is no longer like other people."

The prison in Gerona was so crowded that the cell doors were left open all night so that the prisoners could sleep in the compound.

Benito Vigon waited six weeks to be brought to trial. He was the fourth to appear. Two armed soldiers marched him into the depressing gloom of the courtroom. At the far end under a large photograph of General Franco, three army officers sat behind a trestle table draped with a green cloth. Before each officer was a blotting pad, paper, a glass and a water jug. To the right of the judge's bench was a smaller table at which sat another officer and two civilians. This table was stacked high with folders, files and papers.

Vigon stood to the left of the judge's bench and his escorts seated themselves on a wooden bench. The judges were discussing a dinner they had attended the previous night and ignored the prisoner. One of them went out to relieve himself and almost a quarter of an hour elapsed before the president asked, without looking at Vigon: "What about this one?"

The officer at the small table referred to a typewritten sheet. "Benito Vigon," he intoned. "Age twenty-four, son of a peasant father, served with the government forces and was captured wearing civilian clothes some months after the end of the war."

The president glanced at Vigon momentarily. "You are Benito Vigon?"

"Yes," he said hoarsely.

One of the guards pounded Vigon in the small of the back with his rifle butt. "Yes . . . *SIR!*" shouted the guard.

"Yes . . . SIR!" said Vigon, arching his spine.

"What else?" asked the president.

The seated officer reached for another typewritten sheet. "He did not surrender and concealed himself from the authorities. He had no documents and had destroyed his uniform. We have twelve depositions from citizens of Escoleras. These state that he has Socialist opinions, approves of the confiscation of private property and has declared himself in favor of trade unions. He has shown sympathy to the Federation of Anarchists." One of the civilians handed the seated officer a sheaf of papers.

"These are the depositions," said the officer.

The civilian gave him another typewritten sheet. "The local Civil Guard report that his family are peasant farmers owning very little property and are without standing in the community. His mother attends church regularly but the father is indifferent and only goes to church when urged by the priest. The accused, Benito Vigon, did not attend church for many years prior to the outbreak of war and has often spoken disparagingly about religion. A number of witnesses affirm he has stated he is agnostic."

"Anything else?"

"That's all," said the officer. He placed all the documents into a manila folder and handed it to the civilian.

The president took a pack of cigarettes from his pocket and offered them to his fellow judges. They all lit up.

"It seems clear enough," said the president.

His companion judges nodded.

"A disciplinary correction camp is the obvious answer."

Again his fellow judges nodded agreement.

"That's all," said the president. "Let's have the next one."

Quite bewildered, Benito Vigon found himself being ushered from the chamber. "Didn't . . . I thought . . . aren't I to have a trial?" he asked one of the guards.

The man chuckled. "That was it."

"But . . . I didn't have a chance to defend myself."

"You're guilty," grinned the guard. "You wouldn't be here if you weren't."

"But . . . what happens now?"

"You heard the judge. A disciplinary camp."

"What's that?"

"You'll find out."

"It was all over so quickly I didn't hear everything. How long must I stay in this camp?"

"He didn't *say*," said the guard. "You stay until they let you out."

For a week Vigon was locked in an underground cell with other men and when there were so many that no more could be packed in, they were marched under armed escort to the railway station, herded into a cattle truck and padlocked in.

They remained seven days in the cattle truck while the train rolled slowly across Spain, lingered in sidings and shunted back and forth in marshaling yards. During the long stops their guards unlocked the doors to let in fresh air, passed around canteens of water and gave them a few stale loaves of black bread. They were not allowed outside to relieve themselves. The heat generated by their close-packed bodies, the jolting in the trucks and the stench of excretion and urine caused nausea and added the smell of vomit to their discomforts. When the train stopped for the last time and they were ordered out of the truck at bayonet-point, many men were too weak to stand.

New guards took over. They were tall, strong men who showed no pity for their hungry, filth-soiled prisoners. They were men from Navarra and Andalusia who nourished a hatred for Catalans. They goaded their prisoners with insults about Cataluña, its people and its traditions, and whenever a prisoner was stung to retort, they beat him.

The prisoners were herded along a highway, along a track and then up a steep path that led to a hill crest overlooking the Mediterranean. The view was magnificent but the prisoners were given no time to enjoy it.

They were hurried on another three kilometers to an enormous open compound surrounded by a perimeter of stakes and coiled barbed wire. The double gates of the compound entrance flew the Nationalist flag and had the words *"Todo para la Patria"* emblazoned above them. Outside the gates was a row of barrack huts where off-duty guards were sunbathing, reading or dozing. They were well-fed, sun-bronzed men who ignored the prisoners herded up to the double gates. The compound doors swung open and the prisoners were driven inside with rifle butts.

Benito Vigon looked around with bitter eyes. The inmates of the compound were scarecrow figures in fluttering rags, their skin burned black by the sun and their limbs so thin and dry they looked as if they could easily snap. He saw gaunt faces, wild eyes set deep in black hollows, ulcerated sores, blood and pus-stained bandages made from ripped-up underclothing.

A bearded man with long, corn-colored hair rose to his feet unsteadily and staggered across to the new batch of prisoners. His eyes were blue and his mouth lopsided as though his jaw had been broken and reset badly.

"Welcome to the camp of no hope," he said in Catalan.

They gathered around him, bombarding him with questions until he raised his hands.

"Please. Please! I cannot answer a thousand questions."

The questions died into expectant silence.

"Understand this, friends," he said bitterly. "We are Catalan swine who must suffer because we perpetuated the war. You are prisoners and must do the best you can for yourselves. There is all the water you need in the communal tap. Food, a little every day. Sometimes a little soup which is no more than hot water. On these rations you must work eight, sometimes ten hours a day. Your clothing is what you stand up in. When it rains you must still sleep on the ground. If you are strong you will live. If you are not . . . you die quickly."

Vigon asked quietly. "How long have you been here, friend?"

The blond Catalan stared at him steadily. "Five months." He raised his hand to his jaw and stroked it tenderly. "My first day here I talked back to a guard. His rifle butt smashed my jaw. I was strong when I arrived. Now look at me."

He held out arms like sticks from which tattered clothing fluttered. His chest was sunken and his ribs stood out starkly.

"This is . . . inhuman!" choked Vigon.

"Our bodies must suffer for our thoughts," said the blond man bitterly.

It was Sunday, a day of rest. But at six o'clock the next morning a siren awakened them. Vigon climbed stiffly to his feet with every joint aching from the chill of the morning and the hardness of the ground. The prisoners shuffled into a long line at the entrance gates. When they were opened the men filed out past a water tap from which each man drank. A prisoner, supervised by a guard, presided over a wooden crate filled with hunks of black maize bread. He gave each man a ration.

The guards shouted orders, the prisoners shuffled into ragged formation and they were marched away from the compound, up over a hill and set to work cutting a road through a mountain.

Vigon thought it looked like a scene out of hell. Starved skeletons wielding picks and shovels, hacking a wide road through solid rock. The work could have gone ahead much more quickly if dynamite had been used. But the road had to be made with men's suffering. So the picks swung, shovels filled wooden wheelbarrows and scarecrow figures swayed as they labored.

Benito Vigon wielded a pickax. He smashed at a boulder, reducing it to a heap of large rocks. Whenever he rested to get his breath or wipe his forearm across his sweat-dewed forehead a guard snarled: "Keep at it. No slacking!"

Benito Vigon glowered and swung the pick but without muscle behind it.

The watchful guard snarled: "That's not the way. Put your back into it. *Cojones* is what you want, man. You Catalans all lack *cojones*. You're a bunch of *maricones!*"

Benito Vigon swung the pick until sweat blinded him. The boulder became the face of the guard and he battered it with terrible fury.

At lunchtime there was a break of half an hour. The wise prisoners had saved their ration of bread and now they gnawed it slowly, savoring every crumb. Benito had eaten his while marching to work and now he could only watch while hunger gnawed at him.

All through the long afternoon they labored on while the sun beat down. At six in the evening, when the whistle blew, a man fainted.

He couldn't get to his feet and was beaten until blood ran from his lips. Benito Vigon and another were ordered to carry him back to camp.

Back at the compound Benito and the other men let their burden fall and sank down exhaustedly onto the hard earth. The bearded, blond man settled down beside them. "What do you think of the Catalan's private hell?"

Vigon said faintly: "When do we eat?"

"Tomorrow morning we get another crust of bread."

Vigon stared disbelievingly. "That's all the food we get?"

"You can live on it. Look at me. I've lived on it for five months."

Benito Vigon gulped. "Is there no way out? No way of escape?"

The blond man nodded. "There is a way," he said. "The way of the *piojo verde.*"

Vigon frowned. "What is the way of the green lice?"

"It is an illness," said the blond man. "Often prisoners suffer from it."

"How does one use it to escape?"

The blond man's deformed mouth tried to smile. "He who catches it is taken away . . . to die!"

Before he had been a prisoner a week, Benito Vigon attempted to escape with a prisoner named Ignacio. For several days they collected every scrap of discarded cloth they could find. One night they bound their hands and wrists and limbs with these rags, crept through the darkness to the barbed-wire perimeter and stealthily wormed their way into it. The long coils of wire were springy and the barbs were long and vicious. They knew the metal thorns would tear their flesh but they had braced themselves to suffer the pain.

A trip wire embedded in the heart of the barbed wire sounded the alarm. A siren wailed mournfully, lights sprang up, whistles blew, guards shouted and powerful spotlights swept over the startled, sleepy-eyed prisoners.

The guards turned out, a sergeant shouted orders, and bayonets were fixed. The guards herded the prisoners into one corner of the compound and stood them at attention. A patrol headed by a sergeant set off at a trot around the barbed-wire perimeter until they found the two escaping prisoners.

Ignacio had made more progress into the barbed-wire forest than

Vigon; only his feet protruded from it. The guards seized his ankles and heaved mightily. Ignacio's tortured scream was a warning to Vigon who had time to clamp his hands over his face before he too was dragged out. Both of them were streaming with blood. They were thrown inside separate punishment huts and the guards went to work on them with boots and rifle butts, leaving them insensible.

For three days and nights they remained in darkness with neither food nor water. Ignacio went out of his mind and raved deliriously.

On Sunday they were dragged out into the sunlight. Ignacio babbled incoherently. His face was a mask of congealed blood and a black scab oozed pus where his right eye should have been. His good eye rolled wildly.

The prisoners had been on parade at attention for three hours, waiting to see the punishment meted out to the would-be escapers. They stared at Ignacio and Vigon with lackluster eyes devoid of sympathy. The night of the attempted escape they had been forced to remain standing until dawn, and they blamed the escapers for their increased misery.

Vigon's mouth was dry and his tongue so swollen it impeded his breathing but he tried to stand upright and glare defiantly at the guards.

"We've our own methods of punishing escapers," said Sergeant Ares. He gestured to the guards. One of them unrolled a canvas flour sack. Baling wire was threaded through its bottom corners and loops of the wire were attached to its mouth. The guards held the sack flat against Vigon's back and passed the wire around his waist and over his shoulders. Pliers twisted the ends of the baling wire together until it cut into his waist, shoulders and armpits.

"Fourteen days," the sergeant told Vigon. "Day and night, asleep and awake, that sack lives with you. Try taking it off for just one minute and it won't be fourteen days. You'll wear it then for the rest of your life!"

Another sack was fastened to Ignacio's shoulders. Then six prisoners were ordered out to gather small rocks to fill the flour sacks.

The sacks were large and as they filled up, Benito's eyes smoldered. When the sack was full and its neck closed with a twist of wire, fifty pounds of rock was bowing him down.

Ignacio was too weak to support the weight. His knees bowed and he sank to the ground. He was booted and butted but not even the steady pressure of a bayonet point could goad him to his feet.

Vigon shouted: "Can't you see you've driven him out of his mind? What do you want to do? Kill him?"

Sergeant Ares was a powerful man. He swung his fist like a professional boxer and Vigon's upraised arm was smashed aside by a blow that stretched him flat on the ground. Vigon stared up at Sergeant Ares with his mouth full of blood. The weighty sack pinned him down and he felt ludicrously like an overturned tortoise.

"Talk back at me and I'll kill you," raged Sergeant Ares.

Ignacio was thrown back into the punishment hut. Vigon rolled over onto his hands and knees, gathered his strength and rose to his feet. He waited with downcast eyes until the prisoners were dismissed and then stumbled across to the water tap.

At first it was the weight of the sack that punished him. He had to work as hard as the other prisoners, swinging a pick or wielding a shovel. If he slacked, he was beaten. At night he could not rest properly: if he lay on his back there was no support for his head; if he lay face down, the weighty sack compressed his lungs. By the third day the baling wire had cut through his clothes and his raw flesh wept blood. During the night scabs formed around the wire which tore away with his first movements the following morning.

Ignacio must have been taken away while the prisoners were out working on the road. They never saw him again.

The next man punished was Ramon Puig, a stocky, slow-thinking youth who had been a butcher's assistant in Barcelona. During the week a guard overheard him speaking Catalan.

On Sunday the prisoners were lined up. Two prisoners were ordered to dig a deep hole. Other prisoners were sent to cut down two slender birch trees, trim them and join them together in the form of a cross.

The cross was laid upon the ground, Ramon Puig was ordered to strip to his drawers, was placed upon the cross and lashed to it with baling wire. A cardboard placard was hung round his neck reading: *I must not speak Catalan!* Then the cross was stood upright in the hole and the earth filled in around it.

All through that long Sunday the crucified Puig hung by his lacerated wrists. The prisoners were forbidden to approach him or speak to him. The sun blazed down upon his tortured body, his thirst increased and he pleaded ceaselessly for water to moisten his lips.

The prisoners tried to put him out of their thoughts but wherever they went within the confines of the compound the tortured figure on the cross couldn't be escaped.

At first one prisoner, then a second, a third and then many went to the compound entrance and stood with their backs to the crucifix as they stared out at the guards. It became a spontaneous demonstration. All the gaunt and weary prisoners stood shoulder to shoulder in close ranks, their eyes a sullen and disturbing challenge.

The guards became uneasy. They swore at the prisoners and made threatening motions.

The prisoners stood firm.

Three of the guards picked up their rifles, fixed bayonets and walked across to the compound gate. They intended to walk in among the prisoners, clubbing with rifle butts and jabbing with bayonets.

But the prisoners stood watching the guards with sullen, hate-filled eyes.

The guards glared in at the prisoners.

The prisoners stared back.

The guards walked away, strangely afraid.

Hour after hour the prisoners stood in silence with their unified hatred flowing out through the barbed wire.

All the guards were turned out and posted around the compound entrance with fixed bayonets. Sergeant Ares was in town, and a messenger was sent to find him. At dusk the searchlights were switched on and in their merciless blaze the shadows were deep and the prisoners' staring eyes became black holes in white skulls. And behind their close-packed ranks the crucifix stood out starkly, towering over them all. Ramon Puig's rasping breathing could be heard clearly as he hung unconscious with black trickles crawling down his arms and his underdrawers stained by his tortured bowels.

Sergeant Ares returned to the compound in a tearing rage, furious that his guards had not used their initiative. But when he saw the silent, close-ranked prisoners and felt their hatred lick out at him, he too was afraid. The seething bitterness of the prisoners was powerful enough to burst apart the entire camp.

Sergeant Ares walked up to the compound and stood with feet astride facing the prisoners. He ordered loudly: "Listen to me, swine. No more breaking regulations and no talking Catalan. Now take that man down. Save the cross. We'll need it another day."

The hostile eyes beat at him savagely. Then the prisoners slowly turned and flooded to the crucifix, swamping around it as it bobbed in the air and then sank down out of sight.

Sergeant Ares ordered crisply: "Double the guard for the rest of the night and keep the searchlights turned on. If anything happens send for me at once. I'll be in my quarters." He frowned as he strode away.

The prisoners destroyed the crucifix but nobody was punished. And afterward the guards drove the prisoners less fiercely and punishments were milder.

It was Sunday in the disciplinary camp and the prisoners sat in the sun trying to draw comfort from its warmth. Vigon took off the filthy rag that was his jacket, picked lice from the seams, squashed them between his thumbnails and listened for the pop as their blood-gorged bodies burst. His chest was shrunken, his ribs stood out and his abdomen was hard and distended.

Vigon had a headache. His limbs throbbed, he felt light-headed and was disinclined to move. He didn't even want to cross to the water tap to slake his thirst. It was the weakness of starvation, he realized. The previous week, despite the bootings of the guard, some men had been too weak to go to work. They had been left lying in the compound in a fevered stupor and had died. Vigon wondered if their illness was contagious and the following morning knew it was. He tried to climb to his feet but could not because of the peculiar muscular rigidity of his limbs. The guards booted him disinterestedly as though knowing it was useless and left him.

Presently the pain of his head and the ache in his bones sent him into a stupor where his thoughts wandered hotly. There were fleecy cool clouds against a pale blue sky and the cool tang of the sea. Cooked meat sizzled succulently, there was the crisp rustle of white linen, lacy edging to dainty underwear and the lavender smell of clean laundry. A great knot was tied in a ship's cable so big that it filled his head. It kept tightening, groaning and expanding. Thirst burned his bowels and his mouth. He had lucid moments when he was aware of the cold hardness of the earth and the blue of the sky. Then came nightmares of leering faces.

At some time he became aware of the blond bearded prisoner with the broken jaw hovering over him.

"What's . . . what's the matter with me?" choked Vigon.

"It's the *piojo verde*," said the man. "Look at yourself."

With an effort Vigon sat up and looked at the mulberry-colored blotches mottling his chest, arms and stomach. They were great blisters and when he pressed them they ached in his joints and his head.

"Will I die?" he whispered. He was mildly curious.

"Almost certainly," said the bearded prisoner. "But not here. They will take you and the others away. They do not care if prisoners die but they must stamp out the epidemic before it spreads."

He was only vaguely aware of the truck that drove into the compound. Its brakes squealed when it stopped beside him. Strong hands grasped his ankles and shoulders and he was swung up. He landed on something soft that moved and whimpered. The truck jolted on, stopped, and a smothering weight falling upon him jolted the breath out of him and rushed him down into the cool, green sea while silver tinsel flowed along his limbs until he flashed like a mackerel. There were black voids of pain and the huge knot groaned greasily in his head, never disentangling.

Slowly he became aware of white walls, a white ceiling and white-coated orderlies. There was a drainage tube drawing off pus from his infected arm. The wounds caused by the baling wire hadn't healed and during his illness infection had run riot.

He had had typhus, they told him. The doctors were proud of him. All their other typhus cases had died.

They had operated on his arm.

"What do you work at?" asked the surgeon some time later when the arm was healing.

"I help my father. We have a vineyard and an olive grove."

"You are lucky it is your left arm. You'll never use it properly again. The muscles are shriveled."

Vigon's face showed his bitterness. The surgeon said sternly: "You're lucky to have an arm at all. Most doctors would have amputated and saved themselves a lot of headaches."

Vigon's arm healed and he regained strength as the hospital food, although monotonous and inadequate, put flesh on his bones.

There came the day when a doctor told Vigon: "There's nothing more we can do for you. Keep exercising your arm and when you get out of here, feed yourself well."

Vigon asked tonelessly: "Will they send an escort for me?"

The doctor knew he had come from a disciplinary camp. He said quietly: "You won't be going back."

Vigon stared at him hopefully.

"I have your identity card and papers," said the doctor.

"But . . . have I been released?"

The doctor said quietly: "Eleven men were brought here. Typhus is contagious and we put you all in isolation. It was thought you would all die. To avoid complications all you eleven men had your release papers signed and dated the day you entered the hospital." He smiled encouragingly. "You're free to go home, Vigon."

3

Many years had elapsed since Escoleras had been bombed but the rubble of destroyed cottages had not been cleared away. Yellow grass, weeds and nettles grew on the mounds of broken stones and the villagers used the bomb sites as rubbish dumps.

Vicente Serra regularly combed through the rubbish, searching for anything which might have value, and today he was especially lucky. Someone had thrown out a rusted pram. With a hammer he could reduce it to old iron and firewood. The tireless wheels, axles and springs he carried in a sack slung over his shoulder. The firewood was in another sack carried by his daughter, Asuncion. She was now eight years of age, a pale, skinny little girl, surprisingly pretty despite her pinched features. Serra was teaching her how to scavenge rubbish and was confident she would soon be able to do it alone.

Father and daughter walked to the next bomb site. It was surrounded by a dozen or more conscript soldiers who were stationed in the military camp on the hill just outside Escoleras. They shouted excitedly to each other as they cordoned off the rubbish-strewn area. Some flourished wooden stakes and others had gathered rocks to throw.

"It disappeared in there," pointed one soldier excitedly. "It's got a hideaway."

Serra swung the heavy sack down off his shoulder and rested it on the ground. He found a piece of wood to use as a club and picked up a large rock. Asuncion rested her sack on the ground and eased her aching shoulders. She rubbed her bare foot against her other calf and watched the soldiers with dull interest.

They crouched as they closed in slowly over the rubble. Their shabby uniforms were ill-fitting, most of them wore *alpargatas* without socks and their shirts were patched. Added to the thrill of the hunt was their genuine need to eat.

They closed in steadily, reducing the size of the cordon until one soldier was close enough to jab a long stick into a hole in the rubble. He kept jabbing. "There's something here . . . I think," he said.

"Don't jab," advised a companion. "Apply steady pressure."

The soldier probed. "I think I've got it." His eyes gleamed as he increased pressure on the stick, thrusting strongly.

A split second later there was an abrupt animal-squealing explosion which made the soldier jump back. A furry, raging tornado shot out from the hole, spitting and clawing and darting first one way and then another, desperately trying to break through the cordon of soldiers who shouted, whooped, threw stones and slashed wildly with their clubs.

It would have escaped through the cordon but Serra was suddenly there, driving it back with a shrewd blow from his club. The half-starved, half-wild cat drew back, snarling at the circle of men, one claw upraised threateningly. The soldiers were a little afraid and unsure how to tackle it.

Serra called loudly: "You, soldier. You with the curly hair. Keep feinting with your stick so it watches you all the time."

The soldier made tentative jabs at the cat. It arched its back and spat. Serra hefted a heavy rock, aimed carefully and tossed it so it dropped cleanly on the cat's back. It landed solidly and the cat howled in fury. The way its haunches twitched showed it had received a crippling injury. Emboldened, the soldiers pounced and grasped it despite the claws that raked their hands.

One of them drove his thumb into its scrawny throat and squeezed tightly until the convulsive struggles diminished and ceased. He held the cat up by its tail, proudly displaying his prey. Others sucked bites and licked scratches. One took out a penknife, cut the fur at the cat's throat, edged the knife point under the skin and slit it open down to the groin.

Serra claimed: "It's mine."

The soldiers instantly united against him. "We saw it, we hunted it and caught it. We killed it too!"

"It would have escaped if I hadn't prevented it. You didn't know how to kill it until I told you what to do."

They stripped the skin off the dead cat as though it had been a rabbit. "There's not much to eat anyway," said one of the soldiers.

"If we share it what we get won't be worth cooking," said another.

Serra's eyes glinted slyly. "Cook it here. Then we can all have some."

Doctor Aldo was passing and walked over to see what had happened. He heard Serra's offer and took an onion and three potatoes from his pocket, a present from a grateful patient that morning. He said: "I'll contribute these."

The soldiers stared suspiciously. "What do you want in return?" asked one.

Doctor Aldo pointed to Asuncion who was waiting patiently, shyly rubbing the sole of her foot against her other shin "See that she gets a share too. She's hungrier than any of you."

The soldiers agreed at once.

Serra was delighted. "Some of you boys get a fire going." He glowered at Asuncion. "Run to Maria Joncols and ask the loan of a cooking pot."

While the soldiers blew the kindling into flames a soldier tugged at Serra's sleeve. "D'you buy penknives?"

"I buy anything if it's cheap."

"What will you give me for this knife?"

Serra glanced at it and laughed. "Throw it away!'

"Give me *something*," urged the soldier.

Serra shook his head.

The soldier sighed. Then he took from his pocket an oddly designed hexagonal watch charm with the letters SRR embossed on it, curiously entwined. "What about this?"

Serra was fascinated by the object. He turned it over in his leathery fingers, testing its hardness with his thumbnail. He was struck by the coincidence that SRR almost spelled his name. It was very old, he realized. Perhaps three or four hundred years. But it was a common metal and had no value. To his surprise he heard himself saying: "I'll give you a *duro* for this and the knife."

"A deal," said the soldier delightedly.

"Where did you get it?" asked Serra, frowning down at the watch charm.

"When I first came here, a soldier who'd served his time gave it to me in exchange for a book. He said it was lucky."

"And was it lucky?"

The soldier wrinkled his nose as though there was a bad smell. "Not so you'd notice."

Asuncion came running up with a cooking pot.

When Doctor Aldo left the soldiers, he walked on through the village and on to the quay. A fishing boat had recently docked. Doctor Aldo shouted to a fisherman sluicing down the deck with pails of water: "What fish have you got for me, Jaime?"

"It's all sold." Jaime nodded along the quay toward Paco Barras who was standing on the quay looking out to sea with a black cheroot jutting from his mouth. "Barras bought the entire catch."

Doctor Aldo strolled over to him. "What fish have you for me, Paco?"

"It is mostly *merluza,* Doctor. Let's see what takes your fancy." There were half a dozen stacked fish boxes and he took them down one by one. The doctor selected two large codfish. "How much do I owe you?"

"*Nada,* Juan. All you have done for me and you want to pay me?"

Isidro drove up on a motor tricycle which had been converted into a small truck. The engine was twenty years old but overhauled so thoroughly that it would still give many years of service. Isidro unloaded a box of chipped ice and helped his father to cover the fish with it.

"Have you got your travel permit?" Paco asked.

Isidro patted his pocket. "Here, Father."

"You'd better get going. Talk to Apierra in Barcelona. He may have goods to deliver to Figueras that'll help pay for the return journey."

Isidro and Paco loaded the crates and Isidro winked at Doctor Aldo as he climbed on to the saddle of the motor truck. "Seal your ears," he warned and started up the engine. It throbbed deafeningly and the doctor was relieved when the engine *phut-phutted* away into the distance.

Paco Barras grinned contentedly. "Another consignment on its way to Barcelona."

"You're an astonishing man, Paco," said Doctor Aldo. "Apart from

Serra, you are the only man in Escoleras earning money. These are hungry, workless days."

Barras nodded soberly. "I am lucky," he agreed. "Most of my life I've been a fisherman but I have learned to buy fish and know the business by instinct. I look at a case of fish, estimate its weight and bid for it. I rarely make a mistake and succeed because others bid too high and lose money or do not bid high enough and lose the opportunity to buy."

"You will become a rich man, Paco. It pleases me."

Barras's face was moody. "I have no need for money. I am happier fishing. But I have responsibilities, Doctor. I will not live for ever and provision must be made for Pepita."

"It is a responsibility," agreed Doctor Aldo. He tugged out his watch. "I must go." He hurried away, the codfish dangling from his forefinger.

Paco Barras picked up a handful of fish he had placed on one side, took off his clogs and trudged back along the beach to his cottage. Pepita was seated outside in the shade of a cane canopy Isidro had built. The scars on her face were now only hair-thin white lines. But the closed lid of her blind eye was curiously distorted.

"Do look at this, Father," she thrilled. "It's a new one!"

"I'll be with you in a moment, daughter." He went inside the cottage and into the kitchen. He kissed Elisa's cheek dutifully and placed the fish on the table in two heaps. "These are for us," he said. "And these are for Teresa." He went back outside.

Pepita sat at a flat-topped table on which were scattered multi-colored mosaic stones. On the stumps of her arms were fastened tightly laced leather sleeves which ended in hardened points. Between them she could pick up the small stones and arrange them in gaily colored designs. She was engaged now on a view of Escoleras. It showed the beach, the sea, the high mountain behind the village and a sailing boat. It was neatly executed and Paco Barras marveled at the facility with which Pepita picked up the tiny stones and maneuvered them into position. Later on, when she had changed the design until she was satisfied with it, he would prepare the cement into which she set the stones.

"You like the scene?" she asked happily.

"It's . . . excellent."

"Better than the others?"

"Much better."

"Will they pay more, do you think, Father?"

All her work was bought by a customer in Barcelona who was a figment of Paco's imagination. "They're sure to," he said. "I'll certainly ask for more."

"If we can get a lot of orders, Father, and employ other people to work at it too, we might make a big business."

"I certainly hope we can, Pepita."

Since her accident, she avoided meeting people and although she was now twenty-two, she was strangely out of touch with the world around her. She got up from the table, walked across to the cottage and glanced inside. "Has Mother gone out?"

"Isn't she in the kitchen?"

"I can't see her."

"She's taken the fish along to Teresa then."

Pepita said: "Oh!"

"Did you want something, daughter?"

She hesitated. "It's . . . I need Mother. I want to go."

"She won't be long."

"I don't think I can wait."

"That's all right, daughter. I'll go with you."

"I'm sorry to worry you, Papa."

"*Nada,* daughter. We'll all do anything for you, you know that!"

"Thank you, Papa," she said as he helped her.

"Call when you want me. I'll be outside."

Presently she called.

"I feel awful about this, Father. So . . . helpless. This is when I notice it most . . . when even the simplest, natural things I can't do for myself."

"Don't worry, daughter. It gets done, anyway, doesn't it?"

"It's awful . . . for you too!"

"Nonsense. When you were a tiny girl sitting on a potty I looked after you. It's the same now. You're a little older, that's the only difference."

"You always comfort me, Papa."

In Coruna's grocery along the street, Elisa Barras watched her grandson, Leon, march up and down behind the shop counter shouldering a roughly fashioned wooden rifle. He was a well-built child with very fair, curly hair, blue eyes and apple-red cheeks. He bore no resemblance to his father but at times his face held an expression of blue-eyed wonder that was startlingly like his grandfather's.

Teresa gutted the fish while her mother watched. Her father-in-law was bowed over a worn accounts book. These were hard days and those who did buy asked for credit. The Coruna family, like most others, lived frugally. Few people could afford clothes, and meat and fish were luxuries. There was so little work in the shop that Narcissus had gone out with an old shotgun. But so many hunted the valleys and mountains that they were almost denuded of game.

"Are you going to be a soldier when you're a big boy, Leon?" asked his grandmother.

He shook his head. "I want to be a fisherman. I want to go out in Grandpa's fishing boat and catch the *biggest* fish ever caught."

Elisa Barras nodded wryly. "Grandpa will take you fishing," she promised. "When you're older he'll teach you to be the best fisherman in the village." There were tears in her eyes. "Grandpa taught your uncle Miguel to fish and he was an expert."

But Leon had already lost interest in fishing and was using his rifle as a bayonet, attacking an imaginary army and lunging lustily with gleeful shouts.

Elisa Barras sighed. "The war is almost over in Europe, they say. Perhaps Miguel will come home soon."

"If he wants to come home, Miguel will find a way," said Teresa.

It was a moonless night but the men worked swiftly in the railroad yard. They taped plastic explosives to switch points and to the axles of the locomotives waiting in sidings. They had little fear of being caught. They had dropped hints in the right quarters and the French nightworkers had invented excuses to be elsewhere.

The saboteurs completed their work and retreated, reeling out the cable until they reached cover behind a brick wall some hundred yards away.

"All set?" asked Miguel.

His men nodded.

"Blow it, comrade," ordered Miguel.

The men crouched low, the plunger was thrust down and the night was split apart by an explosion. Dust and small stones hailed down like rain and there was a jangling grind of metal as a locomotive crashed over on its side.

"Let's go," said Miguel.

He led the way through the darkness but after a few moment's fast walking he hissed a warning and stopped. His men held their breath and listened. Presently they heard what Miguel's sharp ears had already noticed, the scrape of heavy boots and guttural voices.

There was a soft rustle and a clink of metal against metal as Miguel unslung his tommygun. His men fanned out beside him, holding their weapons waist-high. They would slip away into the night if they could. But if they had to fight, they had the advantage of surprise.

The Germans approached rapidly, shouting to each other. One of them was lighting the way with the feeble, yellow rays of an exhausted battery torch.

The saboteurs tensed in the darkness. The Germans came straight at them.

When they were close enough Miguel shouted: "Now!"

A saboteur blazed a powerful light into the Germans' faces. In the same instant, Miguel and his men fired short, devastating bursts. It was a German patrol of eight and those who did not die instantly were finished off by the saboteurs.

The Germans' weapons were gathered up and twenty minutes later the saboteurs were safely hidden in the cellar of a farmyard barn with concealing bales of hay stacked on the trapdoor.

There were ten saboteurs, all Spanish except René Dalfois, a French Resistance liaison man who spoke Spanish fluently. He was intelligent and fearless, and a member of the Communist Party.

"We can be pleased with tonight's work, comrades," he said with satisfaction. "Germany is being hit hard everywhere." His eyes gleamed. "Hitler is doomed!"

Miguel scowled. "So much talk of destroying Hitler. But what of Fascist Spain? *Now* is the time for the free world to strike. Now Hitler is beaten, the Allies must attack Franco."

René Dalfois's eyes narrowed. "Franco is a minor issue, comrade. First the Allies must destroy *completely* our major menace. Then, at leisure, the Fascist lick-spittles will be mopped up."

"Patience!" sneered Miguel. "Always patience. Meanwhile our people live under a reign of terror."

"It will not be for long," said René Dalfois. His eyes glowed. "When France is free from the German heel, every true Frenchman will fight for the freedom of his comrades on the other side of the Pyrenees."

One day when Felipe and his three sons rode back to the farmhouse, he was suddenly struck by his daughter's appearance. Violante had stooped to lift a carafe of wine and he saw the thickness of her hips and the swell of her belly. Shocked by the enormity of his suspicion, he strode across the stone kitchen floor and placed a calloused, exploratory hand upon her.

She twisted away, her flat, brown eyes glaring and her thin lips drawn back in a snarl, as defensive as a mountain wildcat.

"Come here, girl," ordered Felipe.

"No," she panted. "No!"

She had never before dared to defy him and he felled her with a blow.

She pushed herself up into a sitting position. Then she sprang to her feet, snatched up a pickax handle and swung it at her father. His upraised forearm broke the force of the blow, but it beat him to his knees with blood streaming from his head.

Violante would have struck him again, but her brothers sprang at her and held her while she writhed furiously. Felipe climbed to his feet. "Hold the bitch still," he ordered thickly. "Hold her!"

Violante's eyes smoldered as she strove to break free. But her brothers were strong. Her skirt was lifted and her father's coarse fingers explored her knowledgeably, probing her soft flesh as though she were a farm animal.

"The bitch is with child!" he said.

Violante broke away from her astonished brothers, shook down her skirts and glared at her father.

He wiped his hand across his forehead and flicked it, spraying red droplets around him. "Who's the father, you bitch?" he demanded, his face dark.

Violante's lips clamped shut and her face became impassive.

"You whore!" roared her father. "He'll marry you! There'll be no sin in *my* family!

She held her head high, bracing herself against his anger.

"Tell me!" he roared. "Who is he?"

She faced him, unafraid and defiant.

"You won't deny me, you bitch." He seized her, threw her to the ground and held her down with his foot while he unbuckled his belt. "You won't defy me!"

He flipped up her skirt and slashed. The weal was edged with pinpoints of blood. Violante bit her forearm.

"You'll tell me," thundered her father. "You'll tell me!"

Although Violante's teeth drove into her arm until it bled, she made no sound.

At last he stopped. He wiped his belt and said gruffly: "That's to think about. The next time I ask who's the father, be ready to tell me."

Violante climbed to her feet, made her way to the hayloft and lay there enduring her pain.

During the following weeks she was often beaten but maintained her obstinate silence. But there came a time when her swollen belly proclaimed her motherhood so abundantly that the beatings had to cease.

She retreated into her own maternal world. She moved among her menfolk but was apart from them. Her face was serene, she smiled secretly and held herself with care.

Felipe and his sons spent hours pondering over who might be the father of Violante's child. The farm was isolated and visitors were so rare that they could easily be remembered. A long time ago Benito Vigon had stayed with them for some months, but since then no man had visited the farm.

"Is it a married man?" Felipe raged at his daughter.

She seemed not to hear him and smiled secretly, impervious to blows and insults.

They thought of a shepherd whose goats grazed the valley on the other side of the mountains, and father and sons rode away for three days to visit him. He was a stupid man but although they turned his fool's face into a bruised pulp, he said nothing to betray his guilt.

They remembered a band of Gypsies who had camped for one night a mile away from their farm and racked their memories for dates and made calculations, all of which proved that the Gypsies could have had no part in the affair.

"Tell me, you bitch of a whore," raved Felipe. "Who is the father of the bastard?"

But Violante seemed not to hear him.

"Don't mock me, you bitch," raved Felipe. "No daughter of mine will give birth to a child sinfully. It is against the wishes of God, your own mother and Jesus Christ!"

Violante went about her work serenely.

Father and brothers watched her preparations for the baby. She cut down a thin birch sapling and trimmed it with an ax. She cut the thin trunk into equal lengths and notched the ends. With cords made from esparto grass she made a cot. The slender birchwood branches were its ribs and old sacking stuffed with straw was its mattress.

The happiness shining in Violante's eyes turned her father frantic. "You bitch of a whore!" he raved. He knocked her down and had to be restrained by his sons from kicking her.

They remembered that three herdsmen had driven two hundred goats through the mountain valley and father and sons spent a week searching them out. But the herdsmen were so transparently innocent that Felipe and his sons had to ride away disgruntled.

It was Virgil, the most thoughtful son, who advanced a new theory. It was a startling one but since they could find no other explanation, they finally challenged Violante about her relationship with the stud stallion.

At first Violante seemed not to hear them. Then her lips twitched. Then she laughed and her laughter humiliated them.

"You can laugh, whore," snarled Felipe, shaking his fist. "But I am a man of God. I vow you will not bear a child out of wedlock and sin in God's eyes."

She locked the men out of the secret and mysterious woman-world in which she moved alone. Surreptitiously they watched her peaked but contented face and the steady swelling of her belly. They saw how it grew difficult for her to move around, how stooping made her grunt and, presently, how even simple movements cost her an effort. And they marveled that she was so radiant with happiness. It was a happiness that was infectious and despite themselves they tried to make her life easier. They ran to pick up things to save her stooping and did work which only a woman would normally do.

"Who is the father?" panted Felipe.

Violante looked at him steadily. "If I tell you, you will not believe me."

"Who is he?"

She shrugged her shoulders. "I do not know. He was a man I met in the valley. We talked and he touched me and then . . . this happened." She rested her hand upon her belly.

"You are lying!"

She shrugged her shoulders. "You see, Father. You do not believe me!"

"Who is the man?" he stormed. "We must know who he is. Even if he is married, it matters not. The child must have a father."

"When I tell the truth you do not believe me."

"You are shit upon the name of your mother," he stormed. "You are shit in the eyes of God. You are a whore. You have sinned but I promise God the religion of your mother will be respected."

She turned away from him sadly, hands clasped around her swollen belly. "The will of God and the seed of life are stronger than you, Father," she dared to say.

Three weeks later the severe pains struck her. All day she had borne the minor pains, but when the big pain hit her, she dropped her pitchfork, clasped the underside of her swollen belly and moaned aloud.

Zacarias was working with her. "What is it?"

"It is my time," she choked. Then as the pain tore her apart, she went down on her knees in the hay, biting the stalks.

Zacarias shouted for the others. "It is Violante. It is her time!"

Felipe came running with Tomas and Virgil on his heels. They stood over Violante and watched her roll over on her back.

"Yes," said Felipe sadly. "It is her time. Now we must obey the will of God!"

Felipe and his three sons rode into Escoleras just before dusk. Those who saw them were surprised because on the rare occasions that they came to the village they usually led a caravan of mules and donkeys laden with crops. Now they came empty-handed.

They dismounted in the plaza and tethered their mounts to a plane tree. The three brothers squatted on their haunches in the shade with their wide-brimmed straw hats pulled down over their eyes and Felipe stumped off along the cobbled street to the church. He pushed open the door and plunged inside. A few minutes later he came out and strode back to the plaza. He nodded to his sons and sat down with them. They smoked, talked a little and waited.

The villagers wondered about the four men as they went about their business. Night came and father and sons remained in the plaza smoking, chewing raw vegetables which they took from their panniers, and sleeping.

By midmorning the following day wild rumors were sweeping through the village. Everyone who saw the four men sensed the strangeness of their relentless patience.

José Corbera, the mayor, casually asked them the reason for their visit. They at once became evasive. "We shall be leaving soon," said Felipe uncomfortably.

"You have a great deal to do in the village?" asked Mayor Corbera politely.

Felipe avoided his sharp eyes. "Presently we shall go," he said uncomfortably. "When it is time."

"Then you are waiting for something?"

Felipe felt trapped. "Yes," he said. "When it is time . . ." He broke off and looked away quickly, betrayed by his own tongue.

The mayor told Doctor Aldo of the strange behavior of the mountain men. Other villagers mentioned that Felipe had visited the church.

The mayor and Doctor Aldo called on Father Delbos who received them coldly. "Yes," the priest snapped. "There was a man who stormed in as though he owned the church. He smelt abominably. People should have respect for the Church and wash before they come here."

"Did you talk to the man, Father Delbos?" asked Mayor Corbera.

Father Delbos said tartly: "It was not a conversation."

The doctor took out his watch and glanced at it. There was a sheen of perspiration on his forehead and without knowing why, he was gripped by a sense of urgency. "Please, Father Delbos. Tell us why he visited the church?"

The priest shrugged his shoulders. "Merely to show his contempt for the Church, I imagine."

The mayor sensed the doctor's self-control was escaping him and said tactfully: "Will you tell us exactly what happened, Father?"

Again the priest shrugged. "The man's little more than an animal. He strode in here, stinking like a pigsty, gave me no sign of respect and shouted questions at me."

The mayor asked quickly: "What questions, Father?"

"A ridiculously naïve question. He asked: 'Is it a sin in the eyes of God for a woman to have a child out of wedlock?' "

There was a long silence.

"And you replied . . . ?" asked Doctor Aldo.

"There is only one true reply," said Father Delbos stiffly. "The Lord does not condone immorality. Clearly it is a sin."

"Thank you," said the mayor. He hastened after Doctor Aldo.

When Felipe saw them approaching, he rose to his feet unhappily.

"Felipe," said Doctor Aldo. "Where is your daughter?"

"She is at home, Doctor."

"Why did she not come with you?"

There was a long pause. "Someone must take care of the farm," said Felipe.

"Why do you come here with your three sons, empty-handed?"

Felipe stared over his head and said tonelessly: "When it is the time, I will tell you."

They could get no more from him.

Somebody remembered that Benito Vigon had once spent some months with Felipe in the mountains and he was brought from his labor in the vineyard. He wore a sweaty handkerchief tucked under his straw hat to protect his neck from the sun, his sun-bleached shirt was sweat-rotted at the armpits and the black hairs on his arms glistened moistly. The shriveled muscles of his left arm drew up the limb as though it was in a sling and his fingers drooped like the weeping branches of a willow tree.

He listened to the mayor and Doctor Aldo and nodded understandingly.

Felipe and his sons greeted Vigon without enthusiasm. He sat with them, pulled out his worn pouch of tobacco makings, and while they smoked, spoke of the days he had spent with them. But they wouldn't talk. They stared down at the hard-baked earth, sun-dappled through the leaves of the plane trees, and remained silent.

Presently Vigon ventured: "And Violante. How is she?"

Felipe spat to one side.

His three sons stared stolidly at the ground.

"Violante is well?" persisted Benito Vigon.

Felipe said explosively: "I shit upon my whore of a daughter."

"You are angry with Violante, Felipe?"

Felipe's tongue had betrayed him again and he relapsed into determined silence.

"What is this about Violante?" persisted Vigon.

Virgil eyed him steadily. "Do I inquire for your sisters? Do I ask about your mother? Go away. Leave us in peace. We have no wish to question you . . . nor that you question us!"

Sadly Benito rose to his feet, bid them good day and returned to Mayor Corbera and Doctor Aldo. "They will not talk," he sighed.

"And what of Violante?"

"Felipe is angry with her. He shits upon his whore of a daughter."

"But who . . . ?" doubted the mayor. "What man would want . . . ?"

"Whoever the woman, when she has the need she can always find a man to serve her," said the doctor.

"But why . . . ?" began the mayor.

"I'll talk to Felipe," said Doctor Aldo grimly and hurried over to him. He confronted Felipe challengingly. "What is this of your daughter, man. Is she pregnant?"

Felipe stared impassively. "She is *my* daughter!"

"She is your daughter. But she is also a human being. Answer me, man. Is she pregnant?"

Felipe hesitated a moment. "Yes," he admitted.

"Tell me why you have come to the village."

Felipe stared into the far distance. "She betrayed the law of God. She sinned."

"This may be so, Felipe. But why have you come to the village?"

Felipe rose to his feet, stepped out from under the shade of the trees and looked up into the blue sky. He squinted his eyes against the sun, gauging the time. "It is a sin for a woman to give birth unless she is wed," he said.

"It may be a sin in the eyes of the Church," said Doctor Aldo. "But it is an oft-repeated sin which should make God happy since we are all God's children."

"The mother of my children had a deep reverence for God," said Felipe. His weathered face shone with an uplifting inner conviction. "Her whore of a daughter shall not disgrace her."

Doctor Aldo said in a low voice: "You are the father of Violante and responsible for her. Whatever happens . . . *you* are responsible!"

Felipe nodded his head with grave dignity. "I accept that," he agreed. "I am responsible."

"Then tell me why you are here, man!" thundered Doctor Aldo.

Felipe gently shouldered him to one side and again stared up at the sun. At least thirty hours had passed since they had left Violante and he judged it was sufficient.

"You can go to her, Doctor," he said quietly. "It is her time."

Doctor Aldo paled. "You mean . . . she is in labor?"

"Yes," said Felipe. He stared up at the sun while his sons looked mutely at the hard-packed earth.

Doctor Aldo wiped the back of his hand across his forehead. "You must be mad!" he choked and turned toward home and his medical bag.

Felipe's voice was remote. "You go to tend her, Doctor?"

"As soon as I can get there."

"Take the Civil Guard with you," said Felipe. "It will be right and proper."

A Civil Guard sergeant and two men accompanied Doctor Aldo. Teresa Coruna volunteered to act as midwife.

It was twenty-four hours before they returned.

Felipe and his sons were arrested. They meekly accepted handcuffs and climbed into the truck which took them to the jail in Gerona.

Violante's body was wrapped in a Civil Guard's gray cloak, brought down on the back of a mule and taken to the mortuary.

Doctor Aldo hurried home, poured himself a stiff brandy and sat in his armchair. He drank slowly, glared at a crucifix on the wall and swore softly under his breath.

Teresa kept herself under control until she reached the sanctuary of her kitchen. Then she broke down. Narcissus comforted her. "What is it, my love?"

"They're beasts," she choked. "They're . . . animals!" She looked down at Leon playing happily and her voice trembled. "How could they do such a thing?"

"What did they do, my love?"

"They're not men. They're . . . monsters. Felipe vowed that Violante would not bear a child in sin. So when her labor began, they shackled her ankles together and rode away."

Doctor Aldo dropped a hint to Teresa that Señora Ledesma would like to see her and Leon. It was only then that Teresa realized she hadn't seen Anselmo's mother for almost two years.

She tied her hair in a ponytail with a strip of black velvet and put on a short-sleeved blouse and a pleated skirt. She had had the skirt since before Leon's birth, but it still fitted neatly.

She dressed Leon in white shorts and shirt, combed his hair and put on his best shoes. He strutted proudly beside her as they walked to the Ledesma residence.

Teresa seldom visited this side of the village, but from gossip she knew the Ledesma family were having hard times: the farms had lost money; Anselmo's debts were increasing; he had got rid of the servants and been forced to sell some of the farms for a poor price in order to meet his need for cash.

Even so, Teresa was astonished when she saw the state of the grounds. Weeds choked the once carefully tended herb borders, nettles stood waist-high, the gates hung awry, and more weeds sprouted in the wide cracks and potholes of the drive. On the terrace, tiles were missing. There were broken flowerpots and withered plants, and dirt lay thickly as if it was never swept away.

The door stood wide open. Teresa pushed aside the mosquito netting and called. "May I come in?"

From within a voice called: "Who is it?"

"It's Teresa Coruna."

"Come straight through," shouted Silvana.

Teresa took a firmer grip on Leon's hand as they crossed the threshold. He wrinkled his nose in disgust. "Mama. What a smell of caca!"

"Now don't start," she warned him angrily. "Don't speak until you're spoken to!"

Silvana was in the dining room. It had been an impressive room with a great chandelier, long polished table, high-backed chairs with wine-colored upholstery and long sideboard loaded with delicate china.

Now the dining table was pushed away into a corner of the room, the chairs were stacked against the wall and the middle of the room was a playground for Silvana's three children. They were playing happily amidst their own baby-messes.

"Nice to see you, Teresa," greeted Silvana cosily. "Get a chair and make yourself comfortable." She was sprawled out in a sun-bleached deck chair and made no attempt to get to her feet. She had been steadily gaining weight and now her arms and thighs were fleshily overplump. Her cheeks were moist and beads of perspiration made a glistening moustache across her upper lip. She wore a sleeveless cotton dress and at the armpits her soiled undergarment showed.

Teresa said: "I called to see how . . ."

Silvana gestured with a plump arm and wheezed with the effort. "It's as you see, Teresa. A woman's work is never done." She had grown cheerfully placid as she put on weight, but there was a note of resigned discontent in her voice. "If you feel as I do, Teresa, you wonder why we ever married. Why did we? We were enjoying life and then . . . !" She pointed at her three children. "Now I'm burdened. I don't grumble, because I love them. But they're a big responsibility. They rob you of life."

"But they grow to be part of your life too!"

"Don't misunderstand me, Teresa. I wouldn't be without them. But being tied makes a girl brood. Especially with a man like Anselmo. I often think he only married me to have a son; and here we are with three girls! But I'm not a machine. I won't wear myself out just because *he* wants a son. Perhaps in a few years when these three are off my hands I'll think about it again."

"I can understand Anselmo," said Teresa quietly. "He wants to hand down his name and preserve the traditions of his family."

Silvana nodded reluctant agreement and the flesh under her chin wobbled. "I *know* all that, Teresa. But Anselmo wasn't strictly honest with me. I knew he had property. But nobody pays their rent and the farm barely brings in enough to eat. We've never a peseta to spend. I haven't had a new dress for over a year, and I have to do everything myself . . . Not one servant! It's my own fault; I was stupid. I thought I'd have everything, dresses, parties, nurses to take care of the children and a loving husband. But you can't spend land, and that's all he's got. Anselmo's changed, too, Teresa. He's grown embittered."

"And how is Señora Ledesma?" asked Teresa tactfully.

Silvana raised her eyes to heaven, lifted her plump arms in despair and let them flop back on her fat thighs. She sighed. "I do what I can, but you know what mothers-in-law are like. Nothing is good enough for her son, and without saying a word she faults me in everything. So what can I do? If she chooses to live like a hermit, I can't object."

"It's been a long time . . ." began Teresa. "Do you think I might . . . ?"

"Of course." With a wheeze Silvana lifted herself up out of the deck chair. She crossed to the sideboard where dirty crockery was stacked high and reached for a pot of honey. "You like honey?" she asked.

"We have it from time to time."

"You want some?" She thrust the pot at Teresa.

"No, thank you. Not now. I . . . don't eat between meals."

"It's good honey," said Silvana. She ran her forefinger around the pot, scooping up a great yellow, waxy ball, popped it into her mouth and licked her finger clean. "How about you, Leon?" she asked.

Leon was standing stiffly, acutely conscious of his newly laundered white shorts. He shook his head solemnly. "No, thank you, Señora."

"What a polite little boy. Just look at my girls! Look at Silvana. You'd never think she's Leon's age!"

Silvana was chortling as she played with her sisters. The little girl's dress was torn and dirty.

Teresa looked away quickly. "It's a long time since I saw Señora Ledesma," she said.

"She shuts herself up in her room. I'll take you to her." Silvana beckoned Teresa to follow and shuffled along a corridor to the back of the house. She pounded on the panels of Señora Ledesma's bedroom. "What is it?"

"A visitor," shouted Silvana. "Teresa Coruna."

There was a pause.

"Thank you," said Señora Ledesma.

Silvana smiled. "I'll see you before you leave." She shuffled back to the dining room, her hips wobbling fleshily under her tight dress.

Teresa gently knocked on the door.

The key turned in the lock, the door opened and Señora Ledesma said in a frail voice: "This is a pleasant surprise, Teresa."

The room was the elderly woman's sanctuary and would have been musty had not the French windows been open. There was a four-poster bed with fresh white pillowcases, comfortable chairs, a lace-making pillow and a table with clean crockery.

Señora Ledesma stared down at Leon and her eyes glowed. "What a beautiful child, Teresa. He's *so* handsome!"

"Be careful what you say, Señora Ledesma. He's got a big head."

"What have you got to say to me, Leon?"

He stared at her solemnly. "I'm very pleased to meet you, Señora." He held out his hand.

She shook hands solemnly. "I'm enchanted to meet a young gentleman with such charming manners."

Teresa had a lump in her throat. "Do you think he's like his grandfather?"

"Very much," said Señora Ledesma, staring at Leon intently. "Very much like the grandson I would have liked to have had."

"Leon," said the older woman. "You'll like this book. See . . . here are all the animals of the jungle. You can look at it while I talk to your mother."

"I'm always intending to call and see you," apologized Teresa. "But . . ."

The older woman nodded understandingly and placed her hands together. Teresa noticed how frail and bloodless they had become. "What went wrong between you and Anselmo, Teresa?"

"There was another man. He meant nothing to me. It was a purely physical thing. I wanted to be honest with Anselmo and so I told him about it." Teresa spread her hands ruefully.

Señora Ledesma sighed. "It was a pity. You were right for Anselmo. This other one, she's a child. I do not criticize her. I simply cannot live her way. I cook my own meals and try to close my eyes to the travesty she is making of my son's life."

"It is difficult for her too," said Teresa.

"Yes. Silvana was a butterfly in fairyland who wanted to marry a prince and live happily ever after. The pain of childbearing and financial setbacks demand more of her than she is capable of giving."

The older woman propped her lace-making pillow against the back of a chair and flipped bobbins through her fingers. "Anselmo's handicap is that he is a gentleman. He will suffer and grieve but he will be loyal to Silvana. She's his wife and so he will bear everything, her laziness, her dirtiness, her neglect of the children and her tantrums."

"Tantrums?" asked Teresa.

"You've no idea, my child. She looks good-natured. But when Anselmo comes home she's transformed. You can't imagine it. She screams, shouts insults and uses appalling language. If I had dared once to talk to Baudillo in that way he would have beaten me."

"I cannot comment upon these things," said Teresa.

"I am sorry, my dear. We are talking of something that is too close to the hearts of both of us."

"Anselmo made his decision," said Teresa quietly. "But I do not complain. Narcissus is a good husband."

"I'm sure he is."

"Also I have Leon. He is a good boy."

"I see that," said Señora Ledesma. She smiled at Leon. "He is strong and well built."

"Why is that lady outside so fat?" asked Leon.

Señora Ledesma smiled gently. "Because she is."

"And why does she smell so nasty?"

"She does not always smell nasty," said the older woman gently.

"And why don't those children do it in the bathroom?"

Anselmo arrived home as Teresa was leaving. He had bought an old motorcycle to make the rounds of his properties and was dismounting when Teresa, holding Leon by the hand, came down the steps from the terrace.

He found himself strangely breathless. "Hello, Teresa."

"Hello, Anselmo." She stared at him steadily for some moments and then urged her son: "Say good afternoon, Leon."

"Good afternoon, Señor Ledesma," said Leon solemnly.

"Good afternoon, Leon."

"I have visited your mother," said Teresa.

"Mother is not quite herself," he said uncomfortably. "She hasn't been well for some time."

"She seems very frail, Anselmo."

He looked away from her, acutely conscious of her closeness. "She lets trivial things worry her."

"I will visit her again soon."

"I hope you will. She's always pleased to see you."

There was an awkward silence.

"Your children look very healthy and happy, Anselmo."

"Yes," he said. He was compelled to look at her and saw her flush. "Have you seen Silvana?"

"Of course, Anselmo."

"Silvana has . . . not been well for some time."

"It's a great strain to have so many children so quickly," said Teresa gently.

He was grateful for her understanding. "It *is* a lot for Silvana to manage, isn't it?"

"I've only Leon and he's more than a handful!"

He looked down at Leon and thought of a son of his own who would hand down the family wine and traditions. "I'm sorry I wasn't at home when you called, Teresa. Will you take a glass with me?"

"Thank you. I've already stayed too long. Narcissus needs me in the shop. Say good-bye," she encouraged Leon.

"Good-bye, Leon. Good-bye, Teresa."

"Come again soon," he called after her when she reached the entrance to the drive.

"Mama," panted Leon, trotting to keep up with her. "Why are you crying?"

She wiped her hand across her cheek. "What are you saying, silly boy? I'm not crying!"

4

Julio Garcia was miserable as he sat at the wheel of his taxi.

It was prewar and battered; its upholstery sagged, its rusted mud-guards were paper-thin and the worn engine needed careful nursing. Still it was reliable enough to take a passenger from one side of Barcelona to the other through the almost empty streets. But few people could afford his modest fares. The end of the war in Europe had made little difference to Spain. There was acute depression. There were no exports, people had no money to buy, many factories were closed down and others simply went on in hopes for better times. Even the lucky men who had jobs couldn't live on their wages. A family was well-off if it could taste fish or meat on one day of the week.

So Julio Garcia sighed sadly.

Three men sauntered toward him and he sat up straight, scenting clients. They wore thin, blue-and-white striped linen suits and two of them carried worn leather bags. One man opened the door, the others climbed inside and Julio Garcia threw away his cigarette.

One of the men told him in Catalan where to go and when Julio Garcia repeated the address, the man knew by his accent that he was not from Cataluña and switched to Spanish. "There's no hurry," he said. "We're early for our appointment so take your time."

The three passengers were strangely silent and when Julio Garcia slyly looked into his mirror, he found himself staring into cool, gray eyes. He looked away quickly.

The silence of the three men was ominous, and although it was a cool September day, Julio began to sweat.

"You were here during the war, driver?" asked the man with the gray eyes.

Julio Garcia nodded sadly. "We were bombed. We lost all our windows three times."

"It was better before the war, wasn't it, driver? Then Spain was building a new world but now there's only . . . despair."

Julio Garcia hunched his neck down into his shoulders and stared doggedly at the road ahead of him.

"Don't you agree, driver?" asked the man softly.

Julio Garcia didn't answer.

"Are you deaf, driver? Or are you one of *them?*"

Garcia gulped. He said hoarsely: "Why lose your head for just talking?"

They liked his reply. They chuckled and quite suddenly the atmosphere had changed. They were all friends and the tension had vanished.

"We're still ahead of time," said the man with the gray eyes as the driver pulled up outside a marble-fronted bank.

Julio Garcia stretched his hand toward the meter.

"Keep the engine running, driver. We've got other calls to make."

They waited. The city looked dead. Only a few people were on the streets. A Civil Guard paced toward them, his tommygun slung across his back and his patent leather black tricorn gleaming dully in the sun. He glanced at the men in the taxi and strolled on.

"Wait for us, driver. We won't be long," said the man with the gray eyes. He and one companion picked up their briefcases, unhurriedly crossed the pavement and entered the bank.

The third man sat on the edge of his seat breathing down the driver's neck.

"How long will they be?" asked Julio Garcia.

"Only a few minutes."

"I don't like to waste gasoline. It's rationed." Julio Garcia reached for the ignition key.

"Leave it. Don't turn the engine off." The man's voice was so sharp that Julio Garcia turned around slowly and stared at him.

"Leave the engine running," said the man. His face was pale and beads of perspiration had gathered around the wings of his nostrils.

Julio Garcia sensed his fear. "Don't tell me what to do," he said.

"Don't be difficult, driver. Just leave the engine running."

"It's my cab. I'll do what I want!"

The man's eyes glowed. "I hired this cab and you'll do what I say."

"We'll see about that," said Julio Garcia grimly and reached for the ignition key.

The man slid a pistol over Julio's shoulder. "It'll be the last thing you'll do, driver!"

Julio Garcia's hand fell back. His mouth was dry and tasted of copper. He held his breath until the pistol slipped out of sight again. "Just sit quietly."

Julio Garcia sat as still as a statue.

Only minutes had elapsed since the men had entered the bank, and the Civil Guard who had passed a few minutes earlier was returning.

The Civil Guard drew level and Julio Garcia stared at him.

The man behind warned: "Just sit quietly."

The Civil Guard looked straight at the driver. Then his eyes went to the passenger.

Julio Garcia sweated.

The Civil Guard glanced both ways along the pavement, took a deep breath and, with unhurried stride, paced into the bank.

When the two men had entered the bank they had gone to separate desks, seated themselves and written out deposit slips. There were only a few clients in the bank.

The two men glanced up when the Civil Guard entered. The aged, uniformed porter seated at the entrance door hastily got to his feet. "Can I help you, *Guardia?*"

"Tell your chief I want to see him. It's urgent."

The old man limped away and the two men with briefcases watched him.

The Civil Guard took a small wedge of wood from his pocket and thrust it under the door. He straightened up, unslung his tommygun, held it waist-high and said in a voice that resounded through the bank: "Attention, everybody. This is an emergency. Everyone listen!"

Startled faces turned toward him.

"All of you stand against that wall over there."

After a moment's hesitation there was agitated shuffling and pushing as clients and bank employees moved over to the wall.

The two men with briefcases ignored the order.

The aged porter had found the manager who came hurrying, his face worried. "What's wrong, *Guardia?*"

"Stand to one side. The rest of you back right up against the wall."

The bank manager fluttered his hands nervously. "I'll help in any way I can and . . ."

The Civil Guard had raven-black hair with gray sideburns. A ridged welt like a saber scar ran from the corner of his eye to the point of his jaw. He nodded. "Attend to those gentlemen quickly."

The bank manager looked at the two men. "What can I . . . ?"

"Take us to the vault. Quickly!"

The bank manager's eyes narrowed. "I don't think . . ."

They pulled out revolvers.

"No," said the bank manager flatly. "Don't think I'll . . . !"

The man with the gray eyes pistol-whipped him. The manager clutched at his face. The second man tripped him up and he whimpered as he lay on the cool tiles.

The man with the gray eyes stooped and prodded the manager's chest with the pistol. "Don't waste more time."

The bank manager got to his feet and mopped his cheek as he led the two men to the vault.

The men cleared the shelves of stacks of one-thousand-peseta notes. It had been many years since new currency had been printed. All the notes were old and untraceable. There were not enough to fill the two briefcases, so they crammed in one-hundred-peseta notes. They swept the rest of the currency notes, stacks of bonds, stocks and shares onto the vault's stone floor. They applied a lighted match to the paper mountain and when it was well ablaze they ushered the manager outside and shut the steel door.

The man with the gray eyes left the bank first. He took a firm grip on his bulging briefcase, walked out unhurriedly, crossed the pavement and climbed into the taxi.

The second man followed him a few minutes later.

The Civil Guard waited until they were in the taxi. Then he drew his pistol and held it menacingly while he slung the tommygun over his shoulder. "The first to follow me outside gets shot in the belly."

He walked swiftly across the pavement and slid into the seat alongside the driver. "Get going, driver. As fast as you can."

They sped up the Paseo de Gracia, turned left at the Diagonal and drove hard until they reached the outskirts of the city. Julio Garcia trembled when they ordered him to pull over to the side of the road.

"All right, driver. Get out."

Julio Garcia knew he was going to die and a lump in his throat choked him as he thought of his wife and two daughters.

The man with the gray eyes snapped: "Didn't you hear me, driver? Go behind that hedge." His hand was in his pocket holding his gun.

"I won't talk," panted Julio Garcia. "I *swear* I won't say a word to anyone."

The cool, gray eyes were impatient. "Hurry, man. Hurry!"

Julio Garcia stumbled around to the other side of the hedge.
"Kneel down."

Julio Garcia knew men were killed this way during the war.
"Please don't!" choked Julio Garcia as he sank on to his knees.
"Please don't!"

The man with the gray eyes placed his foot against Julio Garcia's
shoulders and thrust hard. The driver fell forward on his face and lay
still, wondering if he had been shot in the back. The man snapped a
handcuff on his left wrist, doubled up his right leg and snapped the
other handcuff around his ankle.

"This is for your trouble, comrade." The man thrust folded thou-
sand-peseta notes into the driver's pocket.

Julio Garcia was too astonished by his reprieve from death to
understand anything clearly.

"Be a good comrade. We'll borrow your taxi. Give us a fair chance
to get away before you cry for help."

Much later, Julio Garcia's taxi was discovered only a quarter of a
mile along the road.

The four men were playing a card game called Manila. The cards
were Spanish, forty-eight to a pack, and the suit designs were gold
coins, drinking cups, green cudgels and blue swords. It would have
been difficult for a foreigner to understand the game by watching it
because the nine of each suit was the strongest card.

Catalina busied herself at a mahogany-stained buffet, cutting black
maize bread into slices on which she spread mashed potatoes and
beans flavored with garlic. As she prepared each slice she placed it at
the elbows of the players.

The hand of cards ended and Miguel Barras pushed back his chair
and got to his feet. "I've no interest in cards!" He crossed to a
window, edged the curtains to one side and stared down into Barcelona's busy Mayor de Gracia. Up and down the street he saw the gray
uniforms and flat caps of Barcelona's special police. "The sons of
whores! The city's crawling with them!"

"But they've bolted the stable door after the horse has run," said
Adolfo and chuckled nervously, remembering the anxious minutes
he had waited outside in the taxi.

"The horse *didn't* escape," said the man with the gray eyes. His name was Marin and the apartment was rented by his mother and his sister, Helena.

The fourth man, Jaime, complained petulantly: "They're too well organized!"

"What do you expect of a police state?" said Miguel.

"It was madness to show yourself with your scar, Miguel. You're a marked man now." Adolfo glowered.

"So I made a mistake!" snarled Miguel. "But *I'm* the one who'll pay. They're looking for me . . . not you!"

"One minute, comrades." Marin held up his hand soothingly. "The plan was good. Slip across the border, rob a bank, hide out a while and then home again. But we couldn't anticipate a police cordon would be set up around the city."

"Only one thing matters," said Miguel. "The money's got to get back to France to work for the Party."

"Patience," advised Marin. "Even if we have to wait a month. Patience!"

They tensed at the click of a key in the lock but relaxed when Helena shut the apartment door behind her. She came into the room and glared at the men. "Did Mother call?"

Marin's mother was in her eighties, bedridden, deaf and partially blind.

"She's sleeping," said Marin.

She scowled at the invaders of her home, hating them and her brother. "How much longer are you going to stay?"

Marin's gray eyes were as hard as steel. "Who wants to know?"

"I want you all out of here," she said. "Didn't you hear it on the radio? In some districts they've started house-to-house searches."

"That doesn't mean a thing, Helena."

"Why did you come back, bringing us all this trouble? Mother and I were all right until you returned."

"What's happened to you, Helena? You're a Party member. Are you turning traitor?"

She glared. "What's bank robbing got to do with communism?"

"The Party needs money," he explained patiently. "We've got to buy arms and equipment."

Helena pleaded with her brother. "Can't you see it's hopeless? What can a handful of you achieve by making raids across the border? When the Allies didn't turn against Spain after Germany was conquered, our last hope was destroyed. You're crying for the moon, Marin!"

He flushed angrily. "What can you know of these things. You're a woman!"

"Any fool knows a handful of armed men can't overthrow a dictator and his army."

"The masses are suffering," said Marin. "They've not enough to eat and are ripe for revolt. Freedom is suppressed. All we need is a revolutionary situation and they'll rise!"

She said sadly: "Are you so blind you can't see reality, Marin? The people suffer. But anything is preferable to another civil war. Nobody wants all that again, the bombing, the killing and the atrocities."

"Don't argue, Marin," said Miguel quietly. "She's a victim of propaganda. She listens to *their* radio and reads *their* newspapers."

Helena glared. "It's not *your* mother you're putting in danger."

"The cause is important, not individuals."

"I want *that* out of here at once!" She pointed to a brown paper bundle. "If they search here that's a giveaway."

Marin said quietly: "Get rid of it, Adolfo. Leave it somewhere, in a park or in a café."

"Me!" exploded Adolfo. His eyes widened in alarm.

"That uniform doesn't leave," said Miguel firmly. "We got it the hard way and we'll need it again."

"Helena's right. If they come here it will betray us at once," Marin said quietly.

"So would my scarred face," said Miguel. "And so would the money." His black eyes glittered. "Or are you suggesting Adolfo dump the money too?"

Marin dropped his eyes. "I'm thinking . . . of my mother."

Helena glared at Miguel. "He's my brother, otherwise I'd turn you all out. But once you leave here don't ever come back. If you do, I'll call the police at once." She stormed out of the room.

Marin shrugged his shoulders apologetically. "Women!" he said and smiled wryly. Then his eyes met Catalina's and he added: "*You* are different, comrade."

"Not so different that I can't sympathize with Helena," she said. "We've got to be *sure* of our contacts. It's a mistake to get into situations where we can't depend absolutely on everyone."

"I was sure I could rely on Helena," protested Marin. "We were both Party members. Her fiancé was killed leading the attack on the Arcazanos Barracks."

"That was ten years ago!" snapped Catalina. "People change!"

There was a ring at the doorbell and everyone listened while Helena answered it. But it was an expected comrade and they pulled up chairs and sat round the table with him. Nolana was a dark man, thirty-five years of age, who worked in the docks as a ships' carpenter. He was ideally placed to make contact with the crews of foreign boats.

"I've fixed it so two of you can sail tonight for Marseilles." Nolana took a manila envelope from his pocket and drew out two Spanish seamen's identity cards. "These will get you into the docks. A banana boat's leaving for the Canary Islands and you're the new crew."

Miguel examined the documents. They were genuine but the original photographs had been changed for those of Miguel and Marin. "My scar doesn't show in the photograph," said Miguel.

"It would be fatal if it did!"

"How do I get around it?" asked Miguel.

"Take a calculated risk," said Nolana. "I've left a suitcase outside in the hall with sailor's clothes and two sea bags. Fill the bags with the money, put dirty underclothes on top and walk through the dock gates showing the passes."

"And the scar?"

Nolana smiled slowly. "Carry the bag over your shoulder as all sailors do," he said. "Pull it hard up against your cheek."

Miguel grinned. "A nice touch, comrade. Walking straight out under the noses of the bastards with the money in a sea bag!"

"How about the rest of us?" asked Adolfo anxiously.

"You'll have to be patient. They're checking everyone, everywhere, at the railways and the port. They're even stopping cars leaving the city and making spot-searches of cafés. You'll have to wait until they relax their vigilance."

Miguel asked: "Did you learn anything about Gomez, comrade?"

Nolana nodded. "He was arrested three months ago on suspicion. They interrogated him and he wouldn't talk. But another man did. Gomez has been identified as a Party member and sentenced to death. No date's been fixed."

Miguel's eyes smoldered. "There'll be no justice until the workers take power."

A new but dusty coupé lurched along the mud-packed road from Figueras. Long ago the road's macadam surface had been eroded by wind, rain and sun. Now the high-wheeled peasants' carts had worn deep furrows along its center. It was difficult for the driver to avoid dropping his wheels into these deep ruts and when it happened, the exhaust pipe or sump scraped the ground.

The car entered Escoleras at a snail's pace and came to a standstill in the plaza under the shade of the plane trees. At once the villagers came hurrying to see the strange, modern car.

The driver climbed out of the car. He was British and embarrassed by the silently staring crowd. He wondered if he had broken a village tabu. He couldn't understand why they had hurried to watch him and why the crowd was swiftly growing. Their faces were sullen and their manner ominous and he wondered for a moment if they might fling themselves upon him. But he shrugged the thought away. Spain was a civilized country even if it was a dictatorship. So he smiled and said: *"Buenas días."*

It was like pressing a light switch in the darkness. The eyes and faces lit up, delighted smiles greeted him and a dozen villagers tried to talk to him at once, their expressive eyes and actions telling more eloquently than words that they were thrilled to meet a foreigner and awed by the magnificence of his car.

He spoke a strongly accented pidgin-Spanish. He told them he had come from England across the sea and had driven through France. He said it was very hot and that the view of the sea was wonderful. He stooped and spoke to his wife through the car window. "You can get out. I don't think they'll eat us."

Mary Tweed was fair-skinned like her husband, but she was beautifully tanned and proud of it as she stepped from the car, a cigarette in her hand. Her yellow linen dress with slender straps completely exposed her arms and shoulders. Her short skirt showed bare brown knees as she balanced on high-heeled white sandals.

There were gasps from the older women of the village. The men and youths stared blankly, unable to believe their eyes.

But the British couple were unaware of the consternation. Mary took a beach bag from the back of the car while her husband happily interrogated the villagers.

"Swim?" he asked, making swimming motions and looking the question.

A dozen hands were at once pointing, heads nodding, eyes smiling.

"That is the beach, Señor. There are many kilometers of beach."

"Deep?" he asked, hands demonstrating shallowness and then deepness.

"Good for swimming," they encouraged. "Very good."

He nodded his thanks. "My car. It is good? Parked here?"

They were perplexed. Parking was a problem they didn't know about.

He tried again. "The car? Here? It is good?"

They nodded reassuringly. Yes. The car was good where it was. But their assurances were dubious and their eyes unhappy. They felt they had failed him.

The Englishman nodded and took his wife by the arm. *"Adiós."*

"Adiós," chorused the villagers, and stood staring after the couple as they made their way to the beach. After a few minutes most of the younger men set off after them.

Robert and Mary walked some distance along the sand before they sat down.

The village youths sat at a distance and watched the foreign couple do something unheard of. They held towels for each other and changed into bathing suits *on the beach.* The youths watched incredulously when Mary dropped her towel to reveal a skintight crimson suit. The youths watched the couple swim, rub oil on themselves, doze in the sun and then swim again. When the couple returned to the village the youths followed them persistently.

"The way they act you'd think they'd never seen a woman swimming," commented Mary.

"Perhaps they haven't," said Robert.

They wanted to buy food to make sandwiches. Teresa was behind the counter when they entered her store. The villagers followed them.

"Food," said Robert Tweed in his primitive Spanish.

"We have dried sardines and salted cod," said Teresa. "There is also sausage meat and tinned tuna."

He did not understand her so she showed him the goods and then, because she had studied French, which is similar to Catalan, Teresa spoke to him in that language. He answered delightedly, his accent strong and his grammar atrocious but his vocabulary extensive enough for them to converse.

"My wife and I love this village," he said sincerely. "It is like something you read about in a book . . . like a paradise. The blue sea, the deserted white-sand beaches and . . . everything."

"I like it too," smiled Teresa. "We live simply but we are happy."

"Is there a hotel?"

"There's the Hotel Catalana in Figueras."

"I mean . . . *here!*"

She chuckled at his foolishness. "Nobody ever stays here."

"You *must* have some people who visit here. Where do they stay?"

"They can always find a room in the village."

"Will someone in the village give us a room?"

Teresa smiled wryly. Such wealthy foreigners couldn't live in a village cottage. "People here live very simply," she explained. "There are few conveniences."

"We don't mind the simple life." He chuckled. "We've just lived through a war. That wasn't luxury living either."

"But there's no running water, the toilets are in the back yard. . . . It's not what you're used to."

"We won't mind," he assured her. "Who will rent us a double room?"

Teresa took a deep breath as she swiftly rearranged her household mentally, with herself and Narcissus sleeping at the Barras cottage. "I have a double room. Would you like to see it?"

She led them up the steep, narrow stairs and hesitantly showed them her bedroom. They looked around without dismay. "This will do," Mary told her husband. "It's spotlessly clean."

"We'd like to stay," he told Teresa. "How much is it?"

She told him.

She noticed his slight hesitancy and feared she had asked too much but then he astonished her by asking: "Is that each day or for the week?"

"For the week," she said and was surprised when he laughed.

"You're making a mistake," he said.

"Am I?" She checked mentally, adding a little to the normal price charged for a double room overnight. "No," she confirmed. "I haven't made a mistake."

"We won't argue," he chuckled. "We'll square up when we leave. Now what about eating? Is there a restaurant here?"

"A bar or a café will prepare a snack. But if you want regular meals . . ." Teresa took a deep breath and plunged. "You can eat here if you don't mind eating in the kitchen behind the shop."

"I'd love it!" Mary said delightedly. "We'd *much* prefer to live with a family!"

They stayed three weeks. They sunbathed on the beach all day, returning only for lunch. In the cool of the evening they took long walks along the rocky coast, exploring little bays and coves and looking down from the high cliff tops into water so clear and transparent that the seabed could be seen clearly.

Robert Tweed studied Spanish grammar books, showed a remarkable aptitude for the language and practiced on Teresa and the family. Mary was enchanted with Leon, played with him endlessly and bought him sweets. He was seven years old and Mary couldn't get over his blond, Nordic appearance.

"Our family has always been blond," said Teresa proudly. "My father is known as 'El Rubio.' "

Everyone was delighted by the friendliness of the English couple. Teresa tactfully explained that the older women of the village were narrow-minded, and without demur Mary wore a short coat, stubbed out cigarettes before she left the house and used less lipstick. The couple drank a lot of wine, visited the village cafés, stayed until the early hours of the morning and invited fishermen and everybody else to drink with them. They ate all that was set before them, even snails.

Robert Tweed bought one of Pepita's mosaic pictures and asked: "How many pictures can Pepita make a year?"

"It's hard to say," said Teresa. "It's . . . tiring for her." She thought of the leather-tipped stumps of arms painstakingly searching among the stones for one of the right color and delicately edging it into position.

"There'd be a good sale for them back home."

"Pepita does it to pass the time."

"They're not works of art," agreed Robert Tweed. "But the colors are gay and the scenes have charm. They're a novelty. If you like, I'll show them around and get some orders."

"It would make Pepita happy," said Teresa.

On their last night in Escoleras they brought champagne to drink with the family.

Robert Tweed said: "We're coming back. This is one of the most beautiful places I've seen." He eyed Teresa thoughtfully. "Why don't you open a boarding house?"

She smiled tolerantly at his grand ideas. "But nobody ever comes here."

He leaned forward and spoke intently. "They will. I'm employed by a big firm that's started a travel agency. I'm its manager and I know what I'm talking about. People have suffered years of war and want to escape. This place is cheap, the climate's wonderful, the beach is perfect. Believe me, Teresa. This is a tourist's paradise."

"But . . . nobody has ever heard of Escoleras. Why should anyone come here?"

His eyes gleamed. "I did, didn't I? Despite bad roads, language difficulties and frontier guards who kept me an hour."

"You're different," said Teresa slowly. "But most people going on holiday don't want problems."

"The problems will ease," prophesied Robert Tweed. "Spain can become Europe's most popular resort. And as soon as your government realizes it, the frontiers will be thrown open, money will be found to build new roads, transport services will improve and everyone will grow prosperous."

Teresa said thoughtfully: "Supposing I could find some good, clean double rooms . . . would that do?"

"They must be clean. And you'll have to arrange for food."

"I could rent a big room with a kitchen."

"Why not get a loan from a bank and build a small boarding-house?"

Teresa was horrified. "We couldn't afford *that!*"

"Then find out how many villagers have rooms to let."

When the Tweeds left the following day, Robert Tweed paid exactly twice what he had been asked.

"It's too much," Teresa said.

"For us, it's not enough," he insisted. "We've had much more than value for money." He chuckled. "We've been looked after too cheaply and you think you've been overpaid so . . . we're both happy!"

After they had gone, Teresa sat in deep thought. Presently she took a pencil and paper from the sideboard and made calculations.

"What are you up to?" Narcissus asked.

She smiled softly. "Making our fortune."

5

Renato Maroto was shown into a well-furnished office with deep chairs, leather upholstery and oil paintings in gilt frames. An enormous desk was weighed down by files and behind it sat a silver-haired man with a lined face as brown as a chestnut. He was known by his staff as the Old Man.

"Sit down, Maroto."

"Thank you, Señor."

The Old Man referred to typewritten notes. "You've a good record, Maroto. You served as lieutenant in North Africa and at Vizcaya and the Ebro. Twice wounded . . . Where were you wounded, Maroto?"

"In the chest and thigh."

"Badly?"

"The chest wound smashed a rib and collapsed a lung. The thigh wound was shrapnel."

"When you left the army you were recommended for secret police work."

"That's right, Señor."

"You have excellent recommendations. You have influential friends, Maroto?"

"My family has always been traditionalist in politics, Señor."

The Old Man pushed himself back in his chair and looked keenly at Maroto. "I've picked you for a difficult job."

Maroto smiled. "I am honored, Señor."

"These damned counter-revolutionaries."

"Yes, Señor?"

"They want to fight the revolution all over again. It's time we put men with military experience up against them."

"You mean . . . Scarface and his gang, Señor?"

"Catalan bandits," growled the Old Man.

"Yes, Señor."

"They've got to be stopped." The Old Man's eyes glowed. "They're bank robbers and murderers, masquerading as a people's army. We must deal with them in a military fashion. But no publicity. They mustn't be called revolutionaries. They're criminals and that's a job for the secret police."

"What are your wishes, Señor?"

"Stamp them out, Maroto. The Civil Guard will give you any assistance you require. If you have to step outside the law, that's at your discretion. I don't want you hampered by red tape. Make them talk!"

"I'll need your authority, Señor."

The Old Man flipped an envelope across the desk. "Here's everything you need, signed and sealed." He stood up and stretched his hand across the desk. "Good hunting, Maroto."

"Thank you, Señor," said Renato Maroto. He looked very tall and very thin now that he was standing. He held his head slightly to one side with his long neck hunched into his shoulders like a vulture.

The garage was on the outskirts of the town near the main highway to Toulouse. It was a long, two-story building with accommodation for two hundred cars and space for greasing and car-washing. The name painted above the entrance was: GARAGE BACHET and in the office of the town hall the proprietors were listed as Miguel and Catalina Bachet.

It was dark when Jean-Luis arrived. He knocked on the glass window of the garage office and Miguel took off his smock and hung it on a peg. "Take over, Charles," he said in bad French to the balding little man at the office window. "I won't be back tonight."

Miguel and Jean-Luis walked down the path which ran alongside the garage to the rear of the building where a steep flight of steps led up to the second floor. The door was bolted on the inside and didn't open until Miguel had been studied through a spyhole.

The room was wide and spacious and ran almost half the length of the garage. There were racks of rifles and hand grenades, Bren guns and boxes of ammunition stacked neatly round the walls. There were mines, walkie-talkies and sticks of explosives. Most of the materiel was United States issue, stolen by GI's and sold cheaply. Pinned on the walls were detail maps of the mountainous frontier between France and Spain and picture diagrams showing the component parts of weapons so that they could be taken apart and reassembled. A large framed picture of Lenin was draped with red bunting and along one whitewashed wall was the slogan *They Shall Not Pass* printed in blood-red letters. In one corner stood a private transmitter.

Eight men and two women were awaiting them. One of the women was Catalina, wearing a black jersey and ski pants. She smiled at Miguel when he entered and the stern lines of his face softened momentarily. He had visited a plastic surgeon in Switzerland and the ridged, red welt which had scarred his cheek was now only a hair-fine white line.

Jean-Luis said crisply: "I've seen Pivot and clinched the final arrangements, comrades. We'll check once more to make sure everyone understands his part." Jean-Luis crossed to a wall map and the others gathered round him.

"We hit next Thursday afternoon," he said crisply. "We set off tomorrow night, cross the border and hide out during the day on Comrade Pivot's farm. Then we disperse, each group making its own way to Barcelona. It's to be at one forty-five, so everyone please synchronize their watches with the radio. They're making it difficult for us, comrades. An armed guard sits inside all the banks and one stands outside. No car is allowed to park within fifty yards of any bank entrance." Jean-Luis's eyes flicked to Clara and Catalina. "It's up to you two to persuade the Civil Guard who's outside to step inside. When he does, we all go into action. Now . . . we can't expect to make a big haul. The banks now keep their money permanently in a central safety vault. We'll get only the day's takings. But our objective is to show the masses that we mean business. They'll know we're using the money to buy arms to fight for freedom."

The others listened intently.

"Any questions?" asked Jean-Luis.

"If things go wrong, comrade?"

"Use your initiative. Avoid capture at all costs! If they take you alive they'll make you talk!"

"We'll be armed," said Miguel succinctly.

It was nearing the bank's closing time and last-minute clients hurried to get in. There was a rush of businessmen with briefcases, two uniformed messengers and two nuns. Nuns visited business houses pleading for charity for orphans and their requests were seldom refused.

The bank guard eased the strap of his tommygun, squared his

shoulders and glanced casually along the pavement. He stifled a yawn, glanced down at his heavy boots and shiny leggings and spat thoughtfully at a winged ant scurrying across the pavement.

Then he became aware of the nun, eyes wide and worried and hands fluttering nervously. Her face was very white and pure against the blackness of her veil. "Please come at once, guard. Your companion is ill. He's asking for you." She gulped. "He is dying, I fear . . . a stroke!"

He ran up the steps, pushed in through the swing doors and saw Pedro lounging on a wooden bench. He hurried over to him.

"Are you all right, Pedro?"

Pedro looked up in surprise. He drank heavily off duty and his fleshy features were flushed. He said irritably: "Of course I'm all right. Why shouldn't I be?"

"There was a nun who . . ." The guard glanced around and was reassured to see the nun standing behind him. "Didn't you say Pedro was ill?"

The nun frowned. "There must be a misunderstanding."

"I was outside and you came up to me and said Pedro was ill!"

A small crowd was gathering around them.

"I asked if you and your companion would donate to the orphans' fund," said the nun.

The guard stared at her incredulously. Then he became aware of the men who hemmed him in and of the sharp pressure against his back. The shot was muffled by clothing and his shocked brain wondered that he felt no pain until he heard Pedro's choking grunt. It was instantly drowned by another shot which he heard this time with his body. The pins and needles in his spine detached his limbs from the swift darkening of his vision.

Marin, dressed as a messenger, eased Pedro's tommygun from his shoulder and spun around, threatening everyone within range. "I don't want to hurt anybody. Just back up against the wall quickly."

With her nun's robes rustling loudly, Catalina was pushing small wedges of wood under the door. Clara was lowering the blinds as though the bank was shut.

Miguel snatched up the other tommygun when the second Civil Guard went down. The guard's head had hit the marble floor solidly and at once blood ran from his ears.

The onlookers were terrified. They pressed back against the walls, eyes fearful, trembling hands raised high.

Miguel and Marin covered the bank clerks and clients while their companions vaulted the bank counter and scooped currency and coins from the tellers' tills. Clara and Catalina helped, their habits swishing loudly.

"Don't worry, comrades," Miguel reassured everyone. "We won't hurt you. We fight only the people's oppressors." He nodded down at the dead guards.

Nobody was reassured.

"We fight for liberty," Miguel said fiercely. "We rob your Fascist oppressors to buy arms to fight for freedom."

They left the bank as it had all been planned. Miguel first, followed by two businessmen and then a uniformed messenger, all carrying briefcases. The two nuns stood outside the almost closed door of the bank to lull suspicion while Marin and others inside kept the bank clerks covered.

Miguel strode along the road, turned sharply to the left and crossed to a parked car with false license plates. The driver started up the engine as Miguel and his companions climbed inside. "Don't drive like a madman," warned Miguel.

The driver pulled away from the curb and Miguel gave the car parked behind it a signal. The two cars slowly rounded the corner and speeded up. Miguel's car drove on straight past the bank but the second car slowed to a standstill. The bank door opened and other men carrying briefcases hurried down to the waiting car.

Marin was the last to leave. "I don't want to kill anybody," he warned. "But if anyone puts his head outside this door within the next ten minutes, I'll blow it off." He unloaded the tommygun, placed it on the floor and slipped outside. The two nuns followed him across the pavement, their presence reassuring to anyone suspicious of seeing a car parked before a bank.

Marin climbed into the car and beckoned urgently to Clara and Catalina. They crossed the pavement solemnly, serene and pure in their white headdresses and flowing robes.

One of the bank's clients who had found himself lined up against the wall was a Falangist and an ex-Nationalist soldier. He had a gun permit and carried a small automatic. It nestled neatly in his jacket pocket. As soon as the door had shut behind the last of the robbers he raced to the nearest window. It was too high to see out of so he ran for a teller's stool, carried it to the window, climbed up on it and looked out through the thick glass. A car was drawn up at the curb, one nun was climbing into it and the other was behind her, pushing her gently.

The Falangist smashed the window with his pistol butt and aimed carefully. He squeezed the trigger only once. He had cut a tendon, and the gun fell from his hand.

Clara was almost into the car when the shot rang out.

Catalina was just behind her, stooped over. The bullet hit her between the shoulders, ripped through her neck, severed an artery and tore out through the hollow of her throat. She went down on her knees.

Her companions didn't realize what had happened. "Hurry," they urged. "Hurry!"

"She's been hit," choked Clara.

"Pull her inside," ordered Marin.

"We'd better get out of here quick," said Adolfo, the driver. His white face was wet with sweat.

"Grab her," ordered Marin, who was farthest from the door.

Hands reached out to seize Catalina but from down the street came the staccato rattle of a tommygun as an alert Civil Guard fired into the air to raise the alarm.

Adolfo acted without thinking. He slammed into gear, let up the clutch. The car shot away with the open door swinging wildly.

"Are you crazy?" roared Marin. "You've left her behind!"

"Do you want us all killed?" Adolfo hunched over the steering wheel.

They looked behind at the swiftly receding black-robed figure kneeling on the pavement. People were running to her. As the first man reached her, she slowly slid forward on her face into a pool of blood.

The cars raced out of Barcelona and on to Badalona where they were garaged in a warehouse belonging to a comrade.

They waited until the early hours of the morning before they set off again. By then the radio had announced Catalina's death. Miguel hardly spoke. He radiated bitter hatred.

"You left her," he told the others tonelessly.

"There was nothing else we could do, comrade. If we had carried her into the car we would all have been killed!"

They drove on through the night, their headlights boring a tunnel through the tree-lined roads. Presently, ahead of them, a red light was waved from side to side.

Two Civil Guards with bicycles had stopped them. The guards stood on each side of the car. "Your papers, please," asked one, stooping to look inside.

"They're here," said Miguel. He brought up a Sten gun from between his knees and fired a burst which all but cut the man's head from his shoulders. Nolana fired his pistol at point-blank range into the other guard's chest.

They drove on.

Twice more they came upon patrolling Civil Guards. Each time they stopped and, when the Civil Guards came over to them, gunned them down.

"There's only one way to deal with Fascist swine," said Miguel tonelessly. "Kill them!"

Later that night they hid their car in a barn belonging to a sympathizer, changed their clothes and tramped off into the mountains. Twelve hours later they were back in France.

"This way, Señor," said the gray-uniformed attendant and Renato Maroto followed him down the stone steps to the basement and along a wide corridor to the iron door at the far end. The attendant swung the door back slowly and switched on the lights.

The walls were whitewashed, the floor was concrete and the air was dank. Maroto felt the cold strike through his thin, summer suit and the sweat at his armpits turned icy.

There were three marble slabs but only one was occupied. The attendant pulled back the sheet to show the corpse's face.

"Strip her, man," snapped Maroto. "We don't use delicacy with scum!"

The attendant pulled the sheet right down.

Renato Maroto stood staring, his long dark face brooding and his shoulders hunched. His thin nostrils quivered, stung by the smell of formalin and antiseptic, and deep down in his mind a chord of memory was lightly touched.

She was about thirty, a strong, wiry girl with firm flesh. Her body was waxlike and the wound in her throat a small black plug of congealed blood. Her breasts were flabby pouches, pocked and pitted by surgeon's knives. Her abdomen bore the ridged scars of many major operations. The scar on her cheek pulled down her eyelid until it drooped.

"Spawn of a whore," he growled at the corpse. He stooped over her, shoulders hunched like a vulture about to peck at its prey, and spat upon the cold flesh.

The attendant's face was impassive but his eyes were shocked.

"Red scum," Maroto said.

"*Sí*, Señor," agreed the attendant bleakly.

"Cover her up," said Maroto. "I've seen all I want."

All the witnesses of the bank raid had been detained and statements taken. Maroto studied them and personally interviewed some of the witnesses.

"I'll see Señorita Bolero next," he told the guard. "Don't bring her here. I'll see her in private!"

He kept her waiting an hour before he strolled along the corridor to the interrogating room.

At a gesture from Maroto, the guard unbolted the door and held it open. Maroto stepped into a bare, windowless room with a solitary chair bolted to the floor below an arc lamp. The door shut behind him and he studied the seated girl speculatively. She was mousy, wore thick-lensed glasses and had a large mole on her cheek. Her stubby fingers nervously twisted a moist strip of handkerchief.

He said curtly: "I've read your statement and there are some questions I must ask you."

She pleaded, "Will it take long? My parents expected me home long ago. They'll be worried."

"You'll leave when I've finished with you."

"It's almost midnight and Mother will be terribly worried. If I can send a message . . . ?"

"Hold your tongue," he snapped so fiercely that she lapsed into silence.

"You say you recognized one of the men who entered the bank? You say his name is Marin?"

She nodded unhappily, regretting she had remembered anything.

"Tell me about Marin."

"It's all in my statement," she sighed. "He used to live across the road from me just before the war. But we moved away and I haven't seen him since."

"Tell me about him. What does he look like? What did he do? Who are his friends?"

"It's so long ago," she wailed. "It's hard to remember and I'm tired. I haven't had a thing to eat. They wouldn't even give me a drink of water."

He stood beside her and his long fingers gathered up the hair at the nape of her neck and held it tightly.

She sat petrified.

"You'll answer my questions, do you understand?"

"Yes," she whispered.

"Murderers won't run around loose because you're too tired to talk. Understand?"

"Yes." Her eyes watered as he increased the pressure on her hair, pulling her head back.

"Tell me about him. What did he look like?"

She talked, telling all she could remember, even trivial and unimportant details. Two hours elapsed before he was satisfied.

"That's all," he told her. He yawned and stretched himself, then walked to the door and rapped on it.

The girl asked with relief. "May I go now?"

He watched her while the guard unbolted the door. "You'll have to stay," he said.

Her eyes widened. "What more can I do? I've told you everything I know. The only reason I was in the bank is because I work there!" Hysteria edged into her voice. "I've done nothing! I want to go home. I want to see Mother!"

"You'll go home," he promised. "We'll release you in a few days when we capture Marin."

Her eyes rolled. "A few days!" A frantic note rang in her voice. "I've done nothing."

He nodded to the guard. "Keep her." He walked away quickly, leaving the guard to take whatever steps he thought necessary to quiet the girl.

During the following days records were painstakingly checked, dozens of people were interviewed by the secret police, and a thick dossier was built up about Marin. He had been a left-wing university student, president of the debating society and author of articles in a splinter-group political magazine. Official records were searched and photographs of him as a young man were found. These were reproduced. Nearly all the witnesses of the bank raid recognized Marin's photograph.

Maroto spoke to the captain of the Civil Guard. "This is the first time we've had a clue to the identity of any of these criminals. If I get my hands on one, he'll lead me to the others. A dog always returns to its vomit. In a few days, or even a few months, Marin will visit his mother and sister. Their apartment must be watched day and night. Take over three or four apartments with a view of the one we're interested in. Set up a secret day-and-night watch. When Marin shows up I want him taken alive."

The captain said doubtfully: "It's a thickly populated area. Innocent people will get hurt if a gunfight starts."

"As soon as Marin shows up, call me and I'll take over," said Maroto.

Teresa had listed fifteen neighbors with double rooms to let. But Robert Tweed had written that he could send her ten times as many guests. She had a feeding problem too. There was no dining room big enough in the village for more than twenty people. And even if such a room had been available it would still need a large kitchen.

Teresa spent hours figuring with a pencil and paper. One day she left the shop, walked to the far end of the village and along the beach. The silvery sand stretched along the bay as far as she could see. In the other direction, only two hundred yards away, was the village. In the winter when the great gales blew, the sea swamped over the beach and flooded the low land between the village and where she stood. The high ground where she now stood became an island, a long wide bar of sandy soil stretching for more than a kilometer, tufted with coarse, yellow grass and yellow weeds.

The owner of the land was a widow who lived in Figueras. Teresa went to see her.

"But why do you want to buy worthless land, my child?" asked the widow. "Nothing can grow there. Even the weeds are poor, starved things."

"I am thinking of building a house," said Teresa carefully.

"A house! Are you mad, child? Surely you know that with the winter storms the land becomes an island."

"That happens for only a few days each winter. And it is not difficult to wade across to the village."

"If you have thought about it carefully then I will sell." The widow's eyes were sharp. "How much do you offer?"

"As you have pointed out," said Teresa, "the land is useless . . ."

"You don't expect me to give it away!"

"I will pay a good price for the land but I will not pay all the money at once. I will need eleven years to pay you with interest. Each year I will pay a tenth of the purchase price. Any year I fail to pay, the land will revert to you and I will forfeit what I have paid."

"The conditions are fair if we agree upon the price," said the widow. "But have you talked this over with your husband, child?"

"I will do so when I know I can reach agreement with you," said Teresa and smiled.

The widow chuckled. "Since you are set on this madness, go and talk to him because we will not quarrel over the price."

But Teresa did not at once speak to Narcissus. Instead she went to her father.

"Do you know Widow Bruton's land just along the beach, Father?"

He was painting his boat. He stooped to load the brush and then drew it smoothly along the scraped, bare wood until it glistened green. "I know it."

"I can buy it cheaply, paying only ten percent every year."

He glanced up quickly and then deliberately turned back to his work. He made no comment.

"If the land is mine, I can build on it," she said.

He made long, skillful strokes with the brush. The new paint gleamed brightly. "Have you not a house big enough to live in?"

"I want to build a boardinghouse, Father. Twenty bedrooms overlooking the sea with a terrace and a large dining room and a big kitchen."

"What nonsense are you talking now?"

She forced herself to speak calmly. "Big changes are coming, Father. We can be among the first to reap the benefits."

"Have you not learned that the only happy man is one without a shirt to his back?"

"I am not thinking of myself, Father. I have Leon and perhaps . . . there may be other children. There is also Pepita."

"I have two strong hands. Neither Pepita, your mother nor any of your children will go hungry while I can work."

She said quietly: "You will not live forever, Father. What will happen to Pepita then?"

His paintbrush faltered as he drew it along the curve of the bow. "So what do you want of me?"

"Money."

"Money!" he snorted. "What money have I?"

"You have money in the bank."

"If I have money in the bank it's no business of yours, girl!" he said gruffly. "It is for Pepita and you others if the need should arise. It is only a little and not to build great hotels or even think of it!"

"You have more than the money you've saved, Father. There is the cottage, the vineyards and the olive grove. I have talked to the manager of the savings bank and he will lend money against these properties. You take out a mortgage and it is twenty years before you must repay."

Paco Barras exploded. "What is this talk of borrowing money? I owe no man. I'm not a slave or a pauper. . . ." Paco Barras broke off. Teresa had braced herself for this expected tirade and was staring stonily at the sand while his words washed over her.

"Don't wear that face!" he snapped.

"I'm sorry, Father. Don't you think I know how you feel about owing money?"

"Well then?"

He resumed painting. Minutes passed and he still could not trust himself to speak.

"I have talked to Juan the builder," she said simply. "He says that labor is very cheap. Everyone wants work. Materials are not expensive either. There's a quarry on the other side of the village and dynamite will break out the rock needed for construction. He too will mortgage his house and his vineyard to get the capital. Then when the house is built it can be mortgaged and the builder paid!

"Juan the builder will give me credit and Narcissus can get loans against the shop and the olive groves. I've calculated it a hundred times, Father. If we get tourists, we'll soon pay back every penny."

"And if it is a failure, daughter?" He recklessly spattered the sand as he slapped the brush furiously up and down the woodwork.

"Then we will be unhappy, Father," she admitted. After a pause she added. "But we will not have been afraid to take the risk."

Paco Barras scuffed the sand with his bare foot, covering up the fallen paint. Then with great care he trimmed the brush on the edge of the paint pot and drew the bristles along the side of the boat in a swift, sure stroke which left no bristle marks.

"Well, Father?"

"Don't come here arguing with me, daughter," he stormed. "You know you can wheedle anything you want out of me."

Teresa smiled. "Then I can go ahead, Papa?" Calling him Papa was like a hug of gratefulness.

"You're a mad one, daughter," he said, shaking his head in despair. "A mad one!"

Paco Barras had enough money to pay the first installment on the land. The mortgages on his house and vineyards plus the property of Narcissus's family got the building started.

Juan the builder had a friend in Barcelona who was an architect. He was young and bursting with modern ideas. He visualized for Teresa a hotel with streamlined curves and walls of glass.

"It will cost you more," he warned. "Also you must look ahead. You must prepare for success. Dig your foundations deep and make them wide and solid. Cement beams are not good enough. Use iron girders. If you build only one story it is expensive. But if you build six, seven or eight stories, as they build on the French Riviera, you will have your solid foundations already laid."

"Iron girders then," said Teresa recklessly. "Deep foundations."

Workmen grew suntanned as they labored in the hot sun and expensive iron girders were brought down from Barcelona.

Every day Teresa walked along the beach and watched her dream take shape. Every day, too, Paco Barras came to see the building and walked away shaking his head.

But Teresa's correspondence with Robert Tweed was reassuring. The hotel must be ready for June, he insisted. He guaranteed every room would be occupied until the end of September. She must not fail him, he urged. The hotel must have all conveniences and showers in every double bedroom.

Juan the builder worked his men sixteen hours a day. All through the autumn and winter the work went on ceaselessly and in spring the painters, decorators and electricians were encouraged by an untiring Teresa.

On the first of June the first group of English tourists arrived in Escoleras escorted by a Spanish-speaking English guide. They were welcomed by a smiling Teresa and Narcissus.

A dozen village girls were dressed in white-and-blue striped dresses with big red bows in their hair and lacy white aprons around their waists. They lacked experience but made up for it with enthusiasm. They talked to the tourists in Catalan and with smiling gestures. And the tourists, enchanted by the sun, the blue Mediterranean and the simple friendliness of the Catalans, delighted in trying to understand them.

"How goes the business?" Paco Barras asked Teresa one day.

"We've twenty double bedrooms. That means forty guests. They pay us double what it costs to have them. It's good business and we shall grow rich."

"I do not wish to be rich, daughter. I want only that my children are happy."

"I've more than a hundred orders for Pepita's mosaics."

"Then I am happy too, Teresa. Talk to your mother and tell her how good things are."

"And how are things with you, Father? Are you still fishing?"

He looked at her laughingly. "I have no need of a hotel to bring a happy flush to my cheeks!"

"You do not yet need the money I borrowed?"

"Have you not said things are going well. So why can you not repay me?"

"Business cannot stand still."

He eyed her warily. "What now then?"

"Another twenty bedrooms. A playground and a wading pool for children at the back of the hotel. An open-air dance floor for dancing in the evening under the trees."

"Trees!" he scoffed. "Where are the trees?"

"I'll bring palm trees from Andalusia where they have so many they give them away. I'll sink their roots deep and pack good fertile soil from the valley around them."

"Forty bedrooms," he snorted. "Trees. A garden and a dance floor! What do *you* know about the hotel business and its problems?"

"This is only the beginning, Father. Our guests are delighted. They love our food. Meat is still rationed in England, Father. Here they can eat as much as they want."

"Only because it's too expensive for most of us to buy," said Paco Barras quickly.

"But to the English it's cheap, Father."

"Do what you will then," he sighed. "Use my money if you must. I urge only that you do not ruin me."

"Do not worry, Father. Your money is safe."

"When you have lived as many years as I have, you will know nothing is safe."

"All the Costa Brava is being opened up for tourists. The land I bought on the beach is ideal for building apartments."

"Apartments!" scoffed Paco. "A handful of tourists in the village and suddenly it's a European invasion."

"I've been offered a good price," said Teresa placidly.

"Then sell it and make a good profit."

She shook her head, smiling secretly. "I'll be offered more, next year."

Paco Barras threw up his hands. "How can I understand such madness when crazy people buy worthless land."

Leon came running up, his fair hair gleaming in the sun. He was a beautiful child and Teresa watched him fondly as he piped excitedly: "Take me fishing, Grandpa. *Please* take me fishing."

The boy spoke in English and ruffling his hair, Paco Barras asked gruffly: "What's all this gibberish you're talking?"

"It's English, Grandpa. I can speak English now."

"He spends all day with the English," said Teresa. "They make a great fuss of him. He shows them the best places to swim, how to find cockles in the shallow water and takes them for walks along the cliffs to see the caves. He's becoming bilingual."

"Can you count to ten in English?" asked Paco Barras.

Leon made a disparaging gesture. "I can count to a thousand!"

"You'll need to and many times over if your mother has her way," said Paco Barras. His blue eyes twinkled as he held out his hand. "Come, Leon. You can row while I bait the hooks."

6

Two men waited in the stuffy room with the curtains drawn to keep out the sun. Although they were stripped to their underpants sweat gleamed moistly on their bodies. One was stretched full length on an iron cot, the other sprawled in an armchair. Two tommyguns were propped against the wall.

Both men were drowsy. When the knock came upon the door, rapping out the signal, neither of them stirred.

The knuckles rapped again, urgently.

"All right, Alfonso," said the man sprawled in the chair. "I'll get it." He padded barefoot to the door of the apartment and opened it cautiously.

The caller slipped inside quickly, his black eyes bright with excitement. "He's here!" he choked. "He's *here!*"

"Who's here?"

"Who do you think, Pedro. It's Marin. He's here!"

Pedro stared at him. He wiped the palm of his hand on his hairy torso. "Marin's here?" he said dully. Then he spun round, raced to the living room, crouched down at the window and stared out through a peephole cut in the curtains.

The window of the apartment opposite was curtained as it usually was.

He straightened up. "You startled me, Juan."

Juan said grimly: "We haven't all been taking a siesta. Marin's in there, I tell you. Marin . . . or some other man. I saw him myself!"

The man on the bed swung his legs off it and sat up. "Are you sure, Juan?"

"I can't swear it's Marin. But I saw a man."

Pedro groaned. "The entire gang might be in there!"

The man on the bed said quietly: "This could be the end of all of us."

"Don't be so ghoulish," snarled Pedro.

"These men are mad," said Alfonso. "They're not afraid of dying and want everyone to die with them! There's something . . . uncanny about them. They never get hurt although dozens have shot at them."

"There's enough of us," argued Juan. "Alberto's in our apartment keeping the window covered. Then there's the upstairs apartment, too. That makes six of us!"

"It's one thing waiting for Marin when he's a sitting duck," said Alfonso darkly. "But it's a different thing taking him alive! Do you know how many Civil Guards have been murdered these last few weeks? Do you know how many have been shot in the back at night, up in the mountains? If Marin's in there he won't be taken without a fight."

Pedro was staring through the peephole. "No sign of him."

"What do you expect?" growled Alfonso. "A red flag waving from the balcony!"

"You'd better phone headquarters," said Pedro.

Juan frowned. "I only got a quick glimpse." He smiled wryly. "You know how it is if you alert headquarters for nothing. They shout as though you don't know your job."

"Is his sister in there?" asked Alfonso.

"She hasn't moved out of the apartment all day."

"Nobody else saw Marin?"

"Rudi was downstairs in the café. But you know how careless he is. He could have been reading while Marin slipped past."

Alfonso sighed. "We'll keep watching until we're sure. Perhaps you made a mistake."

Pedro padded through to the bathroom and returned with two towels. He tossed one to Alfonso and used the other to wipe his chest.

"Keep watching," said Juan. "I'll warn them in the apartment upstairs. Then as soon as we're sure . . . !"

"Perhaps it was a tradesman," said Alfonso hopefully.

Pedro and Alfonso took fifteen-minute spells watching the curtained windows opposite as the heat of the afternoon diminished into the hot humidity of early evening. It was tiring crouched at the window and the temptation to doze was strong. But as it became twilight, Pedro saw the curtain opposite twitch.

He called in a low voice: "Alfonso. Watch this." At the same time he raised his tommygun.

With one pace Alfonso picked up his tommygun from the table and knelt beside Pedro. Both Civil Guards watched from either side of their window as the curtains opposite twitched and then parted.

They could see the man only indistinctly in the twilight, shirtless and with his arms spread, holding apart the curtains as though he was drinking in the cool evening air.

"Is it Marin?" whispered Pedro shakily.

"I can't see him clearly," said Alfonso.

"Step forward, you bastard," whispered Pedro fiercely. "Let's look at you!"

As though he had heard him, the man opposite stepped forward until the failing daylight dispersed the shadows that concealed his features. They saw the face they had seen so many times in blown-up photographs.

"Holy Jesus Christ! It is Marin!" choked Pedro and leveled his tommygun.

"Look at him," choked Alfonso. "*Look* at him!"

The man opposite leaned forward slightly, drawing in the cool air and relishing it. Then he glanced up and his eyes stared straight at Pedro, riveted upon the curtain peephole as though he could see the two men crouched behind it.

Without moving his gaze, Marin's hand went to his trouser pocket.

In that instant of panic the guards were convinced Marin had seen them. They lost their heads and triggered their tommyguns. When the man opposite was blasted back away from the window, they continued firing. Now all the other guards were firing furiously.

In the street below, women screamed and men threw themselves to the ground. White splinters flew from the shutters opposite, dust and stone chips spurted from the brickwork and bullets riccocheted. The guards' fingers vibrated on the triggers until their weapons were emptied.

Alfonso's gun was hot in his hands. A spiral of smoke curled upward from its muzzle and great drops of sweat ran down his cheeks. His black eyes were glazed as he stared at the room opposite. "Holy Jesus Christ," he whispered. "It's Marin. *It's Marin!*"

"Do you think he's had it?" asked Pedro anxiously.

Alfonso crossed himself. "Please God he's dead!"

Juan burst in on them wildly. "There'll be trouble about this," he choked.

Pedro said quickly: "We've got to stand together. It was self-defense."

Juan picked up the telephone. "Holy Jesus Christ!" he said as he dialed.

Renato Maroto was icily furious. "My instructions were precise. I was to be called as soon as Marin showed up."

The Civil Guard captain was torn between anger with his men and a duty to defend them. "They explained that . . ." he began.

"We'll deal with the explanations later," said Maroto grimly. "Your men started this. They can finish it. Send them upstairs to take a look around."

A contingent of Civil Guards was sent to seal off the surrounding streets.

The six Civil Guards unhappily reloaded their tommyguns.

Maroto glared at them. "Open up that apartment and arrest everybody."

Apprehensively they climbed the stairs and stood outside the apartment door. They were so cramped in the narrow corridor that their tommyguns were as much a menace to themselves as to others.

They flattened themselves against the walls on either side of the apartment door and Alfonso pressed the button.

A bell rang loudly.

There was no other sound within the apartment.

Alfonso wiped his fingers across his forehead and rang again.

The stillness of death answered him.

From below Maroto called up through the stairwell: "What's happening up there?"

"Sweet Mother of God," prayed Alfonso. Inside the apartment, he knew, crouched down behind a barricade of furniture and mattresses, were desperate men waiting to rip him apart with American-made, steel-jacketed bullets.

"Holy Virgin Mary have mercy upon a sinner," prayed Alfonso devoutly. He nodded at his companions, placed the muzzle of his tommygun against the door lock and fired a burst.

The door vibrated beneath the hammering and swung inward.

The Civil Guards flattened themselves against the walls on either side of the door. They waited, very much afraid.

"What's going on up there?" roared Maroto.

Alfonso drew a deep breath and made a leap through the doorway, tommygun leveled and eyes searching desperately for the target he must fire at before he himself was killed.

"What's going on?" yelled Maroto.

Pedro came to the head of the stairs. There was a bleak note in his voice. "You can come up."

Maroto and the Civil Guard captain entered the apartment, walked along the corridor to the living room and stood staring into it.

Marin lay on the tiled floor in a pool of blood, his chest and head dissolved into a bloody mess. Still seated upright in a chair was Marin's sister. She had received the brunt of the bullets which had blasted through the window. Blood from her snaked toward the door.

"Marin's sister!" said the Civil Guard captain. He felt sick.

"She's Red scum like the rest of them," said Maroto. "There's no need for tears."

Juan called from the next room. "There's an old woman here. She's dead too."

The old, bedridden woman had died because a ricocheting bullet had freakishly spun into her bedroom and smashed through her ribs above the hip.

"We've got one of the gang at any rate," said the Civil Guard captain.

"Precisely," said Renato Maroto icily. "We've got *one!* And if he'd been taken alive, we'd have had the rest of them!"

The men who took away the bodies were inured to unpleasant tasks. They wrapped a cloth around Marin's head, lifted him onto a stretcher and covered him with a sheet. But they were upset by Marin's sister. She had so many bullets in her that she came apart in their hands.

Nothing was published in the newspapers about the incident and it was some days before Miguel Barras learned from underground contacts how Marin had died.

"The Spanish Civil Guards are murderers," he told his comrades fiercely. "Marin and his sister will be avenged."

Señora Cornelia Ledesma was dying.

There was no medical cause. She had lost the will to live. She remained in her room, shut away from the rest of the household, pale, remote and listless. Anselmo tried to comfort her and interest her in everyday events. But she listened to him detachedly, nodded disinterestedly and quietly faded.

She became so weak she couldn't lift her head from her pillow to take nourishment. Pilar and Antonia came from Madrid and spent their days at her side. Manolo, the youngest son, now a student in Barcelona, came home.

Rafael also came.

He swaggered home in his officer's uniform, his riding boots gleaming and his uniform ablaze with medals. He came as a duty, to attend the funeral of his mother and to claim his share of the dwindling estate.

With her family at her side, Cornelia Ledesma died quietly during the night, passing away as gently as a light breeze.

Teresa called to pay her respects, saw the calm, serene features that now knew peace, and cried unashamedly.

Anselmo, dressed in mourning, stood stiffly erect, and received friends and relatives.

"I'm sorry, Anselmo," Teresa choked. It was their first contact in months.

"Thank you, Teresa." His eyes were moist.

Teresa joined the other women. The older women recalled when Ledesmas were lighthearted and gay, remembered the garden parties and barbecues with Cornelia presiding.

The house filled up as more sympathizers called. Silvana wore a black dress and a suitably sad expression, but she had been too lazy to put on black stockings. Her plump white calves and bedroom slippers aroused the resentment of many.

Pilar and Antonia were red-eyed and deeply moved, but Rafael stood apart, smiling sardonically.

Father Delbos and the choirboys lined up outside the house, and pallbearers carried the coffin down to the hearse. The funeral procession set off and all the men of the village walked bareheaded behind the coffin, to the church and then to the cemetery.

The women remained in the house to cry, to comfort each other, to talk reverently about Cornelia Ledesma and to prepare the food and wine for the returning men.

Pilar and Antonia cut the meat and chickens which had been cooked the night before. Teresa helped, making sandwiches and setting out glasses.

Teresa was alone in the kitchen when Anselmo entered. He crossed to the kitchen range, where so often his mother had cooked before the blazing fire, rested his arm and his forehead on the chimney and cried uncontrollably.

Teresa went to him. He held her tightly, his head on her shoulder. "My God, Teresa," he choked. "My mother. My *mother!*"

She pressed him to her.

"I loved her," he whispered brokenly. "I loved her."

"I loved her too, Anselmo," she whispered.

"Yes," he whispered. "We both loved her."

Rosalia had no appointment that evening so she showered leisurely and dressed slowly, admiring herself in her mirror.

Outside, she hailed a taxi and directed it to one of the most fashionable restaurants in Barcelona. She caused a minor sensation as she swept into the restaurant, her platinum hair tumbling down over her shoulders.

But Rosalia was accustomed to being stared at. She walked to her table with queenly aloofness, allowed the headwaiter to take her coat and seated herself with confident grace. When the waiter hurried away with her order, she glanced around the restaurant, coldly indifferent to those watching her.

After she had eaten, Rosalia rose and walked the length of the restaurant to the lounge. She wore a tight-fitting black dress and was aware her movements were being watched admiringly. She settled in a low armchair, gathered her skirt around her and ordered coffee and brandy from a waiter. Rosalia glanced around her as she reached into her bag for her cigarette holder. After a time, she became aware of the man.

There was always a man.

This one stared more intently than did the others. Once, when she glanced toward him casually, his face lighted up eagerly. He would probably be the one, she decided, as she blew a thin plume of smoke toward the ceiling.

She had only a vague idea what the man looked like. But then, she never really saw any of them.

The waiter brought her a note. The man invited her to drink with him.

She glanced toward him and smiled. When the waiter set the drink before her, she gestured that he should join her.

The man sat opposite her and said the usual things; that she was attractive, looked intelligent and that her dress was charming. She said the usual things too, smiled at his comments, occasionally gave a low chuckle and preened herself so that he could study the firm thrust of her breasts.

The man was shy so she raised the subject herself when he casually mentioned that everything was so expensive these days.

"Especially me," she smiled.

"How expensive?" he asked, emboldened by her bluntness. She told him.

"It's too much," he protested.

She shrugged her shoulders and looked through him, suddenly remote and disinterested.

"Why so much?" he asked.

"I give *complete* satisfaction. Of course, you'll have to pay for the room too."

"Can't we go to your place?"

Her face hardened. "I never take anybody home."

As soon as they were in the taxi, he forced her knees apart and slid his hand up between her thighs.

She concealed her annoyance. "Don't rush, darling. We've got all night!"

They went to the Green Sanctuary, an expensive *mueble*. The rooming hotels for lovers took great care that their clients could enjoy their adventures in secret. Wealthy businessmen brought their secretaries to these love nests, a man could bring his best friend's wife, or the wife her best friend's husband. Only high-class whores had clients who could afford to spend the night here.

They were allocated a room and the white-jacketed steward escorted them up a wide, carpeted staircase. There was no chance of meeting other clients on the stairs. No one left his room until the steward had made sure that nobody else was around.

The steward opened a door, ushered them inside and checked that all was in order, clean bedsheets turned back, freshly laundered towels. He pocketed his tip with satisfaction. "Will you be staying the night, sir?"

"We will. Bring up a bottle of champagne and some glasses."

"Very good, sir." The steward smiled. "May I remind you? We ask all guests *not* to leave their rooms without telephoning for a steward to escort you to your car or call a taxi."

"I understand. You'd better bring up some sandwiches with the champagne. How's that, darling?"

She smiled automatically. "Lovely."

The bed was low and wide enough for two couples. The crisp, white linen sheets were monogrammed. The walls and the ceiling were lined with mirrors and a panel of switches at the head of the bed controlled the room lighting. It could be turned from a merciless white blaze to a cozy glow. The background radio music was romantically soothing.

Rosalia was no stranger to the Green Sanctuary. She put her bag on the bedside table, placed her cigarettes and lighter beside the ashtray, checked that the drawer contained tissues and used one of them at once. A smear of lipstick on a shirt collar could arouse the suspicions of a jealous wife.

She threw the stained tissue into a basket and reached for another. She peered into a mirror, arching her eyebrows as she scrubbed them clean, coaxed mascara from her eyelashes and rubbed the coloring from her cheeks.

The man was fascinated, flattered that she was stripping her face for his protection. "You *are* . . . beautiful!" he breathed.

"Make yourself comfortable while I undress, darling."

She posed, stretching her arms above her head and circling her hands gracefully, snapping her fingers like a flamenco dancer.

She unzipped her dress and moved provocatively as she peeled it down over her arms and hips. Her acting was flawless. Her eyes, smile and mock-modesty implied a sensuality he believed she shared with him. She teased him skillfully, unhooking a stocking slowly, peeling the nylon down her shapely thighs. She was unhooking her garter belt, when the steward knocked. She called to him to enter and waited while he placed the champagne and sandwiches on the table. When he left the room she giggled saucily at the man, took off the belt and tossed it to him.

She eased her slip straps off her shoulders and let the black garment fall. She took off her brassiere quickly, knowing that complete exposure brought an end to the teasing. She thrust her breasts at him, laughing joyously as though kneading her nipples into hard prominence gave her exquisite pleasure.

She flipped her filmy pants into his face and giggled girlishly as she posed with legs brazenly astride. He blundered to his feet, his cheeks moist and his eyes gleaming.

"Don't rush, darling. I'll wash while you get ready."

She took a ribbon from her bag and ran into the bathroom. She gathered up her hair, tied it in a ponytail and adjusted the bidet taps to a steady flow of warm water.

He padded into the bathroom and she sensed his moment of surprise when he saw her scarred back. But he made no mention of it as he took the soap from her. "I'll do this, my love."

"Aaayeee!" she whimpered in mechanical ecstasy as he washed her. "Aaaaeeeh!" She leaned back against him, eyes closed, arms hanging limply and his aroused manhood burning against her cool shoulders.

And because she knew his pride would be flattered, she presently whispered: "No more, my love. No more! You'll tire me out!"

She washed him with a matter-of-factness which cooled his passion but as soon as they returned to the bedroom he seized her fiercely. She teasingly twisted away but his hands were strong and his lips whispered down her cheek to her throat. He slobbered when he reached her breast, and she arched away from the inner moistness of his mouth, vaguely hoping that *this* man might have the patience to arouse her. But she was disappointed. All too soon he became compelling and although she used all her skill to prolong his pleasure he was quickly satiated.

Languidly she reached for her cigarette holder and lit up. She blew smoke up at the mirrored ceiling and studied her reflection. She seemed to be looking down on herself with the naked man at her side lying in fetal position.

"How are you, my love?" she asked after a while.

"Wonderful," he murmured. "And you?"

"It's never been so good," she said and watched the secret smile of pleasure which touched his lips.

Presently she tapped the stub of her cigarette from the holder, crossed to the table, poured champagne and carried glasses and sandwiches back to the bed.

She ate and drank with relish but he merely nibbled a sandwich and refused more than one glass of the sparkling wine. She placed the remains of the sandwiches on the table and sat beside him. "How do you feel now?"

"Very happy, satisfied."

She giggled. "You don't look satisfied to me."

"But I am."

"I don't believe it." She touched him. "There. You see?"

"Don't."

She pouted. "I want you."

"I'm longing to awake and find you in my arms!" he said.

"Tonight too!" she urged.

"Darling. I have my limits."

"Not with me." She caressed him.

He became alarmed. "NO!"

"Don't you like it?"

"You're . . . you're wasting your time!"

"Want to bet?" she mocked. "I'm expensive, darling, but I'm worth it."

A little later he was astonished that she had aroused him again and as her gasps of ecstasy synchronized with his own he swelled with masculine pride. After the hammering of his heart had ceased he rolled over on his side and instantly fell asleep.

Rosalia sat up, reached for the glass of champagne and sipped. She fitted another cigarette in her holder and as she lit it she looked down contemptuously at the man.

She would finish the cigarette, she planned, douche, drink a little more champagne and then sleep. She had disposed of the man satisfactorily. Too often in the past she had had her sleep disturbed by the man reaching out for her in the middle of the night. She had learned.

Now the man slept deeply and exhaustedly, his passions so skillfully dispersed that even in the morning he would not be passionate again.

In a plaza just off the Mayor de Gracia a dark-eyed man with silvery streaks in his black hair sat outside a café and moodily sipped brandy. He was at least ten years older than the girl at his side. She had a white, pinched face, strangely burning eyes and thin, colorless lips. They spoke little and when he glanced at his watch and nodded, she got to her feet at once.

She held his arm as they walked along the street and when he saw the distant green light of a cruising taxi, he stepped out into the road and held his hand high.

The taxi took them to the Green Sanctuary.

The man paid off the taxi and as they followed the white-coated steward, the girl looked with shy interest at the gilt-framed pictures on the passage walls, the wine-colored carpeting and the glass teardrop chandeliers which hung from the corridor ceiling.

When they reached the booking desk, the receptionist gave a searching glance at the pale-faced girl who was so obviously embarrassed. He said gently, "We cannot accept guests who are underage. By law a girl must be twenty-five . . ."

"She's twenty-six," said the man gruffly.

The steward sighed. "I do not doubt your word, Señor. But the law requires me to ask for proof . . ."

The girl fumbled in her handbag and pulled out her identity card. The steward was surprised. Her age was twenty-six. She didn't look twenty.

"Thank you, Señorita." He returned the card to the girl and reached for an invoice pad. "Do you require the room for a period or for all night?"

The man glanced at the clock on the wall behind the reception desk. It was two thirty-five A.M. "We'll take it for the night."

The steward totaled the invoices. Cost of room, towels, soap, tips and government tax. "Do you require a condom?"

The man hesitated. "Yes."

The cost was added to the bill which was receipted.

The man paid, thrust the contraceptive into his pocket. As they followed the steward upstairs, the receptionist frowned after them. He was practiced at calculating ages and was surprised he could have been so wrong about this girl.

The steward showed them into the bedroom, pocketed his tip and went away. The man locked the door and relaxed.

The girl put her handbag on the bedside table, took off her coat and smiled wryly. "I felt *terrible!*" she confessed. "I wanted the earth to swallow me up. I know it's *bourgeois* but I can't help my background, can I? I felt . . . ashamed!"

He took off his jacket and threw it over a chair. He crossed to the bed, sat on it and bounced up and down, testing its springs. "Shame is a conditioned bourgois reflex, comrade," he said. "It takes time to escape from conditioning." His voice was patient as though he was bored with giving the same lesson. He kicked off his shoes, lay back, clasped his hands behind his head and stared up at the ceiling. The bright light showed up the wrinkles around his eyes and the hair-line scar which stretched from his cheekbone to the point of the jaw.

"What time is it, comrade?" she asked.

He glanced at his watch. "We've more than an hour. Sleep if you feel tired."

She kicked off her shoes, sat on the bed, drew up her nyloned legs and tucked them under her. "I *couldn't* sleep."

"Too nervous?"

"Too excited."

"Breathe deeply," he said. "Learn to relax."

"When he asked for my identity card I was scared, comrade."

"Don't ever worry about identity cards," he reassured her. "Only an expert can detect that ours are forgeries."

She looked around at the mirrored walls, the chromium-plated bathroom fittings and the erotic symbolism of the furniture. "Have you been here before, Miguel?"

"Twice. I had to study the layout."

"I mean . . . have you ever brought a girl here?"

He hesitated a moment. "Once."

After a while she said softly: "What we're doing is very dangerous, isn't it?"

"I've never pretended otherwise."

"If everything goes wrong we might . . . we might not live through it?"

His dark eyes turned to her.

She looked back calmly.

"Are you afraid?" he asked.

She shook her head. "No, Miguel. I know the risks and I am ready to die for our cause. It's just that in case anything goes wrong, I want you to know I've always admired you, Miguel. So much so that . . . that if you want to make love, I will be happy too."

His black eyes stared at her and into her.

She flushed. "Have I said something . . . bourgeois?"

"No, Maria-Luisa. You're very sweet," he said softly. But when she moved closer to him, he lay quite still.

"Your father was a loyal Party member whom I admired. We fought at the Ebro. I was with him when he died, when the Civil Guard ambushed us in the mountains."

Her eyes burned. "I hate fascism."

He talked on as though she had not interrupted. "Your mother escaped to France with a group of refugees, tugging you along by the hand. That is how I always see you, comrade. As a child who is the daughter of a comrade."

Her cheeks burned.

"Don't be angry," he soothed. "I'm explaining myself. I have always seen you as a child. But tonight you are a woman and I need time to adjust myself to this new idea."

"You don't want me?"

"On the contrary," he said quickly. "I am deeply honored. But I am not a good partner. I am old and scarred in mind and body. Often I feel I am not quite . . . wholesome. There is a hate inside me. I cannot help it. All I have is hate. I've little else to give anyone."

"You are lonely, Miguel, since you lost Catalina. You need a woman at your side."

He stared at her intently.

She said softly: "Miguel, I will try to give you what you need."

He sighed. "This is not the time." His hands clenched into hard fists. "This is the time for hate!"

She watched his face intently. "Yes, Miguel?"

"Afterward, Maria-Luisa . . ." His hand fell back on the bed. "When we have done what must be done . . . later!"

"Yes, Miguel," she said contentedly. She settled herself comfortably and smiled quietly.

At five minutes to four he put on his shoes and jacket and opened his suitcase. He took from it a long-barreled pistol and dropped it into his pocket.

The girl put on her shoes and looked at him.

"Relax," he said. "I'll send for you."

He stepped out into the corridor and made his way to the head of the stairs. When he reached the floor below he met Adolfo. "Nice timing," he said and they went down the next flight to the ground floor.

In the reception office two stewards were playing cards with the receptionist. When they saw the two men they scrambled to their feet and the receptionist said reprovingly: "We ask guests not to leave their rooms unescorted, gentlemen. It can be embarrassing for other guests. There is a telephone and . . ."

Miguel took out his gun. The receptionist's eyes widened and the tip of his tongue moistened his dry lips. The two stewards gaped.

Miguel said softly: "We won't harm you. Cooperate and you'll have no trouble."

Adolfo ran his hands over the stewards. Neither of them was armed. But three long nightsticks hung from leather thongs on the back of the door and Adolfo tucked them under his arm. "These will be useful," he grinned.

Miguel scowled at the receptionist. "A lie will cost your life. How many more of you in the building?"

"Only the relief. He's asleep in the back office."

"Take us there."

The back office was a windowless room with a cot. Miguel ordered the stewards to remove their white jackets, and he and Adolfo put them on.

Miguel asked one steward, "What's your name?"

The man swallowed nervously. "Burgas."

"All right, Burgas. You come with us." He jabbed his gun at the others. "Stay here, keep quiet and you'll stay healthy."

Miguel locked them in the back office and tapped on the door with the barrel of his gun. "Can you hear me?"

"Yes," quavered the receptionist.

"We're going to be around a long time," warned Miguel. "One squeak out of any of you and you get lead!"

Miguel and Adolfo returned with Burgas to the reception office.

"How many rooms are occupied?" demanded Miguel.

Burgas studied the key rack. "Fifteen on the first floor, fourteen on the second and ten on the third."

"Will you get any more callers tonight?"

"It's not probable, but possible," said Burgas. "Perhaps a drunk with a pickup."

"When you're full, how do you indicate it?"

"We turn off the entrance lights over the garages. Then taxis know we've a full house."

"How do you turn the lights off?"

Burgas pointed to the control panel. "That's the switch."

Miguel turned it off and looked up as Greco padded along the carpet toward the office, closely followed by Nolana. Both men carried Sten guns.

"We'll lock the entrance doors, too, Burgas," said Miguel.

The steward's hands shook slightly as he bolted the doors.

"What's the biggest empty room on the second floor?" demanded Miguel.

"They're all the same size."

"Is there one without a window?"

"Room Two-two-two," said Burgas.

They went up to the second floor, the thick carpeting muffling their footsteps. Burgas opened the door and switched on the lights. Miguel glanced around and nodded. "This will do. Now remember. Work quickly but don't run risks by being negligent."

They went down to the ground floor and stopped outside the first occupied room. Obeying Miguel's orders, Burgas inserted his master key and unlocked the door. He looked at Miguel and nodded.

Miguel turned the handle, stepped into the room, switched on the lights and raised his pistol. Adolfo closed the door behind them.

The man stirred, grunted and went on snoring. The girl's eyelids fluttered as she screwed up her eyes against the light.

Adolfo went to the foot of the bed, gripped the sheet that covered them and ripped it down.

The girl sat up, startled into wakefulness. The man groped for the sheet which wasn't there, blinked his eyes and sat up slowly. His face mottled with anger and he tried to cover himself with his hands.

Adolfo grinned savagely and flourished his nightstick. "On your feet, quick," he ordered. "And not a sound!"

The girl's eyes were terrified, her gaze hypnotized by Miguel's pistol. The man said with bravado, "Now what do you think . . . !"

Adolfo swung the nightstick. It cracked against the man's elbow, paralyzing it. "Make a sound and you'll get another," warned Adolfo.

The man hugged his elbow in silent agony.

"Hurry." Adolfo leered at the girl. "You too, big tits. Get moving."

Miguel opened the door so that Adolfo could herd them outside. The girl hung back. "Can't I put something on?"

"It's not cold," grinned Adolfo. He flourished the nightstick and drove them out into the corridor where Nolana was waiting with his Sten gun. His black eyes were so merciless that the naked couple scampered hastily along the corridor in front of him when he gestured. They climbed the stairs to the second floor and into Room Two-two-two where Greco was waiting.

"Stand over there," ordered Greco, pointing with his gun.

The man and the girl crossed the room and stood in a corner. The man rubbed his bruised elbow and the girl swallowed as though about to burst into tears.

"Don't make a noise," warned Greco. "Otherwise . . ." He grinned viciously and swung his gun, spraying the room with invisible bullets.

"Those rings," said Greco, slitting his eyes. "Put them on that table."

Tears filled her eyes. "It's . . . my wedding ring."

"Put it on the table."

"But . . . please. What shall I tell my husband?"

"Tell him the truth."

She was furious then. She stalked to the table, pulled the rings off her fingers and flung them down. One bounced to the carpet.

"Pick it up," said Greco ominously.

His tone frightened her and she stooped for it quickly. Her buttocks were too much of a temptation for Greco. He booted her, sending her sprawling on her face. She scrambled up and flashed him a glance of hatred.

"Now the earrings," said Greco.

She took them off and threw them down.

"Back in the corner," ordered Greco. He leered at the man. "Your ring now."

The man rubbed his elbow and glowered sullenly as he pulled off his ring.

Nolana rejoined Miguel and Adolfo. They had entered a second room and aroused its occupants. Adolfo's swinging nightstick drove them out into the corridor and Nolana herded the naked couple upstairs.

Steward Burgas was cooperative. He had received one clout on the kneecap from Adolfo's nightstick and wanted no more. He unbolted the doors with his master key, turned the door handle, switched on the lights, and stepped to one side so that Miguel and Adolfo could do their work. Couple after couple were herded upstairs by Nolana.

Maria-Luisa and the other girls now played their parts. They ransacked the vacated bedrooms, searched clothing, wallets and handbags and packed money and jewelry into their large handbags.

When Rosalia was awakened, she was so sleep-drugged that she was only vaguely aware of two threatening figures. She thought it was a police raid, checking for girls underage. The man was sleepily befuddled. He whimpered when the nightstick cracked against his shin. When it dawned upon Rosalia that the intruders were thieves she was relieved. The contents of her handbag was all they could steal. She had left her expensive jewelry at home and her savings under the mattress.

It wasn't until she was being herded through the door that she saw the man with the pistol clearly. She recognized the long jaw and flashing eyes. She gasped. "Miguel. You're Miguel!"

His black eyes glittered and the gun jabbed. "Shut your mouth and keep moving!"

Adolfo swung the nightstick and she hurried out. But she dared to glance back at Miguel. His stance was so familiar that she could picture him on the beach outside his father's cottage, trousers rolled up to show his bare, brown legs. It *was* Miguel Barras, she realized with amazement as she was herded along the corridor.

Miguel and Adolfo steadily worked their way up to the second floor. Only one man showed any resistance. He leaped for his jacket where he kept a revolver. Adolfo brought him down in midleap with a cracked skull and he was led semiconscious, to join the others menaced by Greco's Sten gun.

One couple was surprised bathing and were herded along the corridor coated with lather.

Miguel found the man he was looking for on the third floor.

He was fifty-five, bald, athletically slim and with clean-cut aristocratic features. His eyes blazed as he sat up in bed and glared at the intruders.

The girl was about twenty-five. She had a voluptuous figure and a simple peasant face. On the bedside table there was a little mound of bracelets and rings.

Miguel told Adolfo: "Get Nolana."

Nolana came in and covered the pair in bed with his gun. Adolfo took out a camera.

"Move over," Miguel told the man. "I want the two of you side by side."

The girl grinned foolishly. Her sleep-drugged mind didn't yet feel fear. She moved over and embraced the man. He shrugged her away. "This is an outrage!" he stormed.

The nightstick bounced off his elbow and his face turned pale.

"Snuggle up," said Adolfo through his teeth.

The man glared.

The nightstick fell and the man cried out.

"Snuggle up," said Adolfo.

The man leaned against the girl.

"Put your arm around her. Good. Now hold her breast."

The man hesitated.

Adolfo gently swung the nightstick and the man obeyed.

"You, girl," ordered Adolfo. "Get hold of him. You know how."

The girl's eyes showed only mild surprise and her audience did not deter her.

"That's fine," said Adolfo. "Hold it."

He took three flashlight photographs before he put away the camera.

The man glared. "Why do you want those photographs?"

"Blackmail," said Adolfo and grinned.

"You'll be sorry. You won't get away with it."

"Cry for me when I start to be sorry," grinned Adolfo.

"I'll wait here," said Miguel. "You and Nolana finish up quickly and come back."

Miguel held the nightstick in one hand and his pistol in the other. He flourished the nightstick threateningly every time they moved.

"I'll remember you," said the man. "I could pick your face out from a million."

"Shut up," said Miguel wearily.

The girl asked: "Are you going to steal my jewelry?"

"Yes."

"I've a diamond brooch of sentimental value. It belonged to my mother. I'll willingly pay ten times its value not to lose it."

"We'll come to an arrangement," said Miguel bleakly.

"Thank you," she breathed gratefully.

"Why do you want a man old enough to be your father?" asked Miguel curiously.

She giggled. "He's . . . sweet."

"But he's . . . old!" said Miguel. He was thinking of himself and Maria-Luisa.

"That's why he makes love so nicely. He's experienced!" She giggled again and her breasts quivered.

Presently Adolfo returned. "All finished," he reported.

Miguel said: "Tie them up." He gestured to the man. "You first. Stand over there facing the wall."

The man hesitated until the nightstick swung. He walked to the wall and faced it.

"Kneel down."

He knelt awkwardly because of a war-wounded hip.

"Hands behind your back." Adolfo tied them swiftly with one of the girl's stockings.

"Now you," Miguel ordered the girl.

Placidly she rolled off the bed and joined the man. Her ample breasts quivered and she smiled, pleased that men were watching her nakedness.

"Kneel down and hands behind you."

She knelt and Adolfo tied the stocking with a big bow.

"Foreheads against the wall," ordered Miguel.

They obeyed him and Miguel took a quick step forward and locked his fingers in the man's hair. In the last split second the man knew what was going to happen. He had seen it done before. He tried to rise to his feet but the barrel of Miguel's pistol pressed against the bone behind his ear and as the man strained his head away, Miguel pulled the trigger. He saw the girl's astonished eyes staring at him, released the man and locked his fingers in her hair. The upturned eyes and their surprise made him turn away her head before he pulled the trigger.

The man died instantly but the girl still breathed. Miguel fired again and this time she died.

The girl's handbag was turned out on to the bed. Her identity card was placed prominently on her pillow with her jewelry. The man's identity card was placed on his pillow, and to show that robbery was not the motive for the crime nothing belonging to the couple was taken.

Miguel and Adolfo returned to the second floor where the other guests were prisoners. They were cold and tired of standing. They were afraid too because they had heard the muffled shots. They eyed Miguel apprehensively.

He said quietly: "We had to shoot a couple who made trouble. They're in Room Three-four-four. Be warned. We're not leaving yet!" He nodded at Greco. "I need you now."

Adolfo swept up the jewelry on the table and stuffed it into his pockets. He winked at the prisoners and sauntered out after Miguel and Greco. They locked steward Burgas in with his clients.

Their four women companions were waiting in the reception office with their handbags bulging.

"Ready to go?" asked Adolfo.

Miguel nodded. Adolfo picked up the telephone. When a voice answered he glanced at his wristwatch. "Ready in ten minutes." He replaced the receiver.

They waited. The minutes ticked past slowly. Miguel's face was set like stone and Adolfo watched him slyly.

Adolfo glanced at his watch. "It's time."

They unbolted a door, passed through into a garage and out into the gray dawn. Just inside the entrance gates two cars were waiting. Four hours later they were all sound asleep in a barn only two hours climb from a mountain pass leading to France.

The murdered man was an influential politician. He was a pillar of the Church, a leading light in the new Spain, and his wife was related to one of Spain's aristocratic families.

The public would have been shocked to learn that he had slipped away from Madrid to spend a night in a Barcelona *mueble*. It would prove depravity in high places and give anti-Franco agitators a propaganda weapon.

But much more dangerous to the regime was the identity of the girl. She was the daughter of a wealthy family prominent in Spanish society. She was related to royalty and was the niece of an ambassador. Many town and village streets bore her grandfather's name, and she was married to a young member of the government. It would rock Spanish society to learn that she had an elderly lover.

A third factor turned the incident into dynamite. The girl was the wife of the older man's *son!*

Renato Maroto destroyed all evidence of the girl's identity and ordered her body to be removed to the mortuary. It was recorded that she was found in the park behind a clump of bushes with a suicide gun in her hand. She was entombed namelessly. Her husband and relatives would search for her unsuccessfully. In time she would become another of those cases of the inexplicably missing.

The man's body was sent to an undertaker and prepared for a journey to Madrid with all pomp and splendor. According to Renato Maroto's fiction, he died a hero. Singlehanded, he fought murderous criminals he discovered engaged in a robbery and died bravely . . . as he had lived.

A carefully worded news report was issued, Civil Guards who may have seen too much were promoted and transferred to distant districts, and a campaign against Soviet Russia and its unscrupulous criminal agents was launched.

Renato Maroto should have been congratulated but there was a brittleness in the Old Man's voice when he spoke to him from Madrid.

"You have shown great initiative, Maroto. *Great* initiative! But initiative in preventing scandal is not your basic task."

"I understand that," agreed Maroto tautly. He wanted to hurl the telephone across the room.

"Get those men, Maroto. Have no mercy. I don't care *how* you do it . . . get them!"

Maroto was still writhing from the memory of that conversation when the guard unlocked the door of the interrogation room. Maroto stepped across the threshold and the guard shut the door behind him.

The girl slumped on the chair looked up at him with weary, dark-ringed eyes.

He hunched over her, holding his head to one side.

"Your name?"

There was infinite weariness in her voice. "Again! Can't I go home and answer more questions tomorrow. I'm exhausted."

"You'll answer *now*," he said.

She sighed. "Rosalia Prada."

"What do you do?"

She hesitated. "I'm . . . I have independent means."

His long neck craned over her. "I asked what you do."

She said wearily: "I have men friends who give me presents."

"Why do they give you presents?"

She showed a flash of anger. "Lots of men give presents to girls."

"You're a whore," he said flatly.

"All right."

"Now tell me what you are."

"What is this?" she flared. "Music hall comedy? You know what I am!"

"I want to hear *you* tell me," he said softly. "Or are you too ashamed?"

"I'm ashamed of nothing," she flared. "All right. You want to hear it? I'm a whore. A *whore!* Do you hear that? I'm a *whore!*"

He sighed. "I finally got you to make a truthful statement. I hope I won't have as much trouble with the rest of your answers."

She glowered.

"You don't realize the seriousness of your position"—he glanced at the card in his hand—". . . Rosalia." He put one hand in his pocket and toyed with something. "You are a whore," he said flatly. "You should know that girls in moral danger are sent to a correction center for moral reeducation."

Rosalia's face became an expressionless mask. She had heard tales of correction centers.

"We rounded up a batch of girls last week and sent them away," he said casually. He cocked his head on one side. "Do you know about correction centers, Rosalia? They shave your head. No pretty under-clothing. Just a rough canvas smock. And all day long you scrub floors. Your knees grow callused, your nails break and your hands swell. The food's adequate but the girls burn up so much energy that they lose their curves. No man will look at them when they come out."

Rosalia stared up at him.

"You don't want to go to a correction center, do you, Rosalia?"

She slowly shook her head.

"I didn't hear you."

"No," she said loudly.

"All right. Now let's get ahead more quickly. You have scars on your back?"

"Yes."

"Let me see them."

She unhooked her dress, eased it off her shoulders and hunched her back.

"I want to see the scars," he said tonelessly.

"They're the fine, white lines."

"I can't see them properly."

She gave him a hard stare. "You want me to take my dress off?"

"Yes."

She pushed her dress down over her hips and stepped out of it. She pulled the hem of her petticoat up under her armpits.

His voice was toneless. "I can't see them clearly."

She turned to face him, her eyes bitter. "You want me to strip?"

"I want to see the scars."

Nudity meant nothing to her. She removed her clothing and stood with her back to him, wearing only shoes and stockings. She grew impatient of waiting while he studied her and said in exasperation: "What are you doing? Counting the stripes?"

"Who did it?" he asked.

"A lover I had when I was young."

"Why did he do it?"

"He found me with . . . another."

"And then what happened?"

She answered glibly because it was the story she had told many times: "He ran away and joined the army. He was killed."

"You may sit down."

She reached for her clothing.

"You can dress later."

She sat down, watching him curiously, already resigned to accepting him as a lover and wondering how she could turn it to her advantage.

He asked quietly: "Who is Miguel?"

She froze. Panic leaped inside her. She had answered all her interrogator's questions but had made no voluntary statement. She realized the man had not only told about her scarred back but also how Miguel's name had escaped her when she recognized him. She said in disgust: "That big mouth!"

"Is that how you insult a patriot?" he said softly.

"I made a mistake," she said. "I thought I recognized one of the men. But it wasn't him."

"A mistake?" he said gently.

"Yes."

He reached out and she tensed, expecting to be hurt but instead he gently rolled her nipple with his finger and thumb until the stimulation made it stand out starkly. "Who is this man?"

"I . . . er . . . I can't remember where I last saw him."

"You can't?" he said gently. He brought his other hand out from his pocket and she saw the pliers. She watched the open jaws draw closer and shuddered.

"You're not afraid, are you, Rosalia? Only traitors to the State and those who obstruct authority need have fear."

The pliers held her nipple.

"What shall I do, Rosalia? Apply pressure and squash flat? Or twist and tug like pulling a tooth?"

She was petrified.

"Tell me about Miguel," he said gently.

Her voice was husky. "His name is Miguel Barras. He lived near me in Escoleras." Words poured out in a torrent.

He interrupted. "That will do." He squeezed gently with the pliers and she arched forward grasping his wrist.

"All right." He dropped the pliers into his pocket. "Let me see it."

She whimpered and showed him her bruised flesh.

"Stop fussing. I didn't even draw blood. Get dressed."

When she was ready he took her out of the building and flagged down a taxi. He handed her into it and climbed in after her.

"Tell the driver," he said.

"Where . . . where are we going?"

"Your apartment."

She shrank into her corner, unutterably weary and with her breast aching. She was willing to do whatever he wanted.

They reached her apartment building, and he waited while she paid the driver. There were power failures every day in Barcelona, but they were lucky and the elevator took them up to the fourth floor. She opened the door of her apartment and he followed her inside, looked around and nodded approvingly.

Her apartment was her refuge from her public way of life. She had furnished it expensively. Here was home, where she could be completely herself. Apart from workmen, Maroto was the first man to enter it.

He scowled as he browsed around. He opened drawers, upended their contents onto the floor and stirred them with the toe of his shoe while Rosalia watched with dismay.

He turned out the living room and kitchen and in the bedroom found the wooden box hidden in the wardrobe under her shoes.

"The key," he demanded.

She took the key from her purse.

He opened the box and examined the necklaces and brooches, bangles and earrings. "It's profitable being a whore," he said coldly. He locked the box and tossed it back into the wardrobe.

"What . . . what are you looking for?" she ventured timidly.

"Anything that's interesting."

He found her savings, notes of large denomination, wrapped in brown paper and thrust away under the mattress. He riffed through the wad, grunted and replaced it in its hiding place. "How long did that take to earn?"

"Since I came to Barcelona. I was nineteen then."

He nodded, took off his jacket, slung it across a chair and flopped down on her bed. He cushioned his hands under his head and the heels of his shoes soiled the delicate handmade lace covering on the bed. "This room's seen action!" he said and chuckled.

She stared down at him expressionlessly. "This is my private apartment. I never bring anyone here."

"I'm here," he said.

"Please be careful with your shoes. You're tearing the cover."

"You mean . . . like this?" He snagged his heel in the open lacework, ripped and laughed at her pained expression. "Take my shoes off."

She sat on the foot of the bed and drew off his shoes.

"A nice place," he said approvingly.

She said nothing.

"I'm tired of living in a boardinghouse. This will suit me fine."

She was numb with dismay.

"How are you at cooking?"

"Very bad."

"You'll learn."

Her shoulders drooped.

"Don't just sit there," he said. "You know why I'm here."

Tiredly she reached behind her and unhooked her dress.

"What's the matter?" he asked after a while.

"I'm tired. No sleep last night and I've been interrogated all day."

"You can do better than this!"

"I'm doing my best."

"It's a lousy best for an expensive whore. Relax and leave everything to me."

She feared she might fall asleep while he amused himself with her.

But his hands were a soothing rhythm and sleepiness became dreaminess, his knowing touch invading until abruptly she was sharply aware of her alerted pleasure. She had never known anything like it. Every pleasure nerve responded to the rhythm of his hands. Never before had she had a lover patient enough to arouse such sensations. He brought her to the brink of frenzy and she cried out, drove her nails into his shoulders and jerked convulsively until the tempest slowly died and became peace.

"Happy?" he asked.

"I . . . it's never been like that before."

"Do you love me?" There was a mocking note in his voice that rang alarm bells.

"I like you when you're making love."

He chuckled. "Don't be so sure. I'll pleasure you until you're in heaven, at first. Then I'll ration you until you'll do anything I want."

"You conceited bastard."

She felt his hands on her and stiffened to ignore his caress. But she was aroused again until she clung to him fiercely.

A little later he took her bruised nipple between finger and thumb and twisted until she moaned.

"Tell me more about Miguel Barras," he urged.

The Civil Guards came for Teresa just after lunch.

"The captain would like to see you at headquarters."

Teresa was checking stock. "I'm busy now," she explained. "I'll come down within an hour or so."

The young guards were embarrassed. "The captain wants to see you *at once*, Señora."

Then she understood. One Civil Guard could bring her a message but two were an escort! "What wicked thing have I done? Am I arrested?" She chuckled.

They were shocked. "You're not arrested, Señora."

"Wait a minute while I comb my hair."

They allowed her to walk ahead of them to the Civil Guard headquarters, but as soon as she entered the vestibule she sensed trouble.

Captain Romero was worried. He bowed formally. "Thank you for coming, Señora."

Teresa knew the sergeant and most of the Civil Guards quite well. During their long, weary hours of patrolling they often dropped in at her hotel and could count on a sandwich and a drink. Now they eyed her anxiously.

"What's the trouble, Captain?" she asked.

"There's . . . there's somebody from Barcelona to see you. Come this way, please."

She followed him along a corridor. He knocked on a door and ushered her inside to meet a tall, thin man with a long, dark face. "Señora Teresa Coruna?" he asked.

"That's right."

"All right, Captain." When the captain closed the door behind him, Maroto locked it and dropped the key in his pocket. He turned to face Teresa and stood with his head cocked to one side, scrutinizing her intently. "Police," he said and turned back the lapel of his jacket to show a small badge. He pointed to a wooden chair.

"Sit down."

Teresa perched on the edge of the chair and looked up at him curiously. "Is there trouble?"

"No," he said gently. "Just a few questions. You have a brother . . . Miguel Barras?"

Her eyes lit up. "You have news of him?"

Maroto took a blown-up photograph of Miguel from his pocket. He had found its original in the Admiralty files with Miguel's application for a fishing license. Teresa said at once, "Yes. That's Miguel."

More than thirty witnesses had identified the photo despite its being twenty years old.

Maroto returned the photo to his pocket. "Where is your brother now?"

Teresa was dismayed. "Don't you know? I thought you had news of him."

"How did he get the scar on his face?" he countered.

"He was wounded . . ." Teresa broke off. "None of us has seen Miguel for many years."

"You know about the scar?"

She was puzzled by his manner. "I was told by friends who met him."

"You've heard of Scarface?"

"You mean the bank robber . . . the murderer?"

"I mean Miguel Barras, your brother!"

She was incredulous. Gentle Miguel, so slow-thinking and placid

. . . a bank robber! It was impossible. She knew only that he had turned Communist, had been in the Steel Corps, and had retreated to France to carry on the war.

"When did you last see him?"

"Before the war. He enlisted and we haven't heard from him since."

"How about your Catalan friends who bring you his messages?"

"Tell me who they are," she asked quietly. "I'd like to meet them."

"They are scum who hide him when he crosses the border, traitors who conspire with him to destroy their country."

"I know nothing of Miguel. Tell me where he is and I will talk to him and learn the truth."

"The truth!" he sneered. "The truth from a ruthless murderer who kills, tortures, steals and rapes." Maroto lashed himself into a fury. "Scarface and his followers are monsters. They destroy and defile everything that's good and decent. Only when they are buried will Spain know peace."

She turned pale, shocked by the accusations.

"And you will help me to trap him," he said.

"I can't believe . . ."

"You will answer my questions?"

She nodded bleakly.

"Tell me who brought you his messages."

"We've had no messages from Miguel."

The blow was totally unexpected. His knuckles hurled her to the floor. Half-dazed she got to her knees and stared stupidly at the red drops falling on the mosaic tiles.

He gathered up her long hair, wound it around his hand and strained her head back until her eyes looked into his.

"Listen, you Red whore. I'll get the truth if I have to tear you apart."

"I can only tell you what I know," she whispered.

"You'll tell me . . . everything!" he said grimly.

Juan Prenga was the only Catalan Civil Guard in Escoleras. He hovered in the corridor and heard Teresa's cry of pain. He hurried to the vestibule where Captain Romero was talking to the sergeant and reported breathlessly: "She cried out, Captain."

Captain Romero scowled. "This is not our affair," he said bleakly. "It's out of our hands." Then he stared thoughtfully at Juan Prenga and said deliberately: "Take a couple of hours off, Prenga. You may have friends you want to talk to."

"Thank you, Captain," said Juan Prenga and hurried away.

He went to his good friend, Enrique Godes, and talked to him earnestly. Godes got out his bicycle and pedaled along the dusty road to the Marvista Hotel. Narcissus was entering accounts in the ledgers and was astonished to learn that Teresa was at Civil Guard headquarters. "What's it about?" he asked.

Godes hurried him to the door. "Nobody knows," he said. "But it's the secret police from Barcelona!"

"I'll go and . . ."

"No," said Godes. He tightened his grip on Narcissus's arm. "First get the priest. You've got to have somebody with some standing to back you."

Father Delbos was sleepily relaxed after a well-cooked lunch and good wine. He was irritated by the visit of Narcissus and Godes. "What is it?" he snapped.

Narcissus said: "If you please, Father . . ."

Enrique Godes broke in: "It's about the wife of Narcissus. The police from Barcelona are interviewing her. Narcissus wishes to be present and asks you to intervene, Father, so his request may be granted."

Father Delbos eyed them slyly while his thoughts raced. He burned for an appointment in Barcelona. If he interfered with the Barcelona police, word of it might spread and prejudice his hopes of a transfer. He scowled at Narcissus. "When did you last come to church?"

Narcissus gulped. "Since the tourist season began, Father, we've been very busy and . . ."

"I'm sure the police have good reasons for what they do," snapped Father Delbos. "Also it is quite improper to disturb me during my meditation period." He wiped the back of his hand across his moist forehead. "Don't ever worry me again at this hour." He shut the door in their faces.

Narcissus was furious but Enrique Godes was tugging his arm. "Doctor Aldo," he urged. "We've got to find Doctor Aldo."

"But it's the duty of a priest . . ." argued Narcissus.

"We can do without him," panted Godes. "Hurry!"

Doctor Aldo was lancing a fisherman's finger which had been infected by a rusty fishing hook. While he bandaged, Godes talked and

while the doctor washed his hands Godes had a chance to whisper:
"They're beating her up!"

Doctor Aldo's face was set as he hurried along the street with Narcissus and Godes. They went to the town hall where Roca, the new mayor, and Conill, the justice of the peace, were brooding over a disputed land title. Doctor Aldo spoke to them without Narcissus hearing and with grave faces they set off to Civil Guard headquarters.

Already the news had spread magically and a large, sullen crowd had gathered outside the headquarters while Civil Guards stood at the entrance doors trying to look unconcerned.

The deputation, headed by the mayor, Doctor Aldo, Conill, Narcissus and Godes, strode purposefully up to the Civil Guards who saluted and parted to allow them through. In the vestibule, Captain Romero hurried to meet them.

"What's the trouble, Captain?" asked the mayor.

The captain spread his hands. "It's the secret police from Barcelona."

"They've got her in there?" The mayor nodded along the corridor.

"Yes. There's only one man."

"We want to see him, Captain."

The captain scowled. "My orders are not to disturb him under any circumstances."

"I'll accept all responsibility, Captain."

"I've been given my orders. You can't relieve me of that responsibility, Señor Roca."

Doctor Aldo pushed forward. "Teresa Coruna is my patient. Excessive nervous strain can make her seriously ill. I insist that this officer from Barcelona is warned of it."

"As justice of the peace I must be informed about every infringement of the law in the area under my jurisdiction," said Conill grimly. "I must remind you, Captain, that I am appointed by the governor of the province."

Captain Romero smiled with relief. "In these circumstances, gentlemen, I *must* comply with your wishes." He led them along the corridor and knuckled the door loudly. Maroto called sharply: "What is it?"

"A deputation wishes to see you and Señora Coruna. It's the mayor, the justice of the peace and the doctor. Señora Coruna's health may be endangered."

There was a pause. "Tell them to come back later," said Maroto.

"They insist that they see Señora Coruna at once." The captain moistened his lips. "A large crowd has gathered outside . . . we want to avoid public unrest."

There was a long silence. Then Maroto said quietly: "Very well, Captain." The key turned in the lock and Maroto stood on the threshold, his dark face sullen and his black eyes smoldering. "I'm to be snarled up in red tape, am I, gentlemen?" he said bitterly. "Murderers escape so that you can uphold the letter of the law!"

Narcissus choked: "Teresa!"

She appeared behind Maroto, swaying. Her hair was disheveled, the bruise on her cheek had half-closed her eye and blood trickled from the corner of her mouth. Her blouse was torn and a shoulder strap was snapped.

They stared at her in shocked silence. Then Narcissus sprang at Maroto. They went down together, Narcissus hitting out wildly. Captain Romero and Enrique Godes fought to pull the enraged Narcissus away and Civil Guards came running to hold him.

Maroto got to his feet, scowling.

"I'll kill you," panted Narcissus, struggling furiously. "I'll kill you!"

Captain Romero took Maroto by the arm and urged him along the corridor toward the rear of the building. "Let's talk this over and see if we can handle it differently," he soothed.

"Are you all right, Teresa?" Doctor Aldo asked anxiously.

She held her breast. "He hurt me a little."

"If you wish, Teresa," said Conill, "we'll prepare an official complaint and take statements from witnesses."

The doctor and the mayor frowned and shook their heads quickly, advising against it.

"It's up to you, Teresa," said Doctor Aldo.

She tried to smile.

"What was it all about, Teresa?" asked Mayor Roca.

"My brother, Miguel," she said slowly. "They say he's . . . Scarface!"

7

The Civil Guards patrolling the foothills of the Pyrenees were doubled, strict discipline was enforced, and day-and-night vigil was kept.

Two Civil Guards first saw the man through their binoculars. He trudged over the loose, dry soil of the vineyards and they studied the direction in which he was heading and circled around in front to wait for him. One guard concealed himself behind a clump of bushes and his companion stood out in the open. "I can see him clearly now," he said. "I don't recognize him as from around these parts."

"I'll keep him covered."

The man trudged on and when he saw the Civil Guard his stride didn't falter. He wore a faded blue shirt, black corduroy trousers and rope-soled *alpargatas*. He greeted the Civil Guard in Catalan.

"Bon día."

"Can't you speak Spanish?"

"Esclar que sí. Buenas días. Can you understand me now?"

"Papers," demanded the Civil Guard.

The man raised his eyes to heaven in mute disgust and drew out his identity papers from his breast pocket. The Civil Guard scrutinized them. They were quite in order. The man lived in a small village some five miles away and had received permission to travel to Figueras. The guard returned his papers. "Where are you going?"

"To Figueras."

"For what purpose?"

"To buy seed."

"You intend walking?"

"I missed the bus. But if I walk to a highway I may get a lift."

The guard gestured. "All right. Carry on."

The man grinned slyly. *"Bon día,"* he said in Catalan.

The guard scowled after him. He called sharply: "Just a minute."

The man stopped and half turned. He still grinned.

"What's that in your back trousers pocket?"

"Food. A hunk of bread and a piece of sausage meat."

"Let me see it," said the guard.

"You won't make me go hungry, will you, *Guardia?*"

"Let me see it."

The man shrugged his shoulders and thrust his hand into his pocket. He pulled out a black object, leveled it and fired so casually that the guard knew no danger until lead smashed into his chest.

With one burst of his tommygun the guard concealed in the bushes brought down the killer. He ran to him and stood over him trembling with anger. Only obedience to orders, hammered into him again and again, that such men must be taken alive, stayed his finger on the trigger.

The Civil Guard died before he reached the hospital. His killer was badly wounded, his legs smashed and the tendons severed. He was taken to Barcelona, his wounds were treated and a blood transfusion given. While he was recovering from the anesthetic, witnesses filed past him, studied his pale features and unhesitatingly identified him as a Scarface accomplice. He was removed to a private room and two plainclothes policemen guarded him day and night. A news flash was released that an unidentified man had fought a gun duel with a Civil Guard and both had died after admission to hospital.

Some days later when the man was stronger, Renato Maroto visited him. He visited him every day, steadily extracting more and more information. And each day when Maroto left, Greco wept, not only for his own suffering but for the comrades he had betrayed.

Renato had telephoned that he would arrive early for dinner and while Rosalia basted the roasting chicken a thoughtful frown wrinkled her forehead. She closed the oven door, went to her bedroom and took out her savings. The postman had just delivered a bill for the quarter's rent and she was shocked to find that she had only just enough to pay it.

It was amazing how swiftly her savings had dwindled away. Renato liked to eat well and food was expensive. He also liked whiskey which was a prohibitive price. She had no income now. When Renato had first moved in with her she had tried to keep going but he had so often made her stay home and disappoint her regulars that she had lost them all. She didn't regret it. The thought of other men now filled her with revulsion. But Renato was so unpredictable. He always expected her to be on hand when he needed her, but once she had waited three days and nights without a word from him. Then he had arrived as though he had just stepped out for a packet of cigarettes. The previous week he had brought back a slip of a girl with terrified eyes and had insisted that Rosalia watch him make love to her. She had been sickened and angry.

Rosalia took out her jewels, calculated what she had paid for them and was reassured that she had reserves to depend on until she could summon the courage to ask Renato to contribute to the household expenses.

Renato was in a vile mood when he arrived home. She scurried around anxiously, serving the dinner and trying to appease his bad temper. She opened a bottle of excellent wine and this mellowed him. By the time she had got him seated in his comfortable armchair with black coffee, an overgenerous tot of whiskey and a Havana cigar, he was feeling better.

She washed up quickly, took off her apron, prettied herself and went to him. "More whiskey, darling?"

"All right."

She poured.

"More coffee?"

"No."

"Do you want more ice?"

"No."

"Why were you bad-tempered, darling?"

He scowled. "Inefficiency makes me angry." He shrugged. "It doesn't matter. I couldn't have got much more out of him."

Her face became impassive.

"He managed to steal a small plate off his dinner tray," said Maroto disgustedly. "He broke it under the bedclothes and cut his wrists. With two trained policemen in the room all the time, mark you. Yet they noticed *nothing* until the blood soaked through the mattress and dripped on the floor. By then it was too late!"

"He must have had a great wish to die," she said quietly.

"Naturally. That was why he was being watched."

She sighed. "You frighten me, Renato."

He chuckled. "Sit down?"

She placed a cushion at his feet and half-sat, half-knelt on it, resting her arm on his thighs and her chin on her clasped hands.

He tapped an inch of white ash from his cigar. "I didn't tell you what I did to him yesterday."

Her face was pale. "Don't tell me, Renato. *Please* don't tell me."

"You're too squeamish."

"I worry about *you*," she said seriously. "You're . . . sadistic!"

He drew on his cigar and considered what she had said. He exhaled blue smoke thoughtfully. "I wonder if I am? I don't derive sexual satisfaction from inflicting pain. But afterward I discover my love-making has been stimulated."

"Must you be cruel, darling? Aren't I stimulating enough?"

"A man likes variety."

She pleaded. "Please, darling. Be nice tonight. I've waited so long."

He reached for his whiskey and sipped it. "It won't be long before we have your friend Scarface."

"He means nothing to me," she said. *"Nothing!"*

"Stimulate me," he suggested. "Stimulate me until I want to give you what *you* want."

Six came through the mountain pass, all Spaniards. Miguel carried the rucksack of explosives to destroy a train viaduct built high across a gorge. In winter it bridged a foaming torrent. Its destruction would sever rail services between France and the Costa Brava and deal a crippling blow to Spain's booming tourist industry.

Adolfo and Nolana carried walkie-talkies and the other three men had Sten guns. Their hideout was a farmhouse belonging to a secret member of their band. They arrived early in the morning and at once rolled themselves up in blankets in their host's hayloft. They were tired by their long trek over the mountains and slept soundly, unaware that their arrival had been observed through powerful telescopes.

Telephone calls were made, ammunition was issued, jeep tanks were filled up and pale-faced Civil Guards shivered in the night air, with fear like a stone in their bellies.

Just after dawn Miguel's host shook his shoulder vigorously. "The Civil Guard," he choked.

Miguel threw off his blankets, snatched up a Sten gun, leaped the stairs and ran to the nearest window. He saw at one glance the hopelessness of their position. The farmhouse was surrounded. Civil Guards' patent-leather tricornes could be glimpsed behind mounds of earth thrown up during the night; in hedgerows, ditches, behind trees and within the shelter of farm outbuildings.

The men looked to Miguel for leadership.

Miguel picked up a shepherd's staff, placed a hat on it and showed it at a window. Glass splintered and plaster spurted from the walls.

Miguel's face was grim. They could be starved out or with artillery the farmhouse could be reduced to rubble.

Miguel said without hesitation: "We've only one chance, comrades. To attack and break through their lines."

Adolfo was pale. "They'll cut us down before we get halfway."

"It's our *only* chance," said Miguel.

"He's right," agreed Nolana. "The longer we wait the more men they can bring up!"

"It's suicide," protested Adolfo.

Miguel stared at him steadily. "Are you afraid to die?"

Adolfo gave a sad smile. "Yes, comrade. Nevertheless . . ."

They armed themselves, each man taking a pistol, a Sten gun, two hand grenades and ammunition.

Miguel placed six hand grenades on the floor. "If we're fearless we've a good chance to break through," he said. "I'm going to open the door. From time to time I'll lob out a hand grenade. They're too far away to be hit but the explosions will worry them.

"The shortest distance between us and *them* is to our right. They're sheltering in a shallow ditch and that's the side we'll attack. I'll lob out three hand grenades at five-minute intervals. Let them get used to it. Then I'll lob out three more, one on top of the other. While they're still exploding we get out through the door . . . fast! Turn right around the house and run for the ditch. Fire short bursts to make them keep their heads down. Once you're over the ditch keep running on into the trees. There's a steep slope down into the valley. Go down it on the seat of your pants. Losing skin off your ass can save your lives. There are pine trees at the bottom of the slope and they'll give shelter along the valley. Make for the railway, cross the tracks and we'll meet in the sidings. Any questions?"

"It's all too clear, comrade."

The man who owned the farmhouse went to the fireplace, took down a crucifix and put it in his pocket. "It's all I've got left of my wife's," he said apologetically. He cast a sad glance around him. "I knew this would happen sometime but it's still sad, leaving your home."

"Don't worry, comrade," Miguel assured him. "Party funds will recompense you."

"How about French papers? Will I get French citizenship?"

"Don't worry, comrade. We'll fix it." Miguel looked around. "Are you ready?"

The men nodded grimly.

"Stand back while I open the door."

After a time the Civil Guards tired of firing into the empty doorway.

The first hand-grenade was lobbed out and exploded close enough to spatter some of the Civil Guards with earth. They poured lead into the open doorway until their gun barrels were hot.

A second hand grenade was lobbed outside and trigger-happy Civil Guards whose nerves were sorely strained fired at windows and doors until their magazines were empty. A haze of smoke hung on the air.

The third hand grenade exploded.

Only a few Civil Guards reacted, firing unenthusiastically through the whirling dust, vaguely wondering why hand grenades were being thrown which could injure nobody.

Miguel nodded grimly at his men and they tensed. The next three hand grenades exploded quickly, one after the other. Earth geysered and smoke swirled thickly.

Miguel went through the door in a fierce leap with the others following. They were deafened, smoke was in their eyes and soil pattered down like rain. They ran around the farmhouse and fanned out, firing as they attacked.

The Civil Guards sheltering in the ditch were taken by surprise. A few fired overexcitedly and then the Sten guns hammered viciously. A raw guard lost his head and fled, spreading panic among his comrades, some of whom followed him and became clear targets for the desperate men.

Miguel and his men ran fast. Already they were more than halfway to the ditch. But the smoke was clearing and now the guards on their flanks could see them. Rifles cracked and tommyguns chattered.

The owner of the farmhouse was the first to go down. He fell like a stone, his Sten gun flying from his hands. The man behind tripped over him and was riddled with lead as he tried to scramble to his feet.

The firing was deafening as Miguel reached the ditch and leaped it. He plunged into the undergrowth beyond, and hurled himself down the steep slope, rolling and sliding. He pounded against rocks, tore through trailing vines and thorn bushes, ripped his flesh and his clothes and came to a stop in the protective screen of the dwarf pine trees. He had kept his grip on his Sten gun and he lay panting, gritting his teeth against the pain of the bullet which had torn through his shoulder. His shirt was blood-soaked and he needed swift medical attention.

There was a crashing through the shrubbery close to him and he raised his Sten gun and aimed it. But it was Adolfo and Nolana. Nolana grinned wolfishly and managed to stand up. Blood soaked his trousers from a wound in the thigh. Adolfo had fallen down the slope. He stared at them unseeingly, the dark blood that ran from his mouth and the gaping wound in his chest showing that he was beyond human aid.

Miguel offered Nolana his good shoulder and they stumbled along the floor of the valley.

They heard orders being shouted across the valley and jeep engines revving up. Police cordons were being thrown up all around them.

Nolana came to a standstill.

"Keep going," growled Miguel.

"Leave me, comrade," said Nolana quietly.

"Don't be a fool. We can make it."

"Look at my leg."

Nolana's boot was full of blood and left a red trail which was easy to follow.

"Sit down, you fool," growled Miguel.

Although he scowled with the pain of his own wound, he ripped open Nolana's trouser-legs, tore off a strip to make a bandage and used a stout twig to apply a tourniquet above a severed artery. "That's the best I can do," panted Miguel.

"Go," said Nolana. His face was pale with pain. "This is the end for me, Miguel. If I move I'll lose more blood. There's a chance you can make it . . . alone!"

"Don't be a fool. I'll help you up."

Nolana was determined. "I'm done. But *you* can make it. You're more important to the cause than any of us."

Miguel glanced all around him and far behind them. The undergrowth crackled as men forced through it.

Nolana patted his Sten gun. "I'll wait and take some of the bastards with me." He raised his clenched fist. "They shall not pass, comrade."

Miguel stared at him unhappily.

"I shit upon your stupidity, comrade," said Nolana. *"Go!"*

Miguel clenched his fist and choked: "They shall not pass!"

He stumbled away without looking back, heading along the valley toward the railway track. When he reached it he limped along beside it until he came to a siding and a gravel quarry. An old steam engine huffed black smoke. There was no sign of the driver and stoker but Miguel found them on the other side of the train, seated on a stack of old ties with napkins spread over their knees.

They stared as though he was an apparition. He gestured threateningly with his gun and, as though in a trance, they stood up and raised their hands above their heads. Their food cascaded to the ground.

"Is this your train?" demanded Miguel.

The driver nodded stupidly.

Miguel backed to the iron steps and climbed up into the cabin, keeping the men covered.

"Come on up."

They climbed up reluctantly.

"Start her up," ordered Miguel. "Take her out on the track."

"I can't do that," protested the engine driver. "It's a single line. I haven't got a clear way until two o'clock."

Miguel turned his face slightly so they could see the hairline scar. "I'm Scarface. Now . . . get this train moving!"

The driver flung a startled glance at the stoker, pulled levers and spun handles. Slowly the train pulled out of the siding. "Give me more steam, Pedro," said the driver.

The stoker opened the furnace door, threw in a shovelful of coal, expertly blocked the flame backlash with the flat of the spade and drove it deep into the coal again.

"Open her out!" ordered Miguel. Sweat ran down his face, pain made his heart hammer, and his thoughts were hazy, as though he was drunk.

"We have to build up steam," said the driver. "It takes time."

The stoker's strong arms rippled powerfully as he shoveled.

The driver eased the train out onto the main track. He warned unhappily: "We might meet a passenger train!"

"That's a chance we'll take," said Miguel grimly.

Above the noise of the engine they couldn't hear the sound of firing, but bullets spanged loudly on the metal roof.

"They're shooting at us," choked the driver.

"The sooner you get beyond range the better," said Miguel.

The stoker redoubled his energies and the driver crouched low. The train rocked on and presently there were no more bullets.

Miguel was trying to concentrate but thoughts eluded him. He wondered if they would be waiting at the next station or if they could shunt him off into a siding. He swayed as a black wave washed over him, and he closed his eyes, fearing he would faint. He exerted willpower, opened his eyes and saw the driver staring at him hopefully. The man's eyes slipped away guiltily.

Miguel looked down at the embankment sliding away past the train. "Tell me how you stop?"

"You spin this wheel and then pull this lever."

"How do you reduce steam pressure?"

"It's this lever here."

"All right," said Miguel. "Jump."

The driver gaped. "What?"

"Jump!"

"You mean . . . leave the train running by itself?"

"That's right."

The driver shook his head. "I won't leave a runaway train on the line."

Miguel raised his Sten gun. "Have it your way."

The driver looked at the gun, crossed to the steps of the cab, descended them and stood on the bottom step. He looked up at Miguel, wanting to say something but not daring. When Miguel pointed the Sten gun at him he shrugged his shoulders and jumped.

He jumped badly, with both feet together and forgetting to throw himself backward. He was hurled forward on his face and lay making feeble movements as the train rumbled on.

A few minutes later Miguel told the stoker: "You jump now."

Without a word the man crossed the cab and went down the steps. He jumped, rolled over and over, climbed to his feet and stood watching the train disappear.

Miguel watched the countryside sliding past. Pain surged up in another wave of dizziness and he knew he must act soon. He sat on the floor of the cabin with his feet on the iron steps. The swaying jolted his smashed shoulder agonizingly but he peered ahead until he saw the landmark he was awaiting.

He prepared to jump. He was vaguely aware that the train was going much faster and remembered he had anticipated this and asked how to reduce speed. But it didn't seem important now.

He jumped without thinking, feeling himself flying and then smashing against the gravel in black, splintering agony, rolling down the embankment with a thousand knives tearing at his shoulder until he screamed aloud. There was a long drop, a hovering in space and another smashing impact which numbed all awareness.

He recovered consciousness lying on his back in tall grass. The late afternoon sun beat down on his exposed face and the world swam sickeningly. He wanted to lie still but the instinct to escape goaded him to his feet and the crawling black mass on his shoulder and chest buzzed angrily. He smeared away the great clot of ants and blowflies, reeled in the wrong direction for many paces before he realized it and painfully retraced his steps. He saw his gun lying on the ground, stooped to pick it up; his head swam and he almost fell.

He stumbled on, his sunblistered eyes painful and his vision blurred. Vaguely he wondered where he was going. Then a little later —or was it a long time later?—he suddenly knew where he was going.

He was going home!

He stumbled on, eager to reach the beach and show his mother the fish he had caught. A great fish, all silver and alive and leaping in the bottom of his boat while his strong brown calves were cool in the sea and the boat's painter cut painfully into his shoulder as he hauled the boat up the gently sloping beach.

The sand was hot and heavy and clung to his feet so it needed a great effort to lift them. He plodded along the beach interminably, the hot sun burning his shoulder and the sea a black, buzzing cloud. He saw a figure ahead of him and it was his father. He stumbled on more quickly then, wanting to shout. But his mouth was so dry he could only croak. Then when he got closer, he saw it wasn't his father. In a moment of lucidity he recognized the face.

Benito Vigon's back ached as he stooped and swung his sickle, trimming the grass lining the shallow ditch. He could have set fire to the grass, but there had been no rain for many months and a spark could start a fire which would consume crops and olive groves.

His sickle flashed and the curling black hairs on his arms glistened with sweat. With every stroke the long grass fell and the cropped stubble was as yellow as straw. Vigon had been married nearly two years and as he labored he thought of his baby daughter in her crib, cooing with pleasure.

Vigon straightened up, eased his aching back and reached for the sharpening stone. He passed the sickle to his bad hand. Shriveled muscles drew his arm up against his chest but the fingers that hung from his curved wrist could hold the sickle firmly while he honed its gleaming edge.

The stone rang against the metal like a high-pitched bell. He tested the blade, tucked the honing stone into his sash and took the sickle in his right hand.

It was then he saw the man. He was the width of a field away and stumbled drunkenly. His head was lowered and he peered through half-closed eyes as though his vision was blurred.

Vigon watched the man approach, and knew who he was when he saw the Sten gun slung over his shoulder and the blood-encrusted shirt. He dropped his sickle and waited for the man with a breathless constriction in his chest. He had heard on the radio at lunchtime of the battle between the Civil Guards and a gang of criminals.

When the man drew close he unslung his Sten gun but was so weak that he held it with the barrel pointing at the ground. He swayed to a standstill, peered hard and croaked, "Benito!"

Vigon recognized the careworn face, the swarthy skin, the raven-black hair and the long Barras jaw. "Miguel!" he said quietly.

"Thirsty," croaked Miguel. "Mouth . . . parched."

Vigon stooped for his wineskin lying in the shade of a bush and gave it to Miguel. Miguel rested the barrel of his gun on the ground and used his teeth to unscrew the stopper. He raised the bottle to his lips and gulped greedily. Wine ran from the corners of his mouth and dripped onto his bloodstained shirt. He sighed and wiped the back of his hand across his mouth. He said hoarsely: "They're after me, Benito. They . . . got all the others."

"I heard it on the radio."

"Help me, comrade. Hide me. Take me home with you."

"Why don't you give yourself up, Miguel?"

Miguel said, "They'd shoot me on sight!"

"What would happen to my family if I hid you? What would happen to *your* family if they sheltered you? Go away, Miguel. You'll bring bad trouble to everyone."

"I don't understand," Miguel panted. "We're friends, Benito. We're comrades of war. I'm hurt. I need a doctor. You can't deny me."

"Come with me, Miguel," persuaded Vigon. "I will take you to a doctor."

"No! My mother will care for me."

Vigon shook his head. "Your family are my friends. I won't bring your troubles on them. They are good people."

Miguel swayed. "What have you against me? That I killed? We all killed, didn't we? Can you refuse help to a comrade?"

"We've stopped speaking the same language, Miguel. You've stopped being a fighter for freedom. You're a murderer!"

Miguel's face set hard. "Is that what you think?"

"It's what you've proved yourself to be, Miguel."

"If I'm a murderer I'll kill you . . . now!"

Vigon drew himself up.

"Leave me," choked Miguel. His vision was blurred and he was unutterably weary. "Go away," he croaked.

Vigon stared at him steadily for some seconds then turned deliberately and walked away. He walked fifty paces before he looked back. Miguel was sitting on a flat rock with the gun across his knees and his chin on his chest.

Vigon reached the highway and followed it toward the village. Presently a jeep packed with Civil Guards lurched toward him over the potholed road and without hesitation Vigon stepped into its path and spread his arms.

The jeep squealed to a standstill. A sergeant demanded: "What's the trouble, man?"

"I've seen Scarface."

There was instant tension.

"Where?" panted the sergeant.

Vigon pointed. "Take the path a hundred yards along on the right which leads to the Vila farm. The second path on the left leads through an olive grove to a meadow. He's badly wounded. He's sitting there on a rock armed with a Sten gun."

"Your papers," demanded the sergeant.

A corporal said: "I'll vouch for him. He lives in Escoleras."

The sergeant slapped the jeep driver on the shoulder. "Let's go."

The jeep roared off and Vigon watched it come to a standstill farther along the road. Civil Guards leaped from it and ran along the path he had indicated. When they were out of sight he turned and walked on toward the village.

He walked slowly and presently he heard the distant rattle of small-arms fire. The firing didn't last long.

Benito Vigon kept walking and wiped his hand across the corner of his eye.

Rosalia sold her jewelry reluctantly. When she returned to her apartment with the money, she knew at once that Maroto had been home and gone out again. He had left the telephone standing dangerously close to the edge of the table.

She showered leisurely, painted her toenails and fingernails, perfumed herself and put on fresh underwear. She loved the touch of dainty garments on her skin.

There was a worry nagging at her but it was some time before she realized what it was. Maroto's slippers were not under the bed and his dressing gown was missing. She opened the door of the wardrobe and stared in astonishment at bare shelves. His two suitcases had gone too. He had taken everything that was his.

She searched the apartment for a note but all that remained was his hair-oil stain on the pillowcase and the stale scent of cigar smoke.

She sat down calmly and reasoned it out. He had been elated since he had destroyed Scarface's band. Without doubt he had been promoted and switched to other work. He had probably had to pack and leave at a moment's notice. Rosalia resigned herself to patience, anxiously awaited the postman and spent long, lonely nights watching the telephone.

There was not a word from Maroto.

The electricity bill was heavy and the telephone bill with Maroto's many long-distance calls aroused new money worries. It was ironic that when she had resolved to discuss money with him he should have left so unexpectedly.

She knew he would resent her intrusion into his professional life but after two weeks she went to the commissary. The officials were polite to an attractive young woman but not helpful. She showed her identity card to a succession of different officials, answered many questions but could learn only that Maroto had been recalled to Madrid. Nobody knew his address.

Bills came for wine, whiskey and cigars, an invoice for new curtains she had put up the previous week and a reminder from her landlord that the next quarter's rent was due. Rosalia was in pressing need of money. If she worked again it would take time to build up a clientele and she would have to borrow money until she was earning it again. But the very thought of *working* filled her with revulsion. What she wanted more than anything was to have Maroto to care for.

She decided to join Maroto in Madrid. She sold her furniture and adornments for almost nothing. Shopkeepers shook their heads sadly. Times were bad, they complained, nobody had any money and stock stayed in the shops gathering dust. It was the same with her expensive dresses. They brought her very little. She used most of the money to pay outstanding debts. She traveled to Madrid by train with only two crammed suitcases and a slender purse. She told a taxi driver she wanted cheap accommodation for a few days and he took her to a modest boardinghouse.

It was difficult to trace Maroto. Government offices opened in the mornings only and there were always long lines. Often she waited an hour or more, only to be told to try another office where another line was waiting and where the doors closed before it was her turn.

Finally she found him. The uniformed receptionist said: "He's very busy now. You must telephone later."

She walked the streets waiting for time to pass and phoned him from a café. But he had left the building and wouldn't be back until the next day. She telephoned many times the next day but he was never there. Finally she called again at the office.

"He can't see you now," said the receptionist. "Will you call back?"

"It's very important that I see him. I'll wait."

"You may have to wait a long time."

"I don't mind." She crossed to a bench and sat down. After two hours she persuaded the receptionist to ring through again.

"The young lady is still waiting," he reported. "She says it's very important. She doesn't mind how long she waits." The receptionist listened. "All right." He nodded at Rosalia encouragingly and beckoned a uniformed guard. "Take the Señorita to Room Fourteen."

Room Fourteen was a windowless interrogation room. She sat on a chair under an arc light and remembered that it was in just such a room she had first met Renato.

He kept her waiting an hour. When he stepped into the room he was a stranger. She wanted to embrace him but his icy coldness rebuffed her. She stared up at him with pained eyes.

"What do you want?" he demanded tonelessly.

"I . . . didn't know what had happened to you. You left without a word!"

"Was there anything to say?"

Her eyes swam with tears. "I want you, Renato. I *need* you. I'll cook for you, clean for you, care for you."

He stared bleakly over her head. "That's all over now. This is Madrid."

"Please, Renato. Let me be with you. I'll do anything you say."

"Go back to Barcelona."

She choked. "That's all I mean to you?"

"Is there anything else you want?"

"I've given you my love, my money. I've sold my jewelry and my clothes for you. You can't cut me off this way, Renato. I've got nothing . . . *nothing!*"

He frowned, pulled out his wallet and took out two notes. "Here. Is that enough?"

She threw the notes at him. "Don't treat me this way. I'm human!"

He carefully picked up the money. "Why refuse payment? You're a whore, aren't you?"

"Let me stay with you, Renato."

"I need a change," he said brutally. "I've got other interests." He nodded casually and strolled out of the room.

She dried her eyes and left the building with her head high. But as soon as she was outside a black loneliness swamped her. She waited on the other side of the road until he came down the steps. She ran after him, caught his arm.

"I've got to talk to you, Renato. There's something I must explain."

He was embarrassed, tugging his arm free and glancing around anxiously, worried that anyone should see them. He flagged a taxi.

"It's important, Renato," she said. "Terribly important."

He jerked open the taxi door but she stood in his way.

"Rosalia," he said urgently. "I've got important business. I'll see you later at the Black Sheep Tavern. Be there at ten tonight."

She waited at the Black Sheep for more than an hour before she went back to her room and cried herself to sleep.

The next morning when Maroto arrived at the commissary she was waiting for him. "You didn't come," she accused.

His eyes avoided hers. "I couldn't get away."

"I must see you alone, Renato."

"It's all been said, Rosalia. There's nothing more to talk about."

"There's *much* more!"

"If it's money . . . ?"

"It's not money, Renato. It's *you* I want. We've got to talk about it."

He sighed and glanced at his watch. "Do you know the Nouvelle Bar near the Plaza del Sol? Wait outside at ten tonight and I'll pick you up."

"You promise, Renato?"

"Yes."

"Last night you broke your promise."

"Tonight it will be different."

She arrived at the Nouvelle ten minutes early and walked up and down slowly, ignoring men who ogled her. At a quarter past ten there was still no sign of Maroto.

Two tall men stopped on either side of her. One pulled back his coat lapel to show his police badge and she sighed with relief. "Come with us," he said. He had a broken nose which had been set crookedly.

"Did Maroto send you?" she asked.

He looked at her curiously. "That's right."

"Is it far?"

"Only a few steps."

One walked ahead of her and the other followed, along the main street, up a side street and up the steps of a commissary.

"Identity card," said the man with the twisted nose.

She gave it to him.

"This way." He led her down a long corridor. At the end was an iron door. A guard drew back bolts and opened it. It was a large cell crowded with women of all types and ages. They stared out sullenly.

"Inside," said Crooked Nose.

Rosalia stared in astonishment. "What?"

"Don't get awkward *now*," he pleaded.

"I don't understand . . ." she began.

"Will you step inside like a lady or . . . ?"

"You *can't* do this," she choked. "I demand that Señor Maroto knows about this!"

He eyed her curiously. "He does!" He eased her over the threshold and the cell door slammed.

Some of the women were drunk and sang unmusically until guards came and laid nightsticks across their shoulders. There was only a small hole in the stone floor to serve their physical needs and the air was thick with the stench of vomit and stale urine. Some of the women had sores and those who weren't lousy soon began to scratch. Rosalia's mind retreated to an inner remoteness and although horror touched her, she retained her sanity.

The next morning she was taken to the railway station with five other girls and locked in a compartment. The glass windows were painted so that nobody could see in. The seats were wooden, and the compartment had been left in a filthy condition by previous occupants who had made this same sad journey. But nothing could reach Rosalia through the numbed hurt that gripped her.

At the correction center her long hair was sheared off and her head shaved with a razor. She was given a coarse canvas smock to wear.

Stern women warders kept the prisoners working. Nuns led prayers for sinners a dozen times a day, and there were punishment cells for girls who did not conform, cells where they spent days in darkness with a ration of cold water and stale bread.

Rosalia scrubbed floors. She was on her knees from early morning until bedtime. She scrubbed courtyard flagstones and stone steps with cold water and caustic soda. Her nails split to the quick, her hands swelled until it was painful to hold the brush. She scrubbed every flagstone three times over, rinsed it clean and scrubbed it yet again. When all the flagstones in the courtyard were spotless, sheep from the farmyard were herded across it and scrubbing began again. Her knees were swollen and the skin callused. The food was insufficient, her body withered, and as she scrubbed, her shriveled breasts swung and chafed against her smock.

Each day was an eternity of numbed misery.

8

There was one part of the beach where the younger villagers gathered and swam during the summer months. Silvana Ledesma spent all day there, mechanically scolding the children and then relaxing to read a novelette. Her plump shoulders gleamed with oil and her generous breasts swelled out over the neckline of her swimsuit. She remained on the beach until dusk, wading into the sea whenever the sun was too hot.

Her eldest daughter, Silvana, was fifteen. At lunchtime the girl was sent home to cut bread, smear it with tomato pulp, add olive oil and bring it back in a raffia basket. Spending her days on the sand saved Silvana work. Her older children looked after themselves and the young Silvana was always on hand to keep the little ones from drowning themselves and to wash them in the sea when they were dirty.

Other villagers had caught the sunbathing craze of the tourists. Benito Vigon's wife came to the beach every day with her two children. So did Anita Morales, Camila Vigon, Helena Guitart and a dozen others.

There was a natural pigmentation in the villagers' skins and they tanned easily. They swam like fish and when they waded out of the sea and threw themselves down on the hot sand, they fitted into their background.

But the tourists, a hundred yards along the beach, lived in a different world and stood out starkly from their surroundings. The Marvista Hotel was six stories high now and workmen were extending its foundations to double the length of its facade. A wide, tiled terrace ran the full length of the hotel and tourists sat under gaily colored awnings and sunshades or relaxed in deck chairs while pretty waitresses in crisp linen dresses brought them drinks. Rich black soil had been brought down from the mountains, trees and seeds had been planted, so that cool shade was spread by the foliage and a lawn of lush green grass stretched from the terrace to the sea's high-water mark.

The Marvista accommodated two hundred and fifty guests but there seemed to be many more as they stretched out on the lawn, their white-skinned bodies turning pink. The beach was littered with deck chairs. The tourists romped in the sea like lobster-colored seals, paddling and splashing, learning to swim and floating on inflated air cushions. They rented pedal boats or drifted in glass-bottomed canoes. From breakfast until one o'clock this stretch of beach was filled with them. Then magically, long before the Spaniards thought of lunch, the tourists disappeared, leaving only empty deck chairs and slanting sunshades to show where they had been.

Leon Coruna lived in the hotel during his summer break from school, but he always joined his Catalan friends in the mornings. He was tall for his age. His silver hair and laughing eyes were inherited from Teresa and his grandfather, El Rubio. He was slim but well muscled. He swam effortlessly and when he waded out of the sea, the young Silvana watched him secretly.

Leon walked across to their group. *"Bon día,* Señora Ledesma."

Silvana was reading and glanced up absently. *"Bon día,* Leon."

Leon sat down between Asuncion Serra and Diego Munez, a Gypsy boy who was strumming a guitar and singing softly.

"Have you heard about the new promenade, Leon?" asked one boy.

"I heard Mother talk about it," he said knowledgeably. "But it's still under discussion. They want to build a wide promenade and a road for cars with street lamps and laid-out gardens."

"It'll cost millions," said Jaime Guitart, his eyes wide with awe.

"It's for the tourists and they bring millions into the country," said Leon.

They looked at him respectfully. Although he was one of them, he had a foot well placed in the impressive world of wealth and foreigners.

"My father says it's a boom period," said Asuncion Serra. They listened to her too with respect. Everyone knew her father had made a fortune buying and selling old iron. Now he owned a factory in Barcelona which manufactured chicken wire for all Spain. And on the slopes beyond Escoleras he had bought a vineyard for a song, and an army of workmen were pegging out plots for the bungalow village he was building. With typical frugality Serra had hired a truck, driven to Andalusia where there was acute poverty, signed up laborers for a minimum wage and brought them back to Escoleras.

"Are there *so* many tourists?" asked one girl. "Not everyone in the world will come here."

"This is only the beginning," said Leon. He spoke with conviction because his mother's enthusiasm was contagious. "The government will soon have to open more frontiers. Otherwise there won't be enough to let them all in."

"I don't mind as long as the tourists leave us a little sea to swim in," said Silvana and they all laughed.

Every morning they met on the beach and it was fun because they were young. But the older boys and girls were beginning to show shy interest in one another. Leon often swam a long way out to sea and one day when he came back he found a folded note lying on his towel. It read simply: "*S loves L.*"

Leon glanced around furtively. Maria was being buried in the sand by the others and nobody was watching him. But Silvana was nearest.

A little later he invited: "Walk with me along the beach, Silvana?"

She got to her feet at once.

"Don't go far," snapped her mother. "I can't keep getting up to stop Freda falling in the water."

"You'll look after Freda, won't you, Asuncion?" pleaded Silvana.

"All right," agreed her friend amiably.

They walked along the beach side by side, past the tourist zone and on beyond. "Did you write the note?" he asked.

She didn't ask what note. She said: "No!" and flushed.

"You can admit it."

"It's not up to the girl."

"I . . . like you too, Silvana."

"Do you want to be my boy?"

"All right," he agreed and instantly the decision frightened him because it seemed so binding.

That summer passed happily for them. They swam together and sat next to each other on the beach and took long walks, far enough away from the others to share their secret thoughts.

It was an eventful year. There was an abundance of fish, of ambition, of planning and of social activity. It was a year of great events and of sad happenings.

It was the last year of Hernando and Father Delbos.

Although they were now wealthy, Vicente Serra and his wife were still miserly. They lived in the same old house, never spent a peseta if they could avoid it, and worked from morning to night. Serra had invested a fortune in his bungalow project and was so determined nothing should be wasted that he prowled the site with his wife, retrieving damaged bricks the builder had discarded as useless.

They put Asuncion to work in a grocer's store where she started at eight in the morning and remained until it closed at ten at night. The only concession that Serra made to his affluence was an arrangement with the grocer during the summer months that Asuncion needn't start work until after lunch and could spend the mornings on the beach.

When she was young, Asuncion had been taunted by other children about her parents' meanness. The wounds of the jibes never quite healed and she was always ill at ease with others of her own age. She felt she was looked down upon. But she was astonishingly beautiful. Despite childhood illnesses and chronic lack of nourishment, she had grown fit and strong and although thin, she had delicately lovely features and rich blue-black hair.

Father Delbos noticed her. One day after confession he said before she left the box: "Meet me in the vestry, Asuncion."

It was dark in the vestry and it smelled of the bleaching chemical used to clean the choirboys' surplices.

"Come, Asuncion," said Father Delbos in his fatherly way. "Sit by me." He patted the wooden bench beside him. "You're growing quickly. You'll be a woman soon." She wore a sleeveless cotton dress and his fingers teased her armpit, gently tugging a black tendril of underarm hair. "This shows you're growing into a woman, Asuncion."

"Yes, Father," she said with a note of doubt in her voice.

"It's elsewhere too, isn't it?" he asked and the question was so natural that she answered unhesitatingly and thought he must have some special all-knowing power if he could know about *that*.

"Now, Asuncion," he said seriously. "I want you to grow into a *sensible* young woman. I'll help you as I've helped hundreds of girls. It's my duty."

"Yes, Father."

"Nevertheless, it must be a secret between us because I haven't time to spare for everyone. Do you understand, child?"

"Yes, Father."

"You promise?"

"I promise."

"On the book," he said and held it so that she could place her hand on it when she vowed.

"This is a secret between us two. You must never tell anyone, not even your mother and father. If you do, you will go to hellfire."

"I won't tell anyone, Father."

"Very well. I want you to read the Bible to me while I teach you new mysteries."

"Yes, Father."

"Come here, child." He pulled her in between his parted legs and sat her upon his thigh. She wasn't afraid because he was a priest and good. But she felt strange.

"Can I not sit on the bench, Father?"

"Are you not comfortable, child?"

"Yes, but . . ."

"Read to me," he said, handing her the open Bible.

She read slowly and timidly and her voice didn't falter when his hand rested on her knee. But when it slid higher between her thighs she stopped abruptly.

"What is it, child?"

"Please, Father. It is not right you should touch me thus."

He chuckled. "But I am different, child. I am a man of God. What I teach is with the wisdom of the Holy Spirit."

"Yes, Father." But she clamped his hand tightly between her thighs.

"Don't resist me, child."

She gulped. "I am afraid, Father."

"You must not be afraid, child. You are safe and I will guide you as I have many others."

She yielded to his insistence and he touched her in a disturbing way. She made a sighing sound and he said: "You now feel the secret of becoming a woman."

"Yes, Father. But please stop!"

"Are you afraid?"

"No, Father."

"Is it not pleasant?"

"Yes, Father. But it is not right."

"You are impatient, child. Wait a little and you will learn of the deeper pleasure which will make you happy to be a woman."

And it was so.

Two nights later in the vestry he taught her more. It was difficult to concentrate on reading while he taught her the pleasure of becoming a woman and she was relieved when he took the Bible away and placed it on the bench. "Do you know what is Adam's rib, my child?"

The delight of his touch was marred by his smelly breath.

"The rib of creation," said Father Delbos. "Adam's rib."

Intuitively she knew what he meant, having sensed it while she sat on his lap. But learning about it was prolonged for many sessions in the vestry while her timidity and shyness were lulled and she was slowly lured to the intimacy of mutual caressing.

"You have learned well, child," Father Delbos told her.

Her knees were trembling, she was sticky and wanted to wash her hands. He opened a wardrobe, unlocked a drawer and took out a slab of chocolate. "A present, child," he said.

All her inner guilt feelings dissolved then as she recalled how other girls giggled secretly as though at a great joke while they ate sweets that Father Delbos had given them. She went away reassured. Other girls did it too.

Three weeks later at a critical moment with Father Delbos, the vestry door, which he had forgotten to lock, burst open and they were caught by the woman who had come to clean. She was deeply religious and gave her services freely to the church. After Father Delbos spoke to her long and seriously she was almost persuaded to believe his explanations. She spent days in an agony of irresolution and finally turned to the only other man in whom she had confidence.

Doctor Aldo listened quietly and assured her she could leave everything in his hands.

He called upon the Serras and asked to see Asuncion in private. He talked to her alone, gently breaking down her reticence. She gave him the names of other girls whom she thought had lessons with Father Delbos.

Doctor Aldo talked to all of them. Silvana Ledesma admitted that Father Delbos had once embraced her and touched her but she had pulled free and run away. Other girls had had similar experiences. Two girls were at the same stage of intimacy as Asuncion.

Doctor Aldo and the parents called upon the mayor and the judge and later a small deputation called upon Father Delbos.

Like wildfire the news ran round the village. Father Delbos had left suddenly. Nobody knew where or why.

Three days later another priest arrived. He was a middle-aged Catalan, fat and jovial. He smoked cigars in the street, laughed heartily at doubtful jokes, slapped people boisterously in greeting and wasn't above swearing. He quickly learned everybody's Christian names, joined the chess club, paddled in the sea with his cassock rolled up over his knees and organized picnics for the children every Sunday. Outside the church he never reproached villagers who did not attend Mass but his church filled up and within a month he was holding services for larger congregations than had ever been known.

That year the town hall was enlarged. The house next door was taken over, the intervening walls knocked down and the offices expanded. The council's secretary, a permanent official, engaged an assistant. Businessmen from all over Europe bombarded the town hall with letters asking where they could buy land, the conditions of building permits and the facilities available for water and lighting.

Escoleras was becoming a popular tourist resort and the price of land beside the sea soared. Allotments, disused vineyards and neglected olive groves, once thought worthless, were eagerly sought, while astute Catalan peasants forced up the price. Twice a week a lawyer from Figueras came to Escoleras to untangle land-deed problems and arguments over boundaries.

The governor of the province appointed twelve new councillors for Escoleras, a plan of development was drawn up, and money was made available for the scheme to start at once. The promenade was to be built along the front of the village between the harbor and the beach. Palm trees would be planted, there would be gardens with flowers, public benches and neon lamp posts. The beach in front of the village would disappear and the fishermen would have to draw their boats up out of the water elsewhere.

The work went forward quickly. A long line of stakes was placed from the harbor to the beach. They stood far out in six feet of water. A long armed crane was brought down from Barcelona and great concrete blocks were lifted into position. The blocks made a long wall outside the stakes. Then six dump trucks arrived. They dumped earth and stones into the sea inside the stone wall, steadily filling in what would become the promenade.

Hernando's stone hut on the beach came within the marine zone. He did not own the ground and town development couldn't be held up for one man. Hernando would have to go. Everyone regretted it but it couldn't be helped.

Hernando listened with dignity, stroked his neatly trimmed beard and nodded sadly while it was explained to him by the secretary, the architect and the mayor.

But he didn't leave his stone hut.

Paco Barras, Doctor Aldo and many others offered him the hospitality of their homes.

Hernando thanked them gravely, smiled sadly and rolled the waxed ends of his moustache until they bristled like needles.

But he did not leave his hut.

The mayor and the councillors convened a special meeting. They voted Hernando lifetime use of a piece of land the council owned behind the village. A councillor started a subscription list to build Hernando a small villa. Then the mayor and the councillors visited Hernando and told him what was arranged. He thanked them gravely and offered them his wineskin.

But he did not leave his hut.

The dump trucks had started work at the harbor and steadily filled in the space behind the wall, replacing sea with gravel and building a promenade of earth which marched toward Hernando's hut.

Hernando sat on the beach, baiting his fish hooks, weaving his lobster pots and giving no sign that he would leave.

The mayor and others called to reason with him. But Hernando did not argue. He listened, nodded solemnly and offered them his wineskin. And always when they left they felt ashamed and a little ridiculous. Hernando was solemn and dignified but there was a hint of pity in his blue eyes which made them feel like thoughtless children.

The dump trucks worked on. They reached Hernando's hut, skipped it and filled in on the other side. Finally, Hernando's hut and its strip of beach was surrounded by a high dike. The dumping was concluded but for Hernando's hut.

The villagers gathered early the next morning to see what would happen. But there was an anticlimax. During the night Hernando had disappeared, taking his bedding and cooking pans, his fishing line and his shotgun. All had been loaded into his little fishing boat and he had sailed away. He was never seen again.

The gap was filled in, pickaxes demolished the part of Hernando's stone hut which was higher than the earth around it and steamrollers flattened, leveled and prepared the ground for the New Spain.

This same year Pepita became engaged.

Teresa had built her a small factory at the end of the hotel garden where Pepita worked with six girls making her mosaic pictures. They sold well to tourists and Pepita earned money. She had had attachments made for the leather sleeves laced to the stumps of her arms and could cut up her own food and even write.

Luis Jova was twenty-six and eager to make his way in life. His parents were elderly and poor and Luis worked hard! Teresa had made him her assistant manager. He wore a white suit with a black tie, supervised the waiters, helped at the bar and handled kitchen problems.

At the end of the season when business was slack Teresa invited him up to her rest room on the top floor.

"Pour yourself a drink, Luis," said Teresa.

"How about you, Señora?"

Teresa smiled wryly. He always addressed her as Señora and it made her feel old.

"A small one, Luis," she said and realized with a shock that she would soon be forty. The years had flown. She had been so busy with her son and business that time had concertinaed.

Luis sat on the edge of his chair toying nervously with his glass.

Teresa asked bluntly: "What do you think of my sister Pepita?"

"She's . . . very pleasant, Señora."

"You see a good deal of her, don't you, Luis? You handle the orders for mosaics."

"This year we sold more than last year and I've suggested to Pepita . . ."

"You think Pepita's a nice girl?"

He was startled. The word "girl" bothered him. "Pepita's more than thirty, isn't she?"

"Not much," said Teresa quickly. "I call her a girl because she's unmarried."

"She's pleasant," he agreed carefully.

"She was very pretty before the accident."

"You can see that even now, Señora."

Teresa looked down into her glass. "What plans have you for your future, Luis?"

He smiled. "Work hard; save and get out of the rut."

"Why don't you marry Pepita?"

A flush spread up from his neck and turned his cheeks crimson.

"She's not an attractive proposition," said Teresa bluntly. "She's maimed, she's older than you and she's bad-tempered."

He took out his handkerchief and wiped his forehead.

"They're all valid reasons for not wanting to marry her," said Teresa. "But in Pepita's favor we can say she is a sweet girl who needs a husband's love and children."

He listened miserably.

"I'll tell you something about Pepita. The day she's engaged I'll start building a new hotel as a wedding gift. The day she's married it will be furnished and handed over lock, stock and barrel."

He stared at her with wide eyes.

"There are drawbacks in being married to a handless woman. But in marriage you expect to take the ups and downs."

Teresa finished her drink. "This conversation is private, Luis. Whatever you decide won't affect your future with me."

A month later Luis and Pepita became engaged. Teresa gave a dinner party for friends and relatives. Pepita sat at the head of the table and was so radiant that her guests failed to see her disfiguring scars.

When she left the correction center, Rosalia was given a train ticket to Barcelona, a little money and a letter of introduction to the mother superior of a convent which might give her shelter. It was early evening before she reached Barcelona.

Rosalia stepped out into the station hall and looked around slowly as though coming back to life after a long, long death. The familiar smell of scorched iron, burnt coffee and stale tobacco rushed in on her. Scurrying crowds, the anxious voices of passengers hurrying for trains and the static loudness of the station loudspeaker were warmly familiar.

She went to the station café and recklessly spent some of her money on coffee and a roll, standing at the counter while she sipped the rich, milky liquid and relished the soft pastry.

Her hair had grown and been shaved off many times in the correction center and now it was a short bob, a dark lifeless tangle streaked with silver. Combs were nonexistent in the center. The smart clothes she had worn on admission couldn't be found, so they had given her an ill-fitting black skirt, a white blouse and a navy-blue topcoat of shoddy material.

She had nowhere to go except the convent. She showed her letter of introduction, was given a bowl of soup, a piece of bread and a cot for the night. She was sent out early the next morning to find work.

There was severe unemployment and although Rosalia searched diligently the only jobs available paid so little that they could only be accepted by girls living with their parents.

She did not waste too much time on a futile search. She went to an address she knew and asked for La Señora.

La Señora was a plump, middle-aged woman who listened sympathetically but shook her head as soon as she had looked Rosalia up and down.

"You've been in a correction center, dear?"

Rosalia made a face.

"We're full up," sighed La Señora. She eyed Rosalia critically. "I don't want to hurt you, my dear, but you won't get far as you are. You need flesh on your bones. There's not enough of you for a man to get his teeth into. Hair like rat tails and your hands . . . A man wouldn't want you to touch him with hands like those!"

Rosalia flushed. "As soon as I earn a little money I'll look nice again."

"Why don't you go home to your parents and rest."

"I . . . I'm an orphan."

"Haven't you a boyfriend who . . ." La Señora broke off. She saw Rosalia's pinched face. "No. I suppose not."

"All I need is a start and then I'll be all right. I used to earn big . . ."

"Yes," sighed the Señora. "We all used to earn big. There's a time for it but you never know until it's over. It doesn't ever come back. Our profession is unique. We start at the top and there's only one way we can go . . . down!"

"Can't you do anything for me?" pleaded Rosalia.

"I'll be honest, girl. Even if I had a vacancy I *couldn't* have you. My house has to maintain standards."

Rosalia got to her feet sadly. "Can you recommend anywhere?"

La Señora opened a drawer, took out a visiting card and scribbled an address on its back. "Try Lola's. You might think it's beneath you but the way things are you'll be lucky to get in."

"How about going on the streets?"

"Very risky. You don't want to go back to a correction center, do you?"

Rosalia shuddered.

"Perhaps this will help." La Señora thrust a hundred peseta note into Rosalia's hand.

"No. You mustn't. I couldn't," whispered Rosalia.

"Don't be silly, girl. When things get better you can pay me back."

"I will," promised Rosalia sincerely.

Rosalia called at other houses without success. Business was bad and there were more girls than clients. But faced with returning to the convent, Rosalia went to Lola's.

Lola's was in the back streets of the dock area. The madam was a woman of sixty with skin the color of a toadstool and black beady eyes. She looked Rosalia up and down critically. "You haven't much to offer a man."

"I'll be all right when I get started."

"We usually have twenty girls but one left yesterday."

"Will I suit?" Rosalia said quickly.

"We can give it a try," said the madam doubtfully.

"I'd like to," said Rosalia eagerly.

"Each girl has her own room," said the madam. "There's a common room when you're not working where you eat. Don't bring a lot of baggage. There's not room for it."

"I haven't any," said Rosalia quietly.

"We're a fixed-price house. There's a percentage deduction for taxes and living expenses. The balance is shared equally between the girl and the house."

"What's the fixed price?"

"Five pesetas," said the madam.

Rosalia was shocked. "So little!"

"Times are bad."

"When I was working I earned fifty times as much."

The madam smiled venomously. "You can make up for it with the number of clients."

"But . . . it's throwing yourself away."

The madam shrugged her shoulders. "Think it over. But I can't hold it open for you if another girl comes along."

Rosalia thought quickly. It would be a stopgap until she got a start. "I'll stay," she decided. Then seeing the glitter in the madam's eyes, she added humbly: "If you will permit me, Señora."

"Another thing."

Rosalia looked at her anxiously.

"Anything goes. The client pays and you give him what he wants.

A girl who's fastidious about what she does or turns up her nose because she doesn't fancy a client gives us a bad name."

Rosalia nodded. It would only be for a short time, she reassured herself.

Business started at seven in the evening when the twenty girls filed downstairs into a large, dimly lit hall with wooden benches placed round the walls. There were waist-high swinging doors which never stopped flapping until closing time at five A.M. A red light burned above the entrance doors and a placard warned: *"Minors below the age of eighteen not admitted."* The fixed price was painted on each door flap.

In theory the girls sat on the benches while clients strolled around inspecting them. But as soon as the doors were opened, the hall was thronged with men and the girls mingled with them. The smell of cigar smoke blended with the odor of cheap perfume and body sweat. It was the port area and the house catered to lowly paid dock laborers, seamen and lascars.

Rosalia's first customer was a dark-skinned man with thick lips and cropped black hair. He wore a striped sailor's jersey and grubby white pants. She led him through the turnstile, collected her red plastic disk from the madam and ushered him upstairs.

The cot was stripped down with a cotton sheet over the mattress. In one corner was a cracked and brown-veined washbasin and her surprised client had to stand on a chair so that she could wash him.

It was her first physical contact with a man since entering the correction center and his forceful impatience made her cry out. But when he growled: "What's the matter, woman?" she feared he might complain about her. "It's nothing. It's all right."

It was a long night but she learned quickly that for their modest payments clients expected not lovemaking but physical relief and were content with simple climactic satisfaction. They were resentful and even suspicious of her cleanliness. The other girls were slick, leading clients upstairs and bringing them down again with startling rapidity, doubling and trebling her own trade.

She learned that although the hall was always crowded with youths and men, only a few were potential customers. Most drifted from house to house inspecting the girls. She learned she was not expected to wear underclothing. The men pressed around her, face after face stared into hers and it was impossible to know who was a client and who was amusing himself. So the girls held still for them all and smiled mechanically while exploring fingers stroked with an insulting casualness.

Rosalia learned she must encourage the men and brazenly arouse them. Once, that first night, she thought of Escoleras. The man was a big drunken Swede whose weight buried her in the mattress so that she couldn't move. He breathed stale wine and garlic fumes into her face. He was a ship's engineer and his skin smelled of diesel oil. He sweated profusely and great beads of it dripped from his forehead onto her face.

And while she was ground beneath him, she reflected that nothing could be as bad as this. She thought of Escoleras and Josefina. She pictured Josefina, laughing, bright-eyed and big-breasted. She would have opened her arms to Rosalia. Perhaps she still would if she went to her. But Rosalia blanked the thought out of her mind. Escoleras was a part of her life which was dead.

Her last client that night was a lascar with tattooed arms and a shaven head. One of his legs had been crushed and he dragged it when he walked. He watched her undress. "You're not much to look at!"

"I've been ill."

"You're all bones."

"I'm sorry."

"Look at those ribs. Like a scrub board. I can play a tune." He ran his knuckles down them.

"Do you want me to wash you?" she asked.

"I'm sweet enough as I am." He roared with laughter and slapped her hard. "Call that an ass? No flesh."

She glowered and rubbed her haunch.

"Come on, girl." He threw himself down and bunched up the pillow beneath his head. When she stooped over him he grasped the shrunken pouches of her breasts. "What d'you call these?"

"I've been ill," she said. She moved closer to him but he placed his hands on her shoulders and pressed her downward.

"Kiss me, girl," he ordered. "Kiss me!"

After they closed, the madam settled accounts. Rosalia had only eleven plastic disks and the other girls smiled their contempt. She had earned only a few pesetas. Madam explained the accounts. There were many hidden expenses: the rent of the premises, the wages of the cleaners, the doorkeeper, tips to the night guards who were always on hand to quell disturbances, gifts to government inspectors who turned a blind eye to minor infringements of the law and medical fees. A percentage of all these costs was deducted from each girl's earnings and she took fifty percent of what was left.

"You'll earn more when you learn the system, dearie," encouraged the madam. "All the other girls do. Otherwise you won't be much good to yourself or to us!"

Wearily Rosalia made her way upstairs to her tiny room and lay tiredly on her cot with its soiled sheet steeped in the smell of man. She would stick it a while longer, she resolved. And when she had saved enough she would get her own flat.

The doctor came the next day for his weekly checkup. The girls sat in the common room reading, talking, listening to the radio or playing cards while awaiting their turn to be examined. The door was left open and Rosalia saw what was expected of her. The madam gave her a test tube with her name written on it and the doctor didn't even look at her when she entered. She waited until he glanced up. "Ah. You're new." He shredded cotton from a roll and wound it around two fingers. "Brace yourself against the table. That's the way."

He was a middle-aged man with a bony face. He looked tired and hadn't any interest in her as a woman which made her feel less embarrassed while she held her skirt up around her waist.

"Feet astride," he said briskly and his fingers sank deep and then withdrew with a sweeping pressure. Pain hissed out between her teeth.

He looked at her sharply. "Don't move." He thrust the cotton smear into her test tube, corked it and placed it in his bag.

"Sit on the table." He shone a light on her, probing gently with sensitive fingers.

"How long have you been here?"

"I started yesterday."

"Not used to it?"

"I've been in a correction center."

"Is this sore?"

Again she hissed.

"All right," he said.

She stood up and shook down her skirt.

"You'd better rest for a few days," he said. "I'll tell the madam."

"Please don't," she said quickly. "I need the money."

He looked at her unhappily. Then as his hand moved toward his pocket, she said quickly: "It's not only the money. I need the job."

He sighed. "I suppose so." He searched his bag and produced a small glass bottle. "Use this," he said. "It's a soothing lubricant."

His kindness was almost calamitous. Her first client was a German sailor who raged furiously because he couldn't feel anything. She had to wash quickly to appease him.

Rosalia despised the girls she worked with. Most of them came from poverty-stricken villages in Andalusia. They would spit on the floor or unconcernedly break wind at the dining table. Their conversation was filthy and their language vile. Their passions were easily inflamed and they often tore and clawed at each other.

As time passed Rosalia adapted. The food in the house was sustaining and she put on flesh until her hip bones didn't stand out so starkly and her breasts, although still sagging, became pear-shaped. She adapted to her nightly stint. Her calf muscles, strained taut by high-heeled shoes, grew accustomed to the long hours of standing. She had a false smile ever ready. She learned to recognize hundreds of the faces which laughed into hers and even began to remember those who tested the fruit for ripeness but never purchased.

The weeks drifted into months but her savings increased only very slowly. She had had to buy a new dress and shoes—and to visit the hairdresser. There was always something she needed, another dress, cough medicine, headache pills or cosmetics. The lighting in the hall was dim and the girls needed garish makeup to attract attention.

The months passed and one day she realized with surprise that she had been in the house a year. It wouldn't be long now before she got away, she promised herself. Every day she scanned the classified advertisements for furnished apartments, mentally selecting the districts and accommodation which would suit her. An apartment was too much money to manage at the moment but she was saving hard.

She would break free soon, she vowed. She would cut away from the foul-mouthed women she was obliged to live with and become her true self.

9

The speedboat was a crimson splash against the blue of the sea and the youth who weaved across its wake on one ski was like a bronzed god flying across the water.

The speedboat made a curving approach to the sand in front of the hotel and tourists watched the youth with admiration as he swooped in toward the beach and released the tow-cord. He steered the ski across the shallows with such precision that he glided up the sloping beach and ground gently to a standstill. Leon stepped from it, wetting no more than the soles of his feet.

He joined the young people sitting on the hot sand, watching the skiing while they sang. One of them strummed a guitar. They were of mixed nationalities and Leon was their natural leader. He switched easily from French to Italian, to German and into English. The girls gathered around him.

From spring until autumn Leon lived in the hotel like a privileged guest. He was helpful and solicitous to the guests and the mainspring of their social life. He introduced them to other guests, broke down formal restraints, organized outings, arranged beach sports, taught water-skiing, encouraged elderly couples to dance and was never without attractive girls at his elbow.

Leon lay back on the sand with his eyes closed and the English girl beside him watched the rhythmic rise and fall of his chest.

Abruptly Leon sat up. Silvana had stared hard at him as she walked past. She looked away from him quickly.

He got to his feet. "Excuse me, darling," he said to the English girl with the musical accent she found so enchanting.

He followed Silvana along the beach, caught up with her and walked at her side. The surf washed in and lapped around their ankles. "You were looking for me, Silvana?"

"You flatter yourself."

"Then . . . you object to my being here with you?"

There was a pause. "You know that's not true, Leon."

"Why are you angry?" he asked.

"I have no right to be angry? Is that it?"

"I know of no reason," he said quietly.

"You never have time for me, Leon. Always you are with other . . . friends!"

"Then join us," he encouraged. "Come now and sit with us. My friends will be your friends."

She shook her head. "It cannot be, Leon." Her cotton bathing suit was the only one she possessed. It was a year old and she had outgrown it. It cut so revealingly into her crotch that she was continually tugging down its skirt. She had seen how those shameless foreign girls behaved, stretched out on the sand with legs shamelessly flung apart, not caring that their wet bikinis exposed them as though they were naked. Silvana would *never* join such a group.

They had walked a long way along the beach. Leon pointed inland. "Let's walk over there, Silvana."

They would be lost to sight among the sand dunes almost at once. Silvana said: "Let's turn back."

"You see," he sighed. "You dare not walk with me out of sight of your mother and the gossips, for fear of scandal."

"I did not make the laws, Leon. They were made by our parents. A girl may not go alone with a boy and retain her good reputation."

"I want you as my friend, Silvana, but to be your friend I must only sit at your side. We may not picnic without your parents. Your mother's always too tired to come and your father is always too busy. And how can we talk when every word we utter is overheard?"

"It is not as bad as that, Leon. You can sit with my group and swim with us in the mornings. Then in the evenings you can call at home. I would love it, Leon, and I would not expect you to come every night."

He tossed his head, flicking his long, fair hair away from his forehead. "Silvana. I could call upon you for one night, perhaps even two nights. But I could endure no more. I can't bear to be cramped into a mold of convention."

"If you liked me, Leon, you would do it."

He looked at her steadily. "I'm sorry, Silvana. It must be that I do not like you enough!"

When Silvana spoke, her voice was toneless. "I understand. You have everything you want. A good life and . . . friends."

"Yes," he agreed. "I am very lucky."

"But some day you will want to marry?"

He hesitated. "Yes . . . some day . . . perhaps."

They had walked too far along the beach. Silvana turned back and the jealousy simmering inside her could not be restrained. "What do these foreign girls mean to you, Leon?"

"While they are here they are my friends."

"They . . . you kiss them?"

He chuckled. "How different are our two worlds, Silvana. In my world a kiss is a greeting, not a promise of marriage."

"Is a kiss not something more, Leon?"

"It can be," he agreed. "It can be an encouragement to deeper understanding."

"And do you have a deeper understanding with . . . your friends, Leon?"

He said flatly: "Never be surprised that a man has the desires of a man."

Although she had driven him to this admission, the knowledge was a pain. She thought of the shameless girls who, for the brief weeks of their holidays, could see Leon every day. Defiance swelled up in her. She said breathlessly: "I will see you too, Leon. I will enter your world."

He looked at her curiously. "It is what I have always wanted, Silvana. Come, I will introduce you to my friends."

She shrank back. "No. Not *now!*"

"When, then?"

"It must be at night."

"At night it is impossible for you."

"It isn't. I can slip out when everybody is in bed."

He said slowly: "It would be wrong, Silvana. I won't encourage you."

"Tonight," she insisted.

He hesitated. "I've fixed something for tonight."

"And I'm not welcome?"

"There are five of us. Two German boys and a couple of French girls they've just met. We're going out along the coast in my speed-boat for a midnight picnic."

Her voice was dead. "I understand. You don't want me along."

"It's not that, Silvana. It's . . . not suitable for a Spanish girl."

"You want to take another girl," she said bitterly. "I hope you enjoy yourself."

He had intended to invite the English girl but he said quickly: "I have invited nobody. If you want to come you can."

"I do."

He took a deep breath. "It's a big risk for you."

"Where shall I meet you?"

"On the beach. We're setting off at eleven."

The two German boys spoke a little French but neither they nor the French girls spoke Spanish so when Silvana joined them on the beach, she learned only their names. Leon introduced her and then she sat quietly while the others chatted excitedly.

Leon drove with his arm firm against her shoulder as they roared out across the sea. Silvana was thrilled by the breathless beauty of the boat's power. She looked back at the wake. It was churned up like milk and when the spray was thrown high it flashed with luminous colors like a handful of scattered diamonds. When it splashed down it turned the sea alive with phosphorous radiance.

"Was it difficult to get away?" asked Leon.

She shouted to be heard above the roar of the engine. "I locked the door of my bedroom and climbed out through the window."

"It's underhand."

"It's the *only* way."

"You should have told your father you were coming and insisted on your right to do so."

"I haven't any rights," she said quietly. "I'm not twenty-five."

They sped on, paralleling the towering cliffs until, far from Escoleras, Leon eased the boat into a narrow channel in the cliff face. Presently the channel widened out into a cove and at the end of it was a tiny beach where they drew the boat up out of the water.

The German boys gathered driftwood and lit a fire while Leon and the girls unloaded the boat. There were plastic-covered cushions, a transistor radio, a picnic basket containing cold chicken, champagne and hot coffee in a thermos flask. It was late, the sea air gave an edge to their appetites and they ate with relish, laughing and joking and drinking a great deal. The French girls behaved as though they had known the boys for years. One girl shared a chicken leg with a boy, teasing him, pulling it away before he could get his teeth into it, shredding flesh from it with her own white teeth and then offering him her mouth so he could take it directly from her.

Leon was strangely quiet as though Silvana's presence subdued his high spirits.

The coffee was rich and black and the brandy was heady. It loosened Silvana's restraint. The French girls had changed partners and embraced abandonedly.

Leon sat beside Silvana with his shoulder touching hers and presently he slipped his arm around her shoulder. She snuggled up to him but when he lowered his lips to her cheek she turned her face away.

They danced and as they danced they sang, and the German boys banged spoons against aluminum picnic plates.

Just when Silvana was thinking it was time to leave for home, there was a wild clamor for a midnight swim. Silvana couldn't believe it when the German boys and the girls stripped off their clothes and stood stark naked in the moonlight.

Leon asked quietly: "Are you swimming, Silvana?"

When she didn't answer, he unbuckled his belt and pulled his shirt over his head.

She looked away quickly.

They waded, swam and splash-fought. The night was warm and so was the sea. Silvana was the only one who was embarrassed.

They frolicked in the water until they were cold. Then a French girl ran from the water shivering, picked up a towel and dried herself. She stood watching the others romp, her firm flesh silvered and the tips of her breasts hard. The others ran out of the water, laughing and shivering. Without bothering to dry themselves, the German boys lay down upon boat cushions with blankets pulled over them. The girls snuggled under the blankets with them, squealing with cold and giggling at the contact.

Leon walked over to Silvana and stood drying himself, making no attempt to conceal his nudity.

She kept her head turned from him.

"This is my world," he said.

"You're welcome to it!"

He lay out on the cushions and spread a blanket over himself.

"It was wrong of me to come," she said.

"I think so, Silvana."

She was furious with him for agreeing.

"If I hadn't come you'd have had some other girl here, kissing her?"

"Yes," he said quietly.

"You think *that's* the way a decent girl should behave?"

"Every generation has a new attitude to life, Silvana. But Spain hasn't moved with the times."

"It's . . . cheap to behave like that."

"No, it isn't, Silvana," he said gently. "Not if you're sincere."

"How can you be sincere with somebody you've only just met?"

"It's easy to feel sincerity quickly. But often it isn't a lasting sincerity."

"I've spoilt your night, haven't I?"

"I'm unhappy for you," he said.

"Why for me?"

"Because . . . you're so repressed you couldn't let yourself go even if you wanted to."

"I can do anything those other girls can do," she said. "It's a matter of what is *decent!*"

"Don't measure them with *your* yardstick, Silvana."

"Would you have all girls behave like prostitutes?"

"Petting is one of the joys of youth. To lie together, to embrace, to caress and arouse emotions!"

"You have a glib tongue, Leon. But once these things start . . ."

"What do *you* know of these things and what happens when they start?" he asked, and he chuckled when she remained silent.

"I am a woman," she said. "A woman knows things by instinct."

"Yet you have never kissed."

"Do you think I do not know how to kiss?"

"I doubt it."

"I'll show you!"

She sat beside him and bent over him. He raised his hand quickly and his fingers covered her mouth. "No, Silvana. I will make no promise to marry. Perhaps . . . perhaps I will never marry!"

"I shall still kiss you. Not to make you my fiancé but to prove I know how to kiss." She stared down into his face.

He smiled and the moonlight gave the whites of his eyes a silvery glitter. She pressed her mouth against his for long seconds.

Leon lay quite still, strangely unmoved, and she too was surprised that she felt so little emotion.

"You see, Leon," she said. "I too know how to kiss."

He shook his head, laughing at her silently.

"Shall I show you again?"

"Shall I teach you how to kiss?"

"I shall show you again that I know how to kiss."

She pressed her lips on his. But again the kiss lacked delight and she thought of the French girls' passion and wondered if it came only after prolonged kissing.

Then Leon's lips swelled up warmly and moistly, parted hers until she was startled by a shaft of emotion. Their tongues clung lovingly until she trembled. She abandoned herself to the pleasure of his mouth and lips; her tongue caressed the contours of his face, the tip of it explored his ear, moistened the line of his eyebrows, brushed gently down across his cheek, neck and throat and then upward again, searching his hot, moist mouth for the sweetness of its hidden recesses. Her long hair hung down curtaining his cheek and she was breathless as his hands stole under her blouse and ran up and down her spine. "Leon. Leon!"

His caresses were heavenly and she made no protest when he unhooked her brassiere so that his fingers could stroke the full length of her spine from neck to waistline. She knew a moment of alarm and tried to stop him when he drew her under the blanket, but she desisted when he cupped her breasts in his hands.

She was drugged by the pleasure of his caresses and every moment her body became more alive and more aware until his hot nakedness became essential. And then a passion-hungry urge swelled up within her and she whimpered while he fought off her searching hands.

He held her in a strong embrace and caressed her until the ecstasy of it turned her tense, deliciously rigid.

After a time she said tonelessly: "You're disgusted with me now?"

He laughed. "Of course not."

"I . . . I . . ."

"It is the first time you've ever kissed?"

"Yes," she admitted softly.

"And the first time you've had . . . these feelings?"

She nodded. There were tears on her cheeks. "I must love you deeply, Leon, to give myself to you thus."

"Do not speak this way, Silvana. A girl does not give herself. Love-making is a mutual pleasure."

"Am I still a virgin, Leon?"

"Have no fear. I only caressed you."

One of the boys called to Leon and he replied in German.

"It is time to go, Silvana." He helped her rearrange her clothing and she was surprised at how natural it all seemed.

They set off back to Escoleras and the sea was smooth and silvery. The engine roared powerfully, wash creamed back behind them into an ever-widening highway, and they sped away from the towering cliffs, out to sea, heading in a straight line to their destination instead of following the coastal contours.

Silvana sat beside Leon and his forearm touched her. They were hissing smoothly across the silver surface of the sea when there was a loud jarring clang. The launch leaped high and then splashed down. The engine roared frenziedly.

Leon righted the boat after it bucked and quickly cut the engine. In the sudden silence the lapping of the disturbed water was loud and mocking.

"What's happened?" she choked.

"We hit something," said Leon grimly.

"We're not sinking?"

"No. But we've stripped the prop." Leon climbed back over the driving seat. His face was grim.

"How bad is it?" she asked anxiously.

"We hit a piece of driftwood. No propellor."

"What do we do?"

"The current's in the right direction. We'll drift with it."

"It'll take hours to reach land."

He nodded. "That's the trouble. I'm worried about you. You'll have to explain at home about . . . tonight!"

She nodded. Her face was composed but there was cold anxiety within her.

The couples behind them were warm under their blankets and they began to sing softly. Drifting was no hardship for them. One of the boys threw a blanket over the driving seat.

"Are you cold?" asked Leon.

"A little."

He spread the blanket over them, put his arm around her and she snuggled up to him.

A fisherman in a small boat came upon them just after dawn and took them in tow. When they saw the fisherman approaching, Leon folded the blanket but as they were being towed to Escoleras she held his hand. The fisherman glanced back over his shoulder and saw it.

Leon detached his hand from hers but she grasped it again firmly. "Don't you like holding my hand?"

"It's you I'm thinking of. It's bad enough as it is. You know the way people talk."

"I don't care, Leon," she said recklessly. "I don't care." Her eyes shone and she held her head high.

When the speedboat was beached in front of the Marvista the other couples hurried away to breakfast.

"They'll know by now what you've done," said Leon.

Silvana nodded.

"I'll take you home so they'll know who you've been with."

"It's better not."

"I'll accompany you," he insisted.

But when they reached the drive she said firmly: "Don't come any further, Leon."

"I'll explain where you've been."

"Later, if you must. But not now. Please. It's better this way, Leon."

"If you're sure."

"I'm sure." Her eyes caressed his face. "Thank you for everything." There was a break in her voice and she turned quickly and hurried up the gravel drive.

Her father was waiting on the terrace. He had watched her arrive with Leon and as she climbed the steps he asked coldly: "Was the boy afraid to face me?"

"No, Father. I begged him to go away."

"Why?"

"Because I'm tired and don't want a scene."

Her mother choked: *"You're* tired! And we were worried out of our minds!"

"Where have you been?" asked Anselmo in a dead voice.

"We went out along the coast. It was a beautiful night."

"Without my permission?"

"It would have been useless to ask you."

"How many were you?"

"Six."

"Three couples?"

She met his eyes steadily. "Yes."

"What happened?"

"We lost the propellor."

"What happened to *you?* Alone with that boy!"

"Leon is a gentleman."

Anselmo's eyes glittered. "I want to know what *happened!*"

Silvana tossed her head and flared: "I'm tired!"

Her mother intervened. "I'll handle this, Anselmo. I'm her mother." She glared. "We'll talk in your room, my girl!"

Silvana held her head high and her mother waddled along behind her. Once inside the bedroom her mother locked the door. "Now," she said. Her black eyes glittered balefully. "Let's have a look at you." She examined her daughter sharply. "How did your blouse get so creased? And your skirt?"

"Sitting in the boat."

"Creased like *that!* How were you sitting then? With your skirt up around your waist? Get undressed."

"Why should I?"

"You're my daughter and I'm telling you. Do what I say or get my hand across your face."

Pale-faced, Silvana took off her blouse and skirt. Her mother snatched them and threw them across the room. "That's a fine way to go out," she said disgustedly. "Practically nothing on underneath. Take *that* off." She examined the brassiere carefully. "What about this hook?" she demanded. "Pulled off!"

"I've been meaning to sew it for days."

"And this broken shoulder strap!"

"It snapped without my noticing it."

"Without your noticing!" sneered her mother. She scrutinized her daughter's breasts intently. "What's this mark here? This red mark?"

"I can't see any mark, Mother."

"And this mark here. You don't deny that's a bruise?"

"Perhaps . . . perhaps I banged myself."

"Perhaps you held yourself too tightly. Those are finger marks as plain as plain."

"Mother . . ."

"Take that off," grated her mother and Silvana stepped out of her last garment and gave it to her mother.

Suddenly her mother lashed out. The flat of her hand slapped the girl's cheek and hurled her back on the bed. She stood over the girl, her fat face working with rage. "You little slut," she panted. "A daughter of mine behaving like an alley cat!"

"Mother . . . please!" choked Silvana. She was crying.

"You think you can hide it from your own mother! You think I've had all my children without knowing what it's all about? Something'll be done about this, my girl!"

"Please, Mother. You don't understand . . . !"

Her mother waddled to the door, unlocked it and flung it open. "Anselmo!" she screamed along the wide, empty corridor, and when he came hurrying anxiously she screamed: "It's that Coruna boy. He's had her!"

Teresa received Anselmo in her office. They had seen little of each other these past few years. Anselmo had never visited the hotel until now and was impressed by the sumptuousness of Teresa's private office.

Teresa ordered the bellhop who had shown him in: "Tell the desk I'm not to be disturbed unless it's urgent."

As soon as the door closed she walked up to Anselmo smiling with such warmth that he was embarrassed. "It's good to see you, Anselmo. You never call on us. It's a pity because we'd be delighted to see more of you."

He said uncomfortably: "It's Narcissus I called to see."

"Make yourself comfortable, Anselmo. What would you like to drink?"

"Er . . . nothing, thanks. It will soon be lunchtime."

"That's why. An aperitif. What was it you used to like? Yes. Now I remember. Black Cinzano, a little gin and a few drops of Picon."

It was years since Anselmo had drunk an aperitif and he was a little awed by Teresa's self-assurance as she prepared the drinks. He was surprised at how young she looked, as though the years had not touched her. Almost, it seemed, she had improved as she had grown older. Yet she must be forty-five.

Teresa turned around from the portable bar and came over to him, carrying two tall glasses. She sat on her desk.

"I'm sorry about your financial troubles, Anselmo."

"Ah, yes!" he said, nodding sadly. He had been dogged by bad luck on his farm and in his trades.

"I was unlucky," he sighed. "I sold off all the land I had near the sea and was paid a pittance. It has changed hands a dozen times since and now they're building on it. If I had held on a few years I'd have been wealthy today."

"Have you thought of leaving farming and doing something else?"

He sighed. "Many times. But I'm trapped. Antonia and Pilar still need help. They're not married and can't make enough to live on teaching. Then there's Manolo. He's not doing well in Barcelona and I send him something. And I have my own family. All these expenses have to be paid by the farm. But unless things improve soon . . ." Anselmo shrugged his shoulders dismally.

"And Rafael?" she asked. "Any news of him?"

He shook his head. "After Mother's death we had a property settlement. Since then we've heard nothing."

"You look tired, Anselmo," she said and he saw she was looking at him tenderly. "Are you sure you're not working too hard?"

"Work rarely kills," said Anselmo. He took out his handkerchief and wiped his forehead. He had put on his best jacket for this formal visit and it was tight under the armpits.

Teresa noticed his discomfort and encouraged him: "Take your coat off, Anselmo. Be comfortable while you're here." She helped him off with his jacket, and hung it in the wardrobe.

He said abruptly: "It is Narcissus I wish to see."

"He's away today. But you can talk to me, Anselmo. Anything which concerns Narcissus concerns me."

She was looking at his arm and he glanced down and saw the long, white scar. He moved his arm slightly. "A constant reminder, Teresa. I was . . . ungrateful to you. I hope you forgive me."

"When we are young we do many things for which we need forgiveness."

The conversation was turning into byways he dared not enter. "I called to see Narcissus about a serious matter," he said.

"Yes?" Her eyes widened.

"Leon, your son. Do you know where he was last night?"

"He said something about a midnight picnic. The engine broke down and he didn't get back until this morning."

"Do you know who was with him?"

She shrugged her shoulders. "He usually takes out a party of guests from the hotel."

"Silvana was with him," Anselmo said quietly. He took out his handkerchief and mopped his forehead. "All night!" he added.

Teresa's eyes narrowed. She studied him thoughtfully but said nothing.

"That's why I want to talk to you and Narcissus."

"Yes?" said Teresa. Her voice was quiet.

Anselmo spread his hands. "You understand. Something must be done. Soon the whole village will know."

"No. I don't understand, Anselmo. What are you telling me?"

He was surprised. "My daughter's reputation is at stake. Your son is responsible."

Teresa picked up a pack of cigarettes, selected one and offered the pack to Anselmo. He waved it away.

Teresa snapped a lighter and puffed her cigarette to life. Only when she was quite sure she was under control did she say: "My son is responsible? For what?"

He was puzzled by her attitude. "For my daughter's reputation."

"Tell me, Anselmo," she said gently. "Did Leon carry her off by force?"

"Of course not."

"She went with him willingly?"

"But without our knowledge and against our wishes."

"But she went with him voluntarily?"

"And . . . they were together all night!"

"Engine trouble was the cause. These accidents happen."

"Teresa. You and Narcissus must talk to your boy and arrange something."

"Arrange what, Anselmo?" Teresa's voice was ominously quiet.

"They must marry," he said flatly.

Teresa arched one eyebrow. "Is Silvana pregnant?"

He flushed. "If she is we won't know for some time."

"What does Silvana want?"

"She's difficult. She won't talk about it. Her mother can't get sense out of her."

"Perhaps . . . nothing happened?"

"What they did doesn't affect the issue, Teresa. Silvana's reputation is in jeopardy."

Teresa turned and paced to the window. She stood staring out and said over her shoulder: "What do you expect me to do?"

"Talk to Leon. He can call and ask for Silvana's hand. I will agree, of course. The sooner they are married the better!"

"Does Silvana want to marry Leon?"

"She'll do what I say."

Teresa turned around and said carefully: "I'll talk to Leon. If he wants to marry Silvana I will raise no objections."

Anselmo gaped: *"If!"* he said. "On an important issue like this the parents make the decision."

"No," she said quietly. "Leon makes his *own* decisions."

"Have you no influence over him?"

"A great deal. Probably too much. That's one reason for not using it."

"You've got to be firm, Teresa. As parents, you and Narcissus have a duty to see that Leon does the right thing."

"I'm sorry, Anselmo," she said firmly. "I won't influence Leon. He must make his own decisions."

Anselmo got to his feet. He breathed hard. "I'm shocked, Teresa," he said bitterly. "I was confident that as a lifelong friend of the family you would do the right thing."

Teresa studied him for a very long time. Then she said clearly: "Long ago I gave way to a natural impulse and became what you called 'soiled.' Now, when you demand that my son marries your daughter I can only ask this: If I was not fit to marry because I was 'soiled,' why should your own 'soiled' daughter be good enough to marry my son?"

Anselmo turned pale. Without a word he got to his feet and put on his jacket. Without another glance at Teresa he strode to the door and went out.

10

It was the worst winter the old people could remember. The rains were heavy, the wind fierce and the cold intense. One morning the Serras rose before dawn, hitched up their skin-and-bone horse to their old cart and set off into the mountains. Some months earlier at an auction Vicente Serra had snapped up a few acres of agricultural land, unwanted because it was too far from the village. Now he and Maria set off to gather its potato crop.

It was a long, uphill journey along rough, rutted paths and boulder-strewn slopes. Their aged mare's bones stood out from its mangy hide as she wearily hauled the cart. On the steeper slopes Vicente Serra walked in front and pulled the lead rein while Maria pushed the cart.

The rarified air on the higher mountain slopes was much colder than at sea level and as they hobbled the mare and took up their tools, the north wind began to blow. They stooped over the furrows and chipped at the frosty, iron-hard earth while the wind cut cruelly through their clothing. At midday, when they stopped to chew a hunk of bread and drink a little wine, the cold was so intense that they were eager to start work again. By late afternoon the cart was piled high with potatoes and could carry no more.

The aged mare had been standing in the shafts all day and they had to rub warmth into her legs before she could walk without stumbling. They had covered only a few hundred yards of their return journey when one wheel skidded off the side of a large boulder and sprang free from its axle. The cart gave a wild lurch and dropped, the hub scored a groove in the earth and the mare was dragged to a standstill. The potatoes avalanched and Serra swore violently as the wheel rolled on for several yards before it toppled on its side.

The fury of the Tramontana eased a little, as it always did before sunset, "showing reverence to the setting sun," as the villagers said, and Serra shouted fiercely: "Hurry, woman. Help me before it is dark."

They gathered large stones and piled them up under the axle. They used a pickax handle as a crowbar and pushed more stones under the axle. It was slow, laborious work and it was dusk before the cart was propped up level. Maria trundled the wheel to Vicente who was working under the cart. They had only to fit the wheel onto the axle, improvise a pin to hold it and they could be on their way. But the axle had to be raised another inch and while Vicente levered with his crowbar, the aged mare, mistaking his grunts of effort for a command, gathered her strength and lurched forward. The cart toppled slowly forward off the small mountain of stones. Seeing his danger, Serra tried frantically to escape, but the full weight of the cart crunched down upon his leg.

"Holy Mother of Jesus!" gasped Serra.

"Your leg. Your leg!" screamed Maria.

"Don't be hysterical, woman," shouted Serra. "Do something."

The mare's ears pricked and she made another half-start, tugging on the shafts and increasing the pressure on Serra's leg. "Hurry!" he choked.

"What must I do, Vicente?" whimpered Maria.

"That whore of a horse is tearing my leg apart."

She loosened the traces and slapped the mare until she stepped free from the shafts.

"Daughter of a whore!" Serra shouted and the mare trotted away apprehensively, ears pricking as she lowered her long, tired neck to graze.

"Have you much pain, Vicente?" asked Maria, white-faced.

"Not yet," he said. "Quick. Before the pain begins."

"What must I do?"

"Get two big boulders. One to slide under the axle as you raise it and the other to brace the pickax handle on."

Maria strained her weight upon the crowbar and raised the cart high enough for him to pull his leg free. It was by now quite dark.

"Are you in much pain, Vicente?"

"Help me mount the mare," he growled.

But the mare was nervous and distrusted the woman's increasingly angry efforts to catch her. Maria stalked her a long time, never able to get close enough to seize her, and finally lost her in the darkness. She returned to her husband.

"Help me," he said. "I'll try to walk."

He leaned heavily upon her and used a pick handle as a walking stick. They made tortuously slow progress. The Tramontana blew again with full fury and cut through their clothing. Its force often threatened to hurl them forward on their faces. There was no moon, the rock-strewn slopes were treacherous and they stumbled often. The temperature went down and down, numbing their limbs until they ached. Presently snowflakes drove against them, coating them and spreading a white carpet on the ground. Half-blinded by whirling snow they didn't see where the earth had broken away, and they fell in a tangle of limbs. Serra screamed.

"I am sorry, Vicente. I lost my footing." Maria had to shout to make herself heard above the wind.

He groaned.

"Come, Vicente. I will help you."

He held back. "It cannot be. The pain will kill me."

She took him in her arms and rocked gently, her back turned to the fury of the wind to protect him. Snow gathered on them and numbness crept through her.

"Listen, Vicente. I will go for help."

He held her tightly. "Don't leave me."

She warmed him with her own thin body and when he began to whimper she crooned to him. The cold penetrated and drained away consciousness until she slept. She was awakened by the slash of an uprooted thorn bush flung against her by the wind. "Vicente," she choked. "Vicente!"

He did not answer. He was breathing quickly, his fingers were icy and she knew he would die if she did not go for help. She tucked his hands into his jacket and covered him with her shawl. She stumbled along on feet so numbed that she lost one rope-soled sandal without knowing it. She fought on grimly through the driving snow, often floundering knee-deep in snowdrifts. Presently she became light-headed and hazy about direction. She saw distant pinpoints of light and staggered on for an eternity before she reached the stream that flowed through Escoleras. There had been torrential rain the previous day and the stream was waist-deep. But its surface was frozen and covered with snow and when Maria blundered onto it the ice broke and she sank to her armpits.

When she reached Escoleras her clothes were frozen stiff, her hair was white with frost and her flesh was blue.

Rescue volunteers prepared warm clothing and a stretcher while others tried to warm Maria. They stripped off her clothing, rubbed her chilled flesh with alcohol and placed her before a roaring fire enveloped in blankets. Her teeth chattered so violently that she could tell where she had left Vicente only with the greatest difficulty.

The rescue volunteers with Doctor Aldo and four Civil Guards set off into the cold night.

After a time, Maria slept. But even in sleep she shivered violently, her teeth chattered and her flesh remained as hard as frozen beef. Presently she began to cough. The cough came from the depths of her being and shook her convulsively.

It was the worst winter anyone could remember. Eucalyptus trees more than two hundred years old perished. Few olive trees survived and the cactus bushes which marked the boundaries between properties turned black and withered.

The rescue party searched all night and most of the next day but Vicente was not found until the snows melted three weeks later. Maria died of exposure, slipping away swiftly.

Asuncion bore the loss of her parents stoically, went on living in the same tumbled-down cottage, was grateful for the sympathy of her neighbors and worked every day in the grocery store.

The Barcelona solicitor who handled Serra's affairs presently informed Asuncion that as Serra's only daughter she inherited everything!

Asuncion Serra called to see Doctor Aldo.

"I trust you, Doctor Aldo. I know nobody else I can ask for advice."

"I'll help if I can, Asuncion. What's your problem?"

"I want to marry."

Doctor Aldo was not surprised. Long before her parents' death, Asuncion had shown her liking for Diego Muñez, the cheerful, dark-eyed, curly-haired Gypsy youth who would strum a guitar for hours but who loathed work. Vicente and Maria Serra had kept Diego away from their daughter but since their death the doctor had often seen them together.

"It is Diego Muñez you want to marry?" asked the doctor.

Asuncion nodded. "I hope I can make him happy and I know he will make me happy."

"You *should* be able to make him happy," said the doctor dryly, thinking of her inheritance.

And then the girl surprised him.

"Diego will want my money, Doctor Aldo. I don't think it's *only* my money he's after, but he'll expect to handle my money as though it's his own."

He was delighted that she could see so clearly. "You could come to a financial arrangement," he suggested delicately.

"I've discussed it with my solicitor, Doctor. I won't deny Diego anything that's reasonable. But I don't want *everything* squandered. My solicitor has listed various ways to invest money so it can't be touched while it yields a reasonable income." Asuncion pushed a thick manila envelope across the desk. "I don't understand these things much and I'd like you to advise me which you think are best."

Doctor Aldo took the sheaf of documents from the envelope and his eyebrows raised. It was hard to believe that Serra and his wife could have made such a fortune. Every peseta the frugal couple had earned must have been invested again and again. Serra had bought land in Barcelona during the depression and had sold it later for a fortune. He owned stocks and shares, houses, apartment buildings and factories. The amount of property he had bought in and around

Escoleras was startling. He had ferreted out the owners of land long disused and bought it cheaply. The solicitor had prepared a number of sound schemes and Doctor Aldo told Asuncion which he thought suited her best.

"Thank you for your help, Doctor."

"I've done very little. But I'm curious, Asuncion. What will you do with the rest of the property?"

Her eyes glowed. "I'll sell it and put the money in the bank for Diego to squander."

"You think you'll be happy, Asuncion?"

"Diego hasn't anything except his sunny nature, Doctor. But I don't mind him having my money if he'll give me a little of his sun."

Doctor Aldo gave Asuncion away at the wedding. The honeymoon was to have lasted a month but within a few days the couple were back in Escoleras. Diego was bored with traveling. The newlyweds rented a luxury apartment with a view of the sea, and the rest of the Muñez family moved into the two apartments above it. The many Muñez children had new clothes and bright new toys and Diego's parents blossomed out like lottery winners. Diego bought a speedboat for himself and another for his parents. He chose a red sports car for his own use and a gleaming six-seater limousine with a chauffeur for his parents. Every night the entire family, including Diego and Asuncion, dined out at an expensive restaurant. In the bars they paid for everybody's drinks and in restaurants sent champagne to other tables. They tipped so extravagantly that worried waiters sometimes begged them to take some back.

One day Doctor Aldo and Paco Barras were strolling along the promenade and came upon Diego in leather jeans and jacket, strumming his guitar and singing softly. Asuncion sat beside him, listening with dreamy eyes. Diego courteously exchanged greetings and resumed playing when they had passed.

Paco Barras shook his head wryly. "Serra would go *mad* if he could see what's happening to his money. He and Maria pinched and scraped and starved and finally died to hoard a few pesetas. And for what? So the laziest people in Escoleras can spend their money like water."

"It may be for the best," said Doctor Aldo.

"You could be right," chuckled Paco Barras. "Sometimes a cat chokes itself with cream."

"I'm thinking of the girl," said Doctor Aldo. "Did you see the look in her eyes? She's sensible. And that's probably why she's one of the happiest girls we've known."

Rosalia's determination to get her own apartment became a forgotten dream. She had tried to save but there were always expenses which nibbled away her reserves. She had lost the will to escape from her environment.

One night Rosalia found herself among a group of students. It was a stifling evening, the air reeked of sweat and scented bodies and she had to shout to make herself heard. The students joked tipsily and laughed uproariously. If a girl took a number of students up to her room for tricks, it was easy money. So Rosalia laughed with them and touched them with quick fingers, smiled and widened her eyes so that their whites would gleam. "All of you together?" she wheedled. "We'll have fun."

"How's that for a geometrical problem?" said one student.

They laughed uproariously. They were quite drunk.

A student fumbled at her and she held still for him, revolving her loins around his touch. "Aaaah!" she panted.

He abruptly tugged hard, uprooting so fiercely she cried out aloud.

"Another for the collection," he chortled, flourishing his wispy trophy.

Rosalia smarted intolerably and drove her knee hard up into the youth's groin. He doubled up and hugged himself in agony. Then her anger burst all restraint. A space cleared around her and she became the focus of all eyes. But she couldn't stop herself. All her resentment of life poured out in a great flood of obscenity. Her fury finally ebbed. "I shit upon all of you and your whoring mothers!" She spat.

"I'll pay you," offered one of the discomfited students.

"Come upstairs and I'll show you what he did."

The student drew back. He was very young. "I'll . . . I'll give you the money."

She took his arm. "I don't want you to *give* me money. Come upstairs."

He tried to pull away. "No."

"What's the matter? Are you a *maricon?*" She touched him.

"Don't," he said desperately. "I'll give you money. What more do you want?"

"*You*, darling." She thrust against him.

His boyish face was flushed and his eyes alarmed. "Let me go!"

She tried to kiss him.

He recoiled. She saw the revulsion in his eyes and the hurt of it was upon her before he shouted: "I couldn't touch an old hag like you!"

She was only vaguely aware he had broken away and was escaping. As though dazed she climbed the stairs to her room, bolted the door behind her, crossed to the cracked mirror and stared at her reflection.

Old hag!

The awful realization that it was true shocked her.

She saw herself through the eyes of the young student. Mascara mingled with perspiration and ran into the crow's feet at the corners of her eyes. Below them hung dark, fleshy pouches. Her mouth was a mean, pinched line and deep creases in her neck ran down to the raddled flesh between her breasts.

I *can't* be old, she thought wildly. I *can't* be! But she was. Not only in age but with the long years of staring up at the ceiling over the man's shoulder, her mind detached from the activity. Nerves, muscle and skin wearing away, senses blunted and existence a perpetual false smile and submission.

She looked at her cracked mirror with horror. *I'm old*, she thought frantically. *I'm on the road to fifty! What will happen to me?*

In the next instant she knew. She remembered the old crones garbed in black who crouched over trays of matches on the pavements outside the brothels.

The meeting was called for eleven. The mayor and the town council secretary were present, the authorized architect and the surveyor. The four businessmen from Barcelona sat on one side of the long table facing Teresa, Narcissus and the bank manager.

After a whispered conference with the secretary, the mayor rose to his feet. "As you know, an official permit has been granted for your urbanization plan. Work can begin at once. Some modifications have been suggested however. I understand they are probably acceptable to the syndicate but we must legalize it. I'll ask Señor Narcissus Coruna to carry on."

Narcissus smiled feebly. "My wife knows this matter inside out so she'll discuss it instead of me."

Teresa smiled, rose gracefully and pressed her chair away with the backs of her legs. The businessmen came to life and listened with interest. Teresa said crisply: "I'm not proposing any change in our plans but I'm suggesting an additional development."

As she talked, the official architect studied her with concealed admiration. Teresa was a remarkable woman and he knew it better than anyone.

He had worked for months with Teresa, producing plans, and had been amazed at the breadth of her vision. When she had taken an option on her land many years ago, it was worthless swamp. But the land flanked the beach and Teresa was now turning wasteland into a garden city. She had formed the syndicate by going after businessmen and convincing them her plans were sound. Now they would be put into practice. Retaining walls would be built along the beach and dumping trucks would fill in the swamp with grit and rubble. Roads would be made, electric lighting installed, water and sewage pipes laid and housing sites marked out. It was a ten-year plan. Escoleras would become a thriving tourist resort with a population of thirty thousand and an industrial center to provide employment during the winter months. The government in Madrid had approved the plan, the Admiralty would contribute a splendid promenade lined with palm trees and three of the big banks would make extensive loans.

Today's meeting was called because Teresa needed approval for a new suggestion. She had a map spread out on the table and everyone gathered around it as she talked.

"The promenade will border the beach," she said, pointing. "Behind it are public gardens where people can stroll in the cool of the evening. Here, we have our building area. Bungalows in the first rank, two-story villas in the second rank and so on, back to the eight-story apartment blocks. A view of the sea for everyone. Here, the hotels and recreation grounds. Then, right back, we have the factory zone which I'd like modified. I don't think we've allocated enough space to it. We should go deeper inland. I've made pencil lines showing this zone can be expanded."

The Barcelona men studied the plan. One asked: "The syndicate land ends here?"

Teresa nodded.

"This other land can be bought cheaply?"

Teresa eyed him steadily. "I haven't inquired."

"Land so far from the sea-front is valueless," he said. "Even when we build up to its boundary it is still worthless without the right to use our roads."

"I feel it's important the syndicate buys this land," said Teresa. "We can afford to pay a good price."

"How much are you thinking of paying?"

"Five million pesetas."

They took out their slide rules, calculated the price per square meter and looked at Teresa in surprise. "It's . . . it's as much as we pay for your land, Señora Coruna!"

"But my land has to be filled in!"

"But it has direct frontage to the beach."

Teresa smiled. "This project is costing hundreds of millions. Need we quibble about the price of a small piece of land, gentlemen?"

"Señora. It's our duty to our shareholders to buy at a good price."

Teresa chose her words carefully so they would not sound like a threat. "My contract with the syndicate gives me the option to retain twenty percent of my land. Our plans have gone ahead swiftly and I shan't exercise this option because it will disrupt our development. But I say this, gentlemen. If I am cooperative, it makes me unhappy that the syndicate is reluctant to respond when I ask for a fair deal for a small landowner."

The men from Barcelona smiled at Teresa. "Buy the land, Señora Coruna. We're sure your judgment is sound."

Before she left the town hall, Teresa took the architect by his arm and led him to one side. "You will call on Señor Ledesma with the documents and complete the purchase?"

"This afternoon if you wish, Señora."

"The sooner the better."

He sensed she was searching for words. "Anything else, Señora?"

"Yes. Don't mention I am connected with the transaction."

"As you wish, Señora."

"One other thing," she said slowly. "You can be useful to Señor Ledesma. When he sells the farm he'll have money to invest. Why don't you suggest he pull down his residence and build a block of apartments. His home and its ground are large enough for a six-story block. You could design them."

"Thank you for the suggestion, Señora." His eyes were shining. Already he was visualizing the tall, proud apartment block he would build where the Ledesma house now stood.

Narcissus was waiting for Teresa outside the town hall and when they arrived back at the Marvista she sensed he wanted to talk to her. She took him into her office. "I know it's early but make me a cocktail, darling."

Narcissus mixed a cocktail and poured from the shaker into cut-glass tumblers.

"To health and money," Teresa toasted.

"To *your* happiness," he said, looking at her intently.

She savored her drink. "What are you thinking?"

"I congratulate you."

She raised one eyebrow. "Why, darling?"

"You've found a way to help Anselmo."

She said slowly: "His farm was always a headache. Perhaps now he'll be able to invest shrewdly."

"You've always worried about him, haven't you?"

"Do you mind very much?"

"I face facts, Teresa. It was Anselmo you wanted to marry."

"That was a long, long time ago, Narcissus."

"He would have been happier with you."

She said quietly: "I think so. But I've discovered something, Narcissus. If I had my time again and could marry Anselmo, I wouldn't. I would marry . . . you!"

Narcissus smiled. "A sweet white lie. I know I've always taken second place to Anselmo."

She smiled softly. "You're wrong, foolish one. Quite wrong. Young girls have their romantic dreams. But few wives enjoy the tenderness and respect you've always given me."

He looked away from her, blinking quickly.

"Anselmo won't ever speak to either of us again because of that business with Leon." She shrugged her shoulders. "It doesn't worry me at all, darling. Not at all!"

Teresa was walking across the vestibule toward the dining room when something strangely familiar about the man standing at the reception desk caught her attention. As though he could feel her eyes upon him, he turned slowly. For a moment her breathing seemed to cease.

He came to her but the recognition in his eyes was veiled. When he drew close he said in a low-toned, excited voice: *"Chiquita. Chiquita!"*

"Mi Capitan!" Her eyes searched his face. His hair was streaked with silver and his sideburns were quite white. His darkly handsome face was fleshy and red-veined and the whites of his eyes were yellowy. *Mother of God,* she thought. *He's old, terribly old!* And she realized he must be sixty. The absurdity of a lover of sixty made her want to laugh.

"Come," she said. "Let us sit and talk."

"Can't I see you later? Privately?"

"If you wish, Captain. But is it necessary?"

He flashed a furtive glance around him. "Have you forgotten? I'm a political refugee."

"But if they allowed you into the country . . ."

"I've a French name and passport."

"If you'd like to come up to my private room?"

"Later," he said quickly. "Later." He looked towards the ladies room. "My wife's with me and she's very inquisitive. I'd rather she . . ."

His nervousness irritated her. "It's up to you, Captain."

"Where can I meet you?"

"Room Sixty-five."

"When?"

"This afternoon."

"What time?"

"Between three and four. Is that all right?"

"She always sleeps in the afternoons. I'll tell her I'm going for a walk." Again his sly manner irritated her. "I'll leave you now, *chiquita.* I don't want her to see us talking."

"As you wish," she said coldly and hurried away.

But from within the dining room she watched him join the plump little woman who came out of the ladies room. She was his own age, Teresa judged. Dyed auburn hair set as hard as bronze and as lifeless. A pronounced double chin, a suit which betrayed she was tightly corseted, and high-heeled shoes which were much too small. She walked to the elevator as though her feet were tender. He followed attentively.

When she was in her room awaiting his visit, she almost regretted having invited him. She lowered the shutters so that the room was in cool shadow. When he knocked on the door, she was relaxed on her lounging couch. She put down her magazine, straightened the cushions and called: "Come in."

As soon as the door was closed behind him, he sighed with relief. "She's asleep."

"Please sit down," she said formally.

He sat down and smiled at her.

"How about a drink?"

"Something long. A mineral water or a beer."

She poured him a San Miguel and mineral water for herself.

"Seeing you again makes it seem that I was here only yesterday. You haven't changed, *chiquita.*"

"You haven't changed much either, Captain."

"I heard about . . . your brother."

"Miguel?"

He nodded. "It must have been a terrible blow."

She said quietly: "He was lost to us long before he died."

"Everything has changed so much, *chiquita.* There's nothing here that I recognize."

She nodded. "Everything's changing. *Everything!*"

"Everything except . . . except the system, the repression and the corruption."

She was surprised. "I don't understand, Captain."

"There's no freedom. You can't speak your mind. It's a Fascist country."

"It's not as bad as that, Captain."

"The things I read about Spain in the newspapers make me ashamed."

"The French newspapers, Captain?"

"Naturally," he said. "The Spanish press daren't print criticisms of the regime."

"Why are you bitter, Captain? You weren't interested in politics. You were simply an officer doing his duty."

"Spain is my country, *chiquita.* I love Spain and her people. I did my duty as a soldier and an officer. But the corrupt men in power have deprived me of my nationality."

"You can come back, Captain. There's an amnesty. Many, many Spaniards have returned."

"How many trusting fools walked into a trap? How many were beaten up, imprisoned and executed?"

"Those were criminals. Murderers who tried to return under the protection of political amnesty."

"It's easy to accuse a political opponent of murder when he is denied a public trial and is found guilty by a secret court."

"Nevertheless, many have returned to Spain and picked up the threads of their lives again, Captain."

He studied her carefully. "I'm risking my life here. I've got French nationality, daughters at college and a sound family business. I'm afraid, *chiquita*. What's to stop them arresting me and charging me with treason, an offense punishable by death?"

"They won't do that, Captain."

"But they did it, *chiquita*. Officers who remained loyal to the Spanish government and refused to revolt were shot by the Nationalists when they were taken prisoner."

"But that was years ago!"

His eyes stared intently. "Do you think things have changed?"

"I *know* they've changed."

He shook his head. "How many are today arrested without charge and beaten up? What happened to you when they learned that Scarface was your brother?"

"All that was so long, long ago."

"What did they do, *chiquita?* Did they tie you down and beat your bare feet with canes? Did they keep you without food and water until you talked?"

"You exaggerate, Captain. I won't deny that sometimes somebody vicious and unbalanced is in authority, and thirty years ago political hatred was so intense that people killed because of it. But things *have* changed, Captain. A new generation has grown up.

"The new generation hasn't any resentment or hatred. It lives in a different world that doesn't give rise to them. Spain is on the crest of a wave of prosperity and there's work for everyone. Spain lagged far behind other European countries but now we're catching up fast. Working people who once couldn't afford a radio are buying television sets and washing machines! There are still many things wrong in Spain, Captain. But nine people out of ten will sign on for another ten years of prosperity like these we've had under Franco."

"You're biased, *chiquita*. You've done well out of the regime."

"We were a simple family of fishermen, Captain. What we did, anyone could have done."

"But Spain is a Fascist dictatorship, *chiquita*. People can't choose their representatives and vote them into the Cortes."

She smiled slowly. "We Spanish are temperamental, Captain. We need firm rule. Left alone, we'd never reach agreement, all of us pulling a dozen different ways."

"The British have learned how to govern themselves."

"But . . . we're Spanish, Captain!" she said and chuckled.

"Perhaps you are right," he agreed reluctantly.

"How long are you staying?"

"I've got to feel my way. I'd like to go home. My parents died but I have a sister."

"How long will you stay in Escoleras?"

"I leave tomorrow." He walked across to the window and stared out. "The sea is the one thing which hasn't changed. After our retreat to France, while I was in a concentration camp, this view dominated my memory, the deep blue of the sea and the softer blue of the sky. You were a part of it all, *chiquita*. Those months I spent here were the happiest of my life."

She too thought back.

"You did not marry Anselmo?"

She shook her head slowly. "I was not worthy of him."

He came away from the window and stood looking down at her hair. "Were you unhappy?"

"Terribly."

"I'm sorry," he said sincerely.

"You needn't be. I know now I couldn't have been truly happy with him. Anselmo is steeped in old Spanish traditions. I'd have been a respected hostess in my home and the mother of his children. I would have had his affection, care and security. But he would never have permitted me to be other than his wife. I would have accepted decisions . . . but never made them. I would never have known the pleasure of accomplishment."

"And your husband. Are you happy with him?"

"He's thoughtful, sensitive and tender."

He moved behind her and too late she realized what he intended. His hand brushed across her shoulder, slipped swiftly down her arm and rested on her breast.

"This is the way I first touched you, *chiquita*. Do you remember? All these years I've remembered it."

"You have a tiresome memory, Captain. Please stop."

"Nothing changes the way I feel about the touch of you."

"Doesn't your wife satisfy you?"

"She's a good wife, helps with the business and is a good mother but . . . she doesn't have enough fire."

"So you want to work off your excess energy on me?"

There was hurt in his voice. "You know how I feel about *you, chiquita*." He started to pull her dress down off her shoulder but she grasped his wrists.

"I asked you to stop. Do I have to become unpleasant?"

He desisted at once. "I did not intend to offend. If you knew how all these years I've relived again and again the memories of the happy times we spent together . . . you would understand better."

"We cannot live with our memories, Captain. We must live in the real world."

"A man likes to dream." His black eyes were compelling. "I long to caress you, *chiquita*. To kiss you and feel you respond as once you did. The desire is an ache. Is it too much to ask?"

For one frightening moment the temptation was enormous. Then she heard herself say: "You've developed into a dirty old man!"

The words wiped away the tender memories like chalk from a blackboard. He withdrew sharply.

"And how is your father?" he asked formally.

"He is well. He will be pleased to see you."

He shook his head. "Before I meet those who know me, I must learn how things are. I have a good friend in Sevilla, a retired officer. I will seek his advice."

"If I can help you I shall be happy, Captain."

"Thank you, *chiquita*." He glanced at his wristwatch. "Yvonne will be awaking soon. I must go."

"Next time you call perhaps Narcissus will be here. I'd like you to meet him."

"I hope so too," he said politely, but she knew she would never see him again.

They shook hands.

"*Adiós, chiquita.*"

"*Adiós, mi Capitan.*"

11

Paco Barras came downstairs in his stockinged feet and grunted as he sat down and pulled on his rubber-soled boots. He crossed to the kitchen and stood staring at Elisa. She looked no different from behind than she had for almost all the years of their marriage.

"What's for lunch, woman?" he demanded.

"Something you like. Paella."

"With *gambas?*"

"Plenty." The crockery rattled. "Did you put on the clean shirt I put out?"

"I did." He chuckled. "I must look my best when I go walking with the doctor!"

"You're a conceited old man," she scolded.

He stole up behind her and slapped her buttock. "And you're a nagging old woman."

"On your way back try to remember to buy a few boxes of matches."

"Ah! Woman! You want to set me on fire and burn you up!"

"Away with you," she scolded happily. "Talking like that at your age."

Paco opened the back door, stepped outside and scowled. Most of his life he had walked barefooted on the beach. He was still not used to the concrete promenade which replaced the sand. He never would be. In summer the promenade was thronged with tourists. They strolled there with their children, sunbathed in deck chairs, shouted and played games. They thronged around the door and windows of his cottage, peering inside with wide-eyed curiosity. If he stepped outside barefoot, they stared at him as though he was a peculiar biological specimen.

Paco sighed, placed his feet astride, looked out to sea and drew fresh air into his lungs. Then he lit a black cheroot. All had changed so much, he thought sadly. The joy of living in Escoleras had dissolved away. All that remained of his happy way of life was this cottage. It was an anachronism now, overtowered by a newly built street of smart shops and blocks of apartments.

It was one of those January days when the sun blazed down hotly, the blue sky tinted the sea and the distant Pyrenees seemed only a few miles away, standing out cleanly with their peaks snowcapped.

Presently he saw Doctor Aldo and the two old friends slowly strolled the promenade.

"Don't walk so fast," grumbled Doctor Aldo.

Paco Barras gave him a sly sideway glance. "What's the matter, Doctor? Getting old?"

"A touch of lumbago." Doctor Aldo frowned indignantly. "What do you mean, old? You're older than me."

"We all have to get old."

Doctor Aldo looked at Paco's sunburned face, his clear blue eyes and his shock of blond hair and realized with surprise that it was almost all silver. El Rubio had been so fair that its change in color had been imperceptible. "How old are you, Paco?" he asked, envious of his friend's effortless gait.

"Seventy-six next Thursday."

"And you still go fishing!"

"That's when I'm happiest." He chuckled. "It gets me away from all this."

They walked on slowly, past the hot-dog kiosk closed for the winter, the small pier where passengers lined up for excursion boat trips and the town hall's information office built squarely in the center of the promenade.

Presently they stopped and watched the Pradas sitting on the promenade wall and eating *garrotas*. They had a *porrón* of wine, a long loaf and gaily-colored napkins. They chopped open the sea urchins with kitchen knives to spoon out the rich, yellow meat. Isabel and Marcel Prada glanced up and saw the two men watching them.

"You are welcome," invited Marcel.

"Thank you," they said, shaking their heads. They walked on.

"What ever happened to Rosalia?" asked Paco Barras.

Doctor Aldo took out his watch and glanced at it. He had been retired a year and the alert young doctor who had taken over his practice rarely called on him for assistance. He sighed. "Serra told me once he'd been with her in a Barcelona brothel. You know how mean-fisted he was, so you can imagine the cheap type of brothel he would go to."

"She was a good girl. It's hard to believe," said Paco.

"If it *was* Rosalia, heaven knows what she's doing now they've cleaned out all those places."

"She'll be getting past that kind of thing anyway."

"She'll be nearly fifty," said Doctor Aldo.

"We were all to blame for what happened to her," said Paco Barras, shaking his head sadly. "One of us should have taken her in." He shrugged his shoulders. "But with the Nationalists occupying the village and . . . everything!"

"Life deals us all a hand of cards," philosophized Doctor Aldo. "Rosalia got a very poor hand." He sighed and thought of Rafael Ledesma's hard, black eyes and sneering lips. "Did I tell you about Rafael?"

Paco shook his head.

"Anselmo Ledesma would not like it to get around . . . !"

"You can trust me."

"Rafael's been put away. There was always something strange . . . even when he was a boy. Did you see him when his mother died? I thought it might be the strain of war service. It wasn't."

"You mean he's . . . loco?"

"I don't know the details. Anselmo isn't even aware I know. A couple of years ago I received a letter from a specialist in Madrid. They were treating Rafael and asked me for his medical history. He was detained because of a pretty nasty business. He and another man had a girl tied up in their apartment for days, cut her about, cigar ends and things like that!"

They came to a standstill at the concrete base of a towering flagstaff and looked up at the red and gold Spanish flag fluttering in the light breeze.

"Our flag, the symbol of nationalism," said Doctor Aldo tonelessly.

"Hernando was a great Anarchist," mused Paco. "This would have been his final humiliation."

The flagstaff was erected on the site of Hernando's stone hut.

The two men walked on toward the Marvista Hotel.

"Do you remember when Hernando caught that two-hundred-kilo tuna three miles off the coast in his rowboat? He fought it for sixteen hours and had to tow it because it was too big to lift into his boat."

"And that wild boar that blundered into the village, fleeing from the hunters?" said Paco Barras. "I was with Hernando. When we saw the boar he snatched up his gun and went after it. I didn't see him again for three days. But he brought it back. He carried it across his shoulders for fifteen kilometers."

"They don't make men like him these days," said Doctor Aldo and shook his head sadly.

"He was the old Spain," said Paco. He paused and then added slowly. "Perhaps . . . the *true* Spain!"

"We've changed our way of life so much that there's no room left for folk like Hernando," said the doctor.

"We live in a different world now," agreed Paco. "But I doubt if it's a better one. Before the war we lived leisurely. We didn't have much money but we didn't need it. Nowadays, everybody works so hard to earn money there's no leisure. The only truly happy man I've ever known was Hernando and he never had a peseta to spend."

They had reached the wide highway that swept past the rear of the Hotel Marvista. A streamlined crimson sports car snarled past and sounded a fierce blast on its horn. A brown arm waved and a shout of greeting was torn away on the wind and floated to them. Leon's hair shone in the sun as silvery as his grandfather's. The girl beside him fluttered a blue chiffon scarf in the slipstream.

"I'm told my grandson is now called El Rubio," said Paco contentedly.

"He's called Young Rubio and you're called Old Rubio."

"He's just off to Barcelona," said Paco.

"And the girl?"

"She's Swiss. Wealthy family. Her father built that big villa with the swimming pool on the slope overlooking the church."

"Leon's a lucky boy. He's got the world at his feet," said Doctor Aldo.

"I hope he knows how to treat it."

"Wasn't there some understanding between him and Silvana Ledesma?"

Paco Barras shrugged his shoulders. "There may have been. Teresa says he's thinking of marrying this Swiss girl. They're a fine couple and go everywhere together."

They reached the Marvista Hotel and a smartly uniformed bellhop took them up in the elevator to the top floor. They walked the last flight of stairs to the roof terrace and seated themselves under gaily colored parasols on chairs placed ready for them. The weekly aperitifs with Teresa and Narcissus had become a regular and pleasant routine.

A white-jacketed waiter served them, setting out dishes of cockles, mussels, baby octopus and other savories. "El Señor y La Señora Coruna will join you at once," said the waiter.

"Thank you," said Paco Barras. He leaned forward, speared three baby octopus with a toothpick, popped them into his mouth and chewed with relish.

Doctor Aldo looked out at the expanse of blue sea flecked with the silver fish scales of sun-dappled water. Then he turned his gaze to the long sweep of beach stretching into the distance. A new wide highway was being made. Tractors, trucks and mechanical shovels were scattered over the area and great cranes reared up like monster skeletons.

"It's hard to realize our village has become a town in a few short years, Paco."

"I want nothing of towns. I wish this tourist boom had never started!"

"Are you really thinking of leaving Escoleras, Paco?"

"Perhaps. It would not be difficult. Every year my neighbors compete for my cottage. Every year they offer me a million more." He chuckled. "With what they will pay me I can buy a large mansion with many acres of good land." He shrugged his shoulders. "But I will die if when I look out of my window I cannot see the sea."

"If you intend to sell your cottage, Paco, perhaps this year is the year to sell. Next year may be too late."

"Too late?"

"Every year we build like beavers and double the number of our hotels and apartments. Every year industry gears itself up to higher production. It can't go on . . . forever! One year there will be only the same number of tourists as the year previously. Then will come disaster because we Spaniards are sublime optimists and will never believe we have overproduced until there are thousands of apartments with no buyers and hundreds of hotels only half full."

"There are already signs of this," said Paco quietly. "I've been told of new apartments which cannot be sold and of builders who cannot pay their debts."

"Everyone owes, confidently expecting to sell and pay," sighed Doctor Aldo. "But when there are no sales there are no payments. And when there are no payments the banks themselves may collapse beneath the strain of unpaid loans."

"Such problems are not new," said Paco Barras. He sounded strangely contented.

"Are you not worried for Teresa and Narcissus? If the hotel business fails they will lose everything."

Paco chuckled delightedly. "Let them fail. What does it matter as long as nobody is injured. They have lived as wealthy people for a time and it will be no hardship for them to become simple people again."

Doctor Aldo strolled across the terrace and looked out in the other direction. "I see Pepita's building another wing to *her* hotel."

Paco joined him, leaning over the stone parapet. "They've had some good years. Luis is a hard-working boy and doesn't squander money. All he earns he plows back. I'm pleased because if things go badly in the future, Pepita is provided for."

Doctor Aldo's gaze wandered on. "They're getting on with Anselmo Ledesma's apartments." He sighed. "All the old landmarks are disappearing, Paco. Another fifty years and the memories will be gone too. But perhaps that's just as well."

Paco shook his head. "We've some bitter memories, eh, Juan? The Communist Committee and that mad fanatic Escudo."

"It doesn't seem possible now that men were shot in cold blood for their opinions, does it, Paco?"

"Don Carlos too," sighed Paco Barras. "A fine old man, murdered because he was a priest."

"And that young priest . . . what they did to him!" Doctor Aldo shuddered. "And poor Morales. Shot because he was mayor when he didn't want to be mayor!"

"We Spaniards are a cruel people," said Paco Barras.

"We are also foolishly proud and ridiculously brave," said Juan Aldo. His eyes twinkled. "All we have in our favor is that foreigners inexplicably find us so charming and friendly that they flock to visit us."

Behind them Narcissus and Teresa came out on to the terrace and the two old men went to join them.

"You're looking lovelier than ever, Teresa," said Doctor Aldo.

"You old charmer," she chuckled.

Paco Barras reached for his drink and stood with feet astride as though digging his brown toes into the hot sand. Raising his glass high he said with a twinkle in his eyes: "A toast to Spain. The old Spain . . . and the new!"

THIS BOOK WAS SET IN

BASKERVILLE TYPES AND BOUND BY

H. WOLFF MANUFACTURING CO., INC.

IT WAS PRINTED BY MURRAY PRINTING CO.

ILLUSTRATIONS ARE BY PAUL BACON